NOTHING IS EVER EASY

Casey Chwiecko

Cover design created using Canva

ISBN 978-1-956160-16-1 (paperback)
ISBN 978-1-956160-17-8 (ebook)

First printing December 2023
Published by Stray Thought Press

For content/trigger warnings please see final page.

To Freya and Tali, may you both
find your own stories someday.

Tira and surrounding area

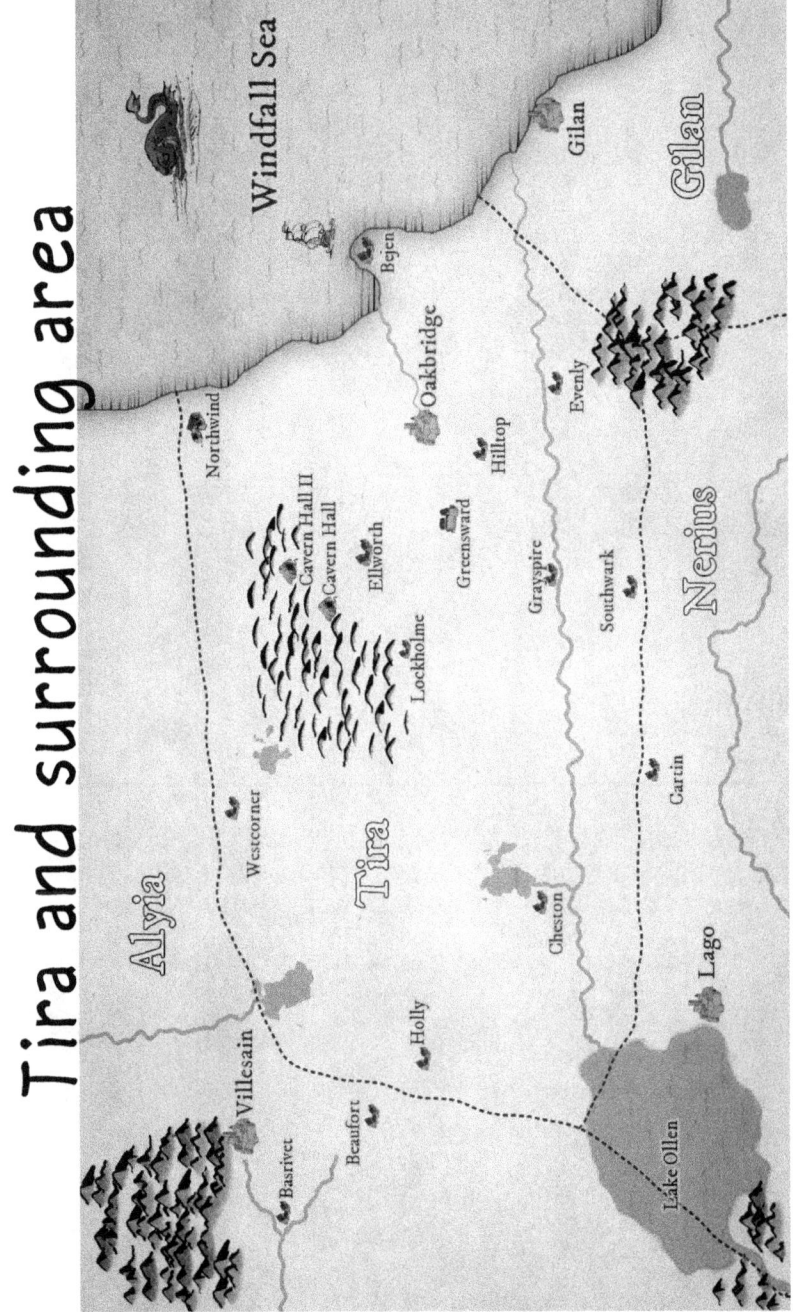

PART ONE

Early December in the Year 292

Chapter One

I HEARD A CLANG AS THE CELL DOOR OPENED. "Move back," the guard in front ordered some unseen person. The guards shoved Jay in and I followed a moment later, stumbling over the uneven floor and grabbing at anything to try to stay upright. As I fell, Jay reached out and caught me.

"Got you," he said, before sparing a glare for the three men as they pulled the door shut with a very final-sounding click. "That wasn't very nice."

One of them grinned. "Welcome to Greensward prison, stupid," he said. The trio disappeared out of sight. I listened to them walk off as I straightened and brushed myself off.

"Are you...okay?" a tentative voice asked. I looked up, a bit surprised they had given us cellmates at all. The jail, from what I'd seen during our trip to this cell - tucked into the far corner of the building - did not seem particularly full.

"Yes, we're just fine, thank..." I took the pair in. The eldest couldn't have been more than nineteen. The young woman peered at us through mussed red hair. Huddled in her arms was a boy, maybe ten, who stared up with the same solemn expression. "What in the name of the gods are you doing in a prison cell?" I asked, unable to help myself. Guilt seeped in as the boy blanched and the girl looked away.

"I'm Jay and this is Jez," Jay said cheerfully to cover the sudden awkward silence. "And you are?"

"I'm Stella. Stella Harper and this is my brother, David," Stella said, forcing a faint smile.

David eyed us. "Are you Freedom Fighters?" he asked bluntly.

I glanced out the cell door to make sure the coast was clear before winking at him.

He brightened, opening his mouth to speak before Stella laid a hand on his shoulder. "Not right now, David." She eyed us, suspicion lurking in her gaze. "They told us they use this cell for people they're going to hang. Did they tell you that?"

Jay and I exchanged a glance. "No, but that doesn't really surprise us," I said before settling myself in a corner of the cell, shifting until I was able to get semi-comfortable. Jay sat to my left with Stella and David across from us in the other far corner. The boy burrowed into his sister's side and continued to regard us curiously.

"How long have you been here?" Jay asked, ever the conversationalist. He had also probably noted the dark circles under Stella's eyes and the smudge of dirt across David's cheek.

"Three days." She looked more tired than anything. "Three *very* long days," she added with a meaningful glance down at her brother.

"Well," I said, "this could take a while, so let's figure out a way to pass the time?"

"I'd suggest a few but I know you'd just shut me down," Jay said, smirking. "Do you have an idea?"

"Have you had lots of adventures?" David asked.

"Yes, lots," Jay said and, suddenly, I had an idea.

"Why don't I tell you a story?"

David pondered that for a moment. "What about?"

"Battles, heroes, villains, lots of adventures," I said with a smile. "Standard stuff."

"Okay," David declared, "you can tell it. But it better be good!"

"David," Stella said, "Jez is being very nice by offering. You could be a little nice in return."

He turned, favoring me with a charming grin. "Please would you tell the story?"

"Since you asked so nicely, it begins just over two years ago, with the assassination of five of the most powerful dukes."

His eyes narrowed. "That's not what happened. Only four of the dukes died! I am old enough to remember *that*."

I grinned. "Mmhmm. That's because there was a young woman named Jasmine. Jasmine was the youngest child of Earl Denham and Countess Alisha Lockholme - minor nobles from a small holding north of Tira's capital. She had four older brothers who loved to spoil her, but her parents were careful to make sure she was educated properly as a young noblewoman. At seventeen, a year before her education would be complete, she was sent by her father to live in the household of Duke Elladan. Elladan's lands bordered Lockholme and were much larger. Her parents thought the experience might do her some good. Jasmine herself didn't mind. Although she would miss her brothers, the newness of it all intrigued her. Plus, the duke's daughter, Virginia, was Jasmine's best friend after her next oldest brother Colin. Lockholme was sleepy. Ellworth, where Elladan held court, was huge in comparison. Within six months of arrival, though, something happened that would change her life forever."

◀ ▼ ▶

Jasmine hummed as she hurried through the now familiar hallways of Duke Elladan's mansion. She knew she was late for her studies with Virginia, but she wasn't too concerned, knowing her friend was likely late as well. With just the two of them in their grade, neither put a lot of stock in showing up on time when other things caught their attention. The conversation she'd just shared with the head of the stables had been far too interesting to cut off early. Her father was a well-known breeder and Jasmine shared his love for the beasts.

She reached the main hall and paused, as she did every time she entered the room. With a high vaulted ceiling and wide windows – some decorated to depict famous events tintd with a popular but expensive staining method – the room was a kaleidoscope of colors on a sunny day. Light would streak through the windows, casting vibrant shadows around the room, often setting the colors dancing.

That was why she heard, more than saw, the duke in the room as she entered, tucking her large history book more securely under her arm. He was standing six or so yards away, discussing some house matters with his advisors. As usual, a few guards were stationed in the room's corners and other household members went about their usual tasks.

Jasmine caught his eye and grinned as he raised an eyebrow at her.

She nodded, acknowledging her tardiness, but didn't immediately move as he returned to his conversation. Instead, she enjoyed the brightness of the room, pushing away the desire to be outside, riding, or just enjoying the wonderful day. She had to finish school. And then have a serious conversation with her parents about what came next.

Taking a deep breath, she started forward and, only then, noticed the man standing in the nearest corner of the busy room. He stared at Elladan with a look of intense concentration. Something about it set her on edge, raising the hair on the back of her neck. She paused again.

Her hesitation only lasted until she realized the man in the corner had pulled a knife and was bringing it up to aim at the duke. Jasmine's breath caught, a combination of anger and panic coursing through her. Indecision gripped her before instinct kicked in.

"Sir!" she yelled as she threw her heavy textbook as hard as she could at the knife-wielder.

Elladan's people spun as the book struck the assassin in the side. The assassin still threw the knife but it went wide, clattering harmlessly off the wall. Elladan's advisors quickly got between him and the assassin, even as the soldiers on duty swarmed the man, subduing him in less than a minute and dragging him off.

Jasmine realized she was shaking only when a hand descended on her shoulder and she jumped violently, looking up into Elladan's gaze. The duke appeared as shaken as she felt. "Thank you," he said softly, as one of his men offered her book back.

"You're welcome, sir." She paused and then, "I don't understand. Why would someone try to kill you?"

"I don't know," Elladan said, "but I mean to find out." His gaze went to the door through which they'd dragged the assassin.

Before she could speak, he held up a hand to forestall her.

"I'm afraid the answer is no, Jasmine. This is not the sort of thing your father would appreciate me exposing you to," he added. "Off to class with you, please."

He squeezed her shoulder and then vanished out the door, leaving a very shaken Jasmine alone, clutching her book.

4

Elladan and his top advisors closeted themselves in with the assassin for almost two full days, taking breaks only to sleep a few hours here and there. Jasmine and Virginia waited in suspense for a verdict or news in any form.

When he finally emerged, looking haggard, Virginia held back but Jasmine approached Elladan, deciding that, since she had saved his life, she deserved answers. "Sir?"

Elladan smiled thinly at Jasmine and his daughter. "It's finished."

"What does that mean?" Virginia demanded.

"He has been executed." Jasmine sucked in a breath but before she could think of something else to ask, Elladan continued. "Jasmine, I received word from your father. He wishes you to return home in two weeks for a ball, to be held in your honor."

"May I go?" Jasmine asked. Something dangerous was obviously going on, so as much as she wanted to see her family, she would respect Elladan's decision either way.

He pursed his lips before nodding. "Yes."

Despite obvious trepidation, Elladan eventually gave in to his daughter's insistence that she accompany her best friend for the occasion. The duke spent the better part of the remaining two weeks impressing upon the girls the potential severity of the situation, but in a vague way that left Jasmine more frustrated than anything. She'd ferreted out that Elladan and the others had gotten no real details from the assassin and they had no idea why. All anyone knew was that four of the other powerful dukes had been killed at approximately the same time as the attempt on Elladan. The only large Dukedom spared an attempt was Northwind, for reasons unknown. At least that meant Colin was safe.

Jasmine spent most of those same two weeks feeling as if she was being watched. As much as she wanted the reassurance of her family surrounding her, Elladan's warnings echoed in her ears and made her sleep less than restful, as she imagined all the things that could happen. Virginia, however, had no such problem and gaily discussed dresses and how much fun it would be to visit the Lockholmes. Jasmine bore it patiently, working hard to try and let it distract her.

Elladan explained to both girls that they would have a hand-picked escort for the entire trip. As anxious as Jasmine was to see her family, she wondered why, if the duke was so worried, he was letting them go.

When she voiced this thought the morning they departed, Elladan smiled. "You know your father is more than just one of my neighbors, Jasmine. He is also an old and trusted friend to both myself and King Patrick. Do not underestimate your father." He paused and looked off in the distance towards Lockholme. "I do not doubt that Lockholme is one of the safest places for you right now." His smile was forced. "You'll be fine. If you do still want to come back, I'll see you in about a week. If you change your mind and want to stay in Lockholme, I totally understand." He'd said this multiple times over the past few days and she knew he meant it.

Jasmine knew she should feel more fear as she mounted, but despite the attempted assassination and her own unsettled brain, Tira'd been at peace for generations. And with no clear threat, it had to just be a weird momentary blip in that peace. There would be new dukes or duchesses and the world would go on.

That all changed when, halfway to Lockholme, the ground under the lead soldiers erupted in a shower of dirt and fire. Jasmine knew instinctively what they were, although she'd only ever seen a demonstration. Balsic contact mines.

As soon as the first mines detonated, the rest began to ignite in a horrid chain reaction, racing towards Jasmine and Virginia, who were ensconced in the middle of the group. Jasmine's horse reared, shrieking with panic. She tugged it around. The mare unwillingly turned, taking Jasmine critical feet closer to the edge of the road and thereby the edge of the mine field. When the explosions reached her, the horse reared again and Jasmine instinctively threw herself from its back. A round of secondary blasts sounded in her ear and she felt pain sear through her side. As she fell over the side of the ravine edging the road, she hit hard and tumbled down the embankment, losing consciousness halfway down.

Later, she found out that her father had sent a group of soldiers to meet their party. They arrived perhaps an hour after the explosion. After a cursory search of the area, Virginia was discovered, still alive. Distracted by the duke's daughter, they never looked down the slope to discover Jasmine.

A short time after they had packed up and left, a mixed group of men and women, with no uniforms or anything to identify them, arrived. Their leader, a young man with blue eyes and a worried frown, was the only one to accurately read the entire massacre and find Jasmine. While her pulse was weak, she was still alive. Working quickly, the group got the young woman out of the ravine and they vanished into the woods.

Jakium McRuoes craned his head back to take in as much of the castle of Oakbridge as he could from horseback as dusk closed in. Home.

"Sir?" one of the soldiers asked.

"Keep moving," Jakium replied, tearing his gaze away from the looming stone structure, and waving the men following him in through the gates. He still found it hard to believe that this was his home, even though it had been for somewhere around eighteen months. He had not wanted this, did not, even now, really want it, but life tended to lead him in odd directions. In a lot of ways, he thought time had passed quickly, but then he remembered what awaited him inside the castle and sighed. The three siblings who now ruled Tira were an odd bunch, strangely dysfunctional when it came to any personal matters, but shockingly apt at ruling the country.

Jakium shook his head, swinging off his horse and passing the reins to one of the stable hands. He let out a breath, glad to be home from a fresh two week stint in the more northern reaches of the country, searching for the Freedom Fighters' hideouts. He was fairly certain there were at least two locations and maybe more, but had no proof.

Running a hand through his hair, he turned back to his weary command. "You're all dismissed. After you get settled, see the sergeant-at-arms, who will give your assignments while you're at the castle."

A chorus of 'yes, sir' or 'yes, lieutenant,' answered and the group of thirty people dispersed out of the courtyard.

As part of his sweep, he had worked his way down south to Greensward, Tira's second largest city after Oakbridge, to meet with Colonel Rees earlier that day. Rees was in charge of both the prison housed there as well as the large garrison. The colonel reported that he'd captured two rebels creating havoc in the town. Jakium hadn't been told the specifics, but he had a decent idea from using his own two eyes. He carried a letter from Rees to General Vladimir Opalin, reporting on everything that had happened in the city.

Jakium glanced down at his filthy uniform and grimaced. If he hurried, he would have time to take a quick bath before reporting to Opalin and his younger brother.

"Lieutenant McRuoes!"

He cringed and turned to face Old Bert, the most annoying of the siblings' many lackeys. "Yes?"

"General Opalin said he wanted to see you as soon as you got back," the man said, giving Jakium the evil eye, almost as if he knew the young lieutenant was debating something else.

Jakium bit back a sigh. "I'm heading that way. Tell the general I'll be up as soon as I wash my face."

"He said right now."

"Yes, I heard you, but I happen to smell and I doubt the general would appreciate it much if he had to be in the room with me. Tell him I will be there as soon as I clean up," he said again, more firmly this time.

Bert eyed him before nodding. "Very well. Your neck," he said primly and stalked off, yelling irritably at Jakium's men as he did.

Uniformly, the soldiers had little respect for the paper-pushers of the castle. They made faces at his receding back. Jakium had to smile at that before he hurried off to get cleaned up and then have a chat with his boss and former guardian.

Chapter Two

"WAIT! JASMINE LOCKHOLME *died*," David said, scowling at me.

I held up my hands in defense. "Can you be patient?"

"No!" he said. At Stella's look, he hunched his shoulders slightly, but stubbornly kept his eyes on me.

"Well, you're going to have to try. Stories don't always give away their secrets at the very beginning, do they?" Which gave me pause. At some point, we would start getting to the secrets and it would be a risk. But so far, there was no sign of the guards since they had thrown us in – no real sounds from the rest of the jail at all. I could easily stop talking whenever we heard people coming. And it would pass the time, of which we now had an abundance.

"I guess not," he said, wrinkling his nose.

"Am I allowed to continue now?"

The boy thought about this. "No. How did the mines explode?"

"You've never heard of Balsic stone?"

He shook his head.

"That's no real surprise, depending on where you grew up. It's a type of stone mostly mined in the area that used to be Elladan's dukedom. It requires a very special way of mining it, because if it comes near fire, it will explode spectacularly. The bombs used in that attack were pressure sensitive, formed so that when pressure is applied," - I illustrated the point with my hands, pressing down between them, - "it knocks two lighting stones together and causes the mined rock to explode. It's not a perfect weapon, but it works more often than not. We tend to use the kind you can set, which has a lit fuse that is outside the casing of the bomb and has to burn for a certain amount of time before it goes off." I paused. "Does that make sense?"

"Yes. Were there a lot of them? The mines?"

"They were thorough. They obviously knew how many people would be escorting Virginia and Jasmine. They covered wide a swath of land strategically with the mines."

The boy absorbed that. "They really wanted Jasmine dead."

I snorted. "Yes, yes, they did."

He frowned but nodded slowly. "Okay, now, you can keep going."

"Thank you." I glanced out the high cell window, assured myself it was still light out, and then continued.

◄ ▼ ►

Jasmine dragged herself back to consciousness inch by painful inch. When she finally convinced her eyes to open, it took a minute to realize she was staring at…stone?

"Welcome back," an unfamiliar male voice said. She forced her head to turn, meeting a bright pair of blue eyes. "Are you feeling better?" the man asked. Although he didn't look much older than her, there was a weariness in those eyes that made him seem many years her senior.

"Yes, sir, I am," she croaked, deciding to err on the side of politeness, not knowing where she was or who this man was.

He smiled. "Good. I was worried about you for a while. Afraid we might lose you. Can you sit up? I have some water for you, if you can manage it."

Jasmine started to push herself up and then stopped, face screwing up with the pain the action brought.

"Steady," he said, putting a gentle hand on her back and helping her the rest of the way up. He handed her the cup and wrapped her fingers around it. "Sip it slowly, okay?"

"Okay," she said. "Where am I?"

"There will be plenty of time for that later," he said, smiling crooking in a slightly sad way. "I have to get back to work, but if you need anything, just yell, all right? I'm Beau."

"My name's Jasmine."

As Beau moved to the entrance of the small stone room, he paused, looking back over his shoulder, expression scarily undecipherable before he vanished out the flap that seemed to serve as a door. Jasmine stared after him for a minute before taking stock of her injuries and her surroundings.

Her left arm was in a sling. It didn't seem to hurt enough to be broken, making her think perhaps it was only a sprain. She had vague memories of landing on it, somewhere in the jumble of fire and screams. Jasmine could also feel bandages across her chest and a few along her legs under the loose clothing someone had dressed her in. Her head was swathed in bandages. She cautiously reached up, biting her lip as she realized that all that was left of her hair was some patchy bits around the bandages. She dragged over the jug of water that Beau had left and peered critically into it. Jasmine stared at the shimmering stranger who blinked back out of the water. Various small cuts on her face had already started to scab over and the bandages reached to her ear on her left side, giving her a distinctively lopsided look.

Swallowing hard, she reminded herself that she was alive after a very serious attempt to kill her. That was what mattered, not the injuries. She hadn't died but so many had. And Virginia, Gods' Breath, was her friend okay? She had to remember to ask. She tried to take a deep breath but that hurt too much, so she settled for working to steady her breathing instead.

To that end, she forced her attention to the small room. She appeared to be in some sort of cave or offshoot of one. The walls, ceiling and floor were rough and she suspected that they were natural. The entrance was covered by a hung cloth and she could hear the sounds of people somewhere beyond, but it was fairly quiet. She lay on a well-padded mattress and other than that, the jug of water, and the cup, the room was empty.

She shook herself and carefully lay back down, too exhausted to even think about moving. Even the act of sitting for perhaps five minutes had severely worn her out. Without meaning to, having a lot she wanted to think about, she drifted off.

The next time she woke, Beau had returned, sitting cross-legged by the door curtain. He had a stack of mismatched papers on his lap that he was slowly working his way through. She watched him silently for a moment. At the same time, she used the silence to analyze how her body felt. She wasn't sure how long she'd slept, but Jasmine was happy to discover she didn't feel quite so worn. Finally, she went to push to a sitting position, making it all the way this time without help, much to her relief.

The movement attracted Beau's attention. He smiled, a small, curious expression that made him look years younger. "Good afternoon. How are you feeling?"

"Better," she said, reaching over to help herself to the glass of water. "Where am I?" she asked again, hoping for an answer this time.

"It's called Cavern Hall by those of us who live here. It has no names on any maps. We're in the hills not far from Ellworth."

"And when can I go home?" she asked softly.

"Someone can take you once you're healthy enough, if you want."

She frowned, bristling a little. "If I *want*?" He just raised his eyebrows and she had the sudden sense of being tested. That there was a wrong answer here. She paused, assessing. "You don't mean it like I think. Like I wouldn't want to go home because I don't love my family. That's…that's exactly why I shouldn't go home, isn't it? Because I do love them and want them safe."

Beau smiled a little. "Yes. Considering they murdered all those guards and tried to murder you and Lady Virginia, it seems they'll kill anyone who gets in their way."

"Which was me, when I saved the duke," she said softly.

He nodded somberly.

"And to try and kill me, they killed all of those men and women." Then the other part filtered in. "Tried? Virginia's okay?"

"She's alive, recuperating at your parents' house. I don't know any details. You had been knocked into the ravine so it appears that your father's people only found her, and not you."

Jasmine pressed her lips together. "So what do I do, then? If I can't go home."

"You're welcome to stay here, as long as you'd like. Circumstances similar to yours was how many of our people came to find us."

"And who *are* you?" She wasn't sure if she was asking about him specifically or the 'our people'.

"We have taken to calling ourselves the Freedom Fighters recently, for lack of better name."

"Freedom from whom?" she asked, frowning. "Because if it's the Highcastles…"

He snorted. "No, the opposite. We'll get into the details later, once you've had some time to settle in and decide if you want to stay, but functionally, we're talking about the assassin's associates and bosses."

Jasmine absorbed that, trying to keep her brain going, even though she was starting to fade. "That's why you gave me that look last time. Because even here it'd be dangerous for anyone to know I'm alive."

She thought she spotted approval in his gaze at that. "It's true. Only Mick and I know for sure who you are. Look at this way. For all intents and purposes, the person you were is dead and gone. You probably won't even look entirely the same once you've fully recovered."

"I can't just…I can't just *not* be Jasmine, though."

He pursed his lips, looking thoughtful. "I think what you need to do is decide who you want to be going forward. I know how nobility in Tira are raised depends greatly on the parents, so I don't know where your skills or abilities fall, but you might need to learn quite a few new things here. While everyone pitches in, most of us have found a couple things we specialize in on the day to day. Either way, I think you'll agree with me that Jasmine is not a safe name to use, but what name you do choose is entirely up to you."

"But I don't know who I am outside of my family, I guess. I'm a Lockholme. I've never been further than Ellworth."

"You're smart and I think you'll adapt. I don't expect you to change who you are inside," he said, reaching forward and gently tapping her chest above her heart. "Think about it. You'll be down for a bit yet, you've got time." With that, Beau stood and brushed off his pants. "Get some rest. We'll speak again soon." Then, he was gone.

She made a concentrated effort to not think of herself as Jasmine the following few days. As predicated, she remained too weak to walk, so she had a lot of time to think, but no names immediately came to her. She had been Jasmine, daughter of Denhem and Alisha, sister to Kent, Jordan, Jonathon, and Colin for eighteen years. Although she understood the point Beau had made – and agreed with him – it wasn't easy to shed the person she had always been, even if just in name. She knew half the reason she was staying was to keep her family safe. She itched to write Colin a letter - she missed him more than any of the others - but that, too, was impossible. She had no choice but to make a complete break from the past.

She trusted when Beau said it wasn't safe for people to know her as Jasmine Lockholme, even here with these Freedom Fighters. She also picked at what he had and hadn't told her, wishing he'd return so she could question him further. She longed to talk the situation over with him. He struck her as incredibly level-headed.

However, he disappeared, leaving the Mick he'd mentioned, in his place. It didn't take long to get the impression that he didn't care for her much. The only thing in his favor was that he was obviously an accomplished healer. Mick was able to give her great advice that she suspected got her to her feet days before she should have been up. When she attempted to question him more about the Freedom Fighters – who the leader was, how many there were, how they existed – he would turn talk back to her healing. The day before she was set to get out of the room, she drew a 'you'll see' out of him, which felt like quite the accomplishment.

Her legs had taken the least beating in her attempted murder, so she'd already been up in the small room a few times. It was stamina and steadiness she'd been lacking. But when she woke up the next morning - she'd managed to adjust to the time despite no sun thanks to Mick - she immediately got herself up. She peeked out of the curtain, not bothering to wait since her legs felt strong enough. He'd probably be happier not having to deal with her anyway. All she saw outside her room was more stone, but definite passages, wide enough for two people.

She edged out, heading towards the voices she could hear to her right. She spotted Beau and Mick first, heading her way. Beau waved and they met her halfway.

"Feeling better?" he asked.

"Much, thanks."

"Figure out who you're going to be yet?"

She sighed. "Not yet. I'm having a hard time deciding where to start."

"Don't worry about it. I have no doubt that it will come to you in time."

"She'll still need a name to use around camp," Mick grunted as he joined them.

14

She looked between them and abruptly understood, wondering why it hadn't occurred to her before. "You're the leader," she said to Beau.

He offered her a nod. "Captain technically, I suppose," he said. "I apologize for not introducing myself as such before this, but I figured you had enough to deal with without trying to be overly correct."

"Thank you," she said automatically and then wondered if she should have added a 'sir.' She became aware of Mick's close scrutiny. "Yes?"

"We need something to call you in the meantime."

She frowned. "I'd rather be nameless than pick something that doesn't work or have to change it after a week or two. I'll figure it out in my own time."

She thought she saw something dart across Beau's face - maybe fresh approval? – but it was gone too quickly to be certain. "Very well, miss," he said, smiling. "Let me know when you've decided. For now, I'm afraid I have work to do. Kitchen is that way. Feel free to explore at your leisure. If you'll excuse me," he said with another small head bow.

"Of course," she said politely.

He turned, moving away. Mick stared at her for another few heartbeats before hurrying after him, talking quietly as soon as he caught up. She watched them go until they vanished from sight. The conversation had taken a lot out of her and she needed the break before she could continue.

The pair had disappeared out of sight by the time she was ready to move again, pushing off the wall. She saw no other ready options, including no people in sight, so she followed them. Her steps started out small and hesitant as she tested her strength, but her legs held, besides than a brief moment when her right threatened to give out. She kept a hand on the stone wall. Noise definitely traveled strangely, because she would have sworn she should be to the voices by then. Another quick turn, and she found herself in a large space. If this was all natural, Beau had found something truly amazing.

Off to her right, a sturdy table held a small group, studying papers spread out among them. They were discussing something in low voices and never even glanced up at her entrance.

In the main center area, a group of around twenty men and women were practicing with wooden swords. "Cross left. Parry. Now block low," an older man bellowed, walking amongst them, correcting postures here and there. As the daughter of a master swordsman, she immediately knew what he was, which only notched up her estimation of these Freedom Fighters. She had no idea

15

where they might have found someone like him, but it certainly lent them some serious credibility.

"Like it?" a new voice asked from behind her.

She jumped, adrenaline pumping. "I, uh, yes?" she managed as she turned, shooting out a hand to stabilize herself on the wall.

The man there raised an eyebrow. "Are you asking me if you like it?"

"What?" She regained some of her poise. "No, I mean, yes, of course I like it," she said. "Whoever found these caves and figured out how to best use them is a genius."

"You can tell Captain Beau that if you'd like. He came first, along with Mick and a couple others." The young man leaned in conspiratorially. "But he's not one to gloat over his accomplishments, you know, which is silly. We're supposed to be egotistical."

"We as in the Freedom Fighters or men in general?" she asked, unable to help a flash of amusement.

Now he grinned, running a hand through his brown hair, causing it to stand up in all directions. "Both work. So you're the woman we saved from the ravine, right? Getting out was fun, even though there were all the dead bodies. We don't leave Cavern Hall often." This was all said quite cheerfully and fast.

She stared at him, not sure whether to be amused at that jumble of thoughts or slightly horrified. "Yes," she finally said cautiously.

"Well, thanks, beautiful," he said, sketching a slight bow. For a moment, she wondered if he knew who she was, but pushed that thought aside. It was doubtful that Beau would have told anyone after specifically making the point that only he and Mick knew.

"You're welcome?"

He waggled his eyebrows. "I'd love to chat all morning, but I'm afraid that spud duty calls. I'm sure we'll see lots more of each other. Enjoy your afternoon!" With that, he snatched up her hand, planted a gallant kiss on the back of it, and then bounded off deeper into the cave.

"Wait!" she called, taking a step after him.

He spun in a full circle and stopped to face her. "Yes?" he asked.

"What's your name?"

"What's yours?"

"I…don't know," she admitted, feeling her cheeks redden.

He winked and then disappeared behind a partition. As she stood, uncertain what to do next or even how to take the rather odd conversation, his head reappeared. "Once you know, tell me, and I'll return the favor. Deal?"

"Deal," she said, unable to stop a smile in return.

"Perfect." He tossed her a salute. "Be good," he said, then disappeared behind the wall. She could hear him singing as he skipped off. She listened until he faded away before looking around again. No one seemed to mind her presence any more than he had, so she picked a random direction, and walked further into the maze of rooms and corridors.

Jakium took a deep breath as he paused outside Vladimir Opalin's office. He checked again to make sure his fresh uniform hung correctly, then knocked.

"Come in."

The lieutenant pushed open the door and stepped inside, offering Vladimir a tired salute. "Hello, sir."

"Ah, Jakium, I'd heard you and your men return. Please, at ease. Have a seat."

"Yes, sir."

"Thank you for coming so quickly after your arrival. I apologize for Bert."

"I can handle Bert," Jakium said, sliding the letter from Colonel Rees across the desk. "Colonel Rees sends his regards and some news. He's captured two rebels attempting to destroy the fort there. He suspects they're Freedom Fighters."

Vladimir's eyes narrowed. "Does he?" he asked, fingering the letter briefly before returning his attention to Jakium. "And your scouting mission?"

"A dismal failure, sir, if I may be so blunt. I couldn't find hide nor hair of their operations anywhere."

He pursed his lips. "And?"

"And, sir?" Jakium asked, fairly certain he had done a good job of hiding his skepticism.

"I think I know you well enough by now to know when you have something else you'd like to say. I'm inviting you to say it."

Jakium blew out a breath. "We're not looking for just one outpost anymore and they're not the ragtag group we fought a couple years ago. They know what they're doing. It's…" *It's time to face that fact.* But he wasn't quite willing to go that far out loud.

"It's?" Vladimir asked.

Jakium could hear the edge in his voice and changed tack. "It's not going to be easy to root them out."

"Yes, they have dug in deep," the general said. He pressed his fingers together. "Any other news?"

"Just a letter from Ani, sir," he said, passing it along.

Vladimir sighed. "Did you speak to her?"

"Yes, your sister wishes to return to the castle. I think she's tired of her, um, vacation."

He frowned. "Sorin doesn't like having her here, but there are plenty of reasons to. I'll write and tell her she can return," he said.

Does blaming it on Sorin make you feel better about exiling your sister? Jakium wondered. Again, he kept his thoughts to himself.

"Thank you for your report, Jakium. I assume I'll see a written version soon?"

"As soon as I've taken a bath and made sure my men have settled back in, sir."

"Good man. I have one more favor to ask."

"Yes?"

"Give your report to Sorin in person."

Jakium couldn't help sighing. "Yes, sir."

Only now did a ghost of a smile flit across Vladimir's normally serious face. "I promise he won't bite."

Jakium knew he wouldn't. That wasn't the problem. He didn't want to disappoint Sorin, which he suspected the news might. He stood and saluted again. "I'll have that report in by tomorrow."

"Thank you," Vladimir said as he returned to his paperwork. "You're dismissed."

Chapter Three

I PAUSED IN THE STORYTELLING, abruptly realizing who my once mysterious Freedom Fighter reminded me of. Maybe, I thought upon reflection, it was actually vice versa. I locked eyes with Jay. I had met Jay over a year after the last time I had seen his brother and, considering the circumstances in which I had last seen Bri, it did not surprise me I hadn't made the connection earlier. I wondered if any of my friends had over the years. I'd have to ask.

I rubbed absently at the scar stretching across my cheek as I, again, assessed the time by the sun filtering through the small window. There was little light left and I could tell it was rapidly approaching night. After the day we'd had, I had to admit I was exhausted.

"It's getting late and Jay and I have had a rough day," I said, "so I'm going to grab some sleep. If you'd like, we can continue once we're all up again."

"Yes, please!" David said.

"Of course."

He yawned and snuggled in next to his sister as I curled up, trying to get comfortable on the rocky floor.

The touch on my arm some indeterminable time later brought me instantly awake. "Shh, Jez, it's me," Jay whispered.

I forced my muscles to relax as I sat up. "What's up?"

"Who knows?"

"Beau and Mick. I suspect Bri did too. You now. Maybe others, especially those who were in the recovery party, considering the timing. Jasmine's 'death' was fairly well publicized. I never asked, though, and they never said. It was safer that way."

He nodded, the motion barely visible in the flickering gloom of the cell. There were torches somewhere in the hallway, but the light only occasionally reached down to us.

"It's amazing how life can change forever in an instant, isn't it?"

"More amazing how the world can," he said.

I chuckled. "So true."

"Think we're getting out of this one, Jezzy?"

"Don't call me that," I said without rancor, enjoying the peacefulness of the deep night, even locked away. Jezzy was Jay's own personal nickname for me and I generally abhorred it, even if I had probably deserved it at the time. "And I don't know. You know Beau, Jessie, and Ry will do their best."

He hummed quietly in response. "Well, we knew the risks coming in, even if we were trying not to get caught," he said quietly. "Good night."

"Night, Jay."

He returned to his stretch of floor and I curled up again, but thoughts of a past that rarely came to mind any more itched at the back of my mind until I finally managed to drift off.

All four of us came awake at the sound of heavy footsteps coming our way. Stella sat up, wide-eyed. "Already?" she asked softly.

Jay and I exchanged a glance, then I shook my head. It was far too early for that. If nothing else, they would want to hang us all as Freedom Fighters, even if Stella and David had nothing to do with it, just so they could say they had. That would require a big to-do and they couldn't have gotten that organized in the less than a day since they'd caught Jay and me.

"Food," a gruff voice announced. A man shoved a bucket of some sort of porridge in along with four wooden spoons and another bucket of water. I smiled grimly at the fact they didn't open the door. I knew after what we had pulled that Jay and I would be considered dangerous. I briefly wondered if Stella and David could possibly have done something to be included in that. I mostly dismissed that idea after another glance at the pair. How anyone could find David dangerous was beyond me.

I snuck a quick look at the guard, but his face rang no bells. I knew the easiest way to free us would be a move like that, but I also, realistically, knew that it was too soon for that.

We made short work of the fare and I had to admit it wasn't very satisfying. After, David turned to me. "I suppose you can continue the story if you want," he said grudgingly, but I could tell his words were an act, considering only the faintest traces of dejection were still evident on his face.

Stella shot him a glare. "David Aaron Harper," she admonished sharply.

"What? S'her choice if she wants to or not," he said with bad grace.

I held up a hand, no doubt saving David from a lecture about politeness. "I would like to continue actually," I said, winking at the boy. "After all, it makes a decent story and passes the time. Let's see how far we get."

His grateful look was enough. I took a deep breath and started back in.

◂ ▾ ▸

As Jez wandered the caves and rooms, she discovered quickly that the group numbered at a little over a hundred able-bodied men and women, along with another twenty or so kids. And the space was clearly busy.

She jumped in surprise when Beau appeared at her elbow about midday, trailed by a rather disgruntled-looking Mick. She'd had no idea he would know where to find her. Her surprise earned another one of his small smiles. "Lunch," he said, gesturing back towards the main room.

She nodded and fell into step beside him. She wondered if she should say something, but Beau seemed content with the silence, so she kept quiet. To her surprise, many tables had been set up during her wandering and she marveled at the multiple ways they used almost every space. Beau went one way, but at Mick's pointed look, she turned and sat down at an empty table instead of following, feeling very out of place and self-conscious of her bandages. As with everything else she had observed, though, there wasn't any excess, so her table soon filled up. She thought they might ask questions, but the others simply accepted her company and filled the area with perfectly normal and cheerful conversation. They demanded nothing of her, which helped her relax.

"Why don't you help in the kitchen to start?" one of the men asked her when the subject came up. She was fairly sure his name was Dunkin. "I'm on

21

kitchen duty during the day this week and we can always use more hands. It's not easy to feed almost a hundred and fifty mouths three times a day. Obviously you won't be locked into that. Either Captain Beau will assign you someplace or, if you find somewhere that interests you, you can always join there too. And who knows, maybe you'll fall in love with the kitchen." He made a face even as he said this. Some of the others chuckled.

"I doubt that," another man said. "She doesn't strike me as the type."

"I don't mind cooking," she protested, not wanting anyone to think she was too good for any job. She hadn't cooked much as the Lockholmes were well off and they had servants, but some of her favorite childhood memories were of baking with her mother.

"Neither do I and I hate kitchen duty," Dunkin said ruefully to laughter.

Having nothing else to do and wanting to feel useful, she took him up on his offer and spent an enjoyable afternoon helping with food preparation and listening to the conversations again, trying to get as much information as possible about this group she now belonged to. It also gave her an opportunity to sit and take things slow, which her body greatly appreciated.

The next five days flew by. She jumped from group to group, trying to find a place to belong. Although she didn't mind the useful work in the kitchens, she saw where it would bore her in no time. Even after almost a week of being up and about, she still felt out of place and had to wonder when and if that would change. The only person who succeeded in taking her mind off it was her mysterious friend from the first day, whose challenge had spread quickly across Cavern Hall. No one would tell her his name, but he had an easy way that made it simple to just be herself without being Jasmine.

A week after her first entrance into the Freedom Fighters, she found herself staring at a sheet of paper. On the top were two columns: Jas and Min. Under those were all the derivations and possible nicknames she could think of. She had started the paper two days previous, but was only just getting down to the business of sorting out her name. Mick's warning echoed in her head – he repeated it regularly – but she was set on not going too far from her old name. It had to be something that would resonate with her, and that she wouldn't have to spend too much time learning to respond to. She absently scratched out and doodled options.

It had been the most recent chance encounter with Mr. Mysterious, along with an interesting session with the master swordsman she'd seen the first morning, which now spurred her to focus on finally coming to a decision.

Early that morning, she had walked into the kitchen looking for a quick breakfast. Somehow, unsurprisingly, he was there, peeling potatoes. She got the distinct impression he did this often and wondered if it was a form of punishment. He had gotten impatient with her lack of name so had shortened 'no name' to Nona, a name that had quickly spread through camp. She could only hope her new name would spread as quickly since Nona was, at best, something one called their grandmother. That morning, most of her bandages had come off, although her left arm remained in a sling. Mick had, cranky as usual, informed her that, while she hadn't broken it, the sprain was bad and she was not to use it all until it no longer hurt in the slightest.

Mr. Mysterious grinned at her and then waved, hand full of potato. "Lookin' good, beautiful!" he called.

She returned the smile, finding it infectious. "Morning," she called back, laughing as she snagged what she needed and headed out.

Later that morning, she found herself watching a group sword practice in the main room. It was a way to pass the time when no one needed her help, as had happened this morning. She probably could have worked in the kitchen, but somehow she didn't want to work side-by-side with Mr. Mysterious yet. Plus, she had to admit that sword fighting interested her. She had spent many hours, as a young child, watching her older brothers train. Her father, when he thought her mother wasn't watching, had taught her a few tricks as well, but nothing that would really serve her in an actual fight. She personally thought she was a decent shot with a bow, though, since hunting was a practical activity and had been acceptable to teach her parents' only daughter.

After watching for a while, she realized the girl closest to her – maybe in her mid-teens – was doing something wrong. At first, she couldn't identify what, though. Every time the girl's opponent pressed, he easily defeated her. More often than not, the attack left the girl on her backside.

She hesitated as she finally spotted it, biting her lip before she rose to her feet and approached the pair. "Excuse me," she said politely, waiting for both to look at her. "I think he's beating you so easily because of your stance. You're standing flat-footed, see," she said, gesturing at the girl's feet. Both looked down. "If you drop one foot back, it'll give you more balance and make it easier to retreat if he's pressuring you."

The girl frowned and then shrugged. "I don't suppose it'll hurt to try. I couldn't do worse against Michael if I tried." The girl reset her feet, dropping one back as suggested.

Jez stepped back out the way to watch. This time when Michael pressed the attack, the girl was forced backwards but managed to stay on her feet, an obvious improvement.

The girl grinned. "Hey, than-" she cut off as she looked over the injured woman's shoulder, seeming suddenly nervous.

"Thought of a name yet?" came the sword master's deep voice.

She spun. "No, sir!" she said crisply, barely remembering they didn't salute here.

"Well, then, Miss Nona, would you mind telling me why you told Rylia to stand that way?"

After a second of indecision, she decided it was probably safer to tell the truth with no details. "It just makes more sense, sir. Because of where your center of gravity is, it gives you more balance if you don't stand flat-footed. Flat-footed results in you on your butt and that results in you being dead."

The big man nodded, studying her thoughtfully before tossing her the extra wooden practice sword he held.

She fielded it easily but with no little surprise. "Sir?"

"Where'd you learn that?"

"My father," she said before she could think to do otherwise.

"Exactly!" he barked, causing her to jump. He turned and she realized, to her great chagrin, they had been addressing the whole group of trainees. "See! This girl just picked up what few of you have managed to do in weeks. Use your brains and if I catch any of you flat-footed again, there will be consequences," he ordered, scanning them all with a dangerous look. "Now, back to work!"

A few present chorused a proper but unenthusiastic response as they moved to do as told. He spun and slashed down at her with a second wooden sword.

She was ready for him, having been on her guard since he'd tossed it to her, suspicious of his reasoning. It proved to have been a good idea as she threw up the sword haphazardly to block and dodged back out of reach at the same time.

He grinned. "Well done, lass. Figured an impromptu lesson was in order. How much skill do you have with that?" he asked, nodding towards the practice sword.

"Very little, sir. I know how to hold it and a few basic blocks, but that's all, I'm afraid."

"Well, people here know how to fight, so I'd say it's about time you started to learn. You fit?"

"I'm one armed for another couple of weeks, but my right works fine."

He chuckled. "Then we'll take it easy to start with. Teach you the basics and we'll switch to the hard stuff once you're back up to full strength. We'll begin now."

"Now, sir?" she asked in surprise.

"No time like the present, lass. I'm Jack Reardon, but call me Reardon. Everyone does, since it seems there are too many Jacks in the world." He winked.

She smiled tentatively back. "Nice to meet you."

"And you're still Nona?"

"For now."

His eyes sparkled at her resigned tone. "All right, lass, Nathaniel can watch this group for a bit while I work with you. Ready?"

"Yes, sir!"

"That's the spirit," he said, then stepped behind her to move her into position. "We'll start with your stance, although you're already most of the way there."

She came back to the present and stared down at the single name that remained after her half-hearted scribbling. She read it once, twice, and then smiled. Yes, that would do nicely. It fit her, but also this new, more complicated world she found herself in.

Jez hurried out of her sleeping space – she'd been able to keep her small room for the time being due to still healing – and headed for the kitchen, which had the best fireplace. Once there, she made straight for the hearth and tossed the paper in, making sure it burned fully. The others present eyed her a bit, but made no comment. She knew it was important to heed Beau's advice on not letting anyone know who she had been. She suspected one day her anonymity might matter. As soon as the paper was gone, she went looking for Mr. Mysterious. She was pointed to what ended up being a partially empty storage room. Attempting to ignore the snickers and whispers that followed her, she headed in that direction.

It took some minutes of searching to find him. When she did, she was a touch surprised to find him practicing with his sword, moving confidently in a definite pattern. It was the expression on his face that really got her, however.

25

Grim and focused, his usual, seemingly trademark grin and roguish twinkle were gone. She stopped dead, just in the doorway. For a moment, she could only watch his movement with awe, before deciding she could as easily talk to him later and moved to creep away.

He stopped his routine mid-swing, barely out of breath. "Nona."

It wasn't a question, but she stepped forward, raising her chin. "That's not my name."

He now turned to face her, eyes calculating. "Oh? Then what is?"

"Jez. My name's Jez," she said firmly, rising to the challenge she heard in his voice.

His face broke into a delighted smile and he thrust out his free hand. "I'm Brighton, but everyone tends to call me Bri. I have been known to answer to 'hey, you' too."

She laughed, taking his hand firmly, not at all surprised when he then shifted their grip and kissed the back of her hand just as he had the first time they'd met a week prior.

A tentative tap on his doorframe brought Sorin Dakamar's head up, wondering who was disturbing him. Upon recognizing the young lieutenant, he nodded. "Back from up north, I see."

"Yes, sir," Jakium said, now stepping inside and snapping off a tired, but respectful salute. "General Opalin asked me to report to you directly."

"Appreciated," Sorin said dryly. "Well?" he prompted when the young lieutenant didn't immediately continue.

"To be honest, sir, there isn't much to report. My scouting mission was a complete failure. We didn't even see an echo of what might have been the Freedom Fighters. They've disappeared from the map entirely."

"Not unexpected," Sorin murmured, glancing down at the paperwork spread neatly across his desk. "Thoughts?"

Jakium eyed him. Sorin kept his face studiously blank. He and Jakium had known each other for a while and he respected the young man, tried to nudge him in the right direction, but they both had parts to play in all this. "I think, sir, that just like us, they have taken the time since our last encounter to…well, this isn't the same group, even if it consists of some of the same people, if that

26

makes sense." He spoke hesitantly, but Sorin suspected that was more from an uncertainty over his potential reaction than a hesitation over his own thoughts.

"It does. And?"

"They know what they're doing and they've got the advantage of also knowing what we do."

Sorin tapped his fingers on the desk as he regarded the lieutenant. "Do you think we're in trouble, Jakium?"

Again, that brief hesitation. "I don't know. It's hard to say when we know so little about them."

"Very well. Remind Vladimir when you turn in your report that I'd like to see it when he's done. In the meantime, you're dismissed. There will be new orders for you in the morning."

"Yes, sir," Jakium said, saluting again. He shot Sorin a brief, unhindered smile before disappearing back out of the door.

Sorin stared after him for a minute, fingers still unconsciously beating out a rhythm on desk. He looked at the papers directly in front of him and shuffled them around, straightening them into a neat, even pile. Sorin, again, scanned them and then leaned back in his chair.

"Is it possible there's another Highcastle?" he murmured aloud.

There had been vague rumors for years that when Elizabeth Highcastle left Oakbridge over twenty years prior, she had been pregnant, but it had never been confirmed. Technically, it was impossible to confirm, considering it was reported and widely publicized that the queen and her retinue had been killed on their journey north for a vacation. Sorin had never fully believed the rumors, since Edward would never have stopped bragging if he had managed to kill the queen. He knew Edward had already been working on things then. He'd set the stage and started a quiet campaign to destabilize things because the bastard had up and decided he'd make a better ruler than the Highcastle family. Vlad had taken over after Edward's death and, as far as Sorin knew, that was when things had started to really move forward. At the thought of his father, or step-father, or whatever Edward would be considered, Sorin shuddered slightly. Thrusting the old fears aside, the point remained.

What if Elizabeth Highcastle had been pregnant when she left? What if she had survived and had a second child?

There was only one person to ask. Sorin pushed back from his desk. It was time to have a chat with Prince Renier.

Chapter Four

DAVID CHEERED AND THEN WENT ABRUPTLY silent, head whipping around. A second later, I heard it too. Footsteps. It took another before I realized it was more than one person coming our way. I glanced at Jay in surprise and held up three fingers. He nodded. Stella, at the same time, pulled David to her, a stubborn fear on her face.

The trio reached the door and I took a good look at them. The shortest was probably Ry's height, so shorter than average. The larger two were obviously the muscle, which was not a good sign at all. Shorty stuck the keys in the door and pulled it open. The two brutes pushed inside and turned to Jay and me.

Not good, I thought with a tinge of panic. Like David, they had to be assuming we were Freedom Fighters or they wouldn't bother to question us at all. Still, they certainly weren't letting the grass grow under their feet. Sure, we'd tried to blow up the garrison and *had* blown up the weapons depot, but it hadn't even been a day. I mean, we hadn't planned on being caught, although it had always been a risk. It didn't completely surprise me they were going to ask questions in general, but we were definitely considered more of a threat than David and Stella. The pair had clearly not been worked over.

In all, this wasn't going to be pleasant.

"You," Shorty pointed at Jay, "up. We've got some questions for you."

Jay stood slowly and was grabbed by the brutes and tugged from the cell. I leapt up, finally forcing my muscles to respond, but I was too late. The cell door slammed in my face - not that I could have done anything anyway. I pressed against the bars, watching them pull my friend down the hall, tension rippling through me.

"Damn it," I whispered. I wasn't particularly worried about Jay telling them anything vital, at least not this time, but still. I let out a breath, slumping against the wall.

"Jez?"

I looked up, my heart going out to David, who once again looked terrified. Stella wasn't doing much better. "Is…" she didn't finish her thought.

I shrugged, forcing down the guilt at increasing their concern. "I'm just worried about all of this."

She nodded, glanced at David, and changed the subject. "Is it safe for you to tell us the story?" she asked. "Couldn't it be dangerous for you and Beau and the rest of the Freedom Fighters?"

"I suppose in some ways it could," I said. *Like if they decide to ask David the questions instead of Jay and me.* I resolved right then to make sure that never happened. "The Three, the people who hated a girl who threw a book, they finally have me. If they find out that's who I am, does it really matter in the long run? At this point, I'm dead anyway. But I'll know to the very end that they got me on *my* terms, because I fought them all the way. In the past two years, I've created more problems for them than I ever would have if they'd left me alone. That's something they can never take from me, no matter what questions they ask or answers they receive." I shrugged again and smiled. "And anyway, it *is* a good story and will help pass the time."

She glanced at the door. "Will Jay be all right?"

"Hope so," I said.

Stella nodded and we fell silent as I kept watch for Jay's return. It seemed to take forever until I spotted the four of them – Shorty leading the way with the two brutes hauling Jay between them. My breath caught and I scrambled to my feet. Jay's head rose. He looked me straight in the eye and shook his head just enough for me to see. I breathed a sigh of relief. That meant two things: there was nothing worse than bruises and he hadn't said a word.

Shorty glared at me as they drew level with the cell door. "Move, prisoner," he snarled.

I merely stared at him, keeping my hands down at my sides in an unthreatening gesture. I was curious what the man would do. He glared and inserted the keys, swinging the door open. Before I could have done anything, even if I had wanted to, the brutes shoved Jay into me. I stumbled backwards and let myself fall rather than trip over Stella and David. Jay helped catch both of us and, after a stunned moment of pain radiating from my backside, I dragged myself out from underneath him. The door clanged shut to Shorty's laughter. I managed to glare at him as Jay pulled himself into a sitting position against the wall.

As soon as Shorty and the brutes had moved off, I turned to my friend, getting my first good look at him. His right eye was already darkening and he was in the process of wiping blood from his nose and lip. I suspected he had various other, similar bruises that we couldn't see, as well. He grinned almost sheepishly at Stella and me through the blood. I scooted forward to help him, but Stella got there first. I raised an eyebrow, unable to help a flash of amusement. Only Jay. His grin widened.

Stella now spoke up, her back to me as she dabbed at his bloody lip. "Why don't you continue the story, Jez? If you don't mind, that is."

I glanced at David and winked. "Should I continue telling it in the third person?"

"Obviously," Jay piped up. "It adds so much drama to the telling."

I rolled my eyes even as David giggled. "Oh, thank you for your wonderful input."

"You asked," he pouted and that alone convinced me he was fine.

"My mistake," I replied dryly and decided it best to pick up the story before we got into one of our typical arguments, or before he started calling me Jezzy again.

Bri's gaze searched her face. "I like it. Jez," he repeated.

"I didn't mean to interrupt," Jez said, "but I wanted to tell you and…" She shrugged. "Sorry. I'll let you get back to it."

He stretched out his shoulders. "It's quite all right," he said. "I was almost done anyway."

"Where did you learn?" She gestured to try and take in what she had just witnessed.

His smile immediately vanished. "My father."

"Is he...?"

"They killed both my parents eight months ago."

She nodded. "I understand to a degree," she said. "My parents are still fine, but, well, you saw what they did to all those people who were just doing their job. Your father must have been a very good sword fighter."

That startled a faint smile out of him. "He was. He was in the army when he was younger. He took a lot of joy out of teaching my younger brother and me. My brother never took to it like I did, but," he shrugged. "I like to think I'm pretty good, although both the captain and Mick could beat me pretty easily if they were to ever try. Reardon too probably, although he'd rather teach than wield these days. Normally, though, they stick to sparring with each other."

"Then how do you know they could beat you?"

He laughed. "Trust me, I've seen them go at each other. They're at a whole different skill level."

She hesitated as he sheathed his sword. "Will you teach me?"

"You do know that this is practical. That you will be called on to use a sword if you know how," he asked softly.

Jez knew what he meant. She might well have to kill someone, maybe a lot of someones, down the line. "Yes," she said firmly. "Reardon started teaching me today, but I'm pretty terrible."

He reached out and gently tapped her sling. "That's to be expected, considering you're one-handed right now."

"I don't want to have to wait," she said stubbornly.

Bri studied her for a minute and then shrugged. "Then let's not," he said, flashing one of those trademark grins. "Learning one-handed is harder, but I've never been one to tell someone not to challenge themselves. Go grab two practice swords and we'll see what you can do, one handed or not."

She brightened and hastened back to the main room where the practice weapons were stored. She grabbed two. When she returned, he was slowly swinging his sword as if testing out new moves.

31

As soon as Bri spotted her, he sheathed it again and caught the wooden one she tossed him. He tested its balance, taking a few practice swings. "Ready?" he asked.

"As I'll ever be."

He stepped forward, starting easy. As Jez blocked using what she had learned from her father, and Reardon earlier in the day, he slowly upped the ante.

"Ow!" She shook out her stinging hand a couple minutes later as he snuck through her attempts to guard.

He eyed her. "Was today the first time you'd ever trained with a sword?"

She made a face. "Pretty much. My father taught me a few tricks when I was younger, but nothing comprehensive."

"In that case, color me impressed."

"Impressed?" she repeated, certain she had heard him wrong.

"Yup. Give me a couple of months and you with two hands and I'll have you competing with the best in this camp. Except maybe the captain. To compete with him, he'd probably have to teach you. And even then, most won't reach his skill."

She studied him for a minute. "You're teasing me, aren't you?" she said finally.

He grinned. "Most of the time that would probably be a smart assumption, but this happens to be one of the few times I'm not. You've got some raw skill, Jez, but you're going to need to work at it if you want to be good." He tossed his sword in the air, let it flip twice before catching it.

"Show off," she muttered.

He sketched a smug bow. "Of course I am. Captain Beau's the only person I've ever met who isn't and he only gets away with it because he's a genius and everyone knows it. Now, let's try that again and I'll show you where you go wrong. Tomorrow night, I'll teach you some of the named blocks and strikes. Sound good?"

"Sounds great! Thank you."

He grinned. "My pleasure."

After that, every night, she joined him after dinner to practice, before letting him work at his own level. Some evenings, she stayed and watched – not surprisingly, Bri was the epitome of being unself-conscious. She loved it. Bri was the first real connection she made, other than Beau. But the captain was so often busy that it was hard to find time to talk to him. Although Bri maintained a serious demeanor when they were actually practicing, the rest of the time, it was hard to tell if he was serious or joking.

It didn't take long for the entire camp to learn her name, but a few insisted on calling her Nona anyway. Bri told her to shrug it off. "They're the immature ones. They'll get over it." Then he grinned. "Actually, I should have called you Nona right then. Damn it, the one time I'm not on top of the punchline."

"I would have smacked you."

"I would have deserved it," he said solemnly

"I'll admit, though, I'm more curious about when you became mature."

Now he laughed. "Good point. I suppose it had to happen sooner or later."

Two weeks after the first lesson with Bri, Mick appeared at her elbow. "The captain would like to speak to you," he said stiffly. Despite the fact she had been there for almost a month, Mick had definitely not thawed out. She wasn't sure if it was her background or what, but he didn't approve. Like with the Nona name, she forced herself to shrug it off.

"Yes, sir," she said politely and followed Mick to Beau's office. When they reached it, Mick stopped and motioned her past. She glanced at him, but couldn't get a read off his face about why she'd been summoned. She had a fairly good idea, based on what some of the others had said - that everyone got a formal invitation to join at some point - but would have liked confirmation.

Beau looked up as she paused just inside the door and favored her with that smile. "How are the sword lessons with Bri going?" he asked without preamble.

Somehow, she wasn't surprised he knew. "Well enough, I guess. He says I'm a fast learner, but it can be difficult with only one hand and I guess I leave myself open for retaliation a lot. I'm not sure how much progress I'm making, but he insists it's good and I suppose he knows better."

"Mick and I were just talking yesterday. It's probably past time we gave your arm a thorough check out, since it's been a month. How's it feeling?"

"Pretty good. Occasionally a bit sore, but not like it was."

"Why don't you meet us at the end of lunch and I'll look at it?" he said.

"That would be great. I'd love to be able to use both my arms again."

Now he waved her over, almost looking embarrassed he hadn't yet. "Please, have a seat. I'd like to talk to you for a minute, if you have the time."

"Time is something I have in abundance," she said, amused. She scooped up some paper off one of the extra chairs and straightened it, plopping it on her lap as she sat.

"That is something we can hopefully fix soon," he said, leaning back in his chair and regarding her somberly. "As I'm sure you've noticed, we're a relatively small group and I'm afraid we don't have a lot of detail on who the enemy is that we face yet. Considering their first fully successful move was the assassinations, we have no names or faces. However, we do know that they are quite powerful. There have been small actions for years, many of which have been bested by the Highcastles."

"The assassin's allies and bosses, like we talked about early on."

"Precisely," he said. "The fact they could kill four out of the six most powerful dukes in Tira proves they are getting ready to make a move. We've been aware of the growing threat to Tira since before I was born, but it's obvious they've been searching for leadership for most of that time. I'm afraid they've actually found it now. With less than two hundred people, there's not a lot we can do to prevent anything."

"And you're afraid they'll hit Oakbridge next."

"I'm almost certain they'll hit Oakbridge next," he corrected, a deep sadness flitting across his face so quickly Jez almost missed it. "I can see the writing on the wall and there's nothing we can do."

She let out a breath. "Nothing is ever easy, Beau. We won't give up, though, and our time will come. Whoever they are…" Her gut clenched as she realized that they could do nothing. And, in doing nothing, it was like they were condemning the king and prince to death. Her mind flashed to her own brother, Colin, who was a soldier in Northwind. Colin was right in the way of anyone trying to remove the rest of the dukes and the royal family from the picture.

Beau patted her hand. "I know. But it's not a choice we really have," he said softly.

"Why would anyone…I just don't understand. We don't know enough to warn them?"

"Nothing specific. My network is too small. It's…it's as much a gut feeling as anything confirmed on paper. Not only that, but why would they believe us? And I do believe the king has some inkling that things are not well," he said, gesturing at the full desk.

They both went silent, staring at the jumble.

"We?" he asked finally.

"Absolutely," she said. "They took everything from me without a second thought. And worse, they killed people because of me. Almost killed my best friend. They did the same to Bri and who knows how many others here, probably most of them. I'm in for as long as it takes, Beau. I can't go back. You were right about that, and I don't think I could anyway, not after seeing this. Not after knowing about the threat. Not after the last month." She ran a hand over her short hair, feeling the scars it was only just beginning to cover. "There's no going back, knowing what I know. I just wish it was possible to protect everyone."

He smiled grimly and offered his hand. "Welcome to," here an almost grimace crossed his face, "the Freedom Fighters, Jez."

She raised an eyebrow, unable to help herself. "Okay, you mentioned being the Freedom Fighters was new, what's the deal?"

"It's Bri's fault. He dubbed us that shortly before we rescued you and it has, unfortunately, stuck. I tried to explain that Patrick Highcastle is still king and it seems a bit…inaccurate, but he argued that it wouldn't be forever, so we might as well get used to calling ourselves that. The others agreed we needed a name and no one could do better."

Jez giggled, covering her mouth. "I'm sorry, but that…I suppose we're truly stuck with it?"

"I think so."

"I feel like I should apologize for him."

A real smile itched at the corner of Beau's mouth. "If you start now, you'll find it's a full time job, so I wouldn't try."

"Good point."

For a moment, they stayed silent and Jez was glad the mood had lightened. Finally, Beau shifted, all business again. "Keep rotating between groups until you find some place to stick. Trust me, we're pretty tight knit here, but it will get easier. Bri will help with that. I'm sure he already has."

She nodded. "He's introduced me to a lot of people and it's nice to have a set place to sit at meals."

"Good, glad to hear it. I promise Mick will eventually lighten up as well. He's-"

"Worried about me?"

"Protective of me," Beau corrected. "He has a hard time with new people, but he'll get there."

She grinned. "I won't take up any more of your time, since I know it's a lot more precious than mine. Thanks."

"You're welcome. I'm glad you're staying."

"Me too," she said, feeling suddenly cheerful as she bounced to her feet, throwing a wave over her shoulder.

Beau groaned in her wake, although she caught it anyway. "Bri's already rubbing off on her."

Jez burst into laughter as she headed out.

"You weren't supposed to hear that!" he yelled, only making her laugh harder.

Sorin waved the guard off and turned the deadbolt on Renier's door before pushing it open. The prince sat in the chair by the window, although he turned at the sound of the door. "Sorin," he said neutrally.

"Hello, Ren."

After a heartbeat of silence, Ren scowled. "Do you want something?"

"I hadn't visited in a while. I wanted to see how you were getting on." To be honest, Sorin was a bit disturbed by how old and tired the prince looked. He and Ren were the same age, their birthdays only a couple months apart.

"Same as last time. Bored, mostly."

Sorin frowned, tilting his head. "Are the books not enough?"

"There's only so much time I can spend reading." There was a dullness to his tone that made Sorin itch.

"Then why don't I give you something else to think about?"

Ren eyed him. "Oh?"

"Do you have a younger sibling?"

Again, silence reigned, although this time the other man stared. "Excuse me?" Ren finally managed.

"Do you have a younger sibling?"

"Gods' Breath, Sorin, you'd think someone might have noticed sometime in the last twenty or so years if I did!"

"It's not as far-fetched as you might think."

"I think I'd know if I had a brother or sister."

"How old were you when your mother vanished?"

Ren's eyes narrowed, as if he could suddenly see where Sorin was going with this. "About four. And my mother didn't *vanish*, she was killed."

"That's what your father told you, and everyone."

A flash of anger darted across Ren's face and he tensed, but managed to pull in whatever he was going to say. "Yes. That's what happened."

For a moment, Sorin debated not pushing. But if there was another Highcastle, he had to know. And even if Ren didn't know it consciously, maybe he'd seen something when he'd been younger. "It has never occurred to you that your father might have lied to you for her safety? And perhaps that of their unborn child? You were barely more than a toddler, Ren. If he had told you the truth, do you honestly think you would have been able to keep it secret at that age?"

"My mother died," he said flatly.

"Those are the facts as we know them," Sorin agreed. He decided it was best not to mention the fact he was almost certain that, if Elizabeth Highcastle had actually died, it hadn't been them. "But there's a logic here." He perched on the edge of the man's bed to look him in the eye. "You've said that your father saw us coming long before Vladimir took control. Wouldn't it be possible that he sent your mother and your unborn sibling away for their safety, and then lied to the world to keep them safe?"

He could see the struggle on Ren's face as the other man worked to keep his anger in check and not admit the possibility Sorin presented. "Where is this coming from?" the prince asked finally.

"I've been analyzing our encounters with the Freedom Fighters, as sparse as they've been, and the overall style they use is identical to that of your father."

"That makes no sense. Even if what you say is true, their leader couldn't have been trained by Father."

"But that doesn't mean they couldn't have been trained in the same style."

"Damn it, Sorin," Ren said, but he sounded more tired than angry. "What do you want from me?"

37

"Is it possible I'm right?"

His jaw worked. "It might be possible."

Sorin nodded, looking past Ren, wondering what to do with this potential information. So far, he had not told Vladimir. "Okay, thank you," he said after a moment and stood, turning to the door.

"If you're right," the prince said, so quietly Sorin almost missed it, "if you're right, then that means my father sacrificed my safety and my life for that of my unborn sibling."

Guilt slammed Sorin hard in the chest, making breathing impossible for a few heartbeats, as he paused. He knew a thing or two about sacrificing safety and life for family. "No, I don't think so," he said once he had regained his breath and glanced over his shoulder, meeting Ren's devastated gaze. "I think the king needed an heir and I think he banked on us needing you…and then to give you a chance, a chance in the form of a built-in, automatic resistance. Whatever you do, Ren, if I'm right, don't hold this against them. Don't let it destroy any remaining chance you have with your family."

Before Ren could respond, Sorin took the last two steps and shut the door behind himself. He paused, head leaning back against the solid wood, before he forced a deep breath and headed back to his office.

Chapter Five

MY STORY HALTED AS FOOTSTEPS ECHOED outside our cell and I glanced at Jay. "Just one," he confirmed.

I breathed a slight sigh of relief, not in any hurry to be interrogated. "Food then."

The same man from before shoved a stew-like substance through the slot in the door, which we all dug into. The three of us silently let David eat more than us. As the boy finished off the last bit, I stood and stretched stiff muscles from the uncomfortable seating and inaction. For the past two years, and even most days before that, I had gotten plenty of exercise daily and this inactivity was already driving me nuts. The others followed my example, David with all the energy only a kid could manage. Then we settled into our selected corners – I was next to the bars, facing down the hallway towards the rest of the jail. David was across from me, which would have made me a bit nervous if I hadn't seen how quickly he moved to Stella's side whenever we heard someone coming. Jay sat next to me on the far side with Stella across from him. Our cell, I had figured out, was the last in the row.

I glanced up at the single, small, barred window set high on the wall between Jay and Stella and was more than a little surprised to find it was already getting dark. "Huh, how time flies," I murmured, half-joking. "I guess it's time for sleep." I had caught a few stifled yawns on David's part, plus I knew it would shortly be too dark to properly see each other.

The boy scooted over to curl up with his sister. I understood the urge for human contact but settled in my corner and closed my eyes. Surprisingly, I drifted off shortly.

Not so surprisingly, I woke at dawn. Jay was already awake, face turned to the weak light filtering through the window. "Hey, you," I said, moving over to lean against him. "Didn't sleep well?"

"Not really," he said. "Been thinking about my brother." I could tell he was trying to find more words so I stayed silent. "I…after Bri left me, I couldn't talk about him. Not even with our own family. When I joined all of you, I still wasn't ready at first, so only Beau and Mick knew. Though Jessie figured it out later."

"Jessie?" I asked. "Really?"

"Yeah, well, she was one of Bri's best friends for quite a while and I did constantly flirt with her. At some point, the similarities were bound to click."

"Don't rub it in," I said dryly at the probably unintentional reminder that I hadn't figured it out until it had smacked me in the face.

That startled a grin out of him. "Still, by the time I realized Beau had nudged me into the same group of friends, I couldn't…I couldn't figure out how to tell you. It wasn't something I felt I could just blurt out. Beau expressed his condolences, as Beau would, but he never really told me about him. I think Jessie would have, but I never…I just didn't ask. To be honest, I'm still mad at him, even though he's dead. It had always been the two of us against the world, but he left without even saying goodbye. The day after our parents were killed. What kind of decision was that? I had no idea where he was or how to follow him. The first time I knew, it was the letter Beau sent me to say he had died." He stopped and I put an arm around his shoulders, sensing he needed the comfort.

"I'm sorry, Jay," I said quietly. "I can't even imagine losing my whole family. It's bad enough that I don't know either way about my brother, Colin." At his questioning glance, I shrugged. "He was part of the guard up at Northwind when the Three attacked and killed the duke and duchess. I have no idea if he survived or even where he might be if he did."

Jay nodded. "I guess my question is: did he change? What was he like?"

I snorted. "I could entertain you with Bri stories for hours if you really wanted, but my guess is he didn't change. There are a lot of similarities between you two and he was, well, a piece of work."

"Yeah, what's up with you people and being blind to the obvious?"

"I suppose I saw the similarities. You definitely filled a gap in the group like Bri, but I suppose I never thought 'little Jim' would follow in his footsteps. Or would be my age. As for specifics, I don't know. He was always upbeat and positive and the only time he was serious was when he held a sword. Although he was surprisingly modest about it, he was an excellent swordsman and, Beau's probably told you, but he rivaled him and Mick, mostly out of sheer determination. He could shed his somber mood, though, in an instant when he wanted to. I think he preferred to focus on the immediate and the future, in making Tira safe again."

"So, I've always gotten the impression you two were an item for a while."

I smiled. "We were. We'll get there soon since it started a few months after I joined and lasted until his death. Beau wasn't thrilled with it, but couldn't complain considering we made a good team and never let it get in the way of our duties."

He smirked. "I bet Beau didn't like it. And who'd have thought Bri would actually be important."

I punched his shoulder. "Shush you. Your brother was a good man and brilliant in his own way."

"Well, damn, and it turns out I could have learned from him."

"Learned from him?" I echoed, confused.

"Yeah, and done whatever he did to get you with Jessie."

I stared and then burst out laughing. "Except you never *actually* wanted to get with Jessie."

He shushed me and I heard another snorted laugh. Stella was already awake and watching us as David now stirred and stretched, yawning widely. I felt momentarily bad for waking him, but couldn't have kept the laughter in even if I had wanted to. "Good morning," I greeted them.

"Morning," Stella said, now sitting up and wincing as she rolled her shoulders. "You two been up long?"

"Not too long. We were having a perfectly normal conversation until James ruined it."

He cringed. "I liked it so much better when you didn't know my full name."

I grinned. "And I'm just starting. I think Jamesy has a very nice ring to it."

The Harpers both snickered as he shuddered. "I think it's time to pick the story back up," he said loudly.

"Breakfast should be coming soon," I started, determined not to let him off too easily.

"Story, now, please? David agrees with me, right, David, old buddy, old pal?"

David gave him an appraising look that only made me more amused. "Yeah, I suppose I'll save you, but you owe me."

"Deal," Jay said.

"Jez, will you please continue the story?"

"Since you asked so nicely, of course," I said, ignoring Jay as he stuck his tongue out at me.

Jez rummaged through one of the storage rooms deeper in the bowels of the cave system. They had limited storage space and most was packed to the brim, making it a chore to find anything. Gradually, she became aware of someone watching her. She glanced up, not surprised to find the teen girl she had helped with her footwork a few weeks before. The girl had been following her, mostly at a distance, much of that time. She decided it was past time she addressed this so she straightened, brushing off her hands. "Rylia, right?"

The girl nodded, eyeing her warily.

"Can I help you with something?"

The teen's eyes narrowed. "No."

"Then can I ask why you're following me around?"

"Who said I am?"

Jez barely bit back a smile. "It's pretty obvious. How old are you?"

"Fifteen."

She reappraised the teen as she would have placed her younger than that. "Oh, you're only three years younger than me."

"What's that supposed to mean?"

She realized belatedly that she probably shouldn't have said that out loud. "Uh, nothing," she backpedaled, trying to come up with something else to say, when she was saved from the need.

"Rylia Schid, if I find you have been skipping lessons again, you will regret it! The captain'll hear about it this time." Even Jez jumped at the loud voice that echoed down the hallway towards them.

Rylia, however, looked downright panicked. "Shit, Iris. Help," she gulped, quickly scanning the area.

Jez did too. "Quick, Ry, in there," she said, giving the girl a shove towards a nearby partition that was large enough for her to hide behind. Then Jez quickly bent back down to a random box and started going through it, as she heard approaching footsteps. When they stopped, she looked up, and up, finally meeting the eyes of one of the tallest and broadest women she had ever seen. It took a moment – along with Rylia's comment – to equate the seeming giant at her side with the children's schoolmistress. Jez quickly jumped to her feet to try and create some sort of even footing. It only partially worked. At least now she wouldn't get a crick in her neck.

"Jez, right?" Iris said, peering down her nose.

In that instant, Jez remembered that she was not yet nineteen and therefore not immune to Iris and her classes. She crossed her fingers behind her back, hoping that Iris didn't know that. "Yes, ma'am," she said.

"Have you seen Rylia Schid?"

"No, ma'am."

"Do you even know who Rylia is?"

"I do, ma'am, and I haven't seen her," Jez said, having no issue with telling a convincing lie. She'd had plenty of practice with her brothers over the years. Plus, she had picked up a few tips from Bri's excellent innocent expression. "No one's been by," she added when Iris didn't appear convinced.

"Are you sure?"

Jez was about to answer when they were both interrupted by a muffled, but distinct sneeze.

"What was that?"

She cursed fluently in her head as she strove to come up with an answer that wouldn't get both her and Rylia in trouble. "What was what?" she managed brilliantly.

"That was definitely a sneeze."

"I didn't hear anything," Jez said.

Iris shot her an entirely too skeptical look. "It was a sneeze and it was coming from-"

"Me."

Jez jumped, spinning to find another woman, maybe a few years older than her, coming out from deeper in the storage area. She carried a rather large box. It took a second to place her, but then she recognized the newcomer as Bri's friend, Jessie. She had often been jealous of their little side conversations during some of the tactical meetings, where she had been spending more time. The pair could often be found snickering in the corner.

"Jessica," Iris said flatly. "What were you doing back there?"

"Reardon asked me to find some of his old practice books for his beginners. Top priority, very important."

The giant of a woman looked between Jessie and Jez suspiciously for a minute. "If I find out that either of you are hiding something from me, especially something in the form of a particular fifteen-year-old, the captain will hear about it."

"I'm sure he will," Jessie said pleasantly. She set her box down. "Jez, there are two more back here, will you help me?" she asked pointedly.

Iris aimed one last glare at both and stomped back off the way she'd come.

The two young women watched her go and then heard Rylia. "Is the coast clear?"

"Free and clear," Jessie said. "Come on out."

She clambered out from behind the partition and boxes. "Thanks for the save. She would have had my hide."

"Because you're following Jez around instead of going to classes?"

Rylia made a face. "It's stupid. I can read and write just fine. It's okay for the little kids, but the rule's eighteen and younger because the captain says you can go that long out there so we should here too." She rolled her eyes and then paused, studying both of them. "You're not going to turn me in, are you?"

"If you don't tell Iris I'm still eighteen, I won't tell Beau that you're skipping lessons."

The girl grinned. "Deal!" Then she looked at Jessie nervously.

"Far be it for me to give Iris any satisfaction. She hates my guts."

"Why?" Jez asked.

Jessie grinned. "Bri and I might have done a few things to get on her bad side at various points in time. So, Rylia's got a new nickname?"

"Nickname?" the other two said.

"Ry?" she prompted.

"Oh." Jez reddened. "I might have forgotten Rylia's full name in my panic to get her hidden." She snuck a glance at the girl to find her looking thoughtful.

"My brother used to call me Ry-Ry. I kinda like the ring of Ry," she said and grinned. "I'll let you off the hook this once."

"Gee, thanks. Jessie, don't let us keep you. Don't you need to get those papers to Reardon?"

The other woman looked blank before she laughed. "Oh! Sorry, I lied. These are some old scraps for the captain and the tactics team."

"Why'd you lie? It would seem to me that having to get something to Beau would have been an even better excuse."

The other two glanced at each other and grinned. "Jez, let us fill you in on a particularly amusing piece of Cavern Hall gossip," Jessie said.

Ry leaned forward conspiratorially. "Iris has a huge crush on Reardon."

That took a moment to sink in and then Jez burst out laughing. "Ah, that makes so much sense."

"Just remind me to fill in Reardon on my excuse at lunch."

"He won't mind you used his name to lie?"

"Of course not. Reardon and Iris personify the idea of a love/hate relationship. Reardon's not her biggest fan and purposely schedules beginning lessons during her school time. And fighting lessons trump schoolwork," Ry said with some relish.

"And yet she has a crush on him?"

"Don't you love irony?" the girl giggled. "Anyway, thanks again for saving me. I just couldn't take her today."

Behind her, Jessie looked amused, clearly thinking that wasn't the real reason Ry had skipped lessons.

Jez reddened slightly and quickly redirected, not wanting any sort of hero worship. Better just regular friendship. "Not a problem, but next time you sneeze, I'm turning you in and claiming ignorance."

"Next time, don't hide me in the dustiest corner in the whole cave!"

They all laughed. "Let's hope there isn't a next time," Jez said and then gestured to the box at her feet. "I was actually looking for some old maps for Beau and the team and it turns out I found them in the box I was using as cover. Why don't you come with us, Ry? We'll put you to work and then no one can accuse you of not being productive."

Ry's face lit up. "Really? But I don't know anything about maps and tactics and stuff."

"Neither did I when I started a couple weeks ago. I'm sure you'll be able to pick it up."

The girl glanced at Jessie who nodded her agreement. "Then what are we waiting for?" she asked, taking off down the hall.

"Slow down!" Jez called after her as the two hefted their boxes. "We're burdened with heavy loads," she said, both of them pretending to stagger under the weight.

"Slowpokes," Ry teased even as she fell into step.

After that day, life became easier. Jessie and Ry were almost inseparable immediately and the two of them, Bri, and Jez spent most of their free time together. Bri continued to work hard with her to improve her sword fighting and made sure to include her in any activities. He also apologized for not having properly introduced her to Jessie sooner.

During downtime, the two often snuck out of Cavern Hall to sit up on the rocks and chat. Jez knew she shouldn't talk about her past too much and was glad that Bri respected that. Instead, he told her serious, silly, and sometimes downright hysterical stories about his own life, including those featuring his younger brother, Jim.

She managed, on occasion, to tell a story of her own, particularly those relating to adventures or conversations she'd had with one or more of her brothers. Most of these involved Colin, who was only a year older. She always got the impression that Bri knew exactly who she was, despite Beau's claim that only he and Mick knew. She certainly wouldn't have been surprised if he had ever called her Jasmine.

Sometimes, they just sat in silence and Jez suspected that, during those periods, they were both thinking about the family they had lost, even if Jez's weren't dead.

Now was one of those times, so when Bri spoke up, it startled her. "Earth to Jez."

"Yes?"

"Whatcha thinking?"

She grinned, determined not to bring the mood down. "Do you really want to know?"

He eyed her. "I thought so, but now I'm not so sure."

"It's really not bad," she said, although she loved the occasional time when she could make him squirm. "I was just thinking about all I've learned about you and feeling bad I can't return the favor.

"Oh hell," he said, "don't worry about *that*." He grinned, leaning in. "I don't need to know your past to know you're beautiful." Bri then winked and slipped to the ground, heading for the entrance.

"Whoa, whoa, whoa, wait a minute there, mister!" she said, laughing, as she slid down after him. "You can't just say that and then walk away."

He paused, eyes twinkling although his expression was solemn. "Can't I?"

That wasn't exactly what she had expected and she paused, not sure how to answer. "Only if you mean it," she decided on finally, voice quiet and containing more waver than she liked.

He smirked, damn him. "Mean what?"

"You know what!"

"I," he began but was interrupted.

"Bri! Jez!" Both jumped almost guiltily as Jessie and Ry appeared around the corner. "There you guys are," Ry said with a grin. "Captain Beau wanted us to tell you it's time to come in for the night. We're shutting everything up." After connecting with Jessie and Ry, Jez had finally moved from her small room to a shared room with the two of them.

"Okay," Jez said and then aimed a glare at Bri. "This conversation is definitely not over."

"What conversation?" he asked and then grunted as she punched him hard in the arm.

47

"Asshole," she muttered.

"Ow," he managed as Jessie stepped on Ry's foot to keep her from commenting.

She didn't get a chance to ask him about it right away. Cavern Hall was busy and time for just the two of them was in short supply. However, it was only another week until Jez finally made a breakthrough with her sword work. She still, even two handed, had issues covering her weak spots, which gave Bri no end of concern – and mirth on occasion. This night, however, for whatever reason, she remembered, blocking the thrust that usually made it through her guard to leave a nasty bruise.

Bri backed up a step, blinking. Jez beamed in triumph. "The question is," he said, "can you do it again?"

"Try me," she said, not certain she could do it again, but responding to the challenge in his voice.

He did exactly that another half-dozen times. Every time, no matter what angle he attacked from, she blocked. Even with it late fall and a chill seeping into the stone, Jez didn't notice because Bri kept her hopping for the entire two hours. She only let him through two or three times.

Finally, he stepped back and lowered the practice sword, both of them out of breath, him for the first time. "Gods' Breath, Jez, I think it's finally sunk in!" he said.

She started dancing around in victory and cheering. Bri burst out laughing and she wagged a finger at him. "No laughing," she ordered, still bouncing in sheer glee.

He made a valiant effort to stop. "What do you want me to do instead? Join in?"

"Obviously!"

After only a split second of hesitation, he did just that, grabbing her hands and bouncing around with her. Then, with a suddenness that surprised her, he tugged her to him, slipping one arm around her waist. "You know our conversation last week? Out on the rocks?" he asked, eyes dancing.

"As if I could forget."

He grinned. "I meant it," he said before leaning forward and pressing his lips to hers.

She absently threaded her fingers into his hair, quite content to deepen the kiss. Finally, after what seemed like both an eternity and far too short a time, he gently stepped back, pushing a stray lock of hair out of her face.

"I take it you're okay with this."

She laughed, even more out of breath than before. "I am so okay with this," she said, then yelped in surprise as he dipped her down and pecked her again on the lips.

"Good, because I think we had visitors."

She went scarlet. "Gods' Breath, I hope it wasn't Mick."

It was his turn to laugh.

At breakfast the next morning, Jessie nudged her in the side. "So, you and Bri, huh?"

Jez fought back a fresh blush. "Bri thought someone had seen us. Why were you peeking?"

"When you both stopped cheering so abruptly, I thought something might have happened, so I poked my head in." She groaned and Jessie grinned. "Hey, no worries, I completely approve. You *are* making it official or whatever, right?"

"You mean dating? I think we have more important things to worry about."

Jessie rolled her eyes. "You're giving me that speech? At least make it original."

"Make what original?" Ry asked as she plopped down on Jez's other side with a wide yawn.

"Her excuse for not officially dating Bri."

"Dating? Did I miss something?" the girl asked, instantly more awake.

Jez dropped her head onto the table with another groan.

"Just quite the kiss last night," Jessie said, taking far too much pleasure in this, in Jez's opinion.

Ry's eyes widened and unholy glee spread across her face. "So," she started, raising her voice, "you and-" That was as far as Jez let her get before slapping a hand over her mouth and pushing her off the bench and under the table with the other. The teen didn't give up, though, taking a deep breath and continued, "you and Bri-"

Jez ducked down to shush her, an opportunity that Ry exploited, dragging her under with her. What resulted was a short, laughter-filled tussle that ended with Jez sitting on Ry's chest, trying to glare at her.

"Nothing to see here!" Jessie called from her seat still on the bench. Jez suspected she was talking to most, if not all, of the rest of the Freedom Fighters and her cheeks heated.

Ry sucked in a breath and Jez punched her in the shoulder. "One word out of you," she started. Jez finally jammed her hand over Rylia's mouth as the teen persisted. "Look, I win since I'm on top. That means you have to do what I say until I get off you."

Ry reached up and pried the hand off. Jez kept it close in case it was needed. "No fair, you're bigger than I am!"

"Not much and anyway, you started it so no whining." While Ry digested this, Jez continued. "Raise your right hand and repeat after me."

Jessie snickered from her spot on the bench as the girl grudgingly did so.

"I hereby solemnly swear that I will not tell anyone what Jessie told me, or anything else relating to Bri and Jez, unless under strict, prior permission from Jez, which will only be granted under extreme circumstances."

Ry did as ordered between giggles.

"What's going on?" Bri asked, sounding confused.

Jez looked up between the bench and table, hastily slapping a hand over Ry's mouth yet again as a safety precaution. "Nothing," she said innocently.

He stared at them for another minute before lighting up. "I get it! Picnic under the table! What a great idea. Can I join you?"

There was an instant of silence before the three burst into laughter, all arguments instantly forgotten.

Prince Renier Highcastle spent most of the following day pondering Sorin's assertions. Almost instinctively he wanted the other man to be wrong, but the idea of a sibling intrigued him. If nothing else, Ren was grateful Sorin had planted the seed in his mind. It did indeed give him something to dwell on other than how incredibly bored he was and how sick he was of the same few walls and the same view. His prison consisted of his childhood rooms – a sitting room and a bedroom, although his bedroom now consisted only of an old bulky family heirloom dresser that Sorin and Vladimir's men had deemed too large to move. The only thing it was good for was getting to his bathroom now. His bed had taken the place of an old conference table near the door, meaning he was almost always under scrutiny, or could be at any moment by opening his door.

The only window provided some source of interest as it looked down over the castle's main courtyard, which allowed him to watch the comings and goings. Most meant nothing to him, although he had recognized Jakium McRuoes when he arrived the day before.

Ren was again at his window, staring at the outside world as he flipped idly through one of the books the brothers provided. A commotion below drew his gaze. As soon as he recognized the redhead dismounting, he groaned. Things had been rather peaceful, and maybe far too quiet, while Anica Opalin had been out of the castle and presumably out of Oakbridge, but now things were likely to get exciting again. A part of him, larger than he liked to admit, was actually okay with this. If nothing else, Ani was a source of entertainment. Often over-the-top, not-sure-how-to-deal-with-it entertainment, but it was probably better than being incredibly bored with only bad books for company.

Ani chatted cheerfully with the men taking her horse and then disappear into the castle somewhere below him. He gave her maybe an hour until she appeared in his doorway. It had taken all of two seconds upon meeting Ani to realize her crush on him was a mile wide and probably about three times as deep.

He got lost back in his thoughts and was just getting up to put his book away when the door burst open. "Ren!" Ani launched herself into his arms. Luckily, he was ready for her and managed to mostly catch her even as he sunk back into his chair.

"Oomph," he grunted. "Hello, Ani. Can you get off now? I think your elbow is in my bladder."

"First you have to say you missed me!"

He rolled his eyes. "And if I don't?"

Her face scrunched in thought. "You know, I'm not sure." Then it fell. "You did miss me, right?"

"Of course," he said quickly, not liking to see her upset, despite everything.

"Good!"

"Now can you get off?"

"Maybe," she sang and then grinned as two equally familiar voices floated down the hallway. Ren glanced that way, always amused by anything that got either of the other two members of their little trio annoyed.

"You did what?" Vlad.

"I wrote Anica four days ago and told her she could come back." That was Sorin.

"Jakium just came yesterday."

"So I preempted you. I'm sure Anica won't hold it against you, at least not for long."

Ren happened to look at Ani to catch something heart-twistingly sad skim across her face. She didn't seem to notice his gaze, watching the doorway.

"Why did you do that?"

"Because it didn't make sense to have her there any longer and I know she would rather be here."

"You gave me Ani years ago, Sorin," Vlad said, voice dropping, although it still carried clearly into Ren's room. "Don't think you can just take her back now." Ani tensed, almost seeming to press herself closer to Ren.

"I didn't say that." If Ren didn't know better, he would have thought Sorin sounded defensive. "I just wrote her a letter, Vladimir, get over it."

The pair appeared in the doorway.

"You should shut the door when you come in here," Vlad said to Ani.

"Welcome back," Sorin said, his look spelling incredible patience.

Ani launched herself off Ren's lap at long last and threw her arms around first Vlad and then Sorin. "Hi, Vlad! Hi, Sunshine!" Her nickname for Sorin never failed to make Ren want to laugh. Sorin awkwardly returned the gesture and Ren smirked. Her half-brother broke the hug quickly and stepped back. Ani grinned at both of them. "Anyway, Renny's not going anywhere. You've always got someone watching the door."

Ren's face tightened in a combination of anger and humiliation. Vlad laughed. "Remembering the first and only time you tried that, Ren?"

"I learned my lesson," he said stiffly.

"Of course you did!" Ani said brightly, bounding back to sit on the arm of his chair and rested her elbow on his head. "My Ren's very smart."

Ren made a slight face and patted her gingerly on the shoulder. "Since when was I yours?"

"I think you were screwed on that front the first time you met," Sorin pointed out dryly from where he leaned against the doorjamb, arms crossed.

"He's got a point," Ani agreed, beaming down at him.

"I'm…not sure how to respond to that."

"Best just leave it at that, Renny," Vlad said.

"Don't call me Renny," he said with a fierceness that surprised him. "It's only fine from Ani." She actually had asked way back after it had slipped out the first time. He could tell she didn't mean anything by it, unlike Vlad, and had consented. Now he was used to it from her.

"Oh really?" Vlad said.

Ren regarded him levelly. Sorin might drive him wild, but Vlad pushed his buttons much quicker.

"Best leave it alone, Vladimir. I think he means it," Sorin said, expression giving nothing away. "So let's leave the nicknames to Anica, and Ren to some peace and quiet while we chat."

This time, Ren felt Ani tense at her full name, something about her definitely screaming unhappiness for that split second. He frowned as he tried to decide if she had ever had that reaction before. He hadn't come to a conclusion when Ani patted him on the head. "I'll be back soon. Have fun while I'm gone!"

"I'll do my best," he said dryly.

She flashed him another grin and then bounced out the door after her older brothers. Ren watched them go, wincing slightly as the lock clicked into place, more an automatic reaction than anything.

He stayed in his chair for a long time, still clutching his forgotten book, trying to decipher Ani's odd reactions to her name, Sorin's possibly true deductions about his hidden sibling, and, a thought that often hit him at random times: a curiosity about why he was still alive that he didn't want to pick at too hard. Because there was a logical conclusion. And he didn't like it.

Chapter Six

ONCE AGAIN, I CUT OFF AT THE SOUND of approaching footsteps. David twisted to look over his shoulder. I spotted them at the same time he scooted back to Stella's side. "It's those three men from yesterday," he whispered, eyes wide.

Jay and I looked at each other and then I stood, watching them as they came. Shorty smirked as he opened the door. "Your turn," he sneered.

As they moved to grab me, I slid past, shrugging out of their grasp. The injuries from my almost death had left me with a slight limp for a while, a reaction to being injured more than out of actual necessity. But it had become such a habit that I often defaulted to it. Now, though, I straightened to my full height - taller than Shorty, much smaller than the brutes - and raised my chin the way Virginia had taught me. Then I started to stroll down the hall.

I could feel Shorty's attention on my back before I heard him scurry after me.

Jay's quiet chuckle echoed after us as we headed down the hall. A short walk later, Shorty gestured me into a small, windowless room containing a single door. As soon as I was inside, the thugs grabbed my shoulders and spun me around to face the door as another man entered. For at least a minute, the two of us appraised the other. I had no doubt this one was the head of the prison at the very least and possibly higher ranked than that. Shorty left the room, pulling the door shut behind him.

"Well, you already have me intrigued," he said, smiling with all his teeth. "That walk screams of nobility." He looked me up and down again before meeting my eyes. "Let's start with an easy one. What's your name?"

I couldn't help the small, amused grin that slipped onto my face. If he thought that one was easy, I couldn't wait until we got to the difficult stuff. "Jack," I replied blandly, thinking of Reardon.

He rolled his eyes. "And where did you learn to walk like that?"

"Same place I learned to walk at all," I said.

He opened his mouth and then shut it again, eyeing me curiously. "I was about to accuse you of being difficult, but I suppose, in a way, you answered that question quite truthfully, just not the way I'd meant it. That, in of itself, is very interesting indeed."

I was not a fan of the knowing look on his face and I had to actively work to squash the first stirrings of nerves. It immediately got worse.

"Get her out of her shirt," he ordered. "I want to see the extent of the scarring."

I struggled as best I could, but the brutes were both quite a bit larger and stronger than I was. Shortly, I stood pinned and half-naked. I glared full-force at him as his eyes widened and he let out a low whistle. "Extensive indeed," he said. "Was it us?"

Although the scars on my scalp were mostly invisible because of my hair, those on my torso, arms and legs were still as vivid as the day my bandages had come off. It was these he studied. "What do you think?" I asked flatly.

He grinned. "So, how did we do it?"

I stared at him as evenly as I could, distantly aware that I was shaking, although whether out of cold or fury, I couldn't say.

He reached towards a particularly deep one on my side. I jerked back into one of the thugs. "Don't," I warned.

He cocked his head. "Or what?"

"Trust me," I said, voice brimming with anger, "you won't like the consequences."

"I'll take my chances," he said, taking his eyes off mine as he again stretched out a hand.

I pressed back against the brute holding me, watching his hand creep closer. Then something in me snapped.

My vision cleared, brain actively processing again, a few seconds, minutes, sometime later and I discovered, with no little surprise, that I had my hands around the man's throat. I sat on top of him, banging his head into the wooden floor. As my brain continued to clear, I became aware of him screaming for the guards. I paused, more than a bit unnerved by my reaction. Granted, few people had ever seen my scars and even fewer had touched them. Still.

He used my pause to secure his grip on my arms and roll onto his side, thrusting me from him. I rolled a few feet and then went to get up, not sure what to do next. That dilemma was solved for me as he screamed, "Grab her!"

While I was still regaining my balance – both mentally and physically – the guards caught me by the arms and slammed me, face first, into the wall. My eyes crossed and the world went a bit crooked. Before I could recover, they threw me across the hallway. I hit the ground and skidded a few feet before bouncing against the far wall with enough force to further drive the breath from my body. I could feel the burn from fresh scraps as I lay there, trying to both figure out what had happened and catch my breath. I determined the former well before I managed the latter.

Somehow, the two of us had slammed into the door with enough force to splinter the area surrounding the knob. I mentally whistled in surprise before the guards reached me again and jerked me back to my feet. One of them twisted my arm back behind me, pinning me in place unless I wanted to snap my own limb. My sense of self-preservation kept me still.

My victim got back to his feet, satisfied that I was under control. He looked a bit worse for wear – one of his eyes was already blackening and he was bleeding from multiple head wounds. I suspected it was his back that had gone through the door, so that probably was spectacularly bruised as well. He moved forward, eyes narrowed as he regarded me. "Remind me to try a less painful way to get that out of you in the future," he said before, without warning, planting his fist deep into my stomach. I gasped as the guard kept me upright. He swiped at some blood that threatened to drip into his eyes. "I want you to remember one thing when you go back to your cell," he said quietly.

"What's that?" I managed.

"That your fate lies in my hands. Every day you live is at my whim, under my orders. I would tread carefully and think about your answers and reactions to my questions. Who's Brighton?"

His question threw me completely off-guard and I blinked owlishly at him.

He favored me with a bloody smile. "Well, I'll admit, you're better than many. Most people would have answered that without thought."

"Where'd you get that name?" I said, angry at myself now. I had made it altogether too clear that I knew a Brighton.

"It's what you screamed at me while you were trying to crush my head," he said dryly.

I winced. "If you must know, he was a close friend who your employers murdered."

"I had guessed that," he said, but looked surprised I'd supplied him with any information regardless. "If you'll answer that, then do you feel like answering your name truthfully?"

"You wish."

He only stared at me until I squirmed, uncomfortable with his scrutiny, and one of the brutes shifted. "Colonel Rees?" he grunted, to my surprise. I'd kind of thought the pair of muscle weren't smart enough to manage speech. It also took a second before I recognized the name. Colonel Rees was in command of the entire city and here he was questioning me.

The colonel stirred and then nodded. "Take her back to her cell," he ordered before looking at me. "We'll continue this soon."

"Great," I said and then gritted my teeth as the brutes twisted my arm even further back and marched me to our cell. Shorty was there and he opened the door, shoving me as hard as he could as soon as the door was open. Luckily, Stella caught me from falling on the unyielding packed dirt – I'd already done that enough today – and David scooped up my shirt, which one of the three had grudgingly thrown in too.

As soon as they were gone, I tugged my shirt back on over my head.

"Okay," Jay said slowly, "something must have happened. You're bleeding all over and, at least with me, our lovely interrogator stuck to fists."

"I think I might have won round one against good Colonel Rees."

"How do you figure that?"

I forced a smirk, even though I was shaken by the entire thing. "He's definitely bleeding more than I am."

Jay stared at me. "What did you *do*?"

"He tried to touch my scars after I warned him not to. I lost it and taught him that that was a very bad idea."

"Okay, this requires more explanation. Details, please!"

I briefly sketched out my encounter with Rees and Jay whistled. "You say you've only done that one other time."

I nodded.

"Bri's death?"

"Yeah." I kept my answer short, not particularly wanting to discuss that, even if I would have to when we got there in the story. I carefully settled myself down, grimacing as my body protested. While none of the injuries were serious, I was good and battered.

"They brought breakfast while you were gone. We saved you some although it's probably cold," Stella said.

I smiled gratefully, accepting the bowl. "Thanks." I gobbled it down, barely noticing the temperature. I doubted it had been all that warm to start with, considering previous fare. Setting the bowl down, I shifted to try and get more comfortable. My back and side burned from being tossed around the corridor. Luckily, an easy distraction presented itself. "Shall I continue?" I asked.

"Yes!" David said and then tried to look like he didn't really care.

I squashed a smile, took a second to remember where I had left off, and then continued.

◀ ▼ ▶

"Beau?"

He started, glancing over his shoulder before relaxing, smiling faintly. "Oh, hi, Jez. What's up?"

"I should be asking the same of you. You're looking very serious," she said, coming to sit beside him on top of Cavern Hall. Something about Beau put her at ease even though they hadn't talked much one-on-one. Perhaps it was the fact that he knew who she was, or at least, who she had been. It also might have been that small smile that appeared rarely, but was so heartfelt. Right now, that smile was miles away.

"I look serious a lot," he pointed out, but that typical amused tone was absent too.

"You're looking serious for you," she reiterated, rolling her eyes at him. "What is it?"

"Just thinking."

"About?"

"Is there a reason you came up here?"

Jez grinned. "To think."

"About?" She noticed he seemed unable to resist returning the grin.

"How old are you, Beau?"

"Twenty-one," he said. "Why do you ask?"

"Because you look a lot younger when you grin."

"Do I look old when I don't?"

She chuckled. "No, but quite a bit old*er*."

"I suppose I'll buy that."

"You had better since it's the truth."

He snorted. "Thanks then." They fell silent and the smile almost immediately vanished from Beau's face.

"What is it?" Jez tried again.

The captain stared out into the woods for a very long moment, so long Jez wasn't sure if he'd heard her. "The attack on the dukes was the first big attack by our unknown enemies, as you well know. That being said, it'll probably be less than a year now before they take control."

"And you're positive they'll win?" she asked quietly. She knew the answer, but she had to ask again, for Colin, for the prince, for everyone who would be – and already had been - hurt by what was coming.

He nodded. "Yes." Beau shook his head, a faint, bitter smile appearing on his face. "What a waste my life will have been if they don't, though."

Jez frowned. She wanted to ask, but reassuring him was more important. "It will not have been a waste at all, Beau, and don't you dare convince yourself it has been. Look how many people you've given a second chance after it seemed that everything had been taken from them and they had nothing left. This enemy has already destroyed the lives of so many, but you've helped a group of people salvage something. Look at me, I'd literally be dead if it wasn't for you. I'm on life number two, Beau. A second life is not an opportunity that gets thrown your way very often and it's not something I'll be forgetting in a hurry."

He looked at her in surprise. "I'd…I'd never thought of it that way."

"Well, maybe you should have," she said lightly.

Beau nodded slowly. "I can't help but wonder sometimes. Just…I've spent practically my entire life preparing for this and now it's almost here. Will I be up to the task? Will we? We might very well end up being the only hope Tira has left."

"We'll have to rise to the occasion, now won't we?" Jez said, half-smiling.

He matched it. "I suppose we will." He hesitated and then, "Do you think we can?"

"I know we can," she told him, but could understand his doubt. He had been deep in all this for so long, it could easily cloud judgment. "And so do you."

"I'm sorry. I can't help wondering sometimes. There's still so few of us and it's such a big task."

"Nothing wrong with it, Beau, but remember, you do have friends and we're more than willing to listen and give you the necessary ego boost when needed."

Beau smiled that small smile of his again. "Thanks, Jez, seriously."

"And you know that Bri is wonderful at ego boosts."

He actually laughed, which she considered a serious success. "Brighton thinks he's wonderful at everything!"

"Glad to hear you agree, Beau," Bri said cheerfully as he climbed up to join them. Bri wasn't just rubbing off on Jez. Referring to Beau without the captain honorific was wearing off on her friends too.

"You always need to get that word in edgewise, don't you?"

"Of course," he agreed, shooting them his most charming smile. "So, Beau, I believe I heard you need an ego boost."

"No, I think my ego is just fine now, thank you."

Bri sulked. "But I wanted to help!" he whined.

Jez laughed. "Later, Bri, later."

A night later, Beau found himself sitting with the four friends for dinner after Jez invited him. She thought it might be good for him to see things from their perspective. And she wanted him to truly know he had friends too.

"You know what I think?" Bri asked out of the blue.

"It's often impossible not to know what you're thinking," Beau told him dryly.

"Yet just as often impossible to have any clue how his brain works," Jessie threw in.

Bri sighed. "You people have no appreciation of my genius."

"You can say that again," Ry murmured.

"Jez," he said, appealing to his girlfriend, "you appreciate my genius, don't you?" In the time since the kiss, which had been almost two months now, the pair had quietly made it official.

"Of course," she said, which wasn't exactly a lie. She did appreciate a lot of things about Bri, including his unusual way of thinking. Sometimes, though, it was a bit much.

Beau snorted. "You are such a liar, Jez."

She stuck her tongue out at him. "Stop exposing me, Beau, or I won't invite you to sit with us for meals anymore."

"So what were you thinking?" Ry said quickly.

"I was thinking," here Bri paused and frowned, "I don't remember what I was thinking."

All four groaned. "Brighton, you have to have some inkling," Jessie said.

"I don't, though."

"Think hard?" Beau tried.

He screwed up his face in thought and then suddenly grinned. "I got it!"

"What is it?"

"No, no, now I've lost it again. Jessica, you distracted me."

"Brighton Dall, if you don't tell me what you were thinking right now, or at least make something feasible up, I will cause you pain," she said.

"She looks pretty serious," Ry added.

Bri thought about it for a minute. "That's it! Let's play hide and seek!"

"Hide and seek?" Jez repeated.

"Yeah, and Beau has to play."

"I do?"

"Yes," he said firmly before hopping up. "Let's go!"

"Have we agreed to this?" Jessie asked.

"Of course! You love every last thing I suggest and you know it, Jessie."

Beau and Jez exchanged glances as the other two girls got up. "This has the potential to end badly."

"Tell Mick to kill Bri and not us when it does," Jez replied dryly.

Beau eyed Bri as he skipped out of the dining area. "I think I will," he said. "Do I really have to participate in this?"

She grinned. "That would definitely be a yes."

Beau sighed. "Fine."

The four followed him, finding Bri outside, bouncing with impatience. "Okay! Jessie'll count first. And you are all playing," he added, giving each of them a look.

"We said we would. Jessie, guess you've been nominated. Start counting."

"Are there any rules?"

"No hiding where you're going to get in someone's way and no hiding outside. We need to confine the shenanigans to the inside area," Beau said.

"Deal. One," Jessie said loudly, turning her back to them as she did.

As it turned out, Beau was by far the best at hiding, but Jez figured later that that shouldn't have come as a surprise to any of them, considering he'd spent all of his life in hiding. The game lasted until dinner, when the five had finally found Bri in the last round. He'd actually hidden in the food storage room, which, upon reflection, should have been the first place they'd looked. They came into the dining room, laughing over the weird expressions they'd gotten from the people who had ended up, for whatever reason, caught in the middle of their game at some point. Mick took one look at Beau's flushed, amused face, shook his head, and actually smiled. The expression made Jez want to dance for joy. It seemed the second-in-command actually appreciated their attempts to distract Beau from his job.

"This is stupid," Vladimir muttered.

Sorin shrugged. "It makes sense tactically for them to attack our borders. We're still the weakest link around here."

"That doesn't make it any less stupid," Vlad grumped, clearly not amused by Sorins's attempt at logic. Sorin rolled his eyes as Vlad turned to Ani. "Ani, anything to add? A report on how things went on your mission?"

It was with no surprise to Sorin that she had been unsuccessful, both because of Ani's personality and the Freedom Fighters themselves. "It wasn't a mission, it was an exile," Sorin muttered and smirked at Vlad's dark look.

Ani didn't seem to hear either of them, staring out the window.

"Ani?"

"What?" she asked, finally looking up.

"Were you paying attention at all?" Sorin asked.

"Nope," she said, with no apology. He squashed a smile.

"You, us, report?" Vlad said, sounding exasperated.

"Oh. What do you want other than it didn't work? I never even got a bite." She turned back to the window and began humming under her breath.

Vlad turned to Sorin. "Can't you do something about...?" He gestured at their sister.

"I believe you were the one earlier who said, and I quote, 'You gave me Ani years ago. Don't think you can just take her back now.'" He kept his voice low, hoping Ani hadn't heard either his response now or Vlad's from earlier.

His brother scowled. "Fine. Anica," he said loudly.

She jumped, turning to look at them. "No need to yell," she said. "I'm listening." She had not been but neither pointed it out.

"Look, I know you just got to see Ren again, but I need you to focus for a few minutes, okay?"

"I heard you," she said and, for a split second, Sorin thought he saw something sharp and calculating in her gaze. He suspected he was right.

Vlad missed it, as he always had. Ani's perpetually cheerful act had fooled him for years. "Good. Anyway, we all need to really focus. Alyia and Nerius are still biting at our borders and there is a lot of day-to-day work that needs to be done here. That means we all need to pitch in."

"Don't forget the Freedom Fighters," Sorin added.

Vlad dismissed that with a wave of his hand. "I'm not unduly worried. We can deal with them when the time comes."

Sorin, again, debated whether or not to mention his theory on a younger Highcastle and decided that later would be better.

"If you're so worried, Sorin," he added, inaccurately reading his brother's expression, "I'll put defending against them in your capable hands."

I wouldn't if I were you, but... "Fine," Sorin said aloud.

"I can help, but can I marry Renny first?"

He could audibly hear Vladimir grinding his teeth, so he made himself step in. "No, Anica, you cannot marry Ren yet. Not until the borders are secure and we've gotten rid of the Freedom Fighters. So try to be patient and content yourself with picking on him. I've explained this to you before."

She pouted at him. "I don't pick on him."

Sorin adopted a blatant look of skepticism.

"He likes it," she muttered.

"That being true or not, can we try and stay on topic?" Vlad interrupted.

"I'd prefer if I could get back to work instead of running around in circles with you," Sorin said. "I have a lot of important things to do."

"I'll need suggestions to take Ani's place."

"I can do that. Send Jakium to me later and I'll give you a list." At Vlad's acknowledgement, Sorin nodded to both and left.

It was no surprise that Vladimir appeared in the doorway of his office about an hour later. "Sorin?"

"Vladimir."

"Got a moment?"

"I suppose. How can I help you?"

Vlad came in and settled himself into one of the extra chairs across from Sorin's desk. "You went and talked to Ren yesterday."

Sorin's eyes narrowed. "Is that a crime?" he asked.

"What did you talk about?"

"I fail to see how that is any of your business."

"You've spent the better part of a week researching who the leader of the Freedom Fighters could be and then you go and talk to Ren about that precise subject."

The hairs on the back of Sorin's neck prickled and he absently rubbed them flat. "You were spying on my conversation with the prince? If that's what all this has come to, then the Freedom Fighters have already won."

Vlad made a gesture dismissing his comment as quickly as he had dismissed the Freedom Fighters earlier. "What did you two talk about?"

Sorin eyed him and decided he would let it slide for now. "All my evidence is pointing towards the fact that Patrick Highcastle had a second child, who is now in charge of the Freedom Fighters."

"You think the leader is a Highcastle? How?"

It only took a minute or two to outline it much as he had with Ren the previous day.

When he was finished, Vlad sat back in his chair. "I suppose this does make them a threat."

"Vladimir, they have been a threat since our first encounter with them. That has not changed with time."

His brother's eyes flashed. "I should probably go make sure Ani is not creating any mischief," he said, smirking.

Sorin turned his eyes to his desk. "You probably should," he said, refusing to rise to the not-so-subtle dig.

"Find her a task, will you?"

"I thought she wasn't my job anymore."

For an instant, silence reigned, each acknowledging the jab.

"Just do it," Vladimir said finally as he stood and swept from the room.

Sorin looked up again to watch him go, rubbing again at the back of his neck.

Chapter Seven

My throat was dry from all the storytelling so I paused, taking a drink of the water saved from breakfast. David pressed into Stella's side. "You're allowed to take breaks, you know," he said, in that sage way only a kid could manage.

I smiled at him. "Thanks, David."

"It's Dave. Only Stella calls me David."

"That's a sister's right," I told him. There was no mistaking the pair as anything but – same flaming red hair and blue eyes. "My older brother, Jonathan, prefers Jon and I always called him Jonathan anyway."

"Well," Dave said slyly, "what about half-sisters?"

"You're only half-siblings?" Jay asked in surprise as I laughed.

"It still counts," I said.

"My father died shortly after I was born," Stella said. "Mama remarried a few years later and eventually had David. David's father ran afoul of the Three's men shortly after they took power."

The boy snuggled even closer to Stella. "Yeah, George, that's our older brother, he took care of the family after Dad died." Then he scowled. "Until they killed him too."

"How did you two end up here?" Jay asked, the very question I had on my mind.

"George was working for the Freedom Fighters, apparently," Stella said with a heavy sigh, "but he wanted to protect David, Mama, and me, so he didn't tell any of us." Her face tightened for a minute as she looked down at her brother's head. This all made unfortunate sense to me. Beau's tiny network of the early days had expanded to a complicated system that spread across all of Tira and involved dozens upon dozens of people who didn't live at the second incarnation Cavern Hall or our other location. "Didn't do us any good when they showed up to kill him."

Dave bit his lip, taking her hand. "They came at night," he said in a small voice. "They thought Mama was George…"

Stella squeezed it. "George had just told me what was going on earlier that night. He was planning on making a run for it, banking on the idea that without him there, we'd be safe. It turned out not to matter, but he went to try and hold them off while I took David. They cut us off, though, and…" She shrugged. "I had an old sword of Frank's, that's David's dad, and he had a knife and…things happened," she finished as Dave shuddered, closing his eyes.

Jay winced. "He…"

She nodded. "We were both inexperienced, though, obviously, so they got us by catching David and shipped us off here."

Dave's shoulders hunched. "I wasn't big enough to fight them off," he said fiercely. "It's not fair! Why'd they have to kill them? George was only working against them cuz they killed Papa."

"No, Dave, it's not fair," I said. "But the Three doesn't seem particularly interested in what is fair, just what they want. They gain some of their power through people's fear of doing anything but what they're told to do. That's why those of us who can fight back do."

"Aren't you ever scared?" he asked.

"Sometimes. I'm scared people will get hurt. People I care about or even people I don't know as a result of my actions." I leaned in, dropping my voice. "I'm also scared Jay might get bored enough he starts flirting with me."

Dave giggled despite himself. "Jez," he complained, "I'm being serious."

"So am I, mostly. Some things do scare me, but someone needs to fight. I got nominated for that a long time ago and now anything else wouldn't feel right."

The boy thought about that for a minute. "I think I understand. I know I'm too small to fight, but I would do anything I could to make sure the Freedom Fighters win," he said stoutly.

"That's the spirit," Jay said. "What the Three don't seem to understand is that each time they've hurt lives, they've helped create people who have nothing left to lose, like the four of us. And we'll stop at nothing until they're gone and Tira is safe again."

I reached out and ruffled Dave's hair. "It'll never be quite right again, but someday it will get closer."

"You won't let them win, right?" he asked, patting it down again good-naturedly.

"No way, no how," I promised.

His face fell again. "Except we're all gonna hang."

"Don't give up hope yet," Jay said. "We've got some time and our friends will do everything in his power to get us back out."

"How did you end up here?"

I figured turnabout was fair play in this case. "Well, they don't like people they catch blowing up a garrison and potentially inciting a riot."

His eyes went wide. "*You* caused the big boom right before they brought you in?"

Jay grinned in satisfaction. "Boom," he agreed with relish.

I kicked him in the shin, chuckling. "Yes, that was us."

The boy thought about it for a minute and then turned to me. "I think it's time to continue the story so we can get to the part about explosions!"

I stood and stretched briefly, not wanting my muscles to completely lock up. "Sure. Where was I?"

"You and the others had just played hide and seek!"

I settled back in and let out a breath. "Then, I suppose the next thing was the announcement that the Three had made their move, giving us names."

Four days later, the friends were camped in various locations around Beau's desk. It was a fairly quiet afternoon and they were doing their best to help him get through all the messages and paperwork so they could play another quick round of hide and seek before dinner. Some, not surprisingly, were doing more work than others. Bri pegged Jez, yet again, in the side of the head with a balled up piece of paper.

"Stop," she said.

He hit her with another.

"Brighton," she growled as she looked up and got one square in the nose. "That's it, I'm going to kill you," she said, struggling to get to her feet without dislodging a million papers and making a mess of the place.

Before she could finish, Mick was in the doorway. "Beau," he said, voice filled with such an unusual emotion for him that Jez couldn't immediately place it. Sadness? Apology?

Instantly, the room went silent as all eyes turned their way. Beau bit his lip, looking what could only be described as lost. "It happened?"

"This morning. Word just reached us. Understandably, things have been…" Mick trailed off as Ry let out a quiet gasp.

"The king and prince?"

"Both reported dead."

"And our new rulers?"

"A sibling trio. Vladimir and Anica Opalin and their half-brother, Sorin Dakamar."

Again, silence descended.

"Well," Bri said finally, completely serious for once, "I guess that means our job officially began."

That seemed to spur Beau back into action and he straightened. "Mick, I want to know as much about these three as possible and I want detailed reports from everywhere they hit as soon as possible too. I'll make an announcement at dinner. In the meantime, we'll start writing messages to our contacts and see how many we can get out tonight. Check if anyone knows anything about them."

"Beau," Mick said sternly.

"I'm fine," the captain said. "We knew this was going to happen."

"Knowing and *knowing* are two different things."

"Not now," Beau said fiercely as the other four exchanged glances, not entirely sure what to make of this conversation.

Mick nodded, but he didn't look happy. "Fine," he said. "I'll get things moving."

As soon as he was gone, Beau looked at the others apologetically. "I don't have time for hide and seek, but…"

"Beau," Jez said, already exasperated with his attempt, "what do you need us to do?"

He smiled gratefully, outlined what he needed, and the five friends got to work.

The repercussions of the newly dubbed Three's takeover rippled throughout all their work for days and weeks. Jez's heart seized when she learned Northwind had been taken by force and the ruling family, who Colin worked for, had been killed along with a lot of their soldiers. There was no direct word on her brother, but she had to assume the worst. Most of the rest of the country had gone down without a fight, primed by the assassinations Jez had found herself in the middle of among many other small actions. Since Ellworth was close, they did get word that Elladan was alive but imprisoned and the rest of his family under house arrest. Jez's heart ached for Virginia. She hoped her friend would stay safe until the Freedom Fighters were strong enough to act.

On the lucky side, what contacts they had with the outside world all seemed to escape. And, in those following weeks, the network actually doubled. Not everyone who wanted to help was in a position to move to Cavern Hall and just as many were willing to leverage the fact they weren't being watched to help the cause. Beau mentioned a new recruit in Bejen who had already stepped up to coordinate the region about two weeks after the coup.

In all, it was only just starting to settle down when Jez turned nineteen, marking almost a year at Cavern Hall.

"Jez! Jez, darling, dear, wonderful, beautiful."

Jez blinked sleepily up at Bri, who was crouched next to her, grinning widely. "What? S'too early, Bri. Go 'way."

"Now, it that any way to treat your boyfriend who's getting you up for a very special day?"

She frowned. "What very special day?" Jez asked, yawning as she sat up, rubbing her eyes.

"Jez, it's your birthday. You're nineteen today."

"It's my birthday?" she echoed, doing some mental math before brightening. "It is!"

He snorted. "I wouldn't just make up a date. Beau told me."

"Sorry, Bri, I *do* appreciate you," she said, giving him a quick hug and making a mental note to thank Beau. "Did you have to get me up so early, though?"

Not surprisingly, he ignored her. "Can I sing to you?" he asked.

"I'd rather you passed."

"Oh, but my voice is like blooming flowers on a warm summer morn."

Jez snorted. "Oh, Gods' Breath, Bri. Why do I doubt that?" At his hurt expression, she smiled and kissed him. "How about you sing later?" she suggested, just to get rid of that look.

He instantly perked up. "Awesome! C'mon, Beau and Mick have cooked a birthday breakfast for us. Just them, us, Jessie, and Ry cuz everyone else is asleep."

"Of course everyone else is asleep!"

"Let's go," he said impatiently.

Jez changed quickly before they hiked down to the kitchen.

"Happy birthday, Jez!" Jessie called as soon as they entered the room.

Jez grinned widely. "I completely forgot, but you didn't. Thank you so much!"

Beau looked up from where he was finishing setting the table. "What else would we do? Especially for you, considering who you united," he said with a nod at the other three.

She laughed at him. "I don't know. Throw me out?"

He grinned back. "It's always an option."

"You wouldn't do that to me, would you, Beau? Huh? Buddy? Pal?"

Mick snorted, rolling his eyes.

"Of course not, Bri. I'd throw you both out, obviously," Beau said.

Bri blinked before nodding in approval. "Touché."

"Hey!" Ry came bursting into the room, her face wreathed in a happy smile. "Happy birthday, Jez! You're now officially safe from Iris," she announced as she hugged her older friend. Everyone laughed before Ry's grin widened even further. "Guess what?"

"What?" Mick asked.

"It's snowing!"

"Really?" Beau asked in surprise. "Isn't it a bit early in the year?"

Ry shrugged. "A bit, but that doesn't change the fact it's snowing. They're nice big puffy flakes too. Perfect for playing in!"

"There's your birthday planned for you," Bri said.

"Let's eat first though," Beau said. "Don't want all this food to go to waste."

"Of course not," Jez said, seating herself. The six of them settled into the table and chatted as they ate, steering clear of anything serious.

"We're sorry we couldn't get you any real presents, Jez," Jessie said. "So Ry and I collaborated to draw you a picture." Ry handed it over. Jez blushed, but also started laughing. Bri glanced over her shoulder and his cheeks also tinged red.

"It's our take on your first kiss," Ry said, her grin wide.

"Can I see?" Beau asked. Jez handed it over wordlessly and Beau bit his lip to keep from laughing at them. It showed Bri dipping Jez while kissing her - the funny part was the bright red color of Jez's face, the faces peeking in the doorway laughing, obviously him, Jessie, Ry, and Mick, and the fact that Bri was dressed in a very skimpy looking spotted outfit.

He shook his head, passing it on to Mick, who snorted. "I certainly hope we don't have the outfit Bri's got on in the picture lying around."

Jessie grinned in response, causing him to raise an eyebrow.

"I am not going to ask."

"Good idea," Ry said as she swallowed her last bite of food. "C'mon, let's go play in the snow!"

Jez shoveled down her last couple bites and turned to Mick and Beau. "Are you coming?"

Mick made a face. "No, thank you. Getting wet and cold is not my idea of fun." She rolled her eyes. Beau hesitated before also declining on account of too much work.

Jez waited until everyone else had left before hugging Beau. "Thanks for breakfast and for remembering," she told him.

72

"You're welcome."

"You sure you don't want to come?" she asked again.

He shook his head. "No, I really should do some work."

"You work too much," she said lightly.

Beau snorted. "Probably, but that's what I get for being in charge."

"Which is why it's our job to take care of you," she said. "But, if you're sure, I should probably get going. The others are going to be rioting already."

"Yeah, you should. Go have fun."

Jez nodded and turned to leave.

"Hey, Jez." She turned back around, a questioning look on her face. "Thanks."

She paused, cocking her head at him. "For what?" she asked, puzzled.

Beau pressed his lips together, as if searching for the words he wanted. "For...just for everything you've done for all of us."

Her face blossomed into a smile. "I haven't done anything."

"You'd be surprised, Jez, really. Even Mick commented on it."

She laughed. "I somehow doubt that, but, since you insist, I'll accept the thanks."

"Jez! Come on!" The call echoed down the hallways. They were going to start waking people up.

She glanced over her shoulder and jerked a thumb towards the entrance. "I should get going, they're waiting for me."

"Yeah, go before they wake everyone up. Have fun and happy birthday!"

Jez paused at the entrance to wave at him before disappearing.

"Were we sneaking a few extra bites, beautiful?" Bri asked.

She smacked him. "So what if I was?"

He shrugged. "Respect."

"That's better," Jez told him.

"Hurry up already," Ry said impatiently, pulling a hat down over her ears. Jez quickly threw on a hat and mittens and the four of them piled out the entranceway. She paused just outside and smiled, catching a snowflake on her tongue. Surprisingly, there was already an inch on the ground - pretty unusual for November - and it was still coming down in large flakes that gently coasted to the ground. Beau was right. It wouldn't stay. The weather would get too warm to keep it on the ground, but they could enjoy it while it lasted.

"What are you waiting for, Jez? C'mon," Jessie called, already lying back in the snow, making an imprint of herself. With a wide grin, Jez hurried over to join them. The three girls were starting to try and shape their snow imprints to actually look like people when something hit Jez in the back of the head, something very cold and wet.

"Brighton!" she yelped, turning around to see her boyfriend standing a few paces away, an innocent look pasted on his face as he whistled carelessly.

"Yes, darling?" The return snowball caught him square in the chest. "Hey!" he protested, as if he had any leg to stand on. He scooped up a pile of snow and dumped it on her. She collapsed into giggles before grabbing him, dragging him down into the snow, and sitting on him. "What are you going to do, huh, Jez?" he teased.

She grinned widely, grabbed his shirt collar, and started trying to stuff snow down it.

"Hey!" he yelped again before finally managing to tip Jez over and roll on top of her. She felt a distinct wave of pleasure at how long she'd managed to keep him down despite his larger size. The fighting lessons were paying off in more ways than one. "Got you."

"Do not," she retorted before attempting to shove more snow at him. The two rolled around, trying to see who could get more snow on the other. It was only broken up when Jessie grabbed Bri and Ry grabbed Jez and each shoved a handful of snow down their shirts. "Ry!" Jez squawked as she squirmed to loosen it.

"That's cold! Cold, cold, *cold*!" Bri hissed, scrambling up and then dancing around shaking his shirt. Ry collapsed into a fit of giggles. The couple finally recovered and shot each other a glance before pouncing. Jessie was caught in the side of the head with the first snowball. Ry, a second later, got hit with her own. They froze in surprise, looking at Bri and Jez, both of whom grinned widely and fired off a second shot. Ry ducked, but Jessie wasn't so lucky, getting hit again. Almost immediately, they were involved in an all-out snowball war. At first, it was Jessie and Ry versus Jez and Bri, but Jez couldn't resist hitting Bri with one when he wasn't looking. From there, the teams rapidly disintegrated.

The four friends finally collapsed into the snow, still giggling and very soaked. Jez reached over with a handful of snow and playfully rubbed it into Bri's hair, causing it to stand straight up.

"Look!" he said, "I'm my own snow sculpture."

"Don't tempt me, Brighton," Jez replied, waving a second fistful of snow over top of him.

"Now would I do that?" he asked, voice dripping with innocence.

"Probably," Ry said.

Jez laughed, attention diverted for a moment. Bri used the time to grab her hand and upend it on her. "Hey!" she yelped and would have retaliated if Jessie hadn't laughed and intervened.

"Why don't we build a snowman? You two are even anyway."

Bri and Jez eyed each other before he rolled over and kissed her firmly on the mouth. "We're even," he announced.

Jez grinned widely. "We're even," she said to snickers from the other two. They all got up, brushing themselves off, before collaborating to make a couple snowmen. They weren't very large, especially since they'd spread the closest snow everywhere, but they were cute.

They headed back inside shortly after that, breathless after another furious snowball fight Ry had started by 'accidentally' failing to put a snowman head on properly. Instead, it had somehow ended up splatting into Bri's back. He'd thrown an entirely different mini snowman at her and things had quickly fallen apart from there. Jez had a huge grin on her face.

At dinner, Bri jumped onto the top of the dinner table, sang a song about her birthday, and then dragged Jez up to kiss her soundly amidst rousing applause for the kiss and *not* the song.

They ended the day, just the two of them. They retreated to the storage room they used for sword practice. "Thanks for today. It was really wonderful, Bri."

"It was a group effort," he said, which was surprisingly modest for him.

She raised her eyebrows at him.

"Oh. I meant, why thank you! I planned and plotted and worked at this for days. Had to arrange the snow and the snowman sneak attack and-"

She clamped a hand over his mouth, laughing. "All right, all right, I get the idea! Still, thank you."

75

"I haven't given you my present," he reminded her.

"Present?" she repeated. She assumed the day was the present. Plus her little illustration from Jessie and Ry.

He beamed. "Yup! Stay right here and I'll go get it." He slipped out from underneath her and skipped out the door. Puzzled, she smiled to herself and, very shortly, he was back, quite obviously hiding something behind his back. "I realize it isn't the most romantic birthday present ever, but I did put a bow on it." He paused for effect before pulling it out from behind his back. It was a sword with a bright pink bow – possibly the gaudiest Jez had ever seen – on it. "I asked Beau to add it to the list of things to get during the last provisioning trip. I think it's brand new. Or new enough?" he trailed off, looking anxious. "Do you like it?"

She set it out of the way and pulled him into a hug, feeling a flood of warmth at the thoughtfulness of all her friends. "It's great, Bri," she said, trying not to choke up, "and the bow really makes it."

"It does?"

Thank the gods for Bri as the urge to cry vanished and she laughed instead. "No, not really, but I appreciate the thought."

"I could try for, uh, jewelry or something next time."

"What in the world would I do with jewelry?" she asked. "This is practical and mine and I love it, just like you." She pulled him down for a kiss. "Thank you."

"It was nothing," he said, legitimately modest for once. "I just...I know it means more when it's yours, you know? And you've definitely graduated to a real one full time."

She glanced at the sword and nodded. "I do. C'mon, let's head to bed. Maybe we can break in my birthday present tomorrow." Jez bent down to pick up the sword, briefly running her fingers over it.

"I was hoping maybe we could have a replay of Jessie and Ry's present instead."

She grinned, taking his elbow as he offered it. "Even with the leopard outfit?"

"For you, I'd wear anything," he said gallantly.

"Ani, I'm trying to eat." Ren was also trying to keep his patience.

"Your point? I'm not stopping you."

"You're staring at me."

"That's not a crime."

He almost laughed at that and the unintentional irony, but decided he didn't feel like getting into it. "That may be true, but it still makes it difficult to eat."

"Aw, Renny, but I like watching you."

"I've noticed," he said dryly.

"Are you sure you can't eat while I watch you?"

Even as she asked it, Ren saw the spark of something teasing, like maybe she was riling him up on purpose and not because she just wanted to be Ani and watch him eat. His eyes narrowed and he opened his mouth to ask. "Ani-"

"I see you two are having fun."

"Vlad!" Ani rocketed out of her chair and bounded over to give Vlad a hug.

"Thank the gods," Ren muttered, briefly ignoring what he thought he'd seen, and quickly shoveling food into his mouth, hoping Vlad could keep her attention long enough for him to finish.

"How come you can eat now?" Ani asked with a bit of a pout.

"Found my appetite," he mumbled around bites and then snorted as Vlad let his head drop heavily into the doorjamb. Sometimes it was nice to know that he wasn't the only one left cold by Ani and her logic.

"That sounded like it hurt, Vlad. You should be more careful," she said, grinning happily and bouncing back to throw herself in the chair across from Ren.

Luckily, he had almost finished. "What brings you here?" he asked Vlad.

"I was looking for my sister."

"Ah. You don't happen to need her?" he asked carefully.

"Nope, as long as she's occupied," Vlad said and smirked at Ren's dirty look. "Ani, when you're done here, I'll be in my office. Come find me and we'll get you set up with a job other than following our favorite prince around his room."

Ren bristled, grip on his fork momentarily tightening before he forced it to loosen. "How very kind of you," he said, clipping each word. He wasn't even mad at Ani for it, but it still felt like a sting coming from Vlad.

"You're very welcome," Vlad said, false sincerity positively dripping from each word. "I'll see you in a bit, okay, Ani?"

"Okay, Vlad," she said and turned to Ren. "You finished!"

"Yup, afraid so," he said, swallowing his last bite.

She absorbed that, looking between the plate and his face. "If I got you more, could I watch you eat it?" This time, there was definitely *something*.

So he bit back the immediate, emphatic no. "I'm full. I just ate an entire meal."

Ani sighed. "Fine. I guess I could take your plate and go find Vlad then."

"That would probably be a good idea," he said neutrally. "Vlad's not the most patient of people."

She grinned. "He usually is around me."

"I think everyone is around you," Ren said dryly and then stiffened, watching her face, worried she might take it the wrong way – although he wasn't entirely sure how he meant it. It was getting easier and easier to be patient with Ani, though, even before he'd started to see the hints of something more behind her everlasting cheerfulness.

Thankfully, she giggled. "Good," she said, hopping to her feet, grabbing his plate, and heading for the door. "Makes life more fun," she added over her shoulder with a wink before disappearing out his door.

He sighed, sagging in his chair. In some ways, Ani was a breath of fresh air and, in others, she sapped all the energy from him. After a minute, he roused himself, standing and moving to the window. He wrapped his hands carefully around the bars that had been installed and peered out, letting his mind wander. It kept slipping back to his supposed sibling, most likely male since he was fairly certain he had heard that the head of the Freedom Fighters was male.

Finally, he rested his head against the bars. "Just as long as she doesn't start watching me sleep," he muttered.

"We're not that cruel." Sorin's voice made him jump, cracking his head against the bars.

"Ow! Gods' Breath, Sorin," he growled, turning.

Sorin smirked, looking at least a little sorry. "It's not my fault you weren't paying attention. But don't worry, I doubt Vladimir will be letting Anica watch you sleep any time soon."

"Wonderful."

"I have to admit that I'm curious. Why do you let Anica get away with everything?"

Ren rubbed the top of his head and frowned. At first, it had been because he suspected the brothers wouldn't take kindly to anything else. But that hadn't proven true either. And it wasn't why he did it. Just like letting her call him Renny. "I guess…I guess it's because she doesn't mean anything by it. None of it is an insult. She's just excited. About everything. And she tends to pout a lot if I tell her she can't."

"That's my sister for you."

The prince looked at him in surprise. "I think that's the only time I've ever heard you refer to her as your sister."

To his continued shock, Sorin favored him with a rueful smile. "For better or worse, she is. Sometimes it's better if I don't openly acknowledge it."

"Why did you write to her?"

Something twisted in this other man's expression. "Because, for some misguided reason, she loves all three of us and it was cruel to force her to stay away on a fool's errand."

"You're the only family she's got left, right?"

Sorin's gaze shifted past him, out the window. "Yes. Our mother died shortly after giving birth to her and Edward's been gone a while."

Ren had picked up enough in two years to know that Edward was Ani and Vlad's father and a nightmare to all three siblings, although he knew no details. He also knew Edward had started this whole damn bullshit. "Does it really surprise you that she loves you and Vlad?"

The other man laughed slightly, more an amused exhalation of breath than anything. "No, but it does surprise me a bit that she loves you."

"Me too," Ren said wryly, not denying it.

Sorin eyed him before nodding. "I should be getting back to work. As always, it's been a pleasure."

"Same," Ren said as Sorin turned to leave and was mildly surprised to find he meant it. He also realized they hadn't talked about anything critical, which was strange. Usually Sorin only appeared when he wanted something. Although maybe that, in of itself, was important.

Chapter Eight

DAVE GIGGLED. "You were extremely silly," he informed me.

I got up to stretch. "We were...younger. In more than just age. But not much has really changed, has it, Jay?"

My partner-in-crime matched my grin. "Not at all. Just picked up a few goofballs, and lost a couple."

"You sound like you had a lot of fun," Stella said, looking amused.

"We sort of needed to, as a stress reliever."

"Was it hard being cooped up in just the immediate area around Cavern Hall?" she asked.

"Sometimes. Most of the time we were too busy training, making plans, or goofing off to get any sort of cabin fever."

"Or flirting with cute girls," Jay threw in.

I rolled my eyes. "For you, maybe. Can't say I've ever taken part in that, nor do I want to, thanks all the same."

A wicked grin flashed across his face. "Yes, but-"

I slapped a hand over his mouth. "You do not want to finish that sentence," I said. I didn't even need to know exactly what he'd been planning on saying to know it wouldn't end well. Jay's grin widened, but he nodded, eyes falsely wide and innocent. I snorted. "Jay, I know you well enough to know that look is the biggest load of bullshit."

He laughed, prying my hand off. "You take away all my fun."

I smirked, sitting back down. "I know. How about we grab some sleep before you say something you regret and I'll continue tomorrow?"

Jay tossed me an irreverent salute. "Good plan, ma'am."

"Don't call me ma'am," I said easily as Dave leaned forward.

"Are we getting to any explosions soon?" he asked.

"Not quite, but we are almost to a battle."

"The Battle at Deepen's Crossing?" Stella asked.

I nodded. "Despite how the Three have spun it, it's the only pitched face-to-face battle we've had with them. Our other encounters have all been small skirmishes or ambushes."

She looked surprised. "Really?"

"Yeah, but we've beaten them most of the times since so they want to try and have it reflect better on them. Do you know why it's called that?"

"No," Stella said, looking curious.

I smiled. "Best to just let it come out in the story, then. Always kind of made me laugh that they dubbed it that."

"You lost Deepen's Crossing, right?" Dave now asked.

"How about you listen to the story and wait and see?" I teased.

"Because it's history, Jez," he said with all the righteousness of a child.

That stopped me cold. I guess in all the time since this mess started, I had never really stopped to think about how we were creating history. One day, our kids, or at least the next generation, since who knew what our survival rate might be, would be taught our lives in school. Even to Dave, who was right in the middle of it now, this was more story than fact. "Yes," I said slowly, "I guess it is, isn't it?"

"Sweet, I always wanted to be famous," Jay said. Trust him to keep things light.

Stella laughed. "You'll only be famous if you storm Oakbridge single-handedly, Jay."

He debated that and grinned. "I could do that."

I opened my mouth but Dave cut in. "Bed, please, so we can get back to the story?" He rolled his eyes. "You two are more kids than I am."

"Too true," I said solemnly.

Within a few minutes, all four of us had settled in to sleep.

The moment Dave was up, he turned to me hopefully. Obviously the idea of a battle had grabbed his attention. I hoped I could do it justice, in more ways than one. I glanced at Jay.

"So what are we waiting for?" Dave said.

Jay grinned. "Your sister, not that she needs it, is still getting her beauty sleep."

I laughed as I spotted that Stella's eyes were open. She promptly sat up.

"Oops," Dave said, but looked positively gleeful that his sister had heard. I recognized the look well from my brothers growing up.

Jay flushed bright red.

"Not that I need it?" Stella asked slowly, as if trying to decide whether to take it as a compliment or insult.

"Well, yes, because, um, you're already beautiful?" Jay stuttered. Stella stared at him before blushing as well.

Dave giggled a bit manically.

I unsuccessfully tried to stifle a grin and shook my head.

Jay noticed and looked at me, clearly trying to take the attention off him. "And what are you shaking your head at, Jezzy?" he demanded.

He'd asked for it now. "The fact that only you can make a woman blush even in jail."

"Not cool, Jez, not cool," he grumbled.

Then, with a suddenness that surprised even Jay, Stella leaned over and kissed him square on the mouth. Dave's, and Jay's, eyes went wide, but before any of us could really respond she had already pulled back, her face an even deeper red.

"That was for the compliment," she said and I got the impression the action had surprised even her. Then she quickly looked at me. "So, battle?"

My mouth had dropped open, but I forced it closed. "Right, yes, the Battle of Deepen's Crossing."

As I picked the story back up, I spotted Jay slip his hand into Stella's.

The more time Beau spent with them, the more Jez found she really enjoyed his presence. He was the opposite of Bri in many ways: he thought every word and action through a hundred different ways first, he spoke quietly but with an undeniable force, he was almost always serious and, obviously, quite a bit more low-key. Jez felt a lot of satisfaction watching him slowly open up to her and her friends. She was certain he needed more friends than just Mick and was glad they could provide. On occasion, he would talk seriously with them about the doubts he'd expressed to Jez early on and sometimes even relax enough to fully be himself. He began seeking them out when he had free time and Jez could tell from Mick's continued softening towards them that his old friend appreciated their efforts. There were longer and longer stretches of time when his usual disapproving look vanished completely.

It was hard to believe a year had passed and that Jez had ever thought she wouldn't fit in. She, Bri, Jessie, and Ry had clearly earned even Mick's respect through their willingness to give their all to any task assigned them, big or small. To be honest, they never minded because they always found ways to keep things fun. Bri, in particular, was good at making up games to accompany more boring tasks.

Through all this, the Freedom Fighters continued to grow, with an especially large surge following the Three's takeover. They had almost doubled in size since Jez had first arrived. If Cavern Hall had felt a bit crowded before, it was nothing to now.

Jez even discovered things she excelled at. Not only did she continue to improve with her sword, but she also discovered an affinity for tactics that didn't entirely surprise her. Her father was renowned as a brilliant tactician during his youth when he ran around with King Patrick, Duke Walters, and others of their generation. Some of that skill apparently rubbed off on her. Or perhaps, knowing her father like she did, he had subtly trained them all as children. She could even recall a few times when out hiking or horseback riding when he'd suddenly given them a challenge – many of which now proved handy. This gained her a place of respect within the tactical group, even though she was always careful not to overdo it. She knew she was no match for Mick or Beau, despite the way it came easy to her.

Shortly after her birthday, the quiet life she'd come to appreciate was shattered. "Captain Beau," a messenger yelled, bursting into the room and doubling over, hands on her knees. "Sir, they're coming. The Three's men. I don't know how they found us but they're coming."

"And you're sure they know where we are?" Beau asked, already on his feet.

"Yes, sir, couldn't be anywhere but Cavern Hall."

"So be it," he said, expression hard, although Jez knew him well enough now to see the worry. She couldn't blame him, knowing it was mirrored on every face there. They weren't strong enough to fight a real battle yet. They would need to stall the Three's men long enough to allow the old and young ample time to clear out to the backup caves that had already been selected. "Jessie, Ry, I want you to find Iris and help her gather the young and old. Then find Faranon and Peterson and tell them to keep that group safe. Any parents who feel they need to accompany their children are, of course, more than welcome to. Mick, take Jez and Bri and start getting everyone roused and ready. People are allowed to pack a few personal belongings as long as it won't hinder them in battle or they can pick them up during our escape. The rest of you, let everyone know that we gather in the main room in a half hour. Go gather your things."

A chorus of 'yes, sir' greeted this and everyone hurried off to their assigned tasks. Within the allotted time, everyone but those escorting the young and old were gathered. As soon as Beau hopped onto a table, everyone went silent. "I'm sure, by now, you've all heard that the Three have discovered our location. I know we're all thinking the same thing: it's too early. I hate to admit that it's true. Now is not our time to make a stand, as much as we might want to. We don't have the manpower yet, but we need to make a good showing of ourselves and fight long enough for the others to get to safety. We will not let them break us. Agreed?"

"Agreed!" approximately three hundred men and women bellowed back, crowded shoulder to shoulder in the space and overflowing into the corridors beyond.

Beau quickly outlined a plan of attack that was simple and allowed them plenty of autonomy, since they hadn't done much large group fighting. Such training was difficult to manage without being spotted.

He finally looked out over them, as grave as Jez had ever seen. "Good luck."

The place Beau had chosen to take the fight was an interesting piece of terrain set deep in the forest about two miles from Cavern Hall. The map christened it Deepen's Crossing, which Beau explained was actually an old wooden suspension bridge that spanned a ravine to the west of the site – a ravine that ran miles in either direction as a result of long vanished glaciers. It took them about an hour to reach the location and settle in to wait for the Three's soldiers to catch up.

Jez twisted her new sword back and forth, squinting at her reflection in the bits of light that filtered through the tall trees, glancing occasionally up as she strained her ears for any sounds other than the breathing and quiet conversation of her companions.

"Nervous?" Bri asked, squatting down beside her.

She managed to summon a weak smile. "A little," she admitted, watching Ry stare at her hands from where she sat beside Jessie. "I'm more worried about all of you than me. I don't know what I'd do if I had to start over a third time. I don't think I have it in me."

He leaned over and kissed her forehead. "No matter what happens today, Jez, remember that you are never alone. There is always a reason to live, for good or bad."

"You're going to live, though, right?" she asked, knowing it was a completely irrational question but unable to help it. She gripped her sword tightly enough that her knuckles turned white. Some part of her had hoped, for the few short weeks, that she would never need to sully the gift. But she had always logically known she would and not just once, but probably many times before things were put right again, assuming she lived that long.

"No one beats Brighton Dall and lives to tell about it," he said lightly and she smiled, not realizing until later he never actually promised.

Movement to the left drew their attention. "Beau's group is moving," Jessie said. They had split into three sections of about one hundred each, led by Beau, Bri, and Mick. Bri hopped to his feet, sharp eyes almost immediately picking out the signal. He raised his hand in a fist and twirled it in a circle.

Jez stood, slipping her sword back into its sheath and pulled the bow she wore slung across her chest off, testing the string. She forced herself to keep taking slow deep breaths, pushing away thoughts of all the things that could happen in the coming seconds, minutes, hours. It was a simple plan: hit and run, hit and run, until they'd slowed the enemy down enough that they could make a quick retreat and catch up to the others.

"Nothing is going to happen. We're going to be fine," she whispered.

"What's that?" Bri asked, obviously distracted.

"Nothing. I'm ready."

That drew his full attention, and he smiled at her, almost sadly. "No one's really ready for their first battle."

"When was yours?"

"We had a run in with the Three before we rescued you, before any of us really even knew what we were fighting."

"I'm as ready as I can be," she amended.

He reached over and squeezed her hand. "That's all I can ask. And I might be a tad biased, but I think you've been well prepared."

She cracked a smile. "You might be, yes."

"Okay, everyone, you know our job. Hit their left flank as hard as we can. As soon as you hear the signal, pull back and regroup. There's our sign. Good luck." He made a quick motion and their group fell into three loose rows, creeping forward towards where they knew the Three to be on the march north. Another signal from Bri and they stopped, the first line crouching, leaving room for the second row as they all drew an arrow. The third row were those without bows.

"Ready, aim...fire!" Bri ordered. The archers loosed two quick volleys – rewarded with screams – before they scrambled back to their feet, throwing the bows across their shoulders bandolier-style and drawing their swords. As soon as Jez was up, she threw herself forward, half drawn by the charge of the others around her. A moment later, they hit the small clearing and the chaos that already reigned throughout it. Beau and Mick's group had clearly gotten there seconds earlier.

She had no more time to think clearly as she ran smack into her first opponent. She barely brought her sword up in time to defend herself, feeling her anger grow. This was so completely unnecessary. She exchanged two quick blows with the man before he let out a gasp and sagged to the side. Jez froze, certain she hadn't done it, before Jessie's face appeared before. "Keep moving," her friend ordered grimly, grabbing her arm.

After that, it was all a blur. Parry, slash, block, duck, parry, dodge, stab. The call to retreat came as sweet relief and she managed to disengage from the fray without too much issue, moving with the others in her group back to the relative quiet of the trees. She realized distantly that she was covered in blood – probably some of it her own – and shaking through a combination of adrenaline and fury. Why did they have to lose good people when they were in the right?

"You okay?" Bri was suddenly at her shoulder and she felt a profound relief he was still standing. She searched out Ry and Jessie with her eyes to reassure herself.

She hugged him tightly. "Yeah, enough," she said shakily, accepting the jug of water he passed her. The single sip she took turned her stomach, though, and she was forced to turn away to retch it up. "Sorry," she murmured, handing it back as he squeezed her shoulder. Ry and Jessie joined them. Ry seemed to be having similar troubles, refusing the water.

"Take a breather," Bri said. "We'll attack again soon."

The break included a systematic pull-back, staying just out of the enemy's sight as the others continued to hit them. After far too short a time, Bri held up two fingers. Quickly, their group finished cleaning their weapons and readying themselves for round two. They didn't dare use the bows again for fear of hitting their own in the melee.

When he dropped the last finger, the group charged back into it, slamming the Three's men in the side, although the wall against them barely buckled under the pressure. Jez met another soldier and slashed, surprising herself when he immediately went down.

After that, the battle fell into some sort of strange routine. They were leading the soldiers away from Cavern Hall - that she knew distantly from the plan - but it was still hard to recognize the bigger picture in all the fighting and death and pain. They hit-and-ran twice more, at least, that Jez could remember. The Three had sent an overwhelming force against them, so even on the fourth charge, their line held strong against the Freedom Fighters.

Suddenly, the area directly in front of Jez cleared and she had a moment to study the raging battle. She spotted Bri a short distance away almost instantly. He was deeply involved in a duel against someone wearing officer stripes. Jessie watched his back, fighting off her own opponents. Jez could tell Bri was tiring, though, so she started fighting her way towards her friends. She was intercepted halfway there and it took precious time to dispatch the man. Finally, she ducked beneath his blow and speared him in the stomach. She pushed the leaden body away, moving forward again. A soldier had gotten past Jessie and, although she threw herself on his back before he could stab Bri through his, the pair staggering past momentarily drew Bri's attention.

It was all the officer needed.

A second later, Bri went down.

A second after that, Jessie shoved the first soldier's dead weight away from her, spun, and stabbed her blade deeply into the officer's back.

Another second and it sunk in.

Then Jessie was grabbing her around the middle. "Don't, Jez, don't," she gasped.

"But he's still alive," she said desperately, needing to believe it.

Already, the soldiers closed in on them. Jez was blind to it, gaze focused on Bri.

"Even if that's true, it's too late."

Jez looked at Jessie, then back at Bri, and the world went very crooked.

The next thing she was aware of, someone had grabbed her forearms in a tight grip. "Damn it, Jez, it's me. Stop it. Stop!" The same someone was shaking her and slowly her vision came into focus. Jessie stood in front of her, their faces only a couple inches apart. "Oh thank the gods. Welcome back."

"What…?" Jez asked, voice cracking like she'd been screaming.

"We lost you for a while there." She forced a brief smile. "You were…a lot. We have to go, the call came for the final retreat."

Ry and Dunkin, who Jez had met on her first day in Cavern Hall, were currently keeping their opponents away.

"I can't," Jez croaked.

"We can't hold out much longer," Rylia said, voice as ragged as Jez's heart. "We have to retreat while we still have support."

"We can't leave him."

"We have to. Bri wouldn't thank us if we got ourselves captured or killed for him like this. You know that, Jez. And that cut…" She didn't need to finish the thought for Jez to know she believed there was no chance of him surviving.

Two soldiers broke through Ry and Dunkin's protection and Jez and Jessie quickly finished them off.

"With Bri gone, Jez, we need someone to lead us."

She stared at her friend, not comprehending. Why was Jessie telling her that?

"We need to leave right now," Dunkin said, urgency making his voice higher than usual.

Jez swallowed, looking between them. As much as she wanted to believe Bri was still alive, waiting for them just on the other side of the soldiers, she knew she couldn't sacrifice or even risk the lives of these three, or any of their forces, for that small, small hope. "Let's go," she said, turning away from him, from that still so brand new happiness and towards the forest. She swiped at her face and smeared blood, grit, and tears with no real effect.

The foursome fought their way through another group of soldiers and then were abruptly out of the combat. Dunkin briefly conferred with one of the other Freedom Fighters, then turned back to the trio.

"Jez, Kilo says we're cut off from the others," he said wearily.

"What are you talking about? We can escape the way we came."

"I guess we moved off course. Deepen's Ravine is over there. We're literally trapped."

Jez pulled up a quick mental map of the area. "Ry?"

"I'm not sure," her friend said. "I have no idea how far we've traveled."

"Okay, guys, keep a step ahead of the soldiers. I'll be back shortly."

"Jez…" Jessie started and she abruptly could read all three faces. They thought she was going to go back anyway. To get herself slaughtered. What had she done out there?

"I'm trying to save lives," she said, as gently as she could. "Jessie, you're in charge-"

"No, whatever you're doing, we do it together. Dunkin, can you keep everyone together and retreating?"

"Yes, of course," he said, doubt lurking in the back of his gaze.

Jez was too tired to argue. "Then let's go." She took off at a sprint towards the ravine, her two friends on her heels.

"What are we doing anyway?" Jessie asked.

"If we're lucky, Deepen's Crossing is close."

Her eyes widened in understanding. "That would be incredibly lucky."

"We've earned a bit of that right about now," Jez said grimly.

A minute later, they burst into the clearing along the side of the ravine and all three hastily scanned up and down. "There!" Ry said, spotting it first about a half mile south of their location.

"That might be doable," Jessie said.

"C'mon." They raced back and told Dunkin the good news. "You and Kilo get everyone across and, whatever you do, keep moving. You'll rendezvous with the group a bit further north."

"What about the three of you?"

"We'll catch up, but the army is gaining too fast. We need to slow them down," Jez said.

"Good luck," he said before turning and running off to get the others moving in the right direction.

The trio unslung their bows and Jez quickly tested the string before drawing an arrow. "Ready?"

"Ready," they both chorused.

Before the forerunners met them, she glanced at her friends. "What did I do? After you stopped me from getting to Bri?" she asked quietly.

"Now's really not the time…"

"I need to know. I need to know if there is something wrong with me. And that you two trust me right now."

"Of course we do," Jessie said firmly as Ry leaned into her. "What you did out there, that was a nasty combination of pure anger and grief and I'm not at all worried about your state of mind." She smiled crookedly. "Just get us out of here in one piece."

"Deal," Jez said, relief coursing through her and then she fired off her first arrow. As soon as she reloaded, she sent a second and then a third as the three friends backed slowly away. "And break!" On that, they turned and sprinted back towards the bridge, hoping they had bought the others enough time to get across.

"Stop them!" came a call from behind, but the girls had the lead. Finally, they burst into the clearing by the bridge.

"They're gone," Ry reported.

"Thank the gods," Jessie muttered as they raced up to it. "Mr. Deepen would kill us for this."

"Mr. Deepen is long dead," Jez said. "Get going."

"It makes more sense for me to be last," Ry said. "I'm the lightest and have the best balance."

"We don't have time to argue," Jessie said, darting back across the clearing to take a forerunner by surprise with a sword through the chest.

"Fine," Jez said and grabbed Jessie's collar, heaving her over to the bridge. "Go and take our things." She and Ry shoved their bags into Jessie's hands. "Make sure this stays attached to that side."

Jessie gave her a skeptical look but hurried across the bridge. Before she was even across, Jez chopped through the railings and then started across, arms held out for balance. She didn't think too hard on it, knowing if she did, she'd freeze. Ry moved about three feet out and threw herself down flat. "Get down, Jez!" she yelled. Then she tightened her grip on her knife and, with two swift chops, cut the thing loose.

Jez had just enough time to drop and grab the bridge before the world lurched out from underneath them. She braced herself, her entire body jarring as the bridge hit the far side and bounced off. Instantly, the young woman glanced down, happy beyond words to see Ry still attached, in the process of awkwardly sheathing her knife and starting up.

"Hurry!" Jessie yelled and Jez looked over her shoulder to see archers lining up on the far side of the bank. In the second she looked, one gurgled and toppled off into the ravine. Jessie had their backs as much as she could. Jez returned her gaze up the side of the cliff and began scaling the bridge like a ladder. One of the slats broke underneath her halfway up, but she had a solid grip on the ropes and managed to do nothing worse than swing.

Finally, she was scrambling over the top. She rolled to her feet as soon as she had gained some equilibrium and unslung her bow, helping Jessie keep them at bay while Ry made it the rest of the way up. As her friend's head appeared over the lip of the cliff, Jez dropped her bow and helped haul her the rest of the way up. "You okay?"

"Just wonderful," she grunted. "C'mon, let's get out of here before they figure out some way to follow us."

Jez gestured them ahead of her, scooped up her pack, and followed.

"So what job did you give Ani that she can't screw up?" Vlad asked Sorin as he entered the room.

"If she puts her mind to it, our sister could screw up just about anything," he said. "Is there a reason you're waiting for me in my office?"

"We need to talk."

"Do we?" Sorin said, keeping his voice mild.

"What job did you give Ani?" he asked again.

"She and Jakium will be in charge of morale boosting activities both here and in Greensward for the foreseeable future. I think it suits our sister quite admirably. Jakium, not so much, but that's what he gets for being merely a lieutenant and Anica's favorite."

Vlad frowned. "I can think of much better uses for Jakium."

"I'm sure you could, but for now, he's Anica's assistant. It'll make them both happy."

"I don't like it."

"You gave me the task of assigning her a job. That does not give you permission to whine when it doesn't work out the way you wanted. What do we need to talk about?"

"Ren and our sister."

"What about them?"

"We're using her for our own gains."

"And she gains the man she loves. I see nothing wrong with this equation," Sorin said.

"Except Ren can't stand her."

Sorin made his way to his desk chair and settled back in it, steepling his fingers. "It's a bit late to be thinking this now," he said simply, instead of the twenty things that had immediately crossed his mind. Like the fact that the prince definitely didn't hate Ani.

"We could just kill him. We're doing fine as rulers."

"You can't have it both ways, Vladimir," Sorin said and, at his brother's confused look, he sighed. "First, you're worried about forcing our sister into an uneven marriage and, now, you want to kill the man she loves more than anything, just like that? If we were going to kill Renier, we needed to do it the day we killed his father."

Not surprisingly, Vlad didn't like that assessment. It was clear on his face. But he didn't move or speak.

"Was there something else?" Sorin asked, still leaning comfortably in his chair. He could feel the tension radiating off Vlad, though, and it took all his effort to continue his nonchalant expression.

His brother's eyes narrowed. "Any luck in tracking down Benton Walters?"

"No." He did it just to piss Vlad off further and was rewarded with a passing glimpse of fury. He had to wonder just how far he could push his older brother before Edward emerged. He had spotted the potential almost the day he came back, the day that he'd...Sorin mentally shook himself.

"And why not?"

"Because he's completely disappeared. There hasn't even been a rumor of his presence since we killed his parents. My guess is, he's lying low, assisting the Freedom Fighters in some way. Benton Walters would be a great draw for them, but there has been no announcement. So there must be some reason why. I haven't figured out what yet." He watched the fury slowly fade to embers.

"Well, keep looking. I trust you'll turn up something eventually."

"Don't hold your breath, but I will do my best," Sorin said and then felt a fleeting flash of sadness. "Why don't you take the afternoon off, Vlad?" he asked, using the nickname deliberately. "Go do something fun by yourself or with Anica."

He could tell his question hit home and, for a moment, he held out hope that Vlad might choose the smart move, but his brother just shook his head obstinately. "There's work to do. I'll talk to you later, Sorin," he said and swept out the door.

"Bye, Vlad," his brother whispered after him. One day the fire wouldn't die down, not at the rate his older sibling was going. Sorin wondered what would happen then.

Chapter Nine

"So there you have it," I said, "the Battle of Deepen's Crossing, which no longer exists thanks to us." Then I quickly wiped away the tears that were slipping down my face, knowing my companions saw even in the flickering light. I took a deep breath to calm myself. It had been a long year since Bri had been struck down. I had moved on – we'd had to – as much as I'd loved him. "Sorry," I added, embarrassed for crying over an old event.

"Don't be. You weren't the only one."

I glanced now at Jay who was drying his own cheeks. "What? Me crying? I did no such thing," he said, although I could see that my account of his brother's death had hit him hard.

"Don't be ridiculous," Dave said. "It's okay to cry over stuff like that." He paused there, suddenly uncertain. "It *is* okay, right?" We had heard him twice already in the night, sniffing into Stella's shoulder.

"Of course it is," Jay said, sobering. "It's not an easy thing to lose a parent or a sibling. I'd never heard a real account of how Bri died. Jessie asked me once if I wanted to know the story of Deepen's Crossing and I told her no."

"Oh, I'm sorry, Jay, I should have asked first," I said, immediately contrite.

"No, no, it's okay," he said. "I…I was ready now. You really did love him, didn't you?"

"Yes. Your brother was one of the finest and most amazing men I've ever met. I think a small part of me may never stop loving him and all he did and was."

"Even with Beau?"

"Even with Beau and he understands that. Bri and my relationship was very different from what Beau and I now have, but it was no less potent, all things considered." I had stopped the narrative briefly earlier to eat the evening meal and, not surprisingly, it was now fully dark outside. "We should probably try and get some rest."

Dave sighed. "Are you sure we can't just continue?"

"Jez's voice needs a rest and we need sleep, bud," Stella said fondly.

"It's called eager anticipation," Jay said. "The faster you go to sleep, the faster you wake up and we continue."

The boy eyed him skeptically. "That's not true."

"Cross my heart, hope to die. It always worked with me when I was your age."

Dave frowned. "You don't have to treat me like a child," he said, sounding somewhere between hurt and indignant. "I know what's coming and what I did to try and help Stella." It was no surprise to me that Dave refused to actually spit out that he had, if not killed a man, seriously wounded one. I suspected the soldier was dead.

"I'm not."

"Trust me, he's not," I said dryly. "I suspect Jay still lives by that rule."

"Only sometimes!"

Dave smiled a little, seemingly against his better judgment. "Being silly isn't going to make it better."

I wasn't exactly sure what he was referring to, but I figured I was capable of replying anyway. "Nothing but time seems to make it better, Dave, but in our situation, what would you rather do?" I asked. "Dwell on what's wrong and what's supposed to happen to us or on all the good things we have? We," I indicated Jay and myself, "long ago learned that dwelling on the bad stuff is just plain depressing and does nobody any good and that joking around doesn't really make it better, but does make it easier to live with."

Dave settled more comfortably against Stella's side as he thought about my words before he nodded. "That does make sense. And I like it when you're silly. Makes me forget for a couple minutes."

"Now," Stella said, "we really should get some sleep." She looked at Jay and me. "Goodnight."

"Night," I said, settling down.

I didn't sleep as well as I had previous nights, probably because Bri's death felt raw all over again. Instead, I had odd shifting dreams about my friends and particularly Bri, in which he tried to fly. I woke early, feeling disoriented and off-kilter. Moving quietly so as not to wake the others, I stood and wrapped my fingers around the bars on the cell door, peering out into the silent jail. Behind me, I could hear the first stirrings of Greensward through our small window. After some indistinct amount of time, I heard the quiet rustle of cloth and then Jay joined me at the door.

"You okay?" he asked softly.

"I should be asking you the same thing," I said, drawing my gaze away from the empty corridor to my friend.

"I still miss him and my parents every day," Jay said. "I'm not sure that will ever change, but yes, I'm okay." He smiled faintly. "Your turn."

"I'm fine. Just…wondering if we'll make it out of here. If we'll get to see the Three pay for what they've done."

"Everyone will move mountains to get us out."

"Unless it interferes with the rest of the plan."

"Rees's interest in us has bought us time as well as the bruises," he said.

I glanced briefly at Stella and Dave.

Jay answered my silent question. "They'll wait. They've got all four of us. What's the point in hanging a little boy and the sister who just protected him? They need more than that for it to be effective and, for that, they need us."

I couldn't exactly argue with that logic and I had to hope Jay was right. He reached out and put a hand over mine. We stood there until we heard a single set of footsteps. By the time the food guard appeared, we were seated back in our usual spots and Stella and Dave were sitting up and stretching.

It took only a minute after we finished for Dave to turn on me with an expectant look. I smiled and picked the story back up without further ado.

◀ ▼ ▶

It took a half hour for the trio to catch up with the stragglers, led, perhaps not surprisingly, by Beau. Jez was distantly aware that the small group of maybe

97

fifteen had to have come back looking for them, since Deepen's Ravine still stood between them and the Three's soldiers. He took one look at them and motioned them to sit. "We've got some time," he said, which Jez was fairly certain was a lie, but she was grateful for the chance to rest, sinking to the ground. "Dunkin passed by a little while ago with the rest of your group. They're on their way to the new Cavern Hall. Are you three okay?"

Jez looked up at him and Beau rocked back on his heels at the pain in her eyes before handing her a clean cloth.

"Clean yourselves up and we'll patch up the worst injuries before we move on." He reached out hesitantly and, at the nod from Jessie, placed one hand gently on her shoulder.

"I saved them," Jez said.

"I know. I'm sorry."

She nodded, tears freshly dribbling down her face, and only then moved to wipe off her hands and face.

"How did we fare?" Jessie asked.

"About how we expected," he said heavily. "Our losses were heavy. Just Bri alone…" he trailed off as Jez passed the cloth along. One of the men came over to take care of the bad cut Jessie had on her upper arm. Ry was unscathed enough to not warrant any bandages for now. There'd be time for smaller stuff later. As they got cleaned up, Beau got the story out of Jessie and Ry and he whistled. "You three are amazing," he said.

"We would have been more amazing if we could have…" Rylia said and shrugged. "We should get going."

Beau stood. "Agreed. We need to catch up to the others. It'll take at least a day to get to our new base." They wouldn't be going directly there just to throw off any potential trackers. So coupled with the distance, it wasn't going to be quick. He offered a hand to Jez to pull her up. As he did, she let out a gasp of pain, the blood draining from her face.

"Jez!" Ry yelped, staring wide-eyed at the small pool of blood that had collected where she sat.

The captain peered behind her. "Gods' Breath, Jez, you should have said something."

"I'm fine," she murmured faintly.

"That injury does not look *fine*," he said, lowering her back down.

"You should have said something!" Ry said, voice going high in her panic.

"I'm fine," she repeated as the medic crouched next to her. "They got me climbing up the bridge. Was more important we got away." She had been aware of it the moment it had happened and had yanked the shaft out. After, she just hoped her two friends wouldn't notice, which they hadn't.

"Where's Mick when you need him?" Beau muttered, helping her lie down on her side so the medic could get an initial patch job done. "Work quickly. We don't have much time."

"Yes, sir," the medic said.

The world felt fuzzy and it took all Jez's focus to watch her friends. It was like acknowledging it to everyone had made the pain catch up.

"C'mon, you two. She'll be okay. I've seen worse," Beau told Jessie and Ry, nudging them away.

"You don't have to placate us," Ry said angrily. "It's plain to see it's bad."

"We'll get her to Mick. If he can't do anything…well, we've lost everyone we're going to. We'll take her to one of the towns with a real doctor if it comes to that."

Whatever was said after, Jez lost as the medic hit a particularly sensitive spot and the world swam out of focus.

It didn't return to focus for some time. Jez didn't remember much of the following days. On occasion, she fought through the haze of pain and disorientation to try and figure out what was going on, but it didn't tell her much. She was vaguely aware that at least one of her friends was there all the time and that they somehow managed to reach the new Cavern Hall, even with her dead weight slowing them down.

What she knew of the time and the ultimate decision to send her to a town, she heard later from the others. For the first four or so days, she would often yell and thrash about, words indistinct. Mick reassured everyone that, as yet, she had not picked up an infection and didn't have a fever. He reasoned that the reaction was probably as much due to what must be running through her head as the deep injury. Based on what Jez remembered of her dreams later, he wasn't wrong.

So her friends waited. One hurdle at a time was more than enough, and all their time and energy was taken by setting up the new Cavern Hall for the survivors.

Later, once she was back up, Jessie and Ry filled her in on the ultimate decision. It happened when she abruptly settled down and stayed quiet. Ry recognized the change immediately and sprinted to gather Mick. Upon arrival, he checked her heartbeat and breathing before sitting back grimly. "She's getting worse. I'm afraid it might be infected now."

"I thought…because she'd quieted down, that maybe…"

"Sometimes I would say it was a good thing. A fever broke or something, but I'm afraid that, her heartbeat is…not as steady as I want."

Beau burst in just then. "What's happened?" he asked, coming over to crouch at Jez's side.

"She's getting worse, Beau," Mick said softly, putting a hand on the captain's shoulder.

He took her hand and squeezed it. For a second, Jez's eyes flickered halfway open and she smiled faintly. "'lo," she mumbled.

"Hey, you. Hang in there," he said. Later, they would also tell her she woke up like that at random times, but they all blurred together into an indistinct bundle.

"'kay." She drifted off again.

"We're only about two days from Kol. It should be big enough to have a decent doctor."

"Let's hope so," Mick agreed. "Rylia, get Jessica and get packed. Meet us outside in an hour."

"Yes, sir!" the girl said, rocketing to her feet and out the door.

Beau hesitated. "I don't want to lose her, Mick. Not on top of everything else."

"None of us do," his old friend said. "We'll make it through this. Just don't do anything foolish out there."

"I won't," Beau said before climbing to his feet and stepping over to the bag containing his belongings. None of the friends had settled in much with Jez so injured. He pulled a few things out to leave behind, then shouldered his bag. Together, the pair got Jez up, ignoring her whimper of pain, and got her out to the front entrance. There, Beau waited with her while Mick retrieved and saddled one of the Freedom Fighters' three horses. By the time he made it out with the horse, Jessie and Ry were there and they helped the two men get Jez up on the horse and tied on, so she wouldn't fall off.

"Be careful," Mick said. Since the battle, he had given up any pretense of maintaining an aloof presence, although his stern exterior never wavered.

"We will. We'll be back before you know it."

"Beau?"

"I'll be fine. Won't be my first time on my own," he said and the two men gripped hands briefly before Beau grabbed the reins of the horse and set off towards the town of Kol, Jessie and Ry on his heels.

The first day passed without mishap. Jez drifted in and out of consciousness, aware that something had changed, but couldn't get her lips to form words, her entire back a throbbing pain. It was the next day when the horse jolted more in its step than usual that the same jolt woke Jez up. She blinked blurrily and focused on Beau, who walked alongside her, holding her hand and the reins with the same hand.

"Beau?" she managed hoarsely.

He started and looked up at her. "Hey! How're you feeling?"

"Herd of horses got me," she said, managing a small smile.

"Well, it could be worse," he said in a purposely upbeat tone.

She forced herself to sit a bit more upright despite the shooting pain, staring at the horse's mane. "Where're we?"

"On our way to Kol. You're badly hurt. Do you remember?"

She nodded. "I'm sorry."

"For what?" he asked, but looked generally unsurprised by the apology.

"For letting Bri die," she whispered. "I should've…"

"Should've nothing, Jez. You listen to me: you did nothing wrong and everything right. This is war and war sucks and war means people are going to die and make sacrifices and that sucks too. You know that, I know that, Bri knew that."

"I know." Fresh tears sprung into her eyes and she made a swipe at them and missed abysmally, her coordination off. "He was right there. And I couldn't…I promised myself I would, Beau. No more being helpless. Not after they almost killed me. I knew with you I could accomplish something. And then Bri…"

"It's never a good idea to make a promise that's impossible to keep, Jasmine," he said softly and then held up a hand to forestall any comment, ignoring her surprise at the use of her given name. "I tried that promise on for

101

size when my mother died. She was the only blood family I'd ever known and she got an incurable disease. We tried everything but we lost her anyway. I told myself the day she died that I would never let myself be helpless again and you know what happened instead? I shut myself off and didn't allow myself to open up for anyone. It drove Mick and Reardon crazy. The day we met, the day you woke up, I decided that it was past time to let go of that promise. I haven't regretted it for a second. You, Jessie, Ry, and Bri, Mick and Reardon again. Bri might be gone, but we still have our memories of him and we need to keep going and get the people that killed him and his parents. For ourselves, for him, for his brother, and for everyone."

She stayed silent, aware even around the pain how much Beau had just taken her into his confidence. "What if all I can remember is the battle?"

"That will fade." He tapped her chest just above her heart. "The rest of them are here."

"How do I find them?"

"Make yourself find them. They're all there: the first kiss, your fighting lessons, your birthday, all of it. That's what's important, Jez. With my mom, once I could let myself remember all the good times, it was easier to process the end as well. My mother lived life her way as best she could and she…was proud of the decisions she'd made and why."

"Thanks, Beau," Jez said, feeling the black start to creep. "'m gonna be okay?"

"You'll be just fine," he promised, squeezing her hand as she drifted off.

They reached the town early the next morning. Jez was just enough with it that her friends didn't notice, but she registered the conversation around her.

"I'll leave now before someone sees me. Do you remember that tree we passed this morning that halfway across the path?" Beau asked. A pause. "I'll meet you there when you return. Get her better," he said.

"We will, Beau, promise," Jessie said.

"Be careful!" That was Ry.

"Don't worry, I'm very apt at taking care of myself," he said with some amusement. "Watch yourselves."

With a wave, the girls set off for town. Ry spun a tale of getting caught in the crossfire of two armies to perfection, keeping it sweet and simple without overtly choosing a side. She didn't condemn the Freedom Fighters – stressing that they were still headed north – nor did she say anything particularly in their favor. Almost immediately once Ry's tale was done, Jez was taken to the local infirmary and Jessie and Ry installed in dirt cheap rooms at the local inn.

It didn't take long to learn that they were over a week's hike from Oakbridge, the capital, and, despite being one of the closest towns to the fight, the locals knew little truth about the engagement that was already being dubbed the Battle of Deepen's Crossing. Both girls found it highly amusing and satisfying that a battle that, for all intents and purposes, the Three's men had won had been named after the Freedom Fighters escape route. Jessie suspected there was more than a little irony in that title, which she voiced to Ry and Jez after Jez returned, and that the Three probably didn't like it one bit. They all wished they knew who had coined it.

The popular story around town was that the Freedom Fighters had jumped a vastly outnumbered group of the Three's soldiers and all but slaughtered them. It wasn't too hard to determine which citizens of Kol fell on which side, even as outsiders. Jessie suspected the tension apparent in the town matched that of the entire country.

It took five days before Jez was released, even if she was cautioned to stay close for a few more. In that time, the two other girls took as much advantage of living in a real town for the first time in ages as they could. Jessie loved the real bed while Ry loved daily baths.

When Jez appeared in their doorway and helped herself to the room's single chair, she caught them both off-guard.

"Jez!" Ry cried, all but tackling her in a hug.

Jessie stared. "Where the hell did you come from?"

"They released me twenty minutes ago and I didn't want to wait for you," Jez said, gently pushing Ry off. "Still sore, remember?"

"Sorry!" she said, hopping off.

"How're you feeling?"

"Sore," she repeated, amused, reaching down and gently touching the bandage. "But a lot less like death warmed over."

"You gave us a real fright," Jessie told her.

Jez smiled crookedly. "Well, I'm all better now. How soon do we leave?"

"Not until you're a heck of a lot closer to fully functional again."

"They wouldn't have released me if…"

"So stand up and walk in a straight line across the room." At Jez's sour look, Jessie laughed. "That's what I thought. A few more days will not be the end of the world."

"Oh, fine. I am anxious to get back, though. Things must be wild at the new Cavern Hall."

"It's taking some time to settle in," Jessie granted, "but they can hold down the fort without us. As far as our scouts can tell, the Three's men have completely given up on tracking us for the time being. Apparently the Nerians are getting restless."

Jez nodded. "I also have a conversation to finish with Beau. He gave me a lot to think about and I wasn't exactly at a good point to hold up my end of it then."

The other two exchanged glances, but let it rest for the time being. It took another three days for both the doctor, and Jessie, to declare Jez fit to leave. In that time, it surprised neither of the friends to find Jez often lost in thought and certainly quieter than before. They knew they all had a lot to work through and that job was only just beginning now that things were settling down. Slightly concerned anyway, both brought up Bri at various points. Jez was more than happy to reminisce with them, but never started the conversation. Little did they know, but she spent a lot of her thoughtful time going over all the good memories as Beau had suggested, committing them to as clear a memory as his death.

When Jez wasn't thinking about Bri, she was dwelling on what had occurred on the battlefield. A couple of times she came close to pressuring Jessie to tell her what happened after she'd seen Bri go down, but could never quite bring herself to. If she was honest with herself, which was about half the time, the potential consequences of that mental blank in her memory scared her witless. She knew the fact it was a completely empty period was probably not a good sign. She resolved to speak to Beau about it at the first opportunity and see what he thought.

"Renny!" Ani yelled as she barreled through his door like it didn't even exist.

Ren leapt from his seat by the window. "What? What is it?"

Ani just giggled, screeching to a halt a couple feet from him.

"What?" he asked again, eyes narrowing as his heart slowly returned to a normal speed.

"You look really funny when you do that."

His expression turned sour. "Thanks a lot." She tilted her head and studied him for at least a minute in silence. The long period of quiet from her disturbed him and he finally squirmed. "What? Do I have something on my face?" he asked gruffly, reaching to automatically rub a cheek.

"No. Why are you in a bad mood?"

He blinked. "How can you tell I'm in a bad mood?"

"I just know, Ren," she said. "What's wrong?"

"I wouldn't think that question really would need asking." Then he paused, something striking him. "You called me Ren."

"Am I not allowed to do that?" she asked and he absently noticed her usual overabundance of energy had mysteriously vanished.

"No, of course you are, you just never do."

"I like Renny better," she said matter-of-factly.

He snorted and dropped back into his chair, placing his chin on his fist as he directed his gaze out the window.

After a moment's hesitation, Ani sat across from him. "What's wrong?" she asked again, but gently.

It was that gentleness that got him.

"Where should I start?" He gestured morosely at the window. "I have bars on a window that's already sealed shut. I have a guard posted outside my door all the time. That same guard's sole job is to teach me a lesson if I step one little toe out of line – a line I'm not even sure is always in the same location. Plus, I never know when they're actively listening in. I haven't had a breath of fresh air in almost two years. I haven't been out of these three rooms in just as long. Time has just…" He let out a laugh. "What the fuck is time? If your brother didn't rub the passing of it in once in a while, I could have been here five, six years and never known." He looked her in the eye. "And how about the fact my future is more of the same? This room and this view. Gods Breath, even my thoughts are just shit your brothers have said. Why am I still alive?" He almost told her not to answer that. He really didn't want to speak it into existence. "Do I actually have a younger sibling who is in charge of the Freedom Fighters? I only even know about the possibility because Sorin told me." Even despite how good it felt to get

105

it all out, Ren caught the curious flicker to Ani's expression. "I hate it. There's nothing else left. And it's slowly tearing me apart because I can't do a damn thing about anything." After a long silence, he broke eye contact, distantly surprised, given what he'd seen in her eyes, that Ani hadn't already. An understanding that he wouldn't wish on anyone. "I wish Sorin had killed me when he had the chance," he said softly.

"I don't."

"Ani," he sighed.

"No," she said, firmly. "No, don't ever wish yourself dead. Where there's life, there's hope. I know I'm loud and overbearing," she said, a dry note to her voice. "And I know that everything looks really bleak." Ren shrugged as she reached out and put a gentle hand on his knee. "Look, Ren, I don't know what we've got, but I do know I enjoy seeing you every day and I like to think I make your days better. I...I just get this overwhelming urge to try and cheer you up, see you smile or, gods forbid it, laugh."

That startled a quick smile out of him. She did make his days better. She didn't just need him to throw thoughts at or to confirm anything. She didn't need him at all. And yet, here she was, day after day, patiently - in an impatient way - keeping him smiling.

"You are so incredibly tolerant of me, even at my wildest, and I appreciate that more than words can say. I don't usually get that, even from Vlad, and the fact you are, even with everything else on you, feels like such a gift. I...I guess I want to try and pay you back for your kindness, but I've probably been doing a pretty bad job of it." She paused, seeking out his gaze. "Would it be better if I stayed away?"

He didn't even hesitate, putting his hand over hers. "No! No, definitely not," he added a bit calmer. "I hadn't realized..." He shrugged. "You've been gone." For the first time since he'd been captured. "And things were worse." Mostly he'd been ignored. The return to the constant visits was so much better, even if it included Vlad sometimes. And now, he had Ani again, and the sudden influx of sometimes strangely normal conversations with Sorin. He wasn't sure how to put that into words that made sense, though.

"Good, because I don't want to stay away. I feel the same way." She offered him a tentative smile which he couldn't help but return. "Ren?" she asked after a moment of silence.

"Yeah?"

106

"Can I leave you alone with your thoughts for a few minutes? I gotta go do something really quick."

"I've been alone with them a lot more than that and I haven't cracked yet. Go ahead, I'll be waiting here for you," he said wryly.

She patted his hand and caught his eyes again firmly. "Do not give up, do you understand, Renier Highcastle?"

He was taken aback by how strange his full name sounded coming from her and nodded before he even really processed her words.

Ani flashed him a grin. "Good. I'll be right back," she said, then darted out the door.

Chapter Ten

I TOOK A BREAK THERE, STANDING and stretching. My body was stiff from the injuries and I concentrated on working out all the kinks from the continued inactivity. My scrapes and bruises from my run-in with Rees two days before were all scabbing nicely. Remembering Rees caused me to glance out the cell door. I had a feeling we'd be seeing him again soon, despite the wounds I'd inflicted, and I was intrigued to see how it would play out. I wasn't about to say I was eager to face him again – I had gleaned enough to know he was potentially a very dangerous opponent – but I was definitely curious about how things might go.

Jay took advantage of the break to start giving Dave pointers on acting innocent of all wrongdoing. Stella moved over so she sat across from me. "How long, do you think?" she asked softly.

"No idea. Probably a while. They'll want to get every possible bit of information out of Jay and me and we won't make it easy. And they're in no rush."

She nodded. "You two are rather close, aren't you?"

I squashed a smile, not wanting her to realize I was fairly certain why she was asking. "Yes, of course, but he's like another one of my brothers. He had no problems integrating into our group. Maybe we all subconsciously saw the resemblance to Bri, but either way, we let him right in."

She smiled. "And you and Beau?"

I laughed. "Still going strong as of the day we left. Jessie and Ry knew it long before I did. But I needed time after Bri."

"So, what you do then…" Jay said to Dave, grinning.

"You know, any story that Jay begins that way is a bad idea," I said. "Why don't we continue the story instead?"

"Have you had enough of a break?"

I saluted Dave. "Ready and willing."

"Sweet," he said but Stella stiffened, turning to the door.

"Jez," she whispered, scooting back to Dave's side and I heard it a split second later: multiple footsteps.

Jay's and my gaze met. "Rees."

I stood again. "I guess I'll see you when I return."

He smiled faintly. "Good luck. Try not to piss him off too much."

"Yes, sir."

Shorty appeared, flanked by the two thugs. He opened the door and gestured me out. "Let's go." He led me down the hall again to the small room, which I was amused to discover was currently without a door.

The thugs grabbed my arms, then twisted them tightly up behind my back. I winced despite my best efforts as Rees entered the room. I could immediately see the scabs tracing the top and side of his head, which they had shaved to get at the injuries. His black eye was already a nasty looking yellow and purple, but not swollen shut.

"I have to say you wear the wounds well, Rees," I said with a smirk.

"As well as you do?" he asked even as one of the thugs pulled harder. I was certain for a minute he was going to break it before Rees signaled for him to relax it. I ground my teeth, but was still caught off-guard as he took a quick step forward and planted his fist into my stomach. I doubled over, gasping for breath, before his hand on my chin forced me upright. "I see you're healing well."

"Lots of practice," I managed between sucking in steadying breaths.

"So I'd noticed. Although I won't be so stupid as to try that again, I'm still curious. How did you get all those scars?"

"I fell down," I said dryly.

He raised an eyebrow. "And here I was hoping we might have reached an understanding last time."

I let out a laugh. "In your dreams. Last I checked, that wasn't nearly close to how it worked, Colonel."

He shrugged. "I can always hope. Where did we leave off?" He tapped his chin in false thought. "That's right, your name. So, miss, what's your name?"

I stared at him evenly and he nodded, tightening his grip on my chin. The nod was a signal because one of the brutes twisted my arm behind me savagely, pressing it dangerously close to the snapping point. I yelped in surprise and pain. Rees smiled tightly and the immediate pressure eased, although it remained close to trouble.

"And now?" he asked pleasantly. "You have five seconds."

I held his gaze and ran through my options in double time. If I didn't tell him, I'd have a dislocated arm, maybe broken. That wouldn't be too much of a hardship on death row, but it would be rather inconvenient and give him an easy target for future interrogations. If I did tell him, I might get some serious satisfaction out of his response. And, as I'd said, what harm could it do?

"Time's up." The pressure increased.

"Jasmine," I said in a voice that wasn't firm but at least didn't squeak.

He let go of my chin, taking a half step back to appraise me as the pressure let up, although they kept tight grips on my arms. "Full name," he demanded.

"Jasmine. Jasmine Lockholme." It felt odd to say that. I hadn't been Jasmine for two long years. I could count on one hand the number of times I'd heard it used since my almost-death.

"Jasmine Lockholme? I know that name." Then he snorted. "Nice try, Jasmine," Rees said mockingly, "but we killed you two years ago."

The pressure on my arms instantly began to increase again. I gritted my teeth against the pain. "No, you didn't. You wanted to know how I got the scars, that's how. Most of them came from the day you tried to blow me up. Only my friend, Virginia, survived. Your men came and made sure."

He waved a hand at the brutes, which caused them to stop adding pressure but not let up. "Okay, let's say you are Jasmine. How did you survive? I read that report myself. You were right in the center of the blast site."

This was where the lying started. "I managed to throw myself off my horse and ended up in the ravine. No one thought to check, but eventually a caravan of merchants heard my yells for help. They rescued me and nursed me back to health. As soon as I was healthy, I left because I didn't want to endanger them."

110

"I think you're lying."

"I'm not," I ground out, furious that the brutes continued to tighten their grips. I could barely think straight around the pain radiating from my abused shoulders. I'm sure that was the point, but still. "How do you want me to prove it to you? I can provide any damn detail you want."

I saw his signal and found myself thrust to the ground. Catching myself with my hands, I whimpered as they protested the action. Eyes closed, I focused on deep breaths.

"Look at me."

I didn't see the foot coming, but pain blossomed as it knocked me on my side. The second kick pressed my back against the wall of the small room. I blinked away automatic tears and focused on Rees's face as he crouched a couple feet away.

"Who is Brighton?"

"I already told you," I said, able to see very clearly where this was headed. I curled up to try to protect myself in advance.

"Tell me again," he ordered softly.

It was tempting to tell him, to spare myself at least part of what was coming, but I wouldn't allow it. Bruises I could take. "No."

"No? You could make this so much simpler on yourself, Jasmine."

I summoned a glare. "I'm not going to tell you a damn thing about Brighton. I can't possibly believe your memory is so defective you don't remember a couple days ago, no matter how hard I slammed your head into the floor."

He sighed. "Very well. You have two minutes," he told the brutes.

What I assumed was two painful minutes later, Rees's face swam back into view.

"I'm impressed. Either you're a glutton for punishment or you're telling me the truth."

"So you believe me?" I asked, deciding every inch of me was a bruise.

"I think I do. Everyone knows that Jasmine Lockholme died. Only a complete idiot or Jasmine herself would claim that name, and I already know you're not an idiot by any stretch." He cocked his head at me. "You don't look much like sketches we had at the time."

"I might have survived, but that doesn't mean the blast didn't almost do the task. The merchants didn't even recognize me and they were from the area."

"How'd you survive?"

That hit a nerve and I got snotty. "I'm resourceful."

To my surprise, he smiled and held out a hand, rocking to his feet. "I don't doubt it. Can you stand?"

I eyed him, wondering what the trick was.

"Interrogation's over for today, Jasmine."

I hesitated before taking his hand. "You didn't get much."

"Are you complaining?"

I snorted, despite how it set my body on fire. "No."

"Good. I got something out of you last time, I got a bit more now. These things take time, especially with the tougher opponents." He now pulled me to my feet. My knees wobbled and I used my other hand to brace myself using the wall. "Take her back to her cell," he told the brutes. "Have a nice day," he told me and then vanished through the open door.

If I hadn't felt so incredibly weary and injured, I might have laughed as the brutes grabbed my arms again and escorted me back to our cell. Shorty was waiting. He unlocked the door as the two muscles shoved me in. I caught myself this time. As soon as Shorty and the thugs disappeared, I slumped in my corner, drew my knees to my chest and dropped my face onto them, wrapping my arms around my head. Although I hadn't made a complete fool of myself during the interrogation, I was aware I'd come painfully close and that was almost as bad as the bruises. I didn't bother wiping my eyes from the pain-induced tears and borderline crying, letting the wetness dry on my face instead.

After a few minutes, I heard a shuffling noise and then Jay's arm went around my shoulder. "Hey, don't worry about it," he said softly. I could hear Stella engage Dave in conversation. "Jez, c'mon, kid."

"We're the same age," I said inanely.

"I'm still older."

I lifted my head long enough to glare at him and he grinned.

"You can still talk, that's a good sign."

"Depends on who you're asking."

"Rees is an asshole specializing in assholery," Jay told me. "What did you tell him?"

"My name."

There was a pause. "Your name or your *name?*"

This time I decided the question was too stupid to even deserve a glare and I kept my face buried in my knees.

"You know what I mean," he said defensively, seeming to guess my thoughts anyway.

"My full official name."

"Ah. Let me guess. You chose to tell him your name for the shock value, but despite that, he still managed to make you feel like a helpless moron."

My shoulders tightened despite my best efforts.

"You know, that's really okay."

"No, it's not. He broke through my defenses like they were nothing. What if I can't hold out and I tell him something truly important? Everyone's safety could be riding on me. What if I'm not strong enough?" I said quietly.

"Don't be stupid," Jay said fiercely. "Jez, you are strong enough. We both are. Did you tell him anything else? Anything you didn't choose to tell him?"

"No…"

"And I'm guessing the rest was just as painful, if not more."

"Yes…"

"Then I think I've made my point. If you believe you're strong enough, we will be. Okay? Together, we can keep Rees at bay until our friends orchestrate a daring rescue. Look at it this way, Jez: he's got to be wondering how many others there are that they think they killed, but are still alive. I wish I could see his face when the implications of you being alive really sink in."

"Did you tell him anything?" I asked, peeking around my arms to watch his face.

"I told him my full name too. Let him know in no uncertain terms what I thought of him and the rest of their lot for killing my family. He did the arm thing, right?"

I nodded.

"Then we're even," he said.

"But what if he does it again, but asks something more important?"

"Then we both end up with broken or dislocated arms."

"How can you be sure?" I had to ask.

"Because I know you and I know me," he said with a smile.

I felt myself return it. "Thanks, Jay."

"You're very welcome," he said cheerfully. "What else are the most awesome friends for?"

"Lots of things, especially when it comes to you."

"I'd appreciate it if you spared Stella and Dave the details."

I laughed. "A lot of them will probably come out in the story."

"I can wait that long," he said hastily. "Sheesh, sometimes I don't know why I try and be helpful."

"Because you're sweet like that," I said. "You and Stella?" I asked softly, glancing over at our cellmates.

He winked. "You sure you're okay?"

"I will be," I said with a shrug, regretting the motion instantly as it set my bruises on fire.

"Then I'm going to go back to talking to Stella." On that note, he scooted back over to the others as I burst out laughing.

Shaking my head slightly, I shifted to settle more comfortably against the wall, leaning back and resting my head on the stone. I watched the trio before closing my eyes.

A few minutes later, I heard a hopeful voice. "Maybe telling the story would help?"

I cracked open an eye to find Dave watching me with a half-smile on his face. As soon as he saw me look, he attempted an innocent expression, no doubt coached by Jay. Then, as an obvious bribe, he offered me the water bowl.

"We need to continue to work on that look of yours," I told him, accepting it gratefully. "But you're right, it certainly wouldn't hurt. We were just leaving Kol, right?"

At his nod, I glanced over at Stella and Jay, somehow not surprised to see them sitting side-by-side, Jay's arm thrown around her shoulders in much the same way it had just been around mine. Perhaps there was still hope, even here in a jail dominated by pain and sorrow.

After the three days and thanking the citizens of Kol profusely for their assistance, the trio set out again, back the way they'd come. As they reached the crooked tree, Beau materialized, seemingly out of nowhere. Jez jumped, stumbled, and would have fallen if Jessie hadn't caught her. Ry burst out laughing at the expression on everyone's faces while Jessie looked embarrassed and Beau completely confused. "We forgot to tell her you stayed, I guess. It never occurred to us."

Jez glared daggers at her two friends. "It never occurred to you? You didn't think I might want to know that Beau was living in the woods, waiting for us? And you made me wait three whole days!"

"You weren't physically ready to leave until today," Jessie lectured.

She spotted Beau trying to stifle a smile and aimed her glare at him. "What are you smiling about, mister?" she asked, hands on her hips.

He ducked his head, trying to hide the growing smile. "Welcome back, Jez," was all he said before turning and heading down the path.

Jez blinked after him before turning to the girls. "Am I missing something?"

"Of course you are," Ry said, smirking before slipping past her with the horse.

"Okay, what is it?" she asked, trailing after them.

The two exchanged a knowing look. "Best figure that one out on your own."

"That's really cryptic and obnoxious," she complained before hurrying to catch up to Beau. "Will you tell me?"

"Tell you what?" he asked mildly.

"What I'm missing."

To her everlasting surprise, she was fairly certain she detected a faint blush briefly color Beau's cheeks. "What did Jessie say?"

"That I needed to figure it out on my own."

"Then why are you asking me?" he said.

"Ugh, all of you think you're really cute suddenly." She was rewarded with Beau's trademark smile.

"That's because we're positively adorable," Ry called cheerfully.

Jez rolled her eyes, then sobered, glancing at Beau. "I wanted to speak to you about what we talked about the other day, on our way here."

"I wasn't sure you'd even remember that."

"It's one of the few things I do recall after the escape. I had time in Kol to think about it and you were right, not that that's any surprise. I've been able to focus on some of the good memories along with the end and, as much as I'll always wish it hadn't happened, he went the way he would have wanted."

Beau nodded and waited, seeming to understand she had more to say.

The next part took a moment to put into words. "I've also been thinking about what happened after and I…I think maybe I should leave."

"Leave?" he echoed.

"I don't remember what happened, but I know enough to know I snapped and could have just as easily struck at Jessie or Ry or anyone as the Three's men. I was not in control of myself in any sense. That makes me a danger - to not just myself, but everyone."

"A danger," he repeated flatly.

"Damn it, Beau!" she said, although she still didn't look at him. Then, her shoulders sagged. "I don't want to go, but I think it might be for the best. I can still keep in touch and help where needed outside of Cavern Hall. Jessie said she told you and Mick what happened. She won't give me the details. If it's happened once, it can happen again," she said with as much feeling as possible, although the entire idea depressed her beyond words.

"How many times has it happened?" he asked.

"Once."

"In nineteen years?"

She scowled. "Obviously."

He laughed softly. "Damn it, Jasmine Lockholme, you couldn't pay me enough to throw you out."

Jez looked up at him in surprise as much at the use of her full name as his words. "But if I'm…"

"You're not. I fully believe that you are not, in the slightest, a threat to the Freedom Fighters. I also believe that you are nothing but an asset and a needed spark and so much more. I tried to help support a feeling of informality, but I'm

116

not exactly the best spokesman for it." He smiled slightly. "Especially with Mick always hovering around. You managed in a few short months to create exactly the atmosphere in Cavern Hall that I wanted. By uniting Ry with Jessie and Bri, you allowed for a greater sense of fun and spontaneity. The only way we're going to win this war is by being better than the Three. We'll likely never have superior forces, but what we do have behind us is freedom and creativity and you've brought out both." He held up a hand to forestall her comment. "This is not up for debate. This is plain fact and any current member of the Freedom Fighters will agree with me on this, so ask them if you're uncertain. Losing you, even to be a field agent, would be a blow we might never recover from."

By now, she was bright red at the praise. "Thank you, Beau, but if…"

"If I hear 'but if' out of your mouth one more time, I swear to the gods I will do something about it," he said, nudging her in the side. "Look, I know you're worried about the lapse you had, but the battle was extreme circumstances. Not only that, but Jessie said the instant you heard her voice, you stopped fighting. It took another minute for you to respond verbally, but she felt she was in absolutely no danger from you. The moral of this story is: don't upset you that much. That's something I'm fairly certain we can all manage."

Relief spread through her and she let out a breath. "Thank you," she said again.

"I should be thanking you," he said, patting her shoulder. "Don't dwell on it, okay? I'm truly not worried."

"I won't."

"Good, because if you ever get thrown out, I want to be the one to decide."

"What?" she said and then started laughing despite herself at his smug expression. She slugged him in the arm. "Don't be a jerk."

"Me? Never."

Jez just shook her head and asked how their new home was coming.

It took them two days to return to find Cavern Hall Two still in a state of disrepair. Although everyone was doing their best, things had gotten incredibly jumbled during their flight. Added to that was the fact they were still trying to sneakily smuggle leftover things from the old Cavern Hall. It wasn't easy considering the Three were maintaining a military presence in the area, although they seemed unaware of the caves themselves.

Mick was visibly glad to see them. Ignoring the other three, he walked straight up to Jez and put his hands on her shoulders. "It's good to see you well again."

She smiled, a little surprised despite his thaw. "It's good to *be* well again. Thank you for all your work trying to get me back up."

"I wish I'd been able to, but it seems the trip to Kol did the trick." Now he sent a baleful glare in Beau's direction. "We could have used our captain the past two weeks, but it was worth the risk." On that note, he let go, grabbed Beau's attention, and steered the young captain away with half dozen immediate issues to be dealt with.

Jez was left blinking in his wake. "Did he just…compliment me?"

Jessie chuckled and patted her shoulder. "Don't let it go to your head. It's not likely to happen again," she said. "C'mon, let's see if we can find someone who knows where we can put our stuff."

After being directed to the room they would share with two other women and dumping their bags, the trio immediately got to work helping sort and organize. Jez promptly got lost twice, but had no problem getting directed back to where she needed to be. She fell into bed that night absolutely exhausted and still not fully recovered. She refused to show it unless it got unbearable or the stitches popped, though.

She woke sometime in the middle of the night with the nagging suspicion that something was wrong. Not horribly, dangerously wrong but just off. Wide awake, she decided she might as well spend a bit of time familiarizing herself with their new, larger accommodations before she went back to bed. After twenty minutes, she spotted a room off to the side whose entrance glowed with lantern light. She frowned and approached, somehow not surprised to find Beau also awake and hard at work answering a heaping pile of messages. Without a word, she leaned against the rocky door and watched him. It took a few minutes for him to become aware of her presence and look up. "Oh, Jez, hi." He frowned. "Shouldn't you be sleeping?"

"Shouldn't you?" she retorted.

He waved away the question. "I'm fine," he said even as he yawned. "I've got three weeks of messages and, if we don't respond, people start to worry."

"Beau, you're on the edge of babbling. Don't embarrass yourself and go over it."

He aimed a tired glare at her. "It's true."

"What's also true is there's such a thing as delegating authority. Don't move, I'll be right back."

With that, she turned and hurried from the room, making it back to the room she shared with the others with only one brief wrong turn. She crouched between Jessie and Rylia and then shook them both.

"What?" Ry mumbled sleepily.

"Shh, it's me and I don't want to wake the others."

"What's up?" Jessie asked, sitting up and rubbing sleep out of her eyes.

"I need your help. Any idea where Dunkin and Mick are?"

"Think so, why?"

"Beau thinks he needs to go through all the messages since the battle tonight before he sleeps. We're going to help him so maybe we can all get some sleep."

"I don't like your logic," Ry grumbled, still half asleep.

"Deal with it."

"How can I get volunteered for jobs I don't even know exist?"

"It's called being in the service," Jessie said, hopping up.

It took no time to find the two men and neither protested. Mick merely rolled his eyes and acted supremely unsurprised. "I knew he would do something like this despite his promises."

They returned to Beau's new quarters. He blinked at them, then pushed a pile to each without a word. It took about two hours to shuffle through the pile, discard those already out of date or unimportant, respond to the critical ones, and make a neat pile of those that should be answered soon.

Dunk, Mick, Jessie and Ry all headed back to bed as soon as they were done but Jez lingered, leaning back in her chair. Beau crossed his arms behind his head. "Thanks. Told you that you brought spontaneity to the group."

She chuckled. "I doubt that's what you meant when you said it."

"Probably not," he said easily, "but it was still nice. Think I could get away with firing Mick and putting you in his place?"

"No one would be happy with that arrangement," Jez said, amused, "and you certainly couldn't bear to be parted from Mick."

In response, he reached over with his foot, hooked it around her chair leg and tugged, bringing her chair crashing back onto four legs.

She wrinkled her nose, amused despite herself. "That was an incredibly childish response."

"I felt it was called for," he said with a grin, leaning back.

"You never cease to amaze me, Beau."

"Should I take that as a compliment?"

"See, that's exactly what I mean!" She made a show of looking around the room. "Where did you hide the real Beau?"

He yawned again, stretching. "I think he went to bed."

She laughed. "That might be a good idea for this version too."

He dropped his head down on his desk. "Sounds good. If you'd excuse me, I'm going to sleep."

"Not there you aren't, mister. You've got a bed right there. Use it."

"Yes, mother," he retorted but didn't move.

Jez grinned. "Beau…"

He now glanced up at her, expression surprisingly serious, all things considered. "Both versions of Beau have done a lot of growing up since you first met him. I've found out what it's like to have friends…and really live." He smiled sleepily and Jez might have been more confused if it wasn't so obvious he was almost delirious from lack of sleep. "So let me enjoy it."

"Far be it for me to stop you," she said. "Okay, Mr. Eloquent, it's still time for you to get some sleep." She pointed imperiously at his bed.

"No fair picking on me when I'm exhausted."

"If you'd sleep, you wouldn't be."

He took that in. "Fair point," he conceded, standing and ambling over to his bed. "Good night, Jez, and thanks. Go get some more rest yourself and take it easy until you're a hundred percent again, okay?"

"Yes, sir," she said, tossing him an easy salute before she slipped out the door.

Ani motioned the guard out of the way and burst back into Ren's room, beaming. "Ren!"

He didn't respond, gaze directed out his window.

"Ren," she tried again and then her patience immediately ran out, despite her best efforts. "Highcastle, on your feet," she bellowed.

He shot up and saluted before he recognized what was going on. Then he glared. "That was not funny."

She just grinned. "Sorry, Renny. It was apparently the only way I could get your attention."

To her amusement and relief, he stuck his tongue out at her childishly. "Still not funny."

"I have good news!"

"Yeah?" he asked without energy.

"We're going for a walk."

"We're doing what?" he asked.

"We're going for a walk."

He still gazed at her like he didn't understand the words.

"You, me, out of the room, walking…?"

"I…wait, what?"

She rolled her eyes. "Gods' Breath, Renny, catch up. You and I are going to go for a walk right now around the castle."

His expression darkened. "That's not funny either."

"I'm telling you the truth." She twisted her hands, suddenly nervous. "I thought it…it might cheer you up and make you happier."

A glimmer of hope crackled to life in his eyes. "You aren't kidding?"

"Of course not! I wouldn't do that. Vlad's promised if you behave we can do it at least once a week. I'm sure I can convince him of more with time."

Before she could even finish the sentence, he stepped forward and hugged her. "Thank you," he whispered.

She smiled, trying to contain some of her joy at the simple motion. "Welcome. Oh, and someone's going to come in while we're gone and get your window open. So you'll still have bars, but you'll also have fresh air."

He pushed her back to arm's length, eyes suspiciously wet. "Gods' Breath, Ani, how…"

"Just smile once in a while, okay? And maybe try a laugh once a month," she said breezily, in a way that she knew most people would just ignore. There

121

really was no cost here. She just couldn't bear to see him slowly disintegrate. Ani tugged his hand. "C'mon, let's go!"

He needed no further urging. As they left the room, Ren glanced at his guards, plainly expecting them to follow.

"They're staying there," she told him. "This place is crawling with guards. They're around every corner and through every doorway. If you were to go running off or anything, you wouldn't make it five feet without being tackled by some burly man in too much armor with a big old axe."

Ren paused to look at her.

"What?" She hid a smirk.

He shook his head ruefully but smiled. "Nothing at all, Ani." Then he took a deep breath and sighed happily.

After a few moments, Ani couldn't contain her joy and started skipping alongside his walk, humming under her breath. She finally shot him a mischievous look. "You should skip too."

"Excuse me?"

"You should skip like me. Humming helps too."

"I don't really…I haven't…what?" he managed, sounding desperate.

She grabbed his arm, ignoring his protests, and began skipping again. "Skip, Renny."

He hesitated a second and then tried out a few skips before letting out a true laugh. She skidded to a stop, leaving him to continue a few steps without her. "What? Did I do something wrong?"

"No, no, but…" She smiled. "Ren, you laughed."

He blinked. "I did, didn't I?" He let out another quick laugh. "It feels good…to have something to laugh about." Then he shot her what she could only consider a sly smile. "And someone to laugh with."

She blushed and leaned forward, giving him a quick kiss on the cheek to try and cover the reddening. "You have a nice laugh. You should try and use it more often." She turned to continue, but a hand on her arm stopped her. As far as she could recall, it was one of the first times in their relationship that Ren had initiated physical contact – the hug had also been a shock.

"Thanks, Ani, really. I appreciate this so much."

"My pleasure," she said softly.

He held out his hand. "Let's skip."

She laughed, ducking her head briefly. "Let's," she said, taking it.

The two skipped out to the ramparts where they paused, slightly out of breath, to lean against the wall. "I've missed this," Ren said, gesturing out at the farmyards below. "I've missed the view and being outdoors. It always drove my father nuts that I hated to be inside too long, although he understood and always said I'd grow out of it like he did."

"Makes sense," she said, staring resolutely out at the farms. He was merely grateful for the chance to get outside, but his gratitude would fade and he'd go back to barely tolerating her. Everyone did. Even Sorin could barely deal with her any more. "Would you hate it if you had to marry me?" she asked softly, pursing her lips as soon as the question was out and definitely not daring to look at him now.

His answer caught her by surprise, especially the lack of hesitation. "No."

"But I'm always so..." She waved her hand helplessly to try and illustrate what she meant.

"It's kind of refreshing."

He's just being nice, he's just being nice, because he owes you and he gets no say. "I know I annoy you all the time. I annoy everyone all the time."

"Even assuming that's true, which it isn't, that doesn't mean I'd hate you if I married you."

"You know that's why Sorin and Vlad kept you alive."

"Yeah, I'd figured that one out."

She hesitated and then decided she might as well take the conversation to its logical conclusion. "But you wouldn't love me."

"And how do you know that?"

Ani frowned. "Ren, this isn't funny. I'm one of your captors. My brother killed your father and all three of us have been ruling *your* country for almost two years."

Ren reached out, touching her shoulder and gently turning her to face him. Then he used his other hand to tilt her chin up until they were eye to eye. "Are you really, Ani Opalin?"

She stared at him, speechless and dumbfounded, unable to break eye contact, not sure what to say in light of the intensity in his blue eyes.

Finally, he let go. "Don't worry about it," he said, "doesn't really matter." He turned to look back out, but she shoved her hand into his shoulder to stop him.

"It does matter. I think it matters quite a lot. Are you saying you might... that you could...?"

"Love you?" he asked.

She nodded wordlessly, not sure what to say even if she were capable of words. She stood frozen as he reached up and lightly touched her cheek.

"Think anyone's watching?"

"Probably," she somehow managed to get out.

"Good." Then he leaned forward and pressed his lips against hers. For an instant, she stiffened instinctively before she let herself melt into it. The hand on his shoulder shifted until it was threaded through his mussed hair. Far too quickly, he pulled back, a crooked grin gracing his lips. "I definitely could." Before she could speak, he held a cautionary finger to her lips, his other hand still on her cheek. "That's not a promise. That's a let's see how it goes."

"That's all I want," she said softly and then smiled shyly. "I've never... before...you know, so that's okay, really."

He smiled, resting his forehead gently against hers. "I didn't expect this."

"I didn't either," she said truthfully. She had yearned for it, sure, but expected it? Never in a million years. She knew better than to ever truly hope for anything.

Ren shifted, wrapping one arm around her waist so they were standing side-by-side looking out at the sunset. After a moment, she hesitantly laid her head against his shoulder. He squeezed her waist slightly in response and Ani felt herself smile, feeling like she could light up the whole world with joy.

Finally, as the sun dipped out of sight behind the mountains, she stirred.

"Not used to standing still so long?" Ren teased.

She giggled. "That and we should probably get back. I don't want Vlad to think we're taking advantage of his offer."

"Good point. C'mon, you," he said, tugging her gently. She turned away from the landscape and carefully slipped her hand into his, not missing the smile that spread across his face at the motion.

It seemed far too quick before they reached Ren's room. "I suppose you should probably go," he said.

"Suppose I should."

Neither of them made any motion to move, standing just inside Ren's doorway, the location giving them some foolish sense of privacy from the guard only a couple feet away.

"What do you think your brothers will think of this?" Ren asked, sounding nervous for the first time.

"Don't know and don't particularly care. They *should* be ecstatic we're doing all their work for them." She caught the way he eyed her and knew her tone had come across as perhaps a touch too bitter, a touch too close to the interior.

Before Ren could answer, someone called Ani's name. She recognized Old Bert's voice immediately and sighed. "Yes?" she asked, sticking her head back out the door.

"Commander Dakamar and General Opalin are looking for you, Miss Ani."

"All right, I'll go find them in a minute." She withdrew into the room. "Hey, Renny?"

"Yes?" he asked.

"I'm afraid I've got to go, but I'll be back soon."

"I'll see you in a bit, then."

"Try not to pine away without me, okay, Muffin?"

He did an honest-to-goodness double take. "Excuse me? *Muffin?*"

"Yes, muffin, Muffin."

"Why muffin?" he asked cautiously.

"Because I like muffins. They're tasty."

"I don't want to know the connection."

"Bet you can guess."

"Bet I don't want to."

Old Bert cleared his throat loudly.

"I think we're delaying your friend."

"Oh, are we? So sorry," Ani said with false politeness, knowing Bert would pick up on it. "Well, Muffin, I must be off."

"Just wait until I think of some terrible nickname for you."

"Impossible."

"And why's that?"

"You're too nice to be terrible." She had to grin as his face twisted, trying to follow her logic.

"Wanna bet?" he finally settled on.

"Sure, since we both know I'd end up winning."

"…Not fair."

Chapter Eleven

OUR EVENING MEAL ARRIVED RIGHT on time. I mentally added up the days and sighed, realizing it had only been about four days. It seemed longer.

"You have to let go of Stella's hand if you want to eat easily."

I chuckled as Jay and Stella let go of each other instantly.

"Right you are, Dave," Jay said, trying to play it cool.

"You're supposed to let them suffer until they figure it out themselves," I told the boy as Jay stuck his tongue out at me. "It's part of the learning process." I winked at Stella, who chuckled.

"Jez, I swear to the gods, one of these days I'm going to kill you."

"You'd better hurry up then," I teased.

"Yeah, yeah," he said, waving his spoon in a vaguely threatening manner. Then he looked at Dave and aimed the spoon in his direction as well. "You too, you rascal, I'm also watching you."

The boy grinned. "Don't you just love living on top of each other?" he asked innocently.

Stella and I burst out laughing.

"You're all nuts."

"All of us?" Stella asked, voice just a bit on the dangerous side.

"Um, I mean, they are! Of course not you."

"Really smooth, Jamesy."

"Shut up, you."

Stella fought a smile. "I suppose I'll give you a chance to redeem yourself."

"I feel the intense need to say get a room. Shame you can't," I said mournfully.

Jay threw the spoon at me which I easily ducked, as sore as I was. That reminded me of something, though, and I carefully stood as I tossed it back. I grimaced, already stiff and sore.

"You sure you want to do that?" Jay asked, concern coloring his voice.

"Yes," I said tightly. "If I wait any longer, I won't be able to move for a week."

"I'm moving fine."

"Nothing personal, Jay, but I think he hit me harder than you. All three were smarting after what happened last time." My legs wobbled but held my weight and I carefully stretched out the best I could before returning to the ground with a groan. "Okay, that hurt."

"Idiot."

I made a face at him.

"But I still like you."

"Gee, thanks."

Dave yawned, cuddling up to Stella, before peering cheekily up at Jay. "Am I taking your space?"

"David!" Stella said, but her rebuke was ruined by the fact she couldn't help giggling.

"I hate you," Jay informed him before deliberately curling up with his back to us.

I wasn't particularly tired yet so I stayed where I was, eyes directed out the cell door, although I let myself not focus, mind rolling over recent and past events in my head. Finally, I drifted off.

I woke with a start as pain ricocheted through my body, something connecting harshly with one of my new bruises. I pulled my head off the bars from where it had dropped sometime during the night and looked up. Standing on the other side of the bars was Rees, looking inordinately pleased with himself. "Good morning, Jasmine!"

"I've had better," I said flippantly. Truth be told, I'd never been much of a morning person.

"Each to their own," he replied, undaunted by the fact I was glaring at him. "Can you stand?"

I shrugged, minimizing my movement. "Possibly. Since you woke me, you should be able to tell I haven't tried this morning."

"Why don't you now?"

"Because I'm rather comfortable right here, thanks all the same," I said, keeping things casual.

Rees ruined that. "That wasn't a suggestion." He nodded to his right and, upon peering past him, I spotted my two favorite burly guards.

I sighed and, using the bars, carefully levered myself to my feet. It wasn't pretty and was quite painful, but I got up all the same. "There. Happy now?"

He grinned with what I could only identify as sheer glee. "I suppose so." Then he leaned in. "So, it would appear we're even now."

"It would," I said, not sure where this was going.

"I figured I'd give you a couple days to recover before we had another round with me winning. Don't want to bruise your ego too hard too quickly."

I let out a laugh. "Fine by me. Far be it for me to tell you what to believe."

He smirked. "Stay cocky now, that's fine, but it won't last. We have all the time in the world."

"Think what you like." I leaned carefully against the wall and folded my arms.

Rees opened his mouth and then paused, looking going a bit more wary. Jay's hand landed on my shoulder. "Morning, Colonel."

"Jay," he said with a nod.

"Did you want something?"

"Just to talk to Jasmine."

"Since you have, can you leave now before you stink up the place anymore?"

Rees's expression darkened. "Heal up, Jasmine. Jay, perhaps you might want to hold your tongue next time or I'm afraid when we meet again something might get broken. I'll be visiting you both soon." With that, he turned on his heel and strode off, brutes trailing him.

"Sit," Jay told me and then helped me down, which I was grateful for. My legs really weren't a fan of being used.

"You really shouldn't bait him like that."

"Got him to leave, didn't it?"

I couldn't argue with his results.

"Now there is one who could use a heck of a lot more beauty sleep."

I snickered. On the outside, Rees actually wasn't bad looking sadly and probably only in his late-twenties, but I agreed with Jay's assessment anyway. "I'm not sure all the beauty sleep in the world would help him."

"Did my beauty sleep work?" he asked, striking a pose.

"Absolutely. You're looking as gorgeous as always."

He winked at me as the guard with food arrived, like he had been waiting for Rees to clear out. Jay leaned over to wake the Harpers while I pulled the bowls and utensils to the center of the cell.

I hadn't even put down my empty bowl before I realized Dave's eyes were glued on me, as if he might miss part of the story if he looked away. I was just glad I could distract him. "No need to ask. I'm there." I set my bowl down, took a brief pause to figure out where to pick the story up, and then started.

By the time two months had passed, the Freedom Fighters had swelled to their pre-battle numbers through new recruits and were fully settled in at the new Cavern Hall. Not only that, but their network outside had tripled. They now received frequent communiqués from all the larger towns and cities as well as reports on all the troop movements of the Three's soldiers and the Three themselves. Much of this was thanks to a member of the network named Col, who had appeared right after the takeover in Bejen.

Rylia passed Beau a paper. "Sounds important."

He looked amused and took it.

Jez, meanwhile, crumpled another paper and threw it into the growing pile as she adjusted her position to make herself more comfortable. She had her legs resting on Beau's desk with her chair tipped back slightly. Jessie sat in one of the other chairs, bent over one a particularly long message, reading closely. Ry hopped up, grabbed another pile, and then settled back in against the wall, legs crossed. Beau paced the length of the room as he weeded through the messages the women passed him.

"You get more papers than should be humanly allowed. Think of the trees," Jez said.

"They're trees put to good use," he retorted.

Both ignored the look Jessie and Ry exchanged, used to them.

"Good use. Uh huh. Like this one: everything is calm, awaiting instruction." She snorted. "Really useful."

Beau rolled his eyes at her. "Of course it is, now I don't need to worry about whoever that is."

"Aren't we hoping we don't have to worry about most of them? Shouldn't they only send messages if we need to worry?"

Whatever Beau might have said was stolen as one of their newer recruits burst through the door. "Sir!" He hesitated at the sight of the three women and then threw all four a salute. "Master Mick says that there have been reports of Three scouts within a mile of Cavern Hall, sir."

Beau reached over and snagged a rolled-up map, flattening it on top of his desk. "You," he said, pointing at the recruit, "go get Dunkin Kramer." As soon as the man disappeared, he turned to the map. "Thank the gods we've got a bigger space here," he said to the trio as they gathered around. "We should be able to stay hidden given that and the extra precautions we've put in place. Jessie, Ry, I need you to alert the guards and make sure all the entranceways have extra protection. Then, make sure everyone is inside and accounted for."

The two nodded and Ry tossed an absent salute, as they hurried out the door.

"Jez, I need you to find Iris and get her to gather our young and old and get them to the hiding place. She knows where. Then...actually, can you grab Reardon and Mick first and send them here?" He flashed her a quick grin. "If Iris gives you any trouble, let me know."

"With pleasure," she said and took off. She met Mick halfway to the main area where Reardon could usually be found. "Sir, Beau-"

"I figured," Mick said, patting her on the shoulder as he went by.

It wasn't hard to locate Reardon either, his booming voice echoed through the entire cave system. She waved to get his attention and he immediately set his assistant, Nathaniel, to teaching and came over. "Yes, lass?" he asked.

"Beau wants you. The Three are looking for us."

His expression turned grave. "Okay, thank you," he said before looking at his students. "Class dismissed early," he bellowed, waved away any questions, and hurried toward Beau's office.

Iris was a bit harder, but Jez found her a few minutes later just leaving her classroom. If anything, the large woman's dislike of Jez and the others had grown. Ry attended her classes only three times a week at Beau's orders and Jessie usually forced her to do some learning outside of it anyway. Not only that, but Iris had learned that Jez had spent the better of a year at only eighteen without ever attending lessons.

Jez repeated Beau's orders and got a disgusted look in return. "If the captain wanted me to do this, he would have sent someone responsible. Not one of you."

"Ma'am," Jez said levelly, "I've put up with your bullshit for an entire year and I'm pretty damn sick of it. I'm here to help just like you and just because Beau and I are also *friends* does not mean you have any right to doubt my authority when he sends me on an *important* errand. If you have a problem with this, we can talk about it later or I could throw you outside for the Three to find right now. Your choice."

Iris raised an eyebrow, expression never flickering. "Think you could follow through on that threat?"

"I'd figure out a way, absolutely."

The woman snorted. "Then off you go. I've got a job to do." She cracked her knuckles and stomped off, leaving Jez to stare after her, not sure what to think about that brief confrontation.

She shook herself and headed back to Beau's office to see how else she could help. She reached the doorway and paused uncertainly. Beau had his back to her as he pointed things out on the map to Reardon and Mick, the three highest ranking people in the camp. She felt a twinge of nervousness as she realized how much time she'd been spending with Beau and she had to wonder if she was taking him away from his duties. In the two months since the battle, Beau had slipped into the fourth place in their little group. Jez forced the nerves away. If Mick cared or didn't approve, he certainly wouldn't be shy about letting her know it.

She smiled as she watched Beau point at something and then look to Mick for confirmation. Mick studied it and then nodded, saying something too quiet for her to hear, but she could tell Beau was smiling.

"Hello, Jez. You can come in you know," Mick said, spotting her.

She blushed and slipped into the room, glowering at Beau for his amused smile.

"Okay, I think that about does it," Beau said, winking at her. "Mick, take west. Reardon, east. I'll take south and Reardon, I don't know where that recruit went but grab Dunkin and send him to watch the north."

Jez frowned, opening her mouth but a look from Beau silenced her.

Mick glanced between them, shook his head, and followed Reardon out of the room.

"I could easily take the north," she burst.

Beau stared at the map and refused to look at her.

"Beau…"

"I know you could," he said quietly, "but the risk…"

"The risk? Gods' Breath, Beau, of course there's a risk. Living is a gods-be-damned risk these days. You know I can take care of myself."

He cringed, shuffling some papers around the desk.

She softened. "Look, I appreciate it. I appreciate you care enough to worry, but you can't protect everyone in this business, Beau."

He finally looked up at her seriously. "I know. I just wish I could." They stood silently, eyes locked. "Okay, go tell Dunkin you've got the north. And be careful?"

She smiled quickly. "I will. You'd better follow your own advice as well." She took off towards the northern entrance of Cavern Hall, running into Dunkin halfway there. "Hey, I'm taking over for you," she said.

"But Reardon said," Dunkin started, but Jez cut him off.

"Beau changed the orders. I promise."

"Okay," he said easily. Jez knew he had large, and still growing, respect for her after the way they'd escaped thanks to her quick thinking, but she wasn't sure she wanted it. "Let's get you out there then."

The two slipped out the doorway, listening hard. A minute passed before Dunkin nodded. It seemed they were clear. He then handed her a satchel of food and water and gave her a boost up onto the first branch. She grabbed the next one and swung up, climbing with relative ease. Not only had she climbed plenty of trees with her brothers as a child, but Beau had also made everyone practice for just this eventuality. She reached the platform Beau had ordered constructed and pulled herself onto it.

"He's a genius," she muttered, not for the first time, as she took in the platform. The bottom looked just like a tree branch wrapping around the trunk from below. The design mimicked some of the most populous local trees, so it wouldn't look the least bit suspicious. She dropped to her hands and knees and crept forward until she could see Dunkin. She shot him a thumbs up, even if the height made her stomach twist.

He returned it and disappeared back inside.

Jez scooted against the solid reassurance of the trunk and let out a breath of relief. Luckily, the platform was between two and three feet across which gave her some room to maneuver without getting too close to the edge. She crossed her legs, then cringed when a rumbling, followed by a thump, signaled that she was locked out of Cavern Hall until someone came back for her. It quickly became apparent it was going to be a long wait. The woods were surprisingly quiet – although if soldiers were tromping around, Jez didn't blame the animals for hiding too. She drifted into thought, only snapping back to the present when she heard a noise that might need investigating. The afternoon slowly stretched into evening and Jez chewed on a simple meal of biscuits and dried beef. Evening gave way to night and she began to nod off. She checked the area and then stood and stretched out all her muscles. She then mimed a few of the sword moves she had worked on first with Bri and later with Jessie and Beau, not daring draw her sword and potentially create a reflection.

It was almost fully dark out and she was sitting again, thinking, when another sound drew her attention. She carefully dropped to her hands and knees and inched forward, peering out. Nothing moved and then one of the shadows detached from a tree and slid forward into a faint pool of light. Even as weak as the light was, the form was still identifiable as a man. She scooted around so she could see the stone that marked the hidden entrance to Cavern Hall and watched, pressing herself flat against the wood. The man appeared a moment later, feeling along the rock and peering into every fold. He passed by the door without a pause and she grinned. *Complete success,* she thought with no little satisfaction. She watched for a few more minutes before the shadow disappeared in the opposite direction of Cavern Hall. She waited for a thirty count and then sat back against the tree trunk again. Now, fairly certain the rest of the night would be silent, she let her thoughts truly drift, especially wandering to those lost to her, dead or alive.

As morning dawned, crisp and clear, her thoughts shifted to her current friends. She stood, stretching out cramped muscles from the odd positions she'd forced herself into overnight to stay awake. She finished off her last couple biscuits, suspecting someone would come retrieve her soon. Then she sat back and listened to the sounds of awakening wildlife – the birds singing their morning songs and various animals making their way through the growth beneath her. She relaxed, feeling reassured by the usual forest noises. A frown crossed her face as she abruptly realized that she rarely relaxed anymore and only when she was either alone, which was rare in the tight quarters, or just with her friends. She tried to remember her exact conversation with Dunkin the previous afternoon and figure out if she'd been rude to him. She'd kept conversations and interactions with the others to a minimum and short.

"Am I too afraid that, if I make a friend, I'll lose them too?" she wondered out loud. She debated this, trying to be fully truthful with herself, and arrived at the conclusion it was true. Mentally, she told herself it was time to open up again. That Bri, of all people, would be appalled at her shutting down.

"Jez, you awake?" It was Dunkin. In her musings, she had totally missed the door opening.

"Yeah, I am," she said, "and on my way down!" She slipped the satchel through her belt and carefully reached down to find the next branch.

"Be careful!"

"I will," she said quickly before remembering her mental promise. "Sorry, Dunkin," she said, "just tired."

"No problem. To be expected!" he called up cheerfully.

She carefully climbed down before hopping the last couple feet to land at his side.

"So?" he asked.

"I got a visitor and he passed by the doorway without any hint of identification. Qualified success."

Dunkin let out a whoop and pumped the air.

Jez grinned. "My thoughts exactly." She yawned. "I'd better go report to Beau before I fall asleep standing up."

"Of course," he said, falling into step beside her.

Jez knew she should apologize so took a deep breath and did so.

He eyed her. "For what?"

"For being really short with you and almost everyone else here. I realize I've been really closed off since the battle and you've never been anything but nice to me, starting my first day."

Dunkin shrugged. "Trust me, you weren't that bad, and we all figured you'd snap out of it soon enough. You went through a lot two months ago and sometimes these things take time. I think, of all the people in the world, those of us here understand that better than most."

"Still, that doesn't make my behavior acceptable."

"Very well then, apology accepted, forget about it, and play nice from now on."

She laughed despite herself. "See, this is what I mean about being nice."

"I just can't help it."

"Anyway, I *am* sorry."

"Not a problem." He waved her into Beau's office and then headed off cheerfully, probably to spread the good news.

Beau's head rested on his desk and she was fairly certain he had to be out cold. She quietly took a seat and stuck her feet up on the desk, inches from his head. "What did I tell you about sleeping at your desk?" she asked with mock severity.

His head jerked up and he looked around until he focused on her. "Oh. It's you."

"Who else would it be?"

He yawned. "Don't know. Someone nice?" he asked, poking her feet.

She grinned, dragging them off. "Aw, I thought you'd like them," she said with a yawn of her own.

"Like your feet? Why?"

She shrugged. "Why not? I'll admit, I'm a little hurt you don't."

"I'm not exactly what you'd call a foot person."

Jez stared at him. "I can't believe you said that," she said finally.

He thought about it. "You're not the only one."

"You know, you're actually fun to talk to when you're half asleep."

He glared sleepily at her. "Are you insinuating I'm not fun to talk to when I'm wide awake?"

She adopted a perfect Bri-like innocent expression.

"Oh, ha ha, very funny. You going to give me your report or not?"

"Oh. Right. I saw a man, he felt all around including near the door and never paused or looked twice. I'm positive he was fooled." She stifled another inopportune yawn. "I think you're just trying to change the subject, though."

He attempted to look dignified, but failed considering he was still mostly asleep and his hair jutted in every direction. She reached over and patted it down. "Thank you for the report and good work."

"And what am I supposed to do now? Salute, say 'yes, sir', and wander off to bed?"

"That would be nice. Then I could get back to sleep myself."

"But that's no fun." She stretched, leaning back in the chair.

He dropped his head back onto the desk with a dull thump. "I don't want to talk to you anymore. All you do is make fun of me. So I'm going back to sleep."

"Do we need to restart this conversation?" Jez said, trying to fight how inviting it looked to do the same.

He lifted his head just enough to peek out one eye at her. "Not if your feet are going to come into it." Both of them yawned, almost in concert. "We should really get some sleep."

"I'm going, I'm going," she murmured, pushing herself up before sinking back into the comfort of the chair. "Perhaps I should just stay here. It's kinda comfortable after all."

"So do I get to tease you about it now?"

She waved a hand in his direction as she dropped her head onto his desk. "Sure, go ahead."

Both of them sat in silence.

"What're you waiting for?" she asked, cracking an eye open to look at him.

He peeked back up at her. "It's no fun making fun of someone when you're as tired as they are. I hereby withhold my teasing rights until a more opportune time." He glanced at his bed. "We really shouldn't fall asleep here," he said, making an attempt to rouse himself. Jez didn't bother. "Our friends would never let us live it down if they found us like this. Why don't you use the bed?"

"Because there's only one. You need one too," she replied, quickly fading now that her head was cradled in her arms and she was halfway comfortable.

"That's fine. I've slept in worse."

"I wouldn't be able to sleep in good conscious if you were sleeping here." She glanced over at his bed – which, like everyone else, was a slightly nicer than average bedroll – and squinted. "You've got a big one!"

"Perks of being the captain."

"Then that makes it easy. It's big enough to fit both of us."

Her brain told her that the logic there – and the embarrassment factor – was skewed, but if Beau was thinking the same thing, he was too tired to debate it. Jez slithered out of her chair and went over, flopping on it, asleep almost instantly. Beau was a bit more cautious, but couldn't resist, making sure to leave a little bit of space between them before falling asleep too.

Jez recognized the dream almost immediately. It always started the same way. Bri was there, yelling 'charge' at the top of his lungs. The entire group surged forward, drawing her along with them, despite the fact she knew how it would end. "Bri, no, *no*, come back!" she yelled, fighting towards him. Every time she got close, a new enemy popped up in front of her. Finally, she could see his back as he fought a soldier. She sprinted forward but he went down. Jez stumbled to his side and dropped, abruptly realizing it wasn't Bri at all, but Beau's face staring up at her, unseeing and bloody. This was not how her nightmare was meant to go, though. She jerked backwards, stomach in her throat. The scene around her froze and then it fell back into action and it wasn't just Bri or Beau, but also Jessie and Ry, Dunkin and Mick, even Reardon and Colin lying in front of her.

"No, please, no, someone help, please!" She started sobbing.

"Jez? Jez, wake up."

She knew she recognized the voice, but the context was all off. She woke slowly, disoriented from the dream and blinded by the very real tears that had translated out of her sleep. She fought her confusion, despite the fact someone was holding her tightly and rocking her back and forth. Usually when she had them, Jessie or Ry would wake her and sit with her until all of them were calm enough to sleep again.

"Nightmare?"

She managed to focus on the person who held her. "Beau?"

"Right here. What's wrong?"

Jez leaned against his chest, feeling surprisingly safe and comfortable. "How'd this…" She gestured aimlessly around them.

"As far as I can tell, we were drunk on lack of sleep. I'm sure you'll remember once you wake up a bit more." He gently wiped her tears away. "We both fell asleep on my bed."

"Well, that's rather ridiculous," she said, laughing slightly. "I teased you about my feet."

"And I told you I wasn't a feet person."

"I remember now." She made no move.

"So what's it about?" he asked softly.

"Reoccurring nightmare since the battle. Usually it's a replay of the battle, which is bad enough, but tonight I didn't just see Bri dead, but everyone. You, Jessie, Ry, my brother, everyone." She swiped at her eyes. "Gods' Breath, Beau, that can't be the future, right?" she asked desperately.

"I can guarantee it isn't."

"How?"

"Simple. I have absolutely no intention of dying."

"I doubt Bri or the others we lost did either."

"They can't and won't get all of us."

"We could fail."

"We won't."

"How can you know?"

"Because we're smart and dedicated and we know what we're doing. Add into that the fact that we are gaining new recruits almost daily – we have not just replaced our numbers from the battle but actually increased in size." He grinned crookedly. "Anyway, if we were all dead, you would be too."

"Oh, that's so reassuring," she retorted but smiled.

He shrugged. "It's true."

"Yeah, yeah," she said, yawning as she settled more comfortably against him.

"So don't worry. You're not going to lose me or anyone. I promise."

"Good," she murmured, eyes closed as he continued to rock her gently. "Thanks, Beau."

"You're very welcome, Jasmine," he whispered as her breath evened out. He gently lay her down and covered her with a blanket before settling beside her again, letting just their shoulders touch.

Something bounced off her head, then something else.

"If you don't stop that, she's going to kill you and I won't stop her." That was Beau.

Someone giggled.

Jez forced her eyes open and blinked owlishly just in time for another balled up piece of paper to bounce off her face.

She glared sleepily at Rylia. Her friend whistled innocently and pretended to be very interested in Beau's desk. Then she aimed it at Beau and Jessie. "Maybe I'll just kill all of you, since I see no one stopping her."

Beau grinned. "Glad to see you're more rested."

She sat up and ran a hand through her hair. "What time is it?"

"Just about dinner. Beau suggested we wake you up so your internal clock won't be totally screwed up."

"Ah. Makes sense. What are you three up to?"

"I'm reading the latest batch of messages. Who knows what those two are doing."

Ry smirked. "I'm playing with the rejects."

"I hadn't noticed, except for the fact they all made their way to my head."

The younger girl giggled and balled up another one.

Jez raised an eyebrow, just daring her to throw it at her. Instead, Ry bounced it off Jessie's head. Jessie immediately snagged another and threw it right back. Jez couldn't resist scooping up one of those that had hit her head and throwing it at Ry. This resulted in an all-out war between the trio that only ended when Jez realized Beau was entirely ignoring them. This, unto itself, was not new. But she was fairly certain this was the same message he'd picked up when the paper-war started. Jez caught one of the papers and then held up her hand, turning to Beau. "What is it?"

"You know Col? He previously in Bejen?"

"Of course. Wait, he's moved?" Jez said.

"Yeah, his message before this said they'd relocated to Greensward. But he apparently spent the last week in Oakbridge, observing the Three." He offered her the message. "He's got an interesting perspective on the trio. He also warns we should watch out for Anica, that she's apparently going to, according to rumors, try and infiltrate us."

"That should be easy enough to guard against," Jessie said, accepting the paper from Jez and scanning it. "Who is Col?"

"I'm not sure of his, or her, I suppose, exact identity, but they've been nothing but reliable. There are at least two of them that write under the same pen name, but I consider that handwriting to be the real Col. He writes far more often and seems to get around, where the other writes only about local politics and rumblings."

"Interesting." Jessie handed it off to Ry.

Beau sat back in his chair. "I have to wonder why someone would do what the Three have done," he said, which was a topic change certainly, but Jez could follow.

She shrugged. "We might never know, but I agree with you. I kind of wish we could know."

"It doesn't matter why," Ry said, "because it was still wrong, no matter how you look at it."

None of them could argue with that.

Ani hummed to herself as she stepped into Vlad's office, a rather grand room that fit all three siblings comfortably. "Anica." She froze a step inside the door, sensing as much as she heard something off in Vlad's tone. He'd also used her full name.

"Yes?" she asked cautiously.

"I'd like to congratulate you on a job well done with everyone's favorite prince. I don't know how you did it, but the important question is: will he marry you without a fight?"

Ani stared at her eldest brother.

"Anica?" Sorin prompted and, as she turned to him, she thought she caught something like pain dart across his face.

"I don't know. We didn't…we didn't talk that far." Which wasn't entirely accurate. Distantly, she was glad that *every* word they'd exchanged hadn't been overheard.

"But he admitted he loves you?" Vlad pressured.

"Vladimir," Sorin said sharply, "we have what we want, so leave it alone."

"I'm not making him like me," she said shrilly, feeling like she'd been punched.

Vlad waved a hand dismissively, a new habit these days. "Doesn't matter. What does matter is that he agrees soon and without many conditions."

"Conditions?" Ani echoed, for lack of anything better to say.

"Yes, we need him to peacefully become a figurehead and if we have to bribe him, so be it. Think you could hurry up the agreement?"

Ani stared at him. She had known, in a distant sort of way, that there was something wrong, but there was always something wrong. This, however, went above and beyond the usual. She glanced at Sorin, but his expression was disturbingly blank as he also watched Vlad. "I…maybe I don't want to hurry it up," she said flatly.

"Why wouldn't you? It would work to everyone's advantage. You get the prince. We get the country for good."

"But," she started, not even sure what she wanted to say.

It didn't matter because he cut her off. "But nothing, Ani. Don't be difficult. Once Patrick's younger son sees that his brother is on the throne again, he'll back off."

"That's not true!" she protested, even as she filed that interesting tidbit away for later thought and discussion with Ren.

"It's not?" Vlad's voice dipped dangerously.

"No, of course not," she said, purposefully lightening her voice. The clueless moron act always worked on Vlad. "It's obvious that Renny's brother is smart, so he'll be able to figure out pretty quickly we're just using him."

"All of us?" Sorin asked carefully, rejoining the conversation.

Her gaze darted to him, concerned that she still couldn't read his face, especially since, recently, she'd been able to again. "All of us. I have to go work," she added, more loudly than she meant.

It took another ten minutes before she could extract herself and she paused outside, trying to calm herself. Vlad had shocked her and Ani felt even more unsettled about life than usual. Her conversation with Ren just an hour earlier kept replaying in her head with an overlay of Vlad's almost accusations. She knew she needed to talk to Ren, but Sorin had beat her out the door and she suspected his first stop was Ren's room, although what he might say was a complete and utter mystery to her. As were most things Sorin did these days.

She bit her lip. Never had it been this bad, especially since Edward had died. Ani felt the usual doubts creep in and she fought them and the accompanying tears down. She did not cry. She leaned against the wall, childhood memories inching in at the thought of her father. She swallowed hard. Memories of Edward's fists and the words and the endless nights and how close they had been and how Edward had forced the change and now…now they were holding together by barely a thread. The memories swirled through her mind and she sunk to the ground, covering her face and squeezing her eyes shut. Over the years, she had gotten very good at compartmentalizing the past, shutting it away, but when it came out, it happened with a vengeance. She wondered if Vlad and Sorin struggled with the same issues.

"Ani?"

"What, Vlad?" she asked, voice muffled by her hands.

"What are you doing on the floor?"

"Nothing."

"Nothing?"

"It's nothing," she said fiercely.

"Are you okay?"

"Yes." She listened for his footsteps, but didn't hear them. "Vlad."

"Yes?"

"Go away."

Again, silence. "Is this about Ren?"

That didn't even deserve an answer.

"You're going to run to him and make a fool of yourself again, aren't you? He doesn't really love you."

"You don't know that."

"Do you?"

She bit her lip, still not moving her hands. No, she didn't. He had only said it was possible, not certain. It was enough for her, but now, she wondered. Was Ren playing her?

"See, I know people, Ani. They don't always mean what they say."

"You don't believe in love, do you?"

"No."

She caught her breath. "At all?" she whispered.

"No."

"And that's why we will ultimately fail," she said, standing but not looking at him.

"We will not fail."

"Of course we will. If we weren't already in trouble, you wouldn't need Ren. That's why we need a figurehead. That's why the people don't trust us like they trusted King Patrick."

"Don't call him that."

"That's what he was!" She brushed past him, heading for Ren's room, Sorin or no Sorin.

"You're running to him!"

"Yes, I am," she said, spinning to face her brother. "Because I *do* believe in love and I have faith in Ren that he's telling me the truth."

"There's no such thing as faith either."

"Says you. Damn it, Vlad, Edward sucked, there's no doubt about that, but I've also looked around the world and seen all the people who had good childhoods, loving families, who *fell in love*. I want to be like those people."

He snorted derisively. "You helped us take over Tira, Anica. You will never be like those people."

"Of course not. I have dreams but I'm not deluded. My family sucks, but my future doesn't have to." She turned and started off again.

Vlad's voice, as cold as she'd ever heard it, stopped her dead. "I think you need to analyze where your true feelings lie. Then make a decision and either throw yourself on the mercy of *those* people or start helping Sorin and me with all your heart."

"I do support you and Sorin. I always have and I always will," she said quietly without turning around, "but you're not all there is to my life, as much as you might believe otherwise. If you can't accept that…" she let her sentence hang and turned the corner. A minute later, she reached Renny's room, slowing as she listened for voices. Upon hearing none, she strode up to the guard. He looked surprised at being acknowledged by her. "I'm supposed to talk to Renny without anyone listening in. Make sure it's done, please," she said cheerfully, not wanting to make him suspicious.

"Yes, ma'am," the man said, saluting and stepping across the hall out of hearing range, if the door was shut.

Ani slipped inside, pulling the door shut behind her.

Ren stood with his back to her, clutching the bars on his now open window.

"Ren?"

He glanced back at her thoughtfully. "Hey."

She stepped in a bit more. "I…what did you and Sorin talk about?"

He pursed his lips, turning fully to face her. "I'm not entirely sure. What did you talk to your brothers about?"

"If I can convince you to marry me with only a couple conditions," she said quietly.

"What did you say?"

"Not much," she admitted, wrapping her arms around her middle. "I didn't know what to say. I didn't want to get either of us in trouble and Vlad was so insistent."

"And Sorin?"

"He didn't say much either way before bee-lining it here. How do you not know what you talked about?"

"He didn't say much. I think he was testing me somehow so I mostly listened."

She searched his face. "Ren…are we…?"

"I don't know."

She stepped up to him, grabbed his face between her hands and kissed him firmly. "I love you," she said, holding his gaze. "It's okay if you don't love me back, but I need to say it. I need you to know that nothing my brothers do or say will change that." She held his face, although he made no move to get away. "I know you can't lie when you're looking someone in the eye, so tell me right now that you're not playing me. That the chance we talked about earlier is possible and not sullied by anything Sorin or Vlad might have said or might say in the future."

He reached up and gently tucked her hair behind her ear. "I promise I'm not playing you, Ani. I meant what I said earlier." He bit his lip, eyes darting across her face. "I…Gods' Breath, Ani," he said and huffed out a laugh. "As fucked up as this situation is, I think I love you too."

Her entire face lit up. "Really?"

"Really. You just…make the whole world brighter and, yes, you drive me up a wall sometimes but, the gods help me, I *like* it."

Ani finally let go of his face, dropping her hands, but he caught one, gently entwining their fingers. "We need to get you out of here," she said.

"Excuse me?"

"We need to get you out of here."

"Yes, I heard you, but…"

"I can't let them use you like that. You'll be safe away from here. You can hide with the Freedom Fighters until our base crumbles enough and then you can come be king for real, like you're supposed to." She hesitated. "And I'm afraid what Vlad might do when he finally snaps."

Neither spoke.

"What about you?"

"I'll be fine."

"Ani-"

"Renny, no matter what else happens, they are my brothers and I've made my bed."

"I don't want you to get hurt."

"Drop it, Ren," she said frostily, the whole conversation edging too close to the past and the memories and the distance.

He looked taken aback by her tone and started to nod before horror skirted across his features. "Aren't we being listened to right now?"

"No, I told them I had to talk to you privately."

"What if they came back?"

"Renny, I might be a bit nuts, but I've still got some power around here. They left and stayed gone, trust me."

"What about Vlad...and Sorin?"

He added Sorin almost as an afterthought, which made her all the more curious about what they might have talked about. She left it alone for the time being. "Vlad's concerned about me and my infatuation with you, but doesn't think I'm capable of plotting. Sorin...Sorin just doesn't care." *Or*, she added silently, *if he does care, he's too damn good at hiding it.*

"Okay, then how am I getting out of here?"

She smiled crookedly. "No idea."

"Then we'd best get planning."

Chapter Twelve

I SMILED AS I TOOK A BREAK. "Sorry about that, I just kind of got going, didn't I?"

"Quite all right," Stella said. "It does help the time go faster."

"I think that was the moment when I realized it was time to really move on. I'm not sure I had quite figured out that I liked Beau and I certainly didn't know he liked me, but it was a turning point, nonetheless."

"I have a question," Dave said. "How do you know the little bits of what people said when you weren't there? Like when you were injured?"

"Most of it I learned after Beau and I stopped being blockheads and Jessie and Ry felt they could share. Some of it, Beau told me later. Depends on the tidbit."

Dave nodded, then took advantage of the break to hop to his feet and strain his neck to try and see anything out our small window, which I estimated to be about street level. The corridor definitely sloped down towards the cell. I'd noticed it both times I'd gone to chat with Rees.

I forced myself to stand as well and carefully stretch out bruised and stiff muscles. This time, I heard the footsteps first and tensed, glancing out the door. I dearly hoped Rees wasn't back for more. My body wasn't ready for further punishment yet and he'd said it would be a couple days. The man himself sauntered into view.

"David," Stella whispered and the boy backed to her while I heard Jay get to his feet behind me.

"Good afternoon."

I felt a little reassured by the fact he only had one of the brutes in tow. "Afternoon," I said as Jay stepped to my side, effectively blocking his view of the Harpers. The last thing either of us wanted was him taking an interest in them.

Rees looked between us. "Keep yourselves entertained?"

"Yup. People watching. It's weird, though," Jay said, "we only seem to see assholes."

I bit my lip both to keep from smiling and because, as funny as it was, I wished Jay wouldn't.

"Then perhaps you need a new hobby," Rees said without batting an eye.

"Probably. What d'you think, Je-Jasmine," Jay said with barely any hesitation, "should we take up knitting?"

"Only if the good colonel here would provide us with the supplies."

"I don't think giving the pair of you knitting needles would be good for my health."

"Hm, good point, probably not. What about painting? I've always wanted to do landscapes."

Rees smirked. "Anything I can do to make your stay more comfortable?"

"Go away?" I suggested.

"I would, if you'd just answer my questions."

"You know we can't do that."

He appraised me freshly. "Can't, hm? Not won't. Interesting."

My cheeks heated and I cursed myself for not being more careful with my word choice.

"Same difference," Jay told him. "Both apply."

"I'm not so sure. I think Jasmine said exactly what she meant, which just reinforces the idea that you're part of the Freedom Fighters."

"Think what you'd like," I said. "Far be it for us to stop you." This was not the first or last time I suspected I'd say exactly that to him.

He tilted his head. "I thought the Freedom Fighters were inordinately proud of the fact they were members."

"Anyone fighting against the Three should be proud of it."

"Rumors have it that name originated with them as well."

"Heard the same thing. Can't argue with accurate simplicity," Jay said. "Seriously, Colonel, do you really think we're going to just slip up in casual conversation and say 'yes, we're with the Freedom Fighters' to satisfy you?"

"It would be nice."

"Not going to happen and I think we all know it," I said.

He inclined his head. "Very well. I will talk to you tomorrow, Jay."

"Can't wait."

Rees gestured the brute ahead of him and headed off, radiating smugness.

"Gods' Breath," I murmured as soon he was out of hearing range, leaning against Jay. "We really need to watch every word with him, don't we?"

"Appears so. He's quick."

"Too damn quick." I let out a breath.

He put an arm around me. "We'll be okay. If he's monitoring every last word, maybe we can use that to throw him off track."

"Maybe." I reminded myself of our cellmates and pushed off him, carefully sitting back down.

Dave's eyes were wide and worried and Stella only now drew her gaze away from where Rees had stood. "If he comes after us," she started.

"He won't," Jay said and I suspected we were thinking the same thing: *At least not yet.*

"How do you know?"

"Colonel Rees wants to break us badly. As long as he continues to get snippets from us, purposeful or not, he'll keep at us."

I shifted to settle in more comfortably. "Shall I? We've still got the rest of an afternoon to kill."

"That would be great, Jez, thanks," Stella said with a relieved smile, putting an arm around Dave's shoulders. It was a testament to how nervous Rees made the boy that he didn't protest or squirm away. I took a deep breath, trying to expel Colonel Rees from my mind, and continued.

The next month flew by. Someone had apparently gone looking for Beau and seen the two of them 'sleeping together.' Needless to say, rumors were flying everywhere. Jez did her best to ignore them, but Beau blushed each time someone mentioned it, which, of course, Ry did at every possible opportunity. Although new information came in every day about the Three and their movements, the area where Cavern Hall was remained almost suspiciously quiet. People began to get edgy and jumpy at the silence, so Beau decided a morale boost was in order. Against Mick's better judgment and maybe his too, he put Jez, Ry, and Jessie in charge of it.

He started to agree with Mick's thoughts when, two days later, Ry skipped into his office, followed more sedately by Jez and Jessie while he and Mick talked. The first thing he noticed was each expression: Rylia's face was painted with a wicked grin, Jez's eyes twinkled with suppressed mirth, and Jessie obviously tried not to laugh, while attempting to look apologetic at the same time. The second thing he noticed was that Jez held something out of sight behind her back.

"Hello?" he tried as Mick kicked his foot, in a not-so-subtle 'told you so.'

"Hi, Beau," Ry sang.

"I want it noted that this was not my idea," Jessie added.

"But she's not complaining either," Jez told them.

"I think we can safely end the conversation right there," Beau said. "The answer is an absolute no."

"Aw, c'mon, Beau, you haven't even heard what our proposal is yet. We're only doing our job!"

"I honestly don't think that matters. It's still no."

"Hey, you said we could use any resource we could find as long as it did not get in the way of Cavern Hall's operation."

"Did I?"

"Yes, actually, you did," Mick said. "We were all present."

Beau kicked Mick back with pleasure, but his old friend just smiled, obviously amused.

"Well, I, um, I'm not a resource to be…" He paused. "Okay, bad argument, but the gist of it stands." At the girls' hopeful looks, he sighed. "Okay, fine, I'm not agreeing to anything, but what's the proposal?"

The fact that Ry instantly started to giggle gave him a large sense of foreboding as Jez finally produced the object from behind her back. It took him a long moment to both identify and then recognize it. "Gods' Breath," he said, fumbling it as Jez threw it to him. Mick and Jessie, gods damn them, were both snickering. "No way!" he said, holding the offending object away from him. In his hands was a two piece…outfit, if it could even be called that. The top was a skimpy shoulder wrap while the bottom was a distinctly skimpier bottom, both made of animal skin. It was the same thing that had appeared on Bri in Jez's picture birthday present from Jessie and Ry. "There is no way I will ever, *ever* wear this." He dropped it on his desk and folded his arms in an attempt to look intimidating. Unfortunately, his friends knew him far too well to be fooled.

"Oh really?" Jez asked, looking very assured of herself.

"Why do you want me to wear it anyway?" he asked cautiously.

"We're doing a play!"

"The gods help us," Mick muttered. Beau kicked him again.

"And we want you to play Vladimir."

His jaw dropped. "Excuse me? What kind of play is this?"

"A comedy," Jessie said, speaking for the first time since the outfit had appeared. "It's a two scene play about the Three. Ry's going to be Anica, I think we've convinced Reardon to play Sorin, and we want you to play Vladimir."

"And what about you two?"

"I'm the narrator and Jez is Randy, standing for Random Flunky."

"And Mick?"

"We asked him to play Vladimir, but he said no."

"No one will ever accuse me of being stupid," Mick said, smirking. Beau kicked him yet again before cautiously turning his gaze back on the outfit.

"How in the name of the gods did this make it from the first Cavern Hall?"

"Dunkin scrounged it up. It must have gotten packed by accident," Jez said in all innocence, but he could see the laughter on her face and suspected its appearance was no accident.

Beau sighed. "They were only supposed to bring back useful things."

"I think it's being put to good use right now," Mick said.

Beau barely resisted kicking him a fourth time. "What about Dunkin?"

"What about him?" Jez asked.

"Why can't he play Vladimir?"

"Turns out Dunk's got amazing artistic skills. He's doing our backdrop and scenery."

"Don't tell me," Beau said, "somehow he found paints and things to paint on from what was brought over."

Jez whistled innocently.

"Sometimes," he sighed.

"But that leaves you to be our Vlad."

"It's Vlad now?"

"Well, that's what his siblings apparently call him, so that's what you'll get called in the play," Ry said. "C'mon, Beau, you'll make a great Vlad! Or at least," she clarified, "our version of him."

He glanced again at the outfit, like it might bite him. "Fine, I'll do it."

Ry let out a whoop while Jessie finally gave in to her laughter, sinking into the nearest chair. Jez grinned knowingly, making him squirm.

"But," he added sternly, "there is one condition."

"Yes?"

"I will wear *that* only during the actual play and not a moment before or after. Understood?"

All four present chorused their consent.

"Good, then we have ourselves a deal."

"You should probably try it on at least once for size beforehand," Mick now said.

There was a pause and then all three women burst into laughter. Jessie was wiping tears from her eyes at this point. Mick smirked, threw Beau a salute, and disappeared out the door.

Beau dropped his face into his hands, not sure he had ever been redder. "What do I need to do for this play?"

"We'll do it in a couple weeks. As soon as we're certain about the lines, we'll get them to you, and then we'll need to practice whenever we can squeak in some time."

"Wonderful. How do I let myself get talked into these things?"

"Because you know you love us," Jez said and gave him a hug. "Thanks," she whispered in his ear.

It made him smile. "You're welcome."

Ry opened her mouth but this time she got kicked by Jessie. "Ow! That hurt!"

"Good, it was supposed to," Jessie said.

Jez ducked her head, amused.

It took two weeks of snatching practice time whenever possible before Jessie deemed them ready. They set an evening aside for it and Dunkin and his crew set up the main room all afternoon with a makeshift stage and backdrop. The actors rehearsed one more time and then split to put on their costumes. Beau had told them all they had better not laugh and threatened a painful death if they did. Reardon went to the task as joyfully as he did anything and even Mick was in a good mood, directing people to seats and spots in the room.

Beau appeared with little time to spare, cheeks beet-red. All three tried, rather unsuccessfully, to stifle laughter. Only Jez succeeded.

"I feel ridiculous. Wait, no, ridiculous doesn't even begin to cover it," he mumbled.

"I think you look great," Jez said.

"Yup," Ry said, "really shows off your muscles."

Beau glared.

"She's right, you know, it shows off your assets really well." There was a pause as Jez seemed to realize what she said before blushing and quickly turning to head for the front of the stage. Ry trotted after her, snickering quietly.

Jessie planted her hands on her hips and turned on Beau. "You two are so incredibly unbelievable."

"Who?"

"You and Jez."

"What about us?"

"Either you're both blind, which I don't think I believe, or just too damn stubborn, or scared, to admit it."

"This is a rather inappropriate conversation to be having when I'm dressed like this."

"No, I think it's the most appropriate time possible. Gods' Breath, Beau, just *say* something. I think she's blind and you're scared."

Beau looked away. "I don't want to rush her into anything. It hasn't even been six months since Bri…"

"As much as I loved Bri and love Jez and they were cute together, I suspect you and she were inevitable. You two understand each other on a level that's almost creepy. If you don't take the chance…"

"I'm afraid, you're right. I'm afraid when this all comes to head…she's already scared to death we're all going to die. How much worse would it be if we were an item and I died?"

"That's not your choice to make for her, Beau. Jez is a big girl. What's the point of denying something that everyone here can see? What you two have is already more than just plain friendship. You don't have to get lovey-dovey on us, in fact, please don't, but you still need to admit it. Of course, this is all ignoring the fact you've already slept together."

Beau blushed. "That was…"

"I know, I know, just teasing. Look, if there is-"

Whatever else she was going to say was cut off as Dunkin took center stage. "Before we get started, I'd like to introduce our cast and give thanks to those who helped make this possible. First, Mick for his seating expertise and assistance in getting the captain to join the cast."

"No one will ever respect me after this," Beau muttered as Mick acknowledged the applause with a briefly raised hand.

Jessie tried not to laugh.

"Then, the stage and artistic crew of Dove, Kilo, and Rich."

"Don't forget yourself!" Kilo called from the audience.

Dunkin bowed. "Thanks, Kilo. Now, on to the cast itself. Jez is playing Randy, our random administrative flunky." Jez stepped out onto stage and waved as people laughed, understanding the name.

"Then Jessie as our narrator."

She shot Beau a look that plainly spelled out that the conversation would continue before slipping past Reardon and Rylia to step on stage, amidst yet more applause.

"Ry will be playing Anica Opalin and Reardon, Sorin Dakamar." The pair stepped out on stage. Beau swallowed.

"And now…the person we've all been waiting for," he paused for dramatic effect, "Beau as Vladimir Opalin!"

155

Beau slowly walked onto the stage, cheeks even redder than before, as he focused on Mick in the back. His old friend grinned and shot him a thumbs up.

"You're doing fine," Jez whispered in his ear, earlier embarrassment faded. "No one is laughing too hard."

"Gee, thanks."

She chuckled. "I try my best."

The crowd finally settled down and they began the play. Each of the girls had taken a sibling and studied all the available information on them. Then, they'd gotten together and over-exaggerated their personalities for the sake of comedy. Jessie took her place to the side of the stage and began.

It opened with Anica whining about how bored she was and how everything was dull and why couldn't anyone be interesting. Jez, as Randy, bounded onto the stage and told her that her brothers wanted to talk to her. Anica flailed a bit and went to go after them, but instead tripped and fell off the stage in an exaggerated tangle of limbs. Randy gasped and ran from the room, returning, dragging Vlad – who carried a huge and obviously fake sword – and Sorin – who appeared to be covered in ink – into the room. Vlad complained loudly of not having anyone to fight and almost sliced off Randy's head. Randy cowered while Sorin read a book, talking in an extra intelligent voice about made-up politics. Anica appeared just then, rather battered looking due to her 'fall' and demanded her brothers make things less boring, twirling her hair around one finger. Sorin grumbled about distractions from his precious books while Vlad announced he was going on a crusade. Randy finally shook her head. "I quit!" The three siblings turned towards her and all four froze.

"Those were two words the Three were maybe a little too used to hearing," Jessie said with a wink. The actors quickly rearranged during the resulting applause and then scene two started with Randy skipping off into the sunset (literally – Dunkin painted a gorgeous sunset). The siblings carried on in similar fashions for a bit before Vlad struck a pose. "My crusade begins now!" he said, charging forward before slipping in an imaginary puddle of water and going down. Sorin caught the sword and stared at it before ignoring his brother's troubles entirely and cursing how the sword made it difficult to read. Then, he wandered off towards the same side of the stage where Vlad lay dead and slipped in the same puddle, going down. Anica now danced onto stage, spotted her two brothers and burst out laughing. "Finally, something interesting!" she crowed.

"And so ends another typical day in Oakbridge," Jessie said, signaling the end of Jessie, Ry, and Jez's debut as amateur playwrights.

The entire audience was doubled over in laughter. The cast took their bows. Most of the audience filtered out after, leaving Dunk, his crew, Mick, and the cast behind.

Ren paced his room in a diamond from his bed to his couch, to the door to his old bedroom, to his chairs and back to his bed. He tried to quash his worries about Ani and their plan--or lack thereof. He wasn't sure when he had started to care about Ani, but everything he'd told her earlier in the evening was true. He continued wearing a path in his rug as Vladimir barged into the room. Ren ignored him, because Vlad would say what he wanted no matter what.

"Renier," he snapped.

Ren sighed, stopped, and turned towards him. "Yes?" He had expected a visit from the moment Ani had mentioned that Vlad was worried about her.

"What the hell are you doing to my sister?"

"Nothing."

"You're messing with her mind somehow. Convincing her you care. I know you are."

Ren's stomach clenched as the first spurs of anger flashed through him. "If I was messing with her mind, you'd know, since you listen to every gods-be-damned word I say. Believe me or not, but I do care."

"I don't know what tricks you nobles play."

"Gods' Breath, Vlad. The only one playing tricks or mind games here is Sorin."

With two quick strides, Vlad grabbed Ren by the collar and, with two more, slammed him into the wall. "Do not speak ill of my brother or sister."

Ren clenched his jaw against the spike of pain. "Sorin would be the first to admit he plays mind games. I only speak the truth."

"You weren't supposed to be this much trouble, prince," he said, spitting the last word like a curse.

"How much trouble can I possibly be outside your mind, General?" he asked, giving it right back to him.

Vlad froze and Ren watched the storm break across his face. He knew full well he had pushed the man further than was safe with that one comment.

But he also knew Vlad fairly well after two years. Vladimir Opalin occasionally needed to assert his dominance – prove he was stronger than Ren – and the quickest way for the older man to accomplish that was pound on Ren a bit. He figured he'd be able to get a couple shots of his own off, which would make it worth it.

What he didn't quite account for was Vlad's overwhelming fury. The first fist, which Ren squirmed to try and dodge still pinned against the wall, hit him square in the chest. The prince thought he heard something pop, but dismissed it as his imagination. He did, indeed, get a few good shots in, but went down much sooner than was comfortable. A few short years ago, he wouldn't have been caught dead in such bad shape and he made a promise to himself to do what he could to do what exercise he could. Although, maybe it wasn't so much his fitness as Vlad's rage. The last couple times, the beating had been controlled, purposeful as a method of teaching Ren a lesson. This time contained none of that control.

Finally, Vlad looked down at him in disgust as Ren pushed himself carefully to a seat. "You really aren't much once we get past the words, are you?"

Ren shrugged noncommittally as he took stock of his injuries. They were definitely worse than last time.

The other man aimed a half-hearted kick at him, which Ren easily avoided. "You're despicable." He glared before turning and stalking out of the room.

The prince shook himself as he got to his feet, careful not to put weight on the ankle that already throbbed. "Like you aren't," he muttered to the slammed door, wincing as his body protested. He made his way to his bed and collapsed on it, physically exhausted. Mentally, however, was another story as he found it all but impossible to sleep, his mind racing. His worry for Ani came back three-fold, combined with a swirl of other thoughts from his conversation with Sorin to what had just happened with Vlad. He couldn't believe it had only been a few hours since he and Ani had stood on the rampart.

Eventually, though, he drifted off, lulled by the gentle sounds wafting through his now open window. Suddenly, he snapped awake, blinking in the dark as he tried to keep the dream he'd been having from slipping away. It took a time before his weary brain managed to pull it back up and he realized it was a memory as much as a dream. A couple months before his mother's disappearance, his parents had asked him for a boy and girl name for a potential younger sibling. He felt a deep certainty that this potential younger brother would be Beau, after the name Ren had suggested – his parents' legacy to him.

He scrambled upright, despite the pain it elicited, grabbing a piece of paper and scrawling, *Dear Beau*, across the top.

"Renny!" Ani sang as she pranced into his room far too few hours later.

He rolled over, blinking sleepily at her. "S'it morning?"

"It is! You look thrilled to see me this morning."

He smiled crookedly. "Trust me, it's not you. I was up pretty late last night." He gave her a meaningful look, hoping she'd pick up on it.

"Ah, silly Renny," she said in an overly light voice, "not getting enough sleep. Can I kiss it better?"

"Kiss what? My sleepiness?"

"I can try!"

"Sorry, just a long night last night."

She pursed her lips. "Yes, it was, wasn't it?" Then she paused, grinned, and catapulted herself into his lap. "Hold me!"

He grunted, wincing only a little, but she caught it anyway and immediately slid off. "Why did that hurt?" she demanded, eyes narrowing.

"Just a few bruises, nothing much."

"Bruises?" she echoed, fear brightening her eyes. She glanced away for a split second and, when she looked up again, it was long gone. "Ah, my big brother was being protective. I'm sorry, Renny. He shouldn't have hurt you." Now that he knew to look for it, he could see the force she put into speaking lightly, because even with the fear gone, other emotions weren't. She patted him on the head. "Sorry!"

"It's all right, Ani," he said, amused despite himself. "I'm sure I'll recover with a little time. Just watch the ribs for a few days, okay?"

She eyed him. "They aren't broken, are they?"

"What? No, not at all. Just bruised and uncomfortable." He tucked his injured ankle behind his other leg.

"Can I see?"

He stared. "See what?"

"I wanna see your bruised ribs."

"So, in other words, you want to see my chest?"

"Yup! Are you muscular?"

He'd said that Sorin played the mind games, but this was an entirely different game altogether. He snorted, ignoring how it set his ribs on fire. "I used to be. Doubt it anymore."

"I'm sure they haven't all vanished. Why don't we check?"

He sighed, knowing she was checking up on him. "I'm not sure that's such a great idea."

"Why not?"

"The bruises are...kinda big?"

"How big?"

"Whole chest big?" He pulled his shirt up, though.

"Ren, Gods' Breath, I thought you said they were just bruised."

"Well, they *are* bruised."

"If they're that bruised, they're probably cracked or broken," she said, with a scary note of authority.

"They'll heal. There isn't much you can do to help ribs except take it easy."

Ani studied him closely. "Don't think I haven't noticed the black eye either. What else are you hiding, Ren?"

"Nothing."

"Renny," she growled.

"Okay, so I wouldn't usually mind a role reversal but..."

"Do not try and change the subject. What else is hurt?" She'd clearly given up on the act, definite concern radiating off her.

He shifted his ankle further behind his good leg, but she noticed and looked at it meaningfully.

"Just twisted my ankle."

"You twisted it or Vlad did?" She sighed. "Let me see it."

"It's nothing re-"

"Renny Highcastle, let me see it this instant," she ordered sharply.

He shifted and revealed it.

"Gods' Breath, Ren," she breathed. "That's way too big and looks awful."

He glanced down at it. "It's not that bad."

She poked him in the side of the head, apparently the only space she deemed safe. "Liar. We should get you a doctor."

"I don't need a doctor."

"Fine, but I want Sorin to at least look at you."

"Ani," he protested.

"Don't move an inch. I'll be back in a minute."

"Ani!"

She disappeared out the door, which the guard shut behind her. Ren sighed, slumped a bit to take the pressure off his ribs and waited, having no other choice.

Chapter Thirteen

"THAT WAS OUR FIRST PLAY. I'm sure I didn't do it justice at all and some of it might be a 'you had to be there' sort of thing, but we had a lot of fun with it and it was a great stress reliever. After I finish the whole story, maybe we could try and tell the whole thing. I bet I remember all the parts. We certainly spent enough time with it."

"That would be cool," Dave said. "It sounded really fun!"

"It was. Just what we needed."

"Guess it's probably a good time to get some shuteye and some necessary beauty sleep," Jay said, smiling.

"Speak for yourself," I shot back.

Dave groaned half-heartedly but settled against his sister without further protest. I debated and then carefully wedged myself into my corner. The cell floor had been worn smooth over the years but my cuts and scrapes were not a fan. At least this way, I wouldn't shift in my sleep and make it worse.

I woke early, sometime around dawn, from the weak light filtering in the window. Using the bars on the door, I pulled myself to my feet and carefully stretched out, making sure to take extra care with the sorest spots. I had just finished when I heard footsteps approaching the cell. Apparently I wasn't the only early riser in Greensward prison this morning. I peeked out, spotting Shorty and the brutes, before stepping back. I reached out and nudged Jay with my foot. He woke with a start and blinked owlishly until the footsteps filtered in. Then he rolled away from Stella before standing up in an attempt to not wake her. I was sure it would all be for naught considering Shorty wouldn't likely show the same courtesy.

"Is our buddy getting smarter?" he asked quietly, joining me.

"Or just impatient?" I said and shrugged. It could easily be one or both of those options. It made sense to interrogate someone as soon as they woke up – most people weren't at full mental capacity first thing in the morning. Rees also didn't strike me as the most patient of people.

It was Stella who spoke up next, and probably had it right. "Maybe he's getting pressure from the top." It was true that we were the only potential Freedom Fighters they'd captured, so they'd want as much out of us as possible. She smiled at the unasked question in my eyes, sitting up. "My cold back woke me up."

I returned it as Shorty reached the door. "Jay." He inserted the key and started to open the cell door. From his glare, he seemed less than thrilled to find us already awake. I decided pissing him off more couldn't hurt so I grabbed the door and pushed it back towards him.

"Wait a minute, Shorty," I told him.

He huffed, drawing himself to his full height, which wasn't much. "My name is Dayton."

"I said, wait a minute, Shorty."

"Yeah, you're interrupting the morning séance. Gotta commune with the dead every day or they'll leave your spirit behind," Jay said.

One of the brutes growled, but Shorty held him back, seemingly curious about what we were up to, despite the blatant disrespect.

"I think you should ask him why, but make sure you time it right."

"Righto, when I'm about to get punched, ask the hard stuff. Got it," he said, tossing me an irreverent salute.

"Good luck."

Jay nodded and turned to the door, sketching a quick bow to those waiting. "Thank you ever so much for your patience," he said, false sincerity oozing from every pore. He then pulled open the door and stepped out to join them, glancing back just long enough for me to see the spark of fear in his eyes. I shot him a thumbs-up which he returned with a trademark Dall family grin.

I watched him go before settling back in my corner. Stella and I chatted quietly as she explained in more detail the night they were captured. Dave remained silent, attention darting from our conversation to the cell door and back again.

Jay finally returned, almost an hour later, and slumped to the floor. "He remembered where he bruised last time and they hadn't exactly had time to heal."

"Here, we saved you breakfast," I said, offering him the remains.

"Thanks," he mumbled as Stella settled carefully next to him.

I glanced at Dave, not surprised to find the drawn, worried look back on his face. "Don't worry, kid; Jay and I have lots of experience healing ourselves."

"Still," he said, scrunching down.

I patted his shoulder. "Hey, guess what!"

He eyed me. "What?"

"We're almost to the part where Jay comes into the story." I turned my grin on my friend. "Then he can tell parts and save my voice."

"I like your voice better than mine."

"Like I care."

He stuck his tongue out at me, which was one of the most reassuring things he could have done to convince me he was okay. "Well, you should, as my vocal cords are too important to waste on something as mundane telling stories."

"If I had something heavy to throw at you," I said, picking up my spoon threateningly.

"You wouldn't do it, because I'm an invalid."

"Doesn't seem like it with the way your mouth is going."

"Then because you love me?" he tried.

"Gods' Breath, you two are like an old married couple," Stella said, exasperated. We tended to have that effect on people. "I'm not intruding, am I?"

I had to laugh. "I happened to learn from the best how to come out with the snappy retort, but no, Jay is absolutely all yours."

"Yeah, Jez has got her Beau-bear."

I stared at him. "Jay, I would pay money to watch Beau's expression when you called him that, and the carnage that would follow."

Dave giggled, good humor restored.

"Aw, he wouldn't hurt me that bad. After all, you would protect me."

"In your dreams."

"All right, all right, at the risk of sounding like my brother, can we get back to the story already?" Stella said. "You two are going to drive me up a wall."

Jay had the grace to look sheepish. "Sorry, Stella."

"What are we waiting for?" Dave demanded. Stella smacked him gently on the back of the head. "Please?" he added.

I rolled my eyes. "Part of this, Jessie and Ry filled me in later. And here we go." I picked it up from where I'd left off.

◀ ▼ ▶

Stories of the play somehow made it as far as many of the contacts spread through the country because Col's next message asked for a picture. Beau's response was to spew a collection of impressively colorful curses and then glare at everyone, especially his good friends, for the next twenty minutes.

"I hate you all. All of you," he mumbled.

Mick squashed a smile, but did let go enough to wink at Jez.

"You're allowed to hate us," she said.

He glanced suspiciously up from his paperwork.

"Since you actually did it and did a fine job."

"What she wants to say is that you looked fine too, but wouldn't dream of it," Jessie threw in from where she and Ry played cards in the corner. Jez flushed instantly red and looked at the floor. Beau, meanwhile, smiled for the first time since receiving Col's message, but also looked away. At Jessie's reproving look, he blushed. "You're both so darned…"

"Pig-headed?" Ry suggested.

"Stubborn?" Mick put in.

"Stupid?" Ry tried, snickering.

"I need to, um, go see Reardon," Jez said, beating a hasty retreat.

Mick rolled his eyes and trailed her out of the room.

"I told you our conversation wasn't finished," Jessie told Beau.

"I was hoping it could be put off a bit longer."

Jessie stood, brushing off her pants as she came and perched on the edge of his desk. "Why?" she asked as Ry glanced up from the cards, plainly curious.

"I just...I'm not sure she's ready and...I don't know! Jessie, I don't know anything when it comes to this."

"You'll never know if she's ready unless you ask," Ry said.

"Even after Bri, I would say Jez doesn't know a whole lot more than you. She's obviously nervous too, Beau, but neither of you are going to be comfortable or be able to be yourselves while doing this dance. Plus, it's very obnoxious from the outside."

"But..."

"Beau! Just ask her."

"How?"

"'Jez, will you go out with me?' might work wonders," Ry said dryly.

"Beau, do it any damn way that feels right. Bri and Jez were cute, yes, but there's something very right about you too. I firmly believe you need to be together."

"It's not like she won't say yes. Unless you're an idiot about it."

"Thanks a lot for the vote of confidence," he said nervously.

"Oh, just ask already."

"But..."

Jessie sighed. "I am going to go find her and drag her back here. Then, you two are going to talk. You will figure this out. Then Ry and I will let you out of this room, but not a moment before. C'mon, Ry."

Rylia grinned and shot him a thumbs-up as she followed Jessie. A couple minutes later, Jez was forcefully propelled into the room. "Uh, hey," she said, unable to make eye contact.

"Hey."

Neither of them spoke for an uncomfortable minute.

"What's up with those two?" Jez finally asked, jerking a thumb over her shoulder.

"They're annoyed at us."

"Ah."

Beau waited, but she didn't ask why, even as she continued to find the rest of his room interesting. "Jez, c'mon, look at me. This isn't us."

Her brown eyes came around to meet his. "They're not letting us out of here until we talk about it."

He took a deep breath. "Not sure there's a lot to talk about. I like you," he said, "and I enjoy spending time with you and I know it's only been a few months, but Jessie is right. I can't not tell you how I feel."

"Like," she repeated.

He leaned back in his chair, running a hand through his hair in clear agitation. "What? Would you rather I say that I fell in love with you within days of you being up and functional? Because I can, if you want."

"Only if it's the truth," she said softly. He held her gaze. Her lips quirked up to a smile and she reached out, patting down the hair he'd just spiked. "I like you too."

"Oh, really?" he asked, standing and stepping around his desk so they were eye to eye.

"Mmhmm," she said, heartbeat speeding up, despite her fight to maintain a cool demeanor.

They stared at each other without moving. Then Beau slid forward, threaded a hand through her hair and pressed his lips to hers.

She started but snaked her arms around his neck with little hesitation. When she finally pulled back, her eyes were dancing. "Well, that was unexpected," she drawled.

"But not unwelcome, I hope," he said, nerves instantly flaring again.

"No, definitely not unwelcome." She kept her arms around him and grinned. "Guess this'll make our friends quite happy."

He had to return it. "It makes *me* quite happy."

"Mm, true." Concern sparked in her eyes. "Nothing really needs to change much, right?"

"Except I like to think I have permission to occasionally kiss you," he said dryly.

She laughed. "I think I can manage that." She tucked a lock of hair behind his ear. "I didn't mean that quite the way it came out. It's just…"

"We don't need to be overly showy about it?"

"Exactly."

"I agree. We'd probably kill a lot of people with shock if we tried it."

"If you tried," she corrected mildly. He made a face.

"Are you two okay in there?" Ry demanded from outside. "It's gone awfully quiet."

"There's hopefully a good reason for that," Jessie said.

"Oh, some k-i-s-s-i-n-g?" Ry asked.

"You two can shut up any time," Jez called, "and let us out."

Both of them peeked in. "Do we have a good reason to let you out?"

"You know, Beau's the captain. He could order you to let us out."

"I could. Have you drawn up on insubordination charges and strung up as an example to the rest of our fine crew or something."

"You wouldn't do that," Ry said dismissively. "Well?"

The pair exchanged a glance and then Jez grabbed the back of Beau's head and kissed him firmly. Ry let out a whoop as Jessie beamed at them. Beau rubbed his neck when she pulled back. "That was unnecessarily violent."

"You can't say you didn't enjoy it," she retorted easily.

He shrugged, unable to argue the point. "Are we allowed to leave now?"

"Thank the gods you've finally figured it out," Jessie said. "C'mon, Ry, let's leave them to whatever they were doing before." She grabbed the teen by the collar and hustled her back out of the room.

Jez smirked after them, leaning against him.

"You look far too pleased with yourself."

"Is there any reason I shouldn't be? You've got a smug look going too."

"Point."

"As usual, I'm full of them."

Beau laughed.

In the days that followed, word spread like wildfire around the camp and no one seemed particularly surprised. Jez started spending more nights with Beau. Although they did nothing except cuddle, she was reassured by his presence and found the nightmares less severe when he was curled against her. She also found it refreshing that, at night, when everyone else was asleep, she could be both Jasmine and Jez.

Ren had zoned out, brain feeling sluggish, when his door opened again.

"Good morning, Ren."

It took a minute to drag his attention back and, even then, the world swam a bit.

"I think he might have a concussion," Ani said.

"I'm fine," Ren said, forcing himself to pay attention. The more time he spent awake, though, the more he couldn't ignore that the world didn't feel quite right.

"Did Vlad slam you into the wall?" Sorin's matter-of-fact tone disturbed Ren, but he couldn't quite decide why.

"Only once."

Sorin snorted. "Only once will do it. Ani, I trust you'll keep an eye on him for the next couple days while he recovers from that?"

She nodded. "Will you look at his ankle and ribs too?"

"Of course. Let's start with the ankle." He knelt, then rolled his eyes as Ren automatically tucked it back behind his good leg. "Renier, I can't help if I can't see it."

"It's fine."

Sorin regarded him. "Ren," he finally said quietly, "I may not have been on the receiving end of Vlad's fists, but that doesn't mean I don't know the damage a human can do. I can tell from here that it's not fine. Please let me see it."

A combination of things, including Vlad's nickname and the please, got to Ren and he pulled it out. Sorin smiled faintly and then prodded it, surprisingly gentle. Ren gritted his teeth at the pain, flinching.

"Hold still."

"It hurts," he managed, then felt immediately sheepish as Sorin shot him a pointed look.

"Of course it does." Ani's brother sat back on his heels. "I don't think it's broken but it's at least a nasty sprain. Best put you on crutches for a while." He eyed him. "He lost his cool, didn't he?"

Ren shrugged. "I baited him."

169

"You've done that before without this."

He glanced between the siblings. "Yeah, but I got in a few good shots myself," he added cheerfully, not liking the looks on their faces. "Including a shot to the groin."

"Seems like he deserved it," Sorin said, getting to his feet and brushing off his knees. Ren blinked at him, certain he had not heard correctly. Although, he reasoned, nothing the siblings did should surprise him anymore, if just for the fact their dynamics seemed to be ever-changing.

"The ribs?" Ani prompted from where she hovered nervously at his shoulder.

"I'm getting to those," he said, looking a bit amused. "Shirt off, Ren."

"Are you sure it's just a sprain?"

"Fairly," Sorin told her as Ren clutched his shirt tighter to him. "He'd have reacted a lot stronger to my poking if it was broken. What's the problem now, Renier?"

"You'll just laugh at my scrawny chest."

"That might be the most asinine thing you have ever said."

"It's true."

"I don't laugh at broken ribs," Sorin said. "Now take it off or I'll have Anica do it for you. Your choice."

His sister brightened at the prospect which was all the incentive Ren needed to tug it off, wincing.

Sorin let out a low whistle. "Gods' Breath, he really wasn't pulling his punches," he muttered quietly enough Ren was certain he wasn't supposed to hear that. "You're right. It is a little scrawny," he said instead, perching next to Ren on the bed and examining his chest with more poking and prodding. The prince clenched his hands in an effort to not react to the pain.

"Gee, thanks," he ground out.

Sorin shot Ren an amused look. "It only makes sense. The heaviest thing you've picked up in the last two years is probably a book. Your muscle tone would obviously suffer." After another moment, he nodded. "Definitely broken." He pantomimed a punch. "He got you right about there at point blank range, didn't he?"

Ren nodded, disturbed that Sorin could read the injury that accurately.

"It's still pretty." Both of them looked up to find Ani staring a bit dreamily at Ren's chest. Sorin choked on a laugh as Ren flushed. Sensing their scrutiny, Ani went wide-eyed. "Oops, did that come out aloud?" She grinned briefly at the pair. "So, what do we do about it, Sorin?"

"I'll go get some bandages and patch the prince up. Then we yell at Vladimir for being an idiot."

"I nominate you for yelling at Vlad."

"I can manage that. You keep Ren company while I go get some supplies."

Ren watched him go, then turned to Ani. "Any chance you could explain Sorin to me?" He, of all of them, still confused Ren the most, especially recently.

She pursed her lips. "Sorin's...complicated."

"I'd gotten that much."

She flopped into his chair. "Sorin used to be my rock. The one person I could always rely on." She ran her hand along the chair's arm. "I guess, in some ways, he still is, but it's been different since he came home from school when he was fifteen. I think we'd both changed by then and we could never manage to make the changes...we couldn't get past them to find common ground anymore. Then he left and that was that."

"You saw him after that, though, right?"

"Yeah, sometimes, but never for long enough to even try and really talk. It was always at a function. Until he came back permanently but he was so different then." Her brow furrowed and she glanced again at the door. "He's changing again, though. The Sorin we just saw? He's the closest to my brother that I've seen in a very long time and it's not the first flash."

"And Vlad?"

Ani didn't answer, gaze fixed on the doorway.

"Do you think we're being watched?" he asked softly when it became apparent she wasn't going to. And honestly, no answer to that question was enough.

Ani shrugged, dragging herself back to the present. "Probably. Why?"

"I need you to send a letter for me."

"Oh?"

"You've heard Sorin's theory on the leader of the Freedom Fighters?"

She nodded, understanding breaking across her face. "You're sending a letter to your brother."

"Only if you'll do it for me. I know it's a lot to ask but…"

"C'mon, Renny, it's not like you know any crazy secrets," she said, standing nonchalantly and meandering over so she was between him and the peep hole. He slid the letter out from under his sheets and passed it to her. She slipped it out of sight. "I'll get it out as soon as I can figure out a way. Your brother's group aren't the easiest people to find."

"Guess that means he's doing his job."

She smiled briefly. "Guess so," she agreed, perching on the bed next to him. "Did you know that we met before all of this?"

"We did?" he asked, attempting to quickly filter through his various brief memories of Sorin and Vlad prior to their take over, but nothing stuck out. That had been a lifetime ago now.

"Yeah, in passing. Your father was hosting a ball and Vlad let me come. I was eighteen at the time and somehow Sorin ended up 'in charge' of me. I think Vlad had business to attend to since he was running the business by then. I wanted so badly to dance with you, but Sorin insisted you wouldn't look twice at me since I was just some merchant's little sister. I wanted to ask anyway. I was so sure he was wrong." She studied him. "Was he?"

"Generally. If I hadn't danced with you, it would have had nothing to do with the fact you were a merchant's little sister. As a matter of fact, I liked Sorin all right in those days and your family business was widespread, so for that reason it would have made sense too."

"I think you like Sorin all right these days too," she said softly.

"We do have our moments."

"Oddly enough," Sorin said dryly from the doorway. "All right, Ren, time to bandage you up."

The prince shifted to face him, rolling his eyes as Ani got up and moved around so she could continue ogling his chest. Sorin went to work and pulled the bandages tight around his ribcage. "Ow!" Ren yelped. "That hurt!"

The other man rolled his eyes. "Ren, if I don't tie it tightly, it won't do you any good. This way, it helps keep it stiff so the bones will know what shape to maintain as they heal."

"If my ribs heal in this shape, I'll be deformed."

"Well, I'm sure my sister will like you anyway. Foot up on the bed."

Ren tugged his shirt back on even as he rotated and carefully placed his damaged ankle on the bed, wincing at the contact with the sheets.

"I liked it better off," Ani commented.

"While I appreciate the sentiment, there wasn't much to see."

"It was still pretty."

"Then – Ow! Damn it, Sorin!" he protested, jerking his foot out of reach. "What was that for?"

Sorin smirked, grabbing his calf and pulling the foot back over to him. "Just ensuring it wasn't broken."

"It damn well might be now," Ren muttered.

Sorin ignored him, carefully wrapping up Ren's ankle and immobilizing it. "Look, it's a nasty sprain, Ren, so it's going to take a while to heal."

"Oh good. Well, I have all the time in the world."

Sorin shot him an amused look. "I'll see if I can find you some crutches so you can still be at least somewhat mobile. I know Vladimir promised you and Ani a stroll at least once a week. I'll check it periodically, but for now, no weight on it at all, understand?"

"Yes, sir."

He snorted. "You don't fool me, Ren. I'm serious. Stay off it for your own good. Ani, make sure he behaves himself, okay?"

She grinned. "With pleasure."

"I'll speak to Vladimir later."

"Thanks," Ren felt beholden to say, considering.

Sorin favored him with a crooked smile. "It's no trouble at all," he said and Ren got the feeling there was a lot more behind his words that weren't spoken, although he couldn't, for the life of him, figure out what. "You two behave," he told them and then vanished from the room.

"You're right," Ren said after a moment of thoughtful silence. "I think I do like Sorin all right these days."

Chapter Fourteen

"READY TO START HELPING, JAY?" I asked, taking a sip of water.

"Oh, I suppose, if I must," he sighed. "How long had you and Beau been a couple before I arrived?"

"Officially? Only about two months or so. We never really paid that much attention. It's easy to lose track of time at Cavern Hall, at least accurately," I said, directing the last part towards Stella and Dave.

"Makes sense," Stella said. "I think we would have had the same issue on the farm if David hadn't been in school. That forced us to keep track of the days of the week so we made sure he went."

Dave wrinkled his nose at the reminder. "I would've been fine without school," he said. "George was teaching me all the important things for the farm."

She smiled. "It's good to know more than just how to slaughter a pig." She ruffled his hair.

Irritably, he patted it back down. "Stell," he complained.

I could see my best friend brighten at the nickname and suspected we'd be hearing a lot more of it. He opened his mouth and I decided to cut him off at the pass. "James."

"I really, *really* hate that you can do that to me now."

"Personally, I'm a fan."

"It's rather embarrassing…" he trailed off and eyed me. "You aren't going to tell about my first morning, are you?"

"Of course I am. I think Stella, in particular, will enjoy that one."

He squirmed. "Do you have to? It's not one of my more brilliant moments."

"You have brilliant moments?" Stella asked before I could.

I snickered at his wounded look.

"Stella! You're not helping."

"I definitely want to hear this now."

"How about I just pick up from later?" he suggested hopefully.

"We can't skip things," I told him. "Stella and Dave deserve the whole story."

Jay heaved a sigh. "Fine, but no mocking me afterwards."

"We promise not to do it much," Dave said, crossing his heart with an exaggerated motion.

"Why do I not trust you?" he muttered. "Look, you do that morning, since I don't think I could manage to spit it out and then I'll pick up from there?"

I grinned. "Sounds good to me. That means your embarrassment will be conveyed properly." I picked a good place to start and continued.

There were two skirmishes in the couple months following, but for the most part, the Three had pulled their men back to concentrate on the borders. Both Nerius and Alyia, Tira's two contentious neighbors, had taken advantage of the siblings' preoccupation with destroying the Freedom Fighters to poach Tira's borders. The Three found themselves playing catch-up and, in some places, in pitched battle to defend those borders. In the south, at least Nerius had made serious in-roads and were happily holding quite a bit of Tiran land.

However, in that time, the Freedom Fighters had almost doubled again. The military operations being run were not at all sensitive to the needs or wants of the common person so more found themselves having negative encounters with the siblings or their people. Jez, Ry, and Jessie gained two new roommates – Dunkin's friend, Kilo, and another woman, Ann – as Cavern Hall filled with people, pushed almost to the bursting point. The only good thing in this arrangement was, for the time being, Beau got to keep his office to himself so Jez had an easy escape from the crowded rooms.

One morning, Jez poked her head into Beau's office to ask him something and found him shaking hands with a man about her age. "Hey, you, good timing," Beau said, flashing her a smile. "Jez, this is Jay. He just arrived this morning. Jay, Jez." Beau still made a point of meeting each new recruit, or group of them, personally.

Jez studied him as she offered her hand. There was something about the look on his face that told her Jay would get along well with her and the others. "Nice to meet you."

"Pleasure's all mine. Captain Beau was just telling me that he wanted to introduce us."

"Was he really?" she asked, glancing at Beau.

"He was indeed," Beau said. "I was wondering if you might show him around. I suspect you, Jay, Ry, and Jessie will all get along well."

"Can do. I had a question for you, but it can wait until later."

"Dinner?"

"Deal. C'mon, Jay."

"Thank you, Captain."

Jez made a face. "People still call you that?"

"You do realize that everyone, except Mick and Reardon, did until you came along."

"Details. Jay, to keep Beau from getting a swelled opinion of himself, we've dropped the captain title."

The new man held up his hands. "Don't bring me into this."

She laughed. "C'mon, I'll introduce you to Ry and Jessie." She led the way towards their room, suspecting the others might be there. "So, why'd you join?" she asked, seeking to create conversation.

"A…very good friend of mine joined almost two years ago. He died at Deepen's Crossing. I…have no love lost for the Three and not much to keep me at home, so I figured I'd join. Honor his memory and all that."

Jez nodded, not probing further. That was a common enough tale and they'd lost plenty of good people at Deepen's Crossing – many whom she hadn't even known well. "I'm sorry."

He shrugged. "You move on."

She smiled briefly, agreeing wholeheartedly with the sentiment. "True."

"So, are there a lot of…cliques here?"

"Not many. People usually have a couple really close friends but there's a lot of movement between groups. There's a little less recently since we're growing so fast right now, but it works and no one's excluded." She helped make sure of that considering how lost she'd initially felt. They reached her room and she peeked in past the curtain dividing it from the hallway and grinned. "Hey, friends." She pushed the cloth aside and gestured Jay in. "Jessie, Ry, this is Jay, our newest recruit. Beau asked me to show him around."

The pair looked up from their card game and then Jessie stood, offering her hand. "Hi, Jay. I'm Jessie and this miscreant is Ry or Rylia."

"Does she even answer to Rylia anymore?"

"I do," Ry said indignantly. "Just not quickly."

"Hello," Jay said and then nodded towards the cards. "What're you playing?"

"War."

He took them in. "Jessie's winning."

Ry rolled her eyes. "Don't remind me."

"You also just switched a small pile of the cards while she was shaking my hand, so now you're winning."

Jessie's mouth dropped open. "Why you!"

"How in the name of the gods did you see that?" the teen sputtered.

"Nice sleight of hand," he said, nodding approvingly. "Where'd you learn a trick like that?"

"Street hustling when I was a kid. No one's supposed to be able to see it. Where'd you learn to spot it?"

"Just quick reflexes," he said with a shrug. "Always had them."

"And eyes. Sheesh," Rylia muttered, giving back the stack of cards.

"I'm starting to understand why I always lose when we're playing in Beau's office," Jessie said with narrowed eyes.

Ry grinned charmingly. "I have no idea why that might be. Cross my heart."

Jez clapped Jay on the back. "I think Beau was right. You're going to fit right in with us."

"Yeah, welcome to the club."

"Club?"

"Yeah, we help keep up morale and we're tight with the leadership."

"Except Mick."

"Mick likes us, he just won't say it."

Jay brightened. "Any single female leadership?"

"Jessie," Ry and Jez chorused at the same time, expressions dancing with mischief.

"Wait, what?" Jessie sputtered as Jay grabbed her hand and gallantly kissed it.

"It is a pleasure to meet you, Jessie," he said with basically big puppy eyes.

As Ry burst out laughing, Beau appeared at Jez's shoulder, kissing her on the cheek before taking in the chaos. "Well, Jay's fitting in even better than expected," he said dryly.

"You have no idea," Jez chuckled.

The next morning, the three women joined Mick and Dunkin at a table for breakfast. Ry grinned from ear to ear as Mick glanced at her curiously. "Swimming day," she announced. Scouts, soon after they'd arrived, had discovered a large pond not too far from Cavern Hall. With the Three's presence gone from the woods, Beau allowed small groups to hike to the pond and swim each day. The rules were simple: someone always had to be out of the water, armed and they had to keep the noise level down, just in case. Even for Jez's friends, these were easy enough to follow.

"We should invite Jay," Jez suggested. "We have room for one more, assuming you're still coming, Dunk."

"I'm there," the other man said.

"Do we have to?" Jessie asked. "He's a bit...much."

Ry laughed. "Don't worry, Jessie. Either he'll realize you aren't interested or you'll start to like him." She smirked. "After all, you're two years older than Jez and she's already managed two boyfriends since she got here."

Dunkin snorted into his coffee as Mick rolled his eyes. "Is this conversation necessary?"

The others ignored him as Jez whacked Ry in the back of the head. "Shush you. Dunkin, will you go wake him up and get him in here?"

Dunkin bit his lip to keep from laughing, pushing back from the table. "He's in my room as a matter of fact. I'll go get him."

He reappeared a couple of minutes later, scooping up his plate and glass and moving to the next table over.

"Dunk?" Jez asked.

"I don't think he appreciated my method of waking him," Dunkin said, radiating innocence.

Jay shuffled in then, searching out Dunkin to favor him with a dark glare.

"Morning, sunshine!" Ry said.

He mumbled something indistinct as he grabbed food and plopped down beside Mick. They lapsed into amused silence, listening to Jay's grumbles.

"We're going swimming today and were wondering if you wanted to join us," Jez finally said.

Jay looked up. "Swimming?"

"Yeah, you know, in the water? You, me, Dunkin, Ry, and Jessie."

There was a pause and then a grin crept across his face. "Is it-"

"No, it's not skinny dipping," Jez interrupted, fairly certain that's where he was going.

"Damn. There goes all the fun. You know, Jez, you take all the joy out of the world when you say things like that."

"Good," Jessie said fervently, cheeks a bit redder than usual.

Mick smirked, speaking up. "I think it's way too early in the morning for that sort of thought, Jay."

The newcomer glanced at him, seeming to notice him for the first time. "I don't think we've been introduced?"

"Mick. The second-in-command."

Jay's eyes bulged and he turned scarlet. "I…I…sorry, sir," he managed meekly.

Jez, Jessie, and Ry were cracking up, but Mick, as usual, managed to maintain a straight face. "I do realize it's important to make a strong first impression, but I'm not sure that was quite the way to do it."

"I…" Jay swallowed. "Yes, sir," he said and then looked at the women in hopes they might spare him. "Swimming now?" he asked plaintively.

179

It took another hour for them to all be ready and head out. By then, Jay was fully recovered and awake.

"Dun-can."

"No, it's Dun-kin. Like kin, as in your relatives, relations, family."

"Duncan."

Dunk sighed in frustration and appealed to the girls for help.

"Don't even try," Jez told him. "He's plainly doing it just to annoy you because I won't let him get actual revenge for the wake-up call this morning. Bri used to pull the same shenanigans all the time."

"Or maybe I'm just that stupid."

Ry rolled her eyes. "She was trying to help you, idiot."

"Oh, right. My apologies, Duncan."

"It's…oh, never mind," he growled.

"How about we all call him Dunk and then no one has an issue?" Jessie asked, plainly in a foul temper over Jay's inclusion.

The newcomer bounded over to her. "Someone woke up on the wrong side of the bed this morning," he said sagely.

"I didn't, but I'm heading that way," Jessie said.

"And someone else has gotten over his own poor manners this morning," Ry muttered to Jez and Dunk.

"Oh! I get it." Jay bounced to her other side. "You're actually hopelessly smitten with me and just don't know how to break the news."

She stopped dead and stared at him. "Smitten would not be the first word that comes to mind."

"That's what they all say."

"All?" Ry repeated.

Jay ignored her. "Don't worry. I can wait until you're ready."

"Would anyone mind terribly if I killed him?"

"It'd be a shame if he was a Freedom Fighter for less than a day," Jez pointed out.

"I can handle death threats. It's a start." He crossed his arms behind his head smugly. A moment later, though, he was catching himself from sprawling full out in the dirt.

It was Jessie's turn to look smug. "Best watch your step, there, hotshot," she told him, sauntering past.

Jay stared after her. "She does like me!"

Dunkin shook his head and offered the other man a hand. "Just keep telling yourself that if it helps you sleep better at night."

"I think I will." He dusted himself off. "She initiated physical contact."

Ry choked on a laugh as she tried to keep it in. "She's completely capable of maiming you for life."

"I'll take my chances."

Jez whacked him lightly on the back of the head as she passed. "Keep dreaming, killer."

◀ ▼ ▶

"My turn!" Jay interrupted gleefully.

I gave him a look. "Seriously? That's how we're going to play this?"

"You hadn't taken a breath and I want to go," he whined.

Stella was clearly trying not to laugh. Dave was snickering.

I sighed. "Fine, I'll try and take more deep breaths to let you butt in."

"Why thank you."

"Wait," Stella managed. "You and Jessie?"

He grinned. "Oh, it never happened. And honestly, it is definitely for the best." With that, he picked up the story for the first time.

◀ ▼ ▶

Jay shrugged, not particularly concerned, and let the others draw ahead. The reference to Brighton, by nickname no less, shouldn't have surprised him, but it had caught him off-guard anyway, especially the fondness in Jez's voice. Beau had warned him that Jessie, Ry, and Jez had been Bri's best friends at the camp. He watched them for a minute, wondering if he could handle it, but a part of him thought he could. Even if he wasn't ready to tell them who he was yet, it

181

made him feel closer to the brother he'd known growing up. The one who had turned around and abandoned him immediately after their parents' murder.

He took a deep breath to contain the anger that surged in him at the thought of his brother's desertion. They had been a team growing up and Jay had assumed they would always be a team. Then Bri had left, merely leaving a note that said Jay was too young to follow.

"Jay, come see!" Ry called, ignoring the others as they shushed her.

He brought himself back to the present and realized he'd fallen further behind than he'd thought, so he trotted to catch up. He came to a stop next to the teen, taking in the pond. At the far end, there was a small beach, half-rock and half-sand. Where they stood was a perhaps three foot drop into the deepest end of the water. Ry peered over. "It's about fifteen feet deep here, we figure. It's fun to jump in, but I prefer to wade in and get wet first."

"Really?"

"Yup."

The four of them studied the pond as Dunkin made his way towards the beach to take the first watch. "Good idea," Jay said as she turned to walk away. In one quick movement, he snatched her around the stomach and tossed her calmly, clothes and all, into the water. She yelped before hitting and going under. Jay brushed his hands off and turned just in time to see two hands firmly connect with his chest. He flew off the edge of the rock and hit the water with a loud splash, immediately going under. He came to the surface, sputtering, spotting Jessie at the top, grinning down at him.

Before he could come up with a proper retort, Ry had jumped him from behind, shoving him back underwater. The two commenced a brief but furious fight, during which he heard Jez say, "You do realize he'll take that as flirting, right?"

"The look on his face made it all worthwhile," Jessie said as he got dunked again.

Finally, they both surfaced facing each other. "Truce?"

Ry splashed him, but then took the offered hand. "Truce."

He splashed her with his other.

"Hey! I thought it was a truce."

"It is. We're even now."

"You two look beautiful," Jez said as they waded out, water puddling underneath them at a furious rate.

Jay grabbed Ry and the pair struck a pose. "Why thank you!" he said brightly.

"Maybe you two should be a couple."

"Aw, but we're so cute and fl-"

Jessie slapped a hand over his mouth. "For the love of the gods, please, *please* do not finish that sentence."

He grinned and pried it off. "Promise, cross my heart, hope to die…"

"Good." She turned away to wade in further.

Jez was the only one to catch the mischievous spark.

"Fluffy," he finished.

Jessica turned on him. He only needed one look at her face and sprinted out of the water to cower behind Dunkin. "Help, she's going to kill me!"

"Damn straight."

"Oh, like *I'm* going to help you."

"I swear I know your name! It's Dunkin!"

Jessie continued to advance.

"Congratulations, but that is so not worth facing her wrath."

"You're a traitor to all humankind," Jay pronounced, backing further. "Stay back! I'm warning you!"

"Or what?"

"I'll, um, tell Beau on you!"

"Beau would probably laugh and tell me good job."

"That's no good then." His gaze darted around before he dropped to his knees in supplication, ignoring the attempts by the others to stifle howls of laughter. "I do hereby promise to never try and flirt with you again, unless under pain of death or severe duress or deprivation. I, um," he struggled as she continued towards him, stopping a step away, "will always be nice to puppies and paint rainbows in your honor?" He favored her with his very best winning smile.

She regarded him and then snorted. "Fine. But I promise you that the next time…" She wagged a finger in his face.

"Yes, ma'am, understood, ma'am," he said, hastily saluting.

She didn't move for another minute, so he stayed on his knees, still a bit nervous. Then she burst into laughter. "Gods' Breath, Jay, the look on your face…" she trailed off, unable to continue as the giggles increased.

He rubbed the back of his head in embarrassment as he got to his feet. "Now that we've gotten that over and done with, can we go back to swimming?" He hesitated. "Do I really have to paint rainbows?"

"We'll see, Jay," she managed.

Jez managed to contain her laughter better than the other two. She nudged Ry, who was on the ground, with her toe. "As soon as these two get enough wind back, of course we can."

Jay chortled.

Sorin made sure the smirk was obvious as he let himself into Vladimir's office.

"Yes, Sorin?" his brother asked, a cautious note to his voice. No doubt he was confused by both the smirk and Sorin's unscheduled visit.

"Feeling a little sore today?" he asked with a deliberate drop of his gaze.

Vladimir flushed as Sorin spotted Ani appearing silently in the doorway from the corner of his eye. "I don't know what you're talking about."

"That fairly impressive black eye and the way you're sitting tell me otherwise. You let Ren get you in the eye?"

"I didn't *let* the prince do anything."

"Ah, right, of course not. You were just too damn focused on pummeling the hell out of him to remember that he can hit back."

"Is there something you want?" Vladimir asked darkly.

Sorin shrugged and perched on the edge of his brother's desk. "Not really," he lied, studying the older man. He wondered if it would be possible to bring his brother back from the edge. He still had flashes at times of the Vlad Sorin remembered from childhood, of the boy who always had his back.

"Then why are you here?"

"No reason in particular."

"No reason in particular?" Vlad echoed, raising an eyebrow.

"Why did you beat up Ren?"

"Why? You're really asking me why?" His brother stared at him like Sorin had lost his mind. "How can you ask that? It's obvious he's screwing with her. He's…" As Vladimir struggled to find the words he wanted – Sorin couldn't, in good conscience, call them the right words – Sorin saw his sister shift. Although he was fully aware of her presence in the doorway, Vlad seemed oblivious, his focus on Sorin. He debated alerting Vlad to the fact she was there, but a part of him wanted Vlad to dig the hole he was starting, thought his sister should hear it. He wasn't sure where exactly that part of him even came from, although he suspected it had to do with the way he caught Ren watching Ani as he'd bandaged the prince's foot up. Ren meant every word of what he'd said to Ani the evening before, Sorin was certain. "He's brainwashing her!" Vlad settled on before Sorin could fully finish his train of thought.

The younger brother stared at him, aware his jaw was slack.

"That…that skunk has her believing in love and faith and all that shit, when she should know better."

"Who says they aren't possible?" Sorin's stomach clenched as a fresh pool of memories spread out around him.

His brother's eyes were wild. "I do."

"No, that's Edward talking," Sorin said coolly.

"You can't say he was never right."

He let out an incredulous laugh. "I can't? Vlad, I know you lived with him for four years after I left, but even you can't have sunk so far to believe a word that *ever* crossed Edward's lips, especially about something he so obviously knew nothing about. He never loved anything, not even our mother, for all his words. If he had, he would have done more to keep her alive when Ani was born, not let her waste away to nothing." He didn't dare flick his gaze towards Ani, noticing only after the fact that he'd used her nickname, filing that away for later contemplation.

"What do you know about it, Sorin?" his brother asked scornfully.

Sorin resisted the urge to hit Vlad, forcing his fists to unclench in his lap. "Far more than you know," he said quietly, holding his gaze.

He thought he'd gotten through, could see the energy start to bleed out of Vlad, saw the question in his eyes, but then his brother grabbed hold of his anger with both hands again. "That doesn't change the fact he's using her."

"Are you sure it's not us using her, even with her tacit approval?"

"How in the gods' names can you take his side, Sorin? Have you forgotten who he is? Have you forgotten who we are?"

"I've forgotten nothing, but I also think I see a lot clearer than you do right now, Vlad." The use of the nickname didn't even register, which was not a good sign.

"It was a sound idea. Get things moving, get people used to us, and then use the prince as a final strike to consolidate our hold on the throne. But it wasn't supposed to be at the expense of our sister."

"It's not," Sorin said flatly. "I talked to Ren last night before you beat the shit out of him. I laid it out simply and told him if he even thought about trying to play Anica, I would personally make sure that the rest of his life was a painful, painful mess. He promised me he wouldn't."

Vlad opened his mouth, but Sorin didn't want to hear it and spoke over him.

"I realized something last night, lying in bed. Ren's not like us. He wasn't raised like us. He clearly knows right from wrong, but understands the grey too. He's a good man, despite what we've done to him and, if he says he cares for our sister, then he is telling us the truth. He could no more use her than I could march out of this castle, find the Freedom Fighters, and defeat them single-handedly. Haven't you seen the fondness in him towards Anica for a long time? I have, even if I wouldn't let myself acknowledge it until last night. It just took him this long to figure it out."

Vlad was already shaking his head. "That man wants something so he's pretending to feel for Ani."

"Of course he wants something. He wants to be free, but that doesn't mean he's lying about Anica," Sorin said dryly, but his brother either didn't hear him or deliberately ignored him.

"I say our hold on the country is strong enough."

Sorin stared at him, unable to tear his eyes away, suddenly hyper-aware of Ani's presence at the door. *Don't, Vlad, don't say it, please don't say it,* he thought as strongly as he could, but nothing was going to stop those words.

"We should just kill him and do it ourselves."

For several gut-clenching moments, the office went quiet, the only sound Vladimir's heavy breathing, utterly wound up from his tirade.

186

"You will not touch Ren," Ani said, in a quiet, steady voice.

That in of itself was the scariest thing Sorin could hear, but he unfroze, able to look at their sister and see the disappointment vying with very real fury on her face.

"You touch him and I will…I will kill you."

"Ani," Vladimir started, actually noticing her unnerving calm.

"No." Her voice cracked, emotions finally getting through. "No, no, no," she said, voice rising in pitch with each syllable. "You do *not* get to talk to me. Not right now, maybe never. You…you…" she trailed off, pressing her lips together, the right adjective plainly not coming to her. She stood in the doorway a second longer, trembling, before spinning and sprinting from the room.

"Ani, wait!" Vladimir bellowed, skidding to a stop in the doorway.

Ani said nothing in reply as her footsteps faded from hearing.

Sorin glanced down at his lap, vaguely surprised to find his hands clenched freshly. "You deserved that and more for what you said."

Vladimir dropped his forehead against the doorjamb with an audible thump. "It's true," he said, but the words held no weight.

"It's not and we both know it. Vlad, maybe it's time you took a breather."

"I don't need a vacation. We can't afford a vacation," he said, not moving.

"I don't think you can afford not to have one," Sorin said carefully. "You're falling apart at the seams, Vlad. Take Ani and go to," he cast about in his mind for a suitable normal vacation destination, "the beach or something."

His brother huffed out a laugh. "The beach, Sorin? Honestly?"

It was good to hear him sound at least a bit like himself again, although Sorin didn't like the weariness that tugged at his frame and voice. "It was the first thing that came to mind and seemed properly removed from Oakbridge. I can hold things down here for a few days. Get your head screwed on correctly, take a few deep breaths and come back."

Vlad pushed himself off the wall. "I'm fine, Sorin."

"No, you're not."

He received a disgusted look for that. "Don't give me the 'none of us are fine' spiel. I don't want to hear it." Some of the heat was back so Sorin merely held up his hands in supplication.

"I wasn't going to," he said, holding his brother's gaze as he finally straightened off the desk. "What I will say is this: what you just did here was as bad, in its own way, as most of the things Edward did."

Vladimir opened his mouth to protest.

"Don't bother. Think about it. Everything Edward did was for his own gain, usually at the expense of others. Even the mere idea of killing Ren is exactly that and you know it." He walked to his brother and touched him on the shoulder. "Get your head on straight, Vlad, before you destroy not only what little is left of our family, but before it gets us all killed." Then, using his shoulder, he pushed Vlad out of the way and strode from the room, well-aware that a certain level of shock prevailed on the other man's face. As he headed for his own office, a strange thought crossed his mind: *If I gave you Ani years ago, then you just gave her back to me.* It was somewhat comforting too.

Chapter Fifteen

I sighed. "You chortled? Seriously, Jay?"

"Why yes, I did," he said righteously. "Have you ever tried it? It's a lot of fun."

I made the mistake of asking what a chortle sounded like and got an immediate demonstration, which cracked the rest of us up.

"I don't think I could manage it with the same aplomb, my friend," I told him.

He smirked. "Probably not, no. It does require a special sort of skill."

"You can say that again," Dave muttered.

Stella quickly spoke up before Jay could comment. "So, did you ever renege on that promise?"

"Of course not! There's a reason I add the severe deprivation clause in there."

"That was evil."

"She got over it." He paused. "Mostly."

I glanced at our window, not surprised to find it dark out. The cell never got what I might consider bright and, when we got into the story, I often lost track of time. Mentally, I attempted to add up the days, coming out at around a week already in jail. A week and a lot of bruises. "How long has it been dark out?"

"An hour or two," Dave said innocently.

"You let me waste valuable breath at night?" Jay said, attempting to look intimidating. He failed.

"Yes?"

"I hate you."

Stella gave him a sharp nudge in the ribs, eliciting an 'eep' of surprise. "Be nice to my brother. You seemed to be enjoying yourself. Who were we to stop you?"

"Sleep time," I said cheerfully, cutting Jay off again.

"You get to start tomorrow," he informed me. "My voice is tired."

"After only an hour or so of story? Weak."

"And proud of it," he said, settling down. Stella curled up beside him with Dave on her other side.

I wedged myself into my corner again and watched them for a while before eventually nodding off.

Rees wasted no time. He reached through the bars and shook me awake the next morning before dawn. I struggled to fully wake. The time in jail was definitely weighing on me. Even a week ago, I wouldn't have been caught this sluggish immediately after waking, even not being a morning person, but the bruises and rough sleeping conditions were taking their toll. "Let's go, Jasmine," he said, unlocking the door.

I was a bit surprised, as it filtered in, to find him and not Shorty accompanying the brutes. "Where's Shorty?" I asked as I stood and made a point of slowly stretching.

"It's Dayton's day off. Now let's go."

"In a hurry this morning?" I asked, trying to seem unconcerned, but not sure how well I was doing.

"Something like that. Now, do I need to send Kilgor and Juke in or are you coming?"

"I'm coming." I purposely went to tread on Jay's hand, but he snatched it out of the way at the last second, forming it into a thumbs up. I felt a brief flash of annoyance before reminding myself he might as well get some sleep – nothing was going to stop my date with Colonel Rees. I followed Rees down the hallway, carefully working out some of the kinks in my legs between the bruises and low activity levels.

"After you," he said, motioning me ahead of him. I hobbled into the room and he smirked. "Still a little sore, are we? Maybe not as confident?"

I rolled my eyes. "You wish, Rees. You know, I think I missed your first name. We are on a first name basis, aren't we?" I asked, voice as sweet as possible.

"How about we stick with my title?"

"And show you respect? In your dreams."

He grinned and shook his head. "If nothing else, it's always amusing to chat with you."

"Don't be disappointed that I do not share the same sentiments." I folded my arms across my chest. "Let's move on to the questions so I can refuse to answer and get back to my lovely little cell."

"Why were you planting explosives around the city?"

"It was only around the weapons depot and that is the question, isn't it?" I replied mildly. I was very much aware that the brutes had worked their way around behind me.

"Care to not play semantics and supply me with an answer?"

"What happened to starting with the small stuff?"

He shrugged. "I didn't feel like it today. Enough stalling, Jasmine. Answer me."

"Can you blame me?"

"Now," he said flatly. "Five...four..."

My mind scrambled for an answer. A grin skipped across my face as one occurred to me. "I was trying to blow it up." At his look, I shrugged. "I answered the question. You're the one who failed to specify."

"Very well. *Why* did you want to blow up the depot? Who ordered you to?"

"First question is simple. People like you store your weapons there." I forced a wide smile I didn't feel, since I knew where my answer would lead me. "And I doubted the Three would appreciate it much if the second biggest city, and one of their main strongholds, went up in smoke under their watch because they were too stupid to-" I didn't get to finish my thought as one of the brutes grabbed me by the shirt, spun me, and slammed me face first into the nearest wall.

My breath all left me in a whoosh and I struggled to recover as he set me back down with a thump that jarred my knees. I reached up and wiped my bleeding nose. "Dat was fun," I muttered, holding my hand there. "Any of you have a handkerchief?"

The brutes just stared, but I got a ghost of a smile out of Rees.

"The strangest things amuse you."

"True. Now that we've gotten your impression of both me and the intelligence of our current rulers, how about the second question?"

"Going to need a repeat on that one. It went clear out of my head somewhere around being slammed into a solid wall."

Again, that smile drifted across his face. "Who ordered you to blow up the palace?"

"No one. Jay and I came up with that little treat all on our own." That was actually a flat out lie. The plan had always been to take out the weapons depot and maybe the barracks if we could manage it.

"You're lying."

"Only a little," I said sarcastically, wrist still pressed against my leaking nose. "Honestly, you have no proof that I am. In fact, I think my feelings are hurt that you don't believe I'm capable of trying to blow up parts of Greensward all by my lonesome. Well, okay, with Jay's help."

"What if I said that Jay told me who ordered you to do it?"

"Give me a name and I might believe you." I knew he was bluffing. Disadvantage to them leaving us together, although I'd never say that out loud. If Jay had spilled about Beau, he would have told me.

"So you aren't part of the Freedom Fighters?"

"No." And then I asked for it. "Haven't you realized by now that no one likes you or your employers? Most people think you're all slimy, no good..." His look turned dark and I ducked on reflex, dodging the first swing. Unfortunately for me, though, the second brute managed to snag my shirt and repeat the earlier wall slam. As I stumbled back from that, very off-kilter now, I ran straight into a fist to the gut. I doubled over, wishing I'd been able to curb the temptation to bait them. And here I kept giving Jay crap about it. My feet were swept out from under me and I ended up on the floor in an ungraceful heap. I immediately curled into the fetal position, but not before a boot connected solidly with my stomach, driving what little breath I'd regained out. As I struggled to breathe, I squeezed my eyes shut, trying to focus on anything but the beating, although it was far from easy.

Finally, some indeterminable time later, it stopped. I cracked open my eyes, someone's boots swimming into view.

"Insults get you nowhere, Jasmine." Of course it was Rees.

"No, but they make me feel warm and fuzzy inside," I managed, still trying to catch my breath, which meant not that much time could have passed.

He snorted. "Give me your hand."

I didn't argue, reaching up. He pulled me to my feet. I braced myself on the wall with the other hand, the world spinning unpleasantly beneath, or maybe it was around, me.

"Are you part of the Freedom Fighters?"

"If you're so sure you know the answer, why are you asking me?" I asked wearily. They had definitely re-bruised every bruise and found a few new places for them too. I fought to stay upright.

"I want to hear it out of your mouth."

"Then you're going to be disappointed."

"There's always next time."

"Boy, oh, boy, I can't wait," I said with all the false enthusiasm I could muster. "It's always such a joy to talk with someone as…" I trailed off, realizing now would be a very good time to beat back the temptation. "As wonderful as you," I finished.

One of the pair growled. My catch had fooled no one. I kept a wary eye on all three, but let out a breath as Rees merely said, "Take her back to her cell. Jasmine, we'll talk again soon."

I managed a salute before the thugs grabbed my arms. Even if Rees had managed to brush off my almost-insult, it became apparent the brutes weren't as forgiving. Instantly, they both twisted my arms tightly behind me. I heard two very distinct *pops* before the black rushed up to claim me.

"Jez? Jez, c'mon, you, don't leave me hanging." The voice got more insistent. "Jasmine Lockholme, don't you dare not respond. Wake *up*." Distantly, I knew the voice to be Jay's, but it was too much of an effort to try and pull myself all the way back as pain crawled along my body. There was a pause and then he spoke again and, even as muddled as my mind was, I was certain he was no longer speaking to me. "Aren't you going to do something?"

"There's no reason. She just fainted. Overexertion."

"Overexertion my ass," Jay said in a quiet tone I knew meant danger.

I felt I should warn Rees, but it was a hard enough fight just to focus on the voices and make meaning of the words.

"She would still be able to respond or wake up. For all I know, your damned thugs put her into a coma!" Jay shouted.

I winced, the loud noise cutting through my head and setting it pounding – as if I needed more pain. "Steady, Jez," Stella murmured soothingly from somewhere nearby.

I managed to open my eyes a little, Stella swimming into semi-focus. She smiled worriedly down at me – or at least I think she did, everything was blurry.

"Dislocating a shoulder isn't going to result in a coma."

"Two dislocated shoulders and at least one possibly broken arm might! You've already told me you didn't mean for it to happen, so fix it already, damn it!"

"She'll be fine. As soon as she's back up and moving, I'll have someone check on her, okay?"

"Or you could fix it now."

"She's just fainted, Jay," Rees said more firmly.

"Does that look like a faint to you? She's in shock."

I closed my eyes, my tremulous hold on the real world starting to slip again as my arms continued to throb deeply.

"Which means she'll be just fine given a bit of time."

"Except for the fact your brutish sidekicks just finished using her as a chew toy," Jay growled. It was a bad analogy and I wanted to protest it. "Who knows what they've done to her on top of this. Damn it, Rees, for all I know she could have internal bleeding."

"Now you're overexaggerating just to get a rise out of me."

"A rise out of *you?*" Jay echoed. "Of all the…" I missed the rest of my friend's rant as my hold finally slipped and the darkness reclaimed me.

"Jez? C'mon, Jez, I need you to speak to me. Stella said you were awake earlier. Please wake up." I'd never heard Jay come so close to true pleading as I struggled my way back towards consciousness, vaguely aware he'd been talking to me for a while.

"Hey," I murmured, managing to get my eyes open a crack to squint up at him. The world hadn't steadied much in however long I'd been out.

I couldn't miss his wide, relieved smile. "Hey, you! How're you feeling?"

"Got run over by horses," I said, or tried to. I think only every other word got out intelligibly, but my mind was clearing a bit. The pain was not quite so severe this time. I suspected that meant I'd been out some time. My eyes slid shut again despite my best efforts.

"Hey, stay with me, Jez."

"Am."

"I'm trying to convince Rees to patch you back up, but I'm afraid I ended up just calling him names."

"S'all good." I cracked open an eye. "Good names?"

He laughed, but there was a definite worried tinge to it. "Yes, very creative names. I did us both proud."

"Sleep now?"

"No, I need you to stay awake."

"No coma," I said, feeling like a two-year-old again who didn't know and couldn't find the words she wanted. The pain was too much to allow for any sort of clear thinking, though. "Don't feel good."

"Of course you don't. Two dislocated arms and more will do that to you."

"Still there?" I murmured.

"Yeah, I'm still here."

I wished I had the energy to muster a glare. "Arms still there?"

He frowned. "Yes, of course."

"Get rid of them," I attempted, not at all sure how clearly it came out as the blackness slunk out from the corners of my vision.

"No, Jez, damn it, stay with me."

I slipped off before I could respond. I was aware of waking a few other times and attempting to hold up my end of the conversation, but it never lasted long.

"It's been two days, you gods-forsaken bastard. Do something." That was Jay.

The snort that followed was, without a doubt, even in my beleaguered brain, Rees. "You'd try and kill me if I got within a foot of the door."

"Only because you're just staring. If you were trying to be useful, that would be a different story."

"Sure, a promise that would remain only until I stepped within reach."

"You're just making up excuses now. You *need* to fix her, Rees."

"What were you trying to do the last time I stepped up to the door then?" Rees asked. How he managed to sound smug even with that question, I had no idea, but I wanted to get up and shake it out of him. It only made my head hurt more.

"Kill you," Jay said. I could picture his vindictive smile.

"You call her Jez and yet I thought her name was Jasmine."

"Come off it, Rees. This isn't one of your stupid interrogations. Rest assured, if you don't help her, I will figure out how to kill you. It doesn't need to be pretty."

"Tell me why and I'll fix her."

The silence stretched on so long I almost thought I'd drifted off again before Jay spoke. "Fine."

Now, I did drift off, missing Jay's explanation.

Something nudged me in the side, bringing me back, as conscious as I'd managed so far. "All right. You three in the corner. Jay, you behind the Harpers. One move and we're out of here."

"Don't you dare let the brutes take her."

"Kilgor and Juke are only here to make sure you behave."

"I'm not planning on moving an inch," Jay said.

There was a shuffling noise and then arms encircled my waist, starting to lift me. My right arm flopped listlessly and I whimpered, fresh pain shooting through me.

"Damn you, be careful!"

"I'm being as careful as I can be, James, so be silent." Rees's face appeared in front of me. "Now for the left side."

I braced myself but still yelped as my left arm burst with lancing, white hot pain. I started muttering curses under my breath, although I found that, in all the movement, my mind partially cleared – or at least, I didn't feel quite so close to the darkness. "Hurts," I managed.

"Sorry," Rees said, hefting me upright.

"Not you." I had to wonder why he was being so nice. I did not want to have even the slightest kind thoughts about this man.

"Only a few more feet and we've got a stretcher, okay?"

"'kay."

He mostly dragged me the remaining distance. "You aren't bleeding internally?" he asked me quietly, looking suddenly worried – or maybe nervous.

"Don't think so." My voice cracked. "Why's my voice scratchy?"

"You've been rather, um, noisy the last few days."

I managed to look at him. "Why?"

"You've screamed almost every time you've moved for the past three days."

"You *are* a bastard."

That faint smile skidded across his face. "Probably. You seem better."

"Clarity in pain?" I asked, remembering to catch the automatic shrug before I could try. That would certainly ruin my clarity.

"All right, Jez, I'm going to lower you down. It's going to hurt, so be prepared."

"Already hurts."

He carefully lowered me down to the ground. It wasn't until he went to move my arms that the clarity vanished. I think I screamed as I heard Jay's voice: "Get well, damn you, or I'll never forgive you!" There was something amusing about that, but I was sucked down before I could identify it.

"There, she should be fine now. She'll be right as rain from the dislocations in a few days, but the break in her left arm was bad. It could easily lead to permanent stiffness in the limb. That needs time to rest and heal, understand?"

"Yes, thank you, doctor."

"She'll probably be pretty out of it and sleepy for a few days. I've given her some strong medication to get her through the pain. You have to leave her alone for at least two weeks. Between this and the other injuries, you've weakened her body too much to be able to handle the type of punishment you inflict. I'd prefer a month but understand why I'm sure that's not likely to happen." The doctor sounded decently disgusted.

"I hear you. Thanks again."

I heard the scuff of feet and then the click of a door latch.

"You can open your eyes now, Jez, I know you're awake."

"Barely," I managed, throat dry. "I'm pretty sleepy."

"That will be the medication. How are you feeling?"

"Less like shit an' I want to keep my arms."

He snorted, amused. "Even now, she shows a sense of humor."

"My sense of humor never leaves." I yawned, enjoying the feel of a real bed underneath me.

"So I've noticed. Get some rest, Jez."

"You're calling me" – another yawn – "Jez."

"I've been informed that Jasmine's a bit of an antiquated name for you now. Jay told me you took the name Jez after we killed you."

I now recalled hearing part of that conversation. "Needed something not so obvious."

"Indeed."

Something was bugging me. "Why were you nice?"

He stared at me. "When?"

"When you were pulling me out of the cell to get me here."

"I'm a nice guy at heart."

"Not buying it. Try again."

He shrugged, an action I reminded myself again not to try any time soon, even if the pain had faded to a steady but dull ache. "Maybe I just need you alive."

"After unceremoniously sentencing us to death upon arrival? Still not biting."

"You sure woke up quickly."

"Why?" I pressed, determined to get it out of him before I succumbed to sleep.

He didn't say anything, watching me.

"You got a tip, didn't you?" That had been my gut instinct and now I was sure I was right. "You need to know more about the Freedom Fighters. They've got you nervous because they've been pretty damn successful lately. You think

198

they know a lot more about you than you do about them. And someone put the bug in your brain that Jay and I are with them and can tell you what you want to know."

"Good work, super sleuth, but no tip other than General Opalin," he said dryly. "Plus, my theory actually goes beyond that."

"Do tell."

"You and Jay are not only Freedom Fighters, but highly ranked members."

"Oh, stop. I'm quite flattered, but you're a little off the mark. It's just us. Our mistake was going too far, too fast, and getting caught."

"Now you're making things up. You are definitely not small-time or that stupid."

"Oh?" I prompted mildly, both curious and a bit worried where his deductions might go. The best I could do was play innocent.

"Because you're damn smart. I know stupid small-timers, Jez, I deal with them every day. You and Jay are far too good. In fact…" A surprised look flashed across his face as something occurred to him. "I get it."

I frowned, not liking where this was going.

"You meant to get caught. Or at least knew it was a distinct possibility. You knew you might easily be throwing your life away when you took this job."

I was shocked at his intuition, my opinion of him reluctantly rising a notch. "Now does that make sense?" My voice came out remarkably steady, considering how accurate he was. "I thought you just called me damn smart, thanks by the way. If I'm so smart, why the hell would I put myself in a situation with no way out?"

"I didn't say there was no way out," he said with a smile. "And anyway, it doesn't matter, because you've found something you believe to be bigger and more important than you. I know your type, Jasmine. You're more than willing to sacrifice yourself for the greater good."

"Actually, I'm really as selfish as the next noble, but I'll take that in the spirit in which it was intended."

He didn't even bother telling me he didn't believe me. "But what about Jay?" he mused, actually stroking his chin.

I wanted to push myself up so I didn't feel quite so vulnerable lying down but even the slight movement of my arms increased the dulled pain closer to sharp so I gave up on it. "What about him?"

He studied me. "He's lost someone, like you with Brighton. Someone close."

How right he was. I kept all expression off my face. "Oh?"

"Who is it?"

I laughed, unable to help myself despite the pain. "You have got to be kidding me."

"No, I did not expect an answer, but it was worth a shot. Sleep well, Jez, we'll speak again soon," he said, patting me none-too-gently on the shoulder.

I winced. "Not too soon. I heard the doctor. At least two weeks. And you think you need me, which I'll take."

"I don't need any part of you functional besides your brain and mouth, Jasmine, so I would still caution you to tread carefully."

"Mmhmm, you have wonderful nightmares too, Colonel Rees."

He chuckled and pulled the door shut behind him. I gave into the draw of sleep, although the blackness felt somehow gentler this time.

Early the next afternoon, Shorty appeared to escort me back to my cell. I discovered, upon waking in the morning, that the only actual cast I had was on my left arm, stretching from midway up my upper arm to down to my forearm, mostly encompassing my elbow. I asked Dayton, who bluntly explained that my left elbow had been broken while both shoulders were dislocated. Even with the time delay, the doctor had said there was nothing to be done with my shoulders except limit use until they felt better.

Jay impatiently held himself back as Shorty let me in before all but tackling me in a huge hug. "Gods' breath, Jez, you had me worried," he exclaimed as I gently pried him off after a suitable amount of time.

I felt flattered, tired, and sore. "Thanks, Jay. I promise I'm fine now. Or, well, close to it." I then greeted Dave and Stella as the boy attached himself to me. I let him, glancing out to make sure Shorty was long gone. "Rees had a brainstorm last night."

Jay frowned. "What about?"

"Us, the Freedom Fighters, and our motives." I quickly filled him. "So if he seems like he knows more than he does, it's just conjecture."

"Well, you got to give the man credit. He's smart, if nothing else. Color me impressed. Kinda makes me wish he was on our side."

"Tell me about it. I swear if I hadn't been falling asleep he would have picked everything up just following his stream of thought." I gently convinced Dave to let go of my waist and settled carefully back in my corner, careful not to jostle my shoulders too much. Although the pain was dull for now, I was not anxious to test and see if it would get worse if I stressed them.

After a bit of silence, Dave spoke up. "If it's okay with Jez, maybe Jay could tell the story for now?"

I glanced at my friend. "Where were we? I forgot in all the fun."

He snorted. "We'd just finished at the pond."

"Ah, right. That brings us to Westcorner, considering it was only a couple weeks later."

"Sounds right."

"Then let me do a quick conversation and then you're welcome to it."

He saluted as Dave leaned forward.

Jez headed down the hallway towards Beau's office, able to catch snippets of his conversation with Mick.

"I want to…" That was Beau.

"…untested."

"It'll tell us…"

"What about his…?"

"It'll give me…to see how…is."

"A field test?"

"Yeah, he doesn't…about his…"

"That makes a certain amount of sense," Mick said as Jez entered the room.

"Hi," Beau said.

"Jez." Mick nodded to her.

"Hey. Have you decided on our fifth wheel?"

"I was thinking Jay would be a good choice," Beau said.

She grinned. "Jessie'll hate it. It's perfect."

"Not exactly my thought process, but that works too."

"You do realize I'm still opposed to this, especially when you refuse to take Reardon."

Jez stayed silent, knowing Mick was showing a lot of trust by protesting in her presence. The two of them had come a long way since the early frigid days that seemed half a lifetime ago.

"I need you and Reardon here running things, Mick, you know that. It won't be more than a week, I promise."

"We both know it could potentially be more than a week. This isn't the area around Cavern Hall."

"Mick," Beau said with a sigh, "I need to do this on my own, please."

Mick's gaze flicked from his old friend to Jez and back again. "Jez?"

"We'll take care of him, I promise. We'll all keep our noses clean."

He nodded. "I suppose that's the best I can ask for. Although that is an argument in favor of not taking our newest favorite recruit."

"Jay will behave himself," Beau said, shooting Mick a significant glance that Jez did not understand.

"He'd better or I'll kick his gods-be-damned ass," Mick said sourly.

Jez stifled a giggle, always amused at the few times the second-in-command swore. "I'll go let him know he's coming."

"We're leaving tomorrow morning, bright and early."

She tossed a loose salute. "Sounds good," she said, ducking out of the room and going to find Jay, ready to impress upon him how important his good behavior was. She got distracted by various events and didn't find him until later in the day to let him know about their upcoming trip to Westcorner. She explained, briefly, that every couple of months, Mick or Reardon would take four others and travel to one of the larger villages to meet with one of their local informants and discuss, in person, what was going on in Tira. This would be Beau's first time going since he'd dug his heels in when the topic had come up a week earlier and insisted. Jez understood his need to prove himself away from the two older men.

◄▼►

Jay took a deep breath. I mimed zipping my mouth shut as Stella snorted. My friend beamed and started talking. At least now I knew his signal to let him take over. It was obvious and over-the-top, like most things about Jay, but it worked.

◄ ▼ ►

"So let me get this straight," Jay said. "I get the dubious honor of being one of five people who get to waltz out of our safe hidey-hole into enemy territory to chat up some snitches and then hike all the way back. How many people have *died* doing this?"

Jez laughed at him. "No one has ever died. The Three have never even gotten wind of it."

"I still say it's ridiculous and *dangerous*."

She grinned.

"I'm being ordered to go, aren't I?"

Her grin widened.

"You're all complete bonkers. Utterly bonkers," he said, throwing up his hands.

"Your point being?"

"Just want it on the record before we all *die* of *stupidity*."

She shook her head. "We leave bright and early tomorrow morning, so be ready."

"That leaves scant time for final farewells."

"And who exactly do you need to say a final farewell to? You barely know anyone, but the four of us and Mick."

"There's Dunkin."

"He'll survive. I don't think you and Mick are really close enough to warrant them either."

Jay had the grace to wince. "No, your point is well made. Alas, onward to our deaths, noble friend!"

"It's wonderful you never lose your sense of humor."

"What would be the fun in that?"

"Just try and behave on our trip, okay?"

"Don't I always?"

"No!" Jez said in concert with Jessie as their friend appeared from around the corner.

"I am hurt to the very core. You spear me with your harsh words. Right here!" He clasped his hands over his heart and dramatically collapsed to the floor.

Jessie nudged him in the side with her toe. "Nice acting, killer."

He grinned and hopped to his feet with a flourishing bow. "I do my utmost. My most fair maidens, I will see you anon!" he announced and turned, skipping off down the corridor.

As he did, a frown crossed Jessie's face. "I'll be right back," she told Jez absently and rushed after him. "Jay, hey, Jay!"

He paused and turned, a wide grin on his face. "Have you finally…" he trailed off, taking in the serious expression on her face. "Jessie? Is something wrong?" he asked a bit nervously, grin fading.

"Your friend who died."

Jay's expression went stony as he saw where this was going. "What about him?"

"He wasn't just a friend, was he? He was your brother. You're James, Bri's younger brother, aren't you?"

His jaw worked, silently. "Yes."

"Why didn't you tell us?"

"Because I don't want to. Didn't want to. Whatever. I'd appreciate it if you kept this piece of gossip to yourself," he said stiffly, trying to corral his spinning thoughts. He thought after two weeks without recognition from them, he'd been safe. Something he'd just done had given him away, though, and he resolved to be more careful. "I don't need to be compared to my *wonderful* older brother and spend all my time listening to the darling memories you have of him."

"Jay-"

He cut her off. "I need to go make sure my sword is nice and sharp," he said, spinning on his heel and was, within a few steps, running down the corridor. Before he even realized it, he found himself back in the room he shared with Dunkin, Richard, and another newish recruit. He kicked at his bedroll angrily before glaring around the room. He knew he needed to walk off his energy, though, so he spun, jammed his hands in his pockets, and took off towards the exit.

About halfway there, he heard a familiar voice. "Wait up, Jay!"

He made a face, but slowed.

A moment later, Jessie caught up to him. "Jay, we need to talk."

"Not sure what we need to talk about," he said, speeding back up.

A hand on his shoulder whipped him back around. "Don't be an asshole, Jay."

"Don't be…?" he repeated.

"Look, I didn't mean to hurt your feelings or bring up a sore subject, Jay, and it's clear I did both. I'm sorry, okay? It's your life and I shouldn't have pushed. I promise I won't tell the others. I just…I'm sorry. Now, if you want to go off and be a pisspot, it's your decision, but you don't do angry very well."

But I do hurt really, really well, he thought, studying her face before turning and continuing towards the exit. "C'mon." He'd gone another couple feet before realizing she wasn't following. He rolled his eyes, anger slowly ebbing, as he glanced back at her. "What part of 'come on' do you not understand?"

"C'mon where?"

"For a walk. I need to be outside right now."

She frowned but trotted to catch up with him. He led the way outside into the bright summer sun and found a spot on the rocks near the entrance before sitting down. She settled in beside him silently.

"So how did you figure it out?"

"The skipping, mostly, but once I recognized that, the personality was a dead giveaway too."

"Does anyone else know?"

"I'm assuming Beau and Mick know, but no, I don't think anyone else has made the connection. It's…we've had to grow up and move on a lot in the past six months and it's not something any of us like to think about."

"Did he die…?"

"He saved my life right before he died. The man who got him…he had almost just killed me before Bri intervened." She hesitated, glancing at him. "Why don't you want everyone to know?"

"Bri and I were best friends ever since I can remember. When Opalin's men killed our parents, I thought we'd mourn together and maybe, in the future, join the Freedom Fighters. We were all that was left, after all. Instead, he ditched me the morning after their funeral with no warning, instructing my aunt and uncle not to let me out of their sight and leaving me a note saying I was too young to join, but he couldn't wait. I didn't feel young. Not after losing both my parents at the same time. I was too furious to do anything at first and then my life sort of stalled and I could barely get out of bed some mornings. When Beau's letter came saying Bri had died…it was the kick I needed to get my life back in gear. I waited a few months and got myself in shape, before tracking the Freedom Fighters down. I'm still mad at him, but what I told Jez is true, I want to honor his memory. What we're doing here is right."

Jessie sat forward and hugged him tightly. "I'm so sorry, Jay. I won't lie if someone asks me outright, but I won't go around yelling it either."

"I wouldn't expect you to." He paused. "You're so going to use this as blackmail, aren't you?"

She laughed. "Only sometimes, I promise."

His face fell and he aimed a picture-perfect pout at her.

"You don't stay down long, do you?"

"Dall family trait," he said with a quick smile, hopping to his feet and hauling her up. "C'mon, let's go pack. It's almost time to go hiking to our doom." Before Jessie could reply, he went blithely on, "I'll make eggs one morning. Mm, eggs."

"Eggs?" she repeated.

He grinned. "I make killer scrambled eggs!"

Ani raced headlong down the corridor, choosing turns and stairs at random until she found herself bursting into the main courtyard of the castle. She snuck a quick glance up at Ren's window, hoped he wouldn't see her, and continued her flight past the people working there and out into the main street of Oakbridge. It was somewhere around this point when Ani realized she was crying, big tears rolling down her cheeks. "Damn it," she swore, swiping furiously at them.

She picked up her pace to a jog again, weaving skillfully among the people doing their business along the street. She finally made it to the walls and bounded up the stairs. A soldier stationed there glanced at her, reprimand on his lips before recognizing her. Ignoring her tears, he saluted her and returned his gaze to the area beyond the city. She slowed and headed down the walls, ignoring the soldiers who shot her curious looks. She finally reached a point close to the castle, almost directly below where she and Ren had stood the night before. Once there, she slumped against the wall and buried her face in her hands, allowing the full flow of tears she'd been holding back by sheer force of will.

After a couple minutes, she forced herself to stop, wiped her face, and stood, leaning against the wall to stare out to the farms beyond the city. She couldn't understand how Vlad could even suggest killing Ren. She'd heard his hollow reasoning. She'd heard all the things unsaid and gotten the meanings behind everything that *had* been said – or at least most of them. A few of Sorin's comments had intrigued her, but she pushed aside her curiosity for now, trying to figure out Vlad. They'd all had the same childhood. Granted, she and Sorin had had it worse than Vlad a lot of the time, but her eldest brother's determination as a child to try and protect his younger siblings had landed him in trouble almost as often. None of them had felt a moment's sadness when their father had died when Ani was eighteen.

And yet, somehow Vlad had grasped his legacy with both hands. It had been Edward's idea originally to overthrow the Highcastles and he'd had the backing he'd needed by the time he died. But Edward had wanted it for himself, not for the next generation, but just his personal legacy. Even Ani had seen that. He'd fully wanted the glory for himself.

And yet Vlad had stepped into the leadership role, bringing his siblings along with him. Ani hadn't protested – where else was there for her? Sorin had… been the Sorin she'd gotten to know as an adult, only even worse, and said nothing either way. Now, Vlad was showing Edward-like tendencies more and more and it was getting near impossible to pull him out of them.

Abruptly, the picture of Ren as king popped into her head and she smiled. Ren, she knew, would make an excellent king. He was empathetic, kind, fiercely intelligent – he had all the attributes needed to run Tira well and bring it back from the destruction she and her brothers had wrought. Even as she thought it, she knew there was no place for her beside him. She knew what she had done when she'd stood with her brothers. There were only three options available to her at this point: death, imprisonment - no doubt far worse than Ren's own incarceration - or hiding for the rest of her life. She had to admit she didn't relish any of the possibilities, but forced the thoughts away before they could run to their logical conclusion. At this point, what would happen would happen and there was likely not a damned thing she could do about it either way.

She shifted and felt the jab of paper in her back pocket. She tugged the letter from Ren to his brother out and stared at the plain envelope, adorned in Ren's simple script with the name Beau. She folded it open and began to read:

Dear Beau, I'm sure you know of and about me even though I don't know you. I wish, I guess I wish things had been different and we'd been able to grow up together. I have the feeling our mother is no longer alive, but on the off chance she is, please wish her all my best. Honestly, I don't know what else to say, it seems odd to even believe I have a brother, let alone one who is doing so much to help our country. No offense meant, of course, as it seems to be in Highcastle blood to defend Tira. I know it has been kept silent that I'm still alive, so this letter might come as some surprise. I hope you realize how many tries it has taken me to get this right. It is amazingly difficult to write a letter to a sibling you've never met. Good luck with everything, Beau, and I hope we can meet together on the other side of all of this. Sincerely, your brother, Ren.

Ani liked that he had signed it with his nickname. It seemed appropriate somehow, despite the fact the two never met and, if Vlad had his way, they never would. She scanned it again, running a finger across the tight, almost elegant handwriting. Then she tucked it back in the envelope and sealed it, slipping it back into her pocket. She wasn't sure yet how to get it mailed to the Freedom Fighters' hidden camp, but she was certain something would come to her. Perhaps Trigger Rees's vaulted prisoners down in Greensward could help. She nodded. Jakium was due to head down there any day now. She'd speak to him about it.

In the meantime, she scuffed at the stone childishly with her toes. She still wasn't certain what to do about her elder brother, or even if there was anything she could do. She loved Vlad dearly. After Sorin had escaped their house when Ani was fourteen, Vlad had become her protector full-time and, while he wasn't quite as diligent about it as the middle sibling, he had shielded her more than she could have managed on her own. As such, she found his current thought processes ridiculous. He was leaping to conclusions and acting on stupidity by beating Ren and then threatening to kill him. If he'd come to her she could have…argued uselessly with him, she realized. The brother that had helped protect her, and supported Sorin through thick and thin, was slipping away from them both. Even in the years since Edward's death, since they'd escaped his chains, Vlad had focused single-mindedly on the very things Edward had wanted.

208

Frustrated with the way her mind was moving in circles, she kicked the wall and spun, slumping against it to watch inside the city. She eyed it critically. It didn't look any different from the times she had visited with her brothers before the coup but…as she watched a small gathering of men and women, a group of soldiers in their colors bustled up and laid into them with clubs, ordering them to move out. Ani vaguely recalled a recent edict of Vlad's stating that large groups could not meet without prior approval by the city council. She thought that breaking up a group of maybe ten was pushing it. That was something Ren would never allow.

She wondered absently if she should feel more regret over her own actions as she toed at the ground, making patterns in the dust. She'd been all around the country during her exile from Oakbridge and it seemed to her there were less smiles - less hope - on the faces of the people. She'd been able to move almost without recognition and knew she saw things her brothers never would. Ani debated mentioning it to Sorin. He'd taken steps to lend assistance the few times she had insisted when getting a hold of some ignored letter or another.

In a way, she regretted what it had done to the country. Ren would make an excellent king, there was no doubt about that in her mind, but if her brothers hadn't acted, she would have never gotten the chance to spend time with him, let alone fall in love, and have that love returned. She shrugged.

What was done was done. There was no changing the past, only affecting the future.

Which is why she was determined to save Ren, to get him out of the castle, despite the fine line that meant walking between saving the man she loved and betraying her brothers. No, she thought after a minute, *betraying Vlad*, and then she wasn't entirely sure why she thought that. Perhaps it was the changes she could see in Sorin recently, the small little shifts back to the boy she'd known, who she'd crawl in bed with and cry on and who called her Ani when no one else would. An escape by Ren would absolutely spell the end of their time as rulers. Probably spell the end of their lives. Could she do that to them?

She pursed her lips, abruptly realizing she'd walked back to the stairwell she'd come up on. She glanced over her shoulder back at the castle. "Ren's worth it. *Tira's* worth it," she said to herself as she bounded down the stairs. Maybe it was her task to finally right the wrongs she and her brothers, and ultimately her father, had caused.

Ani slipped in among the crowd, threading her way back towards the castle.

No matter what she did, she thought – as she smiled at the guard for one of the side entrances and walked in, heading for Ren's room – change was coming to Tira.

She peeked silently into Ren's room, shutting the door with a quiet click behind her as she spotted him asleep on his bed. She stood, back pressed against the door, watching him. Then she nodded decisively.

This Change would be for the best.

Chapter Sixteen

"I GUESS I CAN'T BE MAD THAT Jessie knew but still. I never asked her outright, so she never lied to me *and* kept her word to you," I said as Jay took a quick break to grab some water.

"Yup, you were pretty clueless."

"Thank you ever so much for your words of wisdom," I said before yawning.

"Why don't you get some sleep, Jez?" Stella asked. "We'll wake you if anything happens, not that it's likely to until we get breakfast tomorrow." Dinner had arrived without ceremony as usual while Jay was talking. He'd paused for the minute so the guard wouldn't overhear and then picked right back up.

I settled back in my corner, wishing for a better place or way to sleep, but I knew curling up on the stone would only be uncomfortable and potentially impossible, even with how exhausted I was. Despite my discomfort, I drifted off rapidly to the sounds of the other three chatting.

Somehow I slept through the arrival of breakfast because I didn't wake until Jay gently shook me. "Wake up, breakfast's here."

I straightened up, wiggling myself backward using my legs, which were still, by far, the most undamaged part of me, and then eyed the wooden spoon and bowl.

"I could spoon feed you," my friend said.

Just the suggestion was enough for me to carefully reach out with extremely sore arms and pick them up as I glowered balefully at him. To my amusement, Stella punched him in the arm hard, winking at me.

He yelped and rubbed it with a hurt look.

"Jez can't right now," she said. "How's it feel?"

"I'm stiff and it hurts to move, but if I'm slow, it's okay." Add to that the fact I was starving, since I hadn't eaten much in the previous five days and nothing at all for three of them.

"I think you shoulda gone with the spoon feeding," Dave said wickedly and received a punch of his own, no doubt gentler, from his sister.

"Behave," she admonished.

"Not fair!"

"I could punch you again," she offered sweetly.

He quickly scooted over to the door. "No, thanks!"

She smirked. "Then it's fair."

"I hate being the youngest," Dave muttered.

Jay reached over from his position at my side and ruffled his hair, which only earned another protest. "There's nothing wrong with being the youngest. Jez and I both are."

"But I'm a whole nine years younger."

Jay absorbed that and then nodded. "True. You are."

Dave eyed him expectantly. "And?"

"Was there supposed to be an and?"

I choked back laughter at the indignant look on the ten-year-old's face. "Yes!"

"Oh. Afraid I'm fresh out of ands."

"Not *fair*."

"No need to get excited about it, ladster."

"But," Dave sputtered, "aren't you going to offer me some words of wisdom on being a much younger sibling?"

"Can't say as I can, considering Bri and I are only a couple years apart. Jez?"

I started, having been absorbing the words but zoning out, still sleepy. "Huh?"

"You're not a much younger sibling, right?"

"Nope, Colin's only about eighteen months older than me. Well, okay, technically I am a much younger sibling, considering Kent is ten years older than I am, but I never spent much time with Kent in general, let alone by myself. I make a great younger sibling, but don't know much about being significantly younger."

"Well, there you go, ladster, we can't help you."

Dave heaved a sigh as Stella cocked an eyebrow. "Ladster?"

"Yup! Like it?"

"It's…interesting," she said diplomatically.

He grinned. "At first, I was thinking youngster, but then I liked lad better, so when they actually came out of my mouth, they got all twisted and combined to ladster."

Silence greeted that statement.

"Did he really just say that?" Stella finally asked me.

"I always knew he spoke without thinking, so I guess this just confirms it."

"Disrespectful, the lot of you," Jay muttered.

"It's not like I said anything we all didn't already know."

He pondered that, nose wrinkling. "Point."

"So if the first time for ladster was an accident, why did you use it again?"

Instantly, my friend brightened. "I thought it had a nice ring to it! Don't you agree?"

I hid a smile by focusing on my bowl. Once I had it under control and had finished eating, I looked back up. "Did you get any further in the story last night?"

"No, I figured it wouldn't be nice to leave you out, considering you might have wanted to add something, so I entertained our illustrious companions with stories of my childhood, including a few focusing on escaping Marguerite's clutches." Marguerite was, I knew, Jay's older, very much on the straight and narrow cousin. I'd first heard her name shortly after Jay's arrival, on our journey to Westcorner ironically. I wondered if he'd mention her.

"Why thank you."

"You're very welcome, Jezzy."

"Hey! I did absolutely nothing to earn the nickname," I complained.

"Sorry," he said in a tone that sounded anything but, "just where we are in the story reminded me." At my glare, he gulped. "Okay, let's get back to the story!" he said with false cheer and charged ahead.

Jay joined the others in the main room for breakfast early the next morning. Beau smiled at his disheveled appearance. "Not a morning person?"

"Actually, I love mornings," he lied, stifling a yawn. He did not, as proven by his initial meeting with Mick. After his conversation with Jessie the previous afternoon, his brain had refused to turn off for hours. When he'd finally gotten to sleep, he'd been restless, plagued by uncertain dreams.

"Ready to go then?"

"Let's!" he said, forcing a falsely cheerful note into his voice.

Jessie lightly whacked the back of his head. "We're not going to die, genius."

He grinned. "Aw, too bad."

His soon-to-be traveling companions exchanged amused looks as he plopped down between Jessie and Ry to grab a quick bite.

"What am I getting myself into?" Beau wondered out loud.

"You can still back out," Mick said.

The captain shot him a glare. "Mick."

The other man shrugged. "Just saying, that's all."

"Let's go. The quicker we get moving, the quicker we're back and the less likely I am to go insane," he said, sliding off the bench and offering his hand to Jez.

She took it. "Are you implying you're still sane?"

"Are you implying I'm not?"

She smirked, nudging him in the side.

"I hate you."

"No, you don't."

"I most certainly do!"

"No, you really don't." The two turned, still arguing, and headed for the exit.

"Do they do that often?" Jay asked as he jammed one last bite of bread in his mouth.

"Often enough," Jessie said, hopping up. "C'mon, at this rate, they'll leave without us."

Jay shrugged, shouldered his pack, and went to follow, but a hand on his shoulder stopped him.

"You keep them safe, you hear?" Mick asked gruffly, concern reflecting in his eyes.

"Yes, sir," he said with a brisk nod. "We'll get back safely, I promise."

"Good," he said and then turned to speak to Reardon.

Jay watched him for a moment before hurrying to catch up with the others. He met them just inside the entrance, each with a pack like his slung over their shoulders. "So where are we headed again and how long will it take?"

"Good sized town called Westcorner. Probably a solid three days of hiking, maybe a bit more, depending on weather and the like," Beau said, stupid argument with Jez either somehow resolved or forgotten.

"And chances of us getting caught?"

"Slim to none."

"Great," he said as he fell into the rear. Jez and Beau led the way, talking quietly, while Jessie and Ry trailed them, mostly silent. He suspected at least one of them was not a morning person and the other respected that. It didn't take long for him to start humming, even though it was early. It was a gorgeous early summer day, but the tree cover of the forest kept it from getting too warm as it edged towards noon. Without consciously thinking about it, he began to bounce and skip in time with his humming.

"I love the skill. You should be a dancer."

He froze at the end of a hop and looked up, turning scarlet as he realized all four had stopped and were watching him. "Why thank you, Jessie. I appreciate the spirit in which that was intended." As they all continued to stare at him, obviously fighting laughter, he made a shooing motion with his hands. "Get on with you, we've got a lot of walking ahead of us!"

Jez finally gave in to her grin, but obligingly turned and continued. Beau waited until he was level with Jay, then fell into step beside him. "You don't mind that I dragged you along with us, do you?"

"Of course not, boss. I get horrible cabin fever if cooped up too long, and can't control it."

"You can sometimes," Jessie threw over her shoulder.

Beau raised an eyebrow.

"When she's coming after you with death in her eyes, it's best to retreat," Jay told him solemnly.

"Ah, yes, I know what you mean," he said, gaze going to Jez's back.

"So you should!" she called, like she could tell what he was thinking.

The five lapsed into an easy silence, Beau keeping pace with Jay. He had to wonder if it was to prevent his singing and dancing or for no particular reason at all.

"Your turn to say something, Ry," Jay said finally.

"I have better things to do with myself."

Jay stuck his tongue out at her back.

"Glad to see our maturity level is already rising."

He turned it on Beau, which got him laughing.

They made good progress by the time the sun started to dip close to the horizon and they began a look out for a place to rest. They found a sheltered clearing with about an hour left of sunlight and made a quick camp with a small fire. Beau figured they could risk it considering they were in such an isolated area.

The next morning, they were up with the sun. Jez kicked over the fire until there was little evidence left and the five of them set off. By mid-morning, they were at the shores of a large lake.

"According to the maps, it's called Lake Kirapiry," Beau said with a shrug.

"Kira-what?" Ry asked. "What kind of name is that?"

"Ancient Alyian," Jay said, staring out at the crystal-clear waters, probably untouched by man on this end for years. "Means *Shines Bright*. It was no doubt named during the generations that Alyia occupied Tira before Logan the Liberator and I guess Logan didn't bother to rename it."

Silence greeted that statement and, as he turned to continue, he realized that, once again, all four were staring at him.

"And where, pray tell, did you learn that?" Jez asked.

"My older cousin, Marguerite," he said and then immediately cursed himself in case Bri had talked about her. It seemed he had from the brief expressions on Beau's and Jessie's faces, but thankfully Jez and Ry looked as clueless as ever. "She was obsessed with ancient languages and history. I attended a lot of 'school' when I was little at her insistence."

"And you retained it? That's pretty impressive."

"I fought it, but it was the one activity with her I didn't mind. History's fascinating."

"Why can I picture that?"

"Because my intelligence shows in everything I do."

Honestly, he'd been predicting laughter but the rest took it more seriously than he'd expected, or at least with just smirks and amused looks.

Jez patted him on the head. "Exactly, Jay," she said lightly.

By the time night fell, they were getting close enough to civilization that Beau decreed they could still have a fire but needed to keep watch. Jay drew the short straw and got the middle shift. Jessie shook him awake with a far too cheerful grin. "Your turn, sleepyhead."

"Bah," he grumbled, even if he was instantly awake. Years of mixed success with sleep since his parents' death made it easy enough to wake up at odd hours without issue. He accepted the bow and arrows from Jessie and laid both the quiver and his shortsword down beside him as he settled in. By the time he was comfortable, Jessie was fast asleep.

He was deep into amusing himself by creating song lyrics to some popular musical tunes when something caught his eye. He sat up straighter, nudging the fire with a stick behind him to heighten the small flames. There it was again – a flash of brightness just outside their encampment. Definitely eyes. He slid an arrow from the quiver, notched it and aimed before realizing the pair of eyes were not alone – there were at least a dozen peering in at them.

He carefully reached out and kicked Beau's side.

"What?" he mumbled, still half-asleep.

"There are *eyes*."

That woke Beau up and he sat up carefully, spotting them a second later. He reached over and snagged an unused torch, shoving it into the fire until it sparked and caught. Then Beau waved it towards the eyes, all of which immediately shied back, even as the light exposed the watchers. The captain burst out laughing, hastily covering his mouth so that he didn't wake the others. "Dear gods, Jay, they're rabbits. Little *bunnies*." He grinned even as he snuffed the torch out and settled back in. "Next time, only wake me up if it's people or ravenous wolves, okay?"

"I bet they had fangs."

He yawned. "Uh huh, I'm sure that's it exactly. Fangs. Wake Jez up at the end of your shift. For now, I'm getting some more shuteye."

Before Jay could come up with a suitable retort, Beau was asleep.

When he woke Jez an hour or so later, she stretched. "Anything interesting happen?"

"No, why do you ask?" he said and quickly curled up before she could decide if he sounded a touch too innocent.

Of course, his attempts to salvage his pride were immediately ruined the following morning when Beau regaled them with the entire story over the breaking of the camp. The resulting teasing lasted on and off all morning, before Jez gently redirected the conversation, for which Jay was grateful. Even his long-lasting patience had started to run dry and he appreciated that Jez had noticed.

When they reached the road, Beau drew them aside. "All right, here's the plan. Our cover says we're from Holly. What do we know about it, Ry?"

"Good-sized town. Population of a couple thousand. Mostly specializing in timber and farming. On the banks of the Tiyer River mostly south, but a bit west of here near the eastern Alyia border. Need anything else?"

"Nope, that should be about it," he said. "Everyone got that?"

"Yes, but how in the world do you know that?" Jay asked.

"When I first started sitting on the tactics meeting, most of it went right over my head so I decided to do something useful instead and studied facts on Tira's larger towns and cities."

"Good idea," he murmured.

"Jez and Jay, you two will be twins."

Jessie laughed as identical expressions of distaste appeared on their faces.

"Jay, I want you to act a bit clueless. Like you pay attention to nothing and retain nothing. A real daydreamer looking at the world from a different angle. I'm sure your skills are up to the task."

Jez's expression shifted to amusement.

Jay's scrunched. He wasn't fully opposed and could handle it, but he wasn't sure if it was necessary. "Are you sure? Why?"

Beau's face twitched with a smile. "I think it'll do us some good. You'll hopefully be able to be places and get people to open up in a way we won't be able to. They'll think you aren't paying attention, so not listening."

"Jez and I are a couple."

"Big surprise there," Ry snickered.

"And you two are my cousins and thus siblings."

Jessie tossed him a salute. "No problem."

"Everyone's got their fake names down too, right?" he asked, since brainstorming them had been one of their conversations during the hike.

They all nodded.

"Good, moving on." He crouched, pushing aside some leaves to expose the dirt before drawing a rough map of the area. "We're here. Westcorner's here and the road runs this direction," he said, pointing out the landmarks. "As you can see, we're just south of the city. Considering that Holly is south of here, it makes more sense, since we're supposedly on our way home, to come in from the north and leave to the south. If we cross the road here, unseen, we can cut across the backcountry until we meet up with the road that comes straight into Westcorner from the north. Got it?"

"Looks easy enough," Jessie said.

"We should get there in time for dinner, if all goes off without a hitch," he said, straightening.

"Do we expect a hitch?" Jay asked.

Beau winked. "No one's died yet."

"People keep saying this and yet I'm having a hard time believing it," he complained.

"C'mon, we should still get moving. If there's a lot of travelers, it might take us a while to find an opening to cross. Same goes for the road from the north," Beau said, adjusting his pack and then heading for the crossing.

Ani hesitantly moved over to Ren's bed, reaching down and running her fingers lightly along his hairline, pushing hair that had gotten shaggy with time off his cheek. He stirred, but only shifted positions, a small sigh escaping his lips. She patted his shoulder gently before moving over and settling herself in one of the chairs by the window, turning her gaze to the faint bustle of the courtyard. She was tempted to shut it – winter was not the most conducive time for fresh air – but knew that Ren needed that small attachment to the outside world. It hadn't yet gotten old for him after only a couple days. She was dozing off herself, worn out by her unsettled thoughts and the day's trauma, when she heard a small, familiar yet out-of-place noise. She blinked awake, pushing herself up in the chair, trying to track its source before it came again.

This time she identified it immediately as whimpering. Ren had drawn both legs up close, eyes squeezed shut and a deep frown etched on his sleeping face. He shifted restlessly as she rose and sat beside him on the bed, stroking his cheek. "Shh, it's okay, Ren," she murmured.

His hand shot out and closed around her wrist, tighter than she expected.

Her breath caught, memories swarming her before she pushed it aside. "It's just me, Renny."

At the nickname, his eyes fluttered open, although he seemed confused. "Ani?"

"Yup."

Only now did the confusion fade and his grip loosen before he let go. "Oh. Sorry," he mumbled as he carefully pushed upright, wincing. She suspected the motion tugged at his broken ribs.

"No need to be sorry," she said lightly.

"I was…" he started, not making eye contact.

"Having a nightmare. Honestly, Ren, you think I don't recognize the classic signs of a nightmare after growing up in *my* family? Be serious. There isn't a night that goes by without at least one of us and usually all three having a nightmare, even if my brothers won't admit it. Sorin barely sleeps at all, when he can avoid it."

"Oh." He bit his lip. "Sorry."

"Forget about it. What was it about?"

"Same old."

"Did I miss a conversation somewhere in our relationship? That tells me very little," she said, lightly.

That startled a small smile out of him. "It's of the night my father died." Even half-asleep and obviously disturbed, Ren's ability to be diplomatic never failed to astound her. He hesitated, staring at his hands. "Except, instead of getting waylaid by Sorin outside my father's rooms, I make it in before he's killed, but can't do anything to stop it."

"I'm sorry," she said softly, reaching for his hand. He clutched it.

He shook his head. "It's not…I mean, it's not Sorin and Vlad, in the dream. It's something…vaguer and less human." Ren let out a brief laugh. "It wouldn't be as scary if it were your brothers. I know by now just how human they are."

She untangled their hands so she could wrap it around his shoulders instead, resting her head on top. "My poor Renny Muffin."

He groaned.

"Hey!" she said brightly. "Can I ask you something?"

"Sure?"

"Can I sleep with you?"

Ren turned to face her so quickly he almost slid off the bed, only her arm around his shoulders keeping him up. "Can you *what*?"

"Okay, so subtly isn't my strong suit, but I must say, I'm deeply hurt that you find the idea so outlandish."

"We're being watched," he pointed out, seeming to regain his equilibrium as his tone went dry. "I'm not really into that sort of exhibitionism and I think Vlad would take offense."

She really did try to keep in the giggles but failed miserably. "Okay, okay, you redeem yourself. What I meant was: can I stay in here with you for a few days?"

"Of course you can, but what's wrong with your room?"

"Nothing."

"Then what am I missing?"

"I'd…rather not talk to Vlad for a while. We had a…disagreement."

"What would you definite as a disagreement?"

"I might've screamed at him that I never wanted to talk to him again."

"Might have?"

"Okay, definitely did."

"What in the name of the gods did he say?"

"After I yelled at him? I dunno, I left."

"How about before you yelled at him?"

221

She turned her gaze out the window. She didn't want to answer but she'd started the conversation, not Ren, and it wasn't fair not to warn him. She cringed at her wording, but even more at how true it probably was. What if Vlad went behind their backs and came after Ren? Yet another reason she wanted to stay with him. "He said they should kill you to keep you from hurting me. He didn't realize I was there."

"Kill me?" Ren repeated and let out a low whistle. "I didn't realize he was that serious. I thought it was more of an ego thing than an actual desire to cause me harm."

She shrugged. "He did break your ribs and sprain your ankle, but I think it is still more ego talking." *Ego in the form of Edward*, she thought, but didn't say it out loud, as always aware there could be someone listening in. "The point is, he said it and didn't see anything wrong with it and that's…I'm not okay with that, so I'd rather just avoid him for the next few days, until…" she trailed off, not at all sure what a fitting end to that sentence would be.

"Do you think he'll apologize?"

Ani snorted. "He'll apologize all right, but that doesn't mean he'll mean it."

"And you think hiding in my room will prevent you from seeing him?"

"Not really, but it'll make me feel better." She pointed at the couch. "That'll be fine. I don't need to actually sleep with you in any sense of the phrase."

"If anyone gets the couch, it'll be me."

"If anyone," she echoed and let a mischievous grin stretch across her face, figuring they could do with a little lightening of the tone. "That was a very ambiguous statement. Does that mean we've got a choice?"

He burst out laughing. "I'll take the couch tonight."

"You're absolutely no fun. Think of the guards' reactions!"

"I'm more thinking of Vlad's reaction. No, Sorin's, definitely Sorin's. I would not want to test him if he were to find out we were…up to shenanigans."

She clapped a hand over her mouth to try and contain her giggles at his word choice.

"As you shouldn't," Sorin said from where he leaned against the doorjamb.

It was a testament to how comfortable even Ren was with her brother that neither of them jumped.

Instead, Ren grinned at him. "See, Ani. Justified." Then he glanced at her and she was fairly certain she read it correctly as curiosity over what Sorin had said in response to the threat to kill him.

"How'd Vlad react?" Ani asked her brother.

"I thought for a moment what you'd said had gotten through to him, but when I attempted to convince him to take a vacation and give himself a few days to relax, Edward came out again."

Out of the corner of her eye, Ani saw Ren shift slightly, pursing his lips as he looked between the two.

"So, I told him that he was acting just like Edward and it needed to stop now. Then I walked out and haven't seen him since. I'm assuming he's off sulking somewhere about how unfair the world is being."

She studied him before deciding her instinctive reaction would be well-received. So she walked over and hugged him tightly. "Thanks, Sunshine." The nickname was almost as old as Ani but she had only used it a few times recently and before that, not in years.

He carefully returned the hug and she could feel his smile, even if he rarely let her see it. "He deserved it and more for what he said."

"Still, you defended me and you didn't have to." She stepped back and smiled. "I love you," she said deliberately and saw something relax in his eyes – saw even more of the brother she'd grown up with.

"I did have to, not that you're not very capable of doing it yourself these days." His gaze darted to Ren and then back. "I need to get back to work. One of us needs to be. He'll get around to apologizing."

"We'll see if I get around to forgiving him."

A slight smile, almost more the idea of one, whisked across Sorin's face. "Love you too, Ani," he said softly and was gone.

Ren could no longer contain himself, jaw dropping. "Did he just…? What *was* that?"

"That was Sorin," she said, knowing her grin stretched from ear to ear. "That was Sorin as he should be."

"Gods be damned," he said, sounding impressed.

She kissed his cheek. "So, you never answered if I could sleep here."

"Of course you can," he said and then, inexplicably, started chuckling.

She eyed him. "Did Sunshine's admission throw you for this much of a loop?"

His grin widened at the nickname but he shook his head. "After you watched me eat the other day, I made the comment that next you were going to be watching me sleep. Sorin overheard and said that Vlad wouldn't let you. Guess I've really hit rock bottom, huh? You were obviously watching me before the nightmare."

She stuck her tongue out, then slugged his arm.

"Hey, careful there! I'm an invalid."

"Not too much of one," she retorted, grinning.

"Really?" he asked, waggling his eyebrows in an over exaggeration.

She giggled. "Really. I'll smack you if I want."

"You don't want to try it again."

"Wanna bet?" She snuck out a hand but he snagged it and used the momentum to flip her back onto the bed. He grinned down at her. She came up sputtering but couldn't keep up the annoyance at his expression, temporarily carefree and unshadowed for once.

"That's what you get for not keeping your hands to yourself," he said solemnly.

She giggled, flopping back and watching him out of the corner of her eye. "This is war."

He smirked. "Then it's Ren: 1 and Ani: 0."

"Excuse me? It starts now, mister."

"Nope. It's a well-known fact that battles are often fought before the war officially begins. That means I won the first battle and it's become a campaign now that we've declared it a war."

"Cheater."

"No, I just know my war facts," he said smugly.

"Doesn't make you any less of a cheaterface. Who found it so hard to admit his feelings?"

"I'd say Sorin, but after that last encounter…"

She snorted, plucking a pillow from his bed and flinging it at him. He ducked, easily caught it, and then made as if to pound her with it. She squeaked, squeezing her eyes shut and throwing her hands up in some blind attempt to block. When nothing connected, she cracked open an eye to see him, laughing silently. She lowered her hands, glaring. "No fair. You're cheating ag-oomph!" she said as he smacked her with it the instant her guard was down. "Hey!" she managed before he dropped the pillow and started tickling her in the side. She squirmed, dissolving into giggles as she half-tried to get away, not wanting to hurt him and enjoying herself enough she was in no hurry.

Finally, something occurred to her and she reached up, grasping his cheeks between her palms, and pulling him down to meet her, kissing him firmly. When they finally broke apart, surprise and something like satisfaction spilled across Ren's face. She smirked and slipped out from underneath him while he was still recovering. "One for me!"

He let out a laugh and dropped back onto the bed, much as she'd been a moment before. He held up three fingers. "Three."

"Don't expect your lead to last, mister," she said, still trying to catch her breath and sound stern. "Just you wait."

"Just try it, Ani Opalin. I'm on a roll."

She raised an eyebrow. "I thought I was the devious one."

"I'd say spontaneous," he said, "not devious. And I can be spontaneous when I want."

She made a point of giving him a look and then bursting into laughter. "You? Spontaneous?"

He glared. "Not funny or cute."

She settled herself on the couch. "I'd say that's another point in my favor."

"Now who is the cheater?"

Her eyes widened innocently. "Not me. I never, ever cheat."

He finally sat up, flashing her a grin. "Oh, right, I forgot. My mistake."

"I'll forgive you this once if you promise never to do it again," she said magnanimously.

"Promise, and you're welcome."

"For what?"

"For cheering you up."

"We both needed it," she pointed out, but smiled anyway, taking his point to heart.

"But I started it!"

"Did not. I did when I asked if I could sleep with you."

Ren paused, plainly debating that. "Damn. How come you're always right?"

"It's a gift, Muffin, and, now that I think about it, it's a tied score."

"What? How?"

"If battles can happen before a war, then me asking that definitely counted as a won battle."

He opened his mouth, shut it, opened it again, and then subsided with a slight sulk.

She grinned.

Chapter Seventeen

I WAS JUST DRIFTING OFF WHEN I heard Jay stop the story and speak in a low voice. "Don't tell Jez about those mini-stories I told you yesterday. She can be rather sensitive about them." I could hear the grin in his voice.

Dave giggled. "Okay."

"What mini-stories?" I asked, cracking my eyes open and keeping my voice quiet and rigid.

My friend jumped. "What? I didn't say anything about mini-stories," he said, but his innocent look failed him.

I kept my gaze firmly on him.

"I...merely entertained Dave and Stella with a few anecdotes that have already gotten overlooked or might as we continue. Nothing big."

I raised an eyebrow at him. "Then why would I be sensitive about them?"

"Uh, because they're all about you doing rather, um, you know!"

"Do I?" I asked, amused to see Jay sputtering and knowing it wouldn't last long.

"Yeah, you know, when you do stupid-ish things."

"Stupid-ish?"

"Yes," he said, defensively. "Or, I suppose, just plain stupid."

I wasn't entirely sure what he was referring to and wasn't sure I wanted to, but I asked anyway. "What times were these?"

"Well, like the time you asked Mick if he'd waltz with you at dinner." I only partially remembered that, considering it had been one of the few times we'd let loose with alcohol – both ale and harder spirits had been in abundance as a donation of sorts from a merchant we'd helped. I'd discovered just how low a tolerance I had after almost two years of absolutely nothing. "And when you ran into Iris carrying the pail of meat sauce and she chased you around the caverns for over an hour."

I cringed. That one I remembered far too clearly. "That was an accident."

"I have more," he said brightly. Dave, curse the kid, was giggling like mad.

"I get the idea," I said.

"You asked for it."

"Yeah, well, remind me to never do that again."

"Don't ever do that again," he said solemnly.

"That's not what I meant and you know it."

"You told me to remind you, so I did. Do I need to again? Because I could say-"

At this point, Stella clapped a hand over his mouth, amused. "All right, Jay, we get the point."

He pried it off. "You do? Are you sure?"

"Yes, positive."

"So when should I remind her?"

"When she does it again."

"Is she doing it now?"

Stella favored him with an impatient look.

"How about now?"

"*James Dall.*"

He sat up straight, all but snapping to attention. "Yes, Stell?" he asked meekly.

I ducked my head so he wouldn't see my grin. Dave was still laughing.

"Please just continue with the story."

"Should I remind her now?"

"*Jay!*"

This time, he did salute. I snickered.

228

"One story coming right up, ma'am!"

◀ ▼ ▶

Crossing the first road took no time at all – it was deserted. Beau paused halfway across and scanned the ground, muttering to himself. He straightened, a dark cloud passing across his face. "Let's go," he said, words clipped.

The three women exchanged a nervous glance and Jay's own nerves spiked at Beau's anger, but he kept his mouth closed. He wasn't worried about Beau himself, but what it might mean.

It only took a little while longer to reach the second road, which was just as deserted as the first. Beau motioned that it was safe and the five scampered onto the road and began strolling casually towards Westcorner, not that there was anyone around to be fooled.

"Just act natural," Beau murmured as they reached the first outlying houses.

"Then Jay should have the easiest time of it," Ry quipped.

He glared at her back. "Ha ha, Ry, you are such a comedian."

"I like to think so."

Jessie stepped between them. "Settle down, kids."

Beau sighed. "My mistake. Don't act natural. Act your parts."

Jez giggled quietly as they entered the town proper. Jessie took the lead, heading straight for the town's smaller inn, a place called the Wallowing Swan.

"Excuse me," she said to the bartender, the only person present, as they entered. "May we book two rooms, please?"

"Of course, ma'am, just step over here and we'll get you sorted," he said, moving to the end of the bar. Jessie stepped over to him to go through the ritual of paying while Jay, and the others, studied the room. It was rustic but retained a small, comfortable feel to it. In one wall was a large fireplace, unneeded on such a summer day. Tables sat in a neat pattern, lined with benches and a small sprig of flowers adorned each one, adding a homey touch.

Jay clued back in as the bartender in question spoke. "You'll have rooms 15 and 16, ma'am," he said, passing Jessie the keys, one of which she immediately handed to Beau.

"Much obliged. Meal times?"

"We're slow right now, so whenever you want somethin' just let me or my husband know and we'll make it right up for you."

"That's wonderful." Jessie now leaned forward, as if imparting some great secret. Jay was well able to guess what came next and continued to look around, bored. "My friend, Jamison," she gestured towards Jay, "is a bit…well, look, I'm sorry if he causes any trouble, but he just doesn't pay attention. It won't be on purpose, I assure you. Pay him no mind."

"Not a problem," the man said. "People 'round these parts are pretty laid back. He should have no problems."

"Wonderful! And our rooms are…?"

"Located down the hall, up the stairs, and to the right. Last two rooms."

"Thank you, sir," she said with a smile and led the others down the hall.

Beau and Jay's room was simple, but perfect for their purposes – two twin beds, a small, sturdy desk, closet and dresser. The two tossed their bags on a bed and then joined the women next door in their room, which was only different in that it contained two sets of bunks instead of single beds. Ry, Jay and Jessie settled on one of the bottom beds with Beau and Jez across from them. Jay felt like a naughty kid about to get a lecture from his parents. Ry didn't seem to feel the same, swinging her legs.

"What's the plan?" Ry asked.

"Jay, I want you to wander, keep your ears open and eyes peeled. See what you can find out. You're our best bet if someone is, for any reason, on to us."

Jay tossed him a loose salute.

"Do you expect them to be?" Jez asked.

"No, we've never had troubles before, but…" He pursed his lips and then shrugged. "I don't know, just got a funny feeling." He shook himself. "Anyway, Jez will be sticking with me, for obvious reasons, plus, she might well pick up on something I miss. We'll spend our time at the other inn, mostly, because that's where our contact is supposed to meet us. Ry, Jessie, just act like you're new to the area. Country folk. We want to encourage the idea that Jessie is in charge of the group."

"Got it."

"What sort of funny feeling?" Jez asked quietly.

He glanced between them. "It's just…ever since we hit the road…" He pounded his fist into his knee in what even Jay could guess was a rare gesture of angry frustration. "I don't know. What the hell are the Three doing to our country? There was *no one* on the roads today. Sure, I've pretty much stayed in and around Cavern Hall since they took over, but I did plenty of travel before that and never, never did I get past or on main roads as easily as today. How many people did we see?"

"None," Jessie murmured, even if they were all aware it was a rhetorical question.

"Exactly. At this point, they'll oust themselves."

"Which can't be a terrible thing."

"No, except they'll run Tira into the ground first. Alyia and Nerius are having a field day with our borders – towns like Evenly are under Nerian control. Our economy is stalling and, without intervention, will undoubtedly fail." He let out a breath, forcing his fingers to unclench. "I guess the main question is: are we being set up? Are Opalin and Dakamar really that useless as rulers? Is this trip a waste of time?"

"That's three questions, Beau, that are probably not related," Jez said gently, considering they all understood his feelings.

"Discussing it like this is stupid. We don't know the answers and aren't going to," Ry grumbled, bringing all four heads around to look at her. "What we can do is focus on the job at hand and make sure we do it. I don't blame you for letting it get you down, Beau. Opalin and Dakamar are bastards, through and through, we'll all agree on that, but we will bring them down and put a competent ruler on the throne. Nothing bad will happen to anyone else."

Jay was the first to notice the angry tears before she swiped at them. "Hey, Ry, it's okay, honest. We'll get the bastards. You're right. We'll get them good," he said, patting her knee as Jessie put her arms around her. Ry buried her face in her best friend's shoulder, obviously embarrassed.

"Ry?"

"Yeah?" Her voice was a bit muffled.

"Why do you feel so strongly? I know I can't, and don't, really talk about my past, but…if you don't mind me asking," Jez said.

Ry sat up, but didn't make eye contact with any of them. "My parents deserted my brother and me when we were pretty little. He was only three and I was six. We lived on the streets of Greensward from then on. Opalin spent a lot of time there, in the years leading up to the coup, when no one really knew him except those who knew his father's business. By the time Bean, my brother, was ten, even he was pretty savvy on the streets after seven years and he was a fair pickpocket." She swiped at her eyes. "I had told him, time and again, not to go near the merchant district. Sure, they'd bring in a good haul, but they were also more alert to dangers. They knew better than anyone the value of their money." Ry hunched over, digging the palms of her hands into her eyes.

Jay barely remembered to breathe.

"He went anyway. It was a festival and I had a real working job at one of the booths so I wasn't watching him. A friend, another street kid, told me, told me who, told me how. Guess Bean tried to pick his pocket and Opalin caught him and took the law into his own hands with a knife to the gut. Bean didn't stand a chance. Then...he just walked away. I had no idea it would be the same person, but when I heard about the Freedom Fighters, I knew it was right and I could help, so I joined."

Jay's heart went out to her. He understood well the pain she felt. Bean had obviously been her other half in much the same way that Brighton had always been his, maybe even more since it had been just the two of them for so long.

A minute stretched into two and then Ry stood, still without ever looking at them. "I need some time," she said and fled the room.

"I'm sorry," Jez said, stricken. "I didn't mean to..."

"It's not your fault, Jez. Ry's very protective of her past. If she hadn't wanted to tell you, she wouldn't have, but it also hits her hard, because she still feels like she let Bean down, that she should've been with him." This was obviously not a new story to Jessie.

Beau shook his head. "Those...those *three* will pay for all the hurt and pain they've caused."

"But it'll never make up for it," Jay said, fighting the surge of anger. It would do him no good at that moment. "Trust me, I know, but it will prevent shit like that and what happened to me and all of us from happening again or to someone else. We'll be doing the world a favor when we get rid of them."

His announcement elicited nods out of all of them. "Let's get to it. Keep your eyes open for Ry as you go. I want to make sure she's okay," Beau said.

"I just have to ask," Jez said, putting a hand on her boyfriend's arm to keep him down. "Jessie, is your past horrible?"

She smiled faintly. "Oh, no, my parents are both still alive and I never had siblings."

Beau frowned. "Okay, now you've got my curiosity piqued. I don't usually ask, but most people do have pasts similar to Jay or Ry."

"My parents and I have never seen eye-to-eye about much of anything. When I had the gall to start speaking out against the practices of some of the merchants, including those my parents routinely did business with, they were not pleased. They were even less pleased for me to show off that I had a brain in public. I was told repeatedly to be quiet and let things lie. I thought that sounded incredibly stupid. I was looking for a way out and away and came upon it when I met one of Beau's scouts. When out drinking, I let loose my complaints and moved out the next day to Cavern Hall. I send my parents a letter about once a year to let them know I'm alive, but they've all but disowned me at this point. Can't marry off a daughter living in some hole somewhere."

The captain smiled. "Well, we're glad to have you, no matter how." Then he sighed. "All right, let's see what we can discover before the sun goes down. We'll meet back here for dinner." The four headed downstairs. Jessie peeled away to bend the bartender's ear while Jay ambled out just ahead of Beau and Jez. Jez patted his shoulder as they headed down the street towards Westcorner's other inn. Jay spotted the man with the cows heading his way out of the corner of his eye, purposely didn't look, and stepped out in front of them anyway.

"Hey! Hey, you!" the man called. Jay blinked around and then just looked at the man expectantly. The man gave him an exasperated look and gestured at the cows. "Hello! You don't just walk out into the street like that when things are coming. You'll get yourself run over."

He nodded agreeably. "Okay, sure, what do you think it'd be like? To be run over by cows?"

"What it'd be like?" the man repeated incredulously, staring at him. "Why…what kind of question is that?"

"You've never thought about it?"

"Being stepped on by cows or any large animal hurts. Are you daft?" the man demanded.

Jay shrugged. "Everyone looks at the world differently," he said serenely, patting a cow on the nose before strolling off, leaving the man sputtering in his wake.

Jez rolled her eyes at Jay's antics and turned to Beau as they continued down the street. "Who are we looking for?"

"I shouldn't have exploded like that. It was irresponsible of me."

"It happens, Beau. And it was barely an explosion."

"It shouldn't happen to me! Not when I'm…out and in charge."

"That's exactly the reason why it should happen. With only a few small exceptions, we've been holed up in Cavern Hall since before the Three took over. Sure, we know from the reports what's happening around Tira, but we haven't had the opportunity to witness it with our own two eyes until now. It makes sense it would hit hard now that we can see it. We're your friends, Beau. If you're not allowed to explode on occasion in front of us, who else do you have?" She smiled. "Mick? He's had to live with you for a long time, I'm sure he's happy to pass the burden along. So forget it. It's done, over, and no harm sustained. Ry's right. We need to focus on the task at hand. Deal?"

Beau hesitated.

"Anyway, if anything, it's my fault Ry ran off because I pushed her."

"But," he started.

"But I realize there's nothing I can do about it right now. So we move on and I'll apologize next time I see her. Simple as that. We have ourselves a deal?"

He smiled ruefully. "Deal. Thanks for the pep talk," he said, putting an arm around her shoulders.

"I try to be multi-talented."

"You succeed very well."

She rolled her eyes. "I wasn't kidding."

"Neither am I," he murmured, eyes sparkling as he leaned in and kissed her. "I'm a very lucky man to be able to do that."

"You bet your ass you are."

They arrived outside the larger inn, the Hog's Heel, a respectable enough place despite the not so appealing name. Jez went to find them a seat while Beau approached the bartender and struck up a brief conversation. He joined her a couple of minutes later, scooting a mug in her direction. "Ordered us both the house ale. Hope you don't mind."

"Not at all." She raised it in a toast. "Here's hoping it's half good."

"Anything'll be half good after the usual crap we manage to turn up."

"When we turn it up at all," Jez agreed wryly and took a sip, smiling with pleasure. "So?"

"Apparently we're here early, or our contact is late. No sign of him yet. The barkeep says he hasn't been in."

"He knows?"

"The man's a local. Adds credence and respectability to his story if he's just coming home to visit his mom."

"As good as this ale tastes, I assume we're not going to spend all our time here?"

"Figured we'll have a drink a day, keep an eye out and spend the rest of the time wandering town playing tourist. We don't want to raise too much suspicion and our barkeep friend will let the contact know that we're hanging about. We need to make it sound plausible for us to hang around if it takes him a few days."

"Makes sense."

"So glad you approve," he said dryly and then leaned forward. "What do you think of Jay?"

"I have to say, I like him. It seems like so much more time has passed since he joined us. He makes knowing him easy and his teasing of Jessie never fails to crack me up. I suppose we'll see how his fighting skills are."

"I've heard he's proficient with a sword but a dead shot with a bow and arrow, much like you. He used to train with another kid about his own age and that kid was good with a sword. Jay figured the best way to beat him was to be better at something else."

"Smart idea. I used to do things like that with my brothers all the time, especially Colin."

"Yeah. I'll have Reardon test him out and see where his skills lie once we're back home. If he's the dead shot he says he is, he could probably teach a lot of our troops a thing or two."

"Our troops? Since when did I adopt the entirety of the Freedom Fighters?"

"Since you got their captain to fall in love with you."

"My mistake, plainly. Anything I can do to remedy the situation?"

His eyes sparkled with a glee few ever saw as he leaned across the table, slipping a hand behind her head as he firmly pressed his lips to hers. "Are you so sure you want to?"

"On second thought," she murmured, smiling.

"I thought so," he said, at his smuggest.

They finished their ales slowly, managing idle chitchat, not wanting to raise any suspicions by talking quietly. After about an hour, the duo rose, paid for their drinks and headed out to explore the rest of town.

Jay passed Ry early on, heartened to see her chatting with a few teens her own age for once. He merely shot her a subtle thumbs-up and continued on his way.

"Hey, you."

He glanced up to see a woman standing in her doorway, hands on her hips, jutting out in an expression he remembered well from his own mother. "Yes, ma'am?"

"You the new one in town everyone's talking about?"

"Oh, are people talking about me? I do wonder what they might say," he said, smiling and making sure to keep an absent element to it.

"They're saying you're lost in space," she said dryly. "And not paying attention to even the most routine things."

"It's all a matter of perspective," he said solemnly. "Sometimes it creates the most wonderful new experiences."

She rolled her eyes, but Jay thought he detected a hint of amusement. "I was wondering if you'd be so kind as to help me with a few chores if you like new experiences. My son was supposed to be here this week, but hasn't shown up and I'm getting impatient."

"New experiences are what I live for," he said cheerfully, wondering at the tone in her voice. There was something familiar there. He pushed it aside. "I shall happily do my best to help you with these 'chores'. I'm very good at poetry. I could write you an ode."

There was no mistaking the amusement this time. "No poetry necessary. More like holding things and helping me find the best place to hang things. Come on in. What's your name, son?"

"Jamison."

"Come on in, Jamison, and I'll show you."

"All right."

He spent a surprisingly enjoyable afternoon helping Mrs. Cornwall move furniture and hang pictures as she kept up a steady stream of town gossip, not seeming to expect much out of him. Two pieces of information got Jay's attention. First, that a group of kids, just a few years younger than him, had been creating trouble around town recently and, second, that there had been increased troop movement in the area. He tuned much of it out after that, mind racing. Maybe Beau was right and this was a trap. Either way, his urge to get out of town felt like an itch he couldn't scratch, growing larger and larger.

Mrs. Cornwall offered him dinner and he wasn't about to turn down a homecooked meal by this wonderful woman, even if he made a show of protesting that he had to be back to the inn. She finally flagged down a local child and sent him off the Swan with a note to let his friends know he'd be back late. They had a nice meal, chatting amiably about nothing, Jay making up rambling stories about his family and their adventures in Holly that made little to no sense. Finally, she bid him good night and sent him back. Later, Jay realized she fully didn't believe any of his spaciness, but at the time, he was quite proud of himself.

He ambled down the main street of Westcorner, enjoying the quiet of the night as well as admiring the small town by the light of the street's flickering lanterns.

"Well, hello there, traveler. I was wondering if perhaps I might try and make your stay here more enjoyable."

Jay slowed at the voice coming from a nearby alley. He was well aware from Mrs. Cornwall's gossip that they were the only travelers in town. He also didn't like the tone. It made the hair on the back of his neck stand up.

"That's really okay, thanks. I'm having a grand time without your help." That voice he knew – Ry's tone was tight in barely controlled anger.

"The rest of y'all, scat," the male voice commanded. A group of five teens about Ry's age scampered out and disappeared into the darkness. Jay stole up to the entrance of the alley, clocking the gang of late teens lurking a little ways down the street. He paused, knowing Ry wouldn't want help if she could handle it. "So I'm in charge around here, so you know. Might be helpful to you and your pals if you went along."

"Along with what?"

There was a slight scuffle of feet.

"Get away from me."

"You don't mean that."

"I absolutely do. Get away," Ry bit out.

Jay then heard a dull thump and an involuntary whimper from his friend, meaning it was past time to step in. He whipped around the corner of the building and charged the burly late teen who Rylia's arms tightly, trying to kiss her. Silently, Jay barreled into the teen, separating him from Ry and slamming him into the fence at the far end of the alley with enough strength to knock the breath from the boy's chest. He heard Ry gasp as he glared at the barely shorter teen. "*That* is my friend. We do *not* hurt my friend. Is that understood?" he growled, putting them nose to nose.

The kid stared up at him, stunned to speechlessness – or perhaps he hadn't gotten enough breath back to react.

"Is that understood?"

"Jay…mison," Ry said quietly.

Jay pulled back an inch, but only an inch. "Yeah?"

"He's just a big bully. C'mon, let's go back to the Swan and the others."

"Fine." He shoved his face back in. "You come near her or any of my other friends again and you will regret it for a very long time. Understand?" When the boy still didn't respond, he shook him. "Understand?"

Now the teenager nodded. "Yes, sir!"

He allowed Ry to pull him away, finally removing his arm from the kid's throat, having been barely aware he'd even done that.

"I'm so sorry for Jamison," Ry said sweetly with a tight smile that showed the tone was all an act. "He gets over excited when he sees family in danger."

"I don't think you are who you-"

Rylia backed away, drawing Jay with her. "I will sic him on you again, don't think I won't. Leave us alone and we'll forget this little encounter ever happened."

"Oh, no, we won't."

"Fine. Jamison? Sic him."

Jay stepped forward with a growl. Cover or not, daydreamer or not, Ry's safety – and friendship – was more important.

"No, no, you don't understand." He pointed over their shoulders. "You're outnumbered."

Ry whirled. "Gods' Breath," she muttered as she spotted six other shapes materializing out of the shadows at the far end of the alley. "Jay?"

"I thought maybe they were with him when I first came upon you," he murmured. "Do your best."

Before Ry could ask what he meant, Jay twirled and sprinted towards the newcomers as he let out a bellow at the top of his lungs. The teens all took a step back, as Jay had intended. Ry sucked in her breath as her friend careened into the first teen and the rest converged on him. She moved to react, but the leader grabbed her arm and twisted it savagely behind her. She grunted, refusing to give him the satisfaction of more, and lashed out with her foot, snapping his knee. He loosened his grip, yelping in pain, giving her the opportunity she needed to rip her arm free and spin to face him.

"You bastard," she snarled.

He smirked. "You're too cute to let slip by."

"You touch me and you'll end up regretting it."

"Young and yet so rough. I like that in a girl."

"Let's get this over with then, big shot," she said and then, a moment later, she found herself face down in the dirt, her right leg throbbing from where one of his cronies had gotten her knee, knocking her flat.

"Let's," he agreed with a chuckle as the crony grabbed her arms and hauled her upright. She let him, keeping herself limp like her leg was too hurt to hold her weight. The leader stepped up until they were only a few inches apart. Ry grinned and slammed her knee into his groin as hard as she could. He let out an undignified squeak and doubled over, clutching himself. She then shifted, taking all her weight back and shoved off the ground, rocketing her head backwards. The back of her head connected squarely with the boy's nose. She heard it crack and almost instantly felt the dampness from the blood on her hair. He swore loudly and she tore herself free as he grabbed at his nose. Without pause, she turned and sprinted towards the thrashing pile of limbs around Jay. At full speed, she barreled into one of the teenagers, sending him stumbling into another and leaving Jay with only three to contend with. He didn't waste the opportunity, careening into the remaining three as they all went down in a tumble of limbs.

Sorin leaned back in his chair and crumpled the piece of paper in his hand. Eyeing the basket for garbage, he flicked his wrist, sending the paper soaring through the air to land with a quiet plop. Before it had even landed, he was crumpling the next, face set in a deep frown.

He tried to corral his thoughts, get them to sync into place neatly, but they refused. "Hell of a time to remember how much family matters," he muttered and dropped his head into his hands. In some ways, he felt better than he had in years and he liked being able to let that show to those who mattered most at the moment: Ani, Ren and Vlad. In other ways, though, he knew it was dangerous. His ability to focus and concentrate was shot as all sorts of wayward thoughts of the past, present and future – however limited that may be – crowded his mind.

He needed something to focus on or he might do something rash, not that that wasn't a distinct possibility anyway. A distraction came right on time, though, as a knock sounded on his open door. He lifted his head. "What is it, Lieutenant? I'm busy."

Jakium eyed the overflowing basket but wisely kept his comments to himself. "General Opalin sent me, sir," he said with a salute. "Message from Colonel Rees in Greensward." He offered Sorin a paper. "Details are all here."

"Give me the gist of it," Sorin said, sitting back and resisting the urge to automatically crumple and throw this sheet as well, since he was running low.

Jakium stepped into the room. "As you know, the colonel captured a pair attempting to blow up Greensward Palace about a week and a half ago."

"Indeed. Why the message now?"

"Colonel Rees has been working on them and has been surprisingly unsuccessful. His words, not mine."

"Really?" That was interesting. Rees was frighteningly good at his job. It's why he commanded Greensward, which was Tira's second largest city and honestly a problem in itself. "Go on."

"Regardless, he has garnered enough information to believe they are not the small-timers we usually get, but actually part of the Freedom Fighters."

"And what's he basing this on?"

"Intuition, mostly. The relevant part is that the woman claims to be Jasmine Lockholme and Colonel Rees believes her."

"Jasmine Lockholme?" Sorin repeated, sitting up. His eyes narrowed as he recalled the name. "She's the girl Vladimir ordered killed after she saved

Elladan." And then he also remembered, "Vladimir sent you up to the area to ensure it was done." He frowned. "How is she still alive? You were there."

Jakium, thankfully, didn't take that as a condemnation. Sorin had fought against sending Jakium, who had still been a boy. "Apparently through a lot of luck. I was sure we'd gotten everyone but Virginia Elladan at the time," he said. "Colonel Rees didn't give many details but General Opalin is, understandably, intrigued, especially by the notion they're Freedom Fighters. They would be our first successful capture."

"I'm well aware of that," he said.

"General Opalin is planning to leave in about an hour to visit the prisoners himself to see if he can't scare information out of the pair. He's asked me to accompany him, to see if I can positively identify them from the group up by Westcorner or confirm Jasmine's identity."

"If she'd been at Westcorner, you would've known."

Jakium shrugged. "It was dark and raining, I'm assuming she picked up some souvenirs from surviving a bombing, and I thought she was dead. With these misconceptions, it's very possible I might not have."

Sorin nodded, conceding the point.

"I'm then to stay on permanent loan to help out around Greensward so Colonel Rees can devote more attention to the prisoners. There's been some civil unrest around the city since the explosion and they need more hands."

"It's a shame we'll lose you, but you'll do well there, no doubt," Sorin said mildly.

Jakium grinned. "Going to miss me as a handy distraction for Ani?"

"I feel as if I should give you hell for using her nickname, but considering she wouldn't have it any other way, I have no leg to stand on."

"Greensward is only a day's ride. I'm sure I'll be in and out if you need my services."

Sorin snorted. "I'll keep that in mind, Lieutenant. Good luck."

The younger man managed a wry smile. They both knew his track record wasn't great, but he was somewhere between a nephew and a little brother, considering he'd been Vladimir's ward from the age of fourteen. So that would do it. "I'll do my best, sir."

"Tell Vladimir something for me, would you?"

"As long as it won't get my head bitten off, of course, sir."

"Tell him not to waste too much time before making up with our sister."

Jakium raised his eyebrows, clearly able to tell Sorin had more to say. "And, sir?"

"Take care of yourself," he said, then quickly hurried on, "Ani would be most displeased if you got yourself hurt."

"With pleasure, sir," Jakium said. "I should get going. General Opalin is itching to leave."

"Of course. You're dismissed."

The young lieutenant saluted and vanished out the door. Sorin again leaned back in his chair, absently crumpling the message from Rees before remembering and flattening it back out to skim it. Jakium had covered the important parts.

Sorin traced his finger across Jasmine's name. Her survival startled him. They had been so certain they'd been thorough. *Leave no loose ends* had been Vladimir's order. To have missed their main target entirely. *Well, perhaps not entirely*, he thought, as he scanned the bit about her scars. They'd almost gotten her, but not quite wasn't good enough. He racked his brain for what he knew about Lockholme. Small estate with a decent acreage holding, perhaps a little larger than average. They raised good, solid horses. Those were the only facts Sorin knew about the place or its inhabitants. He couldn't even recall Jasmine's father's name offhand, which was shoddy of him, even after two years.

"Bert!" he yelled.

The cantankerous old man shuffled into the room. "Yes, sir?"

"Find me all the information we have on Earl Lockholme. He's in Hillen's dukedom, which used to be Elladan's."

"I'll get on that as soon as I can."

Sorin favored him with his best predatory smile. "How about now, Bert?"

The old man's face twisted. His devotion to Vlad and dislike of Sorin - and everyone else - was on the extreme side sometimes. "Very well, *sir*." He turned and disappeared, Sorin glaring at his back as he went. As soon as the lackey had vanished, Sorin crumpled Rees's message and tossed it neatly into the basket. He hoped, despite his own lack of knowledge, that their file on the Lockholme family would be sufficient. Something about her survival made him jumpy — made the hairs on the back of his neck prickle. At least Jakium had provided an excellent distraction.

Chapter Eighteen

"I THINK THAT'S AS GOOD A PLACE to stop as any," Jay said. "It's dark out and it's time for our beauty sleep."

"No, it's not!" Dave protested. "You left us in the middle of a fight!"

My friend grinned. "Exactly."

The boy made a sour face, but looked between us. "You know what I think?"

"What's that?" I asked.

"We need to escape and make sure the Freedom Fighters win."

"That's the spirit, ladster, and we agree entirely. Now, though, it's time to sleep. We'll need a little assistance on the escape front so we just need to be prepared."

Dave eyed him, obviously unable to tell if he was joking or not. "Do you really think...?"

"Only time will tell," I said gently, not wanting to raise his hopes too much, although I knew Beau and the others would do all they could to spring us.

"I've spent so much time talking, I shall need to rest my voice tomorrow. Oy, Jezzy!"

"Don't call me that," I said automatically as I gently tested my shoulders, finding them still sore, not that I was surprised. It had only been a day.

"Do you think the poor invalid will be able to talk tomorrow?"

"Jay?"

"Yes?"

"Sod off."

"No problem, Jezzy. See you in the morning."

"James?"

"Yes?" he asked, sweetness positively oozing from his lips.

"You're really asking for it."

"Am I?"

Stella gave us both the stink eye. "Please shut up."

I saluted; Jay pretended to snore loudly before cutting off abruptly when Dave kicked him in the shin. "Ow! Stella, call your demon brother off."

"David."

"Yeah?"

"If he speaks again, kick him harder."

Dave giggled. "Can I kick him anyway?"

"No, you may not."

He sighed loudly "Fine."

Jay grumbled something unintelligible before silence finally descended over the cell. If anyone said anything else, I missed it, having drifted off.

Both Jay and I were up early the next morning. We sat shoulder to shoulder. Jay's attention was on our sleeping companions, while mine alternated between the corridor and the window, which just started to show the light.

"I've been thinking."

"Dangerous prospect," I said glibly.

"Shush, you. I was thinking it might work best if we split the story. Wouldn't it be cool if we could just do it seamlessly? Like we were one person telling it?"

"We have an audience who doesn't really seem to care," I pointed out, testing my right shoulder.

"I care," he said, sticking his lower lip out at me.

"Fine, we can do it seamlessly, although I think you're doing a very good job. Especially when your giant breaths when you want to start talking are a good indicator that it's your turn. This does mean no more complaining about talking, mister."

"But I complain so well!"

"That I can't deny." I winced and dropped my arm after it began to protest the motion.

"Why thank you, milady."

"Don't call me that."

"Would you prefer Jezzy?"

"James."

He chortled – I had no other word for it, especially after the demonstration a few days prior. "Good. So we have ourselves a deal?"

"Deal. Next time you pause, I'll butt right in and pick it up." I mentally shook my head. We'd already basically been doing that, but if he wanted to really go for it, far be it from me to argue.

Jay nodded, leaning his head against the rough wall.

I glanced at the window again. "One of these days, I'm going to sit on your shoulders and see what's out that window."

"On me?" he asked, sounding half-asleep. I didn't blame him. It was hard to fully wake up some mornings when all we had to look forward to was more of the same – same food, same views, same people with the only deviation being whether or not Rees was going to beat the snot out of us.

"Yeah. Then I can describe to you what I see."

"You weigh a ton," he said, teasing by default. "And what if I want to see?"

"You'll have to live."

"I could sit on your shoulders."

"If I weigh a ton, I don't even want to think what you weigh. Anyway, my shoulders hurt enough without adding you."

"What's one or two more broken bones?"

"Gee, thanks."

He snickered. "I fight dirty sometimes."

I nudged him in the side with my cast. "Behave yourself. I know all about you. Including, say, the time Marguerite convinced you that she should dye your hair…"

Jay blushed right to the roots of said hair, sitting up to look back at me. "Where in the-Bri."

I grinned. "Right in one. Don't you love blackmail?"

He slumped. "I don't want to know why that story came up."

"Bri thought it was hilarious."

He made a face. "Of course he did."

"Behave," I told him again, resting my head on his shoulders.

I felt him chuckle. "I am."

"Good. Has anyone ever told you you have comfy shoulders?"

"Can't say as they have, but thanks."

We lapsed into a comfortable silence. It was hard to believe, sometimes, that I had only met Jay six months before. It felt like ages. For a moment, I toyed with the idea that he felt so familiar because of Bri, but I dismissed that as uncharitable. As similar as the brothers could be, they were still their own unique people. It was nice having him with me, even if I didn't wish him the pain that Rees inflicted. Having his ever-cheerful optimism, though, made everything that much easier to bear. I knew he'd always have a ready quip no matter how dire the situation.

"I'm glad you're here," I murmured around a yawn of my own, eyes shut.

"Where else would I be?"

"You know what I mean."

"I do, but I'm trying to keep from being insulted."

"You know what I mean," I repeated, nudging him again, a bit harder.

"Yeah, you want me to die."

"James!" I said, sitting upright to glare at him.

He grinned. "You honestly prefer me over even Beau?"

"Okay, maybe not over Beau." I settled back next to him.

"I think you're lying."

"I most certainly am not. Nothing personal, but my boyfriend comes first in my affections."

"Are too."

"Am not."

246

Stella rolled over to pin us both with a sleepy glare. "Would you two shut up already? You're like toddlers squabbling over last piece of candy."

"It'd be me," Jay said even as I opened my mouth to say the same thing.

I stuck my tongue out at him as Stella groaned.

"Gods' Breath! I can feel the maturity level dropping as we speak."

"Nothing wrong with a little immaturity on occasion," Jay said righteously.

Stella sat up and stretched before shaking her brother's shoulder. "Up and at 'em, kid," she said.

Dave's response was to make a sleepy noise of protest and curl up tighter.

"Wake up, David. It's almost breakfast and then story time."

He yawned but sat up. "I'm up, I'm up. Morning."

"Morning, Dave," Jay said and then poked me.

I retorted in kind and, by the time my arms were protesting too much to continue, Dave was wide awake and giggling and we heard the footsteps signaling the arrival of breakfast. We inhaled the meal, despite our best attempts to take it slow. Then Dave aimed hopeful eyes at us, asking us to continue. Jay and I exchanged a quick glance before I picked it up.

◀ ▼ ▶

Beau, Jez, and Jessie sat at one of the wooden tables, talking quietly and casting increasingly anxious glances at the door. The bartender came to clear away their plates. "You folks need anything else tonight?" he asked, obviously ready to call it a night. They were the only ones left in the place.

"No, we're fine, thanks," Jessie said, drawing her attention away from the doorway long enough to smile at him.

"Your friends are fine. We don't get much trouble hereabouts," he said before nodding to them and vanishing into the kitchen.

"It's getting awfully late for them to still be gone," Jez said, "at least for Jay. The note said he'd be back right after dinner. What do you think could have happened?"

"Westcorner does seem like a really sleepy town," Jessie said but her expression remained troubled. "What if they've run into a problem?" Both turned to Beau.

He nodded without hesitation. "C'mon, let's go find our wayward friends," he said, standing and making sure his sword was secure on his belt before heading for the door.

Jay, meanwhile, used the opportunity Ry had given him to plant his fist into the face of one of the bullies as another hit him from behind. He rolled, coming to his feet, ready for the third. Jay sidestepped, thrusting his foot out and, as the young man tripped, grabbed his shirt and helped him fly even further, using his forward. As the man plowed into the dirt, his four companions backed off to begin a more coordinated attack. Jay realized that Ry was nowhere to be found. Even as that thought filtered in, he heard her swearing loudly from further down the alley. He couldn't hear her clearly but didn't need to. Before the five could fully recuperate, he charged towards a gap between two. Jay slammed his shoulder into one, shoving him aside enough he could just spot Ry down at the far end. She was held fast as the leader approached her. Jay sprinted in that direction but only made it halfway before he was tackled. Squirming, he sought to get back on his feet to reach his friend.

Ry was hauled out of the fray shortly after planting her knee in one of the young men's stomach. Her assailant with the bleeding, and probably broken, nose grabbed her arms from behind and manhandled her back towards the leader, his size working against the smaller, slenderer girl. She struggled to break free, swearing loudly at her inability to do so. The leader glared as he stalked up to her, still a little bent over, no doubt from pain in his groin. With a quick dart forward, he stepped forward so they were nose to nose, not giving her any room to maneuver or repeat her earlier action. "Get away from me, you bastard," she growled, trying to shake her arm free. The goon only twisted it tighter, causing her to gasp as pain shot through the limb.

"Got you," the leader said in smug satisfaction, pinching her cheek hard.

Ry tried to kick him.

He merely laughed and grabbed her chin.

"Save yourself some serious trouble and let us go," she told him coldly, trying to wrench out of his grasp.

"Or you could save your friend some serious bruises. Call him off, do me this little favor, and we'll call it even."

She shook her head vehemently. "No way in hell," she said. "I think you underestimate Jamison's skill."

"Five against one is bound to fall in favor of the five. You're outnumbered, sweetheart," he said with a wide smile, pressing closer, ignoring her squirms as she tried to stomp his feet.

"How about when the odds are even?"

The gang all froze. Jay, relief flooding through him, didn't bother, using the distraction to pop one in the stomach.

"Back away from my friends and I might be convinced to let you all survive," Beau continued, voice icy.

The leader darted out of Ry's reach to assess the trio of newcomers.

The captain folded his arms across his chest, staring the younger man down. "Now, my friend, or else things will get ugly."

"There are still two more of us than you. Plus," he scoffed, "you've got two more girls."

Beau smirked, made a small gesture and, in tandem, the three of them dropped their hands to their waists and drew their knives, although they made it obvious in the motion that they had swords as well. "You were saying?" he asked mildly.

Ry used the distraction to jam her heel into the instep of her captor. He grunted, loosening his grip. It took all of a breath for her to bring her arms around front and grab his shoulders, throwing her weight forward. Caught off guard and still off-balance, he came up over her back and slammed hard into the ground between her and the leader. Still trying to settle her internal panic at what could have happened, she favored the leader with an insolent grin as she casually wiped her hands on her tunic. "What was that about girls?" she asked.

He paled, visible even in the dim light, and stepped back. "Did I say anything about that?" he squeaked. "What I meant was…"

"Give it up," Jay told him, pinching his nose to try to stop the bleeding as he stepped back to join the others, not wanting to give the goons any free shots. "You've lost and you know it."

Beau regarded the group. "What do we do with them now?"

"Stuff him and put him on my mantel," Ry muttered, jogging over to join them.

Jez snickered. "Why would you want his ugly mug up there?"

"Not that you have a mantel," Jessie added.

"True."

"We could turn them in to the local authorities."

"The ones who have been letting him run amuck in the first place? Great idea, Jay."

"No need to be sarcastic," he whined. "I just spent time getting my head mashed in."

"Oh, good point. I'm very sorry," Jez said, smirking.

The gang stared at them in undisguised confusion and surprise.

"Could we at least *try* and act mature, folks?" Beau asked, but the amusement in his voice gave him away.

"He's not dim!" one of the gang sputtered.

The friends exchanged glances. "Never said I was. Just that I'm easily distracted, which isn't wrong," Jay asked, honestly dumbfounded. "I think we know who the stupid one is."

"We'll tell," the leader said quickly, trying to get some sort of footing back.

"And who's going to believe the local bully squad?"

"Plenty of people. If you're lying about this, you're probably lying about other things too."

"Well done," Ry said sarcastically, rubbing her wrists where the one had gripped her. "What are we going to do with them?" she asked Beau.

"We're going to escort these fine gentleman to the town mayor and explain to him that they were making advances on you and beating on Jamison. Then we'll make sure it's understood that if they so much as look at any of us again, we won't go nearly as easy on them. Is that understood?"

"Yes," the leader said sullenly, his cronies nodding and echoing their agreement.

The mayor was properly outraged by the gang's daring and assured the friends that they would be properly dealt with and not give them a moment's more trouble. Within the hour, the five were back at the Swan. Jay and Ry had just given a quick description of what had led up to the fight. Beau lit a couple lamps in the common room so they could talk and Jessie could patch Jay up.

"Ow," Jay whined, fidgeting as Jessie bandaged his head.

She rolled her eyes. "The fidgeting will only make it worse, genius."

"But it hurts!"

"Of course it does. You recently got it slammed into at least one fist and I'm guessing maybe a rock."

Rylia winced, holding a block of ice to the back of her head where she'd cracked it into the one man's nose.

"I did fall a couple times."

"Fall?" Beau repeated.

"Using it as a relative term, of course," he said, taking the ice Jessie offered and gingerly putting it against the bandages on his face, peeking with one eye around it. "I suppose I should figure out a way to thank Mrs. Cornwall tomorrow."

"Who?"

"Mrs. Dolores Cornwall." He yawned then winced. "I think maybe I cracked a rib," he said sheepishly.

Jessie rolled her eyes again. "All right, I know you're going to love this, but the shirt has to come off."

It was a testament to how much Jay hurt that he only grinned a little and made no comment as he set the ice down and carefully worked his shirt off.

"So who exactly is Mrs. Cornwall?" Beau asked.

"She's an older lady who lives just on the edge of the town proper. I helped her do a bunch of chores around her house today that she can't manage by herself any more. In exchange, she talked at me all day."

"Learn anything interesting?"

"I...Ow! Damn it, Jessie," he yelped. "Did you not see the bruise?"

She prodded it again. "You mean this one?"

He gritted his teeth. "Yes, that one," he said tightly.

"Of course I did. I was trying to see if it's just bruised or cracked. It's a little hard to tell just from sight. Now answer Beau. It'll help you ignore the pain."

He glared at her but turned to the captain anyway. "She warned me about our friendly bullies."

"Useful," Ry muttered, which was the first thing she'd said since they'd returned. She shifted her ice to more adequately cover the bruise on her head.

"And she told me there's been an increase in troop movement in the area in the past week." He sat forward, ignoring the protests of his chest. "I really think we should scrap this and head home. I can't shake my bad feeling about all this."

Beau looked between them, taking in their serious and concerned faces.

"We'll do whatever you think best," Jez said softly.

"I'd like to get what information we can, but our safety and lives are more important."

"Too late to totally save those," Ry said dryly.

"We need some time to recuperate, though, and I'd like to give our informant one more chance. We'll leave tomorrow night after full dark."

"I'm fine to leave tonight," Jay said, beginning to stand, then carefully sinking back onto the bench with a groan. "Or not."

"For now, let's catch some sleep," Beau said. "Jessie, got him all patched up?"

She finished wrapping a bandage around his chest to keep everything in line. "Just finished. Jay, I'm honestly not sure what's the matter with your ribs, but as long as you take it easy, they should be fine soon enough."

"C'mon, Jay, I'll help you upstairs," Beau said, offering an arm.

Jez watched them go before standing as well. "Let's go. No point in dwelling on things," she said, herding her friends ahead of her.

Despite the late night, none of them slept in the next morning. Ry was the last one down, only seconds behind Jay who happily snagged a spot next to Jessie, grinning at their younger friend.

"How are the ribs feeling this morning?" Jessie asked.

"Sore, but not too bad," he said, considering he'd slept soundly enough though Beau woke him every few hours in case he had a concussion.

"What's today's plan?" Ry asked.

"Jez and I'll return to the Hog's Heel and then wander town just like yesterday. Jay can do whatever he likes, as long as he doesn't want protection, and I figure you and Jessie can wander town together as long as neither of you have a problem with that."

"Course not," she said.

"In the meantime, Jessie, let's go chat with the bartender. See if he knows anything about Mrs. Cornwall's troop movement." At her nod, Beau and Jessie slid out of the table and headed for the bar.

Jay mumbled something as they left.

"What was that? We can't understand you around your mouthful of food," Jez said.

He swallowed quickly, aiming a look at her. "I said: I do *not* need protection. I can take care of myself, thank you very much."

"And that's why you decided it was such a good idea to go after..." Jez trailed off a little too late, realizing abruptly she was crossing a line.

Ry blanched, rocketed from the table mumbling an excuse about the bathroom and took off through the front door.

Jay's expression darkened. "Here's the deal. I don't give a rat's ass that it's obvious you're protecting your own past. I'm sure you have your reasons and that they're good ones, but you pressured Ry into telling us about her past-"

"I didn't pressure her!" Jez protested.

"You asked. That's enough for her, don't you get that? We're the only family she's got now," he snapped. "If you didn't already know that about her, maybe you're not even half the person I thought you might be. Gods' Breath. Ry's still a kid, not even seventeen, and she's lost everyone she's cared about already once. Do you understand how hard that is on someone? How it *never* leaves them as long as they live? Doesn't matter if they make new friends, new loved ones – the fact that the others aren't there to see it eats at you for life. Half of what Rylia says is merely for protection. She's used to having to watch every word for fear someone will use it against her. I have no doubt she's better than she used to be, that you and the others have helped with that, but it's raw again. Didn't you notice that when she did speak last night, everything dripped with sarcasm?"

Jez again opened her mouth, but he went right on.

"You'll let me finish, Jezzy, because you need to hear this. You're a good person, I'm not saying you aren't, and I think most of the time you're fine, but you need to be as sensitive towards others as we are about your past. I think I can safely include even Beau and Jessie in the fact that all of us have left some sort of issue behind us." He stood now, radiating anger. "You're her friend, Jez," he said flatly and then turned and left.

She stared after him, stomach plummeting somewhere around the region of her toes. She'd known, even as the words had started to come out, that she shouldn't say them and she'd stopped, but…the truth was, Jay was right. And hurt more because she should've understood. She'd lost Bri. They all had, but she and Bri been so close. Still, she clung tightly to the fact there had been no official news of Colin's death one way or another and the rest of her family was safely ensconced in Lockholme, keeping their heads down and staying out of the crossfire. So, she could at least get an inkling through the forced separation, and how much Bri had meant to her, even for just the short time. And her family all thought they'd lost her.

She dropped her head in her hands, knowing she owed not just Ry but Jay an apology. He'd done nothing but help and she had given him grief for being beat up.

"Where'd they go?" Jessie asked as they came back over.

"I'm an idiot," she said by way of answer, standing. "You might want to go catch up with Ry."

Her friend eyed her, but nodded. "I'll see you two later," she said and headed out after the others.

"What did you do?"

"I'll explain on the way to the Hog's Heel," she said and led the way out, quietly outlining her comment and the two responses on the way.

Jay, meanwhile, had headed the opposite direction towards the outskirts of town, knowing he had to regain his equilibrium before he could even think about putting on his jolly good-natured, completely-unfazed-by-anything face. He leaned against one of the trees, taking deep breaths to settle himself. He sympathized with their teenaged companion, considering he'd lost his entire family too, but at least his parents hadn't ditched him, allowing him a pretty normal and conventional childhood. He closed his eyes, letting the quiet warble of birds and rustle of leaves soothe him. He'd always felt at home in the forest and now the familiar sounds allowed him to let out some of the recent stress – from Jessie learning his identity to Jez hitting too close to home.

When the first pitter-patter of rain drew his attention, he still stayed where he was, listening to it hit the canopy above and begin to snake its way down leaves and branches towards the undergrowth where he stood. Finally, a drop splashed off a leaf above him and landed on the tip of his nose. He grinned, feeling composed again. Shaking himself like a dog, he sought to fully separate himself from anxieties – or at least compartmentalize them.

Later, he couldn't say what had caught his attention, but he froze, listening hard. Sure enough, he recognized the quiet crunch of old foliage and the cracking of a stick. He remained slouched against his tree, eyes half-closed, but closely scanned the surrounding area. Determined not to make the bunny mistake again, he peered around. A flash of blue drew his attention. Another twig cracked and a low-spoken oath reached him.

Jay didn't bother to stick around to be sure they were even after him. He knew that blue livery. Like a shot, Jay took off towards town, only slowing fractionally when he reached the main street. He burst into the Hog's Heel and slid into place next to Beau scant moments later.

"Jay?" Beau asked softly.

"The sooner we leave, the better."

"What happened?"

"I went out to the woods to calm down so I wouldn't blow my cover again. Someone was stalking me or at least stalking through the woods."

"It could be bandits or even our friends from last night, not to mention the distinct possibility of rabbits." Beau's words sounded cavalier but even Jay could see the concern on his face.

He sucked in a breath, a little winded from his sprint. "Rabbits don't swear, last time I checked. And trust me, I'd know the uniform of the Three anywhere."

Beau glanced worriedly at the bar and shifted. "We still have a better chance of getting out under the cover of night. Especially if the weather continues to deteriorate. I think we have no choice but to wait."

"What if they come for us?" Jay and Jez asked almost simultaneously.

Jay glanced at the young woman for the first time before returning his attention to Beau.

"I don't think they will. It would involve more trouble than it's worth for potential Freedom Fighters. Westcorner might not be large, but it's an important crossroads town and even the Three need to keep up good relations here so they have unfettered access to the main road along the Alyian border. No, they'll wait for us to bolt."

"And we can't wait them out?"

"I suppose we could try, but we have no idea the strength and stretch of their resources. They might be able to keep up patrols and camp indefinitely. And there's the potential they'll convince the mayor that letting them in to find us is in his best interest, if the town doesn't get tired of their presence first and hand us over. We'll bolt, but we'll make it as difficult on them as possible." Beau looked between his two friends. "I'm well aware there are some issues right now. Please work them out before you both get us killed or worse, understand?"

"Yes, sir," Jay said, keeping his voice low. He shot another glance at Jez before standing and sliding out of the inn, back in full acting mode.

Jez groaned. "How in the world do I apologize?"

"I think you have your answer right there."

She frowned down at her ale. "It can't be as simple as a basic apology."

"Why not? First, it's a good place to start and second, they're your friends. Ry, at least, knows you very well."

"She doesn't know who I am."

"Don't give me that bull," Beau said with feeling. "Jez and Jasmine are exactly the same person and always have been. She doesn't know your birth name. Big difference."

Jez couldn't particularly disagree with his argument. Although she was unable to admit where and how she'd grown up, the only real thing that had changed from her 'death' was that Jez had learned a lot more and had so many more life experiences and skills then Jasmine had ever dreamed about at eighteen. But Jasmine now had just as many skills and freedoms. "Apologies first, then we'll see what other groveling I need to do."

He rather obviously squashed a smile. "Sounds like a good idea to me."

She braced herself as she stood. "Okay. I'm going to go find Ry and then Jay. He'll be harder to apologize to."

"Harder to apologize to, but probably not harder to convince to forgive."

She winced. "Don't remind me. I'm really going to have to grovel for a while."

"Probably," he said easily. "I'll wait here until you're done."

It took her only a few minutes to be directed towards Ry and Jessie by the locals, finding them wandering down the main street, talking quietly. When Jessie spotted her, she nudged Ry, then veered off to look at the window offerings of a dress shop. Ry continued a few steps until the duo were face-to-face.

"I'm sorry," Jez said, scuffing one foot nervously but forcing herself to hold Ry's inscrutable gaze. "And not just for the comment this morning. I should have let you tell us your past only if and when you were ready, not because I was curious. It was hypocritical of me to even ask, all things considered."

Rylia smiled faintly. "Apology accepted and I don't really see it as the same thing. My past is...not good, but it's not important in the grand scheme of things. Yours is."

She opened her mouth and then closed it. She'd always suspected Bri knew. Did Ry and Jessie as well? "It's not that I don't want you to know. It just...can't get out."

"I understand, honest," Ry said. "Whatever your name was before, if it got out, it would bring trouble to others."

"I've got family in a potentially perilous position," she said softly before shaking her head. "But this isn't about me. It's about you and the fact I was a jerk."

Ry laughed. "Which makes it about you too, but I'm serious. Apology accepted. I'm glad you know. Jay too, even. I just can't always control my emotions about it, especially when it comes to Bean."

"Think your parents are still out there?"

"Don't know, don't care," the teenager said firmly. "They're not my family anymore."

Jez hugged her, understanding her sentiments completely. "I'm glad to be part of your family, Ry, and I'm very glad nothing more serious than a few bruises happened to you or Jay last night."

Her friend shuddered slightly. "I'll agree with you there." She pulled back and smiled cheekily. "Just try and think before you speak, okay? I don't think Jay's ego can handle too much more battering right now. Although I heard he was still quite capable of giving you a lecture and a half."

"Yeah, let's not talk about that. You haven't seen him, have you?"

"He was heading back to his Mrs. Cornwall's house. That direction. He said it was because he wanted to feel useful, but I'm guessing he just wants more homecooked, free food."

"Homecooked, free food sounds excellent. I won't argue with it. Thanks, Ry."

"What else are friends for?"

Jez flashed her a grin. Within a couple minutes, she knocked on Mrs. Cornwall's door. Jay's cheerful voice, which floated out the open windows, cut off abruptly.

"Who is it?" an unfamiliar voice that had to be Cornwall called.

"It's Je-Jackie, Jamison's sister. May I speak to him? He's mad at me right now and I need to apologize."

Jay paused, slowly lowering the picture he'd been holding up for Mrs. Cornwall's inspection. The older woman looked at him. "Jamison?"

He nodded pensively, although he was heartened by how little time had passed before she was coming to apologize. To him, that meant her earlier comment and insensitivity had been just a brief blank, not a chronic problem. Which made sense, considering Bri had been attracted to her. "That's my sister."

"Is it okay if she comes in?"

"Oh, why yes, of course."

Mrs. Cornwall opened the door and smiled. "Hello, dearie."

"Hi, Mrs. Cornwall," Jez said, offering her hand. "Jamison told me you've been very nice to him. I'd like to thank you for that."

Jay watched her closely since Mrs. Cornwall's back was to him. Her gaze flicked to him and then back to the older woman.

"It's been my pleasure. Your brother has provided admirable company for an old lady like myself."

Jez smiled. "You don't look that old to me, ma'am. Mind if I borrow Jamison for a moment?"

"Not at all, as long as it's okay with him."

"Sure," he said and wandered out after her.

Jez the door shut gently and moved a couple yards away, keeping her voice low. "I'm sorry, Jay. You are completely right and it was incredibly insensitive of me, especially this morning's comment on top of everything else. I guess I just… didn't think," she said with a rueful smile.

"If there's one thing I understand well, it's not thinking before you speak," Jay said. "Let us not forget my introduction to Mick. I forgive you. Just try and behave yourself, okay, Jezzy?"

Her cringe was quite satisfying. "Jezzy? Seriously? Anything would be better than that."

"Your name doesn't give me a lot to work with so don't blame me for a horrible nickname."

"Why do I even need a nickname?"

He grinned. "Let's call it an incentive not to speak before you think."

"That's grossly unfair!"

"Life," he said. "Now, I really should get back to helping good Mrs. Cornwall rearrange her paintings."

"An honorable duty, I'm sure. Be careful of your ribs."

"Trust me, I'm doing as little as possible that would stress them."

Surprisingly to Jay, Jez reached forward and pulled him into a gentle hug, mindful of his injuries. "I'll see you this evening."

"What was that for?" he asked, aware he wasn't following his own advice to think first and speak after.

She patted his shoulder. "We're supposed to be twins, aren't we? Plus, I owe you one – a small one," she added hastily. "I needed a little kick in the butt this morning." With a wave, she headed back into town, presumably to the Hog's Heel and Beau, while Jay returned to the house, mind now racing forward to the planned escape that evening.

Ren and Ani's ongoing mock-war was cut off by a brief knock at the door before Jakium McRuoes poked his head into the room. "Sir," he said with a nod at Ren. He was one of the few people who consistently referred to Ren as sir anymore, Ani thought, and had to smile. The young lieutenant, who now turned his attention to her, was like the little sibling she'd never had.

"I heard you're looking for me?" he asked. "I'm afraid I'm already heading out to Greensward first thing tomorrow on permanent loan."

"Ah!" she said, hopping up. "If you don't want to go, I can prevail on…" She frowned, abruptly remembering she wasn't speaking to her oldest brother. "I can prevail on Sorin to keep you here."

"There's no need for that," he said. "I already talked to the commander. I can be useful in Greensward and I'm sure I'll be back frequently."

Although Jakium was still just a baby, not even twenty yet, he had a good sense of humor and they'd been friends from almost day one. When she'd first met him, she'd thought he was just a very good actor, but it didn't take long until she realized he genuinely liked her for her. That's why she trusted him with this. He'd understand.

"You'd better be, Jaksie," she said. "C'mon, I won't keep you from packing, we can talk in your room."

He rolled his eyes at the nickname, bestowed by a young Freedom Fighter girl, up north near Westcorner. "Okay," he said and again nodded at Ren. "I promise I won't steal her for long, sir."

"It's not a problem. Take as long as you need," Ren said as the young man stepped back into the hall.

"Ren," Ani murmured as she stood. His eyes darted to her as she subtly pulled his letter out of her pocket and flashed it at him. He nodded in understanding. She bounded out into the hallway and grinned at the lieutenant. "Come along, Jaksie-Jaks."

"Only you would take an already horrendous nickname and make it worse," he grumbled, but smiled anyway. "You'll be okay here, right?" he asked, glancing at her as they set off towards his room.

"Of course I will. I've got Renny."

"I heard about your fight with the general."

"Is there anyone in the castle who hasn't?"

"Probably not. And the commander?"

"What about him?" Jakium raised an eyebrow and she felt herself smile. "Sorin's Sorin. No, to be honest, we're getting along the best we have in a very long time. He's...changing."

"It's a good change, isn't it?" he asked quietly. "I've seen it too."

She elbowed him in the side, grinning. "Anyone ever tell you that you're nosy?"

He laughed. "Not since I was a kid."

"You're still a kid."

"You know what I mean. I promise I won't speak out of turn, Ani, I'm just curious. You know me. All our fates are tied in with your brothers."

The two reached Jakium's rooms in the ensuing silence.

"How soon does the commander think?"

"He won't even admit he's thinking it."

The young lieutenant studied her face, then nodded. "What did you want to talk to me about?" he asked, opening his door and motioning her in. Not surprisingly, the small room was neat as a pin, Jakium's scant belongings all in their place. The only personal items were on his dresser, just as they always had been at the house too – a child's old horse and cart set and a painting of him and his parents.

She pulled out Ren's letter. "I need you to find a way to mail this in Greensward."

He took it, eyeing the name and handwriting, before tossing it on his bed and reaching for his bag. "Why do you say it that way?"

"It has to get to the Freedom Fighters."

He spun back to her. "Excuse me?" he managed, eyes wide, bag dropping to the floor. "Ani, are you…?"

"No! No, no, it's not that. It's…it's clean, Jakium, I promise. You know Sorin's theory, right? That they're run by King Patrick's younger son?"

"It's gotten around, yes," he said carefully.

She pointed at the letter. "Ren thinks his name is most likely Beau and wrote him that." She held his gaze. "Beau deserves to know his brother is alive."

"And that's all it says?"

"Yes, pretty much."

"Pretty much?"

"I swear to you it's clean. Nothing incriminating, nothing dangerous to us. It's just a letter from a man who has never and might never meet his brother."

"You do realize I haven't got the faintest idea how to contact the Freedom Fighters, right?"

She grinned at him. "I know you're very resourceful, Jaksie-Jaks. You'll figure something out, I have faith."

"This is entirely the wrong sort of thing to have faith in me about," he pointed out. "And if I do this, no more Jaksie."

"Aw, c'mon, but it's so cute!"

"No. No more."

She sighed loudly. "Fine, be that way, Jaks. I'll try and curb the impulses."

"I'm sure that'll work ever so well," he muttered but returned her hug. "You owe me."

"I know!" she said. "Take care of yourself in Greensward and stay out of Rees's way."

"Colonel Rees and I have an understanding, but I'll do my best to behave," he said. "If you ever need to talk, write me. I can be here in a day."

"And this is why I like you," she said happily, patting him briefly on the head before dancing out of his room. "Ride safe, Jaksie!"

"*Ani!*" he yelled after her, but she could hear the laughter in his voice.

She made a quick stop in her room to pick up some clothes and a few necessary supplies for the next few days before returning to Ren's room and bounding through the door. "Renny Muffin, what drawer is empty?"

He rolled his eyes. "Bottom one. How'd the chat with Jakium go?"

"Oh, dandy, except I'm not allowed to call him Jaksie anymore."

She could see the smile fighting to escape, but Ren kept it inside. "That's really too bad, Ani. I'm sure it's hard to survive and call someone by their full name."

She grinned. "I haven't called Jaks Jakium since the day I met him. Why in the name of the gods would I start now? Even when I don't call you Renny or Muffin or something else, I still just call you Ren. Same thing. Take that with your attempt at sarcasm. Point for me!"

"You do sometimes."

"Only when I'm exasperated at you," she said, pulling out her night clothes. "And I get exasperated with you far more often than I do with Jaksie-Jaks. I'm going to go change in your bathroom." She tossed him an irreverent salute and disappeared into his old bedroom. Ani poked her head out again. "All things considered, it seems pretty silly that I'm changing in another room."

He smirked, his face lighting with mischief. "As much I wouldn't protest, I'd rather keep you for myself and not for whatever lackey your brothers have watching us right now."

Her eyebrows shot up and she laughed. "Yet another reason why I love you."

"Hey, I have feelings that way," he said, laughing too. "Go change and then I will."

"Do you change in here every day?"

"Mostly, yes. Vlad would rather I didn't and has said so, but the price I pay for my modesty is a small one."

She frowned. "Which is?"

He shrugged. "Every couple of days one of the guards comes in and searches my drawers and goes through all my clothes, in case I've got a weapon stashed in that empty room or that I can craft one in the couple of minutes I'm in there."

It took her a moment and deliberate deep breath to not go ream out her eldest brother yet again. "Guess it is pretty small. Okay, changing time. You know, you could come watch."

"Now that is something I suspect your brothers would both object to rather strongly. I appreciate having my arms in their sockets, thanks."

She snickered and stepped back, pulling her shirt off as she heard a knock at the door.

"Commander Dakamar asked me to give you these," she heard one of the guards say. She peeked out in time to see him pass Ren a set of crutches.

She winced, freshly furious at Vlad, before drawing back into the room to finish changing. As soon as she was done, she let out a contented hum, burying her nose briefly in the shirt before skipping out.

Ren, who had obviously been attempting the crutches, froze, eyes widening a little as he stared at her.

Disconcerted by his actions, she stopped too. "Hi?"

His gaze ran over her and she glanced down too, wondering if she'd missed a stain on the old baggy pants and too-large shirt. When she spotted nothing, she looked back up to realize Ren had closed the gap between them.

"Ren?" she asked when he still didn't say anything.

He reached out and tucked a strand of hair behind her ear before running his fingers down her cheek. He smiled softly, slipping the hand to cup the back of her head before pressing his lips to hers. She melted into it, wrapping her arms around his neck. When they finally pulled back of mutual accord, neither moved except Ren rested his forehead against hers.

"You know," she murmured, sneaking another quick peck, "if I'd known that all I had to do to get you to kiss me was wear old clothes, I would have done it ages again."

He chuckled. "Whose clothes? They don't exactly seem your style."

"Pants are mine, but the shirt is Sorin's. I steal a lot of his old clothes. We're about the same height, even if he's a little taller and definitely broader," – she loosened a hand long enough to pluck at the shoulder of her shirt – "and they smell good."

"Smell good?" he echoed.

"Yeah, of safety, of when we were little and I spent most nights curled up next to him in his bed instead of my own. Even if they stop actually smelling like him, they still feel safe." She smiled at the memories, suddenly ridiculously glad she was getting that brother back again, even if she seemed to be irrevocably losing Vlad at the same time.

Ren kissed her again. "I should go change. And no, you may not come. I wouldn't be surprised if your brothers would have an even bigger problem with that than the other way around."

She laughed and stepped back. "Have it your way then, as long as you acknowledge it would be more fun my way."

"No argument there." He moved awkwardly to his dresser, snagged some clothes and then disappeared into the old bedroom. Ani bit her lip against giggles as she heard a small crash and then a much louder curse.

"Are you quite all right, Muffin?"

"Don't call me that and yes, I'm fine. Stupid crutches."

"Sorin said they'd take some getting used to."

"No really?" he asked, obviously put out.

She decided her better course of action was to not respond so she hummed to herself, moving to his window until he reappeared, looking harassed. "My sprained ankle isn't going to kill me, but these might!"

"Don't worry, you'll get used to them. I broke my knee a few years ago and was on them for what felt like forever. By the third day, I could move freely without them hindering me, which, since you know me, you know how important that is."

"Great, so I still have two days left. That makes me feel so much better."

She rolled her eyes. "I've told you before and I'll tell you again, Renny, sarcasm does not suit you."

"Doesn't make it any less effective for releasing frustration," he said and then pointed at his bed. "Yours."

"With that ankle of yours? Not a chance. You need the space on the bed to be able to stretch it out and not aggravate it and make it worse than a sprain."

"Aggravate it?" he said, smirking.

She poked him in the chest. "Watch yourself, Mr. Highcastle. I have a very good vocabulary when I want to use it, thank you very much."

He grabbed her hand and kissed the back of it. "Yes, ma'am."

"I'm not a ma'am yet, by any stretch," she grumbled.

It was a testament to the fact he now knew her far too well when he only grinned. "Fine, I'll take it tonight." He snagged the neatly folded blanket off the foot of his bed and offered it to her. "In case it gets cold."

"Thanks, Renny." She accepted it and gave it a curious sniff.

He raised an eyebrow. "Does it smell like me?"

"Not as much as your other blanket does," she said, hopping over to the couch and spreading the blanket out, catching the pillow he tossed her too. She was tempted to suggest they share his bed, but had to agree that, at this point, she wasn't at all sure how Vladimir might react to such a situation, even if she was fairly certain Sorin wouldn't care. She watched him lean his crutches carefully against the wall and then crawl into bed. Doing the same, she pulled the blanket up and listened to the quiet sounds of the castle – footsteps passing in the hallway and muted voices echoing up through Ren's still cracked window. Despite the fact it was the dead of winter, she didn't expect he would ever shut it again. "Ren?" she asked into the comfortable silence.

"Mmm?" His sleepily hummed response made her smile.

"Thank you."

He peeked open an eye and peered at her. She was just able to see it from the moonlight filtering through the window. "For what?"

"For letting me stay here."

"My pleasure, Ani," he said.

"Only Sorin used to call me that," she said quietly.

"What was that?" he asked.

"Only Sorin used to call me Ani," she told him. "After he moved out and before Jaks moved in, I could only entice Vlad to on occasion and never in front of Edward. Sorin never cared."

"You were more important to him."

She glanced over at him, unable to deny the truth of that even if she'd never thought of it that way. "I guess I was. It's nice to hear it from him again."

265

He smiled. "Well, I like your full name too, but I'll never stop calling you Ani."

"Good," she said, settling down and letting her eyes close. "I wouldn't want you to." A minute later, she drifted off.

Chapter Nineteen

"THAT'S PROBABLY A GOOD PLACE to pause and let these two storytellers rest their vocal cords," I said.

Dave made a face, but quickly pasted on a fake smile as Stella glanced suspiciously at him.

I chuckled quietly and leaned my head against the wall, exhausted. Although my arms were worlds better, I still seemed to tire easily.

"You should rest," Jay murmured.

I ignored him. "I can't believe we ever fought."

"That was our first and last time."

"Good point," I said, unable to stifle a yawn any longer.

"Sleep," he said, nudging me in the side. "We'll wake you up if anything interesting happens."

I snorted. "The likelihood of that happening?"

"Sleep, Jez. You're still healing."

"Yes, Mother." I closed my eyes. "No telling stories about me while I'm asleep." When I was only greeted with silence, I cracked open an eye to favor Jay with a dark look.

He widened his eyes in innocence. "Okay, okay, I won't tell stories when you can't smack me for it."

"That's better," I said, letting my eyes slide shut. A moment later, I felt Jay's shoulder nudge up against mine and I shifted, settling my head on his shoulder, asleep within minutes.

I woke, feeling much more rested.

"Nice nap?" Stella asked.

I rubbed the remnants of sleep out of my eyes. "Yes, actually. I've told Jay before his shoulders are comfortable and I stand by that. You should try it sometime," I added, as innocently as I knew how.

"I'll have to do that," she said, cheeks reddening.

"Can I try too?" Dave asked wickedly. As both Jay and his sister aimed glares his way, he merely grinned. "Story time? I want to know how you escaped!"

"But we didn't," Jay said.

"Wait, what?" Dave sputtered. "Of course you did! You're here, aren't you?"

"That's a pretty poor comment considering exactly where we are, kid," Jay said.

"But you escaped, right?"

"We didn't escape."

I rolled my eyes, intervening. "Jamesy, stop torturing him."

"You didn't get here because of that, right? That's not what you said, right?" Dave pressured, eyes darting between us.

"Jay's just an idiot. We did not end up here because of that. We've still got about six months to cover before this particular capture. Let me continue while your sister knocks some sense into Jay."

"Uh, that's not necessary, really!" Jay said.

"You dug your own grave," I told him as Stella reached over and patted him on the head. I smirked and picked up the story before anything else could be said.

◄▼►

Only Jay later said he didn't think the day before their planned departure dragged. Helping Dolores Cornwall kept him plenty busy. Finally, as dusk settled, they all met back at the Swan for a quiet dinner. As they finished, Beau suggested they try to get some shuteye before heading out. They paused outside their rooms, exchanging glances, before heading in, leaving Beau and Jez in the hall by themselves.

"Think we'll make it?" she asked softly.

"I don't know. Maybe…maybe this isn't the right decision."

"It's our only possible decision, Beau, and we all know that. If we wait, it's a guarantee we're going to get caught. This way, we take the fight to them. Better that than being cornered."

He smiled faintly. "Doesn't make me any less nervous about the decision."

"Beau, we're all with you," she said. "We can do this."

"I hope you're right."

She leaned forward and kissed him on the cheek. "I know I am, because we're the Freedom Fighters and thus awesome."

He blinked and then chuckled. "If you say so. I'll see you in a couple hours."

"Night," she said quietly and slipped in after the girls.

Beau let himself into their room. Jay was already flopped out on his bed. Beau didn't bother changing and slid between the sheets.

"Are you really going to sleep?" Jay asked after a handful of seconds had elapsed.

"I'm planning on trying."

"Who's going to wake us?"

"Jez will. She won't get a wink of sleep."

Silence reigned for almost a minute before Beau heard Jay suck in his breath.

"Just try."

"You didn't know what I was going to ask!"

"I do too. You were going to ask what to do if you can't sleep."

"Damn, you're good."

"I know. Now sleep."

"But what if I really can't?"

"Then go bother Jez."

Another handful of breaths. "What if I prefer male bonding?"

269

"Jay," he growled.

"Yes, sir," he said meekly before finally staying silent.

Far too quickly, there was a light tap on the door, startling both awake. "Time to go," Jez whispered through the wood. They heard a click as she disappeared back into the girls' room.

"It is time," Jay intoned.

Beau threw his pillow at him as he rolled out of bed, grabbing his sword from where it leaned against the wall and strapping it on in the dark.

Jay caught the pillow, smirking. "Guess I fell asleep."

"Guess so," Beau agreed. "Hurry up, the girls will be waiting." He heard Jay fumble in the darkness before acknowledging he was ready. The pair hurried into the hall. Beau knocked lightly on the girls' door and, upon receiving no response, he moved down the stairs and into the common room. Jessie, Ry and Jez were waiting, barely lit by the coals of the fire, which had died down to almost nothing.

"Ready?" Jez asked.

"Yes. Weather?"

"Still raining, harder than when we went to sleep."

He nodded. "Just remember to watch your step, okay? It'll be slippery in the woods."

"Will do," Jessie said and the others nodded.

"Then let's do this," he said, squaring his shoulders and slipped out of the inn. Jez followed on his heels, Jay settled in behind her, Jessie at his shoulder and Ry, at her insistence, bringing up the rear.

Jez wiped off the first few drops of rain as they landed on her head before realizing it was going to be a losing battle. She checked her sword, more out of nerves than anything, and watched Beau scale the fence in the backyard of the inn. After quite a bit of conversation the night before, they had decided that was the best way to avoid any potential prying eyes. As soon as he disappeared from view, Jez pulled herself up, hopping off the top. Beau shot out a hand and steadied her before she ended up in the mud.

"Careful," he murmured.

She offered a grateful smile, sliding out of the way as Jay scooted over the fence, dropping to the ground with no issues. "Show off," she muttered.

He smirked as they waited for Jessie and Ry to join them, pushing his damp hair out of his face. The duo made it over without mishap and the five set off into the woods, Westcorner fading behind them.

Beau kept the pace slow, stopping often to listen, although Jez could never hear a thing beyond their footsteps and the pitter-patter of rain. Finally, he stopped and turned, motioning them forward. Once they were gathered, he spoke quietly. "Okay, we should be far enough from town. Now's the tough part. If we don't want to get lost in this weather, we need to cut back towards the road, but the Three's presence is likely to be heavier, so tread lightly and stick close."

"We'll be very quiet," Jay said.

"When are you ever quiet?" Ry asked.

"I can be quiet when I want to," he said, affronted.

"There's a first time for everything," Jez said, forcing a cheerful note as she patted Jay on the head with a watery splat.

Beau rolled his eyes. "Let's go."

After that, they moved along in silence. The quiet of the woods put Jez on edge as she strained to hear any possible noises that weren't the occasional scuff of their feet or the sound of raindrops. Time seemed to stand still as they slowly made their way across the increasingly treacherous ground. When Beau signaled caution, she immediately dropped low. He inched forward, then indicated an incline. She moved to his side, only spotting the eroding embankment of a small stream once she was practically on top of it.

"Careful," he murmured in her ear and then started down it. Only two steps in, he slipped, landed hard on his butt, and slid the rest of the way, straight into the swollen stream. She could tell from his body language that he was mentally cursing up a storm. She eyed the embankment. In a near-sitting position, she carefully slide down towards the stream, completely dousing herself in mud. She straightened once down and offered Beau a hand up. He took it, shaking mud off his hands and splattering her.

Jez made a face at him as their friends skittered down after them.

"Was coming down here necessary?" Jay complained.

"The stream runs north to south. The road runs east to west," Beau said. "Inevitable. Come on." He searched the opposite bank, then grabbed a jutting root, hauling himself up and scrambling over the lip. One by one, the others followed.

The trouble came when Ry grabbed the root, pulled herself up, throwing her leg over the edge before the root abruptly broke off in her hand. She slipped on the muddy bank, tumbling, head snapping back to hit a rock, luckily just above the water line. It all happened too quickly for her to make a sound. None of the others thought to check to make sure she'd made it.

They'd gone perhaps another fifty yards, before a voice snapped across the chilly evening. "Freeze!"

Beau immediately stepped towards the voice, hand dropping to his sword. Before he could do anything else, men dressed in the blue livery of the Three materialized out of the woods with arrows notched and aimed at them.

"Weapons down!" the same voice barked. "Hands on your heads."

"As if we weren't dirty enough," Jay muttered to Jez, glancing at his muddy hands.

She snorted, glancing at Beau to give them a lead. His hand was still wrapped around his sword hilt, but before he could speak or move, an order seemed to go through the soldiers and each bow string snuck back even more.

"Now!"

"Do it," Beau said, defeat all over his face and in his tone. He slowly drew his sword and knife and tossed them to the ground a couple feet in front of him, then placed his hands on his head.

Jez and Jay exchanged a glance and did the same. Then she looked to Jessie and Ry. Her heart leapt as she realized Ry wasn't with them, although she desperately hoped it was Ry's quick thinking and not something more serious. "Where's Ry?" she murmured to Jessie.

Her friend's eyes were full of panic. "I don't know. I know she was behind us at least through the stream. I never-" she cut herself off as the Three's men approached.

"Where's your other companion?"

"Who?" Beau asked, his face purposefully blank.

"Your last companion. There were five of you."

"I don't know what you're talking about."

The young soldier – Jez placed him somewhere between herself and Rylia in age – rolled his eyes. "Yeah, I bet you don't." He turned away, raising his voice to unseen men. "Spread out and find her. I don't want any of them getting away."

A group of the soldiers quickly bound each of the four's hands, collecting their weapons and then propelling them quickly through the woods to the road. From there, it was a short walk to their camp. Guilt swept through Jez. How could they not have noticed that Ry was missing?

Her friend was still unconscious, having been just lucky enough to land on the far side of the stream. Most of her body was lying across the water, but her head was free and clear. She became gradually aware of someone shaking her. "Young one, wake up, your friends are in trouble."

"Don't wanna," she mumbled, fighting to get her eyes open, though, as a bit of the other's urgency seeped in.

"You have to. They've been captured."

Ry finally managed to open them, squinting and wiping her eyes to try and clear the water out. "Captured?" she repeated, letting the older woman kneeling next to her help her sit up.

"Yes, Lieutenant McRuoes caught them."

Rylia squinted at her, gaze finally focusing. "Who're you?"

"Dolores Cornwall, a friend of Mr. Jamison."

"Jay," Ry corrected as she fingered the back of her head. "Gods' Breath, that hurts."

"As it should. It would appear you hit it quite hard, dear, considering it knocked you clear out, but we can use this."

"Use it?" Ry asked. She pulled herself from the stream, shivering as she propped herself against the bank.

"To rescue your friends. Jamis-Jay left me a letter last night. I was afraid something like this might happen, but I was too slow to catch you back at the Swan. It took some doing to track you through the woods, so I'm sad to say I was too late to prevent their capture. Now, let's get you on your feet," she said, offering her hand.

Ry took it and allowed the older woman to pull her fully to her feet, wincing and pressing against her forehead as the world swam around her. "Gods' Breath," she grumbled. "I'm going to be no help if I can't walk straight."

"Take a few minutes. It won't be perfect, but you'll be a lot steadier once your equilibrium returns."

"Who's Lieutenant McRuoes?"

"One of the Three's lackeys. He's been lurking around the area for a couple weeks now and someone must have tipped him off to your presence."

"And why do you care?" Ry asked.

"My son is a proud Freedom Fighter. He's the contact you were supposed to meet."

She frowned. "What happened?"

"I don't know. His last letter was downright paranoid and now, him not showing up for this meeting…"

Rylia made a mental note to see if they could find out for her once they were safely back at Cavern Hall. "There's still hope," she said gently and fingered her wound. "All right, I think I can walk again. Thank you for your help. I'm going to go try and figure out how to rescue my friends," she said with a wry smile.

"Who says I'm done helping? I had some time to think while I made it back to you after confirming your friends' capture, dear, and I have a plan that just might work."

Ry raised an eyebrow as Mrs. Cornwall quickly outlined a very simple but potentially effective plan. When she finished, she offered Ry a note. "For the captain," she said. "It explains what I've told you and a bit more. Mostly what I've managed to glean from my son's letters and my own observations. Keep it safe."

"Yes, ma'am," Ry said, then, a touch reluctantly despite the ingenuity of the Dolores Cornwall's plan, handed over her sword and knife.

Dolores carefully stuck Ry's sword through her belt. "Ready, dear?"

"As I'll ever be."

The two, Dolores giving Ry directions, made their way back up to the road and out towards the encampment of soldiers, Dolores appearing to hold Ry at knife point. The teen kept her hands on her head like she was good and captured, but it also kept her brain from feeling like it was going to pop out. Her head still pounded from its unscheduled interaction with the rock. Once they got past the first line of sentries, soldiers materialized from the dark to surround them, saying nothing and letting Dolores lead her in until they reached the actual camp. Waiting for them was a young man, a lieutenant if Ry read his insignia correctly. She guessed it was the aforementioned McRuoes.

"Ma'am," he said politely with a nod at Dolores. "I thank you for your dedication and hard work. We can take the traitor from here."

"Traitor?" Ry repeated, unable to help herself. "*You* are calling *me* a traitor? Where in the-"

Something flashed across his face, but it was too dark to see what it was. Maybe she'd imagined it.

Dolores tapped her back gently with the point of the knife. "She's all yours, Lieutenant. Just happy to help."

McRuoes's men moved towards her and Rylia acted. She sidestepped and spun on her heel, grabbed her knife from Dolores by the blade. Even as careful as she was, and with Dolores giving it up without a fight, the blade scored her hand. Still moving, Ry tossed it in the air, snagging it by the hilt with her uninjured hand, even as she grabbed her sword and drew it from Dolores' belt. Dolores fell back with a convincing shriek. Ry planted her foot and spun back, placing her sword's edge at McRuoes's neck before he'd even half-drawn his own weapon. "Let it go, Lieutenant," she said softly.

For a heartbeat, he didn't move and she was afraid she'd have to kill him, before his fingers relaxed.

"Good choice. Hands on your head and tell your men to back off."

McRuoes waved off the other soldiers as he raised his hands to his head, gaze never breaking from hers. "How old are you?" he asked.

"Take a guess," she said, stepping back a bit, still holding him at sword-point. "Now, take me to my friends, nice and slow with no delusions of grandeur."

He turned and slowly moved off. As word spread, the soldiers around them stopped to stare. None made a move, though, which set Ry on edge. A mere lieutenant, even if he appeared to be in charge, shouldn't be worth the lives of five potentially critical prisoners. So what was going on? It seemed to take forever to reach her friends, each of whom was bound, hand and foot, sitting in a row in the middle of the camp. All four brightened upon spotting her.

"All right," she said, "you're going to order your men to release my friends. And then you're going to order the same men to go get us five of your very best horses for our escape."

"This isn't going to work," he muttered.

"Try me," she hissed. "Now do it."

"Or what?"

She pressed it harder against his neck. He sucked in a breath, eyes widening slightly. "Do you want to be decapitated? Despite what you might think, I could do it before you even had time to react."

She could see his jaw set, half-turned towards hers. His eyes searched her face for a minute. "Free the prisoners," he called.

"Lieutenant," one of their guards started.

"You heard me," McRuoes snapped. "Free them and return their weapons."

"Sir!"

McRuoes aimed a fierce glare at the man. "Do as I ordered."

Reluctantly, the soldiers moved to obey.

"I also need five of our horses," McRuoes ordered, nodding at another man. This one looked between him and Ry and then scurried to comply. The lieutenant shifted, glancing at Rylia again. "This isn't going to work."

"You're just hoping it won't work because then you won't have to explain your failure to our illustrious leaders." At his cringe, Ry favored him with a sunny smile she didn't feel, due to her bleeding hand and pounding head.

By now, her friends had been freed and were accepting their weapons back. At the same time, the toady who'd been sent to fetch the horses reappeared.

"You okay?" Beau asked.

"Fine. I want you four to get going. I'll catch up as soon as I'm sure you're away."

"You don't need to do that," Jez said.

"Yes, I do. I need to ensure the good lieutenant and his buddies aren't going to follow us."

The four exchanged glances before Jessie moved, pulling herself astride one of the horses. The others followed suit. "Don't take too long," Jessie said with a quick smile.

Ry saluted with her knife. "Yes, ma'am." Then, knowing her friends would be able to make it out without issue, she turned her attention back to McRuoes. "Ready to take a ride?" she asked him.

"What?" he sputtered.

"I'm not stupid. If we just left, your men would be after us in an instant. If you come with us as my prisoner, then we can get away unscathed."

His jaw worked for a minute and he started to turn towards the horse. Then, it was his turn to catch Ry off guard, slamming his fist down on her right hand - her sword hand. The hilt, made slick with blood, slipped out of her hand, splattering into the mud. Ry instantly backpedaled, trying to get out of striking range as McRuoes drew his sword.

"Get after them," he bellowed, stepping forward. "I told you it wouldn't work."

"They still have a good chance of getting away."

"But you don't."

"Cocky doesn't suit you," she said, bringing her knife up.

"How would you know?"

"Lucky guess," she retorted as he raised his sword, taking a cautious swing at her.

She dodged to the side, seeking to reach her sword, which lay just behind him, but he shifted, cutting her off again. Ry risked a quick glance to see some of the others moving towards them and she knew she had to end it soon. With a quick flick of her wrist, she sent her knife flinging towards him. He started, slashing at the knife. He missed and recoiled as the knife caught him a grazing blow to the arm. She reacted instantly, darting forward, driving her shoulder into his chest. He stumbled back further as she rolled off him, sliding to her sword's side and whipping it up just in time to catch his downward slash.

"That was risky," he huffed out.

She smirked. "Calculated. Don't underestimate your opponent, Lieutenant."

"Can you stop with the mocking title?"

She raised an eyebrow, finally pushing him back enough she could scuttle to her feet. "No can do, sorry."

"You should have had your friends disarm me while they were still here."

"A less than fatal mistake."

"Now who's being cocky?"

She deflected another blow and pressed the fight, making certain to keep her footing in the mud. He edged backwards, face twisting slightly in concentration. "You know, you're getting beat by a sixteen-year-old."

He managed a one shoulder shrug. "I'm not that much older, so I'm not too offended." With that, he planted his feet to try and push her back.

Ry couldn't resist the grin that shot across her face as she dropped and shot out her leg. Her foot caught him right in the kneecap, snapping his leg straight. Then, before he could even yelp, she twisted, catching his other leg just behind the knee and pulling. He went down hard, sword bouncing from his grip. She hopped back up and placed her sword tip at his throat. "Gotcha."

He blinked at her.

She grinned. "And now you're as muddy as I am. Get up."

He did so slowly, holding his hands away from his body until he was up and then he automatically placed them on his head. "Now what?"

"Now you call off that crew," she said, nodding towards the men who had paused in their advance. "Then you call back the crowd that went after my friends."

"Back off," he told them. "You, call back the men."

"Sir," one of them said, frustration coloring his voice.

"My decision," McRuoes snapped, "and I say call them back."

The man hesitated, while Ry pressed her sword a bit closer to the lieutenant's neck. The soldier glared, but spun to sound the horn. Ry recognized the tone as calling them back.

"Now, on the horse, Lieutenant," she ordered.

His face twisted, but he did as ordered. She risked losing contact to snag her knife off the ground before sheathing her sword and hauling herself up behind him. Her eyes searched the area before finding Dolores Cornwall, who stood off on the edge, still watching. Ry nodded slightly and Dolores smiled.

"Don't try anything stupid," she murmured. "Now steer us out of town."

"And if I don't?"

"My knife works really well, as your arm can tell you."

"Except you need me to ensure your safety," he said, kicking the horse until a trot.

"If you decide to be an asshole, I'll take my chances."

"Trying to free myself means I'm an asshole?"

"Yup."

A minute later, they came upon the soldiers returning from the hunt for her friends. "Sir," one started and then cut off, spotting Rylia. "Oh."

"Head back to camp."

"Are you..." the man trailed off.

"If I don't return by the morning, strike camp and head back."

Ry barely squashed a smile. She had no intention of keeping him. The last thing any of them wanted to deal with was a prisoner.

"Yes, sir," the man said, offering a tentative salute, then motioning the other riders past them.

Rylia watched them go, then nudged the horse back into motion. "So," she said after a couple minutes of silence, "Lieutenant, what's your first name?" Conversation was better than the pounding in her head and the way the world felt more than a little off. She needed to focus until she could release the lieutenant and find her friends.

He twisted slightly to look at her. "Why in the name of the gods do you care?"

"I don't like silence," she said cheerfully.

"Seriously?"

"And I do like small talk."

"You're..."

"Amazing?"

He snorted. "That's one word for it."

"So what's your name?" she asked, prodding him in the side with her finger.

"Jakium."

"Jakium," she repeated. "Bit of a mouthful. That's not a Tiran name."

"Alyian, actually. My parents grew up in Alyia before moving here."

"How about Jaksie? That's more Tiran."

"Jaksie?" he echoed. "A...friend calls me Jaks, but Jaksie is...new."

"I like Jaksie better."

"It's *terrible*," he sputtered.

She laughed. "It's got a nice ring to it."

"What's your name?" he countered.

"Why? So you can track me down?"

"I wouldn't dream of it. I have no desire to ever go up against you again."

"As it should be," she said. "It's Rylia," she added after a minute. She couldn't see any danger in him having her first name. It was fairly unique, but there was little legal record of her, considering she and Bean had spent most of their lives on the streets.

He again twisted, brown eyes seeking hers out. "That's a gorgeous name."

That was possibly the last thing she expected. "I...what?"

"Rylia. It's a beautiful name," he repeated.

She reined in the horse. "You're full of shit, Jaksie, and this is your stop, so get off." She figured by the time he dragged himself, in the rain, back to the camp, she and the others would be long gone.

He shrugged as he carefully slid down, snagging the reins and looking up at her. "Don't believe me if you don't want to, but I was being serious."

Her heart skipped a beat and she was glad that it was still just dark enough to hide her blush. "Good luck with life. If I were you, I'd find retirement a very good idea."

He smiled slightly. "It's not that easy."

"Then maybe I'll see you again, Jaksie," she said lightly, tossing him a salute.

"Maybe you will," he said, returning it and releasing the reins.

Before she could let herself waste any more time, she turned and nudged the horse back into a trot, which was the fastest she could tolerate with her head pounding the way it was. She allowed herself one more glance back, to find him standing where she'd left him, watching her through the rain.

It took another two hours to catch up with the others and by then, the world was legitimately swimming. Her hand burned and she was honestly debating removing her head altogether.

Jessie spotted her first. "Ry!" she called, pulling her horse to a stop. "What took you so long?"

"Ran into a...technical difficulty," she admitted.

"I hope that's not your blood," Beau said as Ry drew even with them, all four having dismounted in the short interim.

Ry followed her gaze to a blood splotch on her arm. "Oh, no, that was Ja-the lieutenant. I cut his arm and then dragged him along for a while for safety. Must've bled on me."

Jay came over, offering her a hand. "Come on down from there, Beau was just saying it was time to send the horses running and head off on foot."

She slid down, glad for his steadying hands. Then she stumbled a step and pressed her good hand to her head. "Sorry, headache. C'mon, let's get moving."

"We should check your head," Jessie said. "You hit it last night and probably when you fell."

"We don't have time. We need to get further away before the good lieutenant can get back to camp and follow us. This rain will help hide our tracks, but it's only good while it's still falling."

"Ry," Jessie started, guilt they all felt coloring her tone.

"Don't, Jessie. Beau will agree with me. I'll be fine until we can stop."

"She's right," Beau said. "With the horses, we made good time, but need to head south now back to Cavern Hall. The sooner we get started, the sooner we'll get back."

Ry forced herself to straighten. "Then what are we waiting for?"

It was still early when Sorin arrived outside Ren's quarters, but he had no doubt that the prince would already be awake. He tapped on the door then pushed it open, poking his head in, just in case his gut was wrong.

He smiled faintly as Ren looked up from his chair by the window. As one, they both glanced at the couch, where Ani was still curled up, fast asleep. "Did she sleep all right?"

"I'm not sure she even moved."

"Good. I need to talk to you."

"Sure, come in. What about?"

Sorin moved into the room, gently shutting the door. Then he moved to Ani's side, gently shaking her awake. "Ani, wake up."

Her eyes blinked open and she stretched. "What're you doin' here?" she murmured, still half asleep as she sat up and rubbed her eyes.

As the blanket fell down to her lap, Sorin realized something. "Is that my shirt?"

She favored him with a brilliant, if sleepy, smile. "You don't mind, do you?"

As if he could answer yes with that smile. "Of course not. Didn't realize you still did that."

"Duh," she said. "What are you doing here?" she asked again, a bit more clearly.

"I need you to run a message for me."

"Why me?"

He ignored the question. "Down to Lieutenant Smith at the city gate."

Her eyes narrowed. "The city gate?" she repeated. "Sunshine, that's clear across town."

"That would be the point," he said, mentally groaning at the nickname.

She frowned. "Sorin, I love you dearly, but I will not let you or Vlad fill Renny's head with any more bull."

He resisted the urge to roll his eyes only because it was Ani. "That's not my point at all. Ren and I just need to talk for a minute."

"About me," she said stubbornly.

"You heard what I told Vladimir yesterday. Look, I'm sure Ren will tell you later if I was a jerk and then you've got every right to yell at me or kick me or whatever you want, okay?"

She eyed him before hopping up and hugging him tightly. "Deal." She waited a beat and then added, wickedly, "Sunshine."

This time he groaned out loud. "Ani!"

She grinned. "Morning, Renny Muffin!"

Ren did roll his eyes. "Good morning, Ani."

With that, his sister danced off towards Ren's closet to change, pausing only long enough to pull some clothes from the bottom drawer of his dresser.

"She has a drawer," he noted.

"Would you rather our clothes be mixed?" Ren asked, with no little amusement.

Sorin decided that definitely did not need a response.

"If I run into Vlad because of this little assignment, I'm going to be most displeased," Ani shouted through the door, luckily sparing him an awkward silence – or at least, an awkward one on his end. Ren was disguising his laughter very poorly.

"Vladimir is in meetings all day," he called back.

"Better be!" she said, her humming filtering out a moment later.

Sorin scanned the room, more out of habit than anything, and his eyes landed on the discarded crutches. "Those should be with you."

The prince grimaced. "I feel like an idiot."

He cocked an eyebrow at him. "You'll feel like even more of an idiot when your insistence on hobbling around causes your ankle to heal poorly." He stepped over, snagged them and offered them to the other man. "Use them. It's for your own good."

"Yes, sir," he grumbled, offering Sorin a half-hearted salute as he leaned them against his chair.

Ani danced back out like a whirlwind, kissing Ren on the cheek and actually patting Sorin on the head, before waltzing out the door. Sorin and Ren exchanged glances as Sorin pulled the message out of his back pocket and tapped it against his palm. The prince chuckled.

Her head reappeared. "I think I forgot something," she said sheepishly.

Sorin offered the message. "Thank you."

She just smiled, waved cheerily at Ren, and darted back out the door.

He turned and sank into the couch, mentally trying to rehearse what he wanted to say. "Come join me."

"Why can't I stay here?"

"Because I want to see you walk with the crutches."

With a sigh, Ren did as asked, tucking the crutches under his arms and making his way over to Sorin. It was immediately obvious that Ren had missed the point of crutches being a substitute for the injured leg and he had to cover his mouth to keep from laughing. From Ren's disgruntled expression, it was clear he hadn't missed Sorin's mirth anyway. "See, these things make me look like an idiot."

"That's because you *are* an idiot. Together, the crutches are your left leg. You move them together. Let me see." Ren collapsed thankfully onto the couch and offered them up. Sorin took them and demonstrated, walking across the room and back. "See?"

"Oh. I guess I am a bit of an idiot."

Sorin handed them back, settling himself on the opposite end with a slight smile. "I guess so," he agreed.

"So," Ren said, after a moment of silence, "what did you want to talk to me about?"

Sorin looked down at his hands. "I'm assuming you have figured out why we've kept you alive by now."

"If I marry Ani, you can use me as a figurehead, but have a legitimate claim to the throne. Yeah, I'd gathered that. Vlad's been less than subtle over the years."

"And yet there's Ani sleeping on your couch."

"Your sister doesn't have a duplicitous bone in her body. If she says she loves me, I feel I can be certain it is because she really does love me, not because of your plans."

Sorin managed not to cringe only through the greatest force of will at the repeated 'yours.' Not that he denied his culpability, because he had helped of his own free will, but now it just seemed like such...overkill, considering. "Do you want to marry her?" he asked, before he could stop himself or think twice.

Ren pursed his lips. "I don't know. We've only just begun to have even the closest we can get to a real relationship and to think about marriage now seems like such a rush."

"At least you know her. You were supposed to marry one of the de Carlins, weren't you?"

The prince took a deep breath. "That was the plan, yes. And no, I didn't know Francine. Still don't and probably never will."

Sorin studied his face. "Ren, I know that you're a lot different from us and not just for the superficial, glaringly obvious reasons."

"You mean like the fact you staged a coup of the kingdom?" Ren asked mildly.

He shot him a dirty look. "Yes, like that. Our childhood was...less than stellar, to put it lightly, while yours wasn't traditional, but you had parents who adored you and gave you the world."

"Tried to."

"Ren," Sorin said, fighting a surge of impatience, "I'm trying to be serious."

"You're always serious."

"Never as much as when I talk about Ani."

"I'll give you that," Ren said magnanimously. He was enjoying Sorin's discomfort far too much.

"I don't know what Ani's told you of our childhood, but you need to know that any person who marries our sister has to be dedicated to her, to care for her always and treat her like she deserves. To just…be a good person."

"I swear to you that I will always treat Ani with the utmost respect and care. And, if I don't, you and Vlad will be here to kick my ass."

Sorin was not at all certain that the second part was true at all, but he was fairly certain Ren was telling the truth. "I'm hoping that need will never arise."

"Cross my heart, hope to die," Ren said somberly. "Wait, are you giving me an 'are your intentions honorable' speech?"

He couldn't disagree. There certainly wasn't anyone else out there who would do it, which left it his job. "Are they?"

"Absolutely."

"Good." Sorin stood. "Knowing Anica, she'll be back soon and I have work to do." At Ren's nod, he turned and made it as far as his hand on the door before he glanced back. "Will you promise me something?"

"Depends," Ren said carefully.

"If Vladimir and I are ever not here, you'll take care of her for us."

The prince held his gaze for a handful of heartbeats before nodding. "Always."

Sorin smiled and let himself out, heading back to his office. Once there, he realized that Old Bert had finally come through with the files he'd requested on the Lockholme family. He settled in, flipping through them quickly, before a frown grew on his face. He rose again, poking his head out the door. "Calip!" he bellowed.

The young man practically sprung from his office down the hall. In a way, Sorin was glad that Old Bert would be busy with Vladimir and his meetings all day. Calip was their bookkeeper and historian so he was the best person to ask. "Yes, sir?"

"Why didn't I get anything on the children of Earl Denham Lockholme? It says he has five, but does little more than list names and ages."

"We have a separate file for the children, since there are so many. Bert didn't tell me you wanted that file as well."

"I would if you could grab it for me."

"I pulled it just in case. Hold on a second, sir," Calip said, disappearing back into his office.

Sorin moved back around his desk and sat back down, toying with the papers as he waited. He felt there was something he was missing in all this. Whether about Denham or one of the children, he wasn't sure. It would appear he had missed something about Jasmine, though, if she had managed to survive their assassination attempt, and had spent the past couple years working for the Freedom Fighters. How many others had escaped their grasp?

Before he could follow that thought much further, Calip entered with a quick knock and offered him another file. "All we have on the children is in here, sir."

"Thank you, Calip."

The man nodded and vanished back out the door quickly. Sorin snorted. Other than Bert, none of the help ever wanted to be in his presence alone too long. He opened the file and began reading it. The eldest three boys were boring. Kent, as the oldest, was being groomed to take over for his father. Jordan and Jonathan, the next two, were beyond boring. Typical younger children of a nobleman, undoubtedly looking for advantageous matches with other noble families. It was when he got to the youngest son that he paused. "Colin," he murmured and traced his finger over the next line. "Sent to Northwind to be in Duke Walters' personal guard." A Colin had helped Benton Walters, Duke Robert Walters' son, escape their attack. That couldn't be a coincidence. He frowned, glanced quickly at the page on Jasmine, which did little more than confirm what he already knew of the young woman.

He returned to the file on the parents, reading with a bit more attention. The beginnings were as boring as the oldest sons: raised horses, rarely left his land, married a long time. Again, he paused part of the way through when he got to Denham Lockholme's military history. "Damn," he murmured. Lockholme had apparently been quite a fighter in his prime, complete with a stint as second-in-command of Tira's armies, under none other than Robert Walters, before he'd taken over as duke from his father. Not only that, but he had been the army's top tactician, a trait, the report read, that his sons had expressed equal skill in.

"Surprise, surprise," he said, shoving both reports away and leaning back in his chair. He laced his fingers behind his head. According to this information, not only were they facing a Highcastle but also two Lockholmes, a family apparently quite skilled at tactics, horses, and fighting - *and* both the Walters kids, who had slipped through their fingers as well. The Walters had always been a powerful family. It was part of the reason Vladimir had decided to do away with them. As a result of his haste, both children had disappeared.

Sorin tapped his fingers together. At some point, he wanted to get to Greensward and have a chat with Jasmine, although he knew Vladimir was insisting he go alone first and scout out their resistance. As if Sorin wasn't entirely capable of doing such things himself. He'd have to get over it and talk to Vlad at some point, unfortunately. He still had a country to help run, after all.

After a minute, he stood and glanced out the window briefly before leaving his office. Calip glanced up as he passed the man's open doorway but didn't say anything. It took Sorin some time to reach the same rampart Ani and Ren had been on a couple days before. He paused just outside, taking a deep breath and expelling some of his frustration. He flopped heavily against the low stone wall, grinding his knuckles into the rough stone. The pain did nothing to cease his feelings of being closed in, of slowly suffocating with no way out. He had long ago promised himself he would never feel that way again. Not since he'd been eighteen and walked out of Edward's house. Yet here he was, in a slowly closing trap of Sorin's design and Vladimir's execution.

He dropped his head in his hands. If Diana saw him now, she'd be beyond appalled. She'd be fully disappointed. Disgusted even. Things had just gotten so out of control after her death. It was impossible to believe it had already been three years. Three long, critical years. He sighed.

"Sorin?" Ani's voice was quiet and hesitant.

"Yes?" He didn't bother to raise his head, hoping his sister would leave.

"Are you...all right?" He heard her footsteps approach until she stopped beside him.

"Fine. Aren't you afraid Vladimir will find you?"

"You're the one that said he was in meetings all day." Silence. And then, "Sorin, don't lie to me. What's wrong? You were fine this morning."

"It's not your problem, Ani. Leave it alone."

"It is my problem. We're siblings and we're in this together."

"You shouldn't be here."

"That is water under the bridge by now. I'm here and I'm here to stay."

"How did you know I was here?"

"Calip was concerned."

"Last I'd heard, none of the minions cared much for me."

"Last you'd heard, you didn't care about anything so why should they?" she retorted.

Only now did he peek up at her. "Sarcasm doesn't become you."

She smiled slightly and leaned against the wall. "I tell Ren that all the time. What happened to your knuckles?"

He glanced down, a little surprised to see them leaking blood. "Nothing. They'll be fine."

Both stared out over the farms for a couple minutes. "You know you're the one who taught me that we're allowed to love and be loved, right?"

He let out an incredulous bark of laughter. "Gods' Breath, Ani, leave me with the delusion I didn't fuck you up that badly."

She punched him in the arm, hard. Surprised, his head shot up. "Don't you dare think that," she growled, poking him in the chest. "You're the reason I'm as normal as I am. Do I look screwed up to you?" He shrugged so she hit him again. "Do I?"

He couldn't resist, despite his dark mood. "You certainly don't look normal."

She glared at him.

"All right, all right, considering our family, you don't look screwed up."

"And that's because of you," she said staunchly. He had a momentary flashback to their childhood and how she'd always been so protective of him regarding the other boys at boarding school. Again, they lapsed into easy silence. To no surprise, Ani broke it first. "But you still can't get out of the original question. What's bothering you?"

He sagged against the wall. He wasn't sure how to begin. He had never told either of his siblings about Diana or anything about his years with her. All they knew was that something had happened, bad enough to result in him moving back in. They hadn't asked questions, so he'd thrown himself into the planning, because it gave him something to focus on other than his life. "Do you know what I did for the years on my own? Other than working with Vladimir?"

"Nothing personal, but I didn't realize you did anything *but* work, to be honest. I guess I'd never really thought about it. It's not like we exactly talked much during those years." She frowned, glancing at him. "Why?"

"I am such a bad person for never telling at least you."

"You're not a bad person," she said, nudging her shoulder into his.

"Yes, I am, for so many reasons, but," he added, forestalling her comment, "I know better than to get into that argument with you."

She smirked. "Because you know I'll win."

He couldn't disagree. Maybe not win but push the argument until he gave in, certainly. "About three years after I left, I met a woman. An amazing woman, Diana. We got married after a year."

"You're married?" Ani said, eyes widening.

He shook his head. "I *was* married."

"What happened?" she asked quietly.

"The first two years were perfect and then we found out she was sick and that there was nothing they could do to help her. That she was going to die."

His sister silently slipped an arm around his waist and leaned against him. He appreciated the gesture.

"I should have introduced you. I know that now, but I was still so angry and when Edward died, I thought I had all the time in the world. After we got the diagnosis, I…she was already being taken away from me and I just decided it was better to keep her separate."

"I remember that. You stopped coming to Alexandria as much."

"It took almost two years before the disease finally took her."

"So that's wh…"

"Yes. Why I came back. Why I agreed to," he waved a hand, "this. Just… nothing seemed to work. I had convinced myself that it was forever and then… it wasn't. And I was tired of trying, so I stopped. And came home." He hesitated and looked down at her. "Are you mad?" he asked, feeling almost foolish for asking, but he wouldn't blame her if she was.

"Of course not. Do I wish you'd told us so I could have met her? Yes, of course. But I knew there was something that had you happy. You were distant

289

but between the little Jaks and I saw you, I could tell. So when you came home and were so despondent, I told Vlad not to bother you, that you'd tell us in your own time if you wanted us to know."

He hugged her a bit closer. "You might be mad at me when you hear the rest…"

Chapter Twenty

"Shh," Dave whispered suddenly, slicing his finger across his throat.

I immediately stopped speaking and pricked my ears, hearing the footsteps now that I wasn't talking.

"Who is it?"

I peeked down the hall. "Rees," I said sourly, not looking forward to a fresh encounter. My shoulders throbbed in response.

"Good afternoon, all," he said as he reached our cell.

"Afternoon," I said neutrally, reassured by the fact he didn't have the brute brothers.

Jay didn't bother with a greeting.

"I don't need the glare to know how you feel, James."

"Mm, but it makes me feel so much better."

Rees's jaw twitched, but he turned to me. "How are you feeling?"

"Tired, sore, now pissed off. You?" I asked, making my voice as sickly sweet as possible.

He didn't rise to my bait at all. "Fine. James, Dayton will be back later to get you. We have an appointment. Just wanted to check on Jez, make sure there hadn't been a relapse or anything."

"Oh, trust me," Jay said with a smirk, "you would have been well aware if there was a relapse. And I think I'll pass."

"Pass?" the colonel repeated.

"I don't think I'll be joining you, Dayton, and the brutes today."

"Did you hear a question somewhere in there? You will be joining us later. I thought a warning only appropriate since I was here anyway."

"Or what? You'll break my bones." Jay waved a hand at me. "Been there, done that. She's fine now and you don't know anything more than you did before."

Rees stepped forward and casually leaned against the bars. Nothing else about his posture was casual, though. "If you push me, I can, and will, personally break every bone in your bone, James," he said, voice low and threatening. I curbed a shiver. "Then I will make sure you're in severe pain for the rest of your excruciatingly life."

Jay flapped a hand again, but I could see the flash of nerves. "Empty threats."

"You don't think I could follow through on that?"

My friend rolled his eyes. "I don't think you're allowed to follow through on that. Vladie and Sorin have you on a short leash when it comes to possible Freedom Fighters, don't they?"

The brief darkening of Rees's expression was all we needed as confirmation.

"You know what, Rees?" I asked, interrupting.

His eyes flashed to mine and he cocked an eyebrow in curiosity. "What's that?"

"You are supremely overconfident. I'd bet you've never had a real challenge before in this job. People usually just cave to you, don't they?"

He said nothing, studying me.

"Now, here's the thing. Jay and I aren't going to just roll over because you look at us evilly or dislocate my shoulders or set some goons on us. We're not your usual clientele."

"Because you've got honor and being on the right on your side," he said with an edge of sarcasm.

"Because we're nobody's grunts or low-level losers."

"That may be true," Rees said, "but I've got all the time in the world to work on both of you, so we'll get to the truth of it sooner or later."

"See, there's the overconfidence again," I said conversationally to Jay. "He honestly thinks he gets us indefinitely."

"Don't I?" Rees asked. "We're closing in on two weeks and so far, no rescue attempts. Face it, your mission failed and now you're caught."

I shrugged. "That's assuming the Freedom Fighters don't kick your ass soon. Personally, I'm betting on them."

"Because you know their plans."

It was my turn to cock an eyebrow in polite confusion.

"Why do you both insist on denying being members of the Freedom Fighters?" he asked, in a tone of long suffering.

Jay and I exchanged amused looks. "Because it's true," he said, snorting.

"All I ask is you tell me what you know," Rees said, ignoring us entirely, "and then we'll let you go."

"That's all? Wow, not asking for much, at all. Sucks to be us," Jay replied. "Wish we could help you, Mr. Colonel, but we're fresh out of Freedom Fighter secrets."

"If you're not Freedom Fighters, then why would you have been attacking Greensward's garrison and weapons depot?"

"Maybe someone pissed us off."

"Or we thought it was a tremendous eyesore," Jay added.

"Both weak grasps to try and cover up the truth."

I knew we had to get out of the conversation. Even if we weren't confirming anything, Rees was very quick. I didn't want him to deduce anything further, because that meant the questions, and presumably the punishments, would get worse. "If you say so," I said, adding an eye roll.

"Everyone has a limit to their endurance and tolerance. It appears I haven't found yours yet. No worries, though. I am *very* good at what I do. It's just a matter of time." He smiled, a predatory expression that set my teeth on edge. "James, I'll see you later." He tipped an imaginary hat. "Have a nice day," he said smugly. Then he very deliberately eyed Stella and Dave, sending a thrill of nerves down my spine. He turned on his heel and left.

I watched him go until I was sure he was completely out of hearing. "He's creepily good."

"At least he can't confirm any of it."

"He can still use it when interrogating us," I murmured and turned to our cellmates. "Dave, you okay?"

"He's pretty scary."

"He's just hot air, kiddo, so don't worry, okay?" I said but exchanged a glance with his sister and Jay over his head. We knew Rees was definitely not hot air and, now with his seeming interest in Stella and Dave, he was more dangerous than ever before. I watched Jay, hoping he wouldn't do anything foolhardy when Dayton and the brutes came. Although I wouldn't argue with the idea of planting a fist or something pointier in one of them, I didn't want Jay to do anything risky.

Jay must have read my expression because he smiled. "Don't worry, Jezzy-poo, I won't do anything stupid."

I raised an eyebrow even as I made a face. "You do realize I'd feel a heck of a lot better about that if we had the same definition of the word stupid, right?"

Stella chuckled.

"Ouch. Fine, point for you."

"I win!"

"No, you don't. It's a tie."

I knew exactly what he was referring to. "It didn't seem appropriate to comment on your use of the juvenile nickname."

"That doesn't change the fact the score is one to one," he said.

"Gods' Breath," Dave groaned. "Do you two ever stop?"

Stella burst out laughing. "Out of the mouths of babes," she said, shaking her head. "Now, since you've both put in your thoughts, let's stop bickering. It's giving me a headache."

Personally, I doubted that that's what was causing her headache and, from the look she gave her brother, I didn't think I was wrong.

"We weren't bickering," Jay protested.

I nodded solemnly. "We're bantering."

"There's totally a difference," Jay said at Dave's skeptical look.

"Fine, then, stop the bantering."

"And get back to the story," Dave added hopefully.

Jay opened his mouth then paused, hearing fresh footsteps. "Guess Rees isn't wasting any time. It appears to be my date, come to pick me up for the ball."

"You've always had such impeccable taste," I told him dryly as Dayton and the two brutes appeared at the bars.

My friend grinned at me. "Always."

"Time to go, James."

"Ain't that official sounding." He stood, brushing off his hands. "Take me to your leader!" he exclaimed.

Dayton's expression barely flickered as he unlocked the door. Jay shot me an easy smirk before heading down the hall, the brutes hastening to catch up as Dayton locked us back in. I shifted to watch them until they were out of sight then closed my eyes, letting out a breath. I wasn't any more worried about Jay than usual, despite him having pissed Rees off. Stella spoke quietly to Dave and I let my mind wander, knowing there was nothing else I could do. I must have dozed, because then next thing I heard was Dave saying, "I think he's nice. A little silly, but nice."

I kept my eyes shut, blatantly eavesdropping.

"He is nice," Stella said, "but why are you bringing this up now?"

"Well, it's hard to talk about it when he's sitting right there," he said, in a 'isn't it obvious' tone. "Anyway, you won't even let yourself admit you like him unless I tell you it's okay, since you're responsible for me now."

It took quite a bit of self-control not to laugh at that.

"David Harper," Stella said, aghast, "I do not need your permission!"

"Well, who else's permission are you going to get?" he asked practically.

"I don't need anyone's permission, David. I'm an adult. But now is not the time."

"Now is the only time," he protested. "They're gonna kill us, Stell. You might as well be happy until that happens."

She sighed, ruffling his hair fondly. "You've had to grow up way too fast the past two weeks, kiddo."

He shrugged. "I'm just glad that George could help Jay, Jez, and the others for at least a while."

"Me too," she said.

"You and Jay would really make a good couple. I could list the reasons if you want," Dave said lightly.

"That's completely unnecessary," Stella replied. "I do not need my little brother matchmaking."

"You might not need me to, but that doesn't mean I can't. Right, Jez?"

Apparently, my faked sleeping had fooled no one. "Of course. Nothing wrong with matchmaking," I said. "Or holding on to hope," I added quietly.

"See," the boy said.

"The longer we can put off Rees, the more time for news to get back to Beau and for a rescue to be mounted."

"Do you really think that's possible?" Stella asked.

"Given some time, yes, absolutely. Beau won't leave us to rot here."

She nodded. She opened her mouth and then shut it as we all heard the distinct sounds of whistling. I instantly recognized the sound and I shifted to peer out the door better.

"Cut the racket." I didn't recognize the voice but guessed it had to be Dayton. The brutes seemed to speak infrequently and mostly in grunts.

"No," Jay said before launching into an upbeat drinking ballad.

I winced. Jay's voice had never been my favorite.

"Shuddup," one of the brutes grunted.

I could now see Jay, skipping down the hall, periodically attempting to twirl one of the brutes. "Why should I?" he asked, spotting me and waving jauntily.

"What's going on?" Stella murmured but I could only shake my head.

"I don't know. Jay doesn't have a new bruise on him."

I scooted away from the door as a smugly satisfied James Dall came to a stop in front of it. "Hi, guys!" he said brightly before one of the brutes pushed him out of the way so Dayton could get at the cell.

"You could have asked," Jay told them.

"Get in," the short man said.

"Little patience, high tolerance," my friend sang, bounding in, grabbing Stella and spinning her.

Dayton slammed the door hard enough to rattle it. "You're going to get it, Dall. The colonel will not let those insults stand."

"Well, pardon me for being happy," Jay retorted.

Dayton aimed one last glare at all of us and then spun, stalking off, trailed by the grunts.

Jay aimed a brilliant smile my way. "I'm not sure he even heard me. We're even now, though."

"What in the name of the gods happened?" I sputtered.

"Tell me I'm a genius. I even got an insult in aimed at his great-grandfather."

"James," I grumbled, more interested in why Rees hadn't pounded the crap out of him after our earlier conversation than Jay's skill at insults. "What happened?"

"I won't tell you until you admit I'm a genius."

I rolled my eyes. "You're an amazing genius, now tell me."

"At least tell me with some feeling, Jezzy."

"Insults are some of the lowest form of payback," I told him loftily, unable to resist despite my curiosity.

"Admit it."

"James."

"Admit-" Jay cut off with a squeak of surprise as Stella grabbed his face and kissed him firmly on the mouth. Dave burst out laughing while I tried hard not to do the same.

"Now tell her," Stella said, stepping back.

Jay blinked at her. "This day is unexpectedly awesome," he breathed.

"Tell her," she said, patting him on the cheek.

"To be honest," he said, sobering a bit, "I was expecting a real bruising after this morning's pissing contest, but…something must have happened in the interim."

"That's not a lot of time."

"News can travel fast," Stella said.

Jay nodded and I had to think that news that had plainly resulted in Rees being so preoccupied he didn't even order the brutes to beat up Jay probably spelled bad news for us. "He was very distracted and kept asking stupid questions and not reacting to my corresponding stupid answers." He shrugged, grin widening. "So, me being me, I took it a step further and insulted him personally. When that didn't get a rise out of him, I moved on to his great-grandfather and mother. Finally, even though the brutes were itching to kick my butt, Rees goes: *I'm not in the mood for this, James, I need to think about things and you're not helping. We'll all chat tomorrow.* Then he looked at the thugs and told them to take me, unhurt, back here, so I had free rein to sing at them all the way back."

"I wonder what sort of news," Stella said.

I exchanged a glance with Jay. The news was undoubtedly bad, but it was the 'all' in Rees's last sentence that concerned me after his pointed look at our cellmates earlier and I could tell Jay shared my worries. I said nothing, though. No need to get Stella, or especially Dave, worked up. Hopefully, we were wrong.

"Well," I said brightly, "there's no use dwelling on things we have no answers to, so let's just be glad Jay's fine."

"And continue with the story?" Dave asked hopefully.

"I believe it's Jay's turn."

"It's always my turn," he said with a heavy sigh, "but I shall do as milady demands."

I rolled my eyes as he picked up from where I'd left off.

Beau finally signaled them to stop, sometime after dawn. The sun was making a weak attempt to push through the continued cloud cover, but at least it had stopped raining. Rylia sunk to the ground, cradling her head, and he moved to kneel beside her. "Sorry we had to push so far," he said softly.

"I understand," she said.

"Let me see your head," he said and she pulled her hands away a touch reluctantly. He caught her right wrist. "What happened here?"

"Oh, it's just a cut."

"Just a cut? It's still bleeding and it's been hours, Ry," Jay said as he passed Beau some bandages.

"Just because I'm stoic and you're not, doesn't mean it's bad," she said.

"I whined about my ribs just the right amount, thank you very much," he retorted as Beau wrapped the teen's hand and returned his attention to her head.

She winced as he touched first one then the other tender spot.

"It doesn't seem to be bleeding. I think the blood here is from your hand," he reported. "I'm afraid we don't have anything cold for them, but," he rustled around in his bag, "drink this with some water and it should at least help with the headache."

She downed it gratefully before straightening a bit painfully. "Okay, let's keep going."

Beau pushed her right back down. "Take a couple minutes," he instructed. "There's no rush right now and we should let that potion settle."

"I could really use a nap," Jay said hopefully, widening his eyes innocently when the rest of them shot him dirty looks. He was saying it for her, though, knowing already that Ry never would.

Jessie passed out some jerky to munch on until Ry rubbed her forehead and stood again. "It's better. I can at least see straight, so let's put some more miles behind us."

Jay groaned. "Slave driver," he grumbled.

Ry poked him in the ribs. He yelped. "Get over it," she informed him and set off.

"You heard the girl," Beau said dryly and fell into step behind her.

"So, what happened out there? With all of it?" Jez asked a few minutes later as the first legitimate rays of sun peeked through the cloud cover.

Ry outlined her version of events, omitting the conversation with the good lieutenant at the end. She also gave Beau Mrs. Cornwall's letter, which he tucked away for later perusal. Jessie gave her a knowing look anyway. "Too bad McRuoes is on the other side."

"Too bad," Ry agreed mildly and left it at that.

About midday, their youngest companion was flagging again. "I think it's time for lunch and a rest," Jez said, trying to stifle a yawn and failing.

Jay nodded towards a large, flat rock formation that would be mostly dry. "How about there?"

"Perfect," Beau said. There were some small bushes and scrub brush, which would afford them protection as well as time to rest.

Jay scrambled up first, looking completely undignified, rolling as he got up. "Looks good," he said, turning and offering Ry a hand up. She managed the ascent a bit more gracefully, keeping her feet the entire way, shooting Jay a smirk. "It's only because I helped," he told her, before assisting the other three.

"Food or sleep first?" Beau asked.

"Sleep," Ry said as she found a comfortable patch of moss and curled up, using her bag as a pillow.

"Deal," he said. "One of us will wake you in a little bit. Your head's still worrying me."

"I'm fine," she said, yawning and closing her eyes. "Bean always said I had a hard head."

None of them bothered to argue with her. "Get some shuteye," Beau told the others. "We should leave before dark. I'll take first watch."

Jay and Jessie spread out and were asleep within minutes. Jez lay there, trying to do the same, since she knew she should, by all rights, be exhausted, but it eluded her. After a while, she heard Beau rise so she peeked open an eye and watched him make his way to the edge of the rock, taking a seat and dangling his feet over. After another minute or two of increasing frustration at herself, she rose and moved to join him.

"Can't sleep?" he asked.

"Guess not." She studied his profile. "What's wrong?"

"Who says anything is wrong?" he asked, attempting innocence.

"Your face. What is it?"

"I did a horrible job as leader yesterday. I led all of you right into an ambush, not to mention the fact I lost Ry and didn't even notice. Then, I had to let a sixteen-year-old save our asses while I sat by and did nothing."

"A very competent sixteen-year-old," Jez pointed out.

"I'm supposed to be your leader, your captain, the one who knows what he's doing. I was supposedly born to deal with this stuff."

Jez kept the frown off her face but filtered that information away for later thought. "We're all in this together, Beau. No one is born to deal with this. Maybe you were raised for it, but somehow I have to doubt you were practicing this precise scenario. You did your best and that's all we ask."

"And Ry got hurt for it! That's not okay."

"Of course not, but look at what we're up against, Beau. People are going to get hurt. People we care about. Not everyone will make it through to the end," she added, quieter.

He reached for her hand. "I should do better."

"No one blames you for what happened to Ry, or what happened to her and Jay the night before. Mick and the rest of the fighters won't either."

"You've got too many answers," he said lightly.

She could tell she hadn't fully convinced him, but his expression had lightened, so she considered it a success. "You have too many doubts."

"It's hard not to."

"Of course it is, but remember when we talked after I got injured? About letting people in?"

He nodded.

"You decided to let us in and let us take some of the responsibility and we agreed to that, maybe not out loud, but certainly in our minds. That means we don't expect you to swoop in and rescue us. Sometimes, we're the ones who will do the rescuing, like Ry last night. No one's foolproof, Beau, not even leaders."

He finally looked at her. "Do you realize how much responsibility we will have if we win?"

"When," she corrected.

"When we win. It's not even certain whether Prince Renier is still alive. None of the rumors can be confirmed by our people. Even Col, who is one of our best, is running up short of any real information. But have you ever thought about who will rule if we win?"

Jez let that start to sink in. "Gods' Breath, it would probably be us, wouldn't it?"

He smiled, just the slightest upward slant of his mouth. "Yeah, interesting thought, isn't it?" He stared off through the trees, temporarily unreachable.

"We'll just have to rise to the occasion."

"I can't be king."

Jez knocked her heel against the rock, wondering why he said it that way. "If Renier is dead as well, the Highcastle line will have ended," she said quietly but frowned. "There must be some distant relative that could do the job and we could just support them, like with King Sek."

Beau nodded. "There are distant cousins. Both Renier and Patrick were only children, so it would have to be Patrick's cousins or their children at this point." He looked at her briefly. "Would they have what it takes? What would be the alternative?"

She leaned over and kissed him on the cheek. "I love you, Beau, and we will win this, but you're worrying yourself a bit prematurely."

"It will go faster now that they've struck. You've seen how our numbers have swelled."

"We'll cross that bridge when we come to it," she said, firmly. "Go get some sleep, I'll take first watch."

"Are you sure?"

She smiled, trying to lighten the mood. "If you're this melancholy, you need sleep. I'm just counting on you to carry me when I fall asleep on my feet tonight."

Again with the bare smile. "Deal," he said, pushing himself to his feet and heading for his pack. She half-watched him as he spread out his bedroll and lay down. After a few minutes of fidgeting, he settled, obviously drifting off. Jez returned her gaze to the woods, keeping herself alert for any unnatural noises, although she suspected the likelihood of accurate pursuit was low between the rain and the false trail the horses created. She couldn't resist sneaking another glance at Beau. There had been an undercurrent in that conversation that she couldn't put her finger on. There was something he wasn't telling her. She had to wonder and hope that whatever it was, it wouldn't be or cause a problem. She wouldn't ask. He'd tell her when it was important.

Jez took a deep breath, letting herself relax as she exhaled. There would be plenty of time to deal with everything when they were safely back at Cavern Hall.

The sunset stretched across the view, lighting the vista with streaks of yellows, oranges, and reds. It turned the simple farmhouses surrounding the castle into beautiful strong buildings, although Sorin had to admit some of that was his imagination getting carried away. He thought perhaps he would feel better after unloading the whole truth on Ani, but it had mostly just brought up unwanted worries, hopes, and dreams. Maybe he could take a couple days off and slip away. Ani would cover his disappearance and…no, he could not let himself. He had made his bed the day he had returned to Alexandria and his siblings. He would not drag anyone else into this mess.

"Why are you out here?"

Sorin looked up at his brother only briefly before returning his gaze to the fields.

"Don't tell me you're still not talking to me," Vlad huffed in obvious annoyance.

"I like a sunset as much as the next person."

"Is something wrong?" At least Vlad still knew him well enough to figure it out after just a few words.

A ghost of a smile flickered across his face. "There's always something wrong, Vladimir."

"What is it?"

"Nothing that concerns you."

Vlad scowled. "If it will affect your work, it most-"

"*That's* what you're concerned with?" Sorin snapped, anger flaring. "Go away, brother."

The older man at least had the decency to wince. "That's not what I meant, Sorin," he said, softly. "You just…you've been more like the Sorin I remember from our childhood recently and I don't want to see you slide back down again."

Sorin worried at the stones with his toe. "I don't think I will." Then he finally looked up, meeting Vlad's gaze. "Promise me you'll be careful."

"Be careful?"

"Don't become Edward. Be better than he was."

"That's a little difficult, considering I've done so much worse than he ever did," Vlad said, sweeping his hand across the vista.

Sorin shook his head. "That's not what I mean. What we've done to Tira is something completely different than what Edward was and did. *Promise me.*"

"I want to apologize to Ani," Vlad said, gaze skipping away.

He studied his brother, but didn't push for the promise. He hadn't expected it anyway, and this was a step in the right direction. "Don't let me stop you."

"I want you to be there. I owe at least some of the apology to you, seeing as you were making sense and I wasn't." Which meant he also wanted him there to run interference if necessary. Very well, then, Sorin could certainly handle that.

"You do realize that your actions did nothing but perhaps increase the bond between Ani and Ren."

"Yes, I do now. I don't like to say it, but Ren is probably good for her."

"There is no probably. When do you plan on making your apology?"

Vlad shifted and sighed. "Now, I guess."

"Good idea." Sorin straightened, flexing his fingers. At least his knuckles had stopped bleeding.

"You would think so," his brother grumbled, but turned and headed for the prince's room.

Sorin trailed him through the hallway. Vlad hesitated only briefly as they reached Ren's door before knocking, obviously counting to five, and then entering. Sorin snorted, knowing full well why his brother knocked and not particularly worried about that himself.

"Ani?" Vlad said, as Sorin slipped in behind him, pulling the door shut. As much as he would enjoy his brother's groveling, the guards didn't need to as well.

Anica was perched on the edge of Ren's bed, facing Ren's chair, where he sat. As both looked up, Ren met Sorin's eyes. Immediately, Sorin knew Ani had told him. His heart seized, but he had to trust that, should the situation arise, Ren would do the right thing, so he merely inclined his head slightly.

"What?" Ani snapped.

Vladimir cringed. "I..." It seemed to finally sink in that he had to apologize to Ren as well.

Sorin smirked. It seemed there was *something* out there capable of amusing him tonight.

"Look, I know you're mad at me."

Ani raised her eyebrows, face impassive.

"I, uh, it's just that I-" he stumbled.

"Spit it out, Vladimir."

"Sorin, you're not helping."

"Yes, he is," Ani said quickly.

Vladimir stopped and looked between Sorin and Ani. "That...seems oddly familiar."

"Welcome back to our childhood," Sorin murmured.

They traded smiles, disagreements momentarily forgotten in the solidarity of their shared history. Vlad took a deep breath. "Ani, I'm sorry I overreacted. Ren, I'm sorry I threatened to kill you and-

He was interrupted as Ani let loose a burst of giggles. "I'm sorry," she managed. "Just…all things considered, that strikes me as kind of funny." She grinned at them. "I am so screwed up."

"No, you aren't," all three said, at the same time.

"Well, at least you boys all agree on something," she said cheerily, ignoring their looks of horror, as she slipped off the bed and plopped herself in Ren's lap.

The prince winced – she undoubtedly hit some bruises – but he still wrapped his arms around her, brightening substantially as she kissed him on the cheek.

"She's got you good," Sorin said, freshly amused.

He shrugged. "I accept this."

"Good," Ani said, leaning back into him.

There was another lull with Sorin surreptitiously checking Vlad's reaction, but he seemed okay this time.

"I really didn't mean it,"

"This time," Sorin murmured. Both Ren and Vlad shot him dark looks.

"I just-" Vlad powered on.

"Lose touch with solid ground every so often," Sorin supplied.

"Sorin," he said, sighing, "could you at least *try* to be helpful?"

"Only if you're being honest."

His brother made a face. "I really am sorry, to all of you. I was out of line. I got…angry and wasn't listening to reason," he finished, glancing at Sorin.

"A promise would be nice," he said, softly enough Ani and Ren weren't likely to hear.

"It's not like I can really be mad," Ren said dryly, "considering you were plotting my downfall and possibly my death for years. It's nothing new."

"It sounds so tragic when you put it that way."

"My poor tragic Renny," Ani said, reaching up to pat him on the head.

He swatted it away. "Don't you dare."

"Tragic Renny," she sang, smirking at him.

"Am I done now?" Vlad said loudly over Ani.

"He's not very good at apologies, is he?"

"Watch yourself, Renier," he shot back.

"No, no, now you have to be nice to him, since you led to the man being dubbed with yet another awful nickname by our sister."

"Poor Tragic Renny Muffin," Ani tried.

Ren just groaned. "Thank you both ever so much for this," he told the brothers.

"Our pleasure, truly," Sorin said.

"Are you going to move back to your room now?" Vlad asked briskly, sibling bonding obviously done for the day, as far as he was concerned.

"Maybe, haven't decided yet," she said, smiling cheerfully at him.

"In other words, be quiet and leave her to it and she might," Sorin said.

"I do not need your translations."

"Are you sure about that?"

Vlad shot him a nasty look. "I have work to do. I will see you all later."

Sorin smirked, waiting for Vlad to exit before turning to the pair in the chair. "I actually do need to talk to him about something. You two will be all right?"

Ani smiled. "Of course we will. See you later."

Ren nodded too.

He tossed them a salute and headed after his brother.

Chapter Twenty-one

OUR LITTLE WINDOW SHOWED IT HAD gotten dark while I had been talking, so I decided that leaving me thoughtful on that large rock was as good a place to stop as any. "I think that's enough for tonight," I said, stretching. Dinner had come during the storytelling, so, unless Rees was planning something bad, even for him, I figured we were safe for the evening. None of us appeared talkative as Stella settled back and Dave tucked in against her. I closed my eyes and let my mind wander as I'd found myself doing multiple times since we had been captured.

I thought about the cold, dark nights of winter in Lockholme, where my parents, brothers, and I would ensconce ourselves in the den - the kids having silent fights over who would get to be closest to the fire for the night. The losers would wrap themselves in blankets and furs. Sometimes, if it got too heated, my parents would intervene, banning us all a certain distance from the warmth.

I missed it.

I missed, however clichéd it sounded, the carefree days of my childhood, where the most important thing I worried about was what game Colin and I would play that day. Those days had literally disappeared with a bang almost exactly two years ago. While there was still hope that I could spend more nights like our childhood, my closest brother would never be able to. I ground my teeth. I would never understand why people had to create trouble when none otherwise existed. I would forever hate the Three for their invasion of Northwind and the slaughter at the castle. I had no direct confirmation that Colin was dead, but word was that very few had survived and no one of any rank or status.

Somewhere in the meanderings of my mind, I drifted off.

I must have been exhausted, because the next thing I heard was the rattle of our breakfast being pushed through the slot in the bottom of the door, startling me awake.

"Mornin', sleeping beauty," Jay said cheerfully as he reached past me to pull the tray further into the cell.

I made a vague attempt to smooth my hair, but it was filthy, so I suspected it didn't do much good. "You're looking fresh as a daisy yourself," I said, yawning.

He inclined his head. "Why thank you, kind lady."

"Okay, that's enough out of you both," Stella said dryly and served up the food. In the two weeks, we had progressed from one shared bowl, to each receiving our own. I'm not sure what that said about the impression we were making on the establishment.

The next couple minutes were silent as we scarfed our meager rations. Then, as I collected the dishes and slid the tray back out the door for pick up, Dave asked Jay a question about some story he must have told about his childhood when I hadn't been there. That led my friend to immediately launching into a related story, which, since it was Jay, actually meant *several* stories.

When I heard footsteps so soon after breakfast, my dread from the day before condensed in my stomach. Jay and I looked at each other as Stella hugged Dave close, pulling him away from the door at the same time. Stella was smart. I had no illusions that she hadn't picked up on the same worrying clues I had.

Dayton appeared at the bars with the largest shit-eating grin I had ever seen, the two brutes flanking him. "Colonel says it's time to get up and go."

"Why don't you tell someone who gives a damn?" Jay retorted.

"I don't find you at all amusing." Dayton attempted to sound lofty, but failed miserably. "On your feet, both of you."

"If you did, I'd be doing something wrong," Jay said, but of mutual accord, we stood as he opened the door. "I really don't want to see Rees's ugly mug again this soon."

"Oh, c'mon, I don't think he's that bad looking."

Jay shot me a look that could only be described as scandalized.

"If he weren't a sadistic bastard," I finished.

"Gods' Breath, Jez, don't scare me like that," he said, holding a hand to his heart even as the brute brothers grabbed us.

"My sincerest apologies, dear fellow," I said, as we were propelled down the hall. To no surprise, but my continued unease, we bypassed the usual room and made our way back towards the entrance, before turning into a new room. Dayton smirked as we went by and closed the door behind us, staying in the hall, obviously not invited to the upcoming party.

I turned my attention to the room, able to identify it almost immediately as Rees's office. Sparsely furnished, it contained only a neatly organized desk, two bookcases with a few maps and wanted posters on the wall. A quick scan revealed no Freedom Fighter faces among them. My gaze then darted to Rees, one of the three men present, as he leaned against the wall. He twitched, rubbing distractedly at his still healing wounds, refusing to meet my gaze. Jay nudged me as the man behind the desk cleared his throat, drawing my eyes, even though his never came up from the paper he was perusing. He lounged in Rees's chair like he owned the joint and it only took a heartbeat for me to realize that, in all the ways that mattered, he did.

"So?" Vladimir Opalin drawled, still not glancing up.

I only realized it was directed at the final man when he shifted from where he stood behind and to Opalin's left, and spoke. "Yes, they were both part of the five near Westcorner."

"McRuoes," I breathed, recognizing the young lieutenant in a heartbeat.

Opalin only then looked up, studying first Jay, then me, like we were a potential purchase. I was suddenly very glad Tira hadn't dealt in slaves for decades. "And the girl?"

"It's been a while, but I would say it was her. Hard to tell for certain, considering the circumstances."

I wasn't sure what he was referring to, but I glared anyway, even as my mind scrambled to piece it together.

"Well, well." Opalin leaned back in the chair, the very picture of ease, and steepled his fingers. "So you're Jasmine Lockholme. And here I'd never dreamed I'd have the pleasure of meeting you."

"The pleasure's all yours," I said, even as I turned my attention back to Jakium. "How do you know who I am?"

"Jasmine, dear," Opalin said, voice still silky smooth and brimming with smug satisfaction. "You aren't asking the questions here." I didn't miss Jakium's decidedly guilty squirm as he found the door behind us suddenly fascinating. Whatever his answer, I wouldn't like it.

"Call me dear again and you'll regret it," I growled at Opalin while staring daggers at the lieutenant.

"I like the answer, though, so I'll make an exception this once. Jakium was one of the men at what I'd assumed was your funeral. It wasn't his fault you somehow survived, though, so I hold him blameless."

My stomach twisted. "Oh, I'm so glad you do, because *I* don't," I spat.

Jakium winced and my brute tightened his grip, physically holding me back.

"Be a sport, my dear," Opalin said.

I was rigid with anger but, despite that, a shudder went clawing down my spine at his words.

"Careful, sir," Rees warned quietly.

Opalin raised both eyebrows, gaze raking my body again. "She looks harmless to me, Trigger."

"She...can be dangerous."

"Yes, so you said in your report. You let a *female* prisoner beat you up. It just reinforces the fact that my visit is a good idea to make sure things are going as they should."

"I think, sir, with all due respect, you would have faired the same."

Opalin's face darkened and he started to rise, but a light cough from McRuoes sent him right back down, very carefully schooling his expression. A bit of my anger faded at that. I was dealing with fire here and needed to be careful. I doubted that Opalin would hesitate to order me executed on the spot.

"I told you, sir, these two are the real deal."

"Hear that, Jez? I think good old Trigger just paid us a really nice compliment," Jay said.

It took me a second to have any idea who Jay was talking about before Rees' first name, as used by Opalin, actually settled in. In any other circumstances, I would have laughed. As it was... "My heart just stopped," I said dryly, unable to summon even false enthusiasm.

Opalin seemed to take Jay speaking as a good time to change the subject. "Ah, Mr. James-"

"Actually, James is my first name," my friend replied, "just, you know, to clear up any confusion."

"Then what is your last name?"

"Oh, no, I think we're all good enough friends here to stick to first names, don't you, Vladie? Trigger? Jaksie?"

The various reactions were almost amusing to watch. Opalin's face twisted as he very obviously fought a surge of fury. Rees winced and Jakium's eyebrows shot together as he met my eyes, looking more confused than anything.

"Very well, James," Opalin said after a significant moment. "How about we chat about your history?"

"Eh," Jay said, waving one hand at his side since his upper arms were tightly held, "nothing too interesting really."

"Unlike the colonel, I do not play games, James."

"Maybe, but you are a poet and didn't know it."

Again, Opalin had to take obvious time to recover his temper. My anger had fled entirely as I struggled not to snicker. Trust Jay to risk so much just to be clever. Opalin stood and made his way around the desk, leaning against it with his arms crossed. I mentally warned Jay to be careful, as he was now within easy striking range and I doubted Opalin'd hesitate with that either. "Let me tell you something, James, Jasmine," he said, voice calm but I could tell he was still simmering underneath. "I am not afraid of you or your little gang of so-called Freedom Fighters. We have been in charge for eighteen months and already, the country is at peace again. No brat of Patrick Highcastle will ever sit on Tira's throne, you can bet on it. So, how about you spare yourselves some pain and just tell us what we want to know?"

I stared at him, mind still processing the part about a child of the last king. Did that mean he knew? Or was Renier Highcastle still alive and being held? I kept my features neutral as I tried to figure out a way to get that information out of him without him realizing until it was too late.

"My turn to tell you something, Vladie. Even if we did know anything about the Freedom Fighters, we wouldn't tell you. Or Rees. Or even Jaksie. The truth of the matter is, you don't deserve to know. You are a bastard who has overstepped and you, and your siblings, will be brought down by people who actually give a damn about Tira and its people," Jay retorted.

"Plus, last we heard, you'd killed Prince Renier, King Patrick's *only* child, eighteen months ago," I said. "Is there something you're not telling us?"

"I don't think you understand the gravity of your situation," Opalin said flatly.

"Wait, wait, I know this one!" Jay said. "If we don't tell you all our secrets and fantasies, you will chop off our heads, right? Or do you go more for the whole short drop, sudden stop sort of methodology?"

"Honestly, you should just leave the interrogation to Rees," I told him. "Not that we've given him much either," I added with a smirk.

"I'll admit," Opalin now said, voice suddenly friendlier. As if the bastard thought that might work. I resisted rolling my eyes. "You two impress me," he continued. "You're right. For the length of time, the amount of information Rees has gotten out of you is limited. True, he has made his usual deductions, but you haven't given him facts to back them up."

"We're talented that way."

He ignored Jay. "Not only that, but you are not cowed by the last two weeks." His eyes darted to my bare skin, all of which contained scars in varying sizes. "This impresses me."

"You said that already."

"Shut up, Jay," Rees said.

Opalin leaned back, drawing our attention freshly. "I have an offer for either or both of you."

"No."

"I haven't given it yet."

"You don't need to. We're here because we believe in something and that is not you, so forgive us for not wanting to join you or not be killed or whatever it is you're about to offer in exchange for us spilling our souls."

"Spilling our souls sounds painful," Jay said. "I'm with her."

"You both think you're rather clever, don't you?"

"Clever is Jay's middle name," I said. "Me, I'm a little simpler."

"Do tell," he said, with an insufferable little smirk.

I stared back levelly.

He waved a hand. "It's no skin off my back if you don't, but it might be off yours."

"Oh, we're going for whips now? Kinky."

Jakium audibly choked and I had to purse my lips tightly to keep from bursting into laughter. Opalin shot a glare over his shoulder at the lieutenant before pushing off the table. "Being clever in this sort of situation can be very dangerous, James."

"Let's make this simple," I said, "since I like simple. We are not going to tell you anything."

"This is why I assume they're with the Freedom Fighters," Rees said. "If they didn't have something important to tell, they wouldn't be so insistent that they're not going to tell us anything. And no other group is big enough to be a threat."

"That's what you think," I said with a winning smile.

Opalin's eyes narrowed. "As I said, it's your choice to make this difficult if you want. So far, Rees has played nice on my orders, but once I walk out that door, the gloves are off. Your lives are the only ones at stake here."

"And that's where you go wrong," Jay said. "There is a hell of a lot more lives at stake here than just ours. Including yours."

"Are you threatening me?"

"Not directly, you idiot." He shrugged, once again drawing attention to the hold both brutes had on our upper arms – grips that had only tightened as the conversation progressed. "I'm unfortunately in no position to do such a thing. Are you really so dense you don't see the distinct possibility that someone will beat you? Deposing and killing the king is easy compared to what it will take for you to keep the throne. You've got the Freedom Fighters within your boundaries, growing larger and stronger every day, and that's not even mentioning Nerius and Alyia. Been having fun with our neighbors lately, Vladie?" He smirked as Opalin's expression twitched. "Thought not. The moral of the story is this: you are a despicable excuse for a ruler and I can't understand how your siblings like you."

In a split second, Opalin launched himself forward, planting his fist deep in Jay's gut. My friend doubled over as much as he could, wheezing for breath. I winced in sympathy.

Opalin grabbed Jay's chin, pulling it up so they were looking at each other. "You are damn lucky we want the information you have, or I would kill you this instant," he growled. "Never ever talk about my siblings."

"You always know the right thing to say to people, Jay," I said dryly. "No wonder you've never gotten married."

313

Jay let out a breathless laugh before disintegrating into heaving gulps of air again. "Yeah, me and my big mouth," he managed, starting to recover. "Did take him longer to explode than I was expecting, though."

"You really need to stop baiting people who have the ability to kick your ass."

"Point made, but it really is fun while it lasts."

"Shut up, both of you," Opalin snapped. "Now listen up. I will be leaving you in the colonel's capable hands. We will get what we need out of you before your precious Freedom Fighters make any moves."

I smiled. "Even if that were true, they'll still make their move and you'll still have to deal with it."

He shifted, running his thumb along the scar on my cheek.

I jerked my head back, trying to dislodge his hand, but the brute wasn't giving me much wiggle room.

"I assume that's from us."

"That and a million others," I said tightly.

He maintained contact, despite my best efforts, and I could see Rees behind him, watching it all through narrowed eyes. "It's a pity really," Opalin said, voice soft. "You would have been a beautiful young lady. As you are now," – he smirked, eyes cold – "I doubt you're worth much. I might be willing to make an excep-"

That's as far as he got until Jay, through some superhuman strength – or a mistake on his brute's part – broke free and slugged Opalin in the side of the head.

Opalin reeled back as everyone jerked into motion. Jay had time to get another good strike in before his brute grabbed him, took two quick steps, and slammed him into the wall. Jakium was around the table in a shot to steady Opalin while Rees caught me as my brute thrust me at him. I stumbled in to him, his grip tightening.

I cringed as both big men set into Jay, trying to shake Rees loose. "You don't want to get in the middle of that," he said as Jakium got Opalin back in the desk chair.

Jay fell to the ground and one of the brutes kicked him in the stomach.

"Let go of me," I yelled, jamming the heel of my foot down and grinding it into Rees's instep, a trick Ry had taught me.

314

He swore, grip loosening. I ducked out of his grasp and moved forward, not sure what I could do but determined to try. Jakium intercepted me. "Jasmine."

"Get out of my way, you, you vile maggot!" I hissed, cursing the fact my arms were still not fully mobile.

"I'm sorry, but I can't." I could almost hear the apology in his voice.

Jay yelped.

"You don't *understand*," I tried. "He's my best friend and they're hurting him because of *me*."

"Stop." Opalin's voice cut through the room and the brutes immediately backed off.

I pushed past Jakium, but Opalin had already made it back around the desk and blocked my path. "You get away from me," I snarled, but he grabbed my wrist in a vice grip. "Let go." I had to make sure that Jay was at least still alive. He hadn't moved yet.

"Well, well," he murmured, "this is interesting."

I kicked him in the shin as hard as I could.

He grunted and shook me. "Violence is not the answer."

"Oh, that's rich coming from you," I spat.

Opalin ignored me, which seemed to be his habit. "Colonel."

"Yes, sir?" Rees asked, moving to my side.

I tried to kick him too, but he sidestepped just out of reach.

"Perhaps interrogating them together might be an effective tactic. Just look at dear Jasmine."

"Fuck you," I snapped, wishing I had a better retort as I twisted to try and get free.

"Let's test it. Jasmine, the game is simple, which you should like. You give me a straight answer and James doesn't get hit."

I took a deep breath, trying to regain some sense of equilibrium. "I won't play your game. Let us go back to our cell."

"Just when it's getting fun? I don't think so. You were in an awfully big hurry to save James a minute ago."

"That was different." That had been directly my fault. This was bigger than Jay Dall and Jez Lockholme.

"So when I do this?" he nodded at the brutes, one of whom had hauled Jay upright. The second punched him. My friend grunted and all I could feel was relief that he was alive and conscious. That either made me a bad person or said a lot about the past two weeks. "You won't care?"

I favored him with my best 'you're an idiot' look. "Of *course* I'll care, although it's something you don't seem to understand. I will not answer your questions. I just hope you realize that given half a chance, I will kill you," I added flatly.

He smirked. "Empty threats get you nowhere, Jasmine."

"Yes, but they make me feel so warm and fuzzy inside," I said, suddenly sick and tired of the runaround and bullshit.

He reached forward and cupped my cheek, stroking it with his thumb.

I couldn't help my shudder, eyes blinking shut for a minute as the hairs on the back of my neck prickled. I stood rigid, waiting for him to stop.

"I love fear," he murmured so quietly I almost didn't hear him. "There is a certain…thrill to it, but you might not understand that."

I thought maybe I did. I certainly knew what fear felt like and it couldn't be too different on the other end. At least not for a man like Vladimir Opalin.

"Are you part of the Freedom Fighters?"

"If you're so sure we are, why do you keep asking?" I shot back.

Opalin heaved a heavy, and very fake, sigh, before lazily signaling the brutes. For the second time in a very short period, Jay had a fist buried in his stomach. This time, he promptly threw up breakfast all over the brute who hit him. I silently cheered.

"Are you with the Freedom Fighters?" he asked again.

I looked past him to Jay, who gave a slight nod, otherwise hidden in his attempts to regulate his breathing. "Yes," I told him.

Opalin blinked at me, jaw dropping, while Rees visibly started. "You are?" Opalin asked, plainly startled.

"And proud of it," I said. "Now can we go back to our cell?" I didn't feel particularly guilty for confirming what they had already strongly suspected. If anything, it raised the Freedom Fighters' threat level in their eyes, and potentially lulled them into thinking Jay and I might continue to be this malleable going forward. Or, at least, I hoped that was how it would work.

"Of course not," Opalin said, literally rubbing his hands together as his shock faded. "We're just getting started."

My gaze slipped past him to Jay, trying to apologize with my eyes. He got the message because he nodded again, wearily, but then someone spoke.

I had completely forgotten about Jakium's presence, which just showed how dulled my senses already were after just two weeks. "Sir?"

"What is it, Jakium?" he snapped, irritably. I filed the fact he called him Jakium, and not lieutenant, away for future thought.

"You told the duke you'd meet with him at noon, and from the sun's position," he gestured towards the large, unbarred windows - another thing I filed away, "it would appear to be that time. The eleven o'clock bells sounded a while ago."

Opalin stared at him like he'd lost his mind. It felt odd to agree with Opalin, but I found myself questioning the lieutenant's sanity too.

"You know Duke Wells doesn't take it well when he is not placated."

Opalin let out a growl. "We are finally getting somewhere," he said, almost petulantly.

"And Colonel Rees is perfectly capable of continuing this method of interrogation, sir. I'm sure he will report promptly should he discover anything of use."

"Of course, sir," Rees said.

"Very well," Opalin said. "Colonel, after my meeting with the duke, I will be reviewing the garrison. I expect you to be there."

"Yes, sir."

Opalin then reached up and briefly touched my scar. "We are not finished, Jasmine, you can count on it."

I shrugged. "Bring it on, Vladie."

He glared. "Come, Jakium," he said and swept out the door, ignoring Dayton who almost fell in, ear obviously pressed against the door trying to listen in.

Jakium pushed off the desk, pausing at me and leaning in to whisper. "Rylia and I are even."

I blinked, but before I could fully process that, he was gone.

There was only the sound of Jay's ragged breathing, as Rees regarded us thoughtfully and Dayton lurked in the doorway.

"I wonder how many of my other deductions are right," Rees said, "but that's enough for now. Dayton, escort them back to their cell."

My brute grabbed me again, pushing me towards the door. Jay and the other brute were ahead of us and I still hadn't gotten a good look at my friend. "Jay?" I asked and then squeaked as my brute twisted my tender shoulder.

"No talking," Dayton said smugly, but subsided and hurried to the front as I aimed a withering glare his way.

The walk back seemed to take forever, probably because I was anxious about Jay. From the back, he slumped, practically dragged along by his brute. Finally, we reached our cell. I heard a gasp from Stella as Jay was thrust in. My escort gave me a shove and I tripped over Jay, who had fallen to his knees. Stella caught me before I could hit the ground while Dave helped Jay stay upright.

"Sorry," I told Jay, patting Stella on the shoulder in thanks as I straightened. "Jay?" I asked.

My friend turned and slumped against the wall. "That was less than fun."

"You idiot," I scolded as I studied his face.

His cheek was already swelling and he had a rather classy black eye – and that was just what was immediately visible. He grinned at me, though, a slightly uncomfortable bloody expression.

I groaned. "I love you dearly, but you're still an idiot." I patted his knee. "Thank you."

He shrugged. "That man is a bastard. I couldn't let him just keep going like that. I had been saving up for my big twist to freedom and that seemed like the perfect time. The look on their faces when my fist connected with his skull..." He let out a happy sigh, grin widening. "It made it all worth it."

"You could have let him keep going. I can take care of myself."

"That wasn't all it was," Jay said, but we both knew it was most of it. "It was also revenge for the fist to the gut, which really hurts by the way. It was very uncouth to hit me there again."

"Because that's the first thing this crowd worries about," I said dryly, "being uncouth."

"Should be. And anyway, I recognized the look on your face. You were going to do something rash."

I laughed, a touch hysterically. "And punching *Vladimir Opalin* in the side of the head wasn't rash?"

"Of course not. I very carefully calculated the best place to hit him and the speed which my fist should be going when it connected to result in maximum injury. Obviously."

"Obviously," I repeated.

"Okay," Stella said carefully, as if afraid to interrupt us. "What happened in there? Did you just say Vladimir Opalin? As in, well, *Vladimir Opalin?*"

Dave, at her side, looked caught between excitement and terror.

"Yes, he came to visit," Jay said but glanced at me. "Jez, I'll be fine, I promise. I know it had to be tough in there, holding back so as not to make your arms worse, but it'll be worth it in the end, I promise."

"I hope you're right," I murmured, my sudden good mood evaporating as quickly as it had come. I had hated the Three before on principle and because it was the right thing to do, but that man defied words and human decency. Now my hatred and revulsion was personal, at least towards Opalin.

I let Jay explain as I allowed some of my despair come welling up. It was barely midday – I'd heard the noon bells as we were let back into our cell – and yet the day had already turned out terrible. Although I was unwilling to give up any large secrets just to see Jay not hurt – and knew he felt the same way – I still didn't want to see him injured. If Rees started interrogating us this way, we were bound to crack, even if it wasn't the way he wanted. I didn't like the sound of that, either.

I had lost control twice in my life and had no desire to do it again. I could only imagine, what I might do if pushed to the brink of endurance or, potentially, even sanity. I hoped news of our capture had gotten back to Beau and that there might still be a chance of getting out of here. I closed my eyes, picturing my friends, and sent up a silent prayer to whichever of the gods might be listening. As a general rule, us Tirans weren't a religious bunch, but I thought if there was ever a time to take the chance the old legends were real, now was it.

"You know, I think I hurt in places I didn't know existed."

I cracked open an eye to look at Jay. "Way to perpetrate a cliché."

He smirked, scooting carefully over to my side. "Why thank you, milady."

I had to smile, even if I hated the nickname. "You're a jerk."

"I might be, but I got you to smile."

319

I blinked. "I'm fine, honest."

"If you say so. No getting depressed, you hear? I'll be fine. It's just a few more bruises. Nothing I wouldn't have gained from a regular session with the illustrious colonel anyway."

"Somehow that doesn't make me feel better."

"Who said I was trying to get you to feel better?"

I punched him in the thigh. "As I said, you're a jerk."

He winked, settling in. "I know you are, but what am I?"

I made a conscious effort not to rise to his bait. "I feel so useless here, Jay," I said softly. "We should be out there helping."

"Well, if we hadn't somehow screwed up and got ourselves caught, we would be," he said dryly, but I knew his tone was aimed as much at himself.

"I still don't get that," I admitted. "I don't understand what we did wrong."

"Might've done nothing. Maybe they were just in the right place at the wrong time for us."

My face twisted, but I nodded. In all likelihood, we would never know why we got caught. "You do serious a lot better than you think you do," I said.

He favored me with one big solemn eye. "Of course I do. Everything else is just an act to cover how very sensitive I am. I do not take criticism well and therefore have created a shield to protect myself from the damaging outside world."

I snorted, although I was fairly certain more of that was true than he ever let on. "Uh huh, James."

"You've gotten used to calling me James far too quickly," he groused.

"It's just nice to have something to call you when I'm annoyed at you, that's all."

"When do I ever annoy you?" he gasped, putting a hand over his heart.

"Or when I need something to call you to get your attention," I said, letting a bit of my amusement show.

"Sadly, that's better," he said with a sigh. "Honestly, Jez, I cheer you up and this is what I get? Maybe I'll go flirt with Stella."

"As if you need an excuse."

"How about you pick up the story instead?" Dave said loudly. "That sounds like a much better plan to me."

I grinned. "I suppose I can do that and spare you. Where were we?"

"You were all sleeping on the big rock after escaping from Westcorner." That reminded me of Jakium's odd comment and wondered how many details Ry had left out.

"Ah yes, then let me continue."

◀ ▼ ▶

Finally, Jez shook herself and got to her feet, nudging Jay with her foot as she passed to wake the others.

True to form, he sat up complaining. "How come I get kicked?"

"I didn't hit your ribs, did I?" she said easily.

He stuck his tongue out but got to work unpacking some of their remaining supplies. She paused to watch, marveling at how quickly he'd fit in, considering how short a time he'd been with them. Something nagged at the back of her mind – a certain familiarity – but then he looked up. "Jezzy, darling, mind fetching me some bread from your pack?"

Annoyance overtook her attempts to divine why. "Do not call me Jezzy."

"Now you're sunk," Ry said. "He's going to call you that for the rest of your days because you said that."

"Damn straight!"

Jez groaned and snagged the requested bread. Within a few minutes, the five were settled in for the best meal they'd had in over a day, even if the bread was slightly stale. At least they'd picked up a few fresh supplies before making their escape.

None were anxious to stick around, so as soon as they were finished and Beau had checked Ry's injuries, they packed and slid off the rock without mishap – perhaps a first for them. They turned in the direction of Cavern Hall with Beau in the lead. Even with Ry's concussion, they made good time, heading almost due south. Being able to ride the horses so far along the northern road had put them closer to Cavern Hall but not by much. Instead of taking the hypotenuse of the triangle, like they had to get there, they were now traveling the second leg.

Beau pushed them past dark, picking their way carefully across the fields. When they hit the forest – the same sprawling one that contained Cavern Hall – he finally called a stop. This time, he insisted on taking first watch, to be followed by Jessie and Jay. Jez was far too exhausted to argue, curling up on her bedroll and falling fast asleep within minutes.

"We did well yesterday," Beau said, once they'd all gotten up. "If we move at the same clip, we should be home shortly after nightfall." He looked between them, since even Jay was being unusually quiet. "I think we're all ready to be home."

Ry nodded tiredly. "It's been a long week."

"Truer words," Jessie muttered. "Jay, how are your ribs?"

He brightened, although it seemed like an effort. "Why thank you for your concern! I'm glad someone is," he added, giving everyone else the stink eye.

Ry kicked him in the ankle.

"Ow!" He glared.

She smiled serenely and shouldered her pack.

"How are the ribs, Jay?" Jessie repeated.

"All right. Walking for a long time starts to aggravate them, as do most other movements," he said dryly.

"So, they pretty much hurt all the time."

"Yup."

"Surprised we haven't heard more whining," Jez said.

"I can do stoic when I want to."

"He doesn't want to be shown up by the teenager," Ry said. "Are we leaving now?"

"Yes." With that, Beau set off into the trees, the others trailing behind.

It was easy to tell they were all tired, because they remained quiet until after a brief stop for food around noon. Then, Jay's spirits seemed to pick up, because he began singing, driving Jessie mad.

"For the love of the gods, would you stop?" she moaned finally.

"Stop what?"

"Singing," said all four in concert.

"But I thought Jessie would love it, what with her undying love of..." He trailed off at the look on her face. "Her undying love of the arts," he finished.

Ry rolled her eyes. "Clever, really."

He gave a little bow, taking his eyes off the crude path and promptly tripping over some scrub brush. He let out a very undignified screech and windmilled his arms, trying valiantly to keep his balance. Jez calmly reached out, snagging his shirt and pulling him back upright.

"Ah, yes, well, thank you, Jez," he said, smoothing out his shirt and attempting to regain some dignity. "Much obliged."

Amused, she patted him on the shoulder and slipped by to join Beau in the lead. "So, feeling better after some sleep?" she asked quietly.

"I think you missed your calling. Persuading people around to your way of thinking seems to be a gift of yours."

"Well, look at it this way, I'll probably end up as an advisor to the future king or queen."

He frowned.

"Oh stop it. I realize you don't want to think about the possibility that we might need to rule, that the prince and the king might both be dead, but if, for some reason, we did have to rule, we could do it together. You'd have nothing to worry about."

Just then, Jay's voice rose above the others. "Just because that plant jumped out and bit me doesn't mean I'm not capable of...of something!"

Beau shot Jez an amused look and she shrugged. "Okay, count Jay out of that equation."

He chuckled, but sobered quickly. "I just...is what we're doing just as bad as the Three if I take the throne? I mean...what if they don't accept me either?" he trailed off, studying her closely. "Jez, I need to-"

"Jez, save me!" Jay yelped, racing forward and hiding behind her.

She broke eye contact with Beau. "What did you say to Jessie now?"

"It's not my fault! I said nothing."

"I sincerely doubt that."

"He would deserve everything he got," Jessie muttered.

Jay pointed an accusing finger. "You are evil, evil people."

"And so very clever," Ry said with a smirk.

323

"I change my mind, Jez. I think we can count Jay in."

"In for what?"

"A special, single-man assault on Oakbridge," Beau said, without a flicker of emotion.

Jay stared at him for a minute and then sputtered, glaring at all of them. "You're not supposed to *help* them."

"I thought it was rather funny."

"You think you're all so funny, but you're not," he whined.

"Why? Because you're the only one allowed to be ridiculous?"

"Obviously," he said haughtily. The young women giggled. "But it is obvious you prefer me not to speak, so I shall oblige and not utter another word."

"Ever?" Ry asked, skeptically.

"Never ever. Starting right now."

"Can I time you?"

He glared but pressed his lips together stubbornly.

"Should we be placing bets?" Beau asked.

"Two bets each," Jessie said, "one shorter and one longer, since there are only three of us."

Jay opened his mouth to protest but snapped it shut as Beau gave him a pointed look.

"I vote one minute from now."

He surprised them, though, by remaining quiet until their late arrival at Cavern Hall. They hadn't even had the heart to pick on him during their meals, since he was actually making an effort.

The man guarding the door let them in without comment even if he gave a long, lingering look at their muddy clothes, the blood on Ry, Jay's still obvious black eye, and their obvious exhaustion.

Somehow, though, word spread ahead of them because Mick was waiting just outside Beau's room. "What the hell happened?" he asked, following them inside.

"Lots," Beau said, letting out a happy sigh as he collapsed into his chair. "You need to look at Ry's hand and head."

Mich eyed Ry's clothing, still mud-encrusted, and the bruise on her cheek. "It also appears she lost a fight with a mud puddle, but that doesn't tell me much."

"I'm fine," Ry insisted, slumping into the other chair.

"Oh, and Jay's ribs. I don't think they're broken, but they still don't look particularly good. Could be wrong about the broken thing."

Mick took one glance at Jay's battered face and turned to the remaining two. "Who is going to explain to me what happened?"

"She will," they said at the same time, pointing at each other.

He rolled his eyes. "This shouldn't be difficult."

The other three had found places on the floor, groaning with relief to be off their feet and truly safe. "I need more chairs in this room," Beau said.

Mick groaned. "Fine." He rounded on Jay, the only one who had not spoken. "I nominate you, as the new member, to tell me, so speak."

Jay did look a bit cowed but just pressed his lips together tighter.

"What the hell is *your* problem?"

"He's not speaking right now. It's a matter of personal pride," Ry said, shooting him a smirk.

Jay preened.

"Oh for the love of the gods," Mick said, making a gesture towards the ceiling. "You want to hear a matter of personal pride? Jay sleeps naked despite the crowded conditions."

"He what?" the four said, with varying volumes and amusement.

"I most certainly do not!" Jay yelped, louder than any of them. "My roommates can speak in my defense."

"Good, you're talking. Now spill."

"Gods' Breath, I do not. I respect my roommates," he muttered, subsiding into a sulk. Or trying to.

Mick was having none of it. "That's true. But it served my purpose of getting you to speak again. So let us move on to what happened."

The others all commented after a moment of contemplation. "Ruthless."

"Cold."

"Low."

"Impressively evil."

"As the lowest ranking member here, he won the nomination. It was just a matter of the right leverage."

"That was mean," Jay opined. "I don't think I should tell you now."

"Need I remind you of your first morning here?"

He winced. "No."

"Then start talking."

He heaved a sigh. "Fine. I just want it noted that I outlasted all of their bets." At Mick's look, he hastily cleared his throat. "Right, one story, coming up."

As Jay started with their arrival in Westcorner, Mick moved over to examine Ry. By the time he finished explaining their escape, Ry had fallen asleep on the desk, Jessie and Jez were leaning on each other, dozing, and Mick had checked out Jay and then perched on Beau's desk.

Ani waited until the door shut, then turned to him. "Aww, Tragic Renny is part of the family!"

"Can we please drop the Tragic part?"

"But I like it!"

"It's horrible."

"Then you can't complain about Renny anymore."

He sighed, but she could see his amusement. "Fine. From you."

"Deal!" They shook on it, even as Ani giggled. "You know, I'm in no hurry to return to my room and the cooks are making two meals for your room," she wheedled.

"Are you hinting at something?"

"Maybe," she sang.

He rolled his eyes. "Of course you can stay the night. Do you honestly think I'd object?"

"Well, you do snore."

He nudged her. "For that, you can go back to your own room."

"Kidding! You don't snore, much."

He tickled her in the side. "Thought you might say that," he said, smugly.

She giggled and caught his hand. "Being smug fits you about as well as being sarcastic, Renny."

"I happen to be a fan of both, thank you very much," he said haughtily, trying to squirm his hand free, but she kept her grip tight, smirking.

"If you want to be either, you need to practice." She cocked her head, adopting a sly look. "You don't practice, do you? Because you're really terrible at it." Sometimes, it was just too easy to tease him.

His face twisted as if he couldn't believe they were having this conversation. "Of course I don't. Who would practice being sarcastic?"

"I still maintain that Sorin does. He's really quite good at it."

"I hadn't noticed."

"See," she said, patting him on the head with her free hand, "stick to the basics and you'll do fine. Or take lessons from Sorin. I bet he'd do it."

"Take sarcasm lessons from your brother?" he asked, incredulously. "I can't believe you just suggested that."

"Oh c'mon, Renny, nothing I say should surprise you anymore."

He relaxed, smiling wryly. "Point taken."

She studied his face, tracing a finger down his cheek, marveling once again that he was okay with her doing that. "Hey, Ren?"

He caught the somber edge to her words. "Yes?"

"We're going to end up married."

"I know."

"Is that...okay?"

He shifted, bringing one hand up to cup the back of her head, pressing a firm kiss to her lips. "There are a lot of things wrong with the world right now, but falling in love with you is not one of them." He let out a breath. "Is any of it the way I might have hoped? No. Are there a lot of things that happened that I wish hadn't? Of course. But I can't blame you for that, and if the world had traveled a different path, I never would have met you. So, maybe, in some strange way, things have happened for a reason."

Considering he had lost his father and a lot of other people he cared about because of her and her brothers, Ani knew how much he had to mean that. "Thank you," she said, snuggling against him.

He wrapped his arms around her. They both knew that, for their marriage to last, it would mean her brothers stayed in control, which would slowly destroy Ren. If the Freedom Fighters defeated them, she'd be lucky if she made it through alive. There certainly would be no happy ending.

The next morning – Ani had again won the argument over who got the couch – she was up before Ren. She slid off the couch and quietly padded over to the window, peeking down at the courtyard before looking out over the buildings of Oakbridge. She wanted to be with Ren and she knew that, even if she were to protest a wedding, it would happen anyway, but she couldn't help feeling she was doing him a disservice. He didn't deserve her baggage and he certainly didn't deserve a short marriage that would probably end with his wife dead. She put a hand on her belly. There would be no children, no future, no building off what they shared. Even if they wanted, even if there was still time for a child, she would not bring one into this situation. No matter how much she loved Ren and wanted that future for them, it would not happen.

She was distracted by the sound of Ren sitting up. "Morning," she said, forcing one of her carefree smiles.

"Morning. Did you sleep well?" His gaze was sharp and she was reminded that he missed little when it came to any of them, but especially her.

She shrugged. "Fine. Sleep…has always been inconsistent."

He snagged his crutches and made his way to her side. "Sometimes sleep is more trouble than it's worth," he agreed, looking out the window past her. "What were you thinking about?"

"What a beautiful morning it is," she said, which was only a partial lie. "This is a Happy Thoughts morning."

"Is it?" he asked, amused. "Like what?"

"Would wedding thoughts qualify?"

Both started, spinning – Ren with some difficulty – to the door where Sorin stood. It never ceased to amaze Ani how quietly Sorin could do things. "Wedding thoughts?" Ren echoed.

"Vladimir believes it is time to announce that Ren is still alive."

"And that I'm marrying Ani."

"Shortly thereafter, yes."

She had to admit the almost genius behind the whole plan, which was no doubt Sorin's idea. With Ren back in place as leader, publicly supporting her brothers and with spin on events to make it look like their assault on the castle years previous had all been a great and justifiable action, it would calm a lot of the public's restlessness and perhaps even make Alyia and Nerius think twice before pressing the border. Of course, Ren would be nothing more than a figurehead. She knew he was resigned to it but she also knew it would drive him mad. Captivity had already taken its toll. It was plain to Ani he found it hard to sit still and the actual scuff lines in the floor were a testament to that.

"I understand that your...well, this is still quite new and for that, I apologize, but the plan must go forward," Sorin said.

"Of course it does," she said. "Renny and I expected that. Right, Renny?"

"Right," he said dutifully. "Don't worry about it, Sorin. It could be a lot worse for me." Ani felt a flash of amusement. He was trying to be smug again. She calmly punched him in the side. "Ow! Damn it, ow, ribs!" He bounced away from her awkwardly and sagged into his chair, clutching his side like she'd taken a knife to it and twisted.

She smirked, able to see the same smirk on Sorin's face out of the corner of her eye. "You deserved that."

"Not in the ribs when they're busted," he whined. She stifled a giggle. "It was a compliment!" At her look, he retreated. "Kind of..."

"Trust me. If I had been aiming for your ribs, you would be in a lot more pain," she told him. "So stop whining."

"Yes, whining is most unbecoming."

"No one asked you," he shot at Sorin, whose smirk only grew.

Ani perched herself on the arm of the chair, secure in the knowledge he wouldn't push her off. "So. Wedding thoughts. How much do Tragic Renny and I get to plan?"

"Anica!" he grumbled.

She patted him on the head. "You're fine, Renny, now shush."

He sputtered indignantly and Sorin spoke right over him. "Why are you asking me that?"

"You're the one with experience," she said softly. Only then did Ren go silent.

He stared at her, expression almost indecipherable, except for the deeply lined sadness. After a minute, he shrugged. "We obviously did it all ourselves, as her parents didn't approve at first. If you want to plan it, feel free." He glanced at Ren. "I'm afraid the invite list is very specific and I refuse to invite your brother."

"I guess I'll accept that the family reunion will have to wait for another day."

Ani watched the pair. There was none of the rivalry and dislike that there was between Ren and Vlad. These were two men who, over the past years, had come to understand the other in very real ways. She looked between them – the two people she loved most in the world – and thought that Ren had to be wrong. This couldn't have happened for a reason, at least not a good one, because no matter what, she would lose one of them forever and all their odds were against her brother. She shook that thought out of her head. "Oh c'mon, Sunshine. You'll practically be family now."

He smiled slightly. "As amusing as the idea is, I still must insist. I should go get some work done. Vladimir went down to Greensward for the day and won't be back until later."

"What's in Greensward?" Ani asked.

"He wanted to speak to our pair of prisoners down there. The two that Rees insists are Freedom Fighters."

"May the Gods be with them," Ren murmured.

"Indeed," Sorin said. "I will speak to you both later." With that, he left, pulling the door shut behind him.

Neither moved until Ren finally broke the silence. "I guess that means we're engaged."

"And that makes you my Tragic Renny fiancé!" she said, pulling her gaze from the door to grin at him.

He stared. "I...suppose comments like that shouldn't surprise me anymore."

She leaned down and kissed his cheek. "No, they really shouldn't."

Chapter Twenty-two

Dave shushed me, nodding towards the door. "Visitor," he murmured, shifting towards Stella.

"Opalin?" Jay asked, a shadow crossing his face.

I peered out the door. "No. Rees."

"Alone?"

I nodded as Colonel Rees stalked up to the door, expression dark. "He's gone," he announced without preamble.

"Well, that just makes my day," Jay said dryly. "It'd make my week if you'd go away too."

"How are you feeling, James?"

"Oh, fine. Bruised, battered, and otherwise beaten up. Same old."

"Anything broken?"

"Like you'd care. You didn't when your goons broke Jez's arms."

"That was a mistake," he said stiffly. "I should have reacted quicker. I am in no mood to play your games. Is anything broken?"

I let out a sharp laugh. "Aren't in the mood? You're kidding, right? You had to have loved that. Got some of your all-knowing hunches confirmed."

Rees hesitated. "I...do not like it when others interfere with my investigations."

"Investigation?" I said incredulously. "Is that what you call it?"

"I-" he started but Jay cut him off.

"Bugger off, Rees," he said tiredly. "You've got your information for the day. Unless you're here to take one of us again, *we* are not in the mood. There is nothing broken."

The colonel hesitated again before walking away silently.

Jay and I exchanged glances. I wondered at the undertones in that conversation. Was Rees somehow not happy with his bosses even though he seemed to take great delight in torturing us? Was it Vladimir specifically? I wouldn't know unless I got the dubious pleasure of meeting the other siblings or unless Rees said something, which I strongly doubted.

"That was strange," Jay said finally.

"That's one word for it. Investigation, my ass," I grumbled, leaning back.

"I'm going to try and nap," he said. "We can continue when I wake up, if that's okay."

"A nap sounds good," I agreed, although I wasn't sure I could sleep – or that it would be restful, considering Vladimir Opalin's face seemed etched on the back of my eyelids.

Stella nodded her agreement and Dave snuggled against her, the two starting to talk quietly.

I settled back and closed my eyes, halfway to sleep before Jay spoke quietly. "Look at how much better your arms are."

I cracked open one eye and smiled, strangely reassured. "Thanks. I knew there was a reason I kept you around."

He snorted. "I love you too, Jasmine."

My full name still sounded foreign to me. I had been Jez for two years. Jasmine still seemed like someone else. Someone who had been too young and naïve to realize what the world could be like. I had certainly seen it all now: war and battle and both the best and worst that mankind had to offer. It made me wonder what might happen next. Hopefully helping rule Tira, which just about blew my mind. Talk about a long road. Somewhere in that, as was becoming the norm, I drifted off.

Stella shook me. "Someone's coming," she reported as I came sluggishly awake, whole body aching. Dave patted my shoulder and scooted back to Stella's side.

"Any ideas?" Jay asked, sounding as exhausted as I felt.

I peered out the door and my eyebrows shot up in surprise. "Jakium McRuoes."

"McRuoes?" he repeated as the young man came to a stop outside our cell. I was glad to notice he had eyes only for Jay and me.

"I need to get in contact with the Freedom Fighters," he said quickly, as if he might change his mind if he waited too long.

I stared at him, truly taken aback by his version of hello.

Jay let out an incredulous laugh. "What? Are you thinking about defecting?"

He looked honestly guilty at that question. "I can't."

"Of course you *can*, if you wanted. Your problem is that you won't. Which is fine. We don't want losers on our side anyway," Jay said.

"I *can't*," he repeated more firmly. "I saved you back there. I wouldn't be too hostile."

"Rees already told us that Opalin left. So good luck threatening us."

Jakium shifted nervously. "That's not what I meant."

"Then give us a hundred good reasons why we should even think about telling you how to contact the Freedom Fighters," I interrupted, before Jay could launch into him more.

"I need to post a letter."

We all stared at him. Jay spoke first. "There is a courier system for that, genius."

"I need to post a letter to your leader," he reiterated. He glanced down the corridor and then pulled a wrinkled envelope out of his breast pocket.

I caught a glimpse of the handwriting and craned to see it more clearly. It looked familiar. "Can I see that?"

His grip on it tightened before he carefully held it through the bars. I plucked it from his fingers and read the front. In handwriting achingly similar to Beau's, it read: Beau Highcastle, my brother. I could only stare, shocked to the core and unable to articulate it.

"Who wrote it?" Jay asked, not having seen it yet.

Jakium squirmed. "I can't tell you."

Jay snorted. "Then we can't tell you how to mail it."

"I need to mail it. Please. Ani will kill me if I…" he trailed off.

At that, even my head came up. "Ani? Anica Opalin? What does she have to do with this?"

He hesitated yet again, looking between us. "She didn't write it!"

So that's why Jakium's expression had flickered earlier when we had mentioned Renier Highcastle being dead.

"No, you're right." I passed the letter to Jay. "Prince Renier did."

"What?" Jay squawked, even as he automatically looked down. "He's dead."

"No, he's not and I think this proves it. Right, McRuoes?"

Jakium looked downright uncomfortable. "They kept him alive to marry Ani."

I let out a low whistle as the implications of that struck me. "That's scarily brilliant."

"Sorin's idea," Jakium said, with just a hint of pride.

I eyed him again, even more curious than before. Ry had eventually told Jessie and I about their conversation, maybe even flirting, while Jakium had been her prisoner. On principle, I didn't like him because he'd been at my planned execution, and yet I couldn't find it in me to hate him. She wasn't wrong. In a different world, she and Jakium might've been friends.

"Wait," Stella interrupted, speaking for the first time, having peered over Jay's shoulder at the letter. All eyes shot to her. "Are you saying you know that not only did the Highcastles had a second child, but his name and you didn't tell your superiors?" I wished she hadn't spoken, knowing that her showing detailed knowledge could be bad. At the same time, I had to agree with the question and it made me feel certain the chances were small Jakium would tell on her.

"I'm not going to betray Ani's trust," Jakium said stoutly. "If she doesn't want to tell her brothers, I'm not about to."

"How honorable of you."

"Look, I promised Ani I'd do everything I could to get this to Ren's brother" – I didn't miss the use of the nickname – "I didn't tell them about Beau or Rylia or that I knew before this that you two were with the Freedom Fighters. Just…give me a place for a drop or something! Write a sealed written note. I won't open it. Let me send this letter." He sounded desperate and I had to agree with him. I knew right then we would give him a way. Beau deserved to know his brother was alive and to read his words. Who knew, it might even prove critical to how he approached our eventual attack on Oakbridge.

"What does Anica have over you?" Jay asked, cocking an eyebrow.

He actually smiled. "Nothing, really. I guess you could say it's my horrible nickname, but mostly, I...owe her this."

"Jaksie?" Jay asked with no lack of glee.

"If I get this sent, she has agreed to stop."

I snorted. "Seems like overkill for the risk you're taking."

"Ani's worth it," he said stoutly, which seemed to be his default when it came to Anica Opalin. I had to wonder what caused the intense devotion.

"Fair enough," I replied, since it seemed we wouldn't get anything else out of him.

"You're really odd."

He shrugged. "It seems to come naturally to us. Now are you going to tell me or am I back at square one?"

I wanted to ask about that 'us' but refrained, not wanting to spook him. "Get me paper, a writing utensil, and a way to seal it and we have a deal."

He slipped his bag off his shoulder and pulled out the requested goods. "Will these do?"

"Perfectly." I took them and passed them to Jay. I knew that writing would still hurt. "Be honest," I murmured.

He nodded and scribbled down a quick note before holding it up for my perusal. Brief and to the point, it basically told our two Greensward contacts to get the letter to Beau post-haste and then move to the secondary location in case the primary one was now compromised. Then, he'd signed it for both of us, which would also let Beau know we were still alive. I had to wonder what he thought after we disappeared. I took it and passed it back to Jakium, who knelt down and sealed it. He offered it back. I tested the seal, found it firm, and returned it. "Now, listen up. I'm going to give you the directions you want, but if that is not sealed, they will kill you on sight and deal with the consequences later, got it?"

"Yes, ma'am," he said quickly, all but snapping to attention at my tone.

"Good." I sketched out the directions and had him repeat them. He made no move to record them, which gave me a bit of hope we were doing the right thing in trusting him. "If something happens and I found out our people have been harmed, I will figure out a way to make you pay for it, understand?"

"Yes, ma'am, fully," he said, tucking the two letters away. "I am in your debt."

"I guess we'll see if you can ever pay up," I said. "As far as I'm concerned, you're in my debt for the rest of your life."

Jakium cringed, eyes darting away. "Yes, ma'am," he murmured.

"Are you stationed here permanently?"

He nodded this time, looking a touch confused.

I didn't elaborate. "Remember what I said."

"I will." With that, he bowed slightly, gathered up his bag, and trotted down the hall.

"Why did you ask that?" Jay said as soon as he was out of hearing.

"He'll be able to recognize at least Ry and probably Jessie on sight. And they're coming soon." If they weren't here already, worried about our disappearance. Our friends were part of phase two of the Greensward plan. We were supposed to meet up with them, but of course couldn't.

"Oh. Oh. That could be bad."

"We're going to have to trust that, despite the side he picked, he means us no harm."

"You honestly think he wouldn't report their presence if he saw them?"

"I don't know *what* to think," I admitted. "It almost seems like he wants to switch sides, but something is stopping him."

"He's risking a lot withholding what information he has," Stella said. "I think you can trust him to at least complete this without telling. And other than that, I think your friends should hope they don't run into him."

"Our luck doesn't always tend to run that way," Jay admitted.

"Not a word out of his mouth was a lie, as far as I could tell. I wonder what his story is."

"We'll probably never know," my friend said.

"He had the facts to back him up," Stella put in. "They obviously don't know about Beau or Ry or they would have been asking already."

We nodded before he fixed her with a stern look. "You need to be more careful. The last thing you and Dave need is to draw their attention. Rees is already too aware of your presence." That worried me too and I wondered if we were playing into Rees's hand by making friends with our cellmates. The rest of our wing of the jail, at least, seemed fairly quiet.

"I'm sorry. It came out before I could stop it. I tried to phrase it like I didn't have additional information except from the conversation and common knowledge."

I replayed her comment in my head. "You might have been okay. Just, be careful," I said. The last thing *I* wanted was for Dave to be hurt on our account.

"I won't say a word," the boy told me, crossing his heart solemnly.

I reached over and ruffled his hair. "Good."

"But now they're gone so we could maybe get back to the story," he said with what he obviously considered a winning grin. It was getting better – Jay was obviously not a good influence on him.

I laughed. "Sure. We had just gotten back to Cavern Hall, right?"

"Yes, and Jay was telling Mick what happened."

I saluted. "Then onward!"

◀ ▼ ▶

Mick remained silent after Jay finished until Beau prompted him. "Well?"

"I had a bad feeling about the trip from the beginning."

"Would've been nice if he'd shared that," Jessie grumbled to Jez. She couldn't disagree. He'd only not wanted Beau to go, not for them to not go at all.

"We did get a new contact, though," Beau said, striving for the positive, as usual.

"We'll send someone out after this dies down to meet with Mrs. Cornwall and see what we can find out," Mick agreed. He glanced around at the trio on the floor, the asleep Ry, and Beau, who was slouched in his chair. "You should all get some sleep."

"How's Ry?"

"Fine enough. They're shallow, luckily. Her hand is a bit more severe but she missed doing any serious damage. Hands just heal slowly because of their heavy use. Jessica."

"Yes, sir?" she asked, stifling a yawn.

Mick looked amused, knowing he would never get a 'sir' out of them under less exhausted circumstances. "Can you carry Rylia or do you need help?"

"I probably can, but I've never tried."

Jay nudged Ry even as he stood. "I can get her."

"Even with your ribs?"

"Piggyback shouldn't put too much stress on them," he said, chivvying Ry onto his back. She did so while still half asleep, wrapping her arms loosely around his neck while he straightened. "Come along, Jessica. I'll need you to make sure she doesn't fall off or cause me further bodily harm."

Jessie snorted but stood. "I think this is a ploy to get me alone."

He winked. "The thought had crossed my mind."

She laughed. "Good, I would have been honestly worried about you if you hadn't."

"Now that just wouldn't do." The good-natured banter continued as the trio moved towards the sleeping rooms.

Jez kept her eyes closed as Mick spoke again. "What did Jay not tell me? His injuries do not add up with his story."

Now she opened her eyes, exchanging a brief look with Beau. "Nothing," they said simultaneously.

"Beau, don't you dare try and lie to me. Same goes for you, Jasmine."

She winced at her full name. "It's just…" she trailed off, looking to Beau for assistance.

"Ry told us her past. I'll tell you the whole thing at some point, but suffice to say it's bad. One of the worst I've heard because she was so damn young. And, that led to complications." Jay had omitted the part that painted Jez in a bad light, a fact for which she'd been grateful.

All Mick had to do was raise both eyebrows and stare them down. They squirmed like schoolchildren.

Beau quickly outlined the consequences of Ry's storytelling, including her and Jay's fight with the band of teenaged thugs and her insensitive comment the next morning and subsequent apology. Jez was glad to skip the telling. Mick's recriminating look was bad enough.

"Very well," he said when Beau finished. "You two both need to get some sleep. Beau, when you're functional again, come find me. We've had some news."

"I could…"

"No, sleep is more important. It can wait," he said firmly. Standing, he patted Beau on the shoulder, then exited, leaving the pair alone.

"I suppose he has a point," Beau said. "It's been a busy few days."

"That's putting it lightly."

"True. I…suppose you'll be following Jessie and Jay."

She snorted. "And interrupt their flirting? No thanks."

"You should just stay here," Beau said. She did often stay, especially if they worked late.

"I'm kind of awake now," she said, ready to leave if he wanted to sleep.

He shrugged. "All right. Just…suggesting."

She had to fight a grin at his earnestness, considering how many times they'd slept curled together on his bed. "There's no hurry for me to get back."

He bit his lip. "We don't need to, you know, do anything." He instantly went red, almost before he'd gotten the rather tame sentence out.

She tried not to laugh, pushing herself to her feet and settling in his lap. She cupped his face, then kissed him squarely on the lips. Startled, he still responded in good time. She pulled back after a minute. "You know, we haven't talked about it, but you're right. We really need to be content with kissing until this is over. The last thing I want is there to be an accident and…" She couldn't even mention the possibility of a child out loud.

"Sometimes I hate the idea of self-control."

"It's a good thing you have it in spades then. Maybe too much. I don't see you kissing me right now."

He laughed. "We shouldn't have this conversation now."

"Why not?"

"Because our conversations when we're exhausted *always* rapidly disintegrate and leave me embarrassed once I'm fully awake again."

She grinned. "Now you're being no fun. I'm suggesting kissing. That doesn't require conversation."

"No fun?" He mock-glared. "You could leave."

She kissed him again. "You don't mean that."

He wrinkled his nose. "No, I don't. It's always nice to have some private time, even if we should sleep."

A yawn interrupted Jez's protest and she smiled sheepishly. "That probably is a good idea."

He immediately wrapped his arms around her and escorted her over to his bed. He nudged her to settle down and then moved away as soon as she did.

"Where do you think you're going?" she demanded.

"Someone's cleaned. My blanket's on the other side of the room."

She watched him before stretching across the entire bed.

He scooped up the blanket, turned, and started laughing. "Where am I supposed to sleep?"

She pointed to the floor. "That looks comfortable."

He promptly threw the blanket over her face and sat on her stomach.

She started giggling. "Gerroff," she said, pushing the blanket off to grin up at him.

"Nope," he said, bouncing a little.

"Fine, fine." She wiggled out from under him. "Here, space to sleep."

He kicked off his boots then slid down beside her. "Goodnight."

She dropped the blanket on him. "Night."

Beau rolled his eyes and shook it out, draping it over them both. For a moment, they just lay there before she rolled onto her side and scooted so her back was pressed against him. This was their usual favorite way of cuddling. Instinctively, he shifted, fitting his body against hers and wrapping an arm around her waist.

"Much better," she murmured, closing her eyes.

"Good."

Within minutes, they were both fast asleep.

The next morning, Beau woke early, as usual. He lay without moving before he slowly began to untangle himself. His arm was underneath her, her arm was thrown across his chest, and he wasn't sure how their legs had ended up so tangled. He had almost extracted himself when Jez cracked an eye open to glare blurrily at him.

"Sleep," she muttered, rolling away.

"Go for it. I've got work to do."

"'m sure Mick has it under control."

"Not enough."

"Close enough," she corrected, grinning sleepily as she tugged him closer to kiss him. "I could think of reasons for you to stay."

He chuckled and finally slipped out from under the blanket. "You and me both, but we did agree that it's better if we don't."

She heaved a sigh, which turned into a yawn. "Was hoping you'd forget that."

"I forget nothing. My mind is a steel trap."

She rolled over and closed her eyes. "You suck."

"Yeah, yeah, go back to sleep. I'm going to get some work done."

"You work too much."

"I know, but that comes with the territory."

She sighed again and sat up, stretching. "Now I'm awake. Not fair. You owe me a nap."

"How does that work?"

"You're smart," she said sweetly. "You can figure it out."

He settled at his desk. "I'm glad you have such faith."

Before she could respond, Mick appeared in the doorway. "Knock, knock." He took in the room and raised his eyebrows. "Am I interrupting?" It was not the first time he'd come in on them just waking up, so the question really was more at the obvious light-hearted bickering.

"No."

"Other than Beau being stupid and waking me up," Jez said, sliding off the bed.

"Shame on you for waking a lady," Mick told Beau dryly, coming in.

"Hey now, she's the one who insisted on talking until she was too awake. Don't blame me."

"And how was last night?"

Jez looked up as she plopped herself across from Beau, snatching a paper. "Are you asking if there was anything inappropriate going on last night, Mick?"

"I would do no such thing," he said stiffly.

Beau grinned. "Don't tease him, Jez. Last night involved a tiny bit of banter and a lot of sleep."

"I was just curious if we should install a bell in the hall," Mick retorted, recovering.

Beau snorted, but Jez beat him to the response. "No, we've agreed it is in everyone's best interest if nothing happens until this ends. All they would have seen is us sleeping, which is not exactly a new thing."

"Felt I should ask," he said, smirking.

"Personally, I think you hope we do to give you and Beau some male bonding time."

"Yes, that's exactly it," Mick said, dodging a crumpled note she tossed casually over her shoulder as he moved to join them. "You caught me."

"See, even when I'm sleepy, I'm smart."

"You're always smart," Beau told her solemnly as they settled in.

A few days later, Jessie tracked Jez down in the kitchen with Jay and the rest of the kitchen staff. "Have you seen Ry today?"

"No, why?"

"I can't find her. She wasn't at the meeting earlier and in none of her usual hidey holes."

"I'm sure it's nothing serious. Maybe she just needed a little alone time. I wouldn't blame her," Jay piped up from where he was peeling potatoes.

Jessie's eyes dropped to the potato and she grinned. "Potato duty, Jay?"

He stuck his tongue out at her. "It is *not* a punishment. I like peeling potatoes. So not another word or I get an hour of free flirting."

"Free flirting?" Jez asked curiously.

"Yes. She is not allowed to cause me bodily harm for an entire hour of flirting if she instigates something."

"An hour seems steep for a little harmless potato teasing," Jessie said.

"Who says it's harmless? My pride can only take so much."

Jez rolled her eyes. "Do you think we should track Ry down?"

"Do you mind helping?" Jessie asked. "I am a little worried. She's been quiet since we got back."

"Not at all. Enjoy bonding with the potatoes, Jay."

"I am not bonding!"

Jez leaned forward and whispered loudly. "He was naming them right before you came in."

"I was not!" he said, throwing the current potato at her.

She easily dodged it, favoring him with a finger wiggling wave and followed Jessie out, both giggling.

The pair asked around without luck until they came upon Dunkin. "Hey, Dunk," Jez called.

Their friend paused in his work to look up and smile. "Hey. Fully recovered yet?"

"Just about. Jay still whines about his ribs when it suits him, but Mick assures us he's healing fine and there really shouldn't still be much pain."

Dunk chuckled. "No surprise there. How about Ry?"

"She's getting there. Mick says she'll have a nice scar on her hand."

"No surprise there either."

"Actually, Ry's why we're here, Dunk. You haven't seen her this morning, have you?" Jessie asked.

"As a matter of fact, I have. She headed outside a couple hours ago while I was on guard duty. Said she needed some fresh air."

"Thanks a million, Dunk," Jessie said, waving as they hurried towards the entrance.

After a brief conversation with the woman on duty, they left Cavern Hall and climbed up to the top of their home. As suspected, Ry sat there, staring off into the forest, seemingly not aware of their presence. The duo plopped on either side of her.

"So gloomy on such a gorgeous day. Real crime."

"What's wrong?" Jessie said, more bluntly.

"Should've guessed you two would come find me."

"Of course. That's what friends do, genius. So what's up?"

She shrugged. "I don't know. I know we're fighting for the right side, but…"

"But?"

"McRuoes was very human."

"And that's why this, at its heart, is stupid," Jez said.

"I just expected him to be meaner or downright evil. How can he support the Three?"

"Who knows. Life obviously threw him a different ball than it did us and he ended up there. Doesn't mean he's not a nice enough person in his personal life."

"But how can you separate them?"

"In war, you don't."

"So when we kill people…Gods' Breath, I hate this," Ry muttered. "I feel like, in other circumstances, we could have been friends. He isn't a whole lot older than me."

"In other circumstances, you probably could have been. There's no harm in that," Jessie said.

"At least he was good looking, so you-"

"Jez! Honestly!" Jessie said but was laughing.

"What? The mood needed some lightening, that's all. And he was cute, if I liked younger men."

"No, you like older men," Ry said dryly. "This must be what happens when she sleeps with Beau," she told Jessie.

Jez felt herself instantly flush. "It's – we - it's *just* sleeping. I swear!"

"What you do at night is none of our concern when you are not sleeping in the same room as us," Ry said with an innocent look.

Jez wrinkled her nose. "We both know that to do anything else would be idiotic."

"Making out does not produce babies."

Jez promptly ground her elbow into Ry's side, causing her to squeak even as she laughed and scooted closer to Jessie. "Not funny!"

"Yet ultimately true," Jessie said easily.

"Just because the two of you don't have anyone does not mean you need to try and dig every detail out of me."

"But it is fun."

"And you turn a gorgeous shade of red."

Jez groaned and flopped back onto the mossy rock.

Sorin didn't know his brother was back until Vlad started speaking, almost before he entered the room. "We need to announce that Ren's alive."

"Why now?" Sorin asked, leaning back in his chair. He'd said the same to Ren and Ani earlier, knowing this would be Vlad's next move. He just hadn't quite expected it to be the first words out of his mouth after the trip to Greensward. "And hello, how was your trip?"

He scowled. "Terrible. Rees seems to have respect," he spat the word, "for the prisoners, Jakium was acting strange, and the two prisoners are remarkably resilient. It didn't help that Rees still looks like shit."

The last part made no sense. "What happened to him?"

"The Lockholme girl."

"Care to elaborate?" Sorin asked, not in the mood to try to follow Vlad's thought processes, especially with them seemingly flitting in every direction.

"Rees was stingy on the details, but the first time they talked, she apparently went crazy. Busted them through a door and almost strangled Rees before Kilgor and Juke were able to pull her away."

Sorin's eyebrows shot up. As a whole, the research he'd found on the Lockholme family placed them as a mild-mannered bunch. "That's actually impressive. Are they Freedom Fighters?"

"Yes. That much we did confirm."

That was no surprise. Sorin would have bet just about anything on it. "And what did Rees have to say about his lack of progress?"

"He promises results soon. I'm willing to let him work. He's never failed us and we've still learned more from them than we have before this." He smiled, widely. "These are the first Freedom Fighters we've gotten."

"That we've confirmed," Sorin pointed out. He didn't mention that it had taken them multiple skirmishes, a full pitched battle, and eighteen months to capture two Freedom Fighters. And at the expense of the Greensward garrison. "Who knows where they are these days."

"He's not going to touch Jasmine for another couple days, due to an unfortunate incident involving dislocating her arms. He's afraid if he presses too hard, he'll push her past the point of usefulness, but he said he'd up the ante with James right away. I trust him to get results."

"All right. So why do we need to announce Ren's survival now?"

"Because you're right."

Sorin mentally filed that one away for future reference. "About what in particular?"

"I don't like to admit it, but the Freedom Fighters are becoming wider spread. Announcing Ren will kill their forward momentum. People will be less likely to rebel if they believe a Highcastle will be on the throne."

Sorin wasn't sure it would work like that. To him, it appeared that Beau Highcastle's motion would never end. They had waited too long to stem that tide. But he could play along. "Those are legitimate reasons."

"I think we should deal with the Lockholmes."

"What?" Sorin said, before he could think better of it.

"Their daughter is a traitor."

"They think their daughter is dead, just as we thought her dead. Because she's supposed to be dead," he said dryly.

"We don't know that."

"If they knew, we would have known. We have people in their household. As far as they know, they lost their two youngest children in a very short period of time. You should know, though, that their second youngest is named Colin. Colin, who was stationed in Northwind at the time of our invasion."

Vlad's gaze finally shot to his. "Colin is the name of the bastard who snuck Benton Walters out."

"Yes, quite the coincidence."

"Are you telling me that neither Lockholme is dead?"

Sorin nodded but also shrugged slightly.

"So Benton and this Lockholme are most likely part of the little Highcastle's merry band as well."

"It would stand to reason. It means that he has some strength and some important names behind him. People respect Denham Lockholme and they certainly loved Walters."

Vlad growled. "We never did find the Walters girl either, did we?"

"No and I would assume she has found her brother in the meantime."

His brother paced the room for a minute. "Do you think they have a chance, Sorin?" he asked abruptly, spinning to face him.

"There has always been a chance," he said mildly and then changed the subject. "We shouldn't reintroduce Ren while he's on crutches."

Vlad's expression darkened. "No one will notice."

Sorin cocked an eyebrow in barely polite skepticism.

"Not a word," he shot.

Sorin ignored him. "There are consequences to our actions, even if you prefer to ignore that fact. If you're insistent that this is the right time, that's fine. I'll do what I can to make sure it is a success, but Highcastle's Freedom Fighters are no longer just a small ripple. They are a significant wave and they will only get stronger, no matter what you say."

His brother stared at him, then spun on his heel and stalked from the room.

"Denial never did much for anyone," Sorin muttered and rubbed his forehead. He'd meant every word he said and many he had bitten back, unsure where Vlad lay when it came to sanity. The only way to stop the Freedom Fighter wave now was to defeat them in their own game or in pitched combat. For the time being, Beau Highcastle would not risk a frontal assault. His numbers were not large enough. At the same time, though, Sorin's own network of spies and informants were being out spied and out informed by Highcastle's. Whoever was in charge on his end was damn good and that would not change.

Chapter Twenty-three

I CAUGHT DAVE YAWNING OUT of the corner of my eye and paused, glancing at the window. Somehow, I wasn't too surprised to find it was night. It felt like today had lasted forever, considering Opalin's surprise visit and then Jakium's even *more* surprising, if less damaging, visit. I found myself yawning too.

"Seems like maybe it's time for sleep," Stella said wryly.

"I think you're right." I still tired easily, probably a side effect of my shoulders healing.

Jay roused himself, half-asleep in his corner. "It's past time."

"Go back to sleep, James."

His nose wrinkled but he didn't protest otherwise. "Already halfway there."

Dave needed no second urging, curling up next to Stella and appearing to instantly fall asleep.

Jay shifted and leaned against me. "Damn, but I'm sore."

"It'll be worse in the morning," I told him.

"Oh, why thank you, Jasmine, for being a ray of sunshine."

I smirked. "It's night out, Jay."

"I hate you."

"I know."

I thought he might have been developing a reply, but I fell asleep before he managed it.

"Wake up, Jasmine."

I blinked groggily, looking up in the direction of the voice. "Oh. Morning, Rees." I yawned, rubbing my eyes. After two weeks, my brain was definitely dulling. "What do you want?"

"Doctor's here and wants to see you. So get up."

"He couldn't have waited a couple hours until sane people were awake?" I asked grumpily, nudging Jay in the side.

"He comes here before he goes to his own practice," Rees informed me.

"How kind of him," I said as Jay sat up, yawning too.

"Up," he told me.

I dragged myself up, imagining that as crappy as I felt, Jay had to feel ten times worse.

"How are you feeling, Jay?"

"Shitty," he replied, sitting up with an involuntary grimace. "But I'm sure you knew that already, considering you witnessed yesterday."

Rees smiled thinly as he opened the door. "I thought you might be more excited, Jez," he told me.

"About what?"

"The doctor thinks you'll be able to start fully using your arms again."

"And this should excite me, why?"

"Because you can move again."

"And you can start kicking my ass again," I said.

He shot me a quick, sharp look. "We'll chat later, James."

"I can't wait," my friend said dryly, standing carefully as Rees locked the door behind me.

Rees fell into step beside me. I did my best to ignore him, but he studied my profile. "General Opalin will be back." I decided that didn't need a response. "So, what did you learn yesterday morning?"

That question caught me so off guard that I stopped dead. "What? What are you talking about?"

"You heard the question."

"Yes, but that doesn't mean it's processing. You are definitely crazier than I thought."

"Think about it rationally. Leave your emotions out of it."

I turned on him. "Did you happen to observe yesterday morning?" I said flatly. "It's a little hard to think about it rationally. Really, thinking about it just makes me want to castrate your boss."

"You're a smart girl, Jez, think about it." He started walking again and I automatically did as well.

"I learned that you're still condescending. *Smart girl.*" I rolled my eyes.

"Wording aside," he said impatiently.

"I learned there is more going on behind the scenes than I'd previously thought."

He frowned. "That wasn't quite what I was looking for."

"Really? Am I making deductions you don't appreciate? My bad." I examined him for a minute. "What's your deal anyway, Rees?"

"My deal?" he asked, almost carefully.

"Yeah, you seem to have no qualms about beating Jay and I up while you take pride in your so-called brilliant deductions. But then, as soon as your boss showed up and started trying to do it his way, you balked."

He glanced at me, as we turned the corner. "Don't be stupid, Jasmine."

"Stupid? Really? Are we resorting to childish names now? As I said, I'm just making some deductions of my own."

"And I have the right to ignore them, as you do for me."

I gave him a wide smile. "Glad to see you understand."

His face twisted but he stopped at a door and motioned me in. "We're here." I stepped inside. "Good morning, Doctor."

"Good morning, Colonel. Ma'am. It's good to see you up and about."

I smiled back. "Feels good to be up. Thank you."

"I have work to do. Kilgor is outside and will escort Jasmine to her cell when you're done," Rees said with a polite nod to the doctor and a significant look at me before he stepped outside and pulled the door shut.

"Please have a seat," the doc said, gesturing. "How are your arms feeling?"

"Still achy, but better."

"Motion?" He jotted down notes on paper, like I was a real patient.

I tried hard not to chuckle or roll my eyes. "I can move it in a full range but it hurts. I've tried to limit it as much as possible."

He set the paper down and stood, indicating my shoulders. "May I? Let me know when and if it hurts."

"Go for it," I told him and he stepped over, carefully prodding my shoulders before rotating them. They felt sore but no explosions of pain.

"It seems better. You're not screaming," he said lightly.

I had to like him, at least a little. He had nothing to do with me being there and he had a sense of humor. "Yeah, it's a definite plus."

He checked the cast on my left arm. "Good, it hasn't cracked. You seem to be a quick healer."

"It's a trait that's come in handy a couple of times," I agreed.

The doctor nodded. "You're looking a lot healthier than you did a week ago."

Had it already been a week? "Being immune to the good colonel does help with that."

He smiled faintly. "I've seen my fair share of the colonel's prisoners and your recovery time is still impressive. You were heading towards death last time I saw you."

"I've sported that half-dead look more than once," I said dryly. "What exactly broke?" I asked, tapping the cast.

"Your humerus. Bone between the elbow and the shoulder. It was a nasty break."

"How long until it heals?"

"Four to six weeks, I'd say. Six weeks is closer to normal, but you *do* seem to be a quick healer, so I'd go on the shorter side. I'll be by a couple times to check on you in the meantime."

"And how long until you give Rees the all clear?"

"A week, max. I'm sorry," he said quietly.

"Don't worry about it." I shook my head. "A week is plenty."

The man pursed his lips but stood. "I should probably get going."

"Thank you, sir. I'll see you at some point, then." I stood as well and offered my hand.

"It's good to shake with you," he said wryly. "Good luck."

"Thanks. We're trying hard to keep our sense of humor."

He smiled faintly, picking up his bag. "I'll see you in a week or so."

I nodded and he exited, briefly greeting Kilgor on the way out. I took a deep breath and moved to the door. Kilgor grabbed my shoulder and gave me a shove back towards the cell. I shot him a glare, but he just smirked and did it again. I ground my teeth but said nothing, speeding up so I was just out of easy reach until we got back to the cell. Dayton stood there to let me in, since they didn't seem to trust their own goons with keys. The short man also smirked at me and I stuck out a foot, tripping him as he stepped forward to shut the door behind me.

Jay snickered as Dayton shot me a nasty look. "Watch yourself, Jasmine."

I snorted. "Shut up, shorty. It's clear that you've got no power. Probably only a little more than we do."

He quivered with rage before slamming the door extra hard, locking it, and stalking off.

My cellmates laughed.

"Well played," Jay said, holding up his hand for a high five. "You seem in fine form this morning."

"My shoulders have gotten the okay. They didn't really hurt at all when I moved them. It'll be another few weeks for my arm."

"And how long for Rees?" Jay asked soberly.

"Another week or so."

Dave smiled widely at me. "That's great! Now let's get back to the story!"

Jay laughed as I raised an eyebrow at the boy. "He's been waiting very patiently for your return," he said as he offered me my portion of breakfast. "He wants to know what happens next but I told him I wouldn't continue until you were back."

"Go ahead while I eat then," I told him, settling back into my corner.

"Jay, wake up."

"Don't want to," he muttered.

"Even if Jessie's dancing naked in the hall?"

Jay bolted upright, suddenly much more awake, but maybe not for the reasons Dunkin would assume.

"I am *not*," Jessie yelled.

Dunkin grinned. "Okay, so maybe she's not naked."

"I'm not dancing either, you jerk."

Jay offered his hand for a high five, even as he yawned. "Wow, you got her to pout. Can you teach me?"

"It's a first," the other man said. "Get dressed and then come meet us in Beau's room." He paused, a sly twinkle in his eye. "Jessie, why don't you come keep Jay company while he changes?"

"Someone once mentioned Jay, sleeping, and nude all in the same sentence. As such, I'll pass."

Dunkin's grin widened.

"Why is Jessie standing outside our room anyway?"

"Why don't you ask her?"

Jay eyed him. "Jessie?" he tried.

"I hate you."

He paused, attempting to figure out what he'd done recently that might warrant that. Nothing sprang to mind. "As such," he said solemnly, "I shall have to drown in a pool of my own sorrow."

"Oh shut up. I don't hate you."

He glanced at Dunkin, who was silently cracking up. "I'm confused."

"I am outside your room," she bit out, "because there was enough debate over whether or not you would murder Dunk for waking you so early that I was worried for our friend's well-being. If I had known what he was planning, I would have gotten to him first."

"Fair enough," Jay said, tugging on a clean shirt. "It's good to know you are kind and caring and put others before yourself."

"I take it back. I *do* hate you."

He smirked as he pushed back the curtain and emerged, Dunkin a step behind him. "So why *are* you getting me up at an ungods-like hour of the morning?"

"Today is Ry's seventeen birthday," Jessie said. "It's not ungods-like."

"Is too," he said around another yawn, then offered a bright smile to Jessie. "So, now that you're stalking my room while I sleep, does that mean you're ready to profess your love?"

She stopped so quickly he almost bumped into her. "Dunkin?" she asked in a scarily even voice. "Continue on to Beau's room. Jay and I will catch up."

Dunkin clamped down on an obvious snicker. "Right," he said, winking at Jay and trotting off.

Jessie turned on him, shoving a finger into his chest. "James Dall," she growled, "I believe we had discussed cutting back on the over-the-top flirting."

He cringed at his name. "We have!"

"And I am *not* stalking you."

"I know!"

She glared.

"That was the only comment I made! The rest was all Dunkin," he said solemnly.

She crossed her arms and stared him down.

"What?" he whined. "Honest, Jessie, I've been really good recently!"

A smile escaped before she brought it back under control. "And what, exactly, is your definition of good?"

He thought about it. "Well, you haven't threatened to murder me in *days*, which is a vast improvement," he said cheerfully.

Now she broke down and laughed. "You are such a pain in the ass."

"But you love me anyway."

She smacked him in the shoulder but took the finger out of his ribs and headed down the hall.

He jogged a few steps to catch up. "How do you know I'm not being serious?"

"What do you mean?"

"How do you know I'm not serious about the flirting?"

She fell silent as they walked, then finally shrugged. "I didn't at first. I'm not sure you weren't, but there came a point when I could tell it was all in fun. I don't really mind."

"Mind?"

"That you don't mean it."

"If I thought you minded, I wouldn't do it," he told her seriously. "If I had been serious about the flirting, I would not be nearly so obnoxious."

"I find that hard to believe," she said lightly.

"It's not like I don't like you," he added. "You're a great friend and it's really nice having someone who knows." He grinned. "I think it's clear that I need a stern 'James Dall' to keep me grounded every so often."

"That I can do."

"Plus, you're the first person who has never smacked me for the flirting, repeatedly. You're a good sport, Jessica Rider."

"You have no idea, James Dall."

He slung his arm around her shoulder. "And hey! You never know. If we just let fate take its course..."

She snorted. "Let fate take its course? Is that what you call it?"

He grinned as they reached Beau's room.

"What took you two so long?" Dunk asked with a wicked grin.

"I think I liked you better when you didn't hang out with us," Jessie told him, shooting him a look.

He laughed.

"So what's the plan for Rylia's birthday?" Mick asked, glancing around. "Any ideas?"

"We've done most of the basic ones." Jez ticked them off on her fingers. "A surprise party, playing in the snow, pretending we've forgotten, and Bri even did that one-man play for Jessie's."

Jessie shot a glance at Jay as the others grinned in memory. He shrugged slightly and she nodded.

"Are the love birds sending signals across the room?" Dunk asked, leaning back in his chair smugly.

Unfortunately for him, he was within reach of Jay, who made a face and kicked the back leg of the chair, tipping it dangerously off-balance. Dunkin yelped as he hastily grabbed the desk to keep from tipping over. The others laughed. He finally regained his balance and shot Jay a look.

Jay grinned smugly. "That's what you get."

"That reminds me," Beau interrupted, before they could get into it. "Iris is working on a play and she wants all of you to perform it."

"Iris is doing it?" Jessie asked, making a face. "Why can't we write it again?"

"Apparently yours was too 'risqué' for our younger residents."

"Does that mean no outfit?" Jez asked, giving him a winning smile.

Jay perked up. "What outfit?"

Beau glowered at both of them. "I will never wear that outfit ever again."

A burst of laughter from the doorway caused them all to turn. Ry stood there, hands clapped over her mouth in an attempt to stifle her laughter.

"Ry!" Jessie exclaimed. "Um, hey, what's up?"

The younger girl rolled her eyes. "As if I didn't notice you both get up and leave. You were like a herd of horses." She then turned to their captain. "Bet you'd put it on if Jez asked you."

Beau blushed a fierce red. "I would not!"

"You sure?" Jez asked mildly. At his horrified look, she relented. "I wouldn't make you wear it." She then grinned mischievously. "But I might ask nicely."

"You all are horrible," he told them. "I will not!"

"So, what are you planning for my birthday?" Ry asked, bounding into the room.

"Nothing," Jessie said.

"Make you attend your lessons. Iris is expecting you," Mick said solemnly at the same time.

Ry made a face. "Not funny."

"Super-secret mission to defeat the Three single-handedly?"

"You tried that on Jay already, Beau," she said dryly.

"Then what do you want to do for the big day?" Jez asked.

"Doesn't have to be anything special," she said with a shrug. "We're all here and safe. That's enough for me."

"That reminds me!" Jez said and produced some paper. "Reminiscent of my first birthday here."

Ry accepted it nervously, but almost instantly grinned as she took it in, giving Jez a hug. "Thank you!"

"I can be considerate sometimes."

"A lot of the time," Ry corrected as Jay plucked the paper from her hands and examined it before squinting.

"Do I have horns and *fangs*?"

Jez's eyebrows snapped together and she frowned. "What?"

Jay handed it to her wordlessly.

"Well, I'll be damned," she said after a minute. "No pun intended. Jessica, you wouldn't have any idea how that happened, would you?"

Jessie did her utmost best to look innocent.

"Ouch," Mick murmured, amused.

Their friend finally shrugged. "I thought it needed a bit of…touching up."

Ry burst into laughter at the incredulous look Jay leveled at Jessie.

"From now on, though, we can leave it to fate," she finished quickly.

"No, no, now we're at war," he said with a wide, almost predatory grin.

"This should be interesting," Beau murmured to Jez and Mick.

The rest of the day passed quietly enough. Ry hung the picture in her room. It showed the whole group, including Bri, standing together, smiling, and in Jay's case, looking devilish for real. They gave her their other small presents after lunch and then went for a walk, Jay especially quiet.

"So, not going to get Jessie back today?" Ry finally asked out of curiosity.

He grinned. "Nah, too soon. Remember how Beau waited forever to get you back? I find revenge served just a little cold is the best kind."

"Properly devious of you."

"I'm good at devious when I want. Plus, I want this to be perfect."

"It really wasn't that bad, was it?"

"No, of course not. I'm actually impressed. Didn't realize she had it in her."

The new seventeen-year-old laughed. "Jessie manages a good one every once in a while."

"I heard that," Jessie said, giving them a look as she approached with Jez and Beau. "What are you two talking about?"

"Cake! It is cake time. And singing time!"

Ry grimaced. "Do you have to sing?"

All four of them grinned at her.

She sighed. "As long as Jay doesn't."

"Hey, now! I sing wonderfully," he protested.

The others exchanged glances. "Jessie will let you sing at her birthday," Jez told him.

"Really?"

"No!"

"Meaniehead," he muttered, glowering at her.

She made a face back.

Ren couldn't quite manage to wrap his mind around the fact that he was about to be officially alive again after almost two years. Mostly, because it had never quite sunk in that he wasn't alive in the first place. He paced his room, as best he could on his crutches. Other than Ani's typical in and out, his only other visitor had been Sorin, who just let himself in without even his usual cursory knock.

"Ren."

He looked up, startled. "Yes?" he asked, cautiously.

"Did you ever meet Ani and Vladimir's father?"

Ren didn't miss the name choice. "Edward, right? He started the family business, before Vladimir took it over."

"Yes."

"I believe so. When I was still fairly young. Father introduced me and then warned him to keep my distance, that he was dangerous. I avoided him. Then one day, Vladimir and Ani came, and eventually you. But my father never warned me away from all of you the same way he did Edward."

Sorin sat in thoughtful silence for a couple heartbeats. "Dangerous fits. He could be very dangerous indeed. Many mourned his passing for just that reason." He looked up, meeting Ren's eyes, quiet intensity burning in them. "Remember that," he said with a brief nod, then he turned and vanished out the door.

Ren couldn't quite figure out the purpose of that short conversation, even pondering it for almost a day before Ani bounded into his room. "Renny, darling Muffin!" she sang.

"Yes?"

"Are you ready to face the great big world?"

"You mean a rather small percentage of Oakbridge's population?" he asked dryly.

"Yes, obviously, but it's now, you know that, right?"

He blinked, startled. "What?"

"They've already gathered, knowing there will be an announcement, just, no one knows what for."

"Kind of your brothers to give me a heads-up," he grumbled.

"When Vlad says soon, he means soon," she said cheerfully and passed him his crutches. "Let's go, Muffin."

"Ani," he sighed, pushing himself up and getting the crutches settled.

"No, I will never stop calling you that," she informed him, falling into step and motioning him out his door – for only the second time – before following him out. They found Sorin and Vlad waiting in a small anteroom off the balcony where his father had always made his announcements. Ren's stomach clenched. Vladimir ignored him but Sorin looked up from their conversation to nod.

As it broke up, Sorin stepped over and clasped his shoulder. "Do what you need to do," he murmured so quietly that Ren wasn't sure he heard him correctly. Then he was past, pulling Ani aside to speak quietly to her.

Vlad was suddenly standing in front of him. "Remember, you're not here to talk. Smile and wave. Look healthy."

Ren barely resisted the urge to snap off a quick retort. Ani had passed those directions on to him already. "I understand."

"Good." With that, Vladimir turned and stepped out onto the balcony. Ren heard the slow hushing of the crowd gathered outside as he moved to the door where one of their lackeys stopped him.

"Vladimir wanted to say a few words first," Sorin said, suddenly at his shoulder again, but with the lackey right there, Ren didn't dare ask about his earlier comment or the conversation about Edward.

Using a speaking horn, Vlad could project his voice far enough that the crowd could hear. His speech was uninspired at best and Ren couldn't help but think Sorin would do better, or Ani. "Today, we have a surprise for you," he said, as if it weren't obvious. "I realize it will be a shock, but please, try not to faint." That got a weak chuckle from the crowd. "I apologize for keeping this a secret for so long, but we had to be sure that we could protect him from those that wish him harm."

"Like you," Ren muttered.

Sorin shot him a look but said nothing.

The crowd murmured, all eyes riveted on Vladimir.

"Sir," Vlad said, all respectful. Ren wanted to gag. "Could you come here please?"

For an instant, he debated ignoring him. Sorin didn't move either, standing almost in solidarity beside him.

"Sir," Vlad repeated, a bit more strongly, shooting him a stern look, something lurking just beneath his almost jovial exterior.

Ren hiked forward on his crutches until he could see the crowd. For a moment, there was complete silence.

"Look!" someone yelled. "It's Prince Renier."

A wild cheer went up, followed by dozens of hats.

Ren felt himself smile, despite everything, and he lifted his hand in a wave, which only made them roar louder. He could feel Vlad glaring at his back, but he ignored him.

"Prince Renier," Sorin said after a minute.

His name and title together startled him so much, he glanced back.

"Now would be a good time to announce your wedding."

"What?" he managed, feeling abruptly like Ren the Prisoner again, constantly on his heels, trying to navigate this set of siblings. He didn't feel quite so surprised when he realized Ani and Vlad were both staring at their brother with shock too.

"He's not supposed to speak," Vlad hissed, suddenly furious.

"I highly doubt that Ren would do something so foolish as to call himself a captive."

"I could do an announcement.," Ren said slowly.

"I don't like it. It's an unnecessary risk."

"Ren could tell that crowd anything right now. Absolutely *anything* and they'd approve. They've got their Highcastle again, at your insistence," Sorin said flatly.

The brothers stared at each other, a silent test of wills that had Ren instantly on edge. Ani felt it too, scooting over to him and sneaking her hand into his. He glanced at her, but her gaze was fixed on her siblings, eyes wider than usual, so he squeezed her hand.

The crowd began chanting his name and Ren could tell from the volume that the news was spreading, the crowd swelling. "We need a decision," he said quietly, but it broke the spell.

"Fine," Vlad growled and thrust the speaking horn into Ren's hand. "Do it then."

Ren's gaze darted to Sorin, who smiled faintly and nodded. He squeezed Ani's hand again and turned with her to face the crowd. "Citizens of Tira! People of Oakbridge!" he yelled, voice carrying easily.

The instant the people below heard him, a hush crept through the crowd, every last one of them staring up at the pair. "I am proud and humbled by your response to my survival. I am so glad to be here and to say I have missed you would be an understatement." He felt Vlad's gaze. "But what's done is done and it had to be done," he said, figuring the lie wasn't too bad. "Now it is time for all of us to move forward and that's why I wish to make an announcement. A happy announcement, one that is reason for joy in all of Tira." A fresh smile blossomed. This, he could do. He lifted their linked hands. "Ani Opalin and I would like to announce our engagement and upcoming wedding. We will let everyone know the dates as we choose them." He hesitated, out of words, not sure he needed more anyway.

Ani tightened her hold on his hand. "What's that?" she whispered suddenly.

His gaze darted back to the crowd.

"Long live the king and queen!" The sound slowly began to swell as more and more of the crowd took up the cry. Ren's eyes went wide as it suddenly clicked. He was King of Tira...not the prince. He hadn't really been the prince in two years. That hadn't hit him until now and he felt like he'd been punched in the stomach. The smile vanished as quickly as it had appeared and the hand holding the speaking horn dropped too.

"Ren?" Ani asked, concerned.

He shook his head. "I...I can't..." he managed before turning away and pulling his hand from Ani's, head spinning uncomfortably as he started walking.

"He can't just...!" Vlad started but Sorin shook his head.

"Let him go. Calip, keep an eye on him but don't disturb him unless he tries to get out."

"Yes, sir!" Calip replied before hurrying off.

Vladimir spun on Sorin angrily. "What do you think you're doing? He can't just walk off like that!"

"Leave him alone, Vlad," Ani spoke up, her voice angry too. "Just because you don't understand personal pain doesn't mean you can't be sympathetic to it!" she snapped before turning and stomping away.

"Have fun with crowd control," Sorin added, smirking a bit although Vlad could tell it was more reflex than anything, as the younger brother also turned and left.

Chapter Twenty-four

"Quiet," Dave suddenly said, interrupting me.

"What is it?" Jay asked.

"Footsteps," he murmured and scooted into Stella's side.

I peeked out and was somewhat surprised to see Rees stalking down the corridor. "Rees."

"So soon? I was really hoping to avoid seeing his ugly mug twice today. Plus, I still hurt pretty much everywhere."

I shrugged, smiling that I didn't have to curb the motion. "I don't know, maybe that's part of his plan."

Rees came to a stop outside the door, looking us all over. His gaze came to a stop on Jay. "You remind me of someone," he said after a minute or two of silent but intent study.

"Oh, that's all? And here I was thinking I had something in my teeth," Jay told him.

"Cute," he said absently but continued to stare, tilting his head back and forth.

"What? Do you want a strip show?"

I couldn't help it and burst out laughing.

Even Rees cracked a smile, the intensity dying. "Truly cute for once, James."

Jay sketched a bow while still sitting, smirking. "Glad I can be of service. So, who do I remind you of?" he asked easily.

"I'm sure you two have never met. He has a similar tendency to be random and ridiculous."

"That's it? That's not much to base something like that off of, Rees. I thought you were going to say he was my handsome spitting image."

"If that were true, he would have gotten all the good looks."

Jay cocked an eyebrow. "Ouch. Playing along for once, Colonel?"

"Getting tired of it," he shot back.

"Didn't think you were that quick on your feet," I said, unable to resist.

"It's a learned skill," he said before taking another minute to study my friend. "You and I will be visiting tomorrow, James. Jasmine, enjoy your vacation while it lasts. General Opalin is getting restless for results."

"Bully for him," Jay said. "Now, if you don't mind, Jez and I were just practicing our tango."

"Your what?" he repeated, startled.

I managed to keep a straight face, nodding solemnly.

"Tango. You know, the dance?"

"Are you planning on attending a ball soon?"

"No, but you can never let your skills go rusty," he said. "It's a damn crime if you do."

"Are you any good?"

"I'm all right. Jez is better, though. Comes from being a noble and all that. I'm just a lowly peasant." He slapped a hand over his heart as if wounded.

"With a big mouth," Rees said dryly. "As much as I'm sure you enjoy the attention, James, I need to go. I do have other commitments to maintain."

"You mean we're not your entire life?" I said with a mournful sigh. "What a shame."

"Your sarcasm is cutting, Jasmine."

I smirked. "I know, Trigger."

He once again could not stop the slight wince at his first name. "I will see you tomorrow," he said flatly, spinning on his heel and disappearing.

Jay and I exchanged a high five in triumph.

"What was that about a strip tease, Jay?" Stella asked.

To my never-ending amusement, my friend went bright red, quite possibly the most vibrant shade I'd ever seen on him.

She smirked and messed up his hair. "You're quite cute red, Jay."

"Thanks," he muttered, flattening his hair.

Dave rolled his eyes and spoke up. "Did Jessie really do that to Ry's present?"

"Yeah, apparently something I'd said earlier in the week had gotten to her and she added it while she was still annoyed. She admitted later that she'd completely forgotten about it until I noticed," Jay said, slowly regaining his proper color.

"So, what was your revenge?" he asked.

"We'll get to it," Jay said cheerfully. "I'll pick it up." With a brief thought, he did just that.

◀ ▼ ▶

A few days later, the play came up again at dinner. "So, how's Iris' production coming?" Jessie asked Beau. "Is it any good?"

"I read her first draft last night. It's all right. It's trying to be serious but sort of hovers near funny without making it."

"Why did she decide we needed another one?" Jez asked.

"She told me she expected you three would get bored and start on one soon. She thought the last one was bad enough without adding Jay's lovely influence."

"My influence *is* lovely," he protested. "I would have kept them in line."

"If you say so, Jay," Ry said with a snort.

"I suppose we can play along, as long as it isn't sappy."

"No, definitely not sappy."

Jay looked thoughtful. "Can we have editing rights?"

Jessie punched him in the shoulder, laughing, but Beau nodded. "I think that's a reasonable request, actually, but no writing in the outfit."

Jez pulled a face. "Beau," she whined.

Mick smirked. "C'mon, you three, let's leave the love birds to their discussion."

The pair sent him dark looks while the others laughed.

His smirk merely widened as he shooed the three away.

Just after they'd left, Beau turned to her. "I'm not wearing it," he said firmly.

She grinned, patting him on the cheek. "I wasn't going to make you, don't worry."

He breathed a sigh of relief. "Oh, thank goodness!"

She laughed. "You don't hate it *that* much."

"You have no idea how much I hate that thing," he said dryly. "If I could figure out where you guys hid it, I'd burn it."

"Then you're never finding out," she told him. "I'm still holding out hope I can get you into it at least once more before it's retired. I didn't get to fully appreciate it, and you, last time," she said with wide eyes.

"I am not falling for that. Bri's innocent look has no power over me."

She giggled. "So you say. I'm not giving up hope either way."

He sighed. "Make Jay wear it. He wouldn't mind."

"That," she said, kissing him on the cheek, "is exactly why we won't."

"Then I guess it won't ever be worn again."

"As much as I would like to continue this conversation, I have hand-to-hand training with Reardon," Jez told him.

"Oh! Let me know how that goes. He's been lobbying me for that for a while."

"It seems like a good idea to me, so I will." She stood but he caught her hand, standing too and bringing a hand up to her cheek, kissing her firmly.

"There," he said. "You can go."

She grinned. "Why thank you, fearless leader, for the permission."

It took some time for Jay to figure out an appropriate revenge for Jessie and by then, to his satisfaction, she had relaxed, seeming to think because it wasn't instantaneous that it wasn't coming. He didn't form the perfect plan until he watched a couple of the others in the kitchen carving off ice shavings from the blocks they carted in to try and keep foods cool. It only worked as well as it did because the caves were naturally on the cooler side. It took a little doing but he managed to sweet talk and barter his way into a small bucket of the shavings early one morning. He pushed aside the curtain to the room Jessie, Ry, Jez, and another young woman shared. "Oh, Jessica!" he cried, noting Jez's absence with some amusement. "Wakey, wakey!"

Jessie rolled onto her back and blinked blurrily up at him. "What are you doing in here? And why are you so cheerful?" she muttered, still half asleep.

"It snowed last night," he said solemnly.

She squinted. "Jay, it's not even September. We're not that far north. Come back again in three months." With that, she rolled back on her side, closing her eyes.

"You're ruining it," he told her. Ry sat up now, looking curious.

"Ruining what?" she asked patiently, rolling onto her back but only cracking open one eye.

"My revenge," he said, calmly dumping the bucket of ice shavings on her.

It took his comment, and the cold, a moment to seep in, then she rocketed to her feet, wide-awake.

Ry burst out laughing, followed by their final roommate, Ann.

"Cold, cold, *cold*," Jessie breathed as she danced around, trying to brush it all off. After most of the slushy, cold water was on the ground, she paused to punch him hard in the shoulder.

"Ow, Jessie!" he whined.

She glared at him. "That revenge was way out of line."

"I don't see how," he whined, rubbing his shoulder. "You're already pretty much dry and your bedroll will dry by tonight. You, on the other hand, permanently defaced an otherwise lovely picture."

She finally let out a laugh, punching him again but not nearly as hard. "Gods' Breath, Jay."

"I think of everything, don't I? Look at me making it snow in August!"

"That's one way to look at it," she grumbled, scooping up her bedroll and shaking it out.

"The only way," he corrected.

She sighed. "You're a pain in my ass."

"Yes, but now that we're all up, we can go play!"

"I hate you," Jessie muttered. "Go see if Jez is up while we get dressed."

"Yes, ma'am!" he said cheerfully and bounded off, content in the knowledge his revenge had been perfect.

They spent the day enjoying the nice weather, even managing to drag Beau out for a while. As the afternoon lengthened, they headed back inside and were gathered in Beau's office doing a bit of work when Mick appeared, dropping a pile of parchment on the captain's desk.

"What's this?" Beau asked.

"Iris's final copy of the play. She made me promise I'd look it over after the edits. She seems to think I'll make sure it remains appropriate. I, on the other hand, am not sure I'd fit it to her standards."

"You probably would. Iris can be quite fierce, after all," Ry said, amused. "I should know."

"How? It's not like you ever attend her classes," Jessie teased.

"I'm almost free!"

"If by 'almost', you mean over eleven months, then yes, absolutely."

Ry stuck her tongue out at her best friend.

Jay flipped through the copy thoughtfully. "Let me rework it."

Beau eyed him. "Then Mick will definitely have to edit it."

"If that's what you think, I'll make you a deal," Jay said, looking hurt.

"A deal?"

"Yeah. I rewrite this on different paper with my edits. Then everyone else here and Dunk get to read it. If they don't change anything of substance, and Dunk won't know about the deal, then you have to cook me dinner."

"Cook you dinner?"

"Yes."

"And they can't change anything?"

"Anything for inappropriate material. Grammar and stupid things don't count."

Beau debated it and then offered his hand. "It's a deal."

"Good. It'll be done by tomorrow afternoon."

"Only a day?"

"I'm good like that," Jay informed them loftily, promptly scooping up the script and disappearing.

"You're going to end up making that man dinner," Jessie said thoughtfully.

"You think so?" Mick asked.

"He wouldn't have made the deal if he wasn't confident he could manage it," Jez agreed.

Beau shrugged. "I'm not sure why he wanted a dinner out of it. I'm a mediocre cook at best."

"Yeah, but then he can say the boss cooked for him."

"Oh, so you still acknowledge that I'm the boss?"

"When I must," Jez said easily, grinning.

Jay reappeared the next day, looking pleased with himself. "Done," he announced, passing the changes to Mick. "Ready for the first read through!"

Mick eyed them, shrugged, and sat down at Beau's desk to read.

Jay managed to be patient for all of three seconds, before he began humming loudly.

"Oh for the sake of the gods," Ry grumbled and pointed at Jay. "You, come."

"What? Where?"

"Apparently we need to occupy you while the process happens, Mr. I'm-a-small-child."

He shot her a sulky look.

"Let's go," Jez said, standing up and pulling Jessie to her feet as well. "You too, Beau."

"Oh really? Are you ordering me around now?"

"Yes, sir," she said with a smirk. "Now move it."

He rolled his eyes but joined them.

"I'll come find you when I'm done," Mick said with a vague wave.

"So, what are we going to do?" Jay asked.

"You tell us," Jessie said. "You're the reason we're need to find something."

He thought about it for a minute. "How about constables and robbers?"

The four stopped and stared. "Constables and robbers?" Beau asked curiously.

"Yeah, you know, like we did as kids."

"That's it!" Beau burst. "That's perfect!"

Even Jay looked surprised at that assertion.

"It is?"

"Mick and I have been talking about how we need to practice working as a unit against opponents more and give ourselves more experience in more realistic melee combat. Why not start now? Jez, go find Reardon and tell him what's going on, see who he has today. The rest of you, track down anyone else who isn't involved in something critical. We'll gather in the main room."

It didn't take long to get everyone in the room, settled at tables and on the floor, waiting for Beau to speak. "We are only months away from what I hope will be a successful bid to clear the Three from the Tiran throne. That being said, we are woefully unprepared for any real combat and working together."

He stepped aside so Reardon could take his place. "So, mostly due to the need for peace in Beau's office and Jay's obvious inability to entertain himself," he paused for the chuckles to fade as Jay waved at everyone cheerfully, "we're going to do some practice. The captain and I will split you into two groups, making you as evenly matched as we can. Everyone will get a wooden sword and/or blunt arrows. Be careful, but don't be afraid to dole out bruises. We want this to feel as real as possible."

"He's right. The better we learn to work together, the more of us will make it to the end. If you have other duties throughout the day, you're allowed to leave and complete them, just make sure your team captain knows so we can replace you with someone who has just come off duty. Once you're split, your team captain will let you know what is considered a fatal blow versus a minor or major injury."

The war games went exceedingly well. By the end of the day, the whole group had read Jay's script. They also all, with the exception of Beau and Mick, were covered in bruises, although they had less than many of the other inhabitants of Cavern Hall.

Dunk read it last, setting it down at their table at dinner. He grinned. "Didn't change a word."

Ry, who was taking up half the girls' side with her feet hanging off the end of the bench, looked up. "You didn't find anything either? Did anyone?"

The other three involved shook their heads.

"Beau!" Jay beamed widely. "You owe me dinner."

"Fair is fair," Beau agreed, amused, scooping up the copy. "We'll copy out pieces tomorrow and we'll figure out when we want to put this thing on."

They spent much of the next two weeks learning their parts and throwing together half-hearted rehearsals when they could carve out the time. Finally, the morning of the play dawned and Beau pulled the blanket off Jez. "Good morning!"

She curled up. "Beau, it was warm," she protested sleepily.

"The play's this afternoon and we have yet to have a good rehearsal. Up so we can!"

"I don't like you."

"I know. Get up anyway."

She opened one eye to give him a baleful glare but forced herself to roll out of bed. The rehearsal went well – not without a hitch or two but with Jay's entrance so perfectly timed, Jez was pretty sure it wouldn't matter if they screwed up the rest.

After dinner, the tables in the main room were pushed aside and everyone gathered, using what seats they could find.

Mick stepped forward once they were settled and held his hands up for silence, which came almost instantly. "Once again, we gather to see a play put on by some of our fellow Freedom Fighters. This time," he said dryly, "they've even given me a part."

"Funniest part!" Jessie called, from where she and Dunkin were ensconced in the audience.

"You'd better hope not."

The spectators all chuckled but quieted quickly in anticipation.

"Anyway, we'd like to end today with a very, very serious play," he continued.

"A drama!" Jay called from off stage.

Mick snorted. "As if we'd believe him. It was written by Iris and edited by Jay."

"Is that even possible?" Jessie asked, which was entirely ad-libbed.

Jez looked at Jay, who made a face through the curtain in the general direction of their friend. "Not funny, Jessica!"

371

"You can dress them up, but you can't take them out," Mick commented, smirking, as many present laughed again. "Now, let's introduce our first star, Beau, our illustrious captain and narrator for the night."

Beau slipped out from behind the curtain to take center stage. "Good evening, everyone! It's great to see so many of you here to watch our little production. I suppose this is as good a time as ever to announce that we have been searching and found an appropriate place for a secondary base. We have gained so many new recruits that Cavern Hall is, as you all know, beginning to burst at the seams. We're hoping to move an initial group there before the end of the month to get it inhabitable."

Everyone cheered. They were all sharing at least four to a room, some more than that, and a small group had been reduced to sleeping in some of the public areas for lack of space. Jez quietly stepped out from the curtain to stand near the back. A lot of people noticed but Beau continued speaking, drawing their attention again. "Thank you! Now, announcements over, so on to the meat of our show. Tonight, Jez and I will be playing ourselves but we are joined by two very special guests. First, Vladimir Opalin."

Rylia bounded on stage, wearing the most formal clothing they could rustle up. She scowled at everyone as Jessie and Dunkin led the boos from the audience.

Beau fought a grin. "And…Anica Opalin!"

Jay waited a handful of beats and then bounded on stage. He wore a knee length dress with a very gaudy floral pattern that had actually belonged to Iris' mother originally. He sported a long blond wig –they couldn't find a red one, so they'd made do - and a pair of heavy boots with no socks, leaving his legs exposed between the boot and the dress.

Everyone roared with laughter and it barely settled as Jay spoke, beaming out at them and offering a passable curtsey. "Oh, Vladie, why do they laugh so?"

"I don't know, Anica, why don't you ask them?" Ry responded.

"But whyyyy? Why, Vladie, can't you tell me?"

"I already said I can't, Anica. Why don't you ask them?" She gestured towards their audience.

"But I want *you* to tell me."

Rylia shrugged and turned to them, deepening her scowl. "Why are you laughing at my little sister?"

"Because that dress is ugly!" Iris hadn't been thrilled with that particular line, but she'd allowed it to remain for the sake of art – her words, not theirs.

Jay adopted an overly prissy voice. "I will have you know that this dress comes from the finest dressmakers in Oakbridge."

Now it was Dunkin's turn to heckle. "They must not like you much!"

"I resemble that!"

Rylia rolled her eyes. "Come now, Anica, we have to plan our attack."

"Against who?" Jay's innocent look came in handy here for once.

"The Freedom Fighters, obviously. Look, there are two now! I will get them!" She drew a wooden practice sword and charged at Beau and Jez.

Jay promptly bumbled forward and tripped her. Ry, as they had rehearsed, made a huge showy fall onto her face.

"Jez, we have them now!" Beau cried.

"Never, scalawags," Ry-as-Vladimir returned, scrambling to her feet. Jay promptly plucked the sword out of her grasp and swung it wildly in Beau and Jez's general direction, smacking Rylia with the flat of the blade.

Jez grabbed Beau's arm. "You know what? I think they're doing a fine job of it themselves today."

"I quite agree," he said. "C'mon, we can finish off what's left later." The pair exited the stage, going back behind the curtain.

Ry and Jay fake wrestled for a minute before Ry held the sword up triumphantly, dragging Jay-as-Anica to the other end of the stage, whispering to him with furtive looks at the audience, tossing them the occasional thumbs up or big grin as if the plans were going well.

The rest of the play proceeded similarly and without any big hiccups. Ry-as-Vladimir did all she could to try and attack Beau and Jez while being thwarted at every turn by Jay-as-Anica. Eventually, Vladimir called it quits and dragged his sister away, leaving the castle to the Freedom Fighters. The play ended with Beau cutting a ceremonial strip of red fabric to signify the threshold of the castle and their win. In all, it wasn't a masterpiece, but everyone had a good laugh – especially with Jay prancing around in a floral dress.

Mick stood up, moving to center stage after the six actors had taken their bows. "Consider this, and the cutting of that fabric, to be a symbol of our cause and our movement into a real offensive against the Three. True, we will be spreading out in the next month, but that just shows how much we're growing and, as you all know, we represent a fairly small percentage of our allies around the country. As we've proven through the recent games, we are strong enough to fight back, make a stand against them, and hold our own."

"We don't have details yet," Beau added, "but things are starting to come together, both here and around Tira through our network of allies. The hope is, by this time next year, we will have defeated the Three and good people will once again be in charge of Oakbridge."

Everyone let out a resounding cheer that echoed through the chamber. A few hats went flying into the air, adding to the general enthusiasm for the mini-speeches. The cast took another round of bows, including Mick this time, and then the crowd slowly began to disperse to either bed or late-night duties.

Jay, bored already, although still graciously accepting compliments on the dress, searched out the other cast members and started to grin when he spotted Dunkin. The other man was chatting animatedly with a young woman named Kilo. As soon as Kilo stepped away to speak to someone else, Jay called over, "Hey, Dunk!"

Dunkin looked up and blushed red when he realized it was Jay calling him. "Yes?" he asked cautiously, approaching.

Jay grinned at him. "Does someone have a crush on K-"

The other man sprang forward to stop him but Mick got there first, clamping a firm hand over Jay's mouth. "Jay, do not do that."

"But it's so much fun," Jay whined twice, since he forgot to pry Mick's hand off the first time.

"No, it's not," Dunk protested, blush spreading towards his ears. "It's embarrassing."

"But it's cute. You got all cheerful and flustered!"

"I hate you."

"You know, I hear that a lot."

"That doesn't mean you need to shout it across the room," Mick told him.

"I wasn't really going to, but I wanted him to know it's so adorable."

"Use an adjective like that again and I will kick your ass," Dunkin said, flatly.

Jay's grin widened.

"Don't worry, Dunkin, she'll notice eventually. Jez did," Beau said, from where he stood on Mick's other side.

"Just try not to force Ry and me to resort to locking you in a room," Jessie said lightly.

"I'll do my best," Dunkin said but still stomped on Jay's foot for good measure.

Ren's eyes registered nothing as he walked headlong through the halls. He finally stopped, staring at the door in front of him. He hadn't consciously chosen the direction, but it didn't surprise him to find himself there. After a deep breath, he pushed open the door and stared around the familiar room. It felt empty without his father or any of his things. It was plain the room had not been used, though, from the layer of dust on everything. Maybe his captors did have a sense of respect. Or Sorin probably did.

He stepped in, not bothering to shut the door. He doubted he'd be left in peace for long. Running his hand along the foot of the bed, his chest and he swiped angrily at his eyes. He would not cry. He had not cried since he'd woken up in the castle's prison and known that his father must be dead with the city under the control of the Opalin and Dakamar siblings. Now, he was an adult and one of the worst kings that Tira had ever seen.

He sunk into the chair by the window. The chair where he had sat on his father's lap so many times as a child, listening to stories from his childhood and from Tira, stories about his heritage. Ren set the crutches on the floor and drew his knees up to his chest, staring out the window over the farms surrounding the capital. The farms in *his* country. That was an intimidating thought. His father had only been in his mid-forties when he was killed, which meant, in a perfect world, Ren wouldn't even be thinking about taking the throne. And here he was, technically two years into his reign. He should have had eight years or more before he had to worry about it.

The tears came, no matter how hard he tried to stop them, as his father's death hit him all over again. He wasn't ready for this burden, to try to be more than he was. He was a pushover, a weakling who didn't even try and fight back. He rubbed his eyes and let his thoughts drift. Slowly, sometime later, the sun descended and he became aware of a presence in the room. He looked up, too drained to be surprised that Ani was in the doorway.

"Hi," he said finally.

"Hey."

"How long have you been standing there?"

She hesitated, then shrugged. "Does it matter?"

"No, I guess it doesn't." He studied her, though, fairly certain she'd been there since he'd first left.

"Bit of a shock, huh?" she said with a small smile.

"Just a little," he said, hugging his knees closer.

"Can I come in?" Ani asked cautiously.

"Why ask me?" he asked, knowing his face clearly expressed his cynicism. "This is your castle now, not mine."

She physically recoiled at his tone. "I'm sorry. I'll leave, I didn't...I'm sorry," she stammered. She immediately turned.

"No, no, wait," he said quickly.

She glanced back.

"I'm the one who's sorry. I know better than that. Just, stay, please?"

Ani nodded and leaned against the doorjamb again.

It took Ren a second to realize she was waiting on him. "Why are you asking my permission?" he asked.

"This is," he noted the present tense curiously, "your parents' room. It's not my place to come barging in, especially when you came here to think privately."

"Come in," he said after a beat.

She smiled and walked in and, as usual, even walking contained a bit of a bounce. She came to stand by the chair, peeking out the window. "This is a wonderful view. Much better than your room or mine, but not as good as the one on the ramparts."

"Why do you like the view from there so much?"

"Because it's so open, you can almost feel free."

Ren stared out at the view before slipping his hand into hers. Her fingers curled around his. "I should have known. Logically, I should have realized that I'm king, coronation or not. I think I didn't want to admit it to myself, because that means it's real and that I'm not fit for this job."

"It's a big burden, but you're by no means unfit for the job, Renny."

"I should have done more."

"What could you have done besides push Vlad to the point where he killed you? Look what he did to you just for doing exactly what they wanted and liking me," she said somberly.

That caught Ren off guard. She had a point. Despite the fact that he had a real bed and wasn't in a cell didn't make him any less a prisoner, at the mercy of Vlad or anyone else in their employ. "You're right," he said slowly, feeling some of the guilt slide from his shoulders. "The best thing I could do for Tira and my people was to stay alive and hold on to hope that there might be an opening."

"And that's exactly what you've done. And now there are the Freedom Fighters and your brother."

There were a lot of heavy topics in that sentence, but now wasn't the time, not with her. Instead, he drummed up a small smile and squeezed her hand. "Well, at least we're now officially engaged. The entire country will know within a matter of days."

She grinned and plopped herself in his lap and, for the moment, things were again as close to good as they ever were.

Chapter Twenty-five

THE SET OF FOOTSTEPS THAT INTERRUPTED us next belonged to the young woman who delivered our meals. She silently set the tray down and retrieved our morning tray, replacing it with the new, full one. I watched her and smiled kindly when I caught her eye. She quickly looked away.

"Thank you," Jay said brightly as I pulled the tray in further to distribute it.

She nodded and hurried away.

"And they're holding hands again," Dave told me in a very effective stage whisper, staring pointedly at Stella and Jay.

I shrugged, fighting a smile. "Some people don't learn quickly."

Stella mostly looked amused, rolling her eyes, and went to let go but Jay deliberately made eye contact with Dave and then me. "The food isn't going anywhere," he said almost triumphantly, like he was winning a point.

"It will if you wait long enough. Dave and I are hungry, right, kid?"

He nodded solemnly, eyes alight with mischief.

"You wouldn't!" Jay protested.

"I can't speak for Dave, but I absolutely would. There's no point in letting food go to waste. Aren't you the one always advocating for eating even when it's boring?"

"Yes, because food is important, but that's not what I meant!"

Stella snorted and gently extracted her hand, patting his arm. "We know what you meant."

"Do we?" I asked.

Dave shook his head.

Jay threw the spoon at me, which I easily ducked.

"Jez, can we distract them with the story?" Dave asked hopefully.

I winked at him. "It's worth a shot. It'll also distract Jay from mourning his spoon."

Dave snickered as Jay realized he'd have to eat with his hands. I grinned and picked the story up.

◄ ▼ ►

The next month passed in a hectic mess of moving and transferring people. Mick, Reardon and Beau left for days at a time. To Ry's sadness, it was established that the small school for the kids and teens would remain at Cavern Hall proper, which meant Iris would stay too. Everyone made multiple trips to the new location, which existed above ground but in a well-hidden area at the base of the mountains west of the current Cavern Hall. By the end of the month they had a third of their forces move. Everyone was exhausted. The logistics of it all, while keeping it quiet, hidden, and not creating any well-worn trails, had not been easy.

The morning after the move was finally completed, the entire group lounged in Beau's office, barely talking, doing no work and mostly half-asleep. Reardon and Dunkin were running a hand-to-hand combat practice that none had felt like attending and everyone else was busy with their everyday tasks.

"I'm bored," Beau said.

"Jay," Jessie started as she looked up. "Wait, Beau?"

Jay gave her his best put-out look. "It's not *always* me."

"Usually is," she shot back.

"I need to do something," Beau continued.

"Do not even think about touching the paperwork," Jez told him.

"Why don't you, Mick, and Jay go do some sort of male bonding and leave us to our quiet time?" Ry said.

"I'm not sure I like the sound of this," Mick replied. "What were you thinking?"

"Fishing!" Jay said. "I used to fish all the time at the river just outside my house."

"Where are we going to go fishing? The stream we use for water can't possibly be big enough to have fish of any size," Beau said.

"There's the stream just east of here. Dunk went fishing there a couple times this summer and caught, um, trout, maybe?" Ry said and shrugged. "Fish are not something I have much knowledge about."

"It's chilly today."

"But sunny! And sunshine is good for you," Jay said.

"Don't push me."

"I wouldn't dream of it."

The others unilaterally favored him with a skeptical look.

He grinned sheepishly. "Let's do it!"

"Sounds like it could be fun," Beau said, nodding to himself. "And we could use a full day off. Do we have fishing supplies?"

"Yeah, somewhere. We can ask Dunkin." Jay stood. "Follow me!" Then, he bounded out of room.

Mick heaved a sigh. "Gods' Breath. What have we gotten ourselves into?"

"Oh c'mon, Mick," Beau said with a laugh. "I'm sure it'll end up being fun. Or we can always push him in. That would shut him up."

"You wouldn't!" Jessie said, but she was obviously squashing a smile.

"Are you sure of that?"

Jez poked him in the side. "Yes, you like Jay too much, even if you won't admit it."

"I'd do it," Mick said as he walked out.

"Now *that*, I don't necessarily doubt," Ry said.

It took the trio about half an hour to track down the fishing poles, pack a lunch, and collect some scraps to use as bait. "Okay, we've got everything," Jay said, peering into the bag and then rustled it. "Why do we have a book?"

"So I can throw it at you when you annoy me," Mick said.

Jay frowned. "Can we leave it home then?"

"No, I need to read it."

"Can we at least promise not to throw it at me?" he asked, smartly choosing not to pout.

Mick swiped it from Jay's hands and tucked it under his arm. "No."

Beau interrupted before they could escalate the argument. "Does that mean we're ready?"

Jay nodded.

"Can we go then?"

He nodded again.

"Well, then, let's. And how about I cook you dinner after we get home? Then I won't have that little obligation hanging over my head."

Jay beamed and did a little dance as he headed for the door. "That'll be fun," he threw over his shoulder.

"I'm so glad Jay's definitions of words never match up with the rest of the world," he muttered to Mick.

Mick grinned and headed out.

Jay hummed merrily, doing a little jig a few feet in front of them on their walk. Beau was relieved when they finally reached the stream. "Whose great idea was this again?" he asked Mick but Jay answered.

"Ry's! Isn't she smart?"

"Brilliant," Mick said dryly.

"We should come back when the stream's frozen," Jay said as he settled on the bank and pulled out the bait. He hummed some more as he got his pole ready and dropped it in a deep pool.

"Why? Then it would be really cold," Mick said.

"Yeah, but ice fishing is a blast. Despite the cold." He passed the bait bucket down to them. Jay leaned back, holding his pole in one hand.

Beau dropped his line in the water and stared at it. After five minutes, he glanced at the other two. Mick held his pole in one hand and his book open with the other. "Is this it?"

"Is what it?"

"We just sit here like this all day?"

"Yes, unless you catch something."

Mick snorted. "It continually surprises me, but patience is not one of your strong suits," he said.

"I can be plenty patient when I want to be. I don't like wasting time," Beau retorted.

"We could have a conversation."

"With you?" the other two asked simultaneously with more than a little skepticism.

"That was low, even for you two," Jay whined.

"Great minds think alike," Mick told him, giving Beau a high five.

Jay sighed loudly and flicked his pole. The other two exchanged grins and fell into an easy silence.

"Jay," Beau said finally, "I hate to be indelicate, but why have you never told the others that you're Bri's brother?"

It took him a moment to compose himself. "It's still a sore subject," he admitted, staring at where his line went into the water. "It's something I'd rather not talk about."

"They'll find out sooner or later," Mick said. "And then you'll have to talk about it, whether you like it or not."

"Jessie knows."

"She does?" Beau said, startled.

"Yeah. She figured it out a while back. She's respecting my wishes to keep it quiet, just like you."

"How did talking to her go?"

"We haven't had a lot of time to speak in private, but she's been good. It's been good."

"Talking about Bri with the people who knew him last might be good too."

He shrugged. "I'm not sure I'm ready to forgive him yet."

"Holding on to bitterness about family members, especially dead ones, never helps," Beau said quietly, as if speaking from experience.

"Do you have family?" Jay asked.

"I did once, but not anymore," he said with a slight smile. "It's just me and Mick."

"You don't have any surviving family either?"

Mick shook his head. "My father died a couple years ago. If my mother is alive or if I have any half-siblings, I don't know about it."

"So we're all orphans."

"No," Beau said. "We're just members of a found family, that's all. But try and let go of it, Jay. He's gone now, just like my family and Mick's father, and it won't do you or his memory any favors to continue with bitterness. That being said, I understand it very well. We all have things we'd rather not talk about."

"And you know them all," Jay said, seeking to add a bit of levity.

"That's my job as captain. I need to understand the people under my command. I would never betray a confidence, though."

"We wouldn't ask you to," he said. "Thank you. I will tell them. Although, I'm kind of amused by the fact none of them have noticed the striking similarities. I know I'm better looking, but that's no excuse. Jessie saw it."

Beau laughed. "Sometimes the most obvious things are those we manage not to see."

"Clearly."

Before anything more could be said, Beau jerked as his line went taut. "What...?" he started in shock.

Jay snorted. "You've got something on your line. No need to panic. Reel it in. Let's see if it's worth keeping for my dinner."

The other man shot him a look but got to work reeling it in. The fish put up a serious fight and, by the time Beau pulled it above the surface, both Jay and Mick were very curious about just how large the fish had to be. When it turned out to be barely more than six inches long, both Jay and Mick burst out laughing. Beau smiled proudly anyway. "Should I keep it?"

"Throw it back. By the time we skinned it and took the head and tail off, it wouldn't be worth it, except maybe as an appetizer," Mick said.

"How do I get it off the hook?" Beau asked after another minute of surveying it proudly.

Jay groaned, reaching out to snag the line. He expertly pulled the fish off the hook and offered it to Beau, who held it with fascination. "How have you never gone fishing before?" Jay asked.

Beau shrugged. "It was never something I felt the urge to do. I can hunt, though," he added.

"So you won't starve in the wilderness, good job. Fishing expends a lot less energy."

"Are you sure I can't keep it?"

Mick and Jay exchanged a glance. "To eat or as a pet?"

"To eat. Well, to feed Jay."

"It's a bass. It would taste good," Jay said and shrugged. "Go ahead and kill it now."

Beau stared at the fish with some horror. "How do I do that?"

"Give me the fish," he sighed and quickly and expertly killed it before nudging the bait bucket back to him. "Now let's see if your beginner's luck will last long enough for me to get a full meal out of it."

Beau eagerly affixed another piece of bait and tossed it back into the water, sitting forward.

By the end of the afternoon, even with a lengthy break, they had caught a small pile of fish - enough for dinner for all three of them. It was the last fish that was the trouble. Beau caught it, the biggest of the day. He pulled it, struggling, out of the water and it wiggled furiously. Although he'd managed to bring himself to kill one, he had yet to take his own fish off the hook, so Jay leaned over the water to grab it. It flapped and wiggled and smacked Jay's hand. With a yelp, he overbalanced and tumbled headfirst into the stream. Luckily, the stream there flowed wide and fairly deep with little debris and no rocks. He stumbled to his feet in the water, which came almost to his waist, already chilled.

Beau and Mick were laughing, even as Mick plucked the fish off the line. He had the experience, plainly, even if he had spent all day pretending he didn't.

"I hate you both."

"We did nothing!" Beau said, fighting to regain a straight face.

"You didn't try and catch me."

"It was a truly graceful somersault into the water," Mick informed him, calmly delivering the killing blow to the fish's head. "If you stay in there, you're only going to get wetter."

"I'm not sure that's possible," Beau said.

Jay eyed them both for only a second before heaving a large splash at them.

Beau blinked water from his eyes, then shrugged pragmatically. "I suppose we deserved that."

"You suppose correctly," Jay said and promptly splashed them again.

This time, Mick's eyes narrowed.

"Go ahead, throw your book at me," Jay said cheekily. "I'll be sure to catch it and use it to dry myself off."

Beau shook his head, not even bothering to cover his amusement as he stood and grabbed the blanket they'd used during lunch. "Here. At least take your shirt off and wrap this around yourself, it'll dry."

Jay clambered back onto dry land with a mournful look. "As much as I like you, Beau, that statement would have been so much more special coming from someone not in a committed relationship."

"That's strangely comforting," he said dryly and handed it to him as Jay peeled off his soaked shirt. "C'mon, I think it's time we headed home." He wrung his own shirt out then moved to collect their things.

They returned a couple hours before dark, still damp. After changing into a dry set of clothes, Jay installed himself in front of the fire in the kitchen and watched with barely contained laughter as the cooks showed Beau how to de-skin and cook his fish. Mick also installed himself in the kitchen, helping with another part of dinner but mostly watching Beau as well. Beau finished with a gusto and the three joined the women for dinner, graciously allowing them to try their fish and regaling them with the tale of their adventure.

The sharp rap on his open door drew Sorin's attention. He wasn't too surprised to find Jakium McRuoes standing there. The young lieutenant had, at Ani's request, been invited back from Greensward to attend the announcement and Sorin had suspected he'd offer a report before he returned to the slightly smaller city.

"Sir," Jakium said with a faint smile.

"Hello, Jakium. How soon are you heading back to Greensward?"

"Tomorrow, sir, bright and early. Colonel's orders."

"Well, make sure you get enough time with Anica before you go."

"I plan on it, sir, only she's still with the pri-king," Jakium said with a shrug. "I'll catch her later."

"Have they returned to Ren's rooms yet?"

"I don't believe so."

Sorin nodded, not particularly surprised. They would return in due time. "I suppose we should go find Vladimir then."

"Would you like me to go find him and bring him here?"

He cocked an eyebrow at Jakium, fighting a chuckle. "That was diplomatically put but would only get you in trouble, so I'll come," he said, standing and walking out the door.

Jakium fell into step beside him as they headed for Vladimir's office. When they reached it, Jakium hesitated, reaching up to rap on the door much like he had with Sorin, but Sorin went around him and headed for a chair at his brother's desk. Vladimir caught the scuff of Jakium's feet and looked up as Sorin settled in, nice as you please, in the chair. For an instant, his expression darkened, but it was gone so quickly anyone who didn't know him as well as Sorin might have missed it. Sorin also snuck a glance at the lieutenant but if Jakium had caught it, he hid his reaction.

"General," Jakium said with a crisp salute.

"Lieutenant," Vladimir said, gesturing him forward. "Did you enjoy today's proceedings?"

"Yes, sir," Jakium said with his very best completely neutral look. "I think the people will accept Ani without hesitation. She has a way with people, after all."

Sorin pursed his lips against a smile. Despite the regret he felt at helping drag Jakium into their world, the boy he'd first met had grown into a competent and smart young man. His diplomacy was also to be admired. He managed to navigate the often murky and dangerous waters around all three siblings while making friends with pretty much everyone he met. Sorin hoped that someday, Jakium would find an adequate outlet for those abilities, far away from them.

Vladimir merely nodded. "That she does, although I can't say as I fully understand it."

"That's because people like her," Sorin said, almost before he'd made up his mind to comment.

Jakium went still.

His brother did too before turning slowly to look at him. "What was that?"

"People like our sister. Ren included," he said, injecting a more mild tone this time. "What do you have to report, Jakium?"

"Colonel Res seems very confident he will begin to get more solid, information out of the Freedom Fighter prisoners soon. The doctor has given him permission to begin again with Jasmine. She's healed enough that he won't break her to the point of no return."

"Anything else?" Sorin asked. Jasmine and James were playing a game that, given enough time, Rees would win.

"No, it's only been a couple days since I was posted there," Jakium said with a smile. "I'm sure there will be more by the wedding."

"No doubt," Sorin agreed. "Shouldn't be too long."

"Very good," Vladimir said, but his eyes were already fixed on Sorin. "I am concerned about you."

Jakium went still yet again.

"Concerned about me? Why? I'm fine, rarely been better, actually. You?" he added, just because he knew it would annoy his brother.

"That's exactly what I mean," Vladimir said, pouncing on the words. "You've insisted on ignoring my orders and acting downright cheerful."

"Is that a crime?"

Jakium edged slowly toward the door. If Vladimir noticed, he ignored him. Sorin suspected his brother didn't even see the young man.

"It is when you deliberately don't follow through on orders. It makes us weak."

"No, what makes us weak is when we give *bad* orders and force follow through on them."

Jakium bolted and Sorin didn't blame him one ounce.

Vladimir started to rise out of his chair. "How *dare*-"

"If you just deferred to my better judgment, this wouldn't be an issue."

"We have almost stabilized the entire country," his brother bit out. "Do not mess this up for us."

"For you. You mean: don't mess this up for you."

"What?" Vladimir asked, voice low and dangerous, so much like Edward's that a shiver fought its way up Sorin's spine.

Still, he acted as if he hadn't noticed, or been bothered. "I mean that this is your dream. Ruling Tira was never something Ani or I wanted." It had been Edward's dream, originally, but Sorin wasn't cruel enough to bring up the man by name, even if he'd never understood why or when Edward had decided he wanted to be king. Vlad wasn't that far gone yet.

"It's all of ours," Vladimir corrected sharply.

"Now, yes. It sort of has to be, doesn't it? If we lose at this point, the game is over and we'll most likely be dead or worse."

"Don't give me that. You helped me, Sorin, every step of the way!" he snapped.

"I let you use me every step of the way."

Vladimir finally got to his feet, looming over Sorin, who leaned back in the chair in studious unconcern. "What are you talking about?" he demanded.

"I let you use me," he repeated, making sure to enunciate each word slowly and maybe a little overly deliberately.

"I don't understand," Vlad said after a minute, deflating to press his palms against his desk.

"No, you wouldn't."

"Why?"

"Why did I let you use me? Because I didn't care if I lived or died. Nothing seemed important, including doing the right thing."

"How could you not care?"

"Name one thing I had to live for when I returned to that house and your plan?"

"Ani. Me."

"Halfway right. I did come back to do my best to keep Ani out of it and, if that proved impossible, to keep her alive."

"What about me?" Vladimir asked, sounding almost hurt.

"You've always been able to take care of yourself," he said quietly. "After all, you had cooked up the majority of this plot without me. So I willingly let you use my brain and resources."

His brother pursed his lips. "So what has changed?"

Sorin's lip curled up. "The willingly part."

Vladimir straightened. "Sorin," he started, a threat inherent in the word.

"Stop acting like your godsdamned father," Sorin shot at him, before he could think better of it. "Edward has been buried for years and the world is a better place when he stays buried."

Vlad went white. "I am not my father," he bit out. "Do not ruin this for any of us, Sorin."

"I wouldn't. I have something very important invested in all our plotting, don't I? If I ruin it for you, I ruin it for myself and my sister."

"Our sister."

Sorin cocked an eyebrow at him, then sat forward and stood, brushing off his pants. "Try not to forget that yourself." He straightened, looking Vladimir in the eye. "I will do my best to make this work, for her sake, but it's about time I started telling you when your plans, ideas, or orders are stupid. So I suggest you prepare yourself for that. I am not afraid of you."

His brother pursed his lips and nodded slowly. "I don't want you to be," he said after a minute.

"That's something," Sorin said. "I have work to do. I shall see you later." He turned, before Vladimir could speak again, and left the room. Once he'd rounded a corner in the hall and was out of sight of the doorway, he slumped back against the wall and let out a long breath, closing his eyes. Vlad was getting worse, almost by the day. Maybe it was time for a contingency plan.

Chapter Twenty-six

APPARENTLY, I'D MADE A FACE WHEN Jay recounted his conversation about Bri. He stopped and grinned crookedly. "Had you forgotten we're related?"

"No, I'd forgotten that Beau and Mick knew. You never mentioned that conversation in the tellings after."

"For obvious reasons," he pointed out. "We couldn't explain the talk without saying what had started it and that would require me to come out as Bri's brother. Honestly, I feel like I should be offended it took you as long as it did. Jessie really showed you up."

"That's nothing new," I said lightly, then nodded towards our little window. "Seems it's gotten to be night again. Shouldn't take us a lot longer to catch up to meeting you."

"Really?" Dave asked, with some surprise.

"It's been at least two weeks," I said, "maybe a little longer. That's a decent amount of time, especially when we're not covering every detail."

"What do we have left?" Jay mused.

"The ambush, my birthday, and the decision to send us to Greensward. And the details of how we ended up in here. We're into last October, story-wise, I suppose." It had to be early January by now, if two weeks had passed.

"That should be easily wrapped up in a day or two," Jay agreed.

"Still never thought we'd get there," Dave said quietly.

"I think we'll not only get there but have to think up other ways to entertain ourselves."

Stella grinned. "Well, we do have Jay. That shouldn't be too hard."

"I don't entertain on command," he said loftily.

I favored him with my very best skeptical face.

"I don't!"

I rolled my eyes and settled back in my corner as Dave picked up my end of the argument gleefully. They were still at it when I drifted off, which made me feel for Stella – especially if we made it out of this.

I was less than pleased when Rees kicked the bars by my head very early the next morning. "The hell you want?" I muttered as I sat up, rubbing my ear.

"James, let's go," he said, ignoring me.

"You're interrupting my beauty sleep. Don't you know that's rude?" Jay complained sleepily.

"James," Rees said, unusually taciturn, even for him.

"Fine, since you asked so nicely," he said, pushing himself to his feet.

I barely squashed a wince at how stiffly he moved. The beating he'd taken on my behalf not even two days ago had obviously fully blossomed. And he hadn't moved as much as he probably should have to prevent the stiffness yesterday. If Rees was in as bad a mood as he appeared, Jay'd feel a hell of a lot worse soon.

Rees opened the door and allowed Jay out. The brutes moving to flank him and they led him off.

Stella and I exchanged a worried look and I sighed. We sat in anxious silence until Dave couldn't take it. "Jez, do you miss your family?"

It took me a moment to draw myself out of my imaginings of what Rees was doing to my friend. Then I frowned. What should have been an easy question wasn't as clear-cut as he made it seem with the asking. "Yes," I said after another pause, "of course I do. I was close to all of them. But I know they've been safer with me in hiding and them not knowing. I do miss Colin almost every day, even now. We were all but inseparable until the day he shipped north and I went to live with Duke Elladan. Overall, though, life's been so busy that I barely have time to miss them most days."

"And Colin's only about a year older than you, right?"

I nodded. "Do you have any family left?"

"As far as I know, our grandparents are still alive, on our mother's side. And some cousins and such, but they live on the other side of Tira, out near Holly."

We sat in silence for a while and Dave dozed, leaning against his sister.

"When we get free, will you go there?" I asked quietly.

"No," she said without hesitation. "We'll go with you. Let them stay untouched until this is all over, if they can. Our place would be with the Freedom Fighters. It's what George and Mom believed in and I do too, although they didn't give me that choice until it was too late."

"You'd be most welcome."

"Do you really think we'll get free?"

I thought back to the plans we had so painstakingly formed and reworked a dozen times and slowly put into action. "Not without help," I said finally, "but our friends will do what they can. If we can put Rees off long enough, Jessie and Ry are both set to come into town, as you know. They won't sit idle when they find out we've been caught."

She nodded, leaning back against the wall.

I couldn't think of anything more positive or upbeat to say so I remained silent as we waited. Finally, I heard the sound of footsteps and leapt to my feet, peering out anxiously. My initial view didn't instill confidence. The brutes held Jay between them, dragging him, and he didn't look up at all as they approached. I couldn't even tell if he was conscious.

Dayton led the way, grinning widely and proudly, like he had helped. I had more than half a mind to grab him while the cell door was open. "What did you do?" I demanded as Dayton reached us.

"It is a welcome change to see the high and mighty brought low," he said with a smirk.

I ignored him, ready to catch my friend, but he gained his feet when they stopped and only stumbled a little when the brutes shoved him in. I noticed, in passing, that Jay's hair was soaked and plastered to his face. That could be dealt with in a minute. For now, I gave in to my desire. I grabbed Dayton and pulled him close, ignoring the twinge in my shoulders.

"Let go of me!" he squawked.

"Or what, shorty?" I growled, but the brutes shifted meaningfully towards me. Furious, I stepped forward and slammed him as hard as I could into cell door. Then I got right in his face. "You so much as open your mouth around me again and I will crush your throat before your pals here can save you, understand?"

He swallowed hard, but opened his mouth to bluster. I promptly slugged him, just as Kilgor grabbed me. Although he swiftly pulled me off, my fist had landed with full force and Dayton looked stunned from the blow. "In the cell," Kilgor grunted.

I shrugged free and stepped back into the confines of the cell, allowing Juke to shut the door. I stared them all down until they disappeared from view, Dayton starting to sputter as the brutes escorted him away. I figured I'd pay for that next time I saw Rees but couldn't bring myself to care.

I turned to find Jay already sitting in his corner, knees drawn up to his chest, face buried in his knees with his hands covering it. Even with him as curled up as he was, I could tell his shirt was soaked through, too. I glanced at Stella to see if I had missed anything, but she shook her head.

I moved to sit by him, careful to be loud about it so I wouldn't startle him. He didn't move as I settled in, putting a hand on his shoulder. "Jay?"

He gave no response at all, not even a twitch beneath my hand.

"Jay?" I repeated quietly.

He didn't move, unnaturally still.

I removed it slowly, even more worried now, but stayed by his side. I looked up at Stella and Dave and knew I should offer a smile, a jaunty comment, and continue the story, but I couldn't bring myself to do it. Rees had won a round and I didn't like the reminder that our health and lives revolved around him. Although logically I'd realized that he would up his game after Opalin's visit, I hadn't really been aware of what it might entail. All I knew so far was that water was involved, but that was scary enough.

"Maybe we should take a break for today," Stella said.

We all probably needed the distraction more than ever but I took the offer, nodding. "Please." I quietly moved just enough to touch my shoulder to Jay's, so he'd know I was near. When breakfast came, I took my portion and ate mechanically, stomach squirming when Jay didn't move even when offered his. Jay not eating just seemed wrong. I settled back against the wall and allowed my mind to wander to memories of our friends and even further back to my family. I spent some time trying to figure out if our capture would screw up the plan too much and hoped it would only cause some delays.

I became aware, at one point, of Stella reassuring Dave, tone upbeat, but couldn't summon the energy to chime in. It was a cold, gray day and the winter's chill didn't lift from the cell, making things even colder than usual. Jay shivered in his wet clothes beside me. Without him cracking jokes or making an idiot of himself, I found it harder than usual to avoid thoughts of our potentially dismal-looking future and I rubbed my throat. A couple times, I nudged Jay, murmuring his name, but he ignored the efforts.

Sometime after dinner, I drifted into a sleep which was unsettled by nightmares, the usuals plus a new one which ended with a noose around my neck and the ground dropping out from underneath me.

Eventually, I woke enough to be mindful of someone staring at me. I opened my eyes to find Rees standing outside the cell. Sometime in the night, I had settled more comfortably against Jay, my back wedged in by him and the wall, which left me facing towards the door. A quick glance to my left confirmed that Stella and Dave were both still asleep. Unnerved, I wondered how long he had been watching us. It sent a jolt of adrenaline through me, though, effectively waking me up. "Good morning, Jasmine," he said.

Full name probably wasn't a good sign. "What do you want?"

"I came to check on James. Seems he's not doing too well. You should have heard him talking yesterday."

"Yes, I'm sure he had a lot of choice words about your relations," I said. The thought that Jay might have spilled something was preposterous.

He smirked. "Is that what you think?"

"Don't bother giving me some cock and bull story about what he might have said. I'm not confirming or denying anything until Jay tells me what he said."

"Doesn't look like he'll be doing that any time soon."

I stood, slowly stretching, but my anger simmered. "One of these days, Rees, you're going to regret all of this. Never should have sided with the losing team."

"Losing? Who is it that's in charge of the country again?" he asked.

I grinned, stepping up to the bars. I could have reached out and grabbed him and, from his slight flinch, he seemed aware of it. Still, he didn't step back. Sometimes I didn't understand the colonel, because even though he wasn't a stereotypical bully, he acted it at times. "You and your masters are merely a bump in the road. It won't last. Not with your policies. You're going to hang a godsdamn ten-year-old. Right, because the people just *love* things like that."

"He killed a soldier," Rees said stiffly.

"Who had just helped kill his brother and mother and were threatening him. Yeah, you *really* have a case there," I said, unable and unwilling to hide my sarcasm.

"Young Mr. Harper aside, you and James are far from innocent," he said, trying to regain the upper hand in the conversation.

I let it slide. I could manage this one, too. "Again, you're really one to talk. Who was it that attacked Oakbridge and killed the king? Yeah, that's right."

"Be that as it may, we are the people in charge now and you're at our mercy. You'll never step foot outside this jail again, except for your execution. I should think you'd realized that by now."

"Oh, I'm well aware of my situation," I said calmly. "But I'm also well aware of yours and the crumbling government you've formed. How *are* our borders these days?"

Rees flushed. "I would not bait me, Jasmine. As Jay could tell you, were he able to talk, I can make things extremely difficult for both of you." His eyes flicked to Dave and Stella meaningfully.

"I have no doubt you're going to do your best to do that anyway, whether I bait you or not. Isn't that your job? Or are you scared of me? You've healed nicely," I said with a wide, fake smile as I rested a hand on the bars.

For a moment, so quickly I might have imagined it, something unsettled crossed his face. "I broke your friend," he started.

"See, you don't know Jay very well, so I'll excuse the ignorance. Only, Dalls don't break, because they always bounce back. This is just a little hiccup and, by this time tomorrow, he'll be fine and you'll be back at square one. Good luck with that."

"Do Lockholmes bounce back too? You still have three brothers at home, don't you? And your parents are still alive?"

I went still. "Leave my family out of this." But something of what he'd said sat funny, tugging at the back of my brain.

"But wouldn't they be thrilled to learn their only daughter was still alive? Assuming, of course, that they don't already know. Maybe I should ask them."

"They don't know anything. I haven't seen them since before the attempt on my life," I said firmly, but my voice shook slightly.

He looked triumphant. "If you won't talk to spare Jay, maybe you will to spare your family."

I grasped at the first straw I could find. "If you had permission to do that, you would have already. You learned my name almost two weeks ago."

"That doesn't mean I can't get it."

As the crow flew, Greensward wasn't that far from my childhood home, but there were no direct routes. Lockholme wasn't particularly well known, mostly because of its inaccessibility by any roads but the one from Ellworth. Even if permission was granted immediately, that would give me over a week. With my estimate of when Jessie and Ry might arrive, let alone be able to act, that put my family in a perilous place. I doubted they'd be here within a week. I could only hope that Opalin and Dakamar wouldn't find it worth the trouble or were too busy to give it due consideration, at least for a time. "If you even try and set foot in Lockholme, you or any of your people, will find it harder than you might think to do what you want. I have faith in my family. And in Jay."

"Faith?" he said and let out an incredulous laugh. "Now that's rich. Faith will not save you from the noose."

Actually, as far as I saw it, faith and some luck might be the only things that could save us. "Believe what you want. Only I get to decide when I die and it will not be in some corner courtyard by a bunch of low life usurpers."

"Oh? I would reconcile myself to that exact death very quickly. Your death sentence has already been signed by the general. It's only being postponed to see if you can be useful and perhaps redeemable."

I laughed. "Redeemable? That's rich." I swept an arm back to show Jay. "You've seen and stared and gotten your satisfaction. Did you want something else?"

"You're deluding yourself if you think this won't end in your death."

"Depends on which *this* you're talking about. If it's my life? Yeah, it will end, some day in the future, surrounded by a husband, couple kids, and hopefully grandkids. I can see it now. Warm fire and a rocking chair. Just fall asleep and never wake up, an old, content woman."

His forehead wrinkled in thought as he studied me.

"Hanging just doesn't do it for me," I added.

Now, he snorted. "Get over that. The doctor might have said a week, but that doesn't mean I need to heed his warning. Your recovery has been quick."

I stared him down, having been expecting something of the sort. I waited until he had turned and gotten half a dozen paces, satisfied he'd gotten the last word, before speaking. "Thank you."

Startled, he looked back. "What?"

"I needed that conversation." I felt strangely lighter, more awake, and far less gloomy than I had the day before.

He opened his mouth, then scowled and muttered an oath, before turning again and stomping off. For now, the last word was mine.

Satisfied he was gone, I moved back over to settle again by Jay's side, allowing myself a thin smile. Although the conversation had reminded me why we were fighting and why we could not give up, it had also unnerved me. Rees would come for me soon, but I figured myself safe for the day. With that thought in mind, I turned to my now awake cellmates. Something from the conversation still niggled at the back of my brain, but it wasn't coming yet so I had to just let it lurk until it came to me. "I think taking a break from the story yesterday was a mistake, so if you want, I can keep going. I don't think I'll miss anything important, telling it by myself. Although I'd welcome the help," I said, nudging Jay gently.

He still didn't respond. His shoulders rose and fell with stronger, steadier breaths. Yesterday, I had barely been able to feel even that. I took it as a good sign.

"Where were we?"

"Jay'd just finished telling us about the fishing expedition," Dave said, relief on his face at the return to the now familiar routine.

I tapped my chin. "Nothing else of importance happened until mid-November, when we pulled off the ambush. I'll pick back up there." After another moment of thought, I did just that.

◄ ▼ ►

About a week after the fishing trip, Jez woke to the flickering light of a lamp. She rolled over and squinted blurrily up at Beau. "What time is it?" she murmured.

He started, looking up. "Oh, I'm sorry. I didn't mean to wake you."

She waved off the apology. "What time is it?"

"A couple hours before dawn. Not sure exactly."

"Have you been up all night?" She thought she had vague memories of him falling asleep beside her, but it was possible she was wrong.

"No, well, yes. I couldn't sleep."

She sat up, eyeing him as he bounced on his toes, like Jay might have. "And?"

"I'm plotting," he said with an overwhelming sense of pride.

She only managed not to laugh because she was still half asleep and it felt like too much effort. "Plotting what?"

"Oh, no, no, I don't want to owe you another nap. You can just roll over and go back to sleep."

Jez gave him the stink eye and stood, stretching before meandering over to join him. "You're too excited for me to be able to go back to sleep," she said, peering over his shoulder at the maps spread out on the desk. "What's all this?"

"The Three sent soldiers up to Northwind two months ago, as a show of force against the de Carlins," he said, tracing his finger up the main road from Oakbridge to Northwind, on the far northern borders. The same city where Jez's brother, Colin, had been stationed before the Three had taken it. Jez also knew that the de Carlins, the ruling family of Alyia, the same northern neighbor, had been making a play to encroach on Tiran lands, figuring them too embroiled in their own internal spats to notice. Sending troops to keep them out was about the only thing Jez suspected the Freedom Fighters and the Three agreed on.

"Okay, and?"

"They've moved west as they've gone and will be returning along this forest route, only a few miles from here. According to orders we've gotten to peek at, they're to take it slow and search hard for us, since they figure we must still be in the same general area as the first Cavern Hall."

"And this gets you excited why?" she asked. That sounded like a bad thing, not a good one.

"To get into the valley here, you have to pass through this gully," he said, stabbing the map. "And if you *have* to pass through that gully..."

"Then that means we'll know exactly where they are and probably a good idea of when too," she finished, the excitement finally dawning on her as well.

He grinned. "Exactly!"

"We've never done anything like this, though. Our work has always been more clandestine. And most of us here, and in the other camp, haven't even done that."

"But we have the training. And there are still many of us who fought in the last battle. Plus, this time, we'll control it and won't just be covering for a retreat. Everyone handy with a bow along the ridges. Groups at each end. We bottle them in."

Jez studied the map, even as she rubbed her chin. "It would work. We have the numbers. How soon?"

"The orders should reach them within the next day or two and then it's a few days march south to here after that. A week, maybe?"

"Do we have a more detailed map of the area that includes that gully?"

He pulled out a new map with a flourish. "So glad you asked."

They were still planning when Mick poked his head in, some hours later. "Breakfast – what are you doing?" he asked, stepping further in. "I was expecting at least Jez to still be asleep."

"Plotting!" they answered in unison, then shared a high five.

He raised both eyebrows and joined them at the desk. "Is this about the news that we're going to have soldiers in our backyard very soon?"

Beau pushed over the paper where they had jotted down their initial thoughts and what they needed to do. Mick scanned it and nodded in appreciation. "An ambush. I like it. It'll show the Three that we're strong enough to come after them in the open, which is precisely what we want. In the meantime, breakfast. We can discuss it with the others over the meal and get things rolling."

The next week was a whirlwind of planning and measuring the terrain. The first order of business was a scouting mission of the gully. Both Reardon and Mick, as the most experienced among them, went, taking Dunkin and Jessie with them. They returned with a detailed description of the gully and the surrounding area. Dunkin, a good artist, had sketched it from a variety of vantages, showing the best places to hide men and angles they needed to utilize.

Almost every day, some group either went out to the gully to mark locations or doublecheck something. There was also a steady stream of people back and forth to their second location. As nice as it was to have breathing room in Cavern Hall, trying to communicate with that group was an unexpected trouble. Luckily, they weren't too far and it was an easy trip by foot. Beau immediately dispatched some of their scouts to track the Three's movements south. The reports they got back indicated that the soldiers had no inkling of what was coming and headed blithely south.

Finally, the morning of the planned ambush dawned. They left early, even though the soldiers weren't expected until later that afternoon. It gave those who hadn't gotten to the site - which due to pre-planning, were only a handful - a look at the area. It also allowed them ample time to set up, in case their enemies arrived early. Beau and his group met with the group from the other camp and he surveyed them. They'd brought less than a hundred men and women, even though there would be some two hundred of the opposition. With their position at the high ground, and the fact they would merely be funneling them south, more than that had seemed unnecessary.

"After this, we need to get even more serious about the plan for the end," he murmured to Jez. She nodded, feeling a surge of anxiety and excitement, and he stepped forward to address them. "This is our chance to strike back hard against the people who have taken so much from each of us. Your group leaders will now break you up and have you sent to your places. Strike hard and fast when it comes time. I have no doubt you will do us proud. Good luck and, if the gods are with us at all, we will all walk home at the end of today."

"If the gods are with us," many of those present murmured with brief glances towards the sky.

As the leaders gathered their groups, Jez nudged him. "You're really good at this leadership thing. Give yourself more credit."

He smiled, but there was a strange quality to it that Jez couldn't identify. "I know. Mick reminds me almost daily that I come by it naturally." Before she could ask about that statement, he continued, "Let's go talk to Reardon, Jessie, and Mick and make sure everything is settled."

Reardon had taken the left side of the ravine, with Beau on the right. Jessie, with Ry's help, had taken the rearguard, which would prevent the soldiers from heading back north again. Mick was in charge of a fourth group that would keep the survivors heading south for at least a day and make sure they had no interest in remaining behind to snoop. Beau knew this ambush was a risk – all but confirming that their location was indeed still in the area – but with their current strength, that seemed less important than it had in the earlier days. Things would begin happening soon and hopefully it would keep the Three and their troops busy enough they would not have time to search too hard.

"You don't mind I didn't put you in command of any of the groups, right?" Beau asked.

"No, of course not. You, Reardon, and Mick were obvious and I'd rather be with you and act as a messenger in case of need."

"I appreciate it," he said as they joined the other leaders to go over the plan one last time. Then they went to join their groups, Beau and Jez climbing up to perch at the top of the ravine's side, along with the eighteen other archers. They had placed twenty archers on each side of the ravine, and around thirty with Jessie and Ry, since they'd see the most direct combat, and about the same number with Mick for his pursuit. The pair settled in after getting a confirming wave from Jay, who was playing the same role as Jez on the far side. They waited for a while then ate a quiet lunch. After, Jez got up and slid down the northern side to the ground where Jessie, Ry, and their force waited. A minute after she appeared, Jay bounced in. "Hi, everyone!" he said cheerfully, but kept his volume low as ordered.

The others murmured greetings and they settled in to wait. Finally, one of the scouts ran in. "They're coming," he panted. "Maybe fifteen minutes out. Marching hard."

"Got it. Take a break," Jez told him with a smile, then she and Jay took off to alert the archers. She reached the top and let out a quiet whistle. The others nodded from their hiding places and gave their bows a last check as she dropped down beside Beau. "Maybe fifteen," she reported quietly.

"Good. Waiting was getting tiresome."

She nodded as silence descended on the troop. Slowly, the birds and other small animals in the trees went silent. She and Beau exchanged a glance and Beau shimmied forward to get a better view. That's when she heard the first sound of many footsteps marching their way. She didn't dare sneak a peek and risk them spotting the movement as the footsteps sounded closer and closer. Jez fingered her bow and envisioned herself moving to a crouching position, notching an arrow, and letting it fly into the men below.

The last bit of waiting was excruciating. Then, just ahead of her, Beau shifted slightly to bring his fingers to his lips and let out a loud three-note whistle, which sounded a lot like one of the local birds.

That was the signal.

She instantly propped herself up on one knee. The ravine was full to the brim with soldiers and, for a moment, all she could do was stare. Then as the first arrows loosed with a twang, she remembered herself and quickly notched her ready arrow and sent it into the men. As the first volley of around forty arrows sunk into their intended targets, pandemonium broke out among the soldiers. The surprise of the attack caused them to break rank like amateurs. Those towards the back and the front immediately fought to get out of the ravine. Already, the fastest archers among them were sending a second flight into the mass of bodies.

Jez notched her next arrow, or tried to. Her hands were shaking too hard to manage it. She flinched at a scream from below and dropped the arrow. Her gaze darted to the panicked men but she didn't see them. Instead, she saw screaming horses and soldiers in familiar livery, and she was in the midst of it. Jez doubled over and retched, stomach heaving with each scream from below. She felt she could hear the sounds of explosions and sense the heat coming from the ground. She lost track of the screams and time, hunched over her knees, hands fastened on her ears.

Finally, she felt a gentle hand on her shoulder, tugging her up. She came reluctantly, keeping her eyes averted from the ravine floor. Then, Beau wrapped his arms tightly around her and held her until the shaking slowly subsided and she released her ears, sagging against him.

"I've got you," he murmured. "It's okay, it's all over, and you're okay." It took a minute for her to realize he had probably been saying things like that for some time.

Jez nodded. "I'm okay," she managed.

"Can you walk?"

"I think so."

He helped her to her feet. "Just look straight ahead, okay? We'll get you down to the rendezvous point and the others."

"Did we get them?"

"Yes. Jez, I am so sorry. I never even thought…"

"I didn't either," she muttered. "If I had, I would have stayed back in Cavern Hall. The ambush against me and the others was so different. The explosions and the horses and…" She shuddered, leaning against him as he escorted her down to the level ground. She hadn't had problems with the Battle of Deepen's Crossing, although the situation had been very different.

"Jez! What happened? Are you hurt?"

Other than the noises and memories still ricocheting around her head unallowed, she was okay. "I'm fine," she said, feeling inexplicably tired. Her stomach still rolled with each flash of memory.

"She had a flashback once the ambush started," Beau said quietly. "Can you guys take her? I need do some things as captain."

"Of course," Ry said, sympathy etched across her face.

Beau nodded, squeezed Jez's shoulder, and moved off to talk to some of the others.

Jessie's eyes rounded and she stepped forward, hugging her tightly. "Oh, honey," she murmured. Jessie wasn't one for terms of endearment so the use of one made Jez smile a little.

"I'm okay," she said. "Just caught me by surprise, but as soon as they started screaming." She swallowed hard and gratefully accepted the water Ry offered, sipping it. "Beau said it was a success."

"It was. We had a fight and a few got through, but it was either let them or risk one of ours getting killed. We'll keep an eye out for them," Ry said.

She nodded. "Did we lose anyone?"

"Couple injuries in our group, but Ann thinks they'll all pull through."

"Good." She let go of Jessie and sagged back against a nearby tree. "Where's Jay?"

"We accidentally captured a few. Jay's poking fun, literally, while they try to figure out what to do with them."

She smiled faintly. "I suspect Jay's version of poking fun means fun for him and not for them."

"Pretty much. Are you sure you're okay? You're still as white as a sheet," Ry said anxiously.

Jez shut her eyes and immediately regretted it as the sights and sounds exploded across her eyelids. "I was fine given time last time."

"Yeah, and you spent most of that time unconscious," her friend pointed out.

"I know. I will be fine. Really, the whole thing just caught me terribly off guard. I wasn't expecting a flashback and certainly not that strongly. It's already better."

Ry eyed her doubtfully, but nodded anyway as Beau joined them. "Dunkin's going to take a few of ours and escort the prisoners south then rejoin Mick's group and return home once they're sure the group stays away and continues south."

"What about J-" was as far as Jez got before the man himself bounded out of the trees and threw himself on her.

"Jez, darling, I heard you are most unwell! How may I be of service?"

"By getting off, to start with," she said dryly.

He grinned and bounced back a couple steps. "You know what's really terrible?"

"What?" she asked, not at all sure where he was going.

But, to her surprise, he sobered. "Seeing you disappear from view and not knowing why, especially when you never came back up. I was worried you'd gotten hurt."

She smiled. "I appreciate the sentiments, but I'm okay now. Didn't mean to scare you."

Not so surprisingly, that mood didn't last and he immediately brightened. "Aw, you're such a good friend, forever thinking of others," he said, patting her on the head.

"You're a terrible friend," Jez told him, pushing his hand away, but the familiar banter had actually helped and she felt a little more grounded in the present. "Can we head home yet?"

Beau nodded. "Reardon and a dozen or so of ours are going to stay. The other camp and the rest of us can head back." He glanced at her, question in his eyes.

She nodded and pushed off the tree, standing steady, even if the memories hadn't faded completely. "I'm good enough to walk and I'd like to get back to familiar ground and away from this place."

"Fair enough. Give me ten minutes or so to get everyone organized and we'll get going," Beau said. "Jessie, mind giving me a hand?"

"Not at all, cap'n," she said with a smirk, ignoring him as he rolled his eyes.

By the time they arrived back at Cavern Hall, an hour after nightfall, Jez felt steady in her mind. Still, she decided to take some quiet time in the near future to mull it over and make sure she had dealt with the flashback enough that she wouldn't be likely to freeze or collapse during another battle. She didn't *think* she would, unless the echoes of the ambush were too strong again, because she hadn't had an issue with the battle where Bri died. Still, it was something she should try and face.

Sorin rolled over and stared up into the dark, barely able to make out the patterns on the ceiling. He heaved a sigh and swung his legs over the side of his bed. He knew this feeling deep in his gut too well. He snagged a pair of pants from beside his bed and tugged them on, slipping out his door and down the hallway. The only sound was his bare feet padding softly against the floor.

He nodded to the single guard who paced the opposite way down the hall. The man nodded back respectfully. Sorin made a note to learn his name. The young guard had been on night duty so long he no longer showed any surprise at the nocturnal wanderings of Sorin and his siblings, even when they were only half-dressed, like Sorin now.

He reached his intended destination and hesitated for a second before silently turning the knob and pushing the door open enough he could peek in. When Ani's bed was empty, Sorin silently berated himself. After the day they'd all had, of course she wouldn't be staying there.

He retraced his steps past his room and up a short flight of stairs to Ren's room. He nodded at the guard on duty and, once again, silently cracked the door open. Even as he did, he saw Ani slip into bed beside Ren.

The king stirred. "Ani?" he murmured.

"D'you mind, Renny?" she asked anxiously.

He shifted to give her more room in response. "Course not." He yawned, propping himself up a bit to look down at her. Neither was the slightest bit aware of Sorin's presence at the door. "What's wrong?"

"Nightmare," she said softly, burrowing into his side.

"You okay?"

"Better now, but the couch seemed empty and cold."

"I'm happy to share space here."

She sighed as he wrapped an arm around her. "I hate nightmares. I've had them as long as I can remember and I'm so tired of it. Sorin used to help. He always seemed to know and he'd be awake before I even reached his room."

Sorin's heart skipped a beat. It had been that way for so many years. Even when other things had slipped between them, he had still known. Would ease into her room while she was still mostly asleep and soothe her. When he'd been at boarding school, he'd known and he'd written so many letters to her during those long night hours when he couldn't settle.

"I wonder if he still would, but I suppose it doesn't matter anymore."

It didn't, and that was okay, because she had Ren now. It felt as if a great weight lifted off his shoulders. He hadn't always been good at it – and sometimes had positively sucked at it – but he had always been Ani's protector. Now, though, he felt he could safely allow that burden to pass to Ren and that the other man would do a capable, loving job of it. Possibly, all things considered, a better job than Sorin had done, even at his best.

"I think he would. Maybe, in his own way, he still does," Ren said softly.

She lay silent. "Maybe. I like to hope so." She yawned. "I love you, Renny Muffin."

"I love you too, Ani," he murmured but Sorin wasn't sure she'd heard. She had already drifted off again, safe in his grasp.

Sorin stepped back, silently shutting the door. He glanced at the guard, but the man kept his gaze firmly ahead. If he had heard any of that, he would not speak of it. Sorin nodded to himself and headed back for his room. His sister was in good hands.

Chapter Twenty-seven

I PAUSED. I HADN'T HAD TO TELL that much on my own since Jay had come into the story. It made me all the more worried for my friend. I looked at him and found he had shifted, wrapping his arms around his knees instead of over his head. Despite the chill in the air, he also finally appeared dry and the periodic shaking seemed to have left him completely. My heart lifted a bit.

Since I paused, Stella spoke up. "Was it really horrible?"

"The flashbacks? Terrible. I felt like I'd just lived through it all over again, only worse, because, the first time, I was in so much pain that there was little clarity. Now, though, I knew what it looked like."

"D'you regret it?"

"Regret what?" I asked Dave.

"Ambushing them like they ambushed you."

I pursed my lips. "I regret that it was a necessary evil and that so many people's family members had to die. I regret that Tira has come to this. But I don't regret that we actually did it. We needed to make a statement to the Three and it was the safest way. We had a few injuries, but no one died or was hurt that badly. And it isn't the same either. Methods, well, an ambush is an ambush, but theirs was pure and simple revenge and they killed a lot of people just to get at me. Ours was more a..." I searched for the word or phrase I wanted.

"A declaration of war," Stella said softly.

I looked up. "Yes, actually, that exactly. It was us officially declaring war on the Three. Telling them that we were strong enough to act and not just react."

"But you still ended up in here," Dave said.

"Not everything goes as according to plan as the ambush did, but that's getting ahead of ourselves a bit. The ambush took place at the very beginning of November and we got caught in late December. I should mention, too, that we had been slowly working on an overall plan of attack for Tira as a whole for a while, but after the ambush, almost all our spare time was devoted to it."

"Almost all?"

I smiled slightly, glancing at my friend again. "Jay refused to let it be all. He said that, if we didn't take periodic breaks, we'd become as boring and stuffy as the Three. And while none of us believed him, it was a good enough excuse to take breaks other than to sleep."

"Of course he did," Stella said, amused. "He doesn't even let things get stagnant here and he doesn't have nearly as much to work with."

"That's a Dall for you," I said dryly, nudging him slightly. At least he gave with the motion, instead of sitting dead against it, but his head still didn't come up. I took a sip of the water we'd saved. "Shall I continue?"

"Yes, please!" Dave said. "Although I still say things are going to get boring once we're done."

I chuckled and decided my birthday was the next moment of any significance, which came only a little over a month before our current predicament. I had finally turned twenty and escaped my teen years. Though, at this rate, I wouldn't come anywhere close to twenty-one. Pushing that particular morbid thought aside, I began again.

Jez's birthday came towards the end of November. Dunkin's birthday fell just a week after hers, so the pair had decided to hold a co-birthday celebration then instead. Beau still wanted to do something special for her birthday, even if it was just the two of them, but when he went looking, he couldn't find her anywhere within Cavern Hall. Finally, he headed outside and climbed to the top of their warren of caves. Ever since the ambush, he knew Jez had taken to spending snippets of time out there alone when she could. "Jez?" he called softly when he spotted her, a few yards away.

She looked up briefly and smiled. "Hey."

He spotted the object set out on her lap and smiled sadly himself as he moved to sit next to her. "He would have been very proud of the way you've used that," he said, nodding towards it.

Jez smiled down at her sword, Bri's present to her a year before. "I haven't had much occasion to use it."

"That'll change."

"I know. And soon, if our planning comes to any fruition."

"It will."

"And then everything will change, not just whether I've used my sword much."

He nodded. "Barring anything unforeseen, we'll be in charge of all of Tira."

Jez ran her fingers along the blade thoughtfully. "There has to be a Highcastle relative or something out there, doesn't there? I mean, King Sek wasn't a direct relative to the Highcastle king before him, but he was still family. Didn't you say there were some distant cousins?"

He nodded. "But they're complete unknowns." Beau looked unusually pensive even for him.

"But we can't just take control. Doesn't that make us the same as the Three? We don't know anything more about ruling than they did and we have no connection to the rightful ruling family."

"Actually," he said slowly, "neither of those things are precisely true."

She frowned. "Ruling I could maybe see, but you just said the cousins are unknowns, which means they're not part of the Freedom Fighters."

"Are you more Jasmine or Jez?" he asked, in a weird subject change. "It's almost been two years. Which one is more you?"

"Jez," she answered without hesitation. "I've changed and that fits me now. I was never a huge fan of Jasmine to begin with. But I'm still a Lockholme, so the point is probably moot. Why?"

He didn't answer right away, shifting to face her. "I've been just Beau since my mother died when I was eleven. And although I left my own last name behind then, it's never really left me. Jez, *I'm* a Highcastle. My mother was Elizabeth. My father, King Patrick. Renier's my brother. Or was my brother."

Although her first instinct was to laugh at the insanity of such a claim, she found that impossible in the face of his utter earnestness. Plus, she had met the king and prince a couple of times – Renier and her eldest brother had been playmates during childhood and the king and her father were old friends. If she looked at Beau with her recollections of them in mind, it was very possible there were strong similarities. "How?" she asked after a moment.

"When the king learned my mother was pregnant with a second child, they came up with a plan to keep her and the unborn baby, me, safe by sending her with a small, handpicked group of men and women up into the hills around here. There were already rumors then that a group was trying to orchestrate a takeover, graffiti on walls, and little skirmishes with guards at obscure outposts. So, my parents decided to protect the line at all costs. After coming up here, they faked their deaths. Then they assumed disguises and settled in a small town about two days north of Ellworth. That's where I was born. Unfortunately, my mother caught a disease, when I was ten, and died. I tried to send all the people who had protected us all that time home, but many of them wouldn't go. Some, like Mick's father, had always been in service to the Highcastle family. Reardon's another one."

"Had Mick's father brought him north with him?"

"Yes. Even back then, no one knew what happened to Mick's mom, so when we left, Mick came too. I always knew of Mick, but when I was three, he became my companion, with the understanding that he'd become my bodyguard when we were both older. We connected pretty quickly. Once my mother died, we moved to the first Cavern Hall. Many of that original group is still involved, although some have died. Most are the root of our spy and recruiting network, sending people like Jessie or Bri here to us."

"This is why you said you couldn't be king. On our way back from Westcorner."

He smiled slightly. "Yes. My mom did her best to teach me everything she could, but it's been a long time since she was around to coach me. And although the others did their best, it wasn't exactly the training befitting a king."

"If you become king, you'll have all of us to help you. And so what if you make some technical mistakes because of lack of training? You're still a hell of a lot better choice than the Three. And who knows, maybe by some miracle, your father or brother is still alive and you won't even have to worry about it."

He shook his head. "I worry about that too. They'll have been held captive for close to two years by the time we hopefully get back in there. That's a long time, by anyone's standards."

"We'll cross that bridge when we come to it," she said firmly. "For now, you're still Beau and we have a job to do."

"You're right. But today's your birthday." He stood and offered his hand. "Let's go for a walk."

She grinned. "Don't you have work to do?" she teased.

He just held his hand out, raising both eyebrows.

She took his hand, letting him pull her up, even as she sheathed her sword. "Let's go for a walk," she said.

With a delighted smile, he led the way down off the rock and into the woods.

The next couple weeks were quiet. But by the time the first week in December ended, there was a steadier than normal stream of people in and out of Cavern Hall, many heading out to do various jobs required for the final push.

"I'm at a loss," Beau said one morning, as the main group gathered in his room, all working on aspects of the plan.

"For which part?"

"The two Greensward pairs. Col's there already as well as our usual recruitment pair but I want to keep these jobs separate so if something happens, we still have them. One needs to be in place by mid-December, the other not until January, three or so weeks later. I just don't know who to send."

The four sitting on the floor exchanged looks. "Send us," Jez said. "Jessie and Ry can do one. Jay and I will do the other."

Beau frowned. "I was going to keep all of you here, as part of our command group."

"Which was all well and good when you didn't need positions filled."

"If anything, you'll know they'll both be done right if we're doing them," Jessie said. "And don't both of those call for early action? So we'll still be back in plenty of time before the main attack on Oakbridge."

"There's a risk," Beau started.

"I wouldn't go there with this crowd if I were you," Mick said, surprising the others. "I think they proved themselves in Westcorner as being very capable of getting out of even serious scrapes. Plus, they can out argue anyone, as a general rule."

"I always said that Mick was brilliant," Jay said. "Do either of these missions result in certain and horrid death?"

Beau rolled his eyes. "Of course not."

"Then we're game."

The captain rearranged the papers on his desk in obvious agitation. "I'll think about it."

Again, the four exchanged a look. "Don't think too long if you need a pair in place soon," Jessie said. Then she stood. "C'mon, guys, we won't get many more nice days like this this winter, let's go outside and get some fresh air." Her efforts weren't subtle, but it was a true enough excuse and even Mick stood up without further complaint. Within a minute, they had left Jez and Beau alone.

"Logically, there's nothing to think about," she said quietly, perching on the desk.

"There's everything to think about. The risk…"

"Is no more than we're asking everyone else to take. I understand your worry - of course I do - but this is something we can do. Something concrete, critical, *and* useful."

He sighed and stood, facing her. "If I lose you," he started huskily, hands coming to rest on her shoulders.

"I know how to take care of myself," she said lightly. "You've taught me very well the past two years, Captain."

He leaned forward and brushed a kiss against her cheek. "I hope I've taught you well enough," he murmured and then dropped his hand to hers. "Come on. Let's go enjoy a little fresh air with our friends."

She searched his face, even as she entwined their fingers. "Be the captain," she said quietly and then slid off the desk and walked outside with him to where the others were sitting up on the rocks.

"Summer," Jay complained as they joined their friends, "is more fun than winter."

"Didn't you say a couple months ago that winter was the best season?" Ry asked.

"Don't mess up my rant," he told her and continued on in the same breath. "In summer, you can go swimming and frolic with daisies."

"And those are the only two things summer has going for it?" Jessie asked.

He made a show of thinking about it. "Yes. But winter! Winter has snowball fights and snowmen and all sorts of fun stuff."

"And it gets really, really cold in our home," Ry said.

"You're messing with my rant again!"

The others exchanged amused looks, considering he'd gone from saying summer was best to defending winter in two breaths.

"Why can't you frolic in winter?" she asked, ignoring him. "With snow instead of daisies."

"But what about the rest of the time when there's no snow or daisies?" Jez asked, settling in between Jessie and Beau.

"It's a travesty," Jay said solemnly. "But!" He now leapt to his feet. "I shall make do."

"Excuse me?"

He hopped down the rocks to the ground. "I will find a worthy substitute for snow or daisies. Who wants to join me?"

"We'll pass," Mick said.

They spent the rest of the chilly morning, talking quietly, watching Jay range back and forth among the trees, occasionally skipping and throwing things from sticks to bark to grass around. They left him to his devices, finding the whole thing too amusing to stop, until Dunkin came to fetch them for lunch.

Beau obviously stewed over the decision for the next couple days and Jez let him, figuring he needed time to come to terms with it. But as the days inched by without him being decisive, she tracked him down. She found him in the map room. Reardon, Mick and a few others were there with him, but the meeting had obviously broken up because they were already filtering out. Reardon headed for the door last – other than Mick – and paused, putting a hand on her shoulder and leaning in to murmur in her ear. "Well done, lass. He hadn't told a soul who he was since his mother died. Always knew you were a keeper."

At the kind words, her cheeks flushed. "Thank you."

He winked and hurried past, calling to someone who had already left.

At her voice, the two remaining men looked up and Beau smiled tiredly. "Hey."

"Hey," she said, not minding that Mick was there. She actually suspected from his previous comment in support that he'd be her ally this time. "I wanted to let you know that Jay, Jessie, Ry, and I are well aware of what the Greensward jobs are. Even if you don't give us permission, we're going to do them anyway."

For a moment, his jaw worked with no sound.

"That's a good point," Mick said mildly. "You *could* do that. Well played, Jez."

Even now, two years on, Mick was not quick with compliments so Jez grinned. "Thank you. I take it you've been working on him on our behalf?"

"Constantly, until he tells me to shut up."

"And that doesn't always stop him," Beau muttered.

"Your mother appointed me your companion and bodyguard. A companion wouldn't shut up. A bodyguard would. So sometimes I can't decide which to do," he said mildly.

"Beau, you have to look at this as our captain. Your job, *our* job, is to do whatever it takes to dethrone the Three and put a Highcastle back on the throne, whether that's you or someone else. No matter what your feelings are, we all agreed to that job when we got here. You need the right people for this and that's the four of us, however painful it is to admit." At the stricken look on Beau's face, she softened. "I don't want to leave you, Beau, even for a day. But someone has to do this."

"What if you don't come back?"

"I don't know," she said honestly. "It's been a hazard of my life for two years and yours for a lot longer. But Jay and I will get the job done, no matter what."

"I don't like it," Beau said, but held up a hand and sighed when both she and Mick opened their mouths to comment. "I don't like it, but I have to admit you're right. I wouldn't trust anyone else to do exactly that. And, the four of you work very well together, so I know both phases will get done, even if they don't go according to plan."

She smiled, hugging him. "It'll work out okay, Beau."

"It'd better, or I'll come find you myself," he said. "We've got some free time. Why don't you go grab the others and we'll go over the plans and Greensward in detail and make sure it's foolproof?"

Jez nodded. "Sounds like a good idea."

Within the hour, they were gathered around one of the tables in the main room, half listening to Reardon teach a class in the rest of the large space. Beau had a detailed map of Greensward's streets laid out on the table along with the drafted plans for the Greensward missions. The first job had the arguably more difficult task of blowing up the weapons storage depot with the Freedom Fighters' limited supply of balsic explosives. The second would come in and start a whisper campaign against the Three's troops and hopefully lead to some tricks and subtle attacks on the soldiers. The first pair would stay and assist in the second's efforts, coordinating also with the recruitment group already in place and Col.

After a brief conversation, they agreed that Jez and Jay would be responsible for the weapons depot and leave within the week. Jessie and Ry would follow to spearhead the whisper campaign about three weeks later. The rest of the afternoon passed swiftly as they tweaked the plans to fit their personalities and work in what they hoped were reasonable safeguards.

Their last couple of days passed in a blur of learning the intricacies of balsic stone and its explosive properties from a Freedom Fighter named Martin as well as packing what they needed. It turned out that the Freedom Fighters, through Mick, had quietly been acquiring a small collection of horses, including a handful from the Lockholme stock, and boarding them in the same small village where Beau and Mick grew up. Therefore, he was able to provide the two with a pair of solid, but not flashy, horses for the journey.

The morning of their departure, their friends, including Reardon and Dunkin, gathered with them outside Cavern Hall. "We'll be in Greensward soon," Ry said, throwing her arms around Jez, "so you only need to stay out of trouble for a few weeks."

"We'll do our best, even if Trouble is Jay's middle name."

"Hey, now," Jay protested, giving Dunk's hand a very vigorous shake. "I can stay out of trouble when I want to. It's just not often that I want to!"

The others chuckled, but there was a strain to it.

They moved around the rest until Jay hugged Jessie. "Now, Jessica, no running off with another man while I'm not around. My feelings would be hurt for all eternity."

She laughed. "I wouldn't dream of it, Jay."

He snuck in a quick pat to the head, all the while grinning like an idiot. "Good, I'll need my Jessie-poo when I get back."

Her eyebrows rose, expression darkening dangerously. "Jessie-poo?" she repeated.

"Did I say that?" He quickly backpedaled. "I said Jessie, just Jessie, that's all."

She punched him in the arm, ignoring his yelped protest. "That's because I'm pretty sure I heard you quite clearly."

"Ears can be deceiving," he said sagely.

Ry laughed. "Jez, try and make sure he doesn't get himself killed, okay?"

"I can't promise anything but I'll do my best," she said and turned to Beau. She placed her hands on his cheeks, kissing him slowly, wanting to make it count. Finally, she pulled back slightly. "I love you."

"I love you too," he said softly. "Forget keeping Jay safe," he tried to keep his voice light, "keep yourself safe."

"I'm sure I can manage both," she said, then gently patted his cheek and stepped back. "C'mon, Jay, it's time to go."

"Ready and willing!" He hopped over to his horse and mounted, waving at the others as Jez joined him astride. Then, they turned and set off for Greensward.

Ani burst through Sorin's door the next day, early in the morning. "Hi, Sunshine!"

"Ani," he said reprovingly.

She grinned and flopped in a chair at his desk. "What? It's a good nickname. Not always accurate, but good anyway."

He sighed, but it was clearly more habit than with any feeling. "Do you need something?" he asked curiously.

"No, Vlad told me to meet him here."

"And why did our brother summon you to my office?" he asked, sounding less than pleased. Which Sorin often sounded, but not often when it had to do with her or Vlad.

"Beats me. I did think it was rude that he didn't summon me to his office," she said with an irreverent grin.

"Only you would find only the location rude," he said dryly. "I'm sure he's well aware I would have ignored him had he tried to summon me to his office."

She frowned, opening her mouth to ask why when Vlad barged in, walking first to the fireplace and dropping a stack of paper there. "This all needs to be burned."

"Hello, Vlad!" Ani said brightly.

"Hello," he threw over his shoulder but otherwise ignored her, immediately bringing up some boring administrative thing. Ani fully tuned him out. At least until things got a little heated, which was really weird, because Sorin was always calm and collected.

"What I think is..."

"Vladimir, I honestly don't care about your opinion right now," Sorin said flatly. "You're going about this all wrong and you need to just admit it and leave it to me."

"I don't appreciate your attitude, Sorin."

"If you weren't going to, you shouldn't have asked me to help you take over the country," he said easily, leaning back in his chair. "What do you think, Ani?"

"Hmm?" she asked, trying to act like she'd been fully listening the whole time and hadn't just clued back in.

"Thoughts?"

"Sorin's right," she said, getting up to warm her hands at the smoldering fire.

"Why the hell is Sorin always right?" Vlad exploded. "And do you even know what we're talking about?"

"Something to do with the Freedom Fighters." It was a valid guess to why the two were arguing. Nothing else could be serious enough. Except Ren's safety. "And Sunshine's always right." That wasn't strictly true but close enough, especially recently.

She glanced back in time to see Sorin smirk. She thought he looked pleased. For once, he didn't even comment on the nickname. "Look, Vladimir, just admit you're wrong and we're right."

"Since when did Anica even get a vote?"

"Don't call me Anica!" she told him, flatly. Vlad knew better. She'd allowed it from Sorin for a time because, well, she forgave Sorin everything and he hadn't really known better for a while in a way.

"You know she doesn't like Anica," Sorin said at the same time.

Vlad glared at them. "You two are impossible."

In the tense silence that followed, Ani realized she was actually absorbing the words in the letter on the top of the to-burn pile. "What's this?" she asked. "Vlad, did you do something about this?"

Taken off guard by her changing the subject, he blinked at her. At least the tension fizzled too. "Did I do something about what?"

"This letter. It's from an Eva Morales, a hostel owner outside Greensward," Ani said, reading it more thoroughly. "She's been having problems with your soldiers. Our soldiers! They're being jerks," she said. It was a parred down version, but accurate enough. They were hassling Eva for running her business and harassing her employees and young daughter.

"Being jerks?" Vlad repeated. "Ani, I don't have time for this."

"Isn't that what's being king or at least in charge all about? Listening to everyone?"

"She makes a good point," Sorin pointed out mildly.

"If she did, we wouldn't be here. Or else...damn it, neither of you are ones to talk. If we did that, then we should just abdicate the throne to the Freedom Fighters, which is a wonderful idea. Let's just throw in the towel and hope they're nice to us after we killed the king," Vlad said, voice dripping with an unreasonable amount of sarcasm.

"That was you," Ani said, keeping her tone absent. Sorin seemed to be deliberately baiting their brother. What had happened between them? She had thought they were okay enough after the Ren Incident. But she must've missed something. She'd ask Sorin later.

"For once, Vladimir makes a good argument," Sorin said, "but he misses the main point."

"I can't respond to every last person who writes me a sob story. Tell them to put down the Freedom Fighters and our soldiers won't need to be in their homes."

"It's not her home. It's her business and they're being jerks to her and her daughter, who is a little girl," Ani said, voice more strident, stepping back over to the desk. "A little girl, Vlad!"

"So I feel bad for her, but they didn't actually hurt her. They have a lot of things to get out of their system, that's all. Let them posture."

"If we help, we look better," Ani argued.

"This is not up for discussion, Ani! Those are just papers that need to be burned."

"It should be. Right, Sorin?"

"Mm," Sorin said, reaching out and delicately plucking the letter from her hands to peruse for himself.

"See, Sorin agrees with me."

"He said no such thing!" Vlad grumbled. "When he doesn't speak, you can't put words in his mouth."

"Why not? I know what he's thinking."

"Anica, it's not up for discussion."

She now glared at him. "Don't call me that."

"It's your name."

"It's what Father called me and I don't want to be called that ever. You know that."

That stopped him for a minute. "The point is, I don't have time to help her. And what do you want me to do? We'll always have more soldiers. I can't watch all of them all the time."

"Their commanders can," Sorin muttered but Vlad ignored him and Ani decided to pretend to do the same, even if she felt a small thrill of triumph.

"If you do something for her, she'll tell all the people who stay with her and people will like us more."

"I..." Vlad trailed off.

"She speaks sense," Sorin put in.

Their older brother let out an inarticulate growl. "I have governing things to do! I will talk to you two later," he said, turning and stomping from the room.

"Vlad's not having a good day."

"Vladimir rarely has good days anymore," Sorin pointed out, staring after their brother.

She frowned. "Can you help that? I've never been good at making Vlad happy. And things have been rocky because of Ren."

He meticulously folded the letter back along the creases. "I don't think there's anything I can do either. Vladimir and I haven't truly seen eye to eye since well before I moved out."

Ani sighed. "I like him better happy." She really meant 'not like Edward' but couldn't bring herself to say it.

"Mm," Sorin said, folding the letter smaller and slipping it into his back pocket.

She watched him out of the corner of her eyes and tried not to smile, only partially succeeding. "Let me guess, Eva Morales won't have any more problems."

Sorin flashed her a momentary and still rare smile. "At least not with this crowd. She very usefully gave me the name of the unit commander. They'll be getting a new deployment within the next day. I'm sure someone's going to Greensward tomorrow."

Ani, unable to resist, jumped up and all but tackled Sorin in a hug. "Thank you!" she sang.

He patted her gently on the back. "You're welcome. But Vladimir is right, in so far as it will be all but impossible to step in on all of these."

Her face fell a bit, even as she nodded her acquiescence.

He glanced over at the pile on the hearth. "But I'll make sure any incoming letters get directed through someone else first. We'll see what we can do."

Instantly, she beamed again. "Love you, Sunshine!"

Amusement flickered across his face. "You're welcome." He started to excuse himself.

She recognized the look so she spoke quickly. "Is there any way to really help Vlad?"

"I don't know," he said. "I suspect it's just a reaction to the stress from the Freedom Fighters' pressure, even if he would never admit it. I'm sure he'll be fine once we defeat them."

She studied him, hearing what he didn't say as clearly as what he had. "Can we beat them?" she asked bluntly.

"Now? I believe so. In a couple of months? I'm honestly not sure."

She pursed her lips, uncertain what to think of that answer or fact. "That's what I thought. Take care of Vlad please."

"I'll do my best," he promised, "which means I'd better go make sure Vladimir doesn't do any poor governing. I'll see you at dinner?"

"You bet!" she said and forced a grin. "If I don't get distracted by Renny."

There was a pause and then he shook his head. "I won't ask, so please don't tell me."

"I'll try not," she said, patting him on the head as she bounced past, heading for Ren's room.

Chapter Twenty-eight

I STOPPED THERE, TAKING A BREAK to drink some water and look at my friend. "I think Jay could use his Jessie-poo right now," I said, forcing a smile.

He looked back at me, gaze dull but still alive. "Too right," he muttered.

I was surprised, and very glad, to see him alert and making eye contact. "Hey."

He managed a weak smile. "Hi."

"Are you…?" I started and couldn't finish. I knew he still wasn't okay, I could see it in the tension in his shoulders and the flatness in his eyes.

"I will be. Dalls always bounce back," he said, but without the usual levity and bouncing that accompanied that statement.

"What happened?"

"When I went into the room, there was a tub of water sitting in the center." That explained why he'd been so wet.

"Gods' Breath," Stella muttered.

Jay winced. "When I didn't answer a question, the brutes held me under."

"How long?"

"Long enough. Usually until I took a breath. Then, Rees would wait until I'd coughed it all out and ask another one." He smiled crookedly. "I think I officially hate water."

"I don't blame you. Now would probably not be a good time to offer you a sip," I said, gesturing at the dish.

"Actually, it sounds good," he said, leaning forward and scooping it up. "It's not a very large quantity. Just don't ask me to go swimming or fishing anytime soon."

I nodded. Jay loved both of those activities. I hoped he could get past this, or it would be different enough it wouldn't bother him. "We'll see what we can do to get you comfortable doing those when we get out," I said lightly.

"If," he said softly.

"When," I told him. "We cannot let a man like Trigger Rees win."

"True. We need to see if we can come up with a possible plan too, just in case Jessie and Ry can't manage it."

I had a lot of faith in our friends, but I agreed that trying to figure out something of our own wasn't a bad idea. I just wasn't sure there was a way. Rees was careful with us, always sending both brutes and they outweighed possibly all four of us. "I'm trying, but I don't see you helping."

"Hey," he protested before he caught sight of my expression and made a face.

"Better."

He rolled his eyes, but I took it as a good sign.

"I'm sorry I can't provide you with your Jessie-poo," I said, teasing.

Jay winced. "Not funny. I strongly suspect she's harboring a grudge for that and will promptly murder me upon rescuing us."

"If she was going to murder you, why would she bother rescuing you first?" Dave asked.

"Astute question, young man," Jay said, pointing at him with a touch of his usual vigor. "Plainly it is my fate to die here in this-"

I clapped a hand over his mouth. "Stop that. Don't tempt the gods."

"Good point," he said, muffled from my hand. "I would very much desire to look upon the outside world again."

"You're such an idiot," I told him, taking my hand away.

He smiled a little. "I know."

"If you two are done once again picking on each other," Stella said, "can I ask a couple questions?"

I turned to her. "Sure, about what?"

423

"Two parts of the last section. I try not to interrupt while you're so involved in the story, but since we've stopped anyway, I thought I'd ask."

"Go for it," Jay said, chin still on his knees, but he definitely held himself less tightly.

"Did the Three not retaliate for the ambush? You seemed to be outside freely again pretty quickly after."

"Oh, I did forget that part, didn't I?" I said.

"The Three tried to retaliate," Jay said. "When their remaining soldiers got back to Oakbridge, or when news reached Oakbridge, they sent spies up into the region. Only, they all went through Ellworth and our people sniffed them out. We captured the first three and convinced them better of snooping."

"Of course, that really only pissed them off more, but we got lucky, because Nerius tried to make inroads even further north than towns like Evenly, since the Three have been unable to push them back to their original borders. All the available spies and soldiers were needed down at the border. We kept scouts out, but the main danger was gone."

She nodded. "Okay, that makes sense and, if I'd thought about it logically, I remember hearing about that thrust by the Nerians. Sometimes, it's hard to remember you're telling a true story," she said, with a sheepish smile.

"No judgment," Jay said. "I routinely used to get sucked into stories, true or imaginary, as a kid."

"What was the other question?" I asked, but I already suspected I knew what it was.

"Telling us about Beau. Here, in this place. I mean, yes, we already knew from conversation and McRuoes, but not that clearly."

I shrugged. "To be honest, if McRuoes is sending letters to Beau from the prince that Anica knows about, then I would suspect that Opalin and Dakamar probably have strong suspicions anyway about Beau as the head of the Freedom Fighters. Plus, I know none of them were around when I said it. I kept a pretty close on eye on the hallway."

"And she lowered her voice," Dave added.

"That too."

Stella nodded. "Makes sense. Just seems a little gutsy."

I grinned. "Gutsy is what we do. We wouldn't be here if we weren't being gutsy."

"And foolhardy."

"And sometimes plain idiotic," I agreed, laughing. "Maybe it's time to finish up the story."

"Yes, please," Dave said. "You both had just left for Greensward."

"My memory's not that bad," Jay said. "Since I ditched Jez for the last few bits, including" - here he sighed dramatically - "my frolicking, which she did not do justice, I'll pick up with our arrival at Greensward." He took a deep breath and launched into the last section.

◀▼▶

It took a couple days to travel from Cavern Hall to Greensward, cutting around the outskirts of Ellworth and then straight south on the road. No one looked at them twice. Their first view of Greensward, which neither had visited before, came maybe a half hour's ride out as they crested a small rise. They reined in the horses.

"I am unimpressed," Jay declared.

"It's Tira's second biggest city," Jez said, startled by the assertion. "I'm impressed."

"Look at it," he said. "It's a total fixer upper. I mean, those walls? Honestly."

The walls stood straight and solid with no signs of decay or crumbling. She rolled her eyes. "I will never understand you."

He grinned and nudged his horse forward. "Good!"

They checked in at an inn a respectable distance from the weapons depot, but close to the apartment the recruitment pair shared. To create a credible cover, they told the innkeeper they were Mr. and Mrs. Dalton and agreed to not tell Beau, not that Jez thought he'd get too jealous, but just in case.

The next morning, they left the inn and wound their way through the busy city streets until they reached the shade of the palace of Greensward. Now, the local duke lived there, but stories had it that it had once been the queen's palace to rival the king's castle in Oakbridge. Or, at least, that's what Jay could recall. The palace was an attraction in the city, with its ornate towers and decorative stonework. The Three had closed it to visitors, but there was still plenty to see from outside the low defensive walls and for a while, Jez and Jay strolled along, taking it all in as if they were really there to just view it and had no other reasons. Eventually, though, their walk brought them closer to the barracks and the weapons depot. Jay tore his gaze away from the palace to casually scan the area, keeping up a steady stream of boring conversation with Jez about their plans, both real and fake, since they had enough time to see the city while they were there.

The area was fairly heavily guarded, considering it would go boom rather spectacularly if the right person, armed with the right weapons, could get at it. Additionally, it hugged the wall of the palace, snug between that and the soldiers' barracks. After Oakbridge, it was the second most heavily guarded town, which made sense, considering its size. There had been multiple riots in Greensward, mostly in the earliest days of the Three's occupation. The most recent had been nudged along by the recruitment team, Adam and Ursula, only about six months prior.

"Not going to be easy," Jez murmured.

"Nothing worthwhile ever is," Jay said. "Beau warned us this would be the case. Think it's more or less heavily guarded at night?"

"Not sure. There are certainly more soldiers on site at night, more weapons too, presumably, but most of the rest of the world is also asleep."

He nodded thoughtfully. A minute later, they both turned away and meandered back through the city.

Throughout the next couple days, they made multiple trips, at various times to try to get as accurate a record as possible of when the soldiers were around. Sometimes, they went alone, sometimes together, not wanting to arouse suspicion.

After the reconnaissance, they sat on the bed and examined the sketches and notes they'd made. Jez pawed through them and frowned. "Late morning or early afternoon seem the lightest times. When most of the soldiers are out on duty and no one's sleeping. But even then, they've got good coverage."

"Whoever set up their guard duties knew what they were doing."

She flipped to another page and read. "That's the local colonel, a, um, Colonel Rees. Whoever he is has knowledge and background."

"So, if there's always good coverage, we need to mess up that coverage. How long do we estimate it'll take us to set the charges?"

"Fifteen minutes with a couple more for getting in and out." Jez tapped one of the papers as she thought. "I think we need to bring in Adam and Ursula. They've caused some riots here before. Maybe they can do the same for us."

"It's only a few days' notice," Jay said, "but most Freedom Fighters are miracle workers. C'mon, let's go see them now and take another stroll by the palace on our way back."

Even though they had detected no signs of suspicion from the Three's men, the pair still took the long way to the apartment Adam and Ursula shared. Jay knocked and greeted Adam with a sunny smile. "Hi! We need your help."

"Oh?" he asked, stepping aside to gesture them in.

The two times they'd met with the recruitment team, it had become abundantly clear that Adam did not know what to do with Jay, while Ursula seemed quite at home deciphering the important things and giving him a quelling look when necessary.

"Hello, you two," the woman said. "Come have a seat. Can I get you anything?"

"No, thank you," Jez said, sitting. "We came to ask if you could set off another riot on a schedule, in a couple of days."

The pair exchanged a look, a look Jez knew well, the kind that passed between best friends, and she suddenly missed Jessie and Ry. "Should be doable. Near the depot?"

"The closer the better," Jay said, "so we can make things go boom." He all but yelled the last word and Adam jumped. Ursula shot him a nasty look.

"Sorry, he's been doing that since we got here. The only time he doesn't is when we're scouting," Jez said apologetically.

"But it's so *fun*," Jay protested. "Boom, boom, *bo-*"

Jez slapped a hand over his mouth. "Stop it." She waited until he'd saluted before releasing him. "Thank you." She turned back to the others. "What do you think? And what can we do to help?"

"Give us the rest of the day to figure things out," Adam said even as he stood and moved over to a well-ordered desk.

Ursula nodded. "Come back tomorrow for breakfast. And you don't need to do anything. This is part of our job description. Yours is to make sure that depot goes," she paused and held up a stern finger to Jay, "up in flames."

He sighed loudly. "That is not nearly as fun!"

"I don't care," she said and glanced subtly over at Adam.

Jez stood and pulled Jay up with her. "We'll leave you to it. Thank you. Please let us know if there's anything we can do now or the day of."

"We will. We'll probably need to arrange some sort of signal for the start and when to abandon ship. We can discuss that tomorrow."

Jay saluted again and bounced out the door, Jez following more sedately. They hit the late morning lull at the barracks and wandered casually by, observing everything. As soon as they were far enough away, Jay glanced at her. His grin came too late for her to stop him. "*Boom*."

The meeting the next morning was concise and to the point. Adam and Ursula were confident in their ability to start a big enough riot to entice the soldiers' attention. Ursula explained that the crackdown following the last riot had been so severe that most of the city had already been hovering at the edge of a riot again, in protest of that treatment. They also agreed that they would head to the area together and Adam and Ursula would start things with a simple count to two hundred after Jez and Jay left them. That would give them enough time to get into position to do their sneaking and setting of explosives once the guards were properly distracted.

They set the date to be three mornings from then, which would put Jay and Jez right on schedule – and give them at least a week of laying low and relaxation before Jessie and Ry arrived and they got put back to work. And that assumed nothing had changed in the plan. Or that nothing *would* change.

As they headed back to their inn, Jay stuck his hands in his pockets and looked up at the sky. "This still might not work. We didn't expect it to be so well guarded."

"No, we didn't, but we probably should've. Either way, we have to try."

"Oh, don't get me wrong. We are absolutely trying," he said with a slight smile. "But that doesn't mean we're not screwed. What happens if we are?"

"Nothing, at least until Jessie and Ry get here. We don't have the numbers locally to rescue us. Adam and Ursula have been here too long and Beau, as much as he'd want us out, wouldn't risk Col's anonymity to have him help."

"Ry and Jessie will move mountains to get us out, though, no matter if the numbers are stacked against them or not."

"Exactly."

Jay walked a few more paces, kicking at stones in the road. "Well, seeing the inside of a jail has never been a dream, but hey, I'm all for trying something new."

Jez snorted. "Let's not get ahead of ourselves. We are good at what we do. It might turn out all right."

"True. I am an even bigger fan of positive thinking!" he said.

"Is there anything you're not a fan of?"

He tilted his head, giving the question due consideration. "Probably. Things with fangs."

"That's your criteria? You like it unless it has fangs?"

"Pretty much."

"Guess that makes you easy to please."

"And entertain." He opened his mouth and she nudged him hard in the ribs.

"Do not say it."

He went into an instant pout, but didn't say it so Jez considered it a win.

The morning of the riot dawned bright but chilly, like many December days. Jez and Jay walked to the apartment to meet Ursula after breakfast, since Adam was out making sure a crowd actually showed up just outside the palace. The key was to have the bulk of the protest far enough from the barracks and depot so the soldiers dealing with the crowd couldn't easily see the area, in addition to the distraction factor it offered.

Ursula was in a good mood. "All indications say it'll be a big one," she told them as soon as she opened the door. "C'mon, let's go meet Adam."

Sure enough, the recruitment team had come through. They could hear the chanting of protest from a few blocks away. When they reached it, Jez and Jay saw that the group wasn't large yet, but people seemed to be continually adding to the numbers. This made sense to Jay, since they didn't want any real rioting to break until a little later in the morning. For now, the soldiers watched the chanting crowd warily from their posts.

It took a few minutes to find Adam, who stood off to one side, leaning against a building, eyes trained on the crowd and the soldiers beyond them.

"Looks good," Ursula said.

He nodded. "Word's spreading. In an hour, it'll be big and primed to explode."

Jay's stomach clenched. "You said the last crackdown was harsh. Are we going to get a lot of people hurt or arrested for this?"

A troubled look skittered across Adam's face. "It's hard to say, really," he said slowly. "They seem to react differently each time. And if the crowd gets big enough that should be sufficient distraction without an actual riot, because they'll need to pull people here to make sure it doesn't explode."

"The crackdown was harsh," Ursula said, "but there were no hangings or long-term arrests. Even the soldiers and their commanders realized that would be going too far. There was a rigidly enforced nighttime curfew and some rules about how many people could gather in one space at a time, rules which lasted really only until the next market day when they saw the impracticality of enforcing it."

Although Ursula slipped off a few times to do something or another, Adam barely moved, watching the crowd carefully. Jez and Jay stayed with him, feeling his tension along with the nerves of what they were about to attempt. Each had a bag slung over one shoulder, carrying their half of the explosives.

Finally, an hour crawled by and Adam turned his attention from the crowd to nod to them seriously. "I wish you the speed and luck of the gods."

"We'll take it," Jay said with a faint smile and led the way around the edge of the crowd.

As they moved, they yelled along with the crowd, throwing their fists up. The guards didn't even look as they broke off down a side alley and emerged two blocks down, near the barracks and depot. The pair looked around, dropping their pretense of being casual and were delighted to realize the area was all but deserted. There were only one or two men talking urgently on the far side of the barracks from the depot and they paid the two pedestrians no mind, especially as they were just two of many – most heading towards the crowd, though, and not away. Jez moved forward, scanning again and still spotting no one.

"Now's our chance," she murmured and slipped towards the depot, eyes darting to and fro, searching for signs of an ambush or anyone noticing them. No cry of alarm came as they slid out of sight. Jez pointed at herself and motioned left.

Jay nodded and pointed right, heading that way at a quick trot.

The act itself took very little time. They had practiced the motions ahead of time, back at Cavern Hall. Jez moved down the length of the depot to the far end, double checking that Jay was opposite her before reaching into her bag and pulling out the top device. She set the small mine-like explosive down, lit the long trigger wick, and hurried a dozen feet to set the next. She placed the last one at the corner and peeked out. There were more soldiers, but still none seemed to be looking in their direction. She suddenly wished they had figured out a way to steal two uniforms, even if it seemed like the Three employed few to no women. With a loose enough uniform and only distant scrutiny, she could have passed. They couldn't delay long, though, or the explosives would go off while she still stood practically on top of one. Being all but blown up once in a lifetime was more than enough for her.

She caught Jay peeking out and nodded. He returned it and stepped out, hands casually finding his pockets as he strolled towards the main streets. Jez fell into step with him, linking her arm through his.

They had almost reached the stream of people when a loud, curt voice came from behind them. "Hey! You two, there! Stop."

They exchanged a brief glance and sped up, aiming to blend into the crowd and escape notice, but luck wasn't with them. Before they got very far, four soldiers appeared in front of them, pushing their way through the crowd, presumably on their way back to the barracks.

Jez yanked Jay to the side, but the yelling voice reached over the clamor, obviously in pursuit. "Stop them!"

To their credit, the four soldiers reacted almost immediately. One shot out a hand and grabbed Jez's upper arm in a vice grip. In the time it took her to twist free, they had loosely encircled the pair.

"What is the meaning of this?" Jay asked, adopting the inflection of a nobleman. Jez didn't think the ruse would fly considering their attire, but could certainly play along.

They ignored him, coming to attention as their pursuer caught up, panting. He was a captain from the look of his uniform. "Sir!" one of them said, saluting.

"Thank you, soldiers," he said and turned to Jez and Jay, who had both adopted looks of semi-polite bafflement. "What were you two doing so close to the barracks? That is not a public area."

Jez increased her puzzled look, heart starting to race. The bombs would go off any moment and she doubted they would get out of this if they were

431

still standing here when they did. "We were just going for a stroll. Weren't we, honey?"

Jay brushed a kiss on her cheek. "Of course, bunny."

Jez almost gagged, despite, or perhaps because of, the situation.

"I am so sorry, good sirs, we're on our honeymoon and don't know Greensward politics, I'm afraid. Our sincerest apologies. You can be quite sure it will not happen again," he said, throwing in a little bow for good measure. "Now, if you'll excuse us, we have a lunch date with an old friend of my father's." With that, he tugged Jez's arm and started to step between the soldiers.

"Why the hurry?" the captain asked.

Jay half turned to face him and the depot and barracks beyond. "I just told you-"

In that instant, the depot blew. Jez felt the heat on her back. Whoever had created the little mines had seriously loaded them with balsic from the sheer size and volume of the explosion. Jay's eyes widened in real surprise. "Gods' Breath," he murmured.

Jez turned. The building simply no longer existed, other than some fires on the few remaining bits of wall. As she saw the destruction, she wondered if part of the force of the explosion might have been because they stored balsic stone of their own there.

All around them, people yelled and pointed.

"C'mon," Jay hissed and tugged at her arm.

The captain reacted at the same time, though, yelling and pointing at *them*. "Seize them!"

Instantly, the four soldiers grabbed them by the arms, allowing no room for escape. They were good and caught, even if they had accomplished their goal.

"What did you do?" the captain hissed, getting right in Jay's face.

Jay tilted his head, not bothering to deny it. "Boom," he said after some seemingly grave contemplation.

Despite everything, Jez let out a snort of laughter.

The captain recoiled and jerked another finger at him. "You will pay for this insult!"

"Insult? Don't you mean explosion? Destruction? Devastation?"

The captain let out an inarticulate snarl but, to Jez's surprise, did not hit him. Instead, he turned to the soldiers. "Take them straight to the jail. Let the colonel know we could use his help until we have this under control."

"Yes, sir!" the four chorused. A few more guards had joined them, forming a decent escort. As the captain stalked away, the men shoved the pair forward, parting the gathering crowd easily. Jez tried some experimental tugs and wiggles, but their grips were firm and there was no escaping. Not only that, but the jail was only a few blocks away from the barracks, so it seemed like all she did was blink and they were there.

Once inside, custody was transferred to the prison guards, after a few cursory attempts to get their names. Then, they were led down the halls to a cell at the far end of one. The rest you know.

"Sir," Old Bert grunted reluctantly as he stepped stiffly into the room, "General Opalin wished me to inform you that he will be stopping by shortly to talk to you." His whole expression went gleeful. "He seems quite displeased."

Sorin gave him a frosty look. "Thank you, Bert, you are dismissed," he said, returning his gaze to the paperwork. He heard Bert stomp away, counted to twenty, and looked up. The doorway and hall beyond were empty.

So he did something childish.

He stood and made his way to the door, peeking both ways before slipping through the halls quietly until he reached Ren's room. He didn't bother to try and hide from the guard – the man might figure out his plan soon enough – and knocked once before pushing the door open.

Ren sat by the window and looked up. "Hello, Sorin."

"Hello. Where's Ani?"

"Am I supposed to know?" he asked dryly.

"I thought she might have said."

"Some errand for your brother."

Sorin nodded. That changed his plans slightly, but there was still Ren. "Where do you want to go?" he asked, before he could think better of it.

"Huh?" the prince – no, king – managed brilliantly.

"Within Oakbridge. Where do you want to go?"

Ren stared.

This had better be worth it. "I am offering you the opportunity to not only get out of your room, but get out of the castle for a while. I would take it, if I were you. So, where do you want to go?" he asked, impatiently. He didn't know how long 'shortly' meant but he wanted to be out of the castle by the time his brother made it to his office. If he was going to run away, he was going to do it right.

"I don't know. Just…outside."

"That is singularly unhelpful."

Ren grabbed his crutches and stood. "Are you hiding from something?" he asked, amusement sparkling in his eyes.

"Renier, if you don't shut up, I will either break you or just throw you out the window."

He grinned. Both of them knew the threat wasn't serious. "Either way, I'd get my trip outside."

Sorin rolled his eyes. "Let's go," he said, swinging open the door. Ren came over, much better on his crutches than last time Sorin had checked and stepped outside, Sorin on his heels.

The guard looked briefly surprised before he managed to check his expression and nod gravely at them. Sorin barely noticed, making sure Vlad wasn't anywhere in sight, before heading for the stairs. Ren fell in step with him. They were on the first floor and headed for the courtyard when the king suddenly froze.

"What is it now, Ren?" he growled, turning. Maybe this hadn't been a decent substitute.

"People out there will *know* me." He sounded on the edge of real panic.

"So?"

"They'll want to talk to me."

"So? Just lie through your teeth or tell the truth, whatever. Now stop worrying about things you can't change and let's go. You know you want to. Please?" Now he was borderline begging, desperate to avoid his brother and another inevitable fight.

The 'please' startled Ren out of his panic and he caught up. "You really are hiding from something. Or is it someone?" he asked knowingly.

434

"I knew Ani was paying more attention than she let on," Sorin muttered. "Where do you want to go?"

"The ramparts, please."

"You haven't had enough of stone and stone walls?"

"Yes, but from there I can see both the city and the farms outside."

"And you don't have to talk to anyone. Now who is hiding?"

"I am not. I plan on walking back through the city," he said. "I refuse to let myself chicken out."

"Good for you," Sorin said, leading the way across the courtyard, ignoring the stares, and up into the guardhouse that blocked the rest of the ramparts from the castle.

Ren followed more slowly, due to the crutches. A smile crossed his face, an expression Sorin didn't recognize.

"What is it?" he asked.

"What's what?" Ren asked absently as he reached the top and directed his gaze out over Oakbridge which sprawled, not always prettily, in front of them.

"The smile."

"Oh. I'm not sure you'd understand," he said, after a moment of thought.

"Sounds like a challenge," Sorin said, leaning back against the wall, facing into the city he currently helped rule and that the man standing beside him should have been ruling. "Try me." He relaxed now that they were out of the castle. He could get lost in Oakbridge for hours if he wanted, even with a gimpy king in tow.

"I'm not sure I can," Ren began, leaning his hip against the wall, so he could look outside or inside the walls with a turn of his head. "There's...freedom. Real, true freedom. Then there's a false sense of freedom. Neither of which really fit me. But there's a third type. And being out here, being able to be out here, it hit me that I have that third type. I'm alive and I'm here right now."

Sorin knew exactly what he meant. That third type was the freedom that Sorin had had most of his life. Even in the years on his own and with Diana, he'd never been fully free of his family, of Edward and his legacy. And now, he was so deeply embroiled in it that...yes, this was something he and Ren had in common, even though they came from two wildly different places and lives. When the king looked at him, seeming puzzled by the silence, Sorin smiled, and started moving along the ramparts again. "You'd be surprised at what I understand."

"Maybe. Just doesn't seem like the type of freedom many have to deal with."

"I think you'd be surprised by that too. I think very few people are fully free, even if they think they are."

"Still, I wonder what it would be like for life to be simple. To make decisions that only affect you, and possibly your family, but not a whole country."

"It's good. It would feel downright liberating right about now," Sorin said quietly. Things had certainly been simpler when it was him and then him and Diana. "You know about Diana," he said, feeling safe bringing it up where his brother could not overhear. He wasn't entirely sure why he didn't want Vlad to know. Diana was dead. And there was no harm he could do, really. But something held him back.

Although it wasn't a question, Ren still nodded. "Yes. Ani told me, after you told her."

He nodded. "I could tell when I saw you next. There was almost pity in your eyes."

"Almost," the other man said, smiling slightly.

Sorin let out a bark of laughter. "Almost, but not quite."

"I would wish that on no one," Ren said quietly. "To lose the people you love, there's nothing worse."

Something else they had in common. He nodded, looking out over Oakbridge again, not wanting to go down that road, even with someone who understood. Finally, he said, "Vladimir wants you to marry Ani soon."

"How soon is soon?"

"A week, two tops."

"Short engagement," he muttered, nudging a stone with his crutch.

"Vladimir is insistent and it won't really change things for you - either of you."

"I suppose not," he said and shoved the stone off the edge.

"I didn't think you minded the idea of marrying my sister," he said. He knew that wasn't Ren's problem, but it was worth the test.

"It's not Ani. I'd rather be able to do it on my – our - own terms."

"If that was the case, you wouldn't be able to marry her."

Ren's lip quirked in a sideways smile. "If you'd done your research, you'd remember my family has had a habit over the centuries of marrying commoners."

"It still hasn't happened in a few generations."

"My reign isn't exactly traditional," he pointed out, very dryly.

"Would you marry her?" he asked abruptly.

"If you hadn't come along, I would have married Francine de Carlin a year ago."

"That's not my question."

"I don't know, Sorin. It's hard to imagine a 'what if' these days."

Sorin knew that answer was true and was the only answer he'd get, so he nodded. "We should probably head back."

"I suppose so." He grinned slightly. "Are you safe from whatever chased you out here now?"

"Shut up, Renier," he retorted, searching out the next set of stairs down the wall and heading for them. "And no, I'm going to have to face it, sooner or later, but I wasn't in the mood."

Ren said nothing immediately as he trailed along behind him. Then, he seemed to have read into the words because he spoke. "You aren't as solid as you've led me to believe."

"If you say so," he said, keeping his tone noncommittal, but he knew Ren wouldn't leave it alone.

"Ani thinks the Freedom Fighters are gearing up for a real assault. And that, other than the two prisoners in Greensward, their efforts in the past few months have all been completely successful."

"I fully expect it this year, probably late spring."

"Wait." Ren reached out and snagged his sleeve. Sorin stopped and glanced back, unable to help it. "That soon?"

"Yes. Certainly within the next six months. But they'll have to wait at least until winter ends. They don't have the means to attack around the snow. They can't move their supplies quickly enough."

"How big are they now?"

"There's no real way to tell. I know they have agents everywhere, plus probably around five hundred now at their camps. If not more. We've been unable to locate their bases since Deepen's Crossing, so an accurate count is impossible."

"Are you telling me you have no spies in their camp?"

"No. All of our attempts to approach what we think are their recruiting teams are rebuffed with no hints given that we're even approaching the right people. Ani tried to work it for a while too with no success."

Ren smiled. "Good for them."

"Don't make me tell you to shut up again, Renier," he retorted and started down the stairs, knowing Ren would be slow enough that he could ditch the king until they were on the ground. Then, hopefully, people would notice him and there would be no more talking. He stopped at the bottom and waited for Ren, wondering if he shouldn't have told the other man that. But maybe, he thought, it would preserve hope for the future, even if it wouldn't be his future.

PART TWO

Mid-January of the Year 293

Chapter Twenty-nine

STELLA GRINNED. "EXCELLENTLY DONE. You should put this all down on paper when we get out of here."

I liked hearing a 'when' and not an 'if', even as I laughed. "Jay's handwriting is atrocious and I'm not writing both parts."

"I'll bribe Dunk."

"With what?" I shot. "A strip show?"

Dave started giggling.

Jay blushed. "Jez," he whined, "that was uncalled for."

Stella chuckled too. "Aw, Jay, I'm sure Dunkin wouldn't want that."

"He is merely a friend!" he sputtered.

"You said he had a crush on another Freedom Fighter. So he's taken too," she continued sweetly.

I held my stomach, unable to stop laughing. "Oh Gods' Breath!"

Jay, though, grinned around bright red cheeks. "Okay, point."

The next week passed quietly. Jay got called in to talk to Rees again, but either the colonel's heart wasn't in it or he felt generous, because my friend came back relatively unscathed. Certainly not like the time before. Other than that, we exchanged stories unrelated to our plight and also discussed what would need to be done, assuming the Freedom Fighters won, to put Tira back to rights.

For whatever reason, Rees waited an extra day before sending the goons and Dayton for me. I expected to be taken to the same small room he'd used previously, but instead they steered me right past the door and back towards his office. My stomach sank. I was not ready to face Vladimir Opalin again, especially not on my own. When Dayton opened the door, though, I breathed a sigh of relief. The only person inside was Rees, seated at his desk, leaning back in his chair, which was half-turned to the window.

"Good morning, Jez," he said, without looking away from the window.

"Morning, Trigger," I replied cheerfully, because I had to.

He didn't reply, continuing to stare out the window. Considering it looked out at the alley between the jail and the next building, I wasn't sure what he could possibly find so interesting, but I let the silence build. It was no skin off my back, literally or figuratively, if we delayed our little chat.

Finally, Kilgor spoke. "Sir?"

I started. It was only the second time I'd heard either of them speak. Deciding I should really start the meeting out on the right foot, I asked about it.

The brutes rumbled, like growling dogs.

Rees's head came up, though. "No, Kilgor, Juke. In fact, let go of her."

Both looked taken aback by the order.

"You heard the man," I said, tugging at my arms.

"That's an order," Rees said and shot me a quelling look that I ignored.

They released their grips on my shoulders uneasily and stepped back.

"Jez, sit down," Rees ordered, gesturing at the chair across from him.

I slid forward and perched on the edge, much to his amusement.

"It won't bite."

"I know that," I said and made myself settle back, even if it put me at a disadvantage if the brutes came after me.

"Neither will I."

"Good to know. I don't like mixing my blood and someone's spit," I said sarcastically.

He smiled slightly and straightened a stack of papers, setting it back down very deliberately and pulling the top paper off. "I thought you might be interested in a piece of juicy gossip that you've probably missed, being all tucked away."

"Oh?"

"Renier Highcastle is alive."

"What?" I sputtered, before I could control myself. I knew that Renier was alive, obviously, thanks to Jakium and his letter, but it was about the last thing I had expected to come out of Rees's mouth. My mind whirled back over his last words. If it was 'juicy gossip' that leaned towards the fact it was public knowledge. Why wait almost two years and then let everyone know? What game were they playing here?

"The prince, or should I say king, is alive and well," Rees continued, his voice calm and calculating as he watched me. "Not only that, but he announced his engagement to Anica Opalin. The wedding will be in just a few weeks."

"Marry Anica?" I echoed. That part was a surprise, but the reasoning hit me almost immediately. "That's why he's still alive, isn't it? He was always very popular. If he marries one of the Three, it gives them a legitimacy they otherwise wouldn't have. It also lends a stability to the throne as well, since none of them have officially taken it." I nodded. "And they would have had him make the announcement himself too, didn't they?"

He grinned. "Yes. My, you are quick, Jez."

I rolled my eyes. "As always, your compliments warm my heart."

"Yes, they had him do it. Let him stand up there all by himself."

"I hate to say it, but sometimes they are brilliant. It's rare, but it happens. Was that Dakamar's idea?"

"Does it matter?"

I supposed not, other than to satisfy my curiosity. Opalin hadn't struck me as that kind of smart.

"Although, I'm sure they would appreciate the compliment in turn."

I let out a laugh. "I sincerely doubt that after the other day, but please, pass it along with my greetings."

He smirked and leaned back in his chair, putting his feet on the desk. He obviously thought me no threat with the brutes still in the room. I would have thought our first meeting might've taught him better than that, unless he was going to drop another bombshell. "You are one curious woman."

I blinked. Not what I was expecting. "Thank you?"

The smile widened. "We tried to kill you by blowing you up. Yet you somehow survived."

I didn't appreciate the reminder.

444

"And now, our soldiers have undoubtedly had run-ins with you upwards of a dozen times and you're still not only kicking but in one piece. Relatively speaking."

I didn't appreciate *that* one either. "I know how to swing a sword."

He snorted. "I don't think that's all it is. Who was Brighton?"

I had to give him credit because the question did take me off guard, but probably not in the way he intended. It threw me right out of the conversation. "Do you really expect me to answer that?"

He shrugged. "It's worth a try. Why not tell me?"

"Any reason to keep you from being smug is enough."

"I'll be smug anyway. It comes naturally. Who was he?"

"I told you already."

"He meant something serious to you, didn't he?"

"He was a very good friend. All my friends mean something to me," I retorted. "Look, we both know I'm not going to willingly hand over personal information, so either let me go back to my cell or let's move on."

He studied me in silence. I had to wonder what, and who, exactly he saw. "Your family."

"What about them?"

"You said they didn't know about you. Do they know about Colin?"

I frowned, freshly on my guard. "What about Colin?" It occurred to me suddenly that, considering it was the Three who invaded Northwind, Rees might actually know what had happened to my brother.

"When was the last time you saw him?"

That seemed like a trick question somehow, but I couldn't see it, so I answered honestly, wondering if I could get some sort of confirmation. "Years ago. When he left for Northwind and I went to Ellworth."

Rees's eyebrows went way up. "That seems like a strange thing to pick to lie about."

I searched his face. "It's not a lie," I said flatly. "Colin was in Northwind as part of the family guard when your bosses sent people in to kill the Walters family. If you're asking me about him, then you know this." I wanted to ask but was pretty sure Rees would give me a taste of my own medicine. If only I could see what he was getting at.

He seemed to sense that because he nodded, a slight smirk on his face, even if something in his gaze seemed puzzled. "Very well. Kilgor, Juke, take her back to her cell please. Gently. I don't want to have to call the doctor again."

As we walked back, I tried to do some mental math. We had probably been there twenty or so days. Was that long enough for Jessie and Ry to arrive? I couldn't remember exactly what the plan had been. But I needed out. Something about his interest in Colin had set off an itch in the back of my brain. And then I realized. During our other conversation, when he'd threatened my family, he'd very definitely said three brothers *at home*. Not three brothers alive or three brothers left but three at home. That monster definitely knew something about Colin. And now he knew I didn't know whatever it was.

Once Dayton let me back into the cell and had disappeared back down the corridor, I turned to Jay. "Remember how I told you I was going to stand on your shoulders one day to look out the window?"

"Yes?"

"C'mon, I want to see."

"Now? But you haven't even said what happened."

"Nothing happened that can't wait," I said with a dismissive hand wave, even though that wasn't true. But I needed another minute. "Please?"

He sighed. "You'll only need to sit on my shoulders."

It took a little doing and, in the end, Stella gave me a boost, but I managed to perch on his shoulders. I had plainly never appreciated Jay's strength enough because he managed to keep upright and I wasn't small or light.

I peered out, my eyes slowly adjusting to the brighter light.

"What do you see?"

"Feet. Lots of feet. Big feet, small feet, feet with-"

"Jez, are you really getting poetic over feet?"

"Is there something wrong with it?"

"Other than it being undeniably strange?"

"You're one to talk," I said, basking in the view of the sun. It had to be edging closer to noon than I thought, from its height in the sky.

I could sense him rolling his eyes. "Okay, time for you to get down."

We managed it semi-gracefully. I didn't kick him in the face or fall so I considered it a win. He peeked up, craning to see out the window. "Think you could return the favor?"

I grinned. "Maybe Stella and I together. I don't know how you managed me."

"Muscles," he said solemnly. "But you do weigh a ton."

"Muscles," I retorted.

His lips twitched in a grin before he could squash it. "My shoulders will never be the same."

"Your fault for letting me up."

Stella chuckled and patted the ground in front of her. "Sit and I'll give you a massage."

In about a second, he was seated cross-legged in front of her, giving me a smug look. I shook my head, but Stella seemed well aware of his tricks and also didn't seem to mind. Far be it for me to intervene.

"So," Jay said, a look of bliss on his face as Stella started massaging his shoulders, "you came back awfully quickly. You owe us an explanation."

"We just talked," I said, still trying to puzzle over the meeting, pushing the last bit of it aside for the moment. It didn't make sense to me that he'd hand me the information about the prince, or king, since technically he was right, and not press harder for something in return.

"And?" he prompted impatiently.

"It is now public knowledge that Renier is alive. It's also public knowledge that he's engaged to Anica Opalin, and their wedding is fast approaching."

"You're kidding!" Stella burst, hands pausing. Dave stared at me in shock.

Jay, though, nodded thoughtfully, after the initial surprise. "Makes sense. Everyone loved Renier before the takeover. They'll love him just as much now. It adds to their hold on the throne. Puppet king."

"And queen, if Jakium McRuoes is at all to be believed," I said.

"Gods' Breath," Stella murmured.

"Can't decide if this is good or bad news."

"Good, still, I think until we can get an accurate view of Renier's state of mind."

Jay scratched his chin. "I'll buy that. Anything else we should know?"

"He asked about Bri again. He insisted he was something special to me."

"Considering you screamed his name as you attempted to both throttle him and bash his head into a hard floor, I would say that would be a logical, and reasonable, conclusion," Jay said.

"But why does he keep asking?" Dave asked curiously.

"It's a trigger," Stella said. "Since she originally said it in a time of very high emotion, he wants to use it to try and throw her off her game and then use the momentum to get the answer to another, less emotional question answered."

"He...didn't really."

"He didn't get any information out of asking?"

I frowned and ran the conversation over in my head. "Oh, damn. He did. I didn't even register giving him anything at the time, but I told him that he was a very good friend, which he probably could guess, and that all my friends mean something to me. It's not much, but it was a subtle probe at my defenses."

"See. And now he knows that next time, maybe he can get something more important out of you, while you're all riled about Bri."

"I'll try and be careful."

"Where did you pick that up?" Jay asked. "Nothing personal, but it doesn't strike me as a normal thing you'd learn on a farm."

Stella reddened, patting his shoulder to indicate she was done with the massage. "George was already into politics and I picked up a lot along the way," she admitted. "And he gained a probably unhealthy obsession with interrogation methods after he joined the Freedom Fighters."

"How many of these interesting tidbits did you pick up?" I asked.

"Quite a few," she told me. "George liked to talk about it and I was the easy, accessible one. Plus, I didn't mind. It's strangely fascinating and an interesting look into how the brain works."

I wondered how we could use this to our advantage. If nothing else, I'd be more on my guard than ever. "Would you mind teaching us? It might make the difference in dealing with Rees in the future."

"Of course. I'm not sure it'll be any help," she said modestly.

"Every little thing helps when it comes to a man like Rees," Jay said, shifting around to sit next to her.

"Okay, um, let's see," she said, leaning back thoughtfully. Then, she launched into a lesson.

I listened closely, hoping to pick up some tips. I didn't mind that the topic had moved without me mentioning Colin. I wanted a bit more time to mull that one over.

Jessica Rider offered her faked papers to the guards at the gates of Greensward. After the explosions that had sent the city to its knees three weeks before, security had been tighter than ever. No one in or out without identifying papers. Jessie's contained the innocuous name of 'Jessica Smith' although she suspected she could have used her real name just as effectively. Beau had not wanted to take the risk, though, which was also why she and Ry were coming in separately. The irony of it all was that once someone was within the gates, most of the eyes were off. It was like they thought they could spot a Freedom Fighter by a guilty expression or something equally obvious. Of course, not a single Freedom Fighter felt the least bit guilty about what they were doing.

She smiled blandly and answered the basic questions about the purpose for her visit and where she'd be staying. She lied, the guard stamped her paper, and she strode into the city. Although she'd been able to come in with only a knife, there would be more supplies stashed at an anonymous safehouse so she wouldn't feel so naked.

Taking a moment to orient herself off the maps she had studied, Jessie turned and headed for the prison. As she walked, she casually observed the city, taking in the heavy presence of soldiers and how the common folks made fairly wide circuits to stay away from them. The tension was so thick it pricked at her skin like lightning. She rubbed her arm and gave the soldiers a wide berth too. There was no point attracting trouble.

It took over an hour to work her way through the city to near the palace and garrison. She didn't pause to take in Jez and Jay's handiwork, but she did whistle under her breath. Despite getting caught, they had done their job very well. The building was leveled. Jessie grinned to herself. Soon enough, a few more would be flattened as well and Greensward all but neutralized. The city, as Tira's second largest and being only half a day's ride from Oakbridge, comprised the largest threat to a direct assault on Oakbridge.

The last thing they needed was to be in the midst of battling for Oakbridge and have a whole host of additional soldiers riding up. Thus, Beau, with the help of their informant, Col, as well as Adam and Ursula – who had sent word of Jez and Jay's capture – they had come up with this new plan. The original had been for Adam and Ursula to lead on this bit, to let them finally get their share of the fun, but when Jakium McRuoes had turned up with a letter for Beau from his *alive* older brother, plans had, understandably, changed.

Now, Jessie and Ry were on their own, although the other pair had done a lot of legwork for them – such as stashing extra weapons and the explosives. Col, although always secretive, had consented to be a backup in case of emergency.

Jessie moved on, eyeing the prison out of the corner of her eye as she passed. It was a squat, ugly building, built practically. It rose little over a story high because small, thickly barred windows rested at street level. Jessie made note of that ridiculousness. Perhaps she could figure out which window might belong to her friends. Still, they needed to know the layout of the prison first and there was a good chance they weren't being kept in one of the windowed cells. If the Three had gathered any intelligence on them in the past three weeks, they wouldn't be that stupid.

Although…

She shrugged and drew her eyes away. The soldiers were so thick here, she didn't dare linger. Jessie turned her attention to finding a place of lodging. Not five blocks from the prison, she found a nice, well-kept inn, three stories tall. It would be large enough that they could blend in, but close enough to be effective for what they wanted on both ends of their job. Tilting her head back, she glanced at the sign. A recently painted wooden plaque proclaimed it the Blue Parrot Inn, featuring a bright blue bird below the name. Jessie snorted. Parrots weren't even native to the region. She pushed the door open and stepped inside, blinking to adjust to the darker interior after the bright sunlight.

Her eyes raked the common room. There weren't many patrons so early in the day, but those present were all male and all soldiers. She supposed there was something to be said about operating right under their noses. She strolled to the bar, which was manned by a woman about Jessie's age, at first glance. Despite the hour, the woman already looked wrung out. She summoned a smile for Jessie, though. "Can I help you, miss?"

"I'm hoping you can. I'm looking to book a room for at least the next two weeks, and maybe as long as a month."

"We can probably do that. Any requirements?"

"Two beds, if at all possible, but we can do without if necessary." Beds at all were a luxury Jessie hadn't had in a while. Not since Westcorner. Before that, she couldn't remember. Maybe Kol?

The woman turned away, scanning a chalkboard tacked on the wall behind the bar. "Room 205 would work perfectly. It's upstairs, so it won't be in the path of most of the soldiers."

"Sounds great. What do I owe you?"

"We'll take it week-by-week, so I'll need a week's now." The woman pointed at a board listing the prices.

Jessie glanced at it, because it gave her an exact amount and it might have been suspicious if she didn't, but knew she had the coin. "No problem." She counted out the pieces and the woman swept them off the bar, making them disappear.

"And names of the people staying?" she asked, pulling out a piece of chalk.

"Jessica and Ryan Smith. My younger sister went to do some sightseeing and left me to do the practical stuff," she said lightly.

The woman grinned. "Being a younger sister myself, I totally understand. I'm Kira," she said, offering her hand.

Jessie liked her instinctively, but she cautioned herself that Kira worked in the most heavily guarded area of Tira besides Oakbridge castle, so she would still need to watch her words. "Nice to meet you."

"If you need anything, just yell. We're a little short-staffed, so it's really just me and the boss, Jacob. We've got one part-timer named Caroline and she's very capable too, but never on when one of us isn't."

"Don't worry. Ry and I are easy to please," she told her with a smile.

Kira plunked two keys down on the counter. "Glad to hear it. This lot can be a bear." She added the last bit louder and the soldiers at the bar all laughed and shot varying degrees of good-natured retorts at the woman.

She grinned, plainly unconcerned, winked at Jessie, and bounded off to fill drinks.

Jessie shook her head, amused, and hiked up the flight of stairs to their room. Before she entered, she wandered the length of the L-shaped hall. The staircase up from the barroom connected at the corner of the L. One way went to the front of the building. The other ended in a large window and, when Jessie peeked out, a fire escape that wound both down to the ground floor and up to the roof. When she checked her room number again, 205, was one of the last rooms in that section of hall, with an easy escape route, should it come to that.

Eyes narrowing, Jessie glanced over her shoulder, back towards the stair. Was it just that the soldiers had been giving unaccompanied women a hard time? Or had Kira surmised more than that? She snorted. Maybe Freedom Fighters did have a look about them and the guards at the gate had just been too stupid to notice. Either way, she didn't think Kira would be a threat. If she had wanted to, she could have called the guards down on Jessie immediately. Or certainly given her a less easily-escaped room.

She shrugged and let herself into the room. It was a medium-sized room and nicely appointed with a chair in one corner and bureau in the other near the door. The far end of the room contained two beds with a small table between them. Perfectly adequate for their uses. She slung her bag onto one of the beds and pushed open the window, peering out. Without too much effort, they could probably even reach the fire escape from this window. She grinned and left it open to get a little fresh air despite the winter chill.

Then, she went back to the hall, locking the door and heading downstairs. She returned Kira's wave and headed for the rendezvous point with Ry. Her first job had been to locate the safehouses and make sure they were still safe, or at least appeared that way.

When Jessie reached the market square, which was still bustling, even on a non-market day, she spotted Ry from some distance. Her friend stood on the edge of a fountain. Both waved at almost the same time. Ry knew her intention to find lodging near the prison, so she'd obviously been watching that direction. The other woman hopped down, disappearing into the sea of people, but they met halfway across the square.

"Any problems?" Jessie asked.

"Nope. For all the hype about security, the guards could have given a shit. Guess I don't look like much of a threat."

"Little do they know," she said, amused, deliberately tousling Ry's hair, like an older sister might.

"Don't make that a habit, please," Ry said with a foul look as she patted it back down.

"Whatever you say."

"I have officially surpassed you at hand-to-hand and don't you forget it."

"I wouldn't dream of it," Jessie said, grinning, feeling more secure with her friend there. Although she felt perfectly confident no one had given her a second glance earlier, it was nice to have backup at hand.

"Find us a room?"

"Yup, five blocks away. Closest place that didn't look like a dive."

"Fair enough. Plenty close. And numbers?"

"Heavy, near both and at the inn, but doable. There are some holes already. How about the houses?"

"Don't seem to be watched." Ry shrugged. "But I only did a quick sweep."

Jessie nodded and turned the conversation to what would sound like innocuous topics, like the state of Greensward. Ry had noticed the same tension and wide berth given the soldiers. "I wonder if there have been riots."

"I'll ask Kira if I can get a good opening," she said and then explained who Kira was, just as they reached the inn.

"Really? Blue Parrots?"

She shrugged. "I've heard they can be. And who am I to question inn names? Maybe the owner, or original owner, was from really far south and had seen them. Or had one as a pet."

"Can we ask Kira that too?" Ry asked, amused.

"I'm not sure she'll know, but I don't see why not."

Kira was busy with the lunch crowd – mostly soldiers, although a few people not in uniform were present too – so Jessie just waved again and led Ry upstairs to their room, showing her the fire escape and admitting her thoughts about Kira and their room placement.

Ry shrugged. "If she suspects something and isn't on our side, she would have just sent that group of soldiers pouncing, since we're both here, so either she doesn't suspect anything or she's a sympathizer and it might work in our favor."

She made a good point so Jessie nodded and sat on her bed.

Ry tossed her stuff on the chair and flopped on hers. Then, the two shared, in more detail, what they had seen on their separate mini-missions. It did sound like the safehouses hadn't been compromised, which was a very good thing, since the supplies they contained were critical to their mission's success.

Then talk turned to what came next. "Tonight we'll both scout out the palace. Tomorrow, we'll split. One of us takes the safehouses, the other the jail and palace, since we don't want to linger at either too long."

"I'll take the safehouses for the first day," Ry said. "I've already been to them and I'm better at spotting lurkers than you are."

"Would you stop rubbing in all the things you're better than me at?"

The seventeen-year-old grinned. "But it's so much fun."

Jessie threw her pillow half-heartedly at her. "Gods' Breath, you are such a baby."

"I know. My youth works in my favor. Well, now that I am and look older than sixteen so I can leave Cavern Hall without people thinking I should be in school."

"You still could be."

"I'm seventeen and a half. I could've been out of school over a year ago. Which is why Iris' rules that it's until eighteen are dumb."

Jessie smiled at the old complaint. "As you said, you're seventeen and a half. And, if Beau's plan goes off as planned, we'll have taken back Tira by the time you're eighteen. Then you can do whatever you want."

"And, in the meantime, we get to make things go boom!" she said with a wide grin.

"Okay, that's enough of that already. Jay did that constantly for a week, I don't need you to start."

"But there is something supremely satisfying about it," Ry protested. "You should try it."

Jessie rolled her eyes. "C'mon, let's go get lunch."

Sorin tapped his finger on the desk as he leaned against it, listening to Vladimir grill poor Calip. "It's going to be a quiet affair. I realize the people want to see it, but now is not the time for a massive, public wedding. Too many things could go wrong. It would be like asking the Freedom Fighters to crash it."

Sorin debated mentioning that it would be nice for Ren to have his brother attend, but knew that Vladimir would react terribly.

"Yes, sir," Calip said crisply. "Any other requirements, sir?"

"We'll need to eventually parade the newlyweds in front of the masses, so that will need to be carefully planned and set up, but the information needs to not be leaked too soon."

"And who will be invited to the wedding proper, sir?" Calip asked, taking industrious notes. Sorin wasn't sure why since Vladimir's instructions weren't particularly difficult. Still, he supposed considering the mercurial mood his brother had been in recently, it was in Calip's best interest to make sure he didn't miss a thing.

"Any dignitaries and noblemen who can get away. No representatives from Alyia or Nerius. I don't want them creating any more trouble than they already have. Plus, any ranking officials who are free, and Jakium. Anica would be upset if he wasn't there. Anyone else, Sorin?"

Having half-tuned him out, Sorin was mildly surprised to be addressed. "Oh, you know best," he said mildly. "But I know Rees has his hands full right now, so I doubt he'll be here."

"How do you know that?" his brother snapped, probably more annoyed by the first part than the information about Rees.

"He sent up a note yesterday. Didn't you read it?" he asked innocently.

"Why?"

"Why is he going to be busy? I don't know, he didn't say, although I have to assume it's the prisoners and his continued efforts to replace the buildings and supplies they blew up. I, of course, sent a return message asking for a more detailed report."

Vladimir grunted. "Those kinds of people, Calip."

"Yes, sir. Is there anything else you need right now or may I go get started on this?"

Vladimir waved a hand and Calip hurried from the room, quietly shutting the door behind him. "Where were you earlier today when I was looking for you?"

"Contrary to what you may believe, brother, it is not my job to always be at your beck and call."

"The guard at Renier's room said you'd taken him somewhere."

"Then you know where I was earlier today, so why bother asking?"

"When I couldn't find you in your office or rooms, I thought perhaps you had gone to speak to Renier. It is not-"

"Don't even say 'safe'," Sorin said, his own anger starting to shimmer before he pushed it away. "Ren is not a docile pet, but he's also on crutches, thanks to you, and can move only at a snail's pace. I'm also perfectly capable of taking care of myself. Ren is no threat to me or to our sister, we've been through this."

As Vladimir stared at him, Sorin thought maybe he'd caught the omission of his name. "Where did you go?"

"For a walk along the ramparts and then, escorted, through Oakbridge, via some of the safe but less traveled back roads."

Instantly, his brother's face went stormy.

"Don't," Sorin said again, cutting him off. "They will get suspicious if we keep him cooped up in here. Ren was never like that before and it's already been two years. We can play the illness card only so far. He was gracious and perfectly well-behaved, not even edging the line." In fact, Ren's behavior had surprised Sorin a little. It seemed he trusted the Freedom Fighters to do their self-appointed job and get him out.

Vladimir waved him off, much like he had for Calip. "Fine," he said, turning away.

Sorin watched him, fighting with himself over whether or not it was worth it to say something. "Vlad, Ani and I are worried about you," he said finally, trying to keep his voice gentle.

"Why?" His brother turned to face him again.

He was fairly certain that should've been painfully obvious, but at least Vladimir was listening again, even if he'd pushed Sorin off the last couple times. "Because you're stressed. You're quick to anger and not as collected as you usually are. You made Ani cry, not too long ago, in case you don't recall."

He scowled. "I had not forgotten," he said stiffly. "You're the collected one, Sorin, not me."

"In an entirely different way," he protested. "You know what I mean."

"Do not push me, I'm fine. Now," he said, "are Anica and Renier working out the details on their end?"

The lack of nicknames for both of them bothered Sorin more than the subject change. The three of them had always been notoriously bad at feelings and sharing them. "I think so. I know they did a bunch yesterday to get it done and over with."

"Good." With that, Vladimir swept out of the office – *his* office – leaving Sorin staring after him.

Sorin ran a hand through his hair. What concerned him most was that his brother didn't seem to even notice that his behavior had changed, that things were not good, that he was becoming what they all hated more than anything. Sorin felt certain he did not have the control not to go too far.

Chapter Thirty

Despite Stella's advice and the interesting tidbits, the day dragged. Finally, our dinner arrived. All of us but Jay stared at it. I was heartily sick of the same old thing. It seemed Dave felt similarly as he sloshed it around his bowl before sighing. "Don't suppose we could ask for something else, do you?"

"It is rather plain." The same bland stew with drops of meat – at least it was consistently warm. "It's not like we're exactly in a position to complain and expect them to listen, though."

"Maybe not, but here's what you do," Jay said, leaning forward as if to invite us in on a secret. He'd scraped his bowl clean already. I found myself leaning in as well, curious where he was going with this. "You think about... *food.*"

"Oh, here we go again," I muttered. If he caught it, he didn't acknowledge it.

"This is food," Dave said, pointing at it. "And it's the same thing we've eaten every night for weeks so I don't want to think about it."

Jay sighed impatiently, like we were incapable of keeping up with his genius. I was incapable of keeping up sometimes, but it had nothing to do with him being a genius. "I meant *good* food. You know, bacon and steak and vegetables or, or the whole entire cow!"

I started laughing. "You wouldn't know what to do with an entire cow."

"I would too! I'd eat it all," he said with relish.

"Oh? *All* of it? Including the skin and hooves and–"

"Do not ruin my fantasy, Jasmine," he said grumpily. "I would butcher it first. Or, well, get someone else to butcher it for me."

"Do you know how?" Dave asked, curious.

"It's been a while, but yes, I probably could. I just don't particularly enjoy it. It's kind of icky."

Stella snorted and I remembered they had both grown up on a farm.

"I've never done a cow, but I've helped with the pigs. George let me last year," Dave said.

"Really? Is that a normal age to start helping?" Sometimes having grown up in privilege did make me feel a little disconnected from the other Freedom Fighters, but mostly for things like how to slaughter an animal. I had watched it a couple times as a child out of curiosity and because my brothers were fascinated.

"It's not unusual," Stella said. "George and I both started when we were a little older, but that's only because our father had more relatives nearby to help and didn't need us. With Frank dead too, it was really just the three of us and a couple part-time farmhands."

Dave nodded eagerly. "One of the ways I could help most was being an extra set of hands." Then he sighed again. "I miss the farm. What do you think happened to the animals and everything, Stella?"

He probably missed a lot more than that, but I could see where it felt safer to talk about the farm.

"I'm sure our neighbors are taking care of them," Stella said. That was if the soldiers hadn't taken them as payment. From the look on her face, which she quickly tried to hide, Stella felt the same way. She put an arm around the boy. "We can start a new farm when this is all over," she said, optimistically.

"Okay!"

I felt a little like I was intruding so glanced at Jay. He looked like maybe he could handle taking up farming if need be. When he caught me watching, he blushed and looked away. I grinned.

"Where are you going to live, when it's all over?" Dave asked.

I blinked then shrugged. "I hadn't thought about it much. Even once we win, there will still be a lot of work to do and I'm sure I can help somehow, so I'll probably stay at the castle."

"She says work, yet I hear 'Beau'," Jay said in a stage whisper.

I punched him.

He rubbed his arm but didn't complain, satisfied that he'd won that round. I silently conceded that he had. I had no intention of living away from Beau and, as the prince and second in line for the throne, I doubted he would be living anywhere else.

"What about you, Jay?"

"I'm figuring Oakbridge too, at least for a while. Can't let Jez and the others have all the fun running the country without me."

Dave looked caught in indecision and he glanced up at Stella. "Maybe," he said slyly, "we could live there too, instead of starting a new farm." Considering I'd already talked to her about it, I knew how Stella felt.

I kept from smiling, but barely. "I don't see why not. The castle in Oakbridge is huge," I confided. I had visited a handful of times as a child.

"Would we really live there? In a *castle?*" He grinned. "That sounds awesome! Let's do that, Stella."

She laughed, ruffling his hair. "Let's leave our options open for now," she said, but caught Jay's eye.

"Who will be in charge after all of you get really old?"

"We'll have kids who can take over," Jay said. "Who, you can babysit when they're small."

Dave made a face. "Why would I want to do that? Little kids are icky."

I laughed. "By the time there are little kids running around, you might not think so any more. Which, the idea of you with kids, Jay, is frightening at best."

He grinned. "No little Jays?"

"Gods no," I said.

"I like the idea," Stella said, reddening.

"Well, Jay's practically a kid himself still, so he'd certainly understand them," I said brightly.

Jay opened his mouth to protest then shut it again.

I grinned at him. "Can't argue with that, can you?"

"Shush," he told me and turned righteously back to Stella and Dave. "I don't think we've ever asked. How old are you two?"

"I'm ten," he said proudly, confirming my suspicions.

Stella smiled fondly. "Double digits already on me. Makes me feel old."

"You *are* old," he said with a smirk.

She poked him in the side. "I'm nineteen. I gather you two are both twenty from the story?"

"Yup, but Jez is still younger than me and a baby."

I rolled my eyes. That was not an argument worth engaging in for long, but I had to however briefly. "I'm only a couple months younger than you."

"So? That still qualifies you as a baby to me."

I decided that the best response to that was to ignore him. That didn't last long, but at least by the time the conversation started back up, he'd gotten off that topic.

Jessie and Ry headed downstairs. The main lunch rush appeared to be over, so they grabbed spots at the bar. A small cluster of soldiers sat at the far end and one single, well-kept man sat three stools down.

Kira came their way as soon as she finished serving drinks to the crowd at the end. "What can I get you two?" she said with a smile, shaking Ry's hand.

"Glass of water and a house special," Jessie said after perusing the board behind the bar.

"Same."

Kira moved off towards the kitchen.

"New in town?" It was the man three stools down.

Jessie looked up. "Yes, we're thinking about making the move to a big city. We're spending some time here and in Oakbridge before deciding."

"Ah, that's a good idea. Where are you from?"

"Up near Ellworth," Ry said, which was true enough these days, considering Cavern Hall sat a little ways north of the town.

"Pretty area," he said. "I've been up there a time or two, but unfortunately couldn't stay long."

Kira returned with their water. "Colonel Rees, are you sure you don't want anything else?" the waitress asked as she passed him.

He turned to her and Jessie and Ry exchanged a very quick glance. Had Kira dropped the name and title on purpose to warn them? It certainly seemed that way, but had been done so naturally, the colonel shouldn't suspect a thing. Jessie knew the name too. Colonel Rees was nominally in charge of Greensward, although he had been active less recently. "No, I'm fine, thank you, Kira," he said politely before turning back to them. "So, how long are you planning on enjoying Greensward? Are you staying here at the Parrot?"

"We're thinking about a month all told, but two weeks for sure," Jessie said.

"A month?" he said, obviously feigning surprise. "I didn't realize the Ellworth area was that prosperous."

"Excuse me?" Ry said carefully.

"I didn't realize the salaries in the area were high enough to support two people for a month here in the city, and presumably another month in Oakbridge."

"We've saved for a while, sir," Jessie said. "And with our parents dead, we have nothing to hold us there. We also figured we could pick up the odd job here and there to make a little more."

"Colonel Rees," Kira interrupted sharply before he could reply. She looked annoyed. "We've told you before that Jacob would appreciate it if you didn't interrogate our customers. We've lost more than one regular because of that habit."

"My apologies, Kira, but it is a habit that's hard to break. I applaud your choice of words, though."

"It's no secret your job over at the jail," she said, a touch sourly. "There is still no reason to pester our innocent patrons, though."

"Guess it's a good thing we have nothing to hide," Jessie said lightly, not wanting Kira to get in trouble on their account. She did file the information away. Sounded like Rees was maybe the head of the jail, which meant he was the one they were directly looking to cross by rescuing their friends.

Rees smiled, but the expression sent a shiver itching down Jessie's spine. She barely managed to hide it. "See, Kira, nothing to worry about. Are you two siblings?"

"Half-sisters," Ry said, "but we've always lived together." They had decided a half-sisters backstory made more sense, since they really didn't look related.

"So we're more like full siblings," Jessie said brightly. "I wouldn't want anyone else."

He smiled slightly. "Siblings are a wonderful thing. Where are you thinking about getting work?"

"We haven't even been here a day, sir. We haven't exactly gotten that far," Ry said.

Kira returned with two heaping plates of food. "We could use the help around here. Winter's our busy season, what with the soldiers all cooped up here due to bad weather. A month would get us out of the busiest part of the season. We'll be heading towards the thaw."

"Can we talk about it and let you know tomorrow?"

"Of course. Jacob will be in then too so that makes more sense. If you do want it, he'll probably have you working mornings or afternoons. Caroline and I cover nights."

"Wouldn't you want nights off? Isn't that when Bri is off too?" Rees asked, finishing off his drink.

"Sometimes. He does work evenings a couple times a week, but I'd love to be home during the day. Our poor apartment is starting to fall apart with neglect. A lot of the things that need to be done, he can't do by himself. We really need four hands and I never have the energy. Plus, then we could still spend more time together while actually both awake," she said dryly and glanced at Jessie and Ry. "My boyfriend," she explained.

Jessie's heart had done a little hiccup at the name, but time – and the fact Cavern Hall contained two Brians – had dulled the sensation so she was able to put on a smile. "Ah, I'd guessed as much."

"He works at the jail, cleaning and delivering food and the like," she said fondly. "It pays well and is reliable, steady work."

Jessie studied her, wondering if this boyfriend, this Bri, would allow them to question him-assuming Kira was guessing about their purpose and supported it, as she appeared to. She also pondered the best way to possibly broach the subject with her.

"Do you come here often, Colonel?" Ry asked Rees politely.

"I try and pop over during my lunch and sometimes in the evenings to chat with the soldiers, get an idea of their states of mind and all. And chat with Kira, of course," he said easily.

"He's definitely a regular," Kira said, from where she was wiping down a section of the bar on his far side. "Want anything else, Colonel?"

"No, thank you. Just put it on my tab."

"Already done."

The man slid off his stool. "It was nice to meet you both…I'm sorry, I never caught your names."

"Jessica and Ryan," Ry said, indicating who was who.

He offered his hand. "Pleasure."

"Same, sir," Jessie said, although taking his hand gave her goosebumps.

A moment later, he strode out the door.

Kira let out a breath. "You're more than welcome to politely dodge his questions instead of answering, especially if you do end up working here, because he'll be persistent, and consistent. He's in charge of Greensward but especially the jail." She jerked her thumb towards the squat building Jessie had scouted earlier. "Thus, in charge of all interrogations of prisoners. He seems to think all civilians are fair game, whether reasonable or not. He knows not to try that shit on me, though."

Jessie could imagine. Kira seemed capable of having a very sharp tongue if she wanted. "Thanks for the heads-up and the warning."

"Of course." She snagged Rees's dirty glass and scrubbed the bar.

"I had a question for you," Ry said now. "Completely unrelated."

Kira raised an eyebrow curiously. "Okay?"

"Why blue *parrots*?"

She laughed. "Reportedly the original owner had a pair of blue parrots imported from somewhere south. He apparently bred them and they lived here, which was quite a draw, since who's actually seen a parrot before? This was our grandparents' time. When Jacob's father bought the place, after the original owner died and the parrots were already long gone, he kept the name because of the local history and the fact it was a successful business. He figured it wouldn't be smart to screw with something that worked."

"Makes sense. Do you get asked about it a lot?"

"Not as often as you might think."

"Kira!" one of the group at the other end called.

She shot them a smile and trotted off.

"A little strange?" Ry muttered.

Jessie had to agree. "A little. But it could also be interpreted as one woman giving others advice. I don't like the phrase 'interrogation of prisoners' though. Considering how Jay and Jez were caught, I know it's likely, but he gave me the creeps and he doesn't have any power over me," she said.

"I know. I wish we didn't need to wait as long as we do to do the boom job properly. I want them out of there, but rescuing them first would put them on too high of an alert."

She nodded. "Did your heart leap when he said Bri too?"

Ry shoveled down her last bite and swallowed. "Yeah, startled me. But it's a common enough nickname for an equally common name. Plus, our Bri never would've been caught dead doing menial work at a Three prison."

She had to smile. "True enough. C'mon," she said, piling the appropriate coin on the bar. "Let's go explore Greensward."

Ren stretched out on his bed and watched Ani. She idly flipped through a book of wedding dress sketches as she sat by his window. "I don't think they realize I don't care."

"I don't think they do," he agreed. "If they want us to get married that quickly, isn't it a little late to start from scratch anyway?"

"I would think so. Maybe they have them all made in almost my size."

He snorted. "That must be."

She slammed the book shut and threw it at him. "You pick."

"I...What?"

"You pick the dress. I don't care. Maybe you do. You're going to get a better view of me in it than I'll get of myself anyway."

He glanced down at the book. "Seriously?"

"I trust your opinions on these matters, Renny," she said loftily.

That was secretly gratifying. He flipped open the book before a thought occurred to him. "Does that mean you picked my outfit?"

"No, sadly. My vote would've been for the one with the least clothes."

"Oh for the sake of the gods, Ani," he groaned. "Now I'm very glad you didn't."

She grinned. "And I know you wouldn't dream of doing such a thing to me. Although, I don't think any of those dresses were even close to scandalous. I'm sure they were vetted by at least one of my brothers before they got to me."

He wrinkled his nose. "Something about that thought gives me the creeps," he said, turning a few pages. "I now officially have no respect for your brothers' taste. Most of these are hideous and the rest are still ugly."

"I know," she said, leaning back and putting her feet up on his window sill. "That's why it doesn't matter."

"Except now I'm screwed either way, because no matter what, I have to pick an ugly one." He kept flipping, hoping to find at least one that wasn't.

She smirked. "Exactly."

"That doesn't seem fair."

"Better you than me."

He turned it again and then paused, tilting his head. "What about this one?"

"Which one?"

"The one on the," he checked, "second to last page. It's way better than the others."

"Oh. I got bored and didn't get that far."

He lowered the book to stare at her. "That should not still surprise me as much as it does," he said and then shut the book and tossed it back. "Look at it. I think it's the one, if you have to pick something out of the book."

She fielded it and flipped to the back, studying it. "You're right. It is. We'll go for it." She casually dropped the book onto the table and slid out of the chair to flop on the bed, nestling in beside him. "Glad that's over with."

He crossed his arms behind his head. "That's all the decision we get to make, right?"

"I think so. Unless Sorin convinces Vlad otherwise."

He hummed in response. Although he felt no qualms about loving Ani or even really marrying her, the reason behind the expedited marriage and the fact they were even getting married while he was still officially a prisoner did rankle him. Yet there was nothing he could do but play along and hope that, at some point, things would change. He glanced down at the top of Ani's head. They both knew their relationship could never last. She was one of the Three and that would never change. If, somehow, she ended up in his position…he couldn't do that to anyone. He didn't know what he'd do when the Freedom Fighters and his brother finally made their move. How could he? He wanted Vladimir captured or dead. Sorin too, if he pushed back his initial reluctance, because no matter how good of a man he had slowly become during all this, it didn't change what he had done. Ani, though, Ani had nothing to do with the planning or execution. At every step of the way, she'd been dragged along behind her brothers because she had nothing and no one else.

"What're you thinking?" she asked quietly.

"About stuff."

"Now I feel fully informed," she said dryly, poking him in the side.

"Parts of this feel right, but other parts feel horribly wrong," he said finally, trying to get his thoughts in line. "It was barely weeks ago that I realized I had feelings for you, let alone even thinking about marrying anyone. I know that if things had gone to plan, I would've been married by now, but marrying Francine for political reasons and marrying you for love *and* political reasons is so different. The speed and the factors just…"

She nodded, curling more tightly into the curves of his body. He slid an arm around her shoulders. "I know. I feel it too, but there's not much either of us can do about it."

Again, here she was caught as a pawn in her brothers' game. And in this one, he couldn't count Sorin out. He had only survived the attack on Oakbridge because of this very play and Sorin had been the one to knock him out while Vladimir had attacked his father. "There isn't anything," he corrected softly.

"I could try whining, but Sorin just shrugs now and looks guilty and -" She cut off there.

Ren pushed himself up to look down at her. "What?"

"Nothing," she said, staring avidly at the ceiling to avoid his gaze.

"Ani, what is it? If it's important, I need you to tell me."

"Did you know you have a particular tone of voice that is extra hard to resist?" she asked.

"Ani."

She rolled her eyes but finally met his gaze. "I was going to say that Vlad is too…stressed these days and I'm not sure he'd react at all well to whining. Even whining with a real purpose." Ren knew that stressed was not her first word choice, but he didn't comment on it. They both knew what she meant and he was pretty sure it worried her too, and Sorin, for that matter.

"Sorin said they're under a lot of pressure. And that he, at least, expects an attack this spring, any time after the snow melts."

"How do you know that?" she asked, eyeing him. "I can never get anything concrete out of Sorin regarding the Freedom Fighters and their chances."

"I use that tone of voice you can't resist. I can be very persuasive."

She tried very hard not to giggle and failed. "Yeah, but it's *Sorin*! Somehow, I can't picture you using that voice on him, and certainly not having it actually work."

He grinned. "To be honest, he volunteered most of it. I think as a heads up. Plus, I'm good at reading people, even Sorin now, and I can usually get a bit out of him. Then I can use that to dig for a little more. He can be a bit of a sucker if you get him talking."

She shook her head. "You're right, you do have Sorin read."

"Told you."

She poked him in the side then rolled off the bed. "C'mon, no use dwelling on it. Let's play chess or something."

He snorted but did as ordered.

Chapter Thirty-one

REES DIDN'T IMMEDIATELY CALL ME in again and reinitiate regular interrogations, much to my surprise. I suppose I should have known it meant serious trouble was brewing, but none of us realized. I visited his office again, but he seemed distracted at best and he asked questions without being disturbed by my lack of a straight answer. He did continue to inquire about Colin, seemingly searching for something specific, but I answered truthfully and couldn't make heads nor tails of his interest. He seemed to know Colin's fate but trying to get it out of him was like talking to a brick wall.

When he called Jay, things went in much the same manner. At that, I did start to feel stirrings of nerves. I didn't think his distraction boded well in the long run. I could only hope he was just busy with rebuilding, but my gut told me that was too much to hope for. I could tell Jay felt the same, but we didn't dare talk about it, not wanting to spook Stella or Dave.

Then, one morning, Dayton and the brutes appeared outside the cell. shorty wore a shit-eating grin that could mean nothing good. "Morning, everyone!" he said brightly as he opened the cell. I should have known then – it was the first time our jailers had openly acknowledged our cellmates.

"Who do you want today?" Jay asked wearily, standing.

"Not you or Jasmine today," he said, gleefully.

It took far too long for that to sink in. "No!" Jay and I said, almost in concert.

Dave shrunk back against Stella and she went white.

"The colonel would like to talk to you two," he said, gesturing at the Harpers. "So, let's go, before Kilgor and Juke have to make you."

So Rees had finally gotten smart enough to question them. My nerves flared sharply. If they asked the right questions or scared Dave enough, we could be in some trouble. They would certainly know a hell of a lot more than they did now. At least we hadn't told them any details of Beau's master plan. Although we'd mentioned that there would be others in Greensward at some point, we hadn't gotten into the details beyond it being Jessie and Ry.

While my mind whirled, Stella took Dave's hand tightly and marched out the door, chin held high. I silently applauded. She'd never asked for any of this. Dayton led the way while the brutes – not touching them, yet – followed.

As soon as their footsteps faded, Jay and I looked at each other. "Shit."

"You can say that again. I hope…" He bit his lip. I agreed with him.

I hoped Stella wouldn't try and fight it. I hoped they answered the questions while giving away as little information as possible. I hoped that Rees would be above hurting a child. I hoped there was some sort of reasonable explanation. And I hoped, above all else, that they would be returned to us, even if it wasn't whole.

Jay paced as I stood by the door, clutching the bars. Neither of us said another word until I spotted Dayton and the brutes coming our way alone. My stomach dropped, heart skipping a beat. That meant one of two things. One was bad, but bearable. The other…

I backed up. "Jay," I croaked.

He stopped dead and turned to face the door.

The trio reached us. Dayton's grin had grown. "Let's go, you two."

"Where are Stella and David?" Jay demanded.

"Otherwise occupied. You'll see them soon. Let's go, before they make you, or decide to take it out on the boy."

So we were going with 'bad but bearable.' I exchanged a look with Jay and stepped forward. He was right behind and the brutes closed ranks. shorty led us to Rees's office and held open the door. I stepped in and my breath hitched. Things had potentially just descended past bearable. Once again leaning against the desk, Vladimir Opalin watched us with an almost feral gleam in his eye. Immediately, I could tell something had changed with him, even in less than a month. It wasn't a good change and my skin crawled. Even worse, though, a new man stood near the window, watching us curiously. A new man, with the same blue eyes, and a definite family resemblance. It could only be Sorin Dakamar. That scared me. While Opalin was clearly dangerous in a physical way, Dakamar was known for his intelligence and ability to out-think others.

No matter how I added things up, it was not a pleasant equation.

"Jasmine, what a pleasure to see you again. It's time for us to get some serious answers." Vladimir stepped into my space as one of the brutes held tightly to my arms. The other secured Jay, who watched warily. "You, and your friend, Jay, will give us those answers now. So, please, follow me."

Kilgor dragged Jay out of the room and Juke followed with me. Rees, Opalin, and Dakamar trailed us. At the first intersection, Kilgor pulled Jay away from us. Dakamar followed him, while Opalin slid in front of us and led the way to a part of the prison I hadn't been to before. Finally, he stopped at a door and pushed it open. "After you, Jasmine."

Juke pushed me in and I stumbled to a dead stop. Even expecting it, to see Dave being held, not ten feet away, with a knife to his throat, came as a shock to my system. The boy stood rigid, clearly petrified past the point of tears. Juke pushed me in further then stepped back, not holding me but standing within easy grasp.

"Here's the deal," Opalin said, voice oily. "Rees mentioned that you appear to be very chummy with your cellmates. You answer our questions truthfully, the boy lives. If you don't…" He shrugged. "We will be checking your answers against those of James to ensure that neither of you are trying to sneak falsehoods past us. But you wouldn't do that with the boy's life on the line, would you?"

I was going to have to try. This was far worse than them asking Dave and Stella the questions. This gave us no time to prepare. I had to trust that Jay and I thought enough alike – usually a scary prospect – to pull this off without anyone dying and without giving anything of dire importance away. I tried pleading anyway. "Let the kid go. He has nothing to do with this."

"He now has everything to do with this. You've made him so important, everything might hinge on that boy's life. And that's on you."

I ground my teeth and caught Dave's eye, trying to look reassuring. Then, I looked past him to where Rees lurked by the doorway. "And I thought *you* were a bastard."

He smiled faintly but without his usual smugness.

Opalin didn't waste time. "Are you part of the Freedom Fighters?"

"Yes." We'd already established that. I had no problem confirming it again at this point.

"And who is the leader?"

I hesitated just long enough.

Opalin raised his hand.

"Beau," I said, before he could complete the motion.

"Is he the son of the former king?"

"You mean like a prince?" I said, hoping I sounded the right mix of startled and incredulous. I suspected I did. I didn't know if he or Dakamar knew Prince Renier had a brother. I still wasn't entirely sure how Renier himself knew, given what Beau had told me.

"Yes, like a prince," he said, sounding annoyed.

I eyed him. "The king only had Renier before the queen died," I told him, knowing I was pushing it, but unable to help it.

"That's not what I asked."

"Beau is Beau," I said with a shrug. "If he is, that's pretty cool. You'd hate that, though, wouldn't you? I mean, another claimant to the throne and one not in your clutches." Now I really was pushing it.

He raised his hand.

"Okay, okay," I said hastily, "I'm sorry. I'll stop."

"Where are you based from?" he asked, expression stony. But, my deflection *had* succeeded in keeping him from realizing that I had never directly answered his question. No lie yet, not that it would do me, or Dave, much good if he got wind of it.

"North, mostly. Up in the hills." That was nothing they didn't already know either, considering the Battle of Deepen's Crossing and the more recent ambush.

"I want specifics, Jasmine."

"That's about as specific as I can get. We don't want to be detected by your men, so things are vague."

"But you came from there, so surely you could get yourself back."

Of course I could. I wasn't stupid, just ballsy. "And by now they know we were captured, so they would not be stupid enough to allow us the opportunity to be pushed into leading you there." I was on a roll.

"I think you're lying."

"Then test me against Jay like you said you would. You'll find his answer similar." At least, I hoped so. If anyone was good at deflection and misdirection, it was a Dall and their ability to talk you in circles without you ever realizing it.

"And what did you hope to accomplish here at Greensward?"

I smirked, because I had to, even as aware as I was of Dave and his guard. "To make things go boom." That answer would probably be verbatim to Jay's.

"Don't get cute."

"I'm not getting cute," I retorted.

He hauled off and backhanded me hard enough across the face that I saw stars and could taste blood on the corner of my mouth. I shook my head dazedly, waiting for my vision to clear.

"I said, do not get cute."

I glared.

"How did you survive? I can't believe that, after all the planning I put into your demise, that you lived." This was a question that had to have been eating at him for weeks. Ever since he'd learned I was alive.

"When the second round of blasts went off, I was flung from my horse down into the ravine that ran along the road at that stretch. No one thought to check down there until Beau and the Freedom Fighters arrived."

He studied me through narrowed eyes before nodding. "And were you part of the group Jakium caught outside Westcorner?"

"Yes." That didn't deserve an explanation unless he specifically asked for it.

"You're doing well enough so far," he said, as if the verbal pat on the back would make me feel better or something. "What's the plan?"

"Which one?"

He immediately raised his hand threateningly.

At this point, I wasn't sure if he would order Dave killed, hit me, or both. I didn't relish any of the possibilities. "No, I mean it, which one?"

"How many do you know?" he asked, sounding honestly curious.

"Quite a few, but the vast majority are over and done with and we succeeded." I didn't bother smirking this time. Enough of my smugness had shifted into my words to convey it nicely.

"The ambush?"

"Of course. Beau and I did most of the planning for that. Went off without a hitch, too. Your soldiers ran scared."

"Do not get cute."

"Actually, those are facts," I retorted coldly. By now, Dave had silent tears streaming down his face, breathing shallow and fast. "What else do you want to know?"

"That's rather rude of you."

"Abrupt. It's abrupt of me," I corrected, as patiently as I could.

Rees snorted.

I started, gaze shooting to him. I'd almost forgotten he was present, in my concentration not to slip up with Opalin.

"Very clever, Jasmine. I have already come to expect as much. And how about the main plan? The one in progress right now."

"Not much." That was pretty much a bald-faced lie, but my first.

His hand inched up. "Do not play games."

"I knew our part. And everything that had happened before we came here."

"And what else?" Idiot didn't even ask about the things that happened before, half of which he had no idea about.

"I know there will be others coming to Greensward. Or maybe they're already here. It's hard to keep track of time down here."

"Who?" he asked, ignoring the rest.

"No idea. Whoever ends up fitting the job, which has probably changed since our capture." Another lie. Ry and Jessie had been pegged for that job since before Jay and I had gotten assigned the first part. Although, the job had probably changed to include some sort of serious attempt to free us.

He tapped his chin, actually walking a complete circuit around me. I stood very still. "Unfortunately," he said finally, "I suspect you're right."

I didn't let the relief show on my face. "I think you know by now that I won't risk David's life by lying to you," I said coldly.

"What are the jobs of the other groups in Greensward?"

"The only one I know for certain was our support group. But they left ages ago, after we got caught." Another half-truth. Adam and Ursula had probably left after our capture, but not because of it. But because of Jakium McRuoes and a certain letter.

"So you know nothing of value," he said, more to himself than anything, sounding disappointed.

If he wanted to leap to that conclusion, far be it from me to stop him.

He shot off a couple more easily deflected questions, not even seeming to try any more. He appraised me one last time. "Very well. Let's see what Sorin has to say, Rees," he said. "Keep her here, Juke."

Immediately the brute stepped up and grabbed my arms. I didn't try and move, watching Dave out of the corner of my eye. His guard lowered the knife, but kept a tight grip on him as Opalin and Rees left. The wait seemed to last forever. I didn't even dare scratch an itch, not sure how quickly they might overreact to any motion.

Finally, Opalin returned, still trailed by Rees. I could get nothing from Opalin's face, although I tried desperately to get a reading. But when my eyes darted past him to Rees, I felt myself relax. It was clear from *his* expression that Jay and I managed it.

"Let go of the boy," Opalin ordered.

Dave immediately rushed to me. I twisted out of Juke's slack grip and hugged the boy tightly. "You're okay, Dave, you're okay," I murmured, rubbing his back as he sobbed, as much out of relief as fear probably.

Opalin said nothing until Dave finally started to calm down, wiping his eyes. "Now, kill him."

"What?" I exploded, pulling Dave back close to my side. "You can't! That's not how you said this worked. He's an innocent *child*." My eyes flicked to Rees just long enough to ascertain that this was as much a surprise to him as me.

"J-Jez?" Dave said shakily.

I pushed him behind me, backing towards the wall, my hands held up defensively. "Don't do this, Opalin. We told you the truth."

"But not enough."

"That's not our fault if we don't know the answers."

He held my gaze evenly, smile widening to a predatory grin that sent a shiver down my spine. "Then you need to give me more."

I took another step back, feeling Dave hit the wall. "Then ask what you want, Opalin," I said, but my voice shook.

"I have asked the agreed questions. Now I just need information. Whatever you have. To save the boy?" His voice was so mild, despite what he was insinuating.

I couldn't say an outright no to that, but there had to be another way out of this. There just had to. "Most of it is old news," I said desperately, racking my brain for something that would slow him down. I shot a pleading glance towards Rees, but the colonel had disappeared. My heart thudded in my chest.

The two brutes were almost upon us, when a fresh voice cut across the room. "Vladimir." Calm, but icy, it froze everyone, myself included.

Sorin Dakamar stood in the doorway, fury etched plainly on his face. "What in the name of the gods are you doing?"

"I'm doing it my way. Leave it alone, Sorin, I'll be done soon."

"No, you're not. This isn't your way," he said flatly. "Colonel Rees, please escort both prisoners back to their cell."

Startled, my gaze jumped and found Rees standing exactly where I'd last seen him, like he'd never left. Did Opalin even know he had?

"You do not give the orders," Opalin snapped.

"I do when you're out of control," he retorted.

"Let me take the boy," Rees interjected smoothly. "His purpose, at least, has been served, yes?"

Opalin's jaw worked, but he didn't disagree as Rees came over. "Let me take him, Jez," he murmured.

I squeezed Dave's hand. "Go with Rees."

"But," he started, weakly.

"Go, please. You'll be safe with Stella and Jay," in a manner of speaking – certainly safer. I ruffled his hair affectionately.

He swallowed but allowed Rees to steer him out of the room without another word.

I turned back to the brothers. Their voices had lowered so I couldn't hear the words, but the looks on their faces told me it was still heated. Juke and the other guard hovered near me in obvious indecision. I stayed very still, so as not to give them an excuse.

Finally, face like thunder, Opalin turned to me. "Grab her. I don't want her to be able to stand on her own when you're done with her."

476

As unpleasant as this was going to be, I vastly preferred it over the alternative.

They did as ordered with relish, just as Rees slid back into the room. "Please be cautious of her arms. They've just healed and I'd hate to have to deal with all of that again. And don't break the cast."

Opalin snorted. I was pretty sure he didn't care if they did. I still wasn't sure why Rees did, at least past the point of me being coherent and functional enough to take some pain. "Colonel, come with me," Opalin said and swept from the room.

Dakamar, though, didn't move right away, eyes locked on me. I couldn't get any read off him – in that, at least, the brothers were very much alike. Then he stepped forward and waved the guards off. "There are some orders I cannot, and perhaps should not, countermand."

I said nothing, not sure what he was getting at.

"Sometimes," he continued, "it's best to let things happen as they will and do your best to pick up the pieces afterwards. Do you understand?"

I nodded slowly.

"Good." Strangely, he smiled. "I think you'll be all right."

"Thanks for the vote of confidence."

He patted me lightly on the cheek. "Sarcasm doesn't suit you any more than it suits Renier," he said, like this was a normal conversation. "You and Jay aren't easy to crack. I know you're both lying."

"About what?" I asked, curious if he actually had picked up on the lie.

"You absolutely know the rest of Beau Highcastle's plans to take back Tira."

"Prove it," I retorted.

To my incredible surprise, he actually grinned for a split second. "That's just the thing. I can't! Despite having no warning, you and Jay managed to successfully lie the same way under serious pressure. I'll admit, I'm very impressed. So, you get the pass for now."

"Thanks, I think."

"We'll leave you to Rees. Eventually, he'll get through both of you."

It was my turn to grin. "Not in time, he won't."

"We'll see," he said, not seemingly overly concerned. He stepped back, turning to the guards. "Follow your orders." He fixed his gaze on Dave's guard.

"But keep that knife sheathed. I want no blood from cuts, understand?" he asked coldly.

"Yes, sir," the guard said.

He left, shutting the door behind him.

Juke grinned as he and the other guard closed in.

They fulfilled their orders to the letter. Juke had to drag me back to the cell because my legs were jelly and my head spun, but my shoulders felt fine. He shoved me in, Jay catching me and helping me to my corner.

Dave immediately sprung on me with a tight hug. I returned it, just glad to see all three of them safe.

"Jez, I…I wanted to say thank you," Stella said, twisting her hands nervously. "David told us-"

"Stella, there was nothing you could do about it. I'm just glad I could, although weirdly it's Dakamar we have to thank. And the fact that Jay and I can think scarily alike in a pinch, apparently."

"Still. I owe you," she said quietly, shooting me a grateful smile.

Then Jay opened his mouth and, as usual, talk turned to lighter matters.

It did not take Rylia long to come to despise Greensward. She'd avoided cities for a long time after her childhood growing up on the streets and wasn't thrilled to be back in one now. Especially this one. She figured she should try and get used to it, though, considering that when they won, they'd all be based out of Oakbridge. Part of the lack of appeal for Greensward too, she admitted to herself, was the sheer number of soldiers. They made her itchy and anxious.

About a week after their arrival, she was hurrying back to the Blue Parrot, wanting to tell Jessie about the modifications to the shift change at the garrison, when she bumped into someone quite by accident.

"I'm sorry," she said, pivoting to go around but a hand clamped on her arm, not tightly, more like the person she'd hit was steadying themselves. Still, she looked up with a polite smile, a thrill of nerves running through her.

Despite the fact that she hadn't seen the man in a solid six months, and then their meeting had been brief, she knew him immediately and her heart plummeted. She looked away, but not quickly enough, as Jakium McRuoes's eyes widened. "Rylia?"

Her mind froze to the point where no sound would pass her lips.

"What in the name of the gods are you doing here?" he hissed. "Don't you realize it's dangerous?"

"Been okay so far," she said automatically. "Let go of me."

"No."

The panic swelled. "McRuoes, let go of me, *now*."

"No."

She would not lose her head. "I kicked your ass once. I'm not afraid to do it again."

"I wouldn't suggest it in this crowd," he said, sounding almost amused, the bastard.

"I'll take my chances. Let go."

To her everlasting surprise, he did. "They're still alive."

"What?" she asked, forgetting to back away.

"Your friends. Jez and Jay."

"How do you know," she began, but eyed him. Did this mean he was willing to give her information? They still hadn't met Kira's boyfriend, who apparently avoided the inn most of the time because the soldiers made fun of him for being slow.

"I want to talk."

"Then talk."

"Not here," he said, almost exasperated. "It's far too open."

"I'm not going anywhere with you," she said, stepping back.

He raised his hand like he might grab her again but restrained himself at the last second, dropping it without contact. "We'll go somewhere public. You can pick."

"Oh, for the sake of the gods, Jaksie, just call the police already and have me arrested since you don't seem to have the balls to do it yourself."

"I don't want to have you arrested," he said, startled. "And don't call me Jaksie. I've finally gotten Ani to stop."

Both parts of that statement got her attention. "What?"

"Don't call me Jaksie."

"Yeah, I got that. I was a little more curious about the not wanting to have me arrested part." She poked him in the chest and then pointed at herself. "Different sides, remember? Didn't think that could slip your mind so quickly."

"Do you *want* me to arrest you? I assume you want to rescue Jez and Jay but that's really not the way to go about it. Rees is…it's not the way to go about it."

That didn't sound like it boded well for her friends' safety.

He continued. "And with Master Vladimir and Mr. Sorin here, it's just not a good idea."

This time, Ry grabbed his arm and pulled him towards the nearest inn. She'd heard a lot of titles for Opalin and Dakamar since their rise to power, but those two, and with that familiarity, were new. To his credit, Jakium didn't fight her grip, hopping twice to keep his balance and then falling in step next to her, looking vaguely confused.

She took in the inn's clientele quickly and was glad to see it was a good mix. Jakium nodded politely to the few other soldiers as Ry headed for a quiet table towards the back. Only once they reached it did she let go of him and slide into a seat.

He sat down across from her.

"Are you insane?" she demanded quietly.

He actually gave that due thought. "It's possible," he said finally, slumping back in his seat as the waiter came to take an order. "Do you want lunch?" Jakium asked her politely.

"Are we going to talk that long?" she countered.

He shrugged and ordered an ale and one of their house specials.

After a moment of studying him, she ordered water and one of the specials too.

When the waiter left, Jakium looked at her. "What are you doing here?"

"Do you seriously expect me to answer that?"

"It's more than just rescuing your friends, isn't it?"

She regarded him levelly but said nothing.

He sighed. "Look, I was the reason your other two had to leave."

Her eyes narrowed. Adam and Ursula had made their way back to Cavern Hall because of a letter to Beau. "Oh?" she asked, not wanting to accidentally give him any information.

"Because of the letter. The letter to Beau Highcastle from his brother."

"You sent the letter?" she said slowly.

"Well, Ani asked me to, and I do most things that Ani asks for."

"Why's that?"

He shrugged. "It's Ani."

"That explains exactly nothing."

He thanked the waiter as he returned and took a sip of his ale contemplatively. "When I was fourteen, Ani and Master Vladimir took me in, out of Holly, and gave me a job."

"Some job," Ry scoffed.

"No, I worked for the family business in Alexandria and got to complete my schooling. It really was pretty good. Ani's the best."

She studied him. "Are you an orphan? Or did your parents ditch you?"

"Orphan, but I think that also qualifies as them ditching me," he said with a crooked smile. "They died when I was nine during an Alyian raid. Then I got sent to Holly until Master Vladimir found me."

"And then he dragged you into a war. Real nice of him, shortening your lifespan like that."

Jakium's expression flickered. "Things happen," he said. "You can't say your reasons for joining the Freedom Fighters are all that different than mine."

It hadn't been out of a sense of loyalty at first, no. She hadn't understood anything about politics when she'd been unintentionally recruited, but now it was. Maybe she did understand. "No, I guess I can't," she said. "So you knew them before."

"Before the takeover, yes but not before the planning. Master Vladimir was already knee-deep in that before I ever came. It worked, though. Meant he wasn't home much, which was okay with Ani and me."

"What about Dakamar?"

"I met him a couple times, but he didn't move in until a lot further on. He tried to protect me," he said, a bit wistfully, "but I was stupid and didn't listen and then, after, it was too late."

481

"After?"

Unfortunately, the waiter chose then to return with their food and Jakium seemed to jerk back to the present, setting into his food almost immediately. Ry didn't push him, eating in silence until they had both made a significant dent in the meal.

"You said something about Opalin and Dakamar being here?"

He nodded, swallowing. "They're questioning your friends today. Mr. Sorin came up with a plan to try and catch them up."

"Did it work?"

He smiled slightly. "I don't know. I've been on duty all morning. I'm supposed to meet them at the palace after lunch. We don't seem to be after you, though, so my guess is it didn't work."

"Maybe they just don't know about us."

"I sincerely doubt that," he said. "I doubt that because there were five of you in Westcorner. One of them was Beau Highcastle and two of them were James and Jasmine."

"What does that have to do with whether or not they know we're here?"

"We? Us?" he asked mildly.

Ry cursed herself and shot him a nasty glare. "What do you want?"

"I've come to the private conclusion that the group of you were some of the top people in the Freedom Fighters. For obvious reasons, I haven't shared that information. Mr. Opalin would probably skin even me alive if he knew I'd let the secret Highcastle slip through my fingers. He was pissed enough as it was."

"You did kind of screw it up."

"I misjudged," he said, "but I suppose it can happen to the best of us. Which reminds me, how's your back? And your hand?"

Instinctively, she itched at her palm. "Fine. Small scars but nothing serious. No loss of motion." She felt no little surprise that he remembered. "I would have thought you might've preferred it if it crippled me."

"If I had wanted you crippled, I wouldn't have chatted when we just ran into each other. I don't wish you personal ill," he said and reached out, taking her hand and folding it open to expose the thin, long scar that ran down the palm.

Ry's breath caught at the gentle touch. "You are insane," she muttered.

He grinned, letting go and looking up. "Maybe, but you do owe me a little gratitude. I didn't tell them your name, didn't give them anything to look up. Or that I knew for a fact that Jez and Jay were Freedom Fighters, although they know now. And, as I said, I didn't tell them about Beau Highcastle."

"Why not?" she demanded.

"It was too embarrassing to admit I was beaten by a teenage girl." His delivery was too smooth for her to buy that, though.

"There were far too many other soldiers there who witnessed it for me to buy that. Someone had to have told."

"Events were recorded in our report, but they didn't want to look too bad either, so certain things were glossed over."

She snorted. "Then why didn't you tell? If you owe them your loyalty."

"Mr. Sorin didn't ask."

"What about Opalin?"

He shrugged. "He never specifically asked either."

She pressed her lips together and studied him thoughtfully. "Sounds like maybe it'd be okay if you just disappeared."

"Maybe. But it's a little late for that," he said, swirling the last of his gravy into his potatoes.

"And you're sure Jay and Jez are okay?"

"I was until today. Not in completely one piece. Jez had issues with her arms last time I saw her, but Rees has repeatedly expressed his frustration that no methods are really working on them. But Mr. Sorin's different and his methods might've worked."

"What was he trying?"

Jakium briefly outlined the idea of using their cellmates.

"That's awful," Ry burst. "Using a little boy like that!"

"Mr. Sorin wouldn't actually let him get hurt," he said, defensively.

"You say that and yet the poor kid's been in jail for over a month! Gods' Breath, you people really are horrible."

He frowned. "I would do something about it if I could," he snapped. "It wasn't that long ago I was his age."

"Then you're a fat lot of good."

"I have absolutely nothing to do with the jail and how it's run. I'm only a lieutenant." He actually looked a little hurt by her accusations. "Rees is a colonel."

"The point still stands," she said flatly, not letting herself be swayed by his pathetic look. "Using children is never acceptable. What if the man in charge of him slips? Or is a giant asshole? Or someone changes the rules on your Mr. Sorin."

Jakium's frown deepened. "He wouldn't let them."

"If Opalin took you in, why does it seem like you," she paused, unable to come up with the proper word. Loyal didn't seem quite right, although maybe. Like was definitely not it. Trusted maybe.

"Because Ani and Mr. Sorin are the only two who tried to keep me out. I didn't listen but that's not their fault," he said quietly, fiddling with his fork, eyes firmly on the table in front of him.

"Gods damn it all, stop making me feel bad for you!" she snapped.

The shithead had the gall to smile. "That wasn't my goal. It just seems to keep coming back to me." He looked up, something almost sly in his eyes, along with the pathetic sorrow. "We could talk about you instead."

She had to fight a smile. That hadn't even been any kind of subtle. "Or we could not." She scooped up the last of the potatoes to cover any expression that might have snuck out. "I should probably get going. I have to meet my 'we'." She reached for her coin bag but he waved her off.

"I'm sure you've come amply prepared but I'm the one who insisted on the talk," he said. "I'll get lunch."

She wasn't going to fight it. She also would never tell her friends. In fact, maybe the whole 'lunch' part could be omitted entirely. "I'm not in your debt."

"Of course not," he said with a wry smile. "I wouldn't dream of thinking such a thing. Or imply it."

Ry nodded and stood, but he reached out a hand and gently caught her arm. "It won't be easy, getting them out. You'll need to have a foolproof plan. Rees isn't taking chances, since they're the first definite Freedom Fighters we've caught." At her nod, he let go, but wasn't quite finished. "Good luck."

Mind reeling, Ry all but bolted from the inn.

Ani watched Ren sleep, a favorite secret pastime ever since he'd mentioned that her brothers had promised him she wouldn't. She didn't think Ren would really mind, as long as she wasn't a total creep about it. She smiled just as he began to fidget, squirming and whining deep in his throat. She had seen enough nightmares and had enough of them too. She went to stand, to shake him awake, but found she couldn't move.

Panic started to swell. She had to wake him up, help protect him. Her Ren shouldn't have nightmares.

"I have to kill him. He's messed with her. It can't be allowed to continue." The voice itself wasn't familiar, but the words held a known flavor.

She screamed but no sound came out, struggling vainly against the invisible force that held her down.

A shining sword appeared over Ren's bed, extra bright in the darkness. It hovered over his heart. Struggling ever more frantically, she watched it descend, horrified.

"Ani? Ani, *Anica*, wake up."

She lashed out towards the voice but something wrapped around her arm. Her eyes shot open, blinking blurrily up at her room.

"Calm down, it's okay, you're okay." She'd know that voice anywhere. "Just a nightmare, that's all."

She pulled her arm away as she went to sit up and he let her. "What…?"

Sorin smiled a little. She hadn't even known he and Vlad were back from Greensward. "Good, you're awake." He stood and headed for the door. "See you in the morning."

He had almost reached it before his presence sunk in. "Sorin! Wait," she called as his hand reached the door knob.

"Yes?"

"Why…what are you doing here?" she asked.

He shrugged without turning. "I've always known when you were having a nightmare. Tonight was no different."

She stared at his back. A part of her knew that. Or at least, she knew that he'd used to. "Why aren't you sleeping?"

"Couldn't." He shrugged again.

"Do you think Vlad's losing it?"

Now he half-turned. "Look, you should try and get some more sleep."

"Sorin!" she snapped, angrier at the dismissal than she expected. "Don't do that. Don't treat me like a child. Do you think Vlad's losing it?"

He pressed his lips together and came back over, perching on the edge of her bed. He still looked like he might flee at any moment. "I do."

"So do I," she said softly, catching his eye.

As they sat there, something flickered in Sorin's eyes. "Ani," he began.

"Yeah?" she prompted when he didn't immediately continue.

Still, he hesitated another minute before nodding decisively. "There's something I need to tell you."

"Besides the fact you were married?" she said lightly, but his expression didn't lighten.

"Yes. More important than that." He took a deep breath. "While I was married, Diana and I had a son. Dean."

Her eyes widened. "What…" she started and then didn't know how to continue. If he had a son, her nephew, then where was he now? Her initial conclusion, she didn't like at all. Had he died, along with his wife? If so, how was Sorin still standing?

"He's still alive," he said hastily, allaying those fears. "The doctors said that Diana's illness wasn't contagious. He's almost five now and lives with Diana's parents, in the next town over from where we lived."

"Do you have contact with them?" she asked. Sorin never left enough to actually go visit. The little town, he'd told her, was a full day's ride away.

He shook his head, shifting to sit more firmly on the bed. "No. I don't dare. If the Freedom Fighters or any number of other people or groups found out…if *Vlad* found out…" He tapped a tight fist against his thigh. "No, it's safer for him if no one knows he exists. Then he can safely stay out of the fray and grow up without my legacy hanging over his head."

"If he's four now, then he was just a toddler when you left."

"Yes. Tiny and pudgy, with our eyes, and a large vocabulary for his age, or so I was told." He smiled a little. "He was the most curious human being I'd ever met. But I couldn't raise a child on my own. What do I know about

486

children? Vlad had already been bugging me for months to join in his crusade and I knew that Cedric and Anna would do a much better job raising him than I ever could."

"I'm not sure you give yourself enough credit," Ani said, although she'd seen him when he'd returned and how wrecked he had been. Maybe, at that point, he couldn't. And that, in turn, had robbed little Dean of ever having parents of his own. That stung. Not that Sorin had kept the secret – she saw the logic in that – but that she'd never get to know their family's future. A child who could, and would, not be like them. Who could step outside the family legacy and be *better*.

"Dean's better off with his grandparents," he said, almost like he was still trying to convince himself.

"Now? Yes, definitely. This is no place for a kid. It's barely a place for us or Jaks," she said quietly, then leaned forward and hugged him tightly. "Thank you for trusting me. No one will hear it from me. I wish I could've met him."

"I'm sorry you didn't. I think you would've adored him."

"No doubt," she agreed and released him. "I love you, Sorin."

"I love you too, Ani."

"Tell me everything. All the details."

"You really should sleep. You're getting married tomorrow."

"I'll be fine. I want to know," she said, shifting to sit next to him properly, feet dangling off the side of the bed.

He smiled. "Okay, okay. Everything, huh?"

She leaned into him. "Everything."

Chapter Thirty-two

I had stopped paying attention to people who delivered our food. Now that we weren't telling the story any more, but merely fun anecdotes and even legends, we didn't bother to pause when they came by. Therefore, I only vaguely registered that it was a new person and kept right on listening to Stella's story.

Dave was the one who let out the gasp as the man straightened after pushing the food tray through the slot. "You look like Jay!"

At that, our heads came up. I got one good look at the man's startled expression and my brain screeched to a halt.

"No," Jay breathed, scrambling to his feet. "It's not possible."

The man took a step back, eyes wide. "Who-" he started.

"Bri, get a move on it! Everyone should be fed by now!" someone yelled from down our corridor, sounding exasperated.

He glanced that way, back at us, grabbed his cart, and hurried out of sight.

Only then did my brain stutter back to life and I spun on Jay. "He's *dead*." And yet, that had unmistakably been Jay's brother, just with a nasty scar splitting his face.

Jay just stared at me, obviously shaken to his core.

Stella silently dished out the food and made sure we took ours. Only once we'd eaten – I didn't taste a bite – did she speak. "He's working for the Three," she said carefully.

"Which makes no sense. He would *never*."

"And he's been missing over a year," Stella pointed out.

"There is certainly something strange about it," I conceded. "He didn't *feel* like Bri. But it explains Rees's interest in the nickname when I gave it." I sat back, mulling that over. "If Bri switched sides, Rees would know a lot more about us then he does. And he would be rubbing Bri in our faces."

"But if he was undercover, first, Beau would have told us he was alive and, second, he would have said something just now to tell us," Jay said.

I nodded slowly.

"What other explanations are there?" Stella asked.

"His undercover is more important than you?" Dave tried but I shook my head.

"He either would have gone out of his way to avoid us or still said something, so we didn't give him away. Plus, it'd be strange for him to use his real name in that case."

We fell silent, pondering that.

"And the way the guard spoke to him," I added.

"If anyone had ever tried to speak to him that way, he would have kicked their ass," Jay said slowly. "Yeah, something very strange is going on here."

Stella looked between us. "Do you think we'll get the chance to find out?"

I thought back, to Bri's expression. That had been all wrong too. "I don't know," I said honestly. "I guess it'll just depend on how things play out."

She squeezed Jay's hand and nodded.

"My brother's alive," Jay said, after a minute, in a stunned voice as it clearly began to sink in.

There wasn't much to say to that and we sat in silence, each of us thinking about this new revelation. I examined my feelings and found that, as glad as I was he was alive – barring no crazy revelations like a friendship with Rees – I felt nothing more than that. Whatever Bri and I once had, it was good and over.

Eventually, Dave and Stella fell asleep, leaning against each other. Jay and I didn't. Sometime later, in the wee hours of the morning, I heard footsteps coming our way. I didn't look up, finally dozing, figuring it was the night guard, until they stopped outside our cell and remained there.

I looked up to find Brighton Dall crouched just on the other side of the bars, staring past me. Barely moving, I peeked to find that his gaze was locked on Jay's.

Bri reached out and placed a hand on the bars. "Hi, James," he said softly.

"Hi, Brighton."

His eyes lit up, momentarily making him truly look like the man I'd known. "Is that my name?"

Jay scooted forward to my side. "Yes, of course. Don't...don't you remember?"

He shook his head with a quick jerk. "No, not really. I'm sorry. Things have slowly come back to me in bits and bobs. I knew I had a brother, but I couldn't remember anything else until I saw you earlier. Even now I know there's a lot missing." He touched the scar that ran from the middle of his forehead, down perilously close to his left eye and across his cheek. "Kira's told me the little she knows. That I lost my memory when I got the scar. And that I'd worked for the Freedom Fighters before the Battle of Deepen's Crossing. I still remember most of the kind of things you'd learn in school, or else Kira's helped me get it back."

Jay tentatively put his hand over Bri's. "I'm just glad you're alive."

His brother smiled.

"Who's Kira?" I asked softly.

His eyes darted to me. There was barely even a hint of recognition, which hurt a little, but I pushed it aside. It made sense he would remember Jay and not me. Jay had been a staple in his life for the vast majority of it. I was just a blip on the timeline. He squinted. "You're...we were friends?" he said slowly. "J-name too!" he added after a minute, looking excited.

"Jez," I said with a nod.

He grinned. "Kira's...the best. My girlfriend. She kept me out of jail for being a Freedom Fighter, not that I remember being one, but I was marked that way when they brought me in, so she knew." He eyed me again. "You and James shouldn't be together, right?"

"We should be now," Jay said dryly, "but I joined the Freedom Fighters after I got word you'd died and got to know Jez and your other friends, so no, in your memory, we shouldn't."

"Oh," he breathed. "Oh, I don't think I wanted you to do that."

Jay pressed his lips together, but he mostly steered clear of his own bitterness, in the face of the amnesia. "No, you didn't, but when you were dead, you didn't get a choice any more. Do you remember what they did to our parents?"

"They're dead," he said promptly. "I remember that." His brow furrowed. "But I don't remember why. Is that why I was a Freedom Fighter? Because of our parents?"

Jay nodded. "They got caught in the middle of a tariff dispute and were murdered."

Bri squinted, absorbing all that. "Does..." he searched his brain, "Beau know you're here? That's the right name, right?"

"It is and we assume so, considering all the facts," Jay said.

"Do you have a plan to get out?"

"No, but Jessie and Ry should be here soon and we figure they'll come up with something."

"Jessie and Ry," he repeated. "I know those names. They're Freedom Fighters too. And friends?"

"Yes."

He frowned. "Kira's brother and his best friend do work for the Freedom Fighters. His best friend is one of the messengers here. I tell him things when I see stuff here. Kira does too, at the inn where she works, just over there." He gestured. "I can see if they'll help. Maybe they'll know where Jessie and Ry are too."

"We would really appreciate that. Can you come by to see us without suspicion?"

He nodded. "I'm on food duty for the next week. Bob, who usually has your part, had to have a minor surgery and is out. So I'll see you at dinner times."

"Good. Be careful, okay?" Jay said.

"I always am, James."

"Jay," he corrected.

"Jay," Bri repeated. "Why?"

He shrugged. "Didn't seem right to still be James or Jim without you."

"Jay," he said one more time, like he was tasting it before nodding approval. "I like it."

"*Bri*, what is taking you so long?" someone yelled from elsewhere in the jail. "Get moving!"

He flinched. "Told them I'd forgotten something," he said. "I'd better go."

Jay squeezed his hand. "We'll see you tomorrow."

He smiled, eyes lightening. "Okay. Tomorrow," he said happily and hurriedly straightened, vanishing from view.

Jay and I watched him go then simultaneously looked at each other. "Not what I was expecting," my friend said finally.

"Me neither. Although it explains how he can be alive but never came back." I also wasn't sure who he was talking about in regards to Kira's brother and his best friend. The only other people we had in Greensward as far as I knew were Col and his friend, who also just signed things Col. That had to be them, then. Col was a messenger.

"Seriously. It hurts to see him like that. So much that I couldn't get angry at him."

"There will be plenty of time for that later," I said, leaning back into my corner.

Jay scooted back to his. "Thank the gods for that."

Jessie worked slowly on her late meal, listening to Ry cover ground she already had three times since returning from her impromptu meeting with Jakium McRuoes. Jessie wasn't sure she realized just how much of the story she'd told, since a little more slipped out each time as Ry tried to puzzle it through. Jessie let her mostly without comment. Her friend needed to figure out what most of that had meant without interference. Instead, she half-watched the coming and goings of the inn's clientele.

She almost missed the man sidle into the common room and make his way to the bar. She might have if Kira's face hadn't broken into the widest, pure smile she'd yet to see on the other woman's face, as she hurried over to greet him. Jessie stared, something in the man's stance seeming strangely familiar. With the inn as packed as it was, she couldn't get a good look at his profile, let alone his face.

After a very brief conversation, Kira gestured towards the back with her head and the man hurried that way.

Kira paused to speak to Caroline then followed him out. Jessie glanced at Ry, confusion gnawing at her, but Ry hadn't noticed, still attacking her food, face screwed up in thought. Jessie frowned, tapping the table. Why had there been something familiar about that man? Was it McRuoes? But then why would Kira seem excited? Her heart stuttered for an instant. Kira had a mysterious boyfriend named Bri, who apparently generally avoided the inn due to the soldiers being jerks. Who else would she light up for? But there was no way Jessie knew Kira's Bri, because it was just impossible.

Still, some bit of her was deeply unsurprised when, about ten minutes later, Kira appeared at their table, smiling politely at a table of soldiers next to them. "Hey, can I talk to you two for a minute in the back if you're done? Seems like we might need to change the schedule next week," she said, her tone deceptively light, but her eyes were sparkling. The man had not emerged from the back yet.

Even Ry seemed to pick up on there being something more going on because she pushed her mostly eaten plate away. "Sure."

Jessie nodded, standing too.

Kira led them through tables and out the back door to the hall. She bypassed the stairs, heading for a small storage area, where the door was cracked open. She paused just outside the door, though, and turned to them. "You better hope I'm right about you, because if I'm not, this will end badly for you both," she said flatly, but in a low voice. Then, before Jessie could even really process that, she pushed the door open.

There were two lit lanterns in the room, both sitting on barrels along one side. On a barrel between them, sat a man.

Jessie stared, jaw slack. Although her mind had made the connection, it was not easy to see an impossibility sitting right in front of her. Ry made a choking noise, eyes all but bursting as Kira silently shut the door behind them.

Brighton Dall stared back at them with only the slightest traces of recognition.

"You *do* know him," Kira said with satisfaction. "Bri?"

"Maybe? Did I know you when I knew Jez?" he asked. "Are you Freedom Fighters? Oh! Are you Jessie and Ry?"

Very slowly, Jessie felt herself nod.

"How?" Ry breathed.

"I was a nurse in the town nearest Deepen's Crossing," Kira said, leaning against the door, as if to fully make sure no one could interrupt. "All the wounded from the battle were brought there. Bri was one of a handful of Freedom Fighters brought in and one of only a couple who survived. We hit it off, so I smuggled him out under the guise of taking care of him at home and, as soon as he was well enough, we moved to Greensward, where it was large enough for us to get lost."

"Except you took a job at the jail," Ry said, half-directing it at Bri.

"I know. Doesn't make much sense, I guess," Bri said, with a self-deprecating smile, "but I thought I could do good and keep an ear to things. Kira's brother helps the Freedom Fighters. Everything I hear, we pass along to him and his friend. I'm sorry I don't remember you really."

"But you know who we are."

"Because I just talked to Jez and James – I mean, Jay." He explained his conversation with them.

"So you still don't remember much?"

"More than I did. A lot of my childhood is clearer. To be honest, I think I'm pretty clear up to joining the Freedom Fighters," he said, with a note of apology.

"I suppose it would make sense that your most recent memories would be the last things to come back," Jessie said. "How did Jay and Jez look?"

"A little beat up, but not bad. I'm hoping to meet their cellmates tomorrow, but they were either asleep tonight or pretending it."

"They have cellmates?"

He nodded. "A young woman and a boy, maybe ten, eleven years old. I don't know their full story, but they're there because of some connection to the Freedom Fighters too. I'll try and find out more tomorrow." He leaned forward with some of his classic intensity. "We have to get them out."

Ry snorted. "Of course we do. Why do you think we're staying here?"

"Really good luck?" Kira asked dryly.

Jessie took a step towards Bri. "I know you don't remember me, but...can I give you a hug?"

"Hugs from friends, even forgotten ones, are always appreciated," he said with a tentative smile and slid off the barrel.

She hugged him tightly, breathing in his familiar scent. "Gods, I am so glad you're alive."

"I'm glad to be alive and free," he said, "and I'm really glad I got my shift changed at the jail, so I saw James – Jay – and could start putting the pieces together."

"This is the most progress he's made since very early on," Kira said. "We wanted to be careful, so we struggled with whether or not to have Colin say anything in his messages."

"Colin?"

"Oh, right! You might know him as 'Col'. He's a messenger for the Freedom Fighters. Done a lot of setting up of a network around here."

Jessie, of course, knew of Col. "How do you know Col?"

"He's my brother's best friend. My brother, Ben, can be a little scattered sometimes, so when Colin's out gathering information, Bri and I keep an eye on him."

"I know we need backstory, but can we get on with the rescue mission?" Bri said, with a hint of a whine in his voice.

Jessie shoved him gently in the shoulder.

He grinned. "Do you have a plan yet?"

"We need another week to two weeks to finish our part of the master plan, but we're thinking the same night we do that would be the best night to break them out." Ry flashed a smile. "We figure they'll be suitably distracted by our actions."

"Well, now you can do the two things simultaneously," Kira said after catching Bri's eye and getting a confirming nod. "We'll be helping."

Jessie wasn't going to argue. They knew Greensward better than she and Ry did. Plus, it was Brighton, even a Bri without all his memories. He wouldn't betray Jay, if nothing else. And it was obvious that Kira wouldn't betray Bri at this point. "Do you know how to use weapons? Bri, do you remember?" Jessie asked.

"I haven't tried, but I think I can. Muscle memory like that doesn't seem to have left me, but I can start practicing at the apartment. Or maybe Ben and Colin's space. It's got a little more open area."

"I had training most of my life on various weapons. I'm probably a little rusty, but I can be ready in that time frame," Kira added.

"What do you want us to do?" Bri asked. "I'll probably be the most helpful in getting you into the jail."

"I won't deny that," Jessie agreed and sat herself down on a barrel near him. "I don't suppose either of you know a way to get to the palace?"

Kira leaned against the wall. "Not me. I avoid it and all the other official military areas."

Jessie studied her. The way she said that implied there was a reason for her avoidance, but if they hadn't figured out Bri was the man they'd saved from Deepen's Crossing, they wouldn't know she was the nurse who had spirited him away. Still, she filed that away for future reference.

Bri shook his head too. "Can we ask why?"

Ry looked to Jessie, clearly thinking they could and should trust the pair. Jessie remembered the way Kira had protected them from Rees's questions and all the little things she'd done since. "Sure. Four minds are better than two," she said easily.

Bri's smile could have lit the room and even Kira couldn't hide the fact she brightened.

Rylia grinned, mind clearly off Jakium McRuoes finally, and started explaining their job.

The wedding would not happen until the afternoon, so Ani spent the morning anxiously pacing her room and doublechecking on preparations. She also attempted to make a break to Ren's room multiple times. Sorin, who was bouncing between the increasing flustered bride and groom, managed to cut her off at the pass each time.

"It might be a forced wedding, but you and Ren mean it, which means he can't see you before the wedding itself and vice versa. It's bad luck."

She gave him an impatient look. "Sunshine, our wedding is already one big pile of bad luck. Me seeing Renny will not make it any worse."

"But maybe you *not* seeing him will make it better in the long run."

Ani growled quietly. "Sorin, why are you taking this so seriously? There isn't going to be a long run, if your predictions are correct."

"Because you love him. And I love you and you deserve to have this go properly. Come on, Ani."

She heaved a loud sigh before turning around and flouncing back to her room.

Finally, and none too soon, they were in the audience chamber. Ren stood in front of the throne, Sorin to his left. Vladimir had claimed, as oldest, that he had the right to walk Ani in. Sorin hadn't fought him. Ren needed someone to stand with him and, other than Ani, Sorin was probably the closest to a friend the man had.

"Breathe, Ren," he murmured.

"I am," he shot back, but kept his voice low too. They lapsed back into silence, half listening to the crowd of about fifty, a mix of nobles and soldiers, who talked quietly. "Am I officially the king?"

Although Sorin had half-expected this question at least a couple weeks before, he had not expected it now. "Officially? I suppose not. The ceremony has never been performed."

"Are you ever going to?"

That was an interesting question. "I don't know," he said honestly. "I suppose at some point people will ask and we will have to. Vladimir will be resistant for the obvious reasons."

"So that will make Ani a princess."

Sorin nodded.

"Okay." If he had been planning on saying more, the start of the music and Ani and Vladimir's appearance cut him off. Sorin snuck a glance at Ren to find a genuine smile spread across his face.

Ani looked radiant in a simple white dress that fell artfully off her shoulders. She positively beamed.

Vladimir passed her to Ren, managing to keep an even expression. The prince offered his arm and stepped up to the officiant. The man cleared his throat and began to work his way through the necessary steps of the ceremony. Sorin listened with half an ear, recalling his own wedding day, and scanned the crowd with the rest of his attention. He felt a momentary foreboding when he realized no one from Greensward was there. More importantly, Jakium wasn't and Sorin hadn't thought anything on the earth could or would keep him away. The young man was family, in all but name. What was going on in Greensward that would keep them away? His mind was so focused on that, he almost missed the vows.

His brother, nervous of what either of them might say, had not allowed the pair to write their own. The officiant stuck to the traditional oaths.

"Do you, Renier Highcastle, take this woman to be your wife, to love, stand beside and cherish for all time?"

There was a pause, long enough for Vladimir to start forward threateningly. He stopped dead, though, at the coldest look Sorin had ever seen Ren favor someone with, and that was saying something, all things considered.

"I do," Ren said, voice clear, head held eye as he kept his gaze locked, full of challenge, on Vladimir.

The officiant shifted anxiously and barreled on. "Do you, Anica Opalin, take this man to be your husband, to love, stand beside and cherish for all time?"

Reaching up to turn Ren's face back to hers, she smiled. "I do."

"Very well. Mr. Dakamar, I believe you have the rings?"

It took a second for that to sink in, because he was so intent on his brother. "Yes, of course!" He stepped forward and offered the rings.

"You may now exchange rings." He waited a beat as they did. "I officially pronounce you husband and wife. Congratulations! You may kiss the bride."

Ren's smile widened and he kissed her with a gusto, adding a slight dip for effect. Ani giggled. Sorin didn't miss the dark look that flicked across Vladimir's face, though, and he had a feeling Ren didn't either. Those in attendance stood and clapped politely as, first Vladimir, and then Sorin hugged Ani. Vladimir's eyes never deviated from Ren.

After Sorin had spilled about his son that morning, Ani had explained her nightmare. Watching this, he resolved to keep a closer eye on Vladimir, as Ani and Ren politely accepted the congratulations of the various attendees.

His brother led the way out and the others followed promptly, probably looking forward more to the party than the slightly strange wedding. Finally, only Sorin, Ani, and Ren remained.

"Congratulations," Sorin said quietly.

"Thank you," Ren replied, with a slight smile.

"Of course. Just…be careful, okay? Especially you, Ren."

"I will be."

"Think we can skip the party for a while?" Ani asked, threading her arm through Ren's and leaning against him.

"I think, after Vlad's behavior, that you can skip the entire thing if you want."

She smiled. "I love you, Sunshine."

"Love you too."

"C'mon, Renny, let's go celebrate out on the ramparts."

"I can get behind that," he said, kissing her cheek and guiding her out of the room.

Sorin stood where they'd left him, one clear thought swirling around his head. One way or another, it would all be over soon. Until, then, though, something needed to be made clear. Sorin left the room, tracking down Calip, who somehow knew that Vladimir had headed for the uppermost balcony, on the opposite side of the castle from the newlyweds. Sorin aimed an absent thank you at him and followed.

Finally, after too many stairs, he pushed open a door to find his brother pacing and muttering to himself.

"I don't know what you're planning, but don't do it," Sorin said without preamble, although he kept his tone mild.

Vladimir whirled on him. "You don't know what you're talking about."

"I don't? According to whom?" Sorin couldn't help the surge of anger that slipped into his voice.

"You don't," he said firmly. "So leave it alone."

"I don't think I shall." He smirked, although he only felt a pit in his stomach.

"Sorin," he threatened, eyes narrowing.

"Don't. You do *not* get to pull that shit."

Vladimir stepped closer, as if he was trying to use his slight height advantage. "Do not presume to talk about things you do not understand."

It felt just like talking to Edward. Only worse. "Things I don't understand?" He forced a laugh. "I understand far more than you seem to think I do. Maybe even more than you, Vlad."

Vladimir snorted and started to turn away dismissively. "Don't talk back."

Like a rising tide, Sorin's anger snapped for the first time in ten years. For the first time since he had been pushed too far and reacted, punching Edward in the face and storming from the house. Before he thought his actions through, he took two quick steps forward, grabbing Vladimir by the shirt collar. He used his anger and momentum to spin him around and slam him back into the wall.

"Do *not* ever say that again," he growled, face scant inches from his brother. "First, you clearly have no idea what I do or do not understand. Second, does it even register that this is Edward talking and not you? Third, you need to step back and stop, before you do something irreversible. Do you understand?"

"Yes," Vlad muttered moodily. Sorin knew he was temporarily cowed – maybe only stunned by the physical impact – but not down yet.

Still, he let go and stepped back. Vlad was his brother, still family, despite recent tendencies, and even that much violence towards anyone – let alone family – made Sorin's hands shake as the anger ebbed. "Good. Leave Ren alone."

"How many times do I have to tell you?" Vlad said, straightening, but a lot of the condescension was gone. "You don't give the orders."

Sorin offered a half-smile. "Don't fool yourself, Vlad. There are few who would take your word over mine anymore." That, in of itself, was strange to contemplate, but Sorin didn't doubt it was ultimately true. The people who worked in the castle were neither blind nor stupid, although Sorin might have classified them all as grossly misguided. They saw the changing tides. "But that's not the important part." *Yet.* "What is important is that you stay away from Renier if you can't handle yourself around him."

"Why are you trying so hard to protect him?" He stepped away from the wall, almost seeming afraid that Sorin might shove him into it again.

"It isn't him I'm protecting." Although, perhaps that had been true at one point. Now, Sorin admitted only to himself, that might not be so true.

Vladimir stared at him before understanding dawned. "Anica? Why?"

"I am protecting Ani because you're currently plotting how to murder her husband."

He visibly started at Ren's new title.

Sorin smiled coldly. "Ani has been beyond loyal from the start, despite what we dragged her into. The least you can do is let her be happy." *For a few months, at least, before we'll have to send Ani away if she's to survive the coming battles.*

500

"She's gotten her fair share of positive things out of this," Vladimir shot back.

"Yes, that would be Ren. Or are you really too blind to see it?"

"Renier isn't important."

"If you think that, you're fooling yourself on a lot of levels. If nothing else, he is important to our sister and therefore important to me, and he should be to you as well."

"I'll kill him if I want to." The comment was barely thought out, just a posturing reaction to Sorin standing up to him, but it still carried weight.

Sorin caught his eye. "You will not touch him. Do whatever you want otherwise. I no longer care, but you will leave our *brother-in-law* alone or face the consequences."

"You would never hurt one of your siblings," Vladimir scoffed, voice laced with confidence.

He held his gaze until Vladimir broke first. "Try me," he said softly and then turned and let himself back into the castle.

Chapter Thirty-three

"I BELIEVE OUR CHANCES OF ESCAPING just increased tenfold," Jay said quietly in the thoughtful silence that followed Bri's departure.

I looked at him. Was escape really possible? "If anyone could do it, it would be Bri," I agreed slowly. Maybe things were looking up. Maybe we had a real chance to get back to our Cavern Hall family. We just couldn't let Rees get a whiff of the fact we knew Bri. "Oh, shit," I breathed as the realization hit me.

"What?" Jay demanded.

"I didn't tell Bri that Rees knows his full name. Bri shouldn't know his full name! If Rees tries anything..."

"My brother is nothing if not quick on his feet and I sincerely doubt that's changed too much. He'll cover if anything happens before tomorrow evening."

I didn't quite have Jay's faith in the matter, but there was nothing I could do about it. I did, however, trust that Bri would come up with a plan to get us out and that it would most likely work. With any luck, he'd be able to find Jessie and Ry as well for backup.

For now, our only big obstacle was the obnoxiously brilliant Colonel Trigger Rees.

His cheery "Morning, Jasmine" came far too soon, considering how long I'd laid awake the night before.

I made myself match his cheeriness. "Good morning, Trigger!"

He raised his eyebrows. "You seem to be in a good mood."

"Is that not allowed?"

Rees merely smirked and turned his gaze to Stella and Dave. I tensed. "Stella and David Harper, yes?"

"Yes," Stella said cautiously.

He studied them for too many anxious heartbeats. "You had a brother who was part of the Freedom Fighters."

Stella lifted her chin defiantly. "We did."

He stroked his chin, nodded, and turned back to me. "Come along, Jez, it's time for us to chat."

"Oh, joy. Just what I was hoping for this morning," I said, getting painfully to my feet. The beating at the hands of Juke and his pal had left my legs feeling weak when I stood.

Rees opened the cell and gestured me out. Juke stood just down the hall and smiled at me with all his teeth. I refused to flinch as Rees put his hand on my elbow and steered me down the hall. For the first time since my shoulder injury, he led me to the small interrogation room. I shot a glare at Juke. I wondered about the lack of Kilgor.

"Remembering our last meeting here?"

"Nope, our first," I told him, turning to face him as he shut the door behind us. To my satisfaction, he paled at the reminder. "What's the question this time?"

"Which question?"

"Whatever your dumb question is for the day. What do you want me to tell you this time?"

"Fine, then. Who's Brighton?"

I think I started a bit, but hoped he'd assume it was due to being annoyed, not anxious. I stared at him, trying to figure out his angle. "Why are you so insistent on getting me to talk about Brighton?"

"Did you always call him Brighton? That seems like quite the mouthful. I'm sure he had a nickname. Bri, perhaps?" His gaze held mine, sharp and ready for the slightest flicker from me.

He'd waited too long for that to happen, though. "And why should I tell you if we did?"

"Why should you tell me anything, Jez? It saves you from some pain. I see you're rather stiff right now."

"That's what getting beat up does to a person."

"How about you answer the question?"

"As if it will ever be that easy." I folded my arms. "Let me go back to my cell if that's all you've got."

He grinned. "Oh, I have so much more, Jasmine. Did Brighton have a nickname?"

Juke stepped closer to me meaningfully.

So I lied. "We only called him Brighton. He loved his name and it's what he'd grown up being called. End of story. Aren't you so glad you've been obsessing over it?"

"And if I were to ask Jay?"

"Brighton died before Jay ever joined," I said, which was not a lie really.

"If you say so," he said before glancing at Juke. "Where's Dayton?"

"Getting the prisoner with Kilgor," he grunted.

I stiffened. "Which prisoner?" I demanded.

"You'll find out soon enough."

"If you touch David again, I swear to the gods," I snapped, taking a step towards him before Juke's hand landed heavily on my shoulder and squeezed. I bit back a squeak as pain shot down my arm.

"I do believe that's the first bit of real anger I've seen out of you since our initial chat. Should I be worried about your control?"

"Why don't you push me a little more and see?" I had no doubt that, should I lose control, he'd be very sorry. Last time I'd broken out of both the brutes' grip. This time, there was only one between us.

He hummed and took a step towards me. On instinct, not nearly angry or off-kilter enough to snap – to be honest, I wasn't sure something even as serious as this would be enough – I backed towards Juke. "What was it last time?" he said. "Ah, yes, I went to touch your scars. You seem rather sensitive about them." He took another step forward.

"I wouldn't suggest trying it again. You're even less defended this time." Now I forced myself to hold my ground, eyes locked on his.

"This is true, but I'm also a lot more prepared. I know what to expect." He twitched his hand, which drew my attention to it. He held a short but sharp knife in one hand. I took a deep breath, cautioning myself to calm. "I don't see why you're so squeamish about them," he said softly, almost gently.

"I'm not squeamish." My voice sounded tight and strained, even to my own ears.

"Then why can't I touch them?"

"Because they're mine. Not yours."

"There is very little that is *yours* right now, Jasmine."

"Don't touch them, Trigger." He stood mere inches from me, almost nose-to-nose.

"Or what?"

"I will kill you," I said flatly and found I meant it, even with my vision clear. I took a deep breath and let it out slowly, holding his gaze again.

"Indeed," he murmured. Then, to my vast astonishment, he reached out toward my face. I knew I had a few scars visible at the edge of my hairline.

I stumbled back into Juke's bulk, not that it was nearly far enough away. Still, it turned out that there was no need. In the second before his fingers landed, Jay grabbed him by the shirt and spun, slamming him into the wall, the knife clattering away. "Or maybe," he growled lowly, "*I* will kill you if you touch her. Got it?"

"Jay?" I managed, mind reeling, trying to come down from the adrenaline too quickly.

"You okay?"

Kilgor and Dayton stood in the doorway, stunned. Juke still had his hand on my shoulder but hadn't moved further.

"Yeah. When did you get here?"

"A moment ago."

"Get him off!" Rees sputtered, trying to pry Jay's grip off his collar. My friend gave no ground.

Dayton, in yet another surprise, was the first to move, but with a slight shift, I snuck out a foot. The short man hit it and went sprawling into me and Juke, but it wasn't Jay and Rees so I considered it a win.

"Careful there, Dayton. Better watch your step," I admonished.

"You," he sputtered, trying to get back up. I shifted, throwing him off balance again as he tried to straighten.

Juke shoved past me, throwing me back towards the corner, to help Kilgor pull Jay off the colonel, pushing him against the wall in turn.

Before the brutes could begin beating Jay, Rees straightened his shirt and held up a hand to stall them. "Juke, please grab Jasmine before she does harm to Dayton."

With a glare, the brute shuffled over, pulling me away from Dayton. I didn't fight it. Shooting me a nasty look, Dayton stumbled but caught his balance again.

Rees returned his gaze to Jay, who was still pressed firmly against the wall. "James, you are very lucky there will be nothing more than a bruise from your little stunt."

Jay still radiated raw fury so I reached out a hand, clasping his. "Thank you."

Although he held me tightly, I could feel some of the tension leak out and he nodded slightly, eyes fixed on Rees.

"Well, now, this is adorable."

"Shut up, Rees," we said in concert. Jay glared. Most of my anger had ebbed away at Jay's arrival – Dave was safe.

His grin widened. "I don't understand you," he said finally. "You are fiercely protective of each other, but when I do this…" He gestured and Kilgor hauled off with his free hand and caught Jay in the face, neatly splitting his lip. Jay wiped at his lip, gaze taking a second to refocus, his own anger draining.

I winced sympathetically and squeezed his hand.

"You don't try and protect him."

"There are levels of protection. To get you to stop now, I'd have to give you something in exchange and that would threaten more of our friends. Here, we can control who is threatened and suffers for it."

"Plus, when we're not visiting with you, we can mock you to our hearts' content and get all the excess anger out," Jay said, swiping at his lip with more direction.

"Along with your cellmates?" I didn't like his interest in Stella and Dave at all and freshly cursed Dakamar and Opalin.

"We're friendly people and we're all in the same boat. Can you blame us?"

"You're also willing to risk your lives for them after a month."

"Month and a half," I corrected mildly. My mental math put us around forty days.

Rees flapped a hand at us. "Semantics. That doesn't explain why. It's just a kid and his sister."

"Whose brother and mother lost their lives to a cause which we've spent months and years working on. Not to mention your attack on them turned a ten-year-old into a killer. It's the least we can do for them."

"And the only thing currently," Jay said evenly, like that didn't bother him.

With any luck, we could do a lot more soon.

Rees pursed his lips, looking us both over slowly, eyes settling on our clasped hands. "Very well. I have some other business to attend to. Dayton, please escort them back to their cell."

Uneasiness settled in my stomach. Had he gotten something out of us that I hadn't noticed?

"You have other business?" Jay gasped. "I am deeply and severely hurt that we aren't your only work right now." He clapped our hands over his heart dramatically. I snorted.

Rees rolled his eyes. "Don't make Kilgor punch you again," he said before turning smartly on his heel and leaving.

Dayton waited a minute after he left, glaring at both of us, before gesturing for the brutes to bring us and stomping out in the lead. He said nothing as we made our way back to our cell and he let us in, slamming the door shut right on my heels.

I shot him a glare of my own as he and the brutes left. "Thanks," I told Jay, "your timing was impeccable as ever."

"I figured you could take him, but it might mean more coming from me, since he is obviously not getting the message from you."

"I don't think anything really will," I said dryly. "You okay?"

"Oh yeah, Rees went surprisingly light considering."

"Yeah, what was that all about?"

He shook his head. "I don't know, but I kind of wish I did."

I had to agree as I settled down in my usual corner. Jay sat too and, at Stella's raised eyebrows, explained what had happened.

I half-expected to see Rees again later, even if just to gloat over picking something up that I'd missed, but there was no sign of him all afternoon, even as the light outside faded.

So concerned over Rees, I'd forgotten that Bri was on dinner duty until he crouched by the bars. "Anyone hungry?" he asked with a wide grin.

"Usually I'd say always, but not with the same old slop," Jay said but took it when I was passed it from Bri.

"Soon," his brother promised. "Hi! You must be Stella and David."

Stella smiled. "Nice to meet you, Bri."

"You look a lot like Jay," Dave said.

"No," Bri said winking, "Jay looks a lot like me. I came first, after all."

The boy grinned. "Good point."

Jay snorted. "Got any news for us?"

"As a matter of fact, I do! It just so happens that Kira works nearby at the Blue Parrot Inn and guess who the newest employees are?"

My eyes narrowed. "Who?"

"Oh c'mon, guess," he wheedled.

"It can't be Jessie and Ry."

He beamed. "Why yes, yes it can be!"

"You're shitting us."

"Nope, they chose the Blue Parrot precisely because it was near the prison. I met with them last night to do some planning. We're going to strike in one week. All you need is to be ready when we come. I got news when I came in that the regular guy will be back tomorrow, so I'm not sure I'll be able to sneak back much at all. But one week."

"Are you sure there's nothing we can do to help?" I asked.

"You're a little stuck," he pointed out.

"Thanks for the reminder," Jay said sourly.

"Fine, you can make sure Colonel Rees doesn't get wind of it."

Dave frowned, shrinking back against Stella. "He won't, will he?"

"No, of course not. We're all very smart people," Bri said solemnly. "And eight brains are smarter than one, even a scarily intuitive one."

"I'm not sure this is making *me* feel any better," Jay muttered.

"Shush," Bri said. "I'm sure it'll be fine, David."

"Do we get to know the plan?"

"It's pretty simple. I distract the guard by pretending I lost something. Kira follows me in and takes him out while I'm being a distraction. We take the keys, let you out, and get to a safehouse to meet Jessie and Ry."

I stared at him and then exchanged a glance with Jay. "Is that…all?"

"Yup."

"But that's really…easy," Jay said, perplexed.

"Hence simple. Do you have a problem with it?"

"No, but your plans are usually more elaborate."

"How do we get out of the city?" I asked at the same time.

"We figure Jessie and Ry's present will send the city into enough chaos that we can sneak out while they're trying to figure out what happened."

"Everything goes boom!" Jay said with satisfaction.

"Boom?" Stella asked.

"They're blowing up the Greensward castle. Or at least parts of it," I said, amused.

"Boom!" Jay agreed.

Bri sighed and shook his head. "And people call me immature."

"There is absolutely nothing immature about liking things going boom!"

I had to laugh. "Of course not, James."

He stuck his tongue out at me.

"I will let you know updates as I can, but I don't guarantee anything. I don't want to be here too often when I'm not supposed to be, at risk of getting the colonel's attention."

"Of course," I said, although I didn't like the idea of being left out of the loop. Still, if it came down to the chance of rescue or no chance at all, I could handle it.

"Hang in there," he said sympathetically.

"We will," Jay told him. "Be careful."

"Always," he said, but he didn't try to fool us with a cocky smile. Rees obviously made Bri nervous too. "I'd better get going. Goodnight, Jay. Jez."

"Goodnight, Bri," Jay said. I echoed him and Dave waved.

A second later, Bri was gone. I watched after him and then set into my food.

Nothing left to do but wait.

Bri did not come back to the Blue Parrot the next night as agreed. He didn't usually come often and two nights in a row might raise some suspicions. Kira promised she'd update them with any information he had as soon as she saw them the next day. Colonel Rees, on the other hand, did appear, settling at the bar towards the tail end of the dinner hour. Ry was out doing some errands, but Jessie sat only a couple seats down from him, having been talking to Kira occasionally and sipping at an ale.

"So," Rees asked Kira as she wiped down the bar in front of him, "what *is* Bri short for?"

"I assume Brian. He's never been able to tell me, obviously, so we don't discuss it much."

"Could it be short for Brighton?"

Jessie was glad that Kira was facing her when he asked because her expression flickered to shock for a split second before she schooled it.

"I suppose it could be," the other woman said.

"What do you think?"

"Brighton is an unusual name. Brian isn't, hence my assumption,"

"But it's possible."

She shrugged, turning to look at him. "Anything's possible, sir," she said mildly.

Rees smiled. "That is very true, Kira. Okay," he waved away her offer to get him a drink, "I have business. I appreciate your time as always." With that he left the bar, although he paused a couple times to talk to various soldiers before disappearing out the door.

Kira and Jessie exchanged a glance, but didn't dare say anything.

The next day, Kira filled Jessie and Ry in Bri's conversation with Jay and Jez. In the late afternoon, while Jessie was also working, Bri skipped in. He settled at an empty space at the bar, said hi politely to Jessie, and then started to draw something on a piece of paper, chatting lightly with Kira as he did.

"Good afternoon, Kira," Colonel Rees said as he strolled in maybe twenty minutes after Bri.

Bri hunched his shoulders, keeping his focus on whatever he was drawing.

"Jessica," he added as he slid onto a seat at the bar as well, waving to the soldiers.

"Sir," Jessie said neutrally.

"Ladies, may I please have a drink? Something stronger than water, but not too strong, as the day's still young."

"What's the occasion?" Kira asked, moving to grab one of their easily watered down alcohols.

"We've finally scheduled the hangings for the four prisoners. We've needed them for a while, but their usefulness is at the end. I'm sure Bri's mentioned them. They've been quite a focus for us recently."

Bri stiffened before he returned to his scribbling. Jessie pretended that all her focus was on a particular spot on the bar, scrubbing at it.

"Yes, he has. Two were the pair who blew up the depot a month or so back, right?"

"Indeed."

"What's the date? Jacob'll want to know, for business."

"Two days from today."

That math was dead simple. Jessie swallowed hard.

"Ah, well, that means business will be good that night," Kira said in unconcern, passing the colonel his drink.

"Indeed. You'll be there, won't you, Bri?" Rees asked, acknowledging the other man's presence for the first time.

Bri scrambled to his feet, practically saluting. "Yes, sir, I will be, sir, unless you want me to cover at the prison, sir."

Jessie eyed him, not particularly liking this side of Bri. It felt too unnatural to her, but Kira glanced her way and winked. Jessie wondered if Bri had cultivated this act from the beginning, even before he knew who he was.

"I don't bite, Bri," Rees said mildly.

"Yes, sir, of course not, sir."

"What about you, Kira?" Rees now asked, turning back to the bar. "Will you be there? I don't think I've ever seen you at one before."

"I normally make sure the Blue Parrot is ready for the crowds that will be here until late."

"I think you should be there."

"I'll try my best, Colonel. But I don't usually have the time to fight my way back here to be here on time. If you've noticed my absence, I'm sure you've noticed Jacob's as well."

"Ah, yes, but you have more staff now. How about you, Jessica? Will you or Ryan be there?"

"I doubt it, sir. If it's going to be that busy, it'll be all hands on deck here, even with the extra staff. Plus, my sister is very squeamish." Ry would have hit her if she'd heard that description.

Rees stared at her evenly for a heartbeat too long. "Very well. Brighton, do you have work tonight?"

Jessie's heart lurched in the intervening breath and Kira froze for a second, but Bri didn't miss a beat. "What did you call me, sir? That's not my name, sir. I mean, maybe it could be, I guess, sir, but I don't know."

Rees now studied him as Bri wrung his hands. "Of course, of course. I was thinking of the prisoners. One of them knew a Brighton a few years back. I must still have that on my mind."

"It's okay, sir, of course. I just don't want to be confused, sir."

He nodded. "Do you think it is? Does it ring any bells?"

"No, sir, none at all."

"Does Brian?"

Bri shook his head in wide-eyed ignorance.

Rees downed the drink. "I'll have a glass of water now," he ordered and returned his attention to Bri. "Either way, are you working tonight?"

"Yes, sir, but I am back to my regular duties. I start in an hour. So I thought I'd come see Kira and do some drawing." There was a note of pride in his voice, like a child's pride.

"What are you drawing?"

Bri held up a surprisingly comprehensive map of Greensward. Even Kira looked a little startled and she'd been watching him. Jessie knew he had a sharp memory and an eye for details. "The city," he said. "Kira worries that I'm going to get lost, so I'm making a map. Does it look right, sir?"

Rees took it, studying it critically and without any seeming suspicion, although he had to have some if he was announcing the hanging. "It looks good to me, Bri. I see you have the Blue Parrot and your apartment starred."

"Yes, sir! To remind me and so I will know how close or far from them I am, sir."

The colonel studied it for another minute and then nodded, handing it back. "I should head back to the prison. I'll see you in an hour, Bri."

"Yes, sir."

"Please add the two drinks to my tab, Kira."

"Of course, Colonel." Jessie knew from the other woman that he always insisted on paying for his water too.

As soon as Rees had disappeared out the door, Jessie drifted towards Kira and Bri. Bri waited until they were both close before saying softly, "He's lying. He has to be."

Jessie marveled at the change in his demeanor as he regarded them. "How can you be sure?" she asked.

"Because hangings for proven Freedom Fighters have to take more time than that."

"Good point. Even hangings for the more run of the mill criminals take longer," Kira agreed, relaxing slightly.

"Exactly. You need to set up the square to start with. And there's been no sign of movement there and Kira and I have to walk through it every day to get to work. And they'd probably want Opalin and Dakamar down here, since they've both visited since their capture."

"They have?" Jessie asked. That was news to her.

Bri flapped a hand at her in a clear 'later' gesture. "And they'd need time to get free and get here."

"Plus, they usually offer more warning than that because the city will pretty much shut down for a couple hours," Kira said.

"Okay, so he was bluffing then. To what end?" Jessie asked. "Does he somehow suspect some of us?"

"I don't think directly, but if one of them mentioned my name like it sounds like, then it's possible that deep down Rees has connected the dots, or at least strongly suspects that I'm the same Bri. That seemed clear enough when he tried to trip me up."

"And, I think he figures if we are innocent, then word will spread of the hangings and it might flush out any actual Freedom Fighters," Kira pointed out. "Bar and wait staff are notorious gossips."

"Then we'll get spreading," Jessie said. "No reason to give him any more reason to suspect us." She polished the bar near them.

"He's already suspicious. We'll need to be even more careful and hope Jez, Jay, and their cellmates are up to the challenge as well," Bri murmured, looking down at his map.

"It's only five more days," Kira said. "That's all we need to hold him off for."

"Thank the gods for small favors."

"Why a map?" Jessie asked.

"It's not suspicious and I thought they might be helpful the night of. I'll make each of us one and mark the important places with some various signs that won't be obvious to anyone but us."

She had to smile. "Brilliant," she told him before moving to respond to the waving from a table of soldiers.

Ren woke the morning after his wedding and found that nothing had changed. He still wore his pajamas and Ani was still tucked under his arm as she often was these days, fast asleep. He supposed the fact that neither had woken up with a nightmare might make it special, but it didn't seem like enough.

Ani seemed to sense the fact he was awake because she rolled over to face him with a sleepy smile. "Morning, husband."

He had to smile back. "Good morning. Sleep all right?"

She nodded. "Would've been better if we could have had a proper wedding night," she said lightly.

"Mm, undoubtedly." He shifted to kiss her gently. "We'll just have to content ourselves with this."

She nodded. They both knew, without even discussing it, that neither would risk her getting pregnant with things as they were now. If she had his child, it would give Vladimir a further hold on the throne. With an heir, he could have Ren killed in an accident and install himself as regent and there would be little that anyone could do. Despite the Three's background, they were now properly married, which made any child of theirs a legitimate heir. That, in turn, would eliminate any of Ren's more distant relatives who might try to make a claim.

And the kissing certainly wasn't bad. They'd done quite a bit of it the night before, after all, until Ani had felt guilty about leaving Sorin to the party wolves and they'd gone to make an awkward appearance.

"Can I move in?" Ani asked after a quiet minute.

"What?" He was caught off guard by the sudden question.

"Can I move in?"

He met her eyes. "Are you sure you want to?"

She poked him hard in the side. "Don't ask me that again."

He squirmed. "You know why I am."

"And I don't care. Renny, I love you and I want us to be able to enjoy this as much as we can while it lasts."

He pressed his lips together. "If you want to move in, I would love it. We can rearrange however you want and I have some drawer and closet space. I don't have much in the way of clothes these days."

She smiled. "I've never been one for a lot of clothes, so we should fit just fine."

"I think we already fit just fine."

"Awww, that was wonderfully sappy of you," she teased, patting his cheek.

"You are evil."

She just kissed him. "Do we have to move anything?" she asked, once she seemed to think she had him properly cowed.

"Well, no, but it might be nice."

Ani stared at him before pushing herself to a seat.

He followed suit, a little concerned now. "What is it?"

"Sorin and I talked yesterday. Early, before the wedding. About a lot of things. But he really thinks your brother and the Freedom Fighters are going to win when they attack. That they have the advantage." She hesitated. "Especially with Vlad not really being himself these days."

"Okay? What does that have to do with rearranging my room?"

"I think Sorin's going to send me away, so I'm not here when that happens."

"So you're safe," he said softly, understanding now. They would have even less time than he had thought, but the chances of her dying either in fighting or being hung as a traitor were also probably now much smaller. And he did not wish that on her at all. He had meant the vows the day before, even if most wouldn't believe him. And who knew if he'd get a chance to argue in her favor when the attack came.

She nodded, reaching out to cup his cheek with her hand. "We knew it wouldn't last."

"I know. I just thought…I guess, for a moment yesterday, I thought maybe."

"I know," she echoed, smiling a little. "But we have for now, so we'll just have to enjoy it as much as we can in the meantime."

He wanted to be free, but he wanted Ani to be there too. The Freedom Fighters' hopeful forthcoming victory suddenly felt a little bittersweet. "You'll take care of-" that was as far as he got before Ani shifted her hand to cover his mouth.

"No. Not now. Not yet. I'm not gone yet."

Ren pressed his lips together. "Okay. Not yet."

She smiled, bringing her other hand up. "I love you, my king," she whispered.

He leaned forward and kissed her hard.

Chapter Thirty-four

THE NEXT WEEK PASSED AT A snail's pace. Rees had Jay and I each dragged out of the cell twice, but despite the obvious pressure from above, he seemed stymied as to what to ask us. He suddenly was stuck on the same few questions, especially about Bri, and his attempts at deduction were strangely off base. Besides a few new bruises for being impertinent, we walked away each time unscathed.

I didn't say anything, but it made me nervous. There was no discernable reason for the change and, although a part of me was grateful for the reprieve, a larger part wondered what Rees had up his sleeve. I could only hope it wasn't somehow an awareness of our plan. Still, I shushed the others whenever it started to come up, even though I had ample reason to believe we wouldn't be overheard, considering a lot of what we'd said before.

The night of the planned rescue, I stood, bouncing in place by the doorway. I wanted to pace but, with Jay and Dave asleep, there wasn't room. Stella alternated between watching me and listening hard for sounds of footsteps.

"I'm sure he'll be here. He doesn't seem the type to renege on a promise," she whispered as the night crept later. It had to be after midnight.

At that precise moment, I heard soft footsteps coming our way and I spun to crane my neck, trying to see down the hallway. Even with only half the torches lit for evening, Bri's familiar outline was unmistakable. He was trailed closely by a woman I didn't know, but I guessed was the aforementioned girlfriend, Kira.

Bri grinned as he reached us. "Ready for an epic escape, my friends?"

"Are we ever," I said, nudging Jay in the side with my foot to wake him.

"Great! Gang, this is Kira. Kira, this is the gang."

She and I rolled our eyes at the same time.

"Where are Jessie and Ry?" I asked, even as Bri slid the key into the door and opened it.

"No worries, Jez, as planned they went to make things go boom!"

"Without me?" Jay said, scrambling to his feet and pasting a pout on his face. "No fair!"

"Would you rather we left you here?"

"As if." He winced a bit and rubbed at his leg. The brutes had obviously done something to it the day before and it definitely still hurt.

"You okay?" Kira asked. I took an instant to study her. She stood at least a half foot shorter than Bri, but wore a sword like she knew how to use it, which was really the only thing that mattered to me right now.

"Just sore," he said cheerfully. "Rees can be a vicious bastard when he wants. And when I get all insulty."

"Can you walk all right? We've got a long night ahead of us," Bri asked, in obvious concern.

Jay wagged a finger at him. "No babying the younger brother. I'll keep up. It's just stiff."

I doubted that part, but I did trust that nothing would hold any of us back from this bid for freedom.

"Yes, sir," Bri said dryly and tossed us each a bundle. "Fresh clothes so the stink doesn't attract attention. We even found some that shouldn't be too big on you, David."

The boy smiled shyly. "Thank you."

It took a few minutes for first Stella and I and then Dave and Jay to change, but I figured it was worth the time wasted.

"All right, gang, let's move out," Bri said, leading the way down the hallway. "Introductions time. Kira, this is Jay, my little-"

"Younger," Jay corrected with a nasty look.

"Brother. And then this is Jez, who is, I now know, one of my best friends. And Stella and David. Everyone, this is Kira, my girlfriend."

"Hi," she said and smiled. "Bri's been telling me a lot about you and Jay," she told me, "since his memories have started to return."

I opened my mouth but Jay spoke over me.

"Wait, let me see the keys," he said, reaching over to pluck them from his brother's hand.

"What? Why?"

"Does anyone have an extra set?"

"Somewhere, sure, but not here at the prison."

"Good. We don't need them again, right?"

Bri shook his head, clearly puzzled.

"And you locked the guard in a cell, yes?"

This time a nod.

Jay tossed them into the nearest cell as we passed. "Guess the guard will be stuck for a while. Pity."

Stella stifled a laugh and offered a hand for a high five.

As we reached the front entry, which I only vaguely remembered from being brought in, Kira pointed at a small pile of weaponry. "I found this tucked behind the desk. I'm guessing some of it's yours?"

"It is!" I said, brightening. I grabbed my sword and strapped it back in place. I felt myself relax a little at its familiar weight. "Although it doesn't have quite the same sentimental value anymore." I patted it and grinned at Bri.

It took him a second. "Oh! Is that the one I got you?"

I nodded as I got my knife settled as well.

"Ready?" Kira asked as Stella finished testing the string on a bow and settling a dagger on her hip.

Dave stood near the window, whose shutters were cracked, hand clenched tightly around the hilt of a knife Jay had found him. "I...I think we're in trouble," he said in a small voice without looking back at us.

"What?" Bri, the closest, moved to his side and peered out. He went pale. "I guess we didn't fool Rees very well after all."

I swallowed hard, fighting against the panic that threatened. We *had* to get out.

"They're sure to have the back door covered too. Godsdamn," Bri muttered, pulling Dave away from the window and back to the desk.

"What about Rees's office?" I asked, almost before my brain had caught up with the why. "That has a big window. Maybe they don't have it covered."

"Brilliant!" Bri said. "It's certainly worth a try. Come on." He led the way through the prison and pushed open the door, peeking in, before beelining for the window. He edged closer, looking out in every direction as the rest of us piled into the room. "No one," he reported, "but as soon as we break the window, they'll come running."

"Who said anything about breaking them?" Jay asked, reaching forward, turning the knob about halfway up and giving it a shove. The window swung silently outward.

"Touché."

I rolled my eyes and slid by them, dropping the couple feet to the ground with ease. I turned to help Dave out as the others followed. So far at least, Rees seemed to have not caught on to this plan.

"This way," Kira murmured and set off. We kept Dave in the middle and Bri brought up the rear. We skipped quickly to the shadow of the next building and crept along it as quietly as we could. As we rounded the corner, I spotted some of Rees's goons lurking further down at what was presumably the back door. It suddenly sank in that, after two horribly long months, we were *free*. I clamped down on the urge to cheer and do a victory dance, contenting myself with a nice, big smile instead. We kept to the shadows, creeping past what Bri informed me in a breathless whisper was the Blue Parrot Inn, before we were able to cut across the main road and were finally fully out of sight of Rees and his men.

"What now?" Jay asked, once we were all safely down the street.

"We split up. It's easier for smaller groups to hide and they'll be looking for five adults and a child. Kira will take Stella and Jay. David and Jez will come with me."

Stella tightened her grip around Dave's shoulders.

"We'll take good care of him, Stella," I said quietly. "Promise. We'll get there safely."

She nodded, hugging her brother quickly before giving him a gentle shove over to us. I took his hand.

Bri thrust his chest out and marched forward. For the third time that night, I rolled my eyes and Dave let out a nervous giggle as we followed.

"So, how's the memory?" I asked quietly as we fell in step with him, Dave between us.

"Better. Not perfect. It's really spotty for a decent portion of my life, but it's not gone anymore, which feels amazing."

"I bet. It's amazing to be having a conversation with you. You have no idea."

"Oh, but I do. I am a stellar conversationalist and, as such, all conversations with me should be truly savored."

I jabbed my elbow into his ribs.

He grinned, unperturbed. Then he sobered abruptly. "Soldiers approaching. Three o'clock. Hide the sword."

How was I supposed to do that? But then I saw that he subtly reached down and pushed the point of the scabbard down so it ran parallel to his leg. I did the same, hoping it was quick enough in the dim light. Dave's grip on my hand tightened to the point of being painful. I squeezed it reassuringly as best I could.

"Evening," one of the soldiers said, looking us over.

"Evening, sir," Bri said, cool as a cucumber.

"Get on back to your house. We're clearing the roads. There are bad folk about."

I almost snorted at that very detailed description.

"Yes, sir. We're only a couple blocks away from our apartment."

"Then get there on the double," another said gruffly.

"Yes, sir," I said, making a show of steering Dave and Bri away. I could feel the boy shaking under my hand. "You okay, kid?"

He nodded. "Are we gonna have to do that again?"

"Quite possibly. Just keep your head down and let us do the talking," Bri said softly.

"Where are we headed?"

"Across town, so a distance, unfortunately, and we can't take the most direct route."

"Why so far? There must be a safehouse closer."

521

"Kira's brother is there. There isn't a safer house. And they're leaving with us."

"They?"

"Her brother's friend works for the Freedom Fighters. He sends a lot of messages to Cavern Hall as Col?"

I knew the name of course. Col was our foremost source for Greensward and Oakbridge news. The man seemed to get everywhere and into everything. It was truly impressive. I nodded and let Bri direct our path. It took well over an hour before we finally reached a nice looking row house. It was dark, the shutters drawn tight. Bri looked both ways then hopped up the stairs to knock three times on the door. He paused and did it again.

Only then did I hear the lock click and the door swung open. A man I didn't know stood there. "Come in, come in," he said, herding us through the door.

"Is anyone else here yet?" Bri asked.

"Kira and your other two friends from the prison just got here. Colin's getting them set up in the kitchen with a snack."

My brain didn't immediately catch on the name.

Then Bri spoke again. "Thanks, Benton."

"Really, Ben is fine."

Benton. And Kira. Benton and Kira *Walters*. *Colin*. I shoved past Benton and raced towards the sound of faint voices, skidding to a stop in the doorway of the well-lit kitchen in the back of the house.

"You made it!" Stella said.

The man at the stove turned at her voice and then he froze as he spotted me, eyes going wide in shock, and he dropped the bowl he was holding with a crash. "*Jasmine?*" he breathed.

A second later, I was hugging my brother tightly. "You're alive!"

"*You're* alive!" he shot back, clinging just as hard. "What the *hell*, Jasmine?"

"You two know each other?" Kira asked, startled.

"From before?" Stella added. She'd obviously picked up on the use of my full name.

I pulled back a little to reassure myself that Colin was really alive and standing right in front of me. "This is Colin. My brother," I explained, as Benton, Jay, and Dave caught up to me.

"How are you here?" Colin demanded, giving me a little shake.

"It's a bit of a long story."

Stella burst out laughing. "A bit? Jez, it took you over a month to tell it!"

"Brief version?"

"I didn't die on my way back home and I was rescued by the Freedom Fighters."

"Sufficiently brief," Bri said in the ensuing silence.

"What about you?"

"I didn't die when the Three invaded Northwind, started working for the Freedom Fightres, and then I moved here with Ben because Kira was already here."

"Jez wins," Jay muttered to Stella. She hit him.

I hugged Colin again. "I can't believe *you're* Col. I've *written to you*, you asshole. Why didn't you ever tell Beau who you were?"

"It didn't seem particularly important."

"The support of a duke would've been nice," Jay piped up, already holding on to Stella's hand, like he expected her to try and hit him again.

"I have helped how I can," Benton said, "but your point is valid. Perhaps I should have done more. I have left most of the hard work to Colin."

"Ben's also recognizable. He's the spitting image of his father, so he needed to lie low," Colin said.

"That's why we have Cavern Hall," I said, but couldn't bring myself to care too much. I had Colin now and Bri had said they were leaving with us, so I wouldn't have to leave him behind.

"We're coming now," Benton offered tentatively, even as we heard a knock back towards the front door.

"I'll get it," Kira said and slipped by.

"Jasmine, if you let go, I'll finish getting all of you a snack. Prison food couldn't have been very good."

"It was bland and icky," Dave said.

"Jez," I said at the same time. It still felt weird to hear my full name from anyone, but even though Colin had never called me anything else, it somehow felt even weirder coming from him.

My brother blinked. "What?"

"I go by Jez now. Jasmine was supposed to be dead and all. And the last person to call me that was Colonel Rees at the jail and I'd rather not remember that." I did let go since my stomach was rumbling at the thought of food.

"Jez," he repeated, trying it out.

A moment later, something rammed into my side and I stumbled a couple steps. "Thank the gods you're all right!" Ry.

I managed to twist in her hug to return it, spotting Jessie similarly engulfing Jay in a big hug.

"I heard you went to make things go boom without me," Jay pouted without missing a beat.

"You'll survive, James."

"Damn, you can use that in the open now, can't you?"

Jessie kissed him on the cheek. "You bet."

"We're fine, Ry," I told her.

"All right," Kira said. "Introductions before we try and get ourselves out of Greensward." She quickly went around and gave everyone's name and couple word background as Colin passed out a simple meal of fruit, cheese, and bread. Even as basic as it was, it was a welcome change. Then Kira turned to Jessie and Ry. "How long do we have?"

Rylia did some quick mental math. "Half hour, tops."

"Good. If we leave now, that should give us enough time to be close to the northern gate when it goes up. Everyone ready?"

I nodded.

"We made everyone a bag with essentials," Colin said, distributing them.

Bri and Kira each got two that looked plumper than ours. Kira caught my gaze and smiled, almost embarrassed. "We've had a lot of time to collect things."

"No judgment here," I said.

"I'll take the lead. Bri, Kira, I want you two in the back. Stay close and stick to the shadows," Colin told us.

Bri saluted.

I fell in step with my brother as we slipped out the backdoor. The streets had been quiet before, but now the entire city was silent. "Did Kira tell you that Colonel Rees knows we escaped?"

"Yeah, in brief. Trust you to screw up something like that."

"Ha ha," I muttered. "Looks like maybe they're trying to lock down the city."

"Probably, but hopefully your friends' explosion will provide enough of a distraction we can sneak out."

"Do you really believe that?"

He shot me a cocky grin that I remembered all too well from our childhood. "There are other ways to get out of the city than the gates if need be."

"Then why are we trying for the gates at all?"

"Kira and Ben hate small spaces. And it would be much quicker if we could get out via the gate. We'll assess when we see what we're up against."

I nodded and we hurried down the dark and quiet streets. Twice we had to duck into alleys to avoid being spotted by groups of soldiers. When we neared the gate, Colin held up a hand and motioned for us to stay, soundlessly disappearing out of sight. Considering the fact the last time I'd seen him, he'd still been as noisy as six horses while doing anything, this stealthy ability caught me a little off guard. I knew *I'd* learned new tricks, but somehow it hadn't occurred to me that I might not be the only one.

Within minutes, he was back, frowning. "It's pretty heavily guarded and I think it includes the lovely colonel."

"So what do we do now?"

"How long until your explosion?" he asked Ry and Jessie, who were right behind us.

"Ten minutes, maybe, probably less."

"All right," Colin said. "We wait until the explosion. Greensward's citizens aren't so well trained that they won't come piling out to see what's going on – they certainly did that with the last set -"

"You're welcome," Jay said.

Stella hit him again and he pouted at her.

"And hopefully in the confusion, the colonel will be distracted and we can sneak out. Everyone good with trying this?"

"The gates were still open?" Benton asked.

"Still open," he agreed.

That made me a little uneasy. Even if it would be easier to sneak out with the gates open, if Rees was there, he had a plan to recapture us. I wasn't sure I liked our odds, considering how he had somehow figured out our escape plan.

Still, none of us protested. I would face Rees head on if it was for a chance to get out of this godsforsaken city. After all, I'd almost killed him while unarmed and held captive. I thought my odds while armed with backup couldn't be that bad.

Colin had us backtrack and take another route until he gestured forward and crouched at a corner, peering around it. I followed, peeking over him. Ahead stretched an open area to the gate, which was heavily guarded. It took a minute of searching to locate Rees, who stood facing our direction, talking to two other men.

"There's the colonel," Colin murmured.

I put my hand on his shoulder and squeezed.

Behind me, I heard Jessie quietly giving an approximate countdown. Less than thirty seconds after her zero, a tremendous boom ripped through the air. I spun in time to see a rather large fireball explode into the sky.

"Gods' Breath. You two do nothing by halves, do you?" Benton said, eyes wide.

Jessie grinned, even as she high-fived Ry without having to look. "It's not the Freedom Fighter way."

"That is one *hell* of a distraction," Kira agreed.

"Boom," Jay said solemnly.

"Look!" Colin hissed.

I peeked back out. Rees was directing at least half his soldiers to head towards the palace. He also turned, though, and yelled something at the guard house. A second later, I spotted a figure move on the top of the gate and the large wooden obstacle began to creak shut.

"Not good," my brother said.

No, it most certainly was not.

Still, people began to pour out of the houses and buildings around us.

"Act natural," Colin said but I saw him cross his fingers as he straightened and strolled out into the open area. I stayed on his far side, keeping his body between me and Rees.

Still, something gave us away because two things happened simultaneously. The gate ground to a halt only halfway shut, still almost seven feet off the ground, and two, one of the soldiers shouted and pointed our way.

I heard Colin curse. There was no way we would make it as far as the gate without having to fight. I drew my sword as Stella put Dave behind her. Jay joined her, followed quickly by Jessie and Ry, forming a shield.

Rees yelled something and his men didn't press us, merely cutting us off from the gate. Rees jogged forward until he stood at the front edge of his men. I did a quick mental count. They only outnumbered us about two to one. I was willing to test those odds.

"I see you've found some additional allies, Jez," Rees said. "Some potentially powerful allies," he added as he caught sight of Benton.

"Just goes to show you're fighting on the losing side, Trigger," I said, spreading my hands. "Don't suppose you'd be up for surrendering. I promise we'd treat you better than you treated us."

Colin glanced briefly at me as if trying to spot the injuries. In the dim light of the house and then darkness of the streets, he'd probably barely even noticed the old scars, let alone the fresh bumps.

Rees laughed. "As tempting as that offer is, Jez, I'm going to pass. Men, I'd prefer Jasmine, James, and the duke alive, please. And send someone to figure out why the gate has stopped."

"Yes, sir," a particularly large man said, the same size as the brutes from the jail, and the soldiers advanced, weapons drawn. One man peeled off and raced for the gate.

Rees's eyes traversed the group again. "Hm, I had figured out that Bri was most likely Brighton and certainly one of yours, but not that he and James were brothers." He spoke like they weren't standing right behind me. "And Kira. Now I see the Walters look, but beyond feeling she looked a little familiar, I didn't make the connection. And this must be Colin. Commander Dakamar knew he and Benton were part of the Freedom Fighters."

My brother offered a slight but flourished bow. "Right in one."

"Pretty pathetic you didn't see a family resemblance between Bri and me, though," Jay said dryly. He had a point.

His soldiers were past him and moving faster.

"So you're a coward now?" I asked mildly. "But then, that shouldn't surprise me. You always were hiding behind Juke and Kilgor." His expression darkened as I brought up my sword. "How about it, Trigger? You and me."

"Jasmine," Colin murmured warningly. I didn't bother to correct him this time.

Rees studied me for a second then pulled his from the scabbard, giving it a fancy twirl. As if sensing his agreement, his soldiers parted, clashing with Colin and the others but allowing me to slide between them to confront Rees.

From the instant our swords met, I was on the defensive, blocking and parrying his strikes and focusing on not losing any ground. I didn't want to risk him pushing me into his men and getting jumped from behind. But as we fought, I became slowly aware that he worked in a very obvious pattern. A pattern I knew well from Beau. Rees had either been trained by a Highcastle or by someone who had been.

"Where'd you learn to fight?" I asked, hoping to distract him.

"The army."

"The *Tiran* army?"

He caught my strike and turned it aside. I had to spin quickly to stay balanced and keep myself protected. "Yes."

"So you're a traitor as well as a coward. I should have known."

His jaw clenched and he threw out a wild shot. I blocked then threw a quick fist, catching him in a sensitive spot on the shoulder. He jerked in surprise and quickly backed away to reset himself. "You fight dirty."

"You're one to talk," I said, pressing my advantage. Still, if he was as traditionally trained as it appeared, I had the upper hand. Even so, I wouldn't put it past Rees to also know hand-to-hand combat, although he'd stayed out of the prison beatings.

He recovered quickly and managed to keep me back, but I pressed, preventing him from setting the pace. I kept an eye on his form, waiting for an opening, because I could feel myself tiring already. My stamina had been sapped from the two months of limited activity and I was still pretty banged up from the brutes' tender mercies. I knew I had to end this soon.

I almost missed it when it finally came. He chopped at me with serious strength, as if not expecting me to dodge instead of block, and he lurched forward with the weight of the strike. Out of instinct, I spun back and, in surprise, watched my sword go deep into his chest.

He gasped, eyes bugging as his sword dropped out of suddenly nerveless fingers. He wasn't the first person I'd killed, but he was the first I'd *known*, and even though I hated him, I also respected him for his intelligence. He stumbled back, ripping my sword from my fingers and toppled over onto his back. With one final pitiful breath, he went limp. I didn't move, the noises of the fighting slowly filtering in now that my focus could expand past my own battle.

I stepped up to him, staring down at his now sightless eyes. He'd been a soldier once. One of our soldiers, a Highcastle soldier. I pulled my sword out, wiping it on my pants. "May the gods take you, Trigger Rees," I said quietly and then made myself return to the events at hand. Most of Rees's soldiers were down, but I had a view of the main avenue to the gate and I could see another group hurrying our way.

"Time to go!" I yelled, checking to make sure the gate hadn't shut in the meantime. By some miracle, it still sat open, so the soldier that had gone to check on it had apparently failed. I tried to remember if we had another ally in Greensward. I assumed we had some, but if this had been part of the plan, one of the others would have told us.

Colin dodged aside and grabbed his soldier around the neck. He did something else so quick, I didn't even see it, and then the man dropped limply. Bri spun and took out the man fighting Jay and suddenly we were free.

"Who organized the gate to be opened?" Colin asked as the rest of them joined me and we hurried towards the gate.

Everyone denied responsibility, shaking heads.

"Someone must have," Colin said, slowing, as if nervous of a trap.

"Gods' Breath," Ry breathed, suddenly at my side. "Look!" She pointed towards the small structure that housed the gate mechanism.

I followed her finger and spotted the familiar form standing next to it. "Is that…?"

"McRuoes," she confirmed with an unidentifiable note in her voice.

Noting that we'd spotted him, Jakium McRuoes stepped forward, the distant firelight flickering over his face. I could get no read from the lieutenant, but something seemed to pass between him and Ry, because after a second, she nodded. "We can go. He won't stop us."

Benton looked between them. "Are you sure? Is he a friend?"

Ry pressed her lips together for a second. "He's not exactly an enemy," she said and offered a surprisingly militaristic salute in Jakium's direction. Then she jogged towards the gate.

I glanced back. The other soldiers were only a couple blocks away now. Depending on Jakium's next actions, it could be a long, long night. I hurried after her and that seemed to be enough for the others. Shortly, we were all outside the gate. As one, we all risked a glance back up at the wall top. Jakium had turned to watch us. He offered a crisp salute in return and then reached over and did something with the gate mechanism.

The gate crashed down with a thud that shook the ground. Not only did it seal us out of Greensward but, more importantly, it sealed the soldiers in. That thud was one of the best sounds I'd ever heard in my life.

We were free and there was no going back.

"C'mon," Ry said, "Jessie and I will lead, since most of you have never been."

A minute later, we were trudging along the rutted and snowy path heading north, back to Cavern Hall and back to freedom.

Sorin became distantly aware of a heavy pounding. It took longer for Calip's shrill voice to sink in. "Sir! You need to wake up, sir."

"Go away," Sorin shot back, rolling over and reaching to pull his pillow over his head. It was a rare morning he slept until dawn and he had been planning on treasuring the extra hours. It wasn't as early as some nights, but it was still dark out.

"The prisoners in Greensward, sir, they've escaped."

That woke him right up and he rolled out of bed, snagging his pants and shirt from the day before. "How?"

"Lieutenant McRuoes is here to report to you and General Opalin. He just arrived from Greensward."

Sorin tugged his shirt over his head, pausing thoughtfully. This was an unexpected turn of events but not as unlikely as many, like Vlad, might have thought. Jasmine and James had both proved themselves incredibly resourceful and it didn't particularly surprise him that they had somehow managed to effect an escape, or rescue. In a way, he was more surprised it had taken two months. He pulled open the door. "Where's Jakium?"

"The conference room, sir. Bert went to wake the general."

"Good," Sorin said and took off at a jog. The door was open but no sounds issued forth, meaning Vladimir hadn't arrived yet. Sorin slowed and stepped inside.

Jakium sat at the table, elbows resting on the surface and hands covering his face. His hands and arms were bright red, as if from sunburn, and dotted with dark splotches like soot. The lieutenant hadn't looked this young – even with his face hidden – in a long time. Not since Vladimir had all but shanghaied him into the cause.

"Vladimir should be here any moment."

Jakium started and hastily scrambled up. Removing his hands didn't help the disheveled look. His face was smeared with a black substance that had to be soot. "Sorry, sir, didn't hear you." He sounded exhausted.

"It's quite all right. Sit. And you don't need to hop back up when Vladimir gets here, nor will I ask you to start your report until then."

Jakium flashed him a smile. "Thanks."

Sorin sat down across from him, leaning back in the chair and stifling a yawn. Despite the news, he still felt half asleep. Or maybe because of the news. The winds were changing.

Vladimir burst into the room a couple minutes later, shirt not even buttoned. "What the hell happened?"

Jakium shot to his feet anyway, saluting. "The Freedom Fighter prisoners are gone, sir, all four of them. The Greensward palace is as good as gone and was still burning when I left. Colonel Rees is dead. Sir."

Vladimir stared at him. Sorin did too as he carefully processed each of those three large pieces of information. The winds, indeed.

"How did this happen?"

"It was Colonel Rees, sir. He suspected the prisoners were planning some sort of breakout. He surrounded the jail after the escape attempt had started, so he could capture their rescuers as well, but he had forgotten about the windows in his office, so they escaped his net. He then initiated a citywide search for them, around the midnight bells. We had already mostly cleared the streets

531

before the escape so we started searching house-to-house in targeted areas, while adding extra guards to the gates."

"Okay, and?" Vladimir prompted impatiently.

Jakium had barely had time to take a breath. "In the midst of the search, the palace just...I've never seen an explosion like it. There was a whoosh and pieces landed half the city away." He gestured ineffectually. "Most of it was gone before we even knew what had happened."

"Interesting choice of payback to cover for Jasmine Lockholme's escape," Sorin murmured.

Vladimir glared at him.

Sorin was pretty sure he didn't miss the ghost of a smile on Jakium's face, as he ignored his brother. "Colonel Rees sent a large portion of his forces, including those at the gate he was guarding, to try and save what was left and put out the fires."

"An effective diversion, certainly. What happened next?" Sorin asked.

"We failed in keeping the explosion away from the armory and the fresh store of balsic stone."

Then it was an absolute certainty little of the palace remained, not after a secondary explosion of a large magnitude. That was a shame. It had been a beautiful old building.

Vladimir clenched his fists.

"It was just starting to be contained when reports came of the escape. I left Lieutenant Jeffers in charge and went to investigate and find Colonel Rees for further orders. I found the colonel and his remaining men all dead, just inside the gate and the gate shut but undefended."

"And you saw Rees's body?"

"Yes, sir," Jakium said.

"This isn't good," Vladimir muttered and began to pace.

"How was Rees killed?"

"Stab wound in his chest. Probably was fatal almost instantly," Jakium said. "As soon as I saw that, I sent the men with me back to tell Jeffers I was leaving straight from there to come here to report."

"But that had to have been mere hours ago," Sorin said, startled as he did the math, guessing it to be around the five bells now, maybe a bit later. Jakium had left well after midnight and four hours from Greensward to Oakbridge, especially at night in the winter, was fast.

"I stopped only when I'd burned out a horse and could find a new one," Jakium said. "I thought you'd want to know as soon as possible."

"Of course we did," Vladimir said.

"Well done, Jakium," Sorin said quietly, catching the young man's eye.

He nodded, exhaustion clear on his dirty face. He hadn't sat back down.

"Well done?" Vladimir exploded, catching it anyway. "Nothing about that was well done!"

"And that most certainly isn't Jakium's fault," Sorin retorted, standing as well. "If it is any one person's fault, it would be Rees and I rarely like to speak ill of the dead. Jakium, you are dismissed. Go get yourself cleaned and rested. Stop by my office whenever you wake up. I'd like to talk to you about a few things."

"Yes, sir," Jakium said in relief and hastily scooted from the room before Vladimir could countermand the order.

His brother turned on him. "You don't give the orders!"

Sorin pinched his nose. "Do we have to have this conversation again, Vladimir? Because I am pretty sure you don't want to lose again."

The glare was back twofold. "This is a disaster!"

"That we can agree on," he said calmly, pressing his palms into the table.

Vladimir whirled away and paced the length of the room and back before stopping. "I'm leaving."

That had not been on the list of things Sorin expected to hear. "What? To where?"

"To find the prisoners and retrieve them."

Sorin had not had enough sleep for his brother's insanity. "Before you do that, let me see if we can sort this out," he suggested.

"Fine," Vladimir grumbled.

"*Why* are they so important?"

"Because they're the only Freedom Fighters we've managed to catch alive."

"Okay. And what have they told us?"

"Their leader's name," Vladimir said promptly.

"Okay. And?"

His brother opened his mouth and then shut it again, brow furrowing.

"Exactly. And, our best interrogator is now dead, so I doubt anyone else would manage to get any further. Plus, I think the Freedom Fighters have well proven themselves able to hide in the wilderness where we can't find them. Clearly Jasmine and James had help, as there is no way they could have escaped and blown up the palace all at about the same time."

"They killed Rees," Vladimir said, like it was a trump card.

Sorin studied his brother silently. Rees had once had the potential to be a good man. He'd been a rising star in the Tiran army before Vladimir had seduced him away. Sorin wasn't sure what kind of man he'd really been when he'd died. "Yes, which is a shame. But Rees's own cockiness killed him just as much. He attempted to defeat Jasmine, Jay, and some number of their allies with only about a dozen men. Doesn't he remember how easily they escaped Jakium's attempt at Westcorner? I have no doubt this was the same group, or at least most of it. And Jakium is far more competent than it sometimes appears."

"But, but, they still need to pay."

"Granted," Sorin started patiently, but was interrupted by a knock on the half open door. "Yes?"

Calip poked his head in. "Lieutenant McRuoes asked me to tell you he remembered something after he left." Smart of Jakium not to put himself back in Vladimir's sight. "A local innkeeper, from an inn just a couple doors down from the prison and frequent stop for many of our soldiers, said that three of his employees left a note saying they had to leave last night. He only knew so soon because he went in to check on the inn after the fire."

"Oh?" Sorin said. "I don't suppose he provided names or even genders."

"Three women. Two in their twenties, one in her late teens. A Jessica and Ryan Smith, as well as a Kira Ricker. Kira had been with him for a couple of years but the other two for not very long and had said from the beginning they were only there temporarily. Lieutenant McRuoes also said that one citizen did admit to seeing the fight and said there were about ten escapees, including one boy and a pretty even mix of men and women."

"Thank you, Calip."

"Yes, sir," the man said and disappeared.

"See, there are three named allies right there, plus another three, possibly all male. Clearly this Jessica and Ryan, or whatever their real names are, were sent to help Jasmine and James escape." Still, something else itched at him.

There was something he should be getting from those facts. "It's a shame Jakium didn't run into them at this inn, he might have recognized them."

"All the more reason to go after them! We could get even more prisoners."

Sorin stared at him, but gave up. At least with Vladimir out of Oakbridge for a while, things might be calmer. And Ani less likely to hide all day with Ren. Maybe. "Very well. Good luck. I'll keep track of things here while you're gone." He had no expectations that Vladimir would actually find them. They were already long gone.

"I'll be leaving later today," he said as he turned to leave.

"Vlad."

His brother glanced back.

"Be careful. And stay safe."

Something flickered in his expression. "You too, Sorin."

He watched Vladimir leave and took a deep breath. Then he headed for his office. There would be no sleep after this. Once there, he sorted through his papers until he came upon the file on Denhem Lockholme and his family. He read through it again slowly, making sure he didn't miss a detail. The file was heavy on Denhem's prime and his friendship with Robert Walters and Patrick Highcastle. He skimmed it, once again pulling out the pertinent details. The man had a mind for tactics and raising horses. And he had his five children. He switched files.

And there it was. What he'd forgotten. A Colin who had gotten Benton out and was no question working for the Freedom Fighters. He stopped. Benton Walters. The elder Walters child. The younger was named Kira. Kira Walters.

"No," he breathed. Could Kira Walters have been living under their noses for two years with only a fake last name to throw them off? "Calip!" he bellowed, knowing the man was never far.

A minute later, the man appeared in the doorway. "Yes, sir?"

"Is this absolutely everything we have on the Lockholme family?"

"Yes, sir, as far as I know."

"I'd like the files on the Walters family. Can you do that for me?"

"Of course, sir. Shouldn't take too long to retrieve them. Everything?"

"Everything, as soon as possible. Also, as soon as Jakium is back upright, send him to see me if you run into him. We need to talk."

"Yes, sir." The man vanished.

Within the hour, after Sorin had gone over the Lockholme papers yet again without finding anything new, Calip was back with a thicker file, which he passed to him. "Anything else, sir?"

"Not right now, thank you."

The man nodded and made himself scarce.

Sorin skimmed the Walters family history until he got to a year before their forces had attacked Northwind. Then he slowed. Kira Walters had fought with her parents and left, disappearing from all sight. If that had indeed been Kira Walters, then it was very possible that Colin and Benton had made their way to Greensward to be near her, and had, just hours before, helped Jasmine and the others kill Rees and escape Greensward.

He sat back, running a hand over his mouth as he stared out the window without really seeing, other than to note it had gotten light out at some point. Maybe, once Vladimir had returned empty handed, he should pay Denhem Lockholme a visit and see what he knew of his children's miraculous escapes from death.

Chapter Thirty-five

SHORTLY AFTER LEAVING GREENSWARD, we struck northeast off the path, which ran due north for some miles longer before splitting, one route going towards Ellworth and Lockholme and the other heading around the hills towards the Alyia border. We would have to cross it again further north near the foothills to make it back to Cavern Hall.

Colin had moved up to the front with Jessie and Ry, talking quietly to them with hand gestures that were so familiar. Although my brain had mostly accepted the fact I had miraculously found my brother *and* Bri, both of whom I had thought dead, it didn't seem fully real yet. But then again, neither did freedom, and here we were trudging through the ankle deep snow on our way home.

When Stella, Jay, Dave, and I started to fall behind after a couple hours, Colin called back that we had to keep going just a little further. That we needed to be sure we were far enough from Greensward to be safe. I made a rude gesture in response, but wasn't sure if it got lost in the darkness. All we had to see by was the stars and crescent moon, so even though it was a clear night, it wasn't very bright. Still, the four of us tried to keep up, Dave hanging off Stella's hand, head bobbing like he might have fallen asleep walking. Colin called back occasional encouragement but other than that, the ten of us were silent.

It was near dawn when we finally stumbled into a clearing that contained an old hunting cabin.

"You're a bastard," I told my brother, who looked far too proud of himself. "You knew about this place, didn't you?"

"I might have."

"And you didn't tell us."

"I wanted to make sure my big brother baiting skills were still up to snuff," he said and grinned. "C'mon, we can't risk a fire but it'll be warmer inside. Also, if I'm a bastard…"

"Don't start with me," I told him and shuffled past to the cabin.

The place was small. It had a two person table and a small bed in one corner, but not a whole lot else. We all found places to sit as Jessie and Kira distributed food. Then, Stella and Dave squeezed onto the bed - which would not have fit two adults - and the rest of us spread out around the floor. I was asleep in minutes, happily squashed between my brother and Ry.

When Colin moved, sometime long after the sun had come up, I woke too, listening to him get up and slip out the door, barely making any noise. After lying there a little longer, I realized the lure to talk to him in private was too strong and I painfully pushed myself to my feet to follow.

He stood just off the front porch, looking south. Without turning around, he pointed. "Still burning."

I moved to stand next to him, shielding my eyes against the brilliant late winter sun. Sure enough, after a moment, I spotted the drifting smoke coming from some miles off, heading with the wind east towards Oakbridge. I hoped they choked on it at the castle. "Jessie and Ry do nothing by halves," I said.

He stuck his hands in his pockets and smiled. "Good. Let the bastards get what's coming to them." He glanced sidelong at me. "Got time for that story now?"

"Do Mom and Dad know you're alive?"

"Don't know. Presumably word reached them that Ben and his bodyguard got out, but I haven't dared try to contact them. You?"

"No, they definitely think I'm dead. I couldn't risk trying to contact anyone."

He nodded. "And look, my little sister all grown up."

I rolled my eyes. "If I'm all grown up, then that makes you positively ancient."

He half-smiled, but took it more seriously than intended. "Sometimes I feel like it."

I couldn't disagree. "Me too." Colin was clearly not the same person he had been when I'd last seen him, years before. Nor was I. Still, it felt easy with him, like it always had. "Everyone who knew about you, about 'Col' in Cavern Hall, was in awe." I'd been in awe. I still was. My barely older brother had become a true hero. A legend. The things he'd pulled off while we'd all been keeping quiet, some of them defied logic. Now, more than ever, I didn't think they were exaggerations. That just wasn't Colin's style.

To my amusement, even though I'd been telling the truth, he blushed slightly.

Before we could talk longer, Kira stuck her head out the door. "Hey, doofus, go get some water if you're going to stand out there in the cold, will you? We're serving breakfast or lunch, I guess, if you want some, Jez." She tossed Colin a pack with our waterskins.

Colin's mouth quirked into a smile as he caught it. "Whatever milady commands," he said, pretending to doff an imaginary cap.

"Shut up," Kira told him, but she grinned. It struck me that Kira, as Benton's brother, was next in line for the Northwind Dukedom, which had long been a stronghold against Alyia and one of our most powerful dukedoms.

I debated helping Colin, but decided I'd had enough of the cold and we'd spend the rest of the day hiking in it, so I headed inside, where the sheer number of bodies meant it was near stifling. It felt good. Again, we all found a perch or spot of floor to eat. Colin returned in good time with full skins of ice cold water. For the first time since the escape, I realized just how hungry I was. When I snuck glances at Dave, Stella and Jay, they were scarfing their food just as quickly.

"Prison rations less than filling, Jasmine?" Colin asked.

"Jasmine?" Ry asked, sounding confused.

My brother looked just as confused. He pointed at himself. "Colin Lockholme." He pointed at me. "My sister, Jasmine Lockholme."

"You're…" Ry stared at me, wide eyed.

"I'm still just Jez," I said. "It's not even like I was the only incognito noble lurking around Cavern Hall."

"Yeah, when Beau announced he was a Highcastle, I thought we were going to lose Iris to a stroke!" Jessie said.

"Wait, *what?*" Colin interrupted now. The Walters and Bri looked just as surprised.

"Beau is Patrick and Elizabeth's second son. Born after Elizabeth went into self-imposed exile and the rumors were spread that she died," Jessie explained. "He's Renier's younger brother."

"Gods' Breath," Benton murmured, clearly trying to absorb that.

"We've been working for a Highcastle this whole time. Fancy that."

"I am losing my touch," Bri announced. "I had no idea of that one!"

"Anyone else have a secret identity they feel the need to share?" Jay asked, looking around at us. He pinned poor Benton with a look. "Are you not really a duke?"

"Um, well, technically, no, there's never-"

"How have you lived with Colin this long and *still* rise to the bait?" Kira asked him as the rest of us started laughing.

Benton flushed as he glared at his sister. Colin gave him a companionable pat on the back.

"What's the plan?" I asked more seriously.

"We walk back to Cavern Hall. Duh," Jay said. He was just close enough to me that I could hit him. "Ow!"

"We cleaned up our tracks when we went off the path yesterday until we were into the trees, so hopefully if there is pursuit they won't find us," Jessie said, "but we should still make all due haste."

Dave sighed at the prospect of more walking. I couldn't blame him. I'd felt stiff enough last night, but moving so far this morning had been its own type of agony. Every bruise seemed magnified from both the hours of trudging through snow and then lying on a hard wooden floor.

"We should leave as soon as we're done eating."

As if that was a cue, we all buckled down to finish our food then pack up the few things needed. Colin handed out waterskins, we all shouldered our packs, and left the wonderfully warm cabin.

"Just so you all know, I don't know any waystations as we go further north. This isn't my usual territory."

"But it is ours," Jessie said. "There probably aren't any others, but by the time we stop, we should be up to the foothills and there should be plenty of dry caves. We can spend tonight in one of them."

"How thrilling," Jay drawled, and got hit again, but not by me this time. "Ow!" He sulked at Stella.

She winked at me. "You're welcome, Jez."

Once my muscles had loosened, I trotted to catch up with Jessie and Ry. "So, how's everyone at Cavern Hall?"

"You mean, how's Beau?" Ry asked.

"And Mick and Dunkin and Reardon," I said defensively.

She just grinned. "Beau's been quiet, more like he used to be before you came along. He was so certain we'd lost you and Jay. He is going to *die* when he sees we not only rescued you two, but found Bri and brought along the Walters and Col in the bargain."

"Yeah, can you believe that Bri's alive? Or that your brother has been working for us all along?" Jessie asked.

"No! I haven't wrapped my head around Bri, let alone Colin. It doesn't seem possible when just over a week ago, I thought I'd lost both of them."

"Miracles do happen."

"Speaking of miracles," I said, lowering my voice so only the two of them could hear me. "What was up with Jakium McRuoes last night?"

"I ran into him, literally, while we were in Greensward."

"Oh?" Somehow that didn't surprise me. Not when Jakium seemed to be straddling an interesting line and appeared quite content in that weird place.

"Yeah. We talked for a bit. He told me about how he was pretty much adopted by the Opalins as a young teenager and a few other things. Anyway, it was kind of strange."

"When he came to us with the letter for Beau from the prince," I started.

"Jakium told me that was him."

I nodded. "Although he confirmed to Rees that I was who I said I was, since he was apparently at my attempted execution. He didn't tell him anything beyond exactly what he was asked. Strange man, your friend."

Ry scowled. "He is not my friend. And yeah, he'd mentioned he was holding back."

"Seems like a friend to me," Jessie said. "Even if he's a strange friend to have."

Ry made a face at both of us. Still, as soon as she thought we weren't looking, her expression went decidedly thoughtful.

I exchanged a wink with Jessie then dropped back to join my brother. "So, have you been based out of Greensward ever since Northwind fell? How exactly did you get out of Northwind in the first place?"

"Hello to you too," he said dryly.

I grinned at him. "C'mon, these are important questions. You owe me an explanation!"

"So do you, sister dearest."

"You first, since I asked first."

"Technically, I asked first. Twice."

"Technically whatever. C'mon, I'm sure yours is more exciting."

At that, he laughed. "Okay, fine. We headed south first and stayed along the Windfall. We skirted Oakbridge and lived in Bejen for a while. I thought we'd be able to hide there easily because of all the ships and people in and out all the time, but folks started to get suspicious anyway. For whatever reason, we didn't have that problem in Greensward, despite the heavier presence of soldiers. So we've been there the vast majority of the time. Or, Ben has. I've been in and out, as you know."

I felt a stirring of jealousy. Despite everything, I'd still seen little of Tira and nothing of any of our neighboring countries. *Someday*, I promised myself. Maybe I'd have Colin show me around. And, presumably in the fairly near future, I'd finally make it to Oakbridge, although not in the best circumstances.

"So how did you manage to escape?"

"Captain Beau,"

"Beau," I said. "We cured him of that 'captain' nonsense a couple years ago."

He raised his eyebrows. "Could have fooled me. I still call him that."

"That's because he gets an ego trip out of it," I said with a laugh.

He eyed me. "Am I getting the vibe that you're really good friends with the prince?"

I grinned. "You have no idea."

His eyes widened. "No!"

"Eight months, give or take."

"My little sister is dating a *prince?*"

"Trust me, I was as surprised as you to learn he's a prince," I said dryly.

"Gods' Breath," he muttered, running a hand through his hair.

"So," I prompted, "how did you escape?"

"Forgive me for getting distracted by the idea of you and Ca-Beau."

I smirked. "I solemnly swear not to interrupt you with declarations of love again."

He shot me a look I remembered well from our childhood. "I think you miss the point."

"Escape?"

Colin flagged down Benton, who trotted up to join us from where he'd been talking to Kira and Bri. "Yes?"

"Jasmine wants to know about how we escaped Northwind. Thought you might like to help with the backstory."

"Jez," I corrected.

"Jez," he repeated, yet again, but nodded.

I offered my hand around him, though. "Not sure last night counts as official introductions or not, but I'm Jez, or Jasmine, Lockholme."

"Ben Walters," he said, taking it in a firm grip.

"Not Benton?"

He smiled. "I figure I'll get enough of that once I'm officially a duke."

"Fair enough. So how did it start? Last I knew, Colin was just a regular old recruit."

My brother's grin was somehow half-smirk, half-nostalgia.

"He didn't start totally at the bottom, considering your father and his friendship with mine. But he was just a foot soldier in the guard until he got himself noticed."

"Oh?"

"He was a smartass," Kira said, joining us.

"That's no surprise."

"It was to my father," Ben said, laughing. "So the Three had just taken over and made one sort of testing foray in the form of a failed diplomatic reach. Kira had already left for Greensward at that point. My father and I were in the courtyard, reviewing the soldiers and everyone passed so we go to leave and this voice from one of the back row goes, very clearly-"

"Only total idiots would do nothing more to protect themselves than just make sure that their troops look pretty in a courtyard. That's no real way to prepare," Colin repeated, grinning.

"You didn't!"

"Gods, I wish I had been there," Kira said.

"He did," Ben said. "Our father was *livid*. He whipped around and bellowed for the coward to show his face. I don't think any of us expected Colin to just calmly elbow his way through and pop out of the ranks and offer us a perfectly normal and respectful salute. Then he goes, clear as anything, 'I did'."

I glanced at Colin, whose grin had widened. "What happened?"

"My father stepped right up so they were nose to nose. Colin didn't flinch. For a couple of minutes, they just stood there, neither even blinking. Then, Father goes, 'Follow me' and stalks off into the castle. Colin followed and I followed them, because I honestly thought Father was going to tear him to pieces. Or, at the very least, send him home to Lockholme. To my utter shock, my father walked right to my room and pointed at the room next door, which was small and had been unoccupied since I'd turned eighteen."

"Then he goes, 'You are in charge of Benton's safety. Should you fail, I will hunt you down and kill you, even if it is in the afterlife, do you understand?'" Colin said. "So, I said yes, sir, and the rest is history. Other than the letter I got from Mom and Dad that was equal parts praise and threats of strangulation."

"Sounds about right," I agreed, suddenly acutely missing the rest of our family for the first time in a long time. I couldn't allow myself to think of it before this and even now I worked to squelch it. There might be a time, maybe even within the year, that Colin and I could safely see them again, but it wasn't now, even though at some point we'd be close to Lockholme on our way back north. Still, it hadn't answered all my questions and I'd even come up with a new one. "Kira, why did you leave?"

"Oh, it's nothing special. I'd always had a desire to see more than Northwind, so before the Three took over, but after I turned eighteen, I left. I'd told them that arranged marriages were not my thing and they sort of tried so I left to prove my point, but I knew they wouldn't have pushed unless I had liked the person. Our parents were furious and I was mad at them too, so I only wrote to Ben but sent the parents messages through him." She sighed, some of the amusement sliding from her face. "I'd apologize now, if I could."

"Except, it turned out to be the right decision."

"Yes, because you're a paranoid bastard," Kira told my brother, with no hard feelings.

"Being a paranoid bastard has proven quite successful."

Ben rolled his eyes. If I had to guess, I suspected Kira and Colin did this often. "Anyway," he interrupted, talking over them before they could descend too far into bickering, "Colin made me burn the letters once the Three took over. And immediately burn all successive ones after they did before Northwind fell."

"So they had no idea where you were," I said with sudden understanding.

"Exactly," Kira said. "I'd already been using a false last name, because it was safer when out in the world without protection. And made it harder for our parents to try and track me, so once Northwind fell, Kira Walters fully dropped off the map."

"So what happened the night the Three's men overran Northwind?"

"Well, I'd already set up a set of signals, with the help of Cap-Beau, for when the attack came. Unfortunately, they didn't work as well as I wanted," Colin said.

"By the time they struck, towards the end of that year, Colin and I were friends, considering he was always following me around like a puppy."

"I resent that comparison."

If Colin was anything like he had been when we were younger, I thought it seemed apt enough.

"I like 'fast friends' better."

"Not too fast," Ben said dryly, but smiled. "I was annoyed at first with my father for saddling me with some green minor noble as a bodyguard. I didn't want a bodyguard period."

Colin waved the comment away. "*Anyway*," he continued, looking mildly annoyed at being interrupted. "Even with the safeguards in place, I only managed to get Ben out because I was awake the evening they attacked. It had been cold for a couple weeks and had even snowed heavily a few days before, but I guess they figured it meant our guard would be down. And it was. I saw the torches coming our way and just knew. So I had a bag packed for Ben and a backdoor. I got back to Ben, woke him, and sent him and his bag down to the kitchen, where my bag was and the way out. Then I tried to save the duke and duchess, but somehow they were already inside and I was cut off at every pass. I knew my first duty was to Ben, so I backtracked and got him out through the kitchens." He shook his head. "I should have recruited others, so we could have gotten the duke and duchess out too."

Ben squeezed his shoulder. "We both know you tried your hardest, Colin. That's all any of us could ask."

"And if it hadn't been for you, I would've lost my brother too," Kira added.

"Still. If I knew then what I know now," my brother said. "Next time, I won't have to leave anyone behind."

"I know," Ben said with a small smile.

After that, the conversation moved to lighter topics. We told competing ridiculous stories from our childhoods. Those of us in the know often called the others out on an exaggeration. Finally, well after dark and in the foothills of the mountains – and probably not too far from Lockholme – we found an empty, dry cave and caught a few hours of sleep before moving on at dawn. With any luck we'd reach Cavern Hall late that evening, although probably not before news of the Greensward explosion reached them through courier – through the system Colin had set up, with some help from us at Cavern Hall.

I did grab my brother by himself in the late morning to tell him a much briefer version of events than I had related to Stella and Dave, and Jay, in the cell. "I hope Mom and Dad and our brothers do know you're all right."

Colin nudged me with his shoulder and offered a familiar crooked grin. "Either way, we should be able to set the record straight soon enough. Let them know they haven't lost any kids yet."

I smiled. "Hopefully. Don't suppose you know how they're doing."

The grin widened. "What kind of master spy do you take me for?" he asked and launched into a description of recent goings-on in Lockholme. And for a moment, everything since the day I had thrown a book faded and it was just Colin and I, gossiping about the locals. Although I didn't really want that time back, it was nice to retreat there, just for a little while.

Sorin rapped on Ren's door, counted to ten, and then pushed it open.

Ani cut off her sentence and grinned at him. "Morning, Sunshine!"

"Good morning," he said easily, settling himself on Ren's sofa. Ani was perched on the edge of the prince's desk - trust her to find what most people would consider the least comfortable seat in the room - and Ren sat in his chair by the window, half-facing Ani.

"Did something happen?" Ren asked astutely.

"I mentioned the prisoners we had in Greensward, right? The Freedom Fighters?"

"Yes. You and Vlad have both been down there. Why?"

"Last night, shortly after you were married, the pair, along with their cellmates, broke out and escaped the city, along with a group of others. Did I ever say who they were?"

Ren frowned in thought and shook his head. "I don't believe so, why?"

"Have you ever met Denhem Lockholme's youngest? Jasmine?"

"A couple times when she was still pretty young. I mostly ignored all the Lockholme kids but Kent. And then, she was killed. Why?"

Sorin briefly outlined the saga of Jasmine Lockholme and then the facts and his suspicions about the previous night's escape. Even as he reported it, he knew that if Vladimir found out, he would go ballistic. All the more reason it wasn't such a bad thing that Vladimir would be out of the castle for a while. Ren wasn't likely to mention it either. If he'd learned one thing from his time as a prisoner, it was discretion.

Ren let out a low whistle. "Well, I'll be damned," he said.

"Do you think I'm right? You knew Benton growing up as well, right?"

He nodded. "Ben and Kira both and better than Kent. The two spent a couple winters here when we were kids. Kira especially hated the fierceness of Northwind's winters. Ben and I wrote regularly and he told me Kira had left after a fight with their parents. In a few of the later letters, he said she was fine." Ren paused, studying Sorin. "Colin Lockholme was definitely his bodyguard. He told me the whole story after it happened. Ben grew to trust him with his life. I hope you're right. It would be nice to not have lost him."

And it was time to drop the last shock. "They also blew up Greensward palace."

"They *what?*" Ren burst.

"You heard me."

"But why? They're supposed to be helping, not leaving Tira in shambles!" he protested.

Sorin tried hard to fight an amused smile. "I presume it was to cripple our hold on the city. It hit the balsic stores too."

It was Ani's turn to whistle. "Ka*boom.*"

"Ani!" Ren protested.

"Muffin," she retorted.

"Obviously I'm no less displeased," Sorin cut in before they could get into one of the inane arguments they both enjoyed so much. "But it is what it is. We'll save what we can. Jakium says there isn't much left. And Colonel Rees is dead."

"They killed Rees?" Ani said, surprised, and clearly a little impressed.

"Yes. Jakium saw the body himself."

"Good riddance," his sister muttered.

Sorin both could and couldn't disagree on that. Ani had never liked Rees's desire and ability to go as far as necessary, even taking joy in it when it involved hurting someone. The two had clashed every time they'd been in the same room. That same trait had made Sorin itchy too. It was a little too reminiscent of Edward, but at the same time, it had been much-needed in their work. He respected Rees as a good commander of his men and for his very sharp mind. Clearly, though, he wasn't supposed to have heard that comment so he pretended he hadn't. "Did I ever tell you we got a name for your brother?"

"No," Ren said cautiously.

"Beau. At least, I assume he's the leader of the Freedom Fighters. It was one of the few things Jasmine and James gave up while we had them."

Ren nodded slowly, but didn't look surprised. "That's what I told my parents we should name a brother if I ever had a sibling. I guess they took it to heart," he explained at Sorin's look.

That was interesting. Sorin wished suddenly that he had known Patrick Highcastle better.

"You mentioned Jakium. Is he here?"

"Here and sleeping. He rode through the night to be here before dawn. I want to talk to him when he wakes, but I can send him your way after that. Although, there's no rush, he'll be here a while."

"You're not sending him back to Greensward?"

"No. Greensward is weakened beyond repair. This was the Freedom Fighters' first big move and it worked. In one night, they neutralized the second most powerful city in Tira."

Ani and Ren shared a glance. "Are you saying their next step is here?" Ren asked quietly, like he was afraid someone might overhear.

Sorin cast a quick look towards the peephole but doubted Vladimir was nearby. He would be too deeply involved in his preparations to chase the former prisoners. "Logic would say so. If they can hit and knock Greensward out of the fight like it's nothing? I would think it would be too hard to pull off this winter, but the thaw will come soon enough."

"Gods' Breath," Ren breathed, looking stunned.

"Vladimir is leaving today, or perhaps has already left, to try and track down our escapees. I suspect he'll be absent much of the coming weeks. I'd like to take Jakium and make a brief sojourn north at some point when he is around."

"North? Why?" Ani asked, but there was understanding on Ren's face. Maybe they hadn't ruined the prince after all.

"I'd like to visit Denhem and Alisha Lockholme about their children, specifically the two youngest."

"Can you try and play nice?" Ren asked, a little dryly. "They both believe their children are dead."

"I will do my best," Sorin promised. "I'll let you know before I plan on leaving," he said to Ani.

"Clearly Vlad doesn't feel the same way," she said lightly, knocking her heel against the desk's leg.

"Vladimir has a lot on his mind." He didn't really know why he was defending his brother. Habit, perhaps.

She nodded, but looked unconvinced. He didn't blame her.

"Why are you telling me all this?" Ren asked finally.

Sorin shrugged and stood. "I wanted to tell Ani," he said blandly, "and she's living with you now." None of them believed that for an instant, but it was what all three would swear to if asked. Still, both Ani and Ren's faces held complete understanding.

The Freedom Fighters were coming for the Three. And Vladimir was the only one who wanted to fight any more.

Chapter Thirty-six

WE MIGHT HAVE MADE IT HOME shortly after dark, but Jay decided our time was better suited to other pursuits. Which he proved when a very wet snowball hit the back of my head. I probably should have let it go, but it made me laugh and that felt so good that I returned the favor. It was not our smartest move ever - most of us had no extra clothes - but it was also *fun* and we hadn't had much of that recently.

The fight lasted over an hour and, when we were done, we decided to call it an early night, already shivering. We found a cave with good ventilation and lit a roaring fire, all crowding around, shoulder to shoulder. Colin and Jay competed over who could tell the scariest stories, trying to get a rise out of Dave - for being scared - and Stella - for telling scary stories in front of Dave - but the boy listened without flinching. When the pair stopped, looking at the ten-year-old in awe, Dave just shrugged. "Those are all fake," he announced and would talk nothing more about it, although we all knew what he meant.

Once we were mostly dry, we settled in, sticking close to the fire and each other. In silent accord, we were up early and had breakfast on the march. By mid-morning, we reached the familiar stretch of woods surrounding Cavern Hall. I couldn't help grinning broadly. I missed Beau, but also Dunkin, Reardon, our roommate Ann, and a variety of others.

"Beau's been keeping the door shut, afraid of reprisals from the Three, pretty much since you two left," Jessie informed us as we approached what appeared to be a solid rock wall. She picked up a rock that sat nearby and rapped out a very particular sequence.

551

After a moment's wait, the wall swung open, revealing Dunkin, whose eyes bugged a bit before beaming. "You all made it out! When word reached us yesterday, we were all hoping you'd appear soon. I see you brought friends. Welcome!" He bowed slightly.

"Dunkin!" Bri burst. "Are you friends with this crowd now? I thought you were too stiff for that. After all, you never seemed to like me much."

"That's because you have a tendency to be a pompous pain in the ass," Ry said dryly.

"Shush you," he said easily.

Dunkin's face drained of color. "B-Brighton?" he stuttered, horrified.

"Hi, Dunk!"

"H-How?"

"He's always had a hard head," Jay said, rapping his brother on the skull.

Bri glared at him, shoving his hand away.

There was a pause.

"Oh. Oh, *Gods' Breath*," Dunkin breathed, recognition setting in. "There are *two of you*."

I grinned, as did most of the others. We'd had some time to process.

Ben looked sympathetic, and he'd only known Jay for a couple days, but then Bri was weirdly respectful to him, so this 'new' Bri had to be a bit of a surprise.

Dunkin now looked at us closer. "There is one hell of a story here," he said slowly. "You must be related to Jez," he said to Colin.

"Yes, I'm Jasm-Jez's brother, Colin. Nice to meet you."

Our friend sighed. "This place will never be the same. Come in, come in."

Colin looked vaguely affronted. I couldn't help but take it as a compliment as we all crowded into the entranceway and Dunkin set the door back into place behind us.

"So!" Bri said, living up to his name once we were in. "Can I? Please? Please," he drew out the last word. In the days walking north, the rest of his memory had slowly returned, helped along by stories the rest of us would start and press him to finish. He was fully back to his old self, and old tricks.

"It's not very nice," I said slowly.

"But it'll be *hilarious*," he replied, as he had the last few times he'd brought it up.

"It really can't do any harm," Jessie said. "We won't leave Beau and Mick hanging for long."

"I don't want to know," Dunkin announced. "That way, I can plead innocence later. But I do want the story at some point." He still seemed stunned. I couldn't blame him.

"Oh fine."

Bri beamed and pounced on me, ruffling my hair irreverently. "You're the best, Jezzy."

I gave him a shove. "Don't make me change my mind."

Bri let go, started forward, and then paused. "Damn it, someone needs to show me the way." I'd almost forgotten that Bri had never been to the new Cavern Hall.

"We can do that," Jessie offered. "C'mon, everyone," she said and led the way through the halls. As it was mid-morning, they were fairly deserted but there were the familiar sounds of various groups working all around us. Jessie led us slightly out of the way to avoid the main room.

When we reached Beau's office, Ry slid forward and shot us a thumbs up. "Just Beau, I think," she mouthed.

Bri straightened himself and marched right into the office. "Beau Highcastle! How can you work on a day like this?"

I barely resisted the urge to peek, listening as we heard a scraping - probably a chair - and then a clunk - most likely Bri putting his feet on Beau's desk.

"But then, you so often were a no play and all work kind of man."

Then silence.

I had to admit that, being on this end, it was pretty funny and I bit my fist to keep from laughing. A quick glance told me my mirth was shared by Jessie, Ry, and Jay. The others all looked more mildly amused, probably more from picturing Bri's glee then anything.

"I didn't realize I was this tired," Beau said finally.

"I bet you're overdoing it with Jez gone," Bri said sagely. "Still, I would think that I would at least rate a 'hello, how are you, Brighton old buddy?' out of you. I'm cut deep, Beau. Cut deep, right here." I could just picture him pointing at the nasty scar.

"Sorry? I, um, figured that 'how are you' would be pretty self-explanatory," he said, words still coming slowly.

"Honestly, Beau. Or is it Beauregard, because that would be awesome!"

"Just Beau," he said faintly.

"Right, well, *honestly*, Beau! Does this scar look gushy to you?" Bri sounded almost offended.

Poor Beau never stood a chance. I was amused by his assumption it was a dream.

"No?"

"Then what's the problem? I feel fit as a fiddle! I could do the jig to prove it."

I wanted to peek so badly, but didn't let myself because I knew if I actually saw Beau, I wouldn't be able to hold myself back.

"Please don't? I...I think it's time I woke up," Beau said, more firmly, as if commanding himself.

"Beau, my friend, you *are* awake."

"No. No, I am not, because you're here. And you died. So I'm not awake and my subconscious decided that you should, you know, appear for some reason." He sounded a little frantic now.

"As cool as that would be, I'm not feeling particularly dead, not that I know what being dead feels like, but I suspected I wouldn't feel so warm. And me-like."

Silence again.

"I can prove it if you want!"

"How?"

"Dead dream people can't hurt you, right?"

"Right?"

"You know, actually, I changed my mind, because a certain someone would then actually at least try and kill me and I really like being alive now that I know I wasn't supposed to be."

"Um?"

"I brought you a present, Beau."

"Okay?"

I giggled, trying hard to stifle it.

"A bunch of presents, actually. Okay, crew, that's your cue!"

I didn't wait, turning the corner first.

Beau's head came up and his eyes popped. "Jez," he breathed, freezing.

"Hi, Beau," I said quietly. "We're home."

An instant later, Beau was around his desk and hugging me fiercely. I returned it just as tightly, reveling in his familiar feel and scent. "Gods, I missed you," I whispered.

His response was to shift slightly and capture my lips with his. I had no complaints with that, melting against him. "Godsdamn, Jez, I thought I'd lost you," he murmured.

I pulled back a little. Not because I wanted to but because there were explanations to be made and people for him to meet. "Not this time. Not ever, if I have anything to say about it."

He smiled broadly at me. "Good!"

I snagged another quick kiss before stepping back entirely, although I took his hand. "Beau, I have some people you need to meet."

"Wait," he gasped suddenly and spun back around.

Bri still sat in the chair, feet on Beau's desk. Jay now perched on the desk beside his feet and was pestering his older brother. Beau looked back at me and then back at the Dalls, physically rubbing his eyes. "How?"

"Yes, that's Bri and, yes, he's alive. Long story. We'll get to that. In the meantime," I tugged his hand, dragging his attention back, "there are some *other* people you should meet." Everyone had crowded in behind me. Dave stood close to Stella's side, eyes wide as he stared at Beau in awe. I started with our two former cellmates and then the Walters siblings. Propriety had Beau stepped forward to shake hands with both, greeting them with respect.

Ben just smiled. "I'm just sorry we never came earlier. We thought we could do more good out in the world."

"You probably did," I told him. "And, Beau, this is Col in the flesh. Also known as Colin, my brother."

Beau had already been turning to offer his hand and he now went still. "Wait, *what?*"

Colin grinned, took his hand anyway, and shook it. "Nice to finally meet you face to face, Captain. Seems like you've been taking good care of my little sister for a while now."

I ground my heel into Colin's instep. He winced but didn't look the least bit sorry.

"Yes, we have," Beau said slowly. "You're…you're…Gods' Breath!" He threw up his hands. "Can we start at the beginning, please? Before my brain explodes?"

"Ry went to grab Mick. We figured it'd be easier to tell the story once," Jessie said. She was trying to keep the Dalls separate as well as prevent them from entirely messing up Beau's organizational system. I wasn't sure she was having much luck.

"I think we broke your boyfriend," Colin murmured.

I dug my heel in harder.

This time he danced away, grimacing. "Godsdamn, I forgot for a minute that you are probably better than me at defending yourself now. Not that you were a slouch before," he added hastily, "it just usually wasn't aimed at me."

"You could make sure it's not by not being an idiot," I pointed out mildly.

"If your brother is here, does that mean everyone knows who you are?" Beau asked, his brain clearly trying to process what it could.

"Yes. Even the Three. No more incognito for me. Colin's actually just a bonus."

"You're welcome," he said.

I smirked. "He and Ben helped facilitate the escape once we were free of the prison."

"Where the hell is Mick?"

"Right here. I see everyone is back." I looked up to see Mick standing in the doorway. Ry scooted by him to rejoin Jessie.

"And then some," Jay said cheerfully.

Bri sprung to his feet and held out his arms, as if for a hug. "Mick! So good to see you!"

I'd seen a fair few expressions on Mick's face, even with him as taciturn as he usually was. The absolute mix of horror and shock, though, was something I doubted I'd ever see again. "Dearest gods above," he breathed. He put a hand on the wall to steady himself. "How?"

"Let's all find a place to sit and we'll explain everything," I said, "from our capture to leaving Greensward."

It took a couple minutes to get everyone settled. I sat on the desk, legs tangled up with Beau's, who sat in his desk chair. Bri still hadn't moved and Kira leaned against his chair, sitting on the floor. The others had spread themselves around the room. The remaining actual chair had gone to Mick after he'd been escorted to it. The older man still looked dazed. "Can we start the explanations, please?"

"Jamesy, shall we?" I asked. Beau shot me a sharp look at that, but he shouldn't have been surprised. Even if I hadn't figured out who Jay was before seeing him anywhere near Bri, I certainly should have once I did see them together. Much like people immediately made the connection between Colin and me.

"I believe we shall, Jezzy," he said.

In the same style as we had in the cell, only a little briefer – details could come later – we outlined our time in the jail, including bonding with Stella and Dave – and learning their history – and meeting Sorin Dakamar and Vladimir Opalin. We covered up until discovering Bri, then Jessie and Ry took over and told of their time in Greensward and the serendipitous meeting with Kira and later Bri. Bri and Kira then told the story of his survival. Kira talked about how she'd smuggled him out of the hospital to keep him from going to jail. He explained that they'd moved to Greensward, where she had taken the inn job and Bri had taken the jail job to be close to the soldiers and be able to hear gossip to pass on to Colin and Ben.

That's when my brother gave a quick outline of his and Ben's escape from Northwind and eventual arrival in Greensward. He did go into a little more outline, almost like reporting to a superior, about his travels and some of his recent findings. Then Jay and I finished with the story of the escape, the killing of Trigger Rees, and how Jakium McRuoes had let us out. Beau, having met the lieutenant as well, seemed especially intrigued by this, much as we had been, but said nothing about it.

We had to pause a couple times as word of our arrival spread and various people stopped in to say hello and see for themselves that we were okay and had brought Brighton Dall back from the dead. Dunkin's initial reaction was a pretty common one. Dunkin himself came in about halfway through the story and stayed, taking Dave at one point to help him fetch lunch.

It was early afternoon by the time all the important information was exchanged. Beau had taken my hand again early on in our heavily edited descriptions of our conversations with Rees and had yet to let go, even while we ate.

He let out a low whistle when we finally finished. "Wow," he breathed.

"Wow seems like an understatement." None of us had known every fact that had come out in all of that, although most of us hadn't had the shock that Beau and Mick did.

"Let me absorb it all and then I might have something more intelligent to say," he told me defensively.

"I'm just glad I'm me," Bri said with a happy sigh.

"In other circumstances, that would make you sound incredibly stupid," Jay said.

"Shush, baby brother."

"I am not a baby!" I could almost hear six-year-old Jay in that protest.

"Oh Gods' Breath, we're not going to have to deal with rampant sibling rivalries, are we?" Mick said, his first words in a long time. He pointedly looked at all four sibling pairs in the room.

"Jez and I rarely bickered growing up and I doubt that'll change now," Colin said.

"If we do, we will be private about it," I agreed.

"I only tease because I love," Bri said, grinning at his brother.

Jay stuck his tongue out at him.

Stella responded in the negative. Dave still looked too awed to speak. Kira and Ben also promised to behave. Kira added that she'd do her best to keep Bri on the straight and narrow too. Or at least, as she put it, the semi-crooked and not-too-wide. We all knew straight and narrow was asking too much of a Dall.

"If Bri is too much of a jerk, I'll just remind him that he left me behind," Jay said loftily.

His brother winced. "Point received loud and clear."

"Which reminds me," Beau started.

For whatever reason, that was what reminded me. "You announced you're a Highcastle to everyone!"

Beau smiled a little. "Once I knew Renier was alive, it seemed like the right things to do. Reardon and Mick are the only two still here that knew, but quite a few members of our extended message system," here he nodded at Colin, "are the old guard that left to protect me and my mother over twenty years ago."

My brother lit up, nodding. "That makes a lot of sense. I'd always gotten the impression they were real veterans."

"It was a shock to get the letter from Renier." Beau smile went crooked. "It's the first communication I've ever had with him. I'm glad he's alive and I'm hopeful we can keep it that way. I have no desire to be king. It will be hard enough to be a proper prince when the time comes."

"At least you're already dating a noble," Jay said cheerily.

"And Renier married the enemy. I'm not sure what your point is," Mick returned, dryly.

"Wait, married? As in, it happened?" I interrupted.

Beau nodded. "Of course you wouldn't know. Earlier the night you escaped Greensward. Word reached us at the same time. Renier and Anica are officially husband and wife."

"Something exciting finally happened and I wasn't there, go figure," Colin said. "That's what I get for helping rescue you," he told me.

"And I love you for it," I said.

"It was also a relief to get the letter because it meant you two were alive. McRuoes told Adam and Ursula, so of course they let us know as soon as they arrived," Beau said. "We hurried Jessie and Ry's departure to make sure we didn't miss out on our chance to spring you."

"You make it sound like we're criminals," Jay said sadly.

"We were trying to blow stuff up."

"We *did* blow stuff up," he said with relish. "*Boom.*"

Stella smacked him in the back of the head. It couldn't have been hard, though, because he just grinned.

"Anyway," Beau said loudly, his usual way of trying to bring us back on topic. I had a feeling that would be much harder in the days to come. "I was just going to tell you that when I got interrupted."

"That was a hell of a short engagement," I said.

"They're clearly worried," Stella said quietly. It was functionally the first thing she'd said since our arrival at Cavern Hall. She seemed more surprised by her words than we did. Jay and I had long since learned not to underestimate Stella's observations and the rest of the crew was used to people speaking their minds, even if they were new.

"What makes you think so?" Beau prompted gently when she didn't continue right away.

She reddened as she realized we were all paying attention. "They're trying to gain legitimacy, right? They waited this long to announce that Prince Renier's alive, then in just a month he's already married? And to one of the siblings? Legally, she's now a princess. It means they've dug their claws in more."

"I agree," Beau said. "Potentially, that makes our job that much harder."

"Or that much easier," Ben pointed out. At Beau's curious look, he explained. "Now we know they *are* worried. They clearly see you, us, as a threat. And they're being reactive for the first time, instead of proactive."

"That's true," Colin said thoughtfully. "They haven't always won, but they've been in charge up until now. This won't be obvious to many as reactive, but it was."

"Can we spread the word?"

My brother nodded. "Absolutely. As soon as we can get messages out."

"Great! I think I'm going to like having all these new minds here," Beau said happily. "In the meantime, how about a tour and then it should be about time for dinner? We'll also introduce you around."

Everyone chorused their agreement in various ways.

"After we eat, we'll sort out places for everyone to sleep. Some of them will be temporary for tonight. Tomorrow, I'd like to meet with you all again so we can figure out where you best fit and fill you in on our plans. It'd be nice to get a formal report from you two as well," he said, glancing at Jessie and Ry, "on how things went, other than well." He didn't sound like he expected to actually get it and I figured his chances were about half and half on that.

"Things *really* went boom," Jay said solemnly.

"Thank you, Jay, for that eloquent and detailed description of events."

He grinned and bowed slightly, even as he stood and offered Stella a hand up. "Any time I can be of service, Beau, just ask."

Beau rolled his eyes. "Jay, Jez, I'd like Ann to check you both out before the end of the night."

"Ann? Has she finally taken over?" I asked.

"Yes," he said and explained to the others. "Ann is our head medical officer now. It was past time we'd made it an official post, but with people in and out on missions, we have more injured than we used to. She's also the fourth roommate with Jez, Jessie, and Ry."

"Does she need any help? I'm no expert but I got a lot of experience after the Battle of Deepen's Crossing," Kira said, "and I kept Bri from dying."

"No small feat," Bri said.

"I'm sure she could. I'll make sure you meet," Beau said.

"Okay, before we go any further," Ry said, "does anyone else have any secrets they want to get off their chests?"

"Secrets?" I asked.

"Kira is a nurse and second-in-line for the most powerful Duchy in the country. You're really Jasmine Lockholme. Bri's alive. Jay's Bri's brother. Beau's a Highcastle. Our Col is not only your brother but some sort of spymaster."

"Why thank you," Colin said, sounding quite flattered.

"I don't think so," Beau said after looking around at us.

"Um," Jessie said, clearing her throat, "I actually come from minor nobility. Merchant nobility. My grandfather got the title after providing timely supplies during the last war with Alyia, back when he was a fairly young man. My father is still active in the business. So, he's an earl too, like Jez's father." She paused again. "Except I'm their only child, so technically I'm the heir too. Or, well, if they haven't disowned me for running away. I don't really care."

We all stared at her, but Ry most of all. "I was *kidding!*"

"I figured it was time."

"That explains your clearly first class education," Beau said finally.

I now looked at him in surprise.

"I had no idea," he said. "Just because I know most of the secrets doesn't mean I know all of them. When Jessie told us her family didn't approve, there's plenty of non-noble families like that. I don't actively pry, but being in charge sort of lends itself to knowing things."

"Anyone else?" Jay asked suspiciously.

"My name's Michael," Mick said mildly, "but if anyone ever tries to call me that, including Beau, as he well knows, I will eviscerate them."

For a dozen heartbeats, there was utter silence and then, "Okay, Mickey," Bri said and then bolted from the room cackling.

Mick just heaved a sigh.

"I think it's time for that tour," Beau said, standing. "We'll catch up with Bri, since I doubt he went far without knowing his way around. In fact," he said and counted down from three with his fingers.

"Am I lost?"

Laughing, I slid off the desk carefully, stiff from the long time with no real motion, and waited for the others to all get up too. I took the time to run my fingers through Beau's hair and kiss him gently. "I love you," I said quietly.

He smiled that little smile of his. "I love you too," he said then led the way out for the grand tour of Cavern Hall.

It took a week before Sorin could leave Oakbridge for the jaunt up to Lockholme. When he approached Jakium about accompanying him, the young man looked mildly confused but agreed readily enough. He had recovered fully from the events in Greensward.

Vladimir hadn't. His brother returned mid-week, empty handed and railing against the Freedom Fighters. To no surprise of Sorin's – or perhaps anyone with an even keel – the escapees had disappeared without a trace. Vladimir didn't seem satisfied with Jakium's version of events either and questioned the lieutenant three more times, but Jakium stuck firmly to his story. Sorin wasn't entirely sure he believed all of it either, but he trusted that if Jakium wasn't telling the whole story, he had good reason. He'd known Jakium for a while and knew the young man thought everything through. Ani also trusted him implicitly and the list of people she felt that way about was painfully short. It was enough for Sorin. But it was also why he'd invited the young man along to Lockholme.

Sorin hoped that Vladimir would stay put after the fruitless search but he was gone again almost immediately. Impatiently, Sorin waited for him to return only to have Vladimir announce he'd be gone again for a couple days. At that, Sorin gave up on the hope that one of them would be in the castle. He had to trust that the Freedom Fighters would truly not be able to mobilize in the winter, even a mild one.

So he picked a day and dragged Jakium with him. It would take a full day to get there. Jakium stayed quiet all morning. Sorin half-expected to catch him smothering yawns at their early start, but mostly he looked lost in thought. Sorin was okay with that. He had a lot to mull over, including what the best approach might be in Lockholme.

Finally, though, after a brief lunch, he broke the silence. "Where did you live before Vladimir took over as your guardian?"

"Holly, Mr. Sorin," he said. "It was the nearest place with an orphanage, after my parents were killed."

"Alyian raid, right?"

"Yeah, which was ironic, considering my parents had both grown up in Alyia and moved to Tira about a year after I was born."

To his shame, Sorin hadn't known that. "Do you ever wonder *what if*?"

Jakium didn't hesitate or ask him what he meant. "All the time. More so recently, I guess, what with Ani marrying the prince and all."

"I'm still sorry that Vladimir did not give you a choice."

"Water long under the bridge. Although hey, Jasmine didn't die after all, so it wasn't quite as horrible as I thought."

Sorin stared at him, smiling despite himself. Jakium often had that effect. His sense of humor was subtle and regularly eclipsed by Ani's more obvious and sometimes overbearing humor. "Clearly," he agreed. "Although it certainly took us long enough to find out."

"Not as long as it could've been."

Jakium also had a sense of optimism that rivaled Ani's, which continually surprised Sorin as well. His own optimism had vanished a long time ago.

"Can I ask you something?" Jakium said after a moment.

"Of course."

"Ani said you think the Freedom Fighters will attack come spring. What are their chances?"

"Do you want an actual number or is 'good' enough?"

"Good is enough," he said, pressing his lips together thoughtfully.

Sorin let the silence stretch. Shortly after nightfall, they came upon a wayside inn and he called a halt. They would get little enough good regard in Lockholme, there was no point in pressing their hospitality by showing up late as well. The next day, they pressed on to Lockholme, getting there by early morning.

Lockholme's soldiers greeted them respectfully and took their horses as they dismounted. Two of the men escorted them inside.

"Did you write ahead of time?" Jakium muttered.

"Why?"

"They didn't seem particularly surprised to see us."

"No, I suppose they didn't," he agreed as they reached a set of double doors. He paused, grabbing Jakium's arm. "I'm sorry."

"What? Why?" the younger man asked as the doors swung open. "Oh," he breathed as he understood.

"Good morning, Mr. Dakamar."

Sorin took a deep breath and stepped into the room. "Good morning, Prince Beau."

Chapter Thirty-seven

WE HADN'T REALLY HAD TIME TO PREPARE. Colin received news from a trusted associate in the capital the morning Sorin Dakamar left Oakbridge. Dakamar, with only our old friend Jakium McRuoes as company, had departed for Lockholme to meet with our parents. Presumably about us. News had spread around the castle and wherever this associate was placed, they had gotten wind just early enough to offer us an opportunity.

Our plan, hastily thrown together on the way to Lockholme, had revolved around the fact we would arrive after Dakamar and Jakium. Cavern Hall was equally as far from Lockholme as Oakbridge. Still, when we arrived at my childhood home well after dark, the place was quiet. After exchanging some glances, we changed the plan and approached.

"Halt and say who you are," the guard at the gate to the estate said.

I wished I could see the mansion better. Surely this would be the strangest homecoming in Tira's history.

Colin, at my side, dismounted. "Colin Lockholme," he said clearly, "accompanied by Jasmine Lockholme, Prince Beau Highcastle, James Dall, Jessica Rider, and Rylia Schid. We wish to see our parents."

"I will never get used to that," Beau muttered from my other side as the rest of us dismounted.

The others had all wanted to come too, but Beau chose our group very carefully.

The guard hesitated but another plucked a lantern off a nearby ledge and held it up to Colin's and my faces. "Great gods above," he breathed, almost dropping it. "Let them in, Hobbes," he said quickly and dropped a half bow to all of us.

"Ooh, we got bowed to," Jay said, in too loud of a whisper. Then he grunted. Good, Jessie or Ry had gotten him.

"I will see to it that your parents are awoken, sir," the lantern guard said.

"They aren't awake already?"

"No, sir, it is rather late."

"Is Sorin Dakamar here yet?"

"Sorin Dakamar, sir?" he said, very startled.

Colin glanced at Beau and me. "We beat him here."

Beau's expression pinched. "Interesting. Either he changed his mind last minute or he chose to stay overnight on the road. Either way, we're in it now, so we might as well see your parents."

"Gods' Breath," I muttered, finding it hard to wrap my head around.

"If you'd all follow me, sirs and ma'ams," the guard said and left Hobbes to watch the gate, muttering to his compatriot that if Sorin Dakamar turned up to turn him away. Hobbes' eyes went wide but he didn't argue. Clearly the lantern guard outranked him.

A sleepy stable boy took all our horses when the lantern guard called for him and then we were inside the house. There were a few torches still burning, but not many and the house seemed dim and unused because of it. I wondered if our three older brothers were still around. As far as Colin had told me, they were all safe and living in Lockholme but it was possible that, with recent events, I had missed things. We were barely a week out from our escape after all.

"If you could all wait here, I will go wake the earl and countess," the lantern guard said with another quick bobbing bow and then he hastily disappeared.

We were in the library. I took a deep breath of the old scent of the books and closed my eyes. For a heartbeat, it was easy to imagine we were still innocent kids, fooling around among the shelves when we were supposed to be studying. Colin, apparently more practical than me, went to light a few more torches, so we could see the room properly. Jessie and Ry helped him.

Jay looked around and whistled. "Your family is pretty well off, aren't they?" he asked me.

"The horse business can be really lucrative if you know how to do it," I said absently, looking around and drinking it in.

By the time the library was brightly lit, our parents burst in, wearing just their dressing gowns and old pairs of slippers. Two steps inside, they both froze.

"Oh, it *is* you," my mother said and a second later, we'd met in the middle, hugging each other tightly. "Oh, Jasmine, my baby."

"Hi, Mom," I managed around a lump in my throat. "Surprise."

"I don't understand it, but I'm not going to argue," she said, crying. Then, she dragged me to the side and pulled my father and Colin into our hug, which was easy considering they already were hugging each other.

"We can explain," I said. I had been so busy I had rarely let myself feel homesick but now, being here with all of them, it was overwhelming. "Are Jordan, Jon and Kent okay?"

"They're just fine, sweetheart," my father rumbled, leaning through the tangle of limbs and heads to kiss my forehead. "Upstairs asleep, I assume, or else the commotion would have brought them running."

That made Colin draw back a little. "We'll have time to talk later," he promised, "but we should explain why we're here. It's a little complicated. We need a favor, but it might put you all at risk."

"All right. The maid is bringing some refreshments," my father said. "Introduce us?" he asked quieter as he scanned our friends. Then his gaze settled on Beau and he went pale. "Great gods above. How...who?" Sometimes I forgot that my father had been friends with King Patrick. He'd visited with fair frequency when we were little, often taking Kent who was about Renier's age, but we'd never gone. The king and Renier had stayed at our house a couple times for an overnight while traveling but never for long and mostly when we'd been young so my memories of both were fuzzy. Still, I suspected that perhaps Beau's familial relation extended to looks as well as blood.

Beau stepped forward, offering his hand. "I'm Beau, sir. Jez, Jasmine, tells me you and my father were good friends in your younger years."

My father, used to required politeness, took the hand and nodded. "Yes, we were. How-" he started again before understanding crashed over him. "Gods' Breath. Elizabeth?" he asked.

"She passed when I was ten."

At that, my mother's eyes widened as she finally caught up with the conversation, although she had been staring at Beau like she felt she should recognize him.

I resisted the urge to take Beau's hand. That might be one shock too many for my poor parents at this point.

"I sense that there is a very long story in all of this," my father said.

I exchanged a grin with Jay. "That's putting it mildly."

My mother, taking a better look at Colin and me, reached out and touched one of the yellowing bruises on my cheek. "Are you okay?" she asked quietly.

I was fiercely glad I'd had a week so didn't look nearly so bad. "Yeah, I am. They're almost gone. Anyway, Mom, Dad, these are some of our other friends." I did a round of quick introductions, both ways.

"So why are you here now?" my father asked.

"We're all part of the Freedom Fighters. Beau's in charge," Colin said, which was such a gross simplification that I almost laughed. "We got word yesterday that Sorin Dakamar and one of his lackeys are coming here to meet with you and Mom. Presumably about the fact Jez and I are alive."

"Jez?" our mother interrupted, like she just couldn't help herself.

"It's a nickname, Mom. Part of the very long story."

She frowned, but didn't protest. I knew she would later. Jasmine was a longstanding family name and she wouldn't be able to resist giving me a lecture about dropping it. Even though it was technically 'safe' to use it again, I doubted I would. I'd become someone other than Jasmine and there was no changing that now.

"Anyway," Colin continued easily, "we figure he wants to fish for information. To be honest, we expected him to get here ahead of us, because where we are is almost as far as Oakbridge, but clearly he didn't. So instead of snagging him when he leaves, we figured we'd ask nicely if we could snag him when he arrives instead."

"If he'd already been here, we wouldn't have seen you," my father said, astutely.

"Probably not, not until this is over for good."

"We don't want you in trouble any more than you already are now that they know I'm part of the Freedom Fighters. And might well know about Colin now too."

My father pursed his lips. "Are you going to kill him?"

Beau answered. "No, sir. We need information from him, but I fully intend for him to stand trial for what he's done once my brother is back on the throne."

"Then you are welcome to him and any lackeys. You're also welcome to use the mansion's lands for as long as you want."

"That won't, can't, be long," Colin said. "We'll have tomorrow and part of the next day before they realize he's missing, at most. We'll take him with us."

Just then, the maid knocked and entered, setting the tray on one of the large tables. My mother pulled her aside, speaking softly to her before the maid nodded and left. Then my mother stepped over and started pouring tea. "Please have a seat and some refreshments. Angie and the rest of the night staff are going to prepare rooms for you all. I assume you're all tired after riding all day."

The remaining bumps and bruises ensured I was more worn out than usual, but seeing *my parents* for the first time in three years was almost more than my heart could take. A quick glance at Colin confirmed he felt the same way as we joined the others at the table.

Colin and I gave the super short versions of where we'd been and gave a brief overview of the Freedom Fighters. Beau finished what was happening at Cavern Hall.

"Rumor has it you had something to do with the big uproar in Greensward a week ago," my father said.

"It's how I found out Jez was still alive," Colin said, "among other things. Except Beau," it hadn't taken long to crack him of the Captain nonsense, "we were all there."

"Is that where the bruises come from?"

I nodded.

Jay covered a yawn just then.

"Oh, forgive us," my mother said. "We're neglecting our hosting duties."

"I think you have good reason," Beau said with his small smile, although it was tinged with sadness. He would never get to have this moment with his parents. Thankfully, Renier seemed open to the idea of a relationship.

"Still, let's show you to the guest rooms."

Without further ceremony, my parents escorted us upstairs, showing the others to rooms. I hadn't mentioned Beau and I yet so he got his own room.

Then, our parents turned to us. "We put you two both in guest rooms. Colin in with Jay and you just down here," my mother said. "But if you'd rather…"

I wanted to visit my room before we left, certainly, but trying to sleep there might be even more impossible then sleeping in general. "This will be great, Mom, thank you. Can you make sure we're up at dawn? Dakamar and McRuoes can't be far."

"Of course, sweetheart," she said and wrapped me in another tight hug. "Oh, this…this…" she trailed off and kissed my forehead.

"I love you too, Mom," I murmured.

After a minute, she peeled herself off reluctantly. "We'll see you bright and early."

"Count on it." Then she took my father's hand and, with many glances back, they left Colin and I standing there.

"Didn't tell them you're in love with a prince."

"Didn't tell them you're a talented super spy."

"Touché. Going to go sleep with him?"

"I'm afraid me not being in the assigned room might freak them out."

"Quite possibly but probably not in the way you think."

I had to smile at that. "Think things will ever slow down again?"

"Doubtful."

I nodded. "Night, Colin."

"Night, Jez." He slipped in after Jay while I retraced our steps a few doors and found Beau.

Far too soon, there was a rap on the door and then everything was a flurry of activity. Our three older brothers appeared to hug the stuffing out of both Colin and me and greet our friends cheerfully. We had a quick breakfast and then, other than my father and oldest brother, who got to stay by right of heirship or some such, they cleared out to potentially safer parts of the mansion. I didn't think it totally necessary. By all accounts, it was only Dakamar and Jakium and I had a gut feeling it wouldn't get nasty.

When my father's scout, who he had sent out early to watch the northbound road, came rushing in, he carried the report we all expected. Just the two of them, riding leisurely this way. Instructions were reiterated to bring them straight to the ballroom, the biggest space our mansion had.

We waited in our own ways. Jay whistled quietly. Jessie and Ry murmured to each other. Colin, standing on our father's left – Kent on the right – didn't seem to move a muscle, eyes fixed on the door. I stood next to Beau, close enough our shoulders touched. Once word came that Dakamar was in the building, I'd join our friends. Just like my gut said it wouldn't get nasty, it also told me to let Beau handle it. I studied his profile out of the corner of my eye, still trying to fully reconcile the fact that he was second-in-line for Tira's throne. It wasn't that I couldn't see it, because I absolutely could. But he was my captain, my friend, and now my second half before he was a prince.

A servant peeked in and nodded.

I reached out and squeezed Beau's hand before moving to stand next to Jay. My friend took my hand silently.

This time, the waiting was short. Within ten minutes, the doors swung open, exposing two familiar men, flanked by some of my parents' people. Dakamar had a grip on Jakium's forearm. Jakium looked shocked. Dakamar did not.

"Good morning, Mr. Dakamar," Beau said.

Dakamar released Jakium's arm and stepped forward, holding his hands away from his sides and weapons. "Good morning, Prince Beau."

Somehow it didn't surprise me that he had put two and two together to identify Beau. Maybe he had at just that moment, or maybe he'd known for a long time.

Beau glanced back and nodded to Colin.

My brother stepped forward and patted Dakamar down. There were no hidden weapons, just the knife and sword on his belt. Jakium now stepped in too, allowing the men to shut the door. Jakium's gaze swept the room, he visibly relaxed at the sight of Ry and let Colin frisk him too without fuss.

Dakamar scanned as well, offering a solemn nod to Jay and I and a more pronounced one for my father. Then his gaze returned to Beau as Colin stepped back and Jakium came to stand at Dakamar's side almost protectively, arms folded.

"You don't particularly seem surprised, Mr. Dakamar."

"I wanted the chance to talk to you. This seemed like the easiest way. Not in the least because it gave you an excuse to visit Lockholme."

I felt a flash of surprise. Dakamar had walked into our trap on purpose. More than that, he'd set the trap for himself. Suddenly his lack of escort made perfect sense, but what was his angle? I didn't deny I had a healthy respect for him. Far more respect than I did for his brother. But in this case, I couldn't see it.

"If you think we're going to thank you, you have another thing coming."

"No, although we are kin now. Does that mean certain niceties have to be followed?"

"I suppose that depends on why you're here," Beau said.

"I want what you want, Your Highness," he said soberly. "I want this to end."

"That makes no sense. Why would you want it to end? You started it."

Dakamar's eyes darted to me. "Let's just say that I'm sick of picking up the pieces."

In a flash, his words at the tail end of our last meetings came back to me. I pressed my lips together.

"That tells me very little."

He spread his arms. "Okay, I want to make a deal."

Beau said nothing, studying him evenly.

"I give you myself and Vladimir, your brother's safety, and Tira, in return for you letting Ren make the final decision regarding my sister, as well as Jakium's freedom."

Silence. Jakium shot him an incredulous look, as if shocked those were his only two terms.

Was he insinuating that Renier and Anica's marriage was more than just a political ploy? Was that even possible? His choice of words made me think he was telling the truth, as did Jakium's reaction. However.

"It can't be that simple," Beau said finally.

"Why not?"

"Because we have fought for *years* and now you're just going to hand it over? Your men...we have lost *good* people!"

"And I'm offering you a way to avoid losing more," Sorin Dakamar said. "You're right. There has been far too much bloodshed over my father's misguided ideas."

"Your father," Beau repeated slowly.

"Technically Ani and Vladimir's father, but considering Edward murdered my biological father before I was born, that's who he always was." He said it so calmly.

Sometimes, I forgot that Sorin was only a half-sibling to the Opalins. Both he and Vladimir must have had a lot of their mother in them, because there was no mistaking a familial relation. I idly wondered if Anica was the same.

"He's the one," Sorin continued, "who started this. Unfortunately, before he died, he passed the concept and what power he'd gained on to Vladimir, who decided to run with it and then actually managed the task, using the business Edward had started as a front."

Although I hadn't heard this before – I doubted many now even knew – it made complete sense. Patrick Highcastle had been worried for a long time, considering he'd sent his wife and unborn child into hiding so long ago. Even though the Three were older than me, they would have been just children then and not capable of being the original plotters.

Beau turned to Jakium. "Do you agree with this plan?" he asked.

It had to be the first he'd heard of it, but he didn't hesitate. "The sooner this ends, the better for Tira. Wherever Mr. Sorin and Ani stand is where I stand," he said firmly and then glanced at Sorin. "I knew they were in Greensward trying to rescue Jasmine and James. And I was there when Rees died. I let them escape the city."

Sorin didn't blink but his face did register surprise. Then he smiled crookedly. "So that's what you weren't telling. I see we've both been working towards the same goal without consulting each other." Then, he murmured something I didn't catch.

Jakium's expression relaxed slightly and he nodded.

"So I heard," Beau said, "and I suppose a thank you is in order."

Jakium shrugged. "I have no doubt they could have escaped without my help."

"But they didn't have to try." Then Beau turned his attention back to Sorin. "I believe we can take Oakbridge and the rest of Tira without you. We've grown strong."

"I don't doubt it and I'd be lying if your strength wasn't some of the reason that I've come now and not before. You need to be strong enough to hold it from any factions that remain once you've taken the country. And from Nerius and Alyia, who will take the change of power as yet further weakness. If you take my way, you'll have even more people to do that because you won't have to fight your way through all of Oakbridge."

The logic was undeniable. The less people we lost, the better, even beyond the fact we would face trouble on other borders besides the Three. Still, it came down to whether or not we could trust him and I couldn't see how we could. Yet, at the same time, I recalled how he had saved Dave, his wry humor, and the things Jakium had done in Greensward to allow our safe passage. My bruises seemed to throb at the very thought of Greensward and Rees.

"Say your terms are acceptable. How do you propose this happens?"

"I have strongly suspected for some time that you have a pretty deeply rooted spy network of your own in Oakbridge." I resisted the urge to look at my brother and I suspected the others did too. "This confirms it, since I kept this trip fairly quiet."

"It was a test."

"Of sorts. I figured you weren't planning on moving against us until the snows melted, since it's easier to move large groups of people on foot without the snow or muds of early spring. I just wasn't sure if you could move quite that quickly. Now it seems I'm right. But that's not important. A network assumes you have safehouses. The trouble, of course, would be getting the supplies and weapons, along with the people, into Oakbridge undetected. I can offer that safe passage. You stash your people and supplies and, once you have the numbers you need, you let me know and I'll open the castle to you. I can also get a couple people into the castle on a permanent basis as well, which I'm willing to bet you don't have."

From the intrigued look on Colin's face, I suspected Sorin was right. Abandoning not calling my brother out, Beau looked back at him with his eyebrows raised.

"Best we've got is the occasional delivery service," Colin admitted. "The castle is a very insular place for the most part. Staff consists of those who have been around. Competition for open jobs is fierce and the vetting process even more so. I haven't dared risk it myself and I'm not sending anyone to do what I'm not willing to."

"Then how did you get word of our coming then, if I may ask?" Sorin asked, gaze sharp. He seemed to have identified Colin easily enough. I had to wonder if he'd known about my brother's job, at least in part.

Colin grinned, a little smugly. "Infirmary."

"Ah!" Understanding spread across Sorin's face. "Of course. Although our vetting process also extends to the infirmary personal, it does not include people from other infirmaries who come for brief learning stints or to bring or take supplies. The infirmary has always seemed too off to the side. I never suspected it could cause a leak." He nodded his head respectfully to my brother. "Well done."

Colin nodded back, with the look of someone who appreciated the work of a fellow professional. I was proud of him. By all accounts, including my own, Sorin Dakamar was undoubtedly brilliant. But Colin had gotten to his world while Dakamar had never managed to crack ours.

Beau rubbed his chin. "As far as I understand your plan, though, this would require us trusting you enough to let you go back to Oakbridge to orchestrate this. We have absolutely no guarantee that we're not going to get people in and set up and you won't ambush them. Or have your soldiers on the watch so they don't even make it through the gates."

"That is the dilemma you face," Sorin agreed. "However, you must know that if you keep Jakium and I as your prisoners, the efforts my brother has so far put into chasing you will triple. Your part of the country will not be safe. The Lockholmes and any other family they suspect might have Freedom Fighter leanings will not be safe. Jay's entire town, for instance." He held up his hand as Jay's grip on my hand tightened. "I am not threatening you. I'm merely stating how my brother will react should I vanish. His assumption will be that I need rescuing. For all his other defects, he will not desert me."

Beau nodded slowly. "And handing over yourself and your brother?"

"When you do come, I won't fight. There are those in the castle, Vladimir included, who will undoubtedly fight to the end, though. All I can guarantee on that score is that he will physically be in the castle when you attack. The rest of that would be up to you."

That seemed fair enough, going back to the assumption that we would trust Sorin enough to go along with this. To take the risk. I had to wonder how much we might stand to lose if it fell through. Colin would lose his infirmary connection, true, but there would be ways to test Sorin's sincerity without risking much, unless he played us for a long time. And, he had come here to us, practically unarmed and unprotected to give us this offer. He wouldn't know where our safehouses were. And there were plenty of ways, with some thought, we could make this backfire on him if it went awry.

I almost missed Sorin and Jakium exchanging a look. Jakium nodded somberly, which is what really drew my attention. "I offer Jakium up as collateral."

I was pretty sure that caught us all off guard. "What?" Beau said.

"One part of my bargain is Jakium's freedom at the end of this. Therefore, it stands to reason I have a vested interest in keeping him alive, correct?"

Beau nodded.

"Then you keep him as collateral. If I show any signs of reneging on the bargain, you do what you see fit to him, as publicly or privately as you want."

I studied Jakium's face, but it didn't contain a hint of doubt. Just utter trust.

"I hate to lose him, of course, as he'd be a useful point of contact between your people and myself, as he has been once before," – how did he know about that, I wondered – "but this seems a fair trade to me."

"Why the vested interest?" Beau asked, as if trying to ferret out a trick. But I knew, at least in part. I remembered the conversation we'd had with Jakium at Greensward prison and his intense devotion to Anica Opalin. And what he'd told Ry.

"Jakium is the younger brother Ani never got. Vladimir took him in when he was fourteen and most of the time, it was just him and Ani around the house for quite a few years. Eventually, Vladimir dragged him into his plans, much as he dragged our sister."

I noticed that he didn't include himself and wondered. Where had he been during those years? And why had he not been dragged in as well? I resigned myself to the fact that there was much about Sorin Dakamar and the entire history of the Three that I might never know.

"And all you ask in return is that my brother gets to decide Anica's fate and that Jakium, assuming you don't betray us, lives?"

"Yes," Sorin said, lifting his chin slightly as he held Beau's gaze.

"Not your own life?"

"No."

"So, if we agree to your terms and Jakium McRuoes stays here with us, how do we contact you once you're back in Oakbridge?"

"I assume that we can sort that before I leave. It certainly seems like the youngest Mr. Lockholme has his ways."

576

Colin smirked a little.

"I have, at bare minimum, a half a day before I should set out again, considering my story, and plan if you had not been here, was to discuss Jasmine and Colin's lack of being dead with their family and see what further information I might be able to get on them."

Beau nodded slowly then turned to my father and Kent. "Can you please keep an eye on them while we talk?"

"Of course," my father said and stepped forward, hand on his sword hilt.

Beau and Colin came to join the rest of us. "Well?" Beau asked, looking around.

"I think we have to take the chance. We can figure out ways to minimize the risk to our people," Colin said.

"I think he's telling the truth," I added.

Jay nodded. "If it works, it's worth all the risks. I think collectively, we can outsmart him if it's a sham."

"Jakium's had ample opportunity to throw a wrench into our plans and hasn't," Ry put in.

When Beau looked at Jessie, she just shrugged. "I can't think of a good objection."

Beau ran a hand over his face. "I don't foresee this speeding things up much, because it'll take time to slip people and materials in, but it does seem like it will make taking Oakbridge much easier when the time comes. I just can't believe we're trusting him."

"We'll have backups and backups of backups," my brother promised. "We'll make this work."

"And you have ideas on how to contact him?"

"Yes and who I want in the castle," Colin said. "I'll have Russ be my contact with him. I think he'll manage Dakamar well and he can take care of himself. He grew up in the Greyspire guild system, which is no slouch."

Beau nodded like he understood the reference, and he probably did. I felt a twinge as my lack of travel caught up with me again. I had no idea Greyspire had a guild system, let alone one that might prepare someone for what Colin was suggesting. "So we're agreed?"

"We're agreed."

The rest of us nodded.

Beau took a deep breath then turned and walked back. "We have a deal," he said and looked to my father. "Can we use the library to talk?"

"Of course."

Beau returned his attention to Sorin and Jakium. "Let's go sort this out then," he said.

"Where is he?" Vlad stomped through the door without knocking, so it was his own fault he got a full view of Ani sitting in Ren's lap, making out with him. Ani felt no shame. Ren's expression went wary but he didn't let go of her.

"Who?" Ani asked mildly, taking her time sliding off Ren's lap to perch on the desk next to him.

"You know who! Sorin. And Jakium, too, I suppose." He scowled. "He can't just take Jakium whenever he wants."

"He asked Jakium if he wanted to go and Jakium said yes. That's kind of the point of him being around Oakbridge." Ani marveled at her own daring. She and Vlad had had a strained relationship for a long time, although not as mixed as her brothers with each other. Still, Sorin's recent warnings and her own observations showed her that Vlad's grip on himself was slipping. By all rights, she should be doing the opposite of riling him, but she found she was mostly mad at him for letting himself go this far.

"Where is he?"

"Everyone around knows where he went. Why are you asking me?" she asked bluntly.

Vlad's eyes flashed but he visibly reined himself in. "Ani."

At her nickname, she relented. "Lockholme, to interview Jasmine and Colin's parents to see if he could get more information."

Vlad's frown deepened. "Okay, that's what Bert said, but the men said he declined an escort."

"He mentioned wanting to travel quietly. Maybe he thought that would bring too much attention when we know the Freedom Fighters' headquarters is up there somewhere," Ani said, but wondered at that a little herself. What was Sorin playing at?

Her brother nodded slowly. "Did he say how long he would be gone?"

"Just a couple days. He was hoping to be there by this morning and then start back this afternoon. So tomorrow late probably."

Immediately, he was annoyed again. "He should have stayed until I was here."

"You weren't around much, and he didn't want to wait too long," Ani said, defensively.

Only then did Ren move, taking her hand and giving a gentle warning squeeze. Without Sorin here, no one was around who was able to bring Vlad off a ledge. Ani hated it but knew it was true.

"Still!"

"He tried to talk to you a couple times but you've barely been around in the last week."

"I have important things to do," he said.

"Like Father always did," Ani whispered.

Vlad's eyes, which had been roaming the room almost absently, snapped back to her. Ren half rose, as if he could get between them.

"Sit down, prince," he said flatly.

Ren glanced at Ani, waiting until she nodded before he settled back. He perched on the chair arm, giving Vlad a dark look.

"You don't know what you're talking about," Vlad told her without missing a beat.

She tightened her grip on Ren's hand, reminding herself to stay grounded. No matter what he said or did, this was *Vlad*, not Edward. "Vlad, don't say that," she said quietly. "I'm not stupid and you're not our father. *Please* be better than that."

After one too many heartbeats, his gaze softened. "Sorry, Ani. I...he thought he'd be back by tomorrow?"

She let out a breath, disappointed, even if his response was better than nothing. "Yeah. He didn't think he'd be welcome even a full day in Lockholme."

"Okay. Thanks."

"Of course. You leaving again?"

"No, I can wait until he gets back. Let me know if you need anything." He nodded to them both a little stiffly and let himself out, closing the door quietly.

Ani turned and hugged Ren tightly. "How did Edward dig his claws into Vlad but not me and Sorin?"

"I can only assume different personalities. Maybe Vlad just got more of his father than you or Sorin."

"Once we were older and especially after Sorin left, Father really did pull him in as his heir." She sighed as Ren slid back to the chair and held her close. "We should have stopped him. Sorin and me. We both knew better, but it was easier then. Now, though…we've already lost Vlad and with the Freedom Fighters…" She snuggled in against him. Ren wrapped his arms around her. "He'll want to send me away sooner."

Ren didn't have to ask who she meant. "And you should probably go. I would never forgive myself if something happened to you."

She nodded, tucking her head under his chin. It felt safe like this. "Sorin doesn't think until spring, so we might have some time."

He just nodded and tightened his grip.

For now, she'd take as much comfort from their time together as she could, and dream of what would never be.

Chapter Thirty-eight

LATE THAT AFTERNOON, I CLUTCHED Beau's hand as I watched the two horses ride through the mansion's gates and out of sight. On my other side, my mother pressed her fingers to her mouth, eyes wide and worried.

"Colin'll be okay, Mom," I said with confidence. If my brother had made it this far without any of us, he could manage to foil any possible double-cross from Sorin Dakamar.

She nodded. "I just hate to see him go so soon."

"With a little luck, soon enough we can come back whenever we want," I told her and transferred my grip to her hand. "Come on, we have some time, let's catch up in a little more detail."

She smiled. "Okay." She squeezed my hand and led me back inside, but my mind was still outside and on the day's discussions. First we'd sorted out all the details with Sorin, which had mostly been Beau and Colin with the rest of us listening for any discrepancies. Not that there were any.

That had been followed by a fierce debate of who would go with Dakamar back to Oakbridge, because none of us were willing to let him go alone and have our people approach him later. This way, no one in place would be exposed until we had a better idea whether he was really telling us the truth.

Ry had quietly bowed out, saying while she wouldn't mind, she preferred to keep an eye on Jakium. This surprised no one. Jessie deferred as well, wanting to back Ry up.

Although I didn't want to leave Beau or the others so soon, I didn't particularly want Colin going into the den by himself. Jay seemed to feel similarly.

Finally, Beau folded his arms and leveled a look at both of us. "Neither of you can go. I don't particularly like the idea of Colin going alone, but he is rather uniquely suited. And he has support in Oakbridge, right, Colin?"

"Of course. We've got quite a few operatives in the city proper. And safehouses galore."

"Why not?" Jay asked Beau, frowning.

"You're a liability. If Dakamar does turn on us, and you two are there, all he has to do is describe you. Or pull some soldiers from Greensward who know you. You'll be trapped."

"So will Colin," I pointed out, even more worried for him.

My brother shot me a confident smile. "Yes, but I'm a mouse, Jez, I can get out of any hole."

I scowled at him. "I'm sure we could manage."

"Opalin has made you his biggest focus right now. Not the rest of them. You and Jay, because you're The Freedom Fighters. You heard what Dakamar said, and it matches our own reports. He is combing the cities and countryside for you two. If he gets wind you're in Oakbridge, there will be no stopping him. People will get hurt."

In a way, I was relieved. Greensward had taken a lot out of me. "You're sure you'll be okay, Colin?"

"Positive," he told me. "I won't take any foolish risks, but this *is* our chance. I want to take it while we can."

There was no arguing with that, so while Jakium stayed, Sorin and Colin rode off. They would stick together until reaching the outer parts of the capital. Then Sorin would take himself back to the castle and, supposedly, tell the others that Jakium had stayed in the Lockholme and Ellworth area to keep an eye out for Freedom Fighters and any dissent, while keeping a low profile. Jakium, on his end, would write dutiful but fake letters from Cavern Hall, which we would make sure reached the right hands for Opalin to believe their authenticity.

We spent the rest of the evening in Lockholme, having an enjoyable dinner with the rest of my family. Not really knowing what else to do with Jakium, my father had invited him. The young man was on his very best behavior and never said a word through the entire dinner, but not in an uncomfortable way. He seemed to be perfectly content drinking things in. That night, he was stuck in a guest room with a two person guard. I didn't think that was necessary. I had the feeling that Jakium McRuoes wasn't going anywhere. Just as we'd all felt that Sorin Dakamar was telling the truth about his offer.

After breakfast the next morning, we got ready to head out. My family didn't throw a fit about me leaving again once I promised regular updates, but were clearly sad about it.

Jakium kept his horse but Ry took the reins. Late in the afternoon, we paused again. Jakium had said little during the ride too, as if still trying to figure out where he stood with us. It was a fair question. I wasn't sure any of us knew the answer to that yet. Still, I gave him credit for taking this all in stride. "I'm assuming I'm getting blindfolded?"

"Yeah, sorry," Ry said with a wry smile.

He shrugged. "I don't blame you. Mind if I tie it on? You can all test it."

Ry glanced at Beau who nodded and passed Jakium the thick strip of cloth.

Jakium arranged it over his eyes and then tied it neatly. Ry leaned forward and tried a few things to test him and he never flinched. She kept her horse even with his, though, going forward, talking to him quietly.

By evening, we'd reached Cavern Hall. Once we had the horses settled at their separate location, we descended into the caves. The rest of the crowd were there to greet us, but they all stopped at the sight of Jakium.

"You can take it off now," Ry told him.

"I take it it was a success?" Ben asked carefully. "Or at least a partial one?"

"A complete success," Beau said. "C'mon, we need dinner and we'll explain what happened and Mr. McRuoes's presence."

"Jakium, please," he said, seeming more relaxed after talking to Ry, but there was still a wariness in his gaze. I didn't blame him for it.

"Or Jaksie," Jay said innocently. Honestly, I was shocked it had taken him this long. His self-control had clearly gotten the better of him for almost a full day. Stella jabbed him in the ribs.

"Please don't," Jakium said, wincing, as he always seemed to at the nickname.

Ry hid a smile.

Bri didn't bother to hide his. "Jaksie," he repeated gleefully.

583

"Brighton," Kira warned. "C'mon, food before you say or do something you regret."

"But Kira, darling, I never do that. I regret nothing."

"Is that another Dall family life philosophy?" Stella asked Jay.

"Yup. Regret Nothing. Bounce Back Quickly. Be a Terrible Singer."

I started laughing. "All three sound damn accurate to me."

Jay sketched a little bow in my direction. "Then we are succeeding at being Dalls. Glad to hear it."

"I'm really hungry," Beau said loudly, much to my continued amusement. It amazed me how he still thought that just talking over us could stop us. Or result in much more than mocking. True to form, both Dalls turned on him. Beau blinked at the dual attention and seemed to have a couple definite regrets right then. "Um, can we have dinner?"

"Can we sing at it?" Bri asked and high fived Jay without even having to look.

Beau sighed, shook his head, and gestured to Jakium. "C'mon, we'll show you where to find food."

Jakium cautiously fell in step with him. I did the same on Beau's other side, since Mick was taking his time, probably trying to figure out if he could feasibly bonk Jay and Bri's heads together. "Sir, I was talking to Rylia and...I'm unclear on my position here. I don't want to be a bother or a drain on your resources, but I understand that, as collateral, I'm no better than a prisoner."

Beau took a deep breath. "For now, that's basically true. You can have free run of Cavern Hall, but with a guard. Any attempts to duck the guard or do something stupid, like touch a weapon without warning, will get you stuck in a room all the time. Once Mr. Dakamar has proven his commitment to the plan, we can relax a little. At that point, I don't really care what you do as long as you stick around Cavern Hall and have an escort if you leave for any reason. I believe you're loyal to both him and Anica and are fully in on this plan."

"Really? That's...that's your version of a prisoner?" he said a little incredulously.

"We're not Rees. Or Opalin," I put in dryly.

"Still!"

"Would you rather we're harsher?" Beau asked.

"No, sir!" he said quickly. "That sounds very acceptable. Thank you, sir."

"Great. Well, this is the main corridor. Most things can be found nearby," Beau went straight into guide mode and I listened absently.

"Jakium," I interrupted, when Beau took a breath, "why Sorin?"

He looked past Beau to me, clearly understanding my question. "Mr. Sorin moved back in when I was sixteen and I was just starting to realize things were, well, not well with Master Vladimir. Or, at least that he was up to things that were big. And dangerous. And treasonous." I noted the names for both of them, a contrast to each other and to just plain 'Ani' for the sister. "Mr. Sorin tried his damndest to keep me out of it. Ani too. But Master Vladimir sucked me in. When I was present for your attempted execution, all Master Vladimir had told me was that he needed me to run a message to Kilburn. I knew a little about the dukes' assassinations but not as much as I should've. The man he sent me to, the man behind the deaths and the whole setup, kept me there and then, when I refused to accompany them that morning, knocked me out and dragged me. It's not an excuse," he said hastily. "I had ample opportunity to run before it went that far, but...I didn't. I did see you that day, down in the ravine, and hoped to the gods you'd survived." His expression was earnest. "Anyway, Mr. Sorin and Ani were the only two in my life, after my parents, who tried to save me. Even if it didn't work."

Beau appraised him. "I'm not so sure it didn't," he said quietly.

Jakium looked clearly startled at that. "You don't have to say that, sir. I've caused a lot of pain for people you care about." He nodded to me. "Beyond Miss Jasmine, I hurt Rylia."

"I'm pretty sure that's between you and Rylia and you've worked it out," Beau said.

"Please don't call me that. Just Jez is fine, Jakium, really. Or 'miss' if you really insist. Plus I'm alive and well, so let's just call that one a draw too." I had hated him for a couple hours, when he'd first identified me, but it hadn't lasted long. All my hate had been needed for Rees and Opalin.

"And I'm not just saying it. I don't just say things," Beau said with one of his small smiles. "Let's get dinner."

Jakium ended up between Ry and Jay at our overfull table. He was quiet again, but seemed a little less nervous. He even made a few comments to those close to him.

After dinner, Dunkin politely took Jakium off on a full tour with some of his other friends and the rest of us adjourned to Beau's office to pass on the full story and explain Colin's absence. Beau apologized to Ben for stealing his bodyguard.

Ben smiled. "Colin hasn't really been my bodyguard since we left Northwind. We decided that it had to be an even relationship to do the work we wanted to do. Now we're just friends and he's the more useful member of the duo."

Beau then explained the rest: the deal we'd made with Sorin Dakamar and the plan that had come out of it. This, of course, included Colin's leaving that morning to be Dakamar's escort back to Oakbridge and to start the process.

"So the question, then, becomes our exact timing. Obviously it will take time to filter people safely into Oakbridge, enough to equalize things, but we've still got part of the winter remaining. I think we can safely stick to our original plan of spring. Two months, give or take. What does everyone think?"

"There's a lot of hard feelings in the cities," Kira said, glancing at Ben for support. "Greensward is ready to blow and this time I don't mean literally. People are pissed about soldiers throwing their weight around. Especially in the last couple months. Rees, for all his faults, was a fair acting governor, but when his focus changed to Jez and Jay, he left things to Mosk. Simply put, Mosk is a pompous asshole, who cares little about the citizens."

Ben nodded. "People are upset and ready for an alternative. From what Colin's said, Greensward is not unique."

"And you don't think us blowing up the palace will change that?" Jessie asked.

The siblings shared a look. "I don't think so. You were aiming at them, not the average citizen."

"Can I log a protest that I don't feel that Rees was particularly concerned with the average citizen?" Jay said, half raising his hand.

"You aren't an average citizen by any scope of the imagination," I told him.

Beau grinned and talked around us, as usual. "So you think a lot of the cities just need a push from our people?"

"Exactly."

Nodding, he tapped a pile of papers on his desk. "We have over seven hundred able-bodied people between the two camps these days."

"Seven *hundred*?" I sputtered.

"Yeah. Recruits have been pouring in. That doesn't count the people we have out of the camps, which is a high number because we can't really house a lot more comfortably right now."

"So how many do you think the day we attack?"

"A thousand out of here, but some of those will go places other than Oakbridge."

"Gods' Breath," I said.

Bri let out a whistle. "Can you even believe it? Considering where we started? Considering where we were when I died?"

Kira punched him.

True to form, Bri whined until she kissed his cheek.

"So what do you need from us?" Ben asked.

We spent the next hour hammering out a timeline we'd follow if all went well in Oakbridge, and one we'd follow if Dakamar foiled our plans. Then the others filtered out. After what felt like forever, Beau and I were finally alone. I yawned. "Bed time, please?"

He glanced at all the unanswered messages.

"No. Bed time," I told him. "I'll help with the messages in the morning, along with whomever else we can convince to help."

He rolled his eyes a little but stood and stretched. "If we get much fuller, we'll need to stick others in here with me."

"We are not fuller yet," I told him, cutting him off on his way to change and kissing him firmly, wrapping my arms around his waist. "You okay?" The previous night, we'd both been still trying to process the entire situation and had said little about it.

"I'm okay. You?"

I nodded. "We okay? You've been jittery."

He smiled a little, but something lurked in his eyes. It wasn't the first time I'd seen it. "I think I have the right to be, all things considered."

"No, something else is bothering you. Has been since we got back at least. What is it?" I couldn't read it, but I knew enough to know it was lasting.

He sighed. "I can't ever get anything past you, can I?"

"No, so stop trying," I told him, running a finger along the edge of his hair and then cupping his cheek. "Talk to me."

He pressed his lips together. "Bri," he said finally.

That ranked somewhere close to the bottom of possible subjects I'd expected, but as soon as he said it I realized that was stupid. I could see where he might feel I had chosen him as a way of bouncing back from Bri\'s death, but the truth was, I had no interest in Bri that way anymore. "You have nothing to worry about, I promise."

He searched my face. "I just…I remember you two before he died," – gods, Bri's casual references to his own not-death were catching, we were all doing it now – "the way you looked at him. And I was jealous back then. I liked you from day one."

"Look, Bri and Kira are very happy, clearly. And I have you. I guess I can't speak for him, but odds are we're both a lot happier now than we were before. I love both Dall brothers, but I couldn't ever see myself spending the rest of my life with them. They take too much work. And, as a bonus, Bri's not actually dead!"

"I think the phrase you're looking for is 'high maintenance'," he said, visibly relaxing.

I kissed him again and, this time, he returned it with due enthusiasm. "I love *you*," I told him, "and if you don't believe me, I will ensure you're wearing the leopard outfit when we take Oakbridge back. And I doubt that's the first impression you want to make on your brother."

I was highly amused by the utter horror on his face. "You wouldn't!"

"I would."

"You and what army?" he said defensively.

I grinned. "Have you met our friends?"

He opened his mouth and then shut it again. "I love you too," he said instead of arguing.

With the plans in place and us waiting on word from Colin, the next few days were shockingly dull after the previous months. I didn't precisely mind, but it felt strange to only have everyday duties and nothing life and death. Seeing Jakium around stopped having a startling effect and he joined us for all meals, mostly because Ry and Jessie had appointed themselves his guards. He continued to mostly listen, but slowly started to comment on things and offer his opinion. He was quizzed a lot and, while he didn't talk much about his early time with the Three, he readily told us anything we wanted to know about the cities he'd been to and their defenses and degrees of loyalty. In that way, he was like puppy, eager to please, only more articulate. In fact, although my initial estimate of Jakium from Westcorner, and even Greensward to a degree, was exactly that of a puppy – eager, sort of bumbling, tail wagging – the man was quick and had a knack for noticing the little things.

He didn't approach Beau and Mick until after we'd gotten word from my brother that things were stable and secure and to send the first batch of troops. When he did, he waited until he thought it was just them, because he looked a little surprised to see me. "Oh, I'm sorry, I can come back another time," he started. I glanced past him but there was no sign of Ry or Jessie, which meant it was serious. Even since he'd gotten more freedom at Colin's letter, he was rarely without one of our group, because many still viewed him with suspicion. I didn't blame them, but I did feel a little bad for Jakium.

"No, it's okay," I said. "I can go."

Beau motioned for me to stay, though. "I think I have an inkling of what you're going to say and I think Jez's opinion might be a good thing to have."

Jakium looked between us and nodded. "Maybe, sir." He hesitated before drawing in a breath and straightening. "I want to make a case for not killing Mr. Sorin."

Beau sank into his desk chair and gestured Jakium across from him. "I make no promises, but convince me."

He sat gingerly. Mick leaned against the desk, just far enough away to be intimidating but not threatening. I sat in the other chair, shifting so I faced him. Jakium clasped his hands together, but his voice was even and he met Beau's gaze. "I know the deal is just for me. And for R-the prince to decide on Ani. But I wanted to request that Mr. Sorin's life be spared as well." I made a mental note to ask him why that phrasing for Anica. Why have Renier decide? I kept forgetting to actually ask.

"Mr. Dakamar didn't seem to think that was an important enough part to add to his deal. Why do you?"

"He blames himself for a great many things," Jakium said, "I think, including this entire mess. He blames himself for your father's death, even if Master Vladimir did the actual killing. Every death that day and since sits heavily on him. He thinks he deserves to die."

"Maybe he should, considering," Beau said flatly, but I could see the calculations in his eyes.

"He's certainly not blameless," Jakium said quickly. "But neither am I. Or Ani. Or any of their foot soldiers either. But that doesn't necessarily mean we're all terrible people who deserve death. Any more than all of you are for opposing us. Everyone does something bad at some point in their lives. And most people do something good too. I'm not saying he's perfect. And I'm not saying he, or any of us, have made the right decisions for a while now. But he's not a *bad* person. Especially now. Ani and I never knew what it was, but for a long time, Mr. Sorin refused to have anything to do with Master Vladimir's plots. Ani told me later, after I got involved. And then, one day, it was like someone had turned him off and he just didn't care anymore. I met him a bunch before he moved back into the house with us, because he still worked for Master Vladimir and the family business. And he *was* different then. He had a sense of humor, he made jokes, he smiled. Until recently, I hadn't seen him smile in years."

"What's changed?"

"I think he's somehow found his way out of the hole of depression, sir, and really looked at what's gone on. What he's helped *do*. And I think a lot of that is because of your brother and Ani and watching them."

"I suppose it's about time I asked," Beau said. "What is the story between my brother and Anica? I didn't question his wording at the time, because it seemed low on the scale of importance, but now I have to wonder."

Jakium smiled. "They fell in love."

"That's the story we've been told, yes."

"No, they really did," he insisted. "They spent a lot of time together because Ani had a crush on him from the first day. Maybe even before that. She always looked a little dreamy when she talked about him before. She so desperately wanted to get to know him. And somewhere in there, fairly recently, they both realized it."

"And you're positive that my brother feels the same way?"

"Yes, sir. Mr. Sorin worded it that way because he knows that the prince will spare Ani. And protect her when the battle comes. He also thought phrasing it that way might help you believe." He shrugged slightly.

Beau glanced at me, then Mick.

"He has a point," Mick said. "If Dakamar had been at all worried that Prince Renier did not feel the same way, he would have outright bargained for her life, much as he did with Mr. McRuoes. As is, he's left Prince Renier the power to keep her alive and safe."

Beau nodded slowly then turned to Jakium. "I withhold my right to make a decision either way until I have time to think it over. And," he added when I gave him a look, "talk to my wonderful and amazing core group."

Jakium nodded and all but shot out of his chair as he saluted. Mick covered his mouth to hide his grin. I didn't bother. "Thank you, sir."

"Did you need anything else?"

"No, sir," Jakium said and actually bowed slightly before disappearing out the door.

I tilted my head as I watched him depart. "Huh."

"What?" Beau asked.

"He bowed to you. Has anyone ever bowed to you before?" I asked, half teasing.

He made a face. "Until my mother died, all our people bowed to me," he said a bit sourly. "I was hoping for something more like words of wisdom on Jakium's proposal."

"I don't know, Beau," Mick said. "It seems too...easy? Plus, being sorry for your actions doesn't absolve you from them."

"No, but helping atone for them certainly helps," I pointed out. "Sorin and Vladimir are very different people. In a weird way, he did save my life while we were in jail."

"And Jakium isn't necessarily advocating for his freedom, just his life," Beau said.

"We can wait and see what Colin and the others who work directly with him in Oakbridge have to say in the end."

"Which reminds me," Beau said and our conversation shifted to who to send in the second batch. Beau was hoping it might be some of our core group. Still, I couldn't help thinking about Jakium's proposal in the following days. Sorin Dakamar certainly had depths I didn't understand, but was it enough?

Sorin could feel Colin Lockholme's burning curiosity on the ride back to Oakbridge, but he ignored it for the first afternoon of riding. But they had an evening to spend anonymously at an inn and it became harder to ignore his stare. It wasn't a rude stare, or even a particularly digging one, but mostly Colin sizing him and finding his ability to read Sorin sadly lacking. In a way, Sorin was glad he still retained the ability to be a little undecipherable, but at the same time, he'd stepped in far too deep now to pull back. So, as they sat at a private corner table and ate, Sorin looked up and met Colin's calculating gaze squarely. "Yes?"

Colin grinned crookedly. "I didn't say anything."

"You don't need to. Your persistence rivals Ani's, only hers is much louder. So what do you want to know?"

"Why are you doing this?"

"I told you."

"You told us generic reasons. Guilt and wrong feelings. But it's more personal than that."

"Why do you say that?" he asked.

"I have talked to a lot of people since leaving Greensward. People who are fighting this for a personal reason have a look. Most of the Freedom Fighters have it. You have it."

"I want to protect Ani."

"You've already said that."

Sorin felt a flash of amusement. "Is that not personal enough? She's my little sister. Surely you understand that."

"I think if I tried to protect Ja-Jez at this point, she would protect herself anyway and then kick my ass."

"But the instinct is there."

"Well, yeah, now that I know she's alive. I also feel the same way about my brothers."

Sorin saw it as the hook it was meant to be. After only a second of contemplation, he took the bait. "I no longer do," he said honestly. "Vladimir has gone too far. He went too far a long time ago."

"So did you, then. What's changed?"

Sorin stared at him and took his final bite of dinner as he debated. "Ani also joined in," he said finally.

"Everyone who has paid any real attention to all this knows that she's never killed anyone or been anything but a pawn. The plan all along was clearly to marry her and the prince off, just without the expectation that they would fall for each other."

Sorin raised his eyebrows, even as his internal estimation of Colin ticked up a bit. Godsdamn but the Lockholmes bred them smart. It was probably a very good thing the older three Lockholme children had not gotten involved in this conflict. "You really have been paying attention."

Colin smiled and shrugged. "You notice a lot when your life and the lives of a lot of others rely on you. And your avoidance only gives credence to my theory."

Sorin let a small smile of his own slip out. "There's a theory?"

"Work in progress. It hasn't been that long since you decided to make an unscheduled visit to my parents' house and I could start working on the whys. And I will admit, I wasn't fully expecting you to be expecting *us*."

"But there's still one."

"Of course. I have a reputation to uphold."

"What is it?"

Colin pushed his empty plate aside, planting his elbows on the table and dropping his chin on his fists. There was something deeply casual and easy about it. Sorin envied it a little. "There have clearly been two catalysts for your involvement. The second was watching your sister and the prince."

"I said as much, so that's not much of a theory."

He grinned, unoffended. "I know, that has to do with the first part. The one that got you into this with your brother." The grin slid away and it was his turn to hold Sorin's gaze evenly. Sorin's heart skipped a beat and he had no idea what Colin's next words might be. Even with the sudden sensation that perhaps Colin's 'theory' wasn't so much theory as somehow, impossibly, the truth, the young man's next words still shocked him. "Your father-in-law died last month and your mother-in-law is not well."

His muscles seized. Cedric was dead? Anna sick? How did *Colin Lockholme* know that when he didn't? How was that even remotely possible? Oh gods. "How?" he managed after far too long of a silence. Surely, somehow, Beau and the others couldn't know. If they had known, they would have known that the best possible blackmail material was out there.

Colin let out a breath that was half laughter. "I've had to get really fucking good at my job very quickly, Sorin."

"How?" he repeated.

"I started digging after the three of you chased us from Northwind. We hadn't yet hooked up with the Freedom Fighters, but I couldn't just sit still in Bejen and keep my head down. So I figured I'd see if I couldn't determine out where you'd all come from, since no one seemed to really know. I thought too, that if I ever needed leverage for anyone, you or the Freedom Fighters, it would give me a powerful starting point. I'd hold the cards, because it was clear a lot of your past had been purposefully buried. Asking around in Alexandria was a tricky proposition. The family business is still going strong and, at that point, the locals were still pretty fiercely loyal to you as a family. After all, the entire town relied on your operations. So I got a job under an alias and, as soon as I was part of the group, I started to hear more. I didn't need too much, but I got the gist of your childhood and your exodus and mostly staying out of family affairs until after Edward Opalin's accidental death. It wasn't pretty but it wasn't anything that I couldn't have figured out a myriad of ways, so I looked at the three of you. Anica was an open book. She'd never officially worked for the business but had always been around and had become a sort of foster mother to Jakium after he moved into the house and none of her time was ever not accounted for. Your brother could have any number of extra skeletons because he was often out of town on business, but from what I could gather, he was a workaholic and serial dater who dropped his significant others as soon as things smelled serious."

Sorin listened through the shock, taking the words in for later absorption. "And me?"

"You disappeared," Colin said, shaking his head in a clearly admiring way. "It was not easy to trace your actions and, by then, we'd hooked up with the Freedom Fighters and there were a lot of other things vying for my time. To be honest, I stumbled upon your marriage almost completely by accident. I was in Holbeck because I'd managed to follow you that far but people were very close-mouthed. The first of the really bad things, the beyond-killing-the-king things, had started to filter out and no one wanted to claim a relationship with any of you without fear of some sort of retribution coming down on them. But I finally got a lead at a bar, late one evening when I was told to look at the public records." He shrugged. "It was easy from there."

"Who knows?"

"Me."

"Benton Walters?"

"Just me," he said calmly and spread his arms, hands palm up and unthreatening.

"Why?" Sorin couldn't understand. He had the ultimate leverage, information that so very, *very* few people had and yet...he hadn't used it? Why? It made no tactical sense and Colin had proved himself a brilliant tactician, just like his father. "And why tell me now? What do you want?"

"Have you had any contact with them since you dropped your son off?"

"No, of course not," Sorin said immediately, because he thought about it every single day and had to convince himself that he could not, no matter what. "It's too dangerous for him."

"If Anna dies, he becomes a ward of the state."

"What do you *want?*" Maybe it did make tactical sense. Colin could still blackmail him to ensure he stuck to his end of the deal. Why else would he tell him?

"I would never hurt a child. Not for any reason, I swear it on my family's lives. I'm telling you this because I want to trust you. And I think I can. Between being a father and the fact you clearly have broken through to remember that the world did not end when your wife died, thanks to your sister and the prince." He shrugged. "But trust goes both ways and I know it might seem like blackmail but I wanted you to know that I've kept your secret. Even though if I had said something to Beau when I first stumbled upon the information, I could have probably ended this entire conflict that much earlier. But using a child in that way, a boy who is barely old enough to go to school, that is a moral line I refuse to cross, even though we never would actually hurt him." Colin seemed to drip sincerity.

Sorin stared at him. Even now, out of the hole he'd lived in for so long, sometimes he forgot to see that level of gray. Colin had not used such powerful blackmail merely because it would have broken his moral code. Sorin let out a laugh that was more sob than anything and buried his face in his hands, struggling to hold it together. What had they *done?* What had Edward turned them into, despite the fact Sorin had been so damned convinced he'd gotten free the day he'd walked out of that house? When he had forced the tears back, he looked up at Colin. "Thank you."

Colin didn't downplay the thanks. "No matter how this turns out, I promise that Dean will be okay."

"I don't deserve that," he said quietly.

"Maybe, maybe not, but that little boy certainly does. No one gets to pick their parents, do they?"

"No, definitely not."

"What are you going to tell your sister when we get back?" Colin asked.

"I don't know. Lying to Vladimir will be easy enough. He's distracted and more Edward than Vlad now. But, even at my lowest, I never lied to Ani."

"Then don't."

"It's not that simple," he protested, but had to wonder if maybe it was.

"Why not?"

Sorin stared at him. "Colin, either we're going to become best friends or I'm going to strangle you very soon."

He burst out laughing. "Ben said something similar once and I'm still alive." He shrugged easily. "You have two options as I see it. Tell your sister just enough of the truth that she knows where Jakium is and won't ask further questions. Or tell her the whole truth. You clearly trust her enough that you're sure she won't go running to your brother."

"No, she definitely wouldn't. She noticed Vladimir's slide before I did. Maybe long before. I don't know, she doesn't really talk about the years at the house in Alexandria after I left."

"So then you just need to decide what your moral compass is good with."

Sorin let out a bark of laughter. "Colin, my moral compass has never been properly aligned."

"In this case, that's not the important part. It's clearly got *some* alignment or we wouldn't be here right now. So use that."

He ran a hand over his face tiredly. "It's going to be friends, I guess. I don't have the energy to fight your damned logic."

"You're welcome," Colin said, with just a hint of smugness.

"Not that you'd want to be friends with me."

"You might be surprised. I like to think my judgment of people is based on their whole self, not just one part or one section of their life. Plus, I have some ideas for our future," he said mildly.

"*Our* future?"

"Let's get Tira back in its rightful hands, then we'll talk."

"You say that like you assume I'll still be alive after Tira gets back to its rightful hands," Sorin said. "You're the one who promised me Dean would always be safe."

"That's a 'just in case' only," Colin said. "Trust me. You really don't think Jakium will advocate for you?"

"Why would," he started then stopped, frowning. Gods damn Jakium. Of course the idiot would advocate for him. He sighed. "I shouldn't survive this, Colin."

"Maybe, maybe not," he said again, "but let's concentrate on one thing at a time. C'mon, I'd like to be on the road early tomorrow." He stood, dropping some coins on the table, enough to pay for the whole meal.

Sorin stared as the last coin rolled to a stop with a clink against his plate. "Okay," he said and pushed himself back from the table.

The rest of the trip to Oakbridge passed in relative silence. As they began the last approach into Oakbridge, Colin reined his horse in. "Do you know the inn The Caroling Son?" he asked.

"It's about two blocks down the main street out of the castle."

"I'll meet you out back, at noon, in two days. Send a rescheduling message through the Son if something comes up and you need to postpone. I'll have someone with me who can act as an anonymous go-between."

Sorin shifted in his saddle and offered his hand. "It's almost done."

"Almost," Colin agreed, taking it.

"Two days." Then he spurred his horse on to the capital alone.

Chapter Thirty-nine

DESPITE HAVING FOUGHT TO GO with Colin and Sorin, I didn't fight to be in the first group sent from Cavern Hall to Oakbridge. I was enjoying the relative downtime after the turbulent months in Greensward and, from Colin's messages, I didn't have to fear for his safety. Beau ended up sending Kira and Bri with the first group and, from all accounts, the infiltration went off without a hitch. Colin had set Sorin up with an Oakbridge friend of his, the aforementioned Russell Darcy. Russ now had an official job at the castle infirmary, where it would not seem at all strange for him to talk to Sorin.

During the rest of March and early April, Beau shifted two more small groups into Oakbridge, messages flying between us and the capital daily. Russell, Colin, and Sorin had almost worked out a fairly foolproof way to get the Freedom Fighters inside the castle. Once that was set, I volunteered for the last group. As soon as I had, Jay did too, citing the fact he was my trusty bodyguard and would not bear to be separated from me. Stella rolled her eyes but looked a little regretful as she said she had to stay with Dave. Ry and Jessie also chose to stay behind, this time because they would be in charge of one of the groups that came from Cavern Hall on the day of the attack.

The ten of us going in were given our various cover stories and were ready to set off the following morning. With a word to Mick, I stole Beau for the late afternoon, while we still had a bit of daylight. We made our way outside, despite the lingering winter chill, because it was the only place we could really find privacy. It took a little searching to find a rock that wasn't damp from the spring rains and we sat side by side, leaning into each other.

"It won't be long this time," Beau said after a few minutes. His breath felt warm on my hair.

"I know. And then it'll be all over." That assumed that we won and, in winning, neither of us died. Despite the extra help that having Sorin on our side gave us, it was by no means a guarantee that any of us would make it through this alive.

"And everything will change," he murmured.

I sat back a little to look him in the eye. "But hey, you won't have to be king since your brother is still alive."

"Yes, thank the gods for small favors," Beau said with a crooked smile. "I sincerely doubt I'm cut out for kingship. I think I'm probably barely cut out to be a prince."

I patted his cheek lightly. "Beau, honey, you already are one of the best princes this country has ever seen. Look at everything you've done for Tira. *Your* determination is why we're this close to taking Tira back. Without you, the Freedom Fighters would not exist."

"Someone else could have and would have done it," he said, almost dismissively.

I raised my eyebrows at him. "Beau Highcastle, don't you dare ever sell yourself short to me. Eventually, perhaps the ragtags would have condensed into something that would pass as a rebellion, but without your leadership, skills, and background, it would not have happened for a lot longer and I, for one, would be dead in a ravine between Ellworth and Lockholme."

"So shut up?" he said dryly.

I grinned. "I do think this means you owe me a kiss," I agreed and laughed as he pulled me forward and our lips met. "Apology accepted," I told him breathlessly minutes later.

"I solemnly swear I will not say such things again."

"Even better. Now, I don't want any more serious conversation tonight. There will be plenty of that as we start putting Tira back together once it's ours again."

"I don't like that we won't be together for all of the battle," he said.

"Aw, I can take care of myself, good sir."

He tickled me in the side, smirking as I squirmed and swatted his hand away. "That's not what I meant and you know it."

"You only meant it that way a little bit," I said, holding up my fingers about an inch apart.

"Well, I'd feel better if I was the one watching your back, that's all. And if you were the one watching mine," he said honestly. "There's no one I trust more in the world."

I knew he trusted Mick equally. The two were bonded and had been since Beau was a tiny child, but Mick wouldn't be with him either – which made me nervous because it meant Beau's back might actually not be adequately watched. I would have to speak to Dunkin before I left. Mick was leading the third attack party.

"You're going to make me blush."

"Is that possible?"

"Bri and Jay have both managed it."

He waved his hand. "Bri and Jay have special magical powers that way. It transcends normal people. They don't count."

I chuckled. "Probably true. They do know how to push."

"And we love them for it," he intoned dryly.

"Sometimes. I'll be fine anyway, Beau. I'll have Jay, Bri, Kira, and Colin to watch my back. I'm far more concerned about yours."

"I'll make sure it's covered."

"Take Dunkin and his buddies in your group?"

"If you insist, honey."

I grinned. "I do, sweetie." Then I leaned into his steady chest and took a deep breath. "I love you, Beau."

"I love you too. Although I'd understand if you ran for it once we're in Oakbridge."

I immediately sat back up, feeling more than a little offended. "What?"

"Well, I'm going to be an official prince once we're there. There's a lot of work and responsibility that comes with that."

"Are you saying that I can't handle work and responsibility?" I asked dangerously.

"You'll be a princess," he countered.

That did actually stop me. "Oh. Oh. Well. Shit."

He clearly couldn't help himself and burst out laughing. "Yes, shit."

"That's...crap, why did I fall in love with you again?"

"I'm offering an out," he said a little tentatively.

"Oh, don't be a moron," I told him.

"You didn't know I was a prince when this started."

"I'm not a moron either," I told him. "I don't like you because you're a prince, obviously, and I'm not going to run away because you are one. You're far too important to me for that."

He visibly relaxed. Idiot. "Okay, I wanted to make sure you knew what you're getting into."

"Do you know what you're getting into? It's not like you've been an official 'everyone knows me' prince before."

He paused. "Good point. I guess we will figure it out together."

"That's the best kind of figuring it out."

He smiled. "Yeah, I think I like that."

"I'll miss you in the meantime," I said honestly.

"I'll always miss you, but I feel a little more confident this time that you will not get yourself caught."

"Cross my heart, hope to die," I said. "Colin will keep me safe." And, if the gods forbid something *did* happen, I could only hope that somehow Sorin could help me. "And you'll have Ben, Jessie, and Ry here with you."

"And our friend Jakium."

"What are you going to do with him when the battle happens?"

"Not sure yet. I suppose that will rely heavily on him," Beau said. "I will probably leave him here with Iris and those who can't fight. I trust him enough now that I don't think he'd come after them and there will be enough guards that he wouldn't stand a chance if he tried it."

"No, I trust him not to do something like that too. He seems like a nice guy whose loyalties just fell on the other side. As if he would have been as loyal to you or Renier if things had played out a little differently."

Beau nodded. "That seems so. He also has a very definite soft spot for our friend Ry."

601

I smirked. "I'm glad I'm not the only one who has noticed. I'm also glad that neither Dall has, or that, if they have, their respective girlfriends are keeping them quiet. I could actually see them working, if they both decided to try."

He pressed his lips together thoughtfully. "What do you think I should do about Sorin?"

Hearing the man's name on Beau's lips made me fully realize that he'd gone from being 'Dakamar' to 'Sorin' to all of us, thanks mostly to Jakium's influence but also Colin's reports. "I don't know. Maybe we let the chips fall as they may and, if he's still alive after the battle, then we decide. See what Renier says. I think Colin has plans." He'd written me a couple letters separate from the reports and he was downright gleeful about something he was plotting even if he was being evasive on the details. I hoped I could pin him down once I got to Oakbridge myself.

He nodded. "I think that's the best decision. Maybe if he survives the battle, he deserves to live."

"Stranger things," I agreed and then shivered. "C'mon, as much as I hate it, the sun's going down and we're going to lose our warmth."

He stood and offered his hand, pulling me to my feet. "I never lose my warmth," he said solemnly, eyes twinkling.

I laughed.

The ride to Oakbridge was uneventful. For most of the trip, the ten of us rode together, but once we got to the edges of the more frequent buildings and inns that marked the final approach into the capital, we split, heading in small groups for the three main gates of the city. Jay and I had decided we wouldn't go to the same gate. I had put my hair under my hat and would be passing for a young man but we still thought the pair of us ran the risk of being identified together. I did miss my partner-in-crime as myself and one other Freedom Fighter approached the gate. Our papers were scrutinized quite a bit, but Colin's information did not let us down and the guards finally waved us through.

Trying not to look as relieved as I felt, I steered my horse down the side streets to the safehouse where half of us – Jay included – would gather for further instructions. We left our horses at an inn with a stable down the street and made our way the rest of the way on foot. I knocked the right rhythm, the door swung open, and I was pulled into a tight hug. "You being alive has not gotten old yet," my brother said cheerfully.

I returned it, glad to see him. "I like to hope that me being alive will never get old," I told him, as dry as he was cheerful.

"Maybe not, but you'll get old!"

"You'll get old sooner," I told him and pushed him back so we could get in the door and shut it behind us. "In case you two didn't meet when Colin was at Cavern Hall, Colin, this is Matthew. Matthew, my brother, Colin."

"I'd gathered that," Matthew said and shook Colin's hand.

"You're the first. Russ is in the kitchen if you want to go in and say hi," my brother said.

"I bet he'll be less rude to me," I said with a smirk and trotted off in that direction before my brother could come up with a suitable retort. Matthew stayed behind to wait with Colin for the others. It took a minute to find the kitchen and I poked my head in. A man about my age with dark shaggy hair was puttering around, putting together a plate of snacks, which my stomach appreciated. We hadn't eaten since breakfast and it was now a little after lunch. "Can I help with anything?"

He looked up and smiled. "Hi, you must be Jez."

I entered and offered my hand. "Nice to meet you. Colin's spoken highly of you in his letters."

"He'd better," Russell said mildly. "There are plates in that cupboard, if you'd get them down."

I moved to do as ordered. "Colin said you're working up at the castle now?"

"Yes. Sorin arranged for me to bypass most of the hiring process quietly. I have a split shift today. Worked early this morning and need to be back a little before dinner until fairly late. I should see him after dinner."

"And he's been fine?"

"He's been a fountain of information. Anything we want, he's happy to provide and then some," he said. "He's clearly decided if he's going to go against his brother, he's not going to hold anything back."

That corresponded with Colin's messages and somehow didn't surprise me. We'd all come to the realization that if he hadn't been serious about this, he would have never gone to Lockholme in the first place.

"Glad to hear it. I think we're all ready for this to be over."

Russell smiled a little. "It won't really be over once we displace them. You realize that, right?"

I set the plates down. "Well, no, of course not. But *this* part will be over." I heard a knock echo down the hall. "You've spent some time with Sorin now. What do you think about his future?"

He grinned. "Ask your brother that question. Far be it for me to intervene in Colin's plots."

"So my theory was right."

"If your theory involves Colin most likely recruiting Sorin when this is over, then yes, definitely."

I shook my head. "At least Colin's staying busy."

Russell blinked and then burst out laughing. "Is that what your family calls this?"

I had to grin too. "And my friends. It's a way of life."

He shook his head. "Clearly."

We were then interrupted by Colin, Jay, Matthew, and our remaining two Freedom Fighters as they entered the kitchen.

"Jezzy!" Jay cried, like he hadn't seen me just a couple hours before. Thankfully he didn't fully throw himself on me, like he had a habit of doing. I gave him a tight squeeze, just to show I was happy he had made it through the guards safely before patting him on the head.

"Down, Jamesy."

He stepped back, grinning. I saw his intention a second before he acted on it and groaned as he threw himself on Russell in much the same manner. "Russell! Hi! Nice to meet you!"

I knew I shouldn't laugh, and yet. Poor Russell was clearly taken aback as he patted Jay awkwardly on the back. "Um, hello?"

"Russ, you've met Jez and this is Jay." Colin did the rest of the introductions. "And everyone, this is Russell Darcy, but he goes by Russ. He's our secret weapon in the castle."

"Were you ever at Cavern Hall?" Jay asked, having politely detached himself from Russ. "You don't seem familiar."

"No, I've been in Oakbridge since before the death of the king," Russ said.

"Russ was an accidental recruit," Colin said and grinned at him. "He's worked at one of the local infirmaries for a while and we met there. I got the vibe he might be receptive so we planned a chat and I dragged him in."

"Why do I have a feeling you have a lot of allies in infirmaries?" I asked dryly.

"Your skepticism hurts me deeply, Jez."

"But is probably not unfounded," Russ said, just as dryly as me.

Jay held up his hand for a high five and Russ returned it after only a moment's pause.

Colin sighed loudly. "Would you all like something to eat?"

"Adopting Beau's habit of talking over us to change the topic is not going to work any better for you," I said but began handing out plates as Russ set the large tray on the table within our reach.

My brother stuck his tongue out at me.

Despite both of us, talk did move to business as we made short work of the fare. Colin gave our three companions their assignments and said that he and Russ would give us all a quick, essential tour of Oakbridge before seeing them off. Jay and I would be staying with Colin, Bri, and Kira even if we'd have to be careful about going in and out. Colin said the building had multiple entrances and multiple apartments so he wasn't too worried about surveillance. At this point, I was willing to take Colin's word on anything covert.

After our tour, Russ had to return to his apartment and then head back to work so we went to see Bri and Kira. Bri's greeting was even more effusive than Jay's, but at least he had reason. We hadn't seen him in over a month. I might have held on an extra minute, just glad to feel his solid form and reassure myself that he wasn't dead.

"I haven't been dead all month, promise," he said cheerfully, ruffling my hair.

I punched him in the arm. "How's Oakbridge been treating you two?" I asked as I turned to hug Kira.

"Great, actually. And Colin's made a decent roommate. I can see why my brother was able to handle him." She grinned past me to Colin as Jay threw himself into Bri's arms – not surprisingly, Bri caught him with ease. "Did you know that Colin and I initially did not get along at all?"

That actually surprised me. Neither had mentioned that previously and they had seemed to have a good relationship the little bit of time I'd spent with both of them. "Really?"

"Oh yeah. She *hated* me," Colin said. "But never for letting her parents down, which always confused the crap out of me."

Kira smiled slightly. "Colin," she started.

He held up his hands. "I know, I know, it wasn't my responsibility and I did the best I could. I know. Still wish I could have saved them too, that's all."

"So why didn't you like him?"

Kira actually reddened. "To be honest, I wasn't used to not being my brother's best friend. I mean, he was also really cocky and annoying at first, but mostly the first part."

"She was jealous," Jay said in a stage whisper, slinging an arm around my shoulders.

"Thank you, James," Kira said dryly.

It made me smile. She was certainly Bri's match and that translated, obviously, to Jay as well.

Jay grinned widely at her. "You're welcome!"

"Let's fill you both in on your jobs while we're here and then we can go grab some drinks and dinner," Kira suggested.

"Good idea," Colin said and led us into a dining room, which was clearly not used for eating, as the table was covered in paper and maps of both Tira and the city of Oakbridge specifically. We spent the next hour or two going over our jobs and then went to a nearby inn, called the Caroling Son, and had drinks and a very delicious dinner. The barkeep clearly knew all three of them and kept up a cheerful banter when she delivered our drinks and food. Colin didn't introduce us and, when I asked later, he explained that she knew full well who they were but, in a public setting, he didn't want to say things where prying ears might hear.

The next two weeks passed in a flash. We scouted various venues, met with locals, watched soldier movements, and a variety of smaller jobs – like moving weapons to certain safehouses – and the like. We saw Russ at least once a day when he stopped by to report on movement in the castle and whatever Sorin said. None of the rest of us saw Sorin ourselves, but Colin did tell us that he left the castle rarely so it was actually safer if he didn't start making frequent trips out for a reason no one knew. I saw the logic but found myself staring up at the castle thoughtfully whenever we were within sight of it. Not only was it my future home – which was strange enough – but there was so much going on in there at any given moment and so much of it was the same sort of activities that would continue after we took it back. After all, a lot of the minutiae of running a country would not change.

After the first week, word came to us from Sorin that he and Renier – Russ told us that Sorin called him Ren – had decided that Anica was safest not at the castle when everything went crazy, just in case a Freedom Fighter not in the know accidentally killed her. They arranged for Colin to meet her and get her settled somewhere safe. So my brother disappeared for the better part of the second week. We all knew our jobs, though, and collected reports as needed.

A couple days after Colin's return to Oakbridge, the six of us – including Russ – gathered in the dining room around the maps and paperwork. Colin had been changing the subject any time any of us asked about Anica, but he constantly looked terribly proud of himself so I figured he'd done a good enough job of hiding her. He looked down at all the papers and then up at us and grinned. "Anyone else notice something?"

"You've called a meeting like you're actually important?" Jay asked mildly.

"Ha ha," Colin said and then pointed at a large chart on the wall. Most of the items there were crossed out. "We're done. Or, done with everything that needs any sort of time, the non-last minute things."

I had noticed but assumed it was not the complete list. It dawned on me abruptly. "Are you saying that we're *done?*"

"Now, Jez, my darling sister, that is-"

"Shut up, you know what I mean."

He grinned. "It's time to send our illustrious leader a message telling him it's go time."

Kira whistled quietly.

"Go time," Bri repeated softly.

"What do you need us to do for the last couple days?" Russ asked.

"That is why I've made a new list," Colin said cheerfully and held up a much smaller and shorter one. Then he went over it, assigning each of us tasks. Russ's list was the longest but at the same time, none were particularly hard given his work environment.

Somehow the next couple days went by in even more of a blur than the previous two weeks. And then there was Stella walking into the Caroling Son to meet us. All of us acted nonchalant despite Jay's obvious desire to do anything. She settled at our table and grinned, although there was tension in her expression. "They're ready. Tomorrow morning, at the dawn watch change."

Jay took her hand and squeezed it.

Colin grinned. "Perfect. Russ?"

"I'm ready. I told you that yesterday. I'll head up there tonight and get a message to our friend."

"The rest of you?"

"Ready," we reported and my stomach fluttered.

The time that followed his visit to Lockholme might well have qualified as the strangest in Sorin's life and that was saying something. He worried constantly about Dean and his mother-in-law's failing health, along with his inability to do anything about it. He worried about Ani, as usual, and the fact she was caught in the middle of this entire mess and that would not change, even with Beau Highcastle's promise. He worried about Vladimir and the long-ago events that had driven him to the point he was at now and whether he, Sorin, was doing the right thing in turning against him.

But he stuck to his promise. Vladimir, in his better days, certainly would have agreed that Ani's safety was paramount to either of theirs. It had always been their rule growing up. Two days after arriving home, with Vladimir safely off on another wild goose chase – the humor of the Freedom Fighters coming to him when Vladimir was trying so hard to find them was not lost on Sorin – he quietly slipped out of the castle and down to the Caroling Son to meet with Colin and his anonymous friend.

Neither were there when he arrived, but that didn't surprise him. Colin would be making damn sure Sorin didn't bring any surprises with him. He waited almost ten minutes before Colin slipped out of a side alley, accompanied by a man a little younger, with very dark wavy hair and a pair of solemn eyes that had clearly seen more than they liked to admit. Sorin knew the look well and wondered if Colin could see it, if that was why Colin had picked this young man.

Colin stepped forward, offering his hand with a smile. "Sorin."

"Colin," he replied.

"Sorin, this is Russell Darcy. Russ, Sorin Dakamar."

Russell's expression was wary but not closed. "Mr. Dakamar."

"Mr. Darcy."

"Russ has been working at one of the Oakbridge infirmaries for a couple years now," Colin said. "I was hoping we might be able to get him a job in the castle, to make correspondence easy."

Sorin sized him up freshly and then shot a series of detailed questions about various injuries and illnesses at him.

After an initial look of surprise, Russ responded quickly and accurately, only getting one wrong and, in all fairness, it was a pretty obscure illness.

"And you don't mind starting pretty low?"

Russ smiled slightly. "I'm not in it for the job. Medical work was...never my end goal."

"Working for Colin was?"

"No, and I'm still not sure it is long term, but I believe in what they're fighting for."

A step behind him, Colin nodded solemnly. Clearly, he wasn't going to let Russ leave easily.

"Then we're in agreement," Sorin said. "Can you come up to the castle tomorrow? I'll let the guards know to let you in and we'll introduce you to everyone. You clearly have learned a thing or two while working in the city so no one will question your ability to do the job. I think it'll be a nice fit and I'm down there fairly often anyway."

"You clearly have knowledge on the topic as well."

"The initial learning was of necessity but I found myself fascinated with the entire concept. To be honest, it might have been my end goal, had things gone differently."

"What time tomorrow?"

"I'm an early riser, so you choose a time."

"Nine?"

"I'll meet you at the infirmary at nine," he agreed.

"Awesome!" Colin said, beaming.

The next day, Russ pretty much got the job of his own accord. If the head doctor thought it weird that Sorin was backing a young person from the city as a potential infirmary worker, he said nothing of it to Sorin or, more importantly, to Vladimir. Russ fit quietly into the infirmary's flow and did a good job. The head doctor had nothing but praise for him after the first couple days and appreciated the extra set of hands.

Sorin stopped by daily and no one seemed to notice that he talked to Russ for longer or more quietly than he spoke to the rest of the staff. Every time, Russ had new questions about things Colin wanted to know and Sorin answered them to the best of his ability, working on finding the answer the next day if he didn't know it immediately. Sorin had to be losing his touch because it took almost two weeks to realize that some of Russ's questions came from general curiosity and not Colin's need to know. When it hit him, they were in the middle of a conversation and he stopped dead, staring at Russ. "Colin doesn't need to know that."

Russ smiled and shrugged. "Maybe I'm just interested at this point."

"In me?"

"That really shouldn't surprise you," he said, but Sorin found that it did. He didn't consider himself particularly interesting and never had.

He shrugged.

"Oh come on," Russ said, sounding amused.

"I'm really not that interesting, despite how everything has played out."

"Okay, then just flat out mysterious."

"That I'll accept," he said with a small smile. "What has Colin told you?"

"He did ask me to pass you a message today, which I don't think is good news."

Sorin was instantly on alert. "What is it?"

"He said to tell you she doesn't have very long, but he's got things taken care of and will talk to you about it when you've got a chance."

He closed his eyes. Colin would make sure that Dean was okay and that was important, although, in a way, he'd miss Anna and already missed Cedric. His in-laws had been good people who hadn't deserved him as a son-in-law. Him or his family. At least Dean was safe from all that. "Thank you, Russ."

"I'm going to assume that means something to you."

"Yes. Tell Colin thanks and I owe him one."

"Of course, no problem," Russ said. "Need any other messages passed?"

"Not yet. I want to talk to Ani first."

"Sure. I'll see you tomorrow," Russ said with a smile.

Something about the way he said it struck Sorin and he realized the wariness that Russ had regarded him with at first had not just faded but completely disappeared. In fact, the smile seemed genuine, like he wanted to see him tomorrow.

"All right, tomorrow," Sorin said, not sure what to make of this weird new feeling of someone other than Ani being happy to see him. And a member of the *Freedom Fighters* no less. Trying not to dwell on it, he nodded sternly and quickly left.

He tried to ignore it from then on out but it was hard. Russ didn't just ask questions but also created conversation that had nothing to do with the troubles at hand, but Sorin didn't feel they were prying questions. A lot were about Ren and Ani and Sorin was happy to not talk about himself. He also found that he sometimes instinctively asked questions of Russ, but the other man dodged anything about his past with a mastery Sorin almost envied.

Then Russ told him that Anna had died and that Dean was safe somewhere. Not so obviously as that, Colin was certainly keeping his secret, but in a way that Sorin knew what he meant. So he finally screwed up his courage and went to find his sister. Not surprisingly, she was with Ren in their room. As he knocked and let them know it was him, he briefly debated trying to draw her elsewhere, but Ren knew about Diana and Sorin had checked the peep holes to make sure no one was spying on them, so he felt relatively safe talking about it. Still. He opened the door and poked his head in. "Hey, you two. Want to go for a walk?" he asked them both.

"Always," Ren said, hopping up and offering his hand to Ani, who took it, and they joined Sorin outside the room. He led them down to a fairly large balcony, where it would be easy to tell if they had listeners and went right to the edge. The pair joined him.

"What is it, Sorin?" Ani asked softly once they were there.

He smiled slightly. "How much have you told Ren about the time when I wasn't with you and Vladimir?"

"She told me you were married, that your wife died of an incurable disease, and that you came back to them after that and were a different person," Ren said.

"She didn't tell you about my son?"

"Your...son? No," he said, drawing out the last word.

611

"We found out Diana was sick, shortly after Dean was born. He's, well, he just turned six. Last week. Since shortly after Diana died, he's been living with my in-laws, Diana's parents. Except I've recently found out that first Cedric and now Anna have died."

Ani gasped quietly. "Where is Dean now?"

"I don't know. What I haven't told you yet is..." He had been putting off this entire conversation, still not sure how much to tell them, but with Dean's future at stake and with a small plan forming in his mind, he had to tell them. "My trip to Lockholme." He quickly filled them in on how things had gone and meeting Ren's brother and his contact with Colin now. "Colin knows. The man is a genius. He followed the trail and eventually discovered Dean's existence. He has safely hidden Dean where no one will know who he is and he's safe, but I can't let it go at that."

Ren held up his hands. "Wait, wait, slow down. That is a *lot* of information to throw at us all at once. You've met my brother?"

Sorin made himself take a deep breath. It *was* a lot of information and he had to let them absorb it enough that neither would make any mistakes with it. "Yes, I met Beau. He has a lot of Highcastle in him. There was certainly no mistaking him for anything but your relation. I've also met the youngest two Lockholmes and Colin has proven reliable and helpful. There is also a man, Russ, working in our infirmary who is a spy for the Freedom Fighters and he got his job thanks to me suggesting him."

"I've met him," Ani said with some surprise. "He seemed really nice."

"He is very nice. I speak to him at some point every day to answer questions and pass information along to the Freedom Fighters."

"Well, *shit*," Ren said, dragging a hand through his hair in some strange combination of agitation and being impressed by the entire thing.

"How did Colin find Dean?" Ani asked, patting Ren soothingly on the arm. She didn't seem the slightest bit surprised and Sorin hated, for just a short moment, how well she knew him. At the same time, though, he was reassured that he was doing the right thing.

He explained it again in more detail then continued, "I made the deal with Beau that Ren gets to decide your fate, Ani, and while I trust my brother-in-law will make the only logical decision-"

Ren looked downright offended. "Obviously."

"I think it would be better if you weren't here when the fighting happens," Sorin finished smoothly, raising an eyebrow at Ren.

"Don't insult my honor," Ren said, almost sulkily.

Ani kissed him on the cheek. "Down, Muffin," she said, amused, before turning back to Sorin. "I take it you want me to go to Dean."

"Yes, please. Through Russ, we can get you to Colin and he can get you to Dean. I'm sure Colin has him safe but…"

"He's already been without family long enough?" Ren said quietly.

Sorin pressed his lips together and nodded.

"Even if Dean didn't exist, I'd still agree with Sorin," Ren told Ani, squeezing her waist. "I'd rather have you far from the fighting. Although I trust you can take care of yourself, I don't trust some of the Freedom Fighters to make the distinction between you and someone they should fight. And if I can't be there to protect you…It would just be until the tide has changed for good."

"They might not want me back after that."

"I don't care. I will," Ren said firmly, cupping her cheek and turning her face to him. "Once the fighting is over, I will make sure you come home, here, with me, where you belong."

She smiled, brushing his hair from his forehead. "I know you will, Renny."

Sorin smiled too to cover the sudden ache in his chest. Most of the time, he didn't let himself miss Diana, but other times it wasn't something he could avoid.

"How soon should I go?" she asked Sorin.

"As soon as I can get everything arranged with Colin and we can make it look natural. We'll say we're sending you out on another secret mission." That's how they'd coded her last, ill-fated attempt to 'join' the Freedom Fighters.

"All right. I'll start packing," she said and sighed, leaning against Ren.

He squeezed her shoulder. "Thanks, Ani."

"You're keeping me safe and yet thanking me?"

"You know why."

Her smile softened. "I'll tell him all about you."

"You should, but then Sorin will be able to too," Ren said.

"I think there are better than even odds I won't make it," Sorin said, keeping his voice light. "So let's consider this a just in case."

Ren let out a low whistle. "Someone's been working on you. That's the most positive I've ever heard you."

"The Freedom Fighters seem to be rubbing off on him," Ani agreed solemnly.

He rolled his eyes. "Yes, you two are very cute."

"Of course we are," she chirped.

He tried to smother his smile with mixed results. "As soon as I've gotten things sorted with Colin, I'll let you know the timing," he said then looked at Ren. It had occurred to him that he might be able to get the prince out as well and he suspected the same had potentially occurred to Ren as well.

"I'm staying," he said simply. "This is *my* castle and I will not abandon it at any time."

"I was hoping you'd say that," he said and inclined his head, "Your Majesty."

Sorin waited to talk to Vladimir until after Ani had left, which took about three days to arrange and execute. He wanted her safely out of Vladimir's clutches, in case his brother got wise to anything, not that he expected him to.

He knocked on Vladimir's partially open door. "Vlad?"

His brother looked up. "Sorin," he said, with a clipped edge to the word. "What do you want?"

"Do I have to want anything?"

Vladimir's eyes narrowed. Clearly that had been the wrong thing to say. "It would seem not. You appear to be very willing to ignore me when you decree something."

It took Sorin a second. "Ani."

Vladimir had gone back to his paperwork with a fake focus.

"Do you have a problem with her being out of the castle?"

"She's not safe out there."

"She's safer there than she is here. Out there, she can be anyone."

"And if some Freedom Fighter recognizes her?"

That's when Colin truly proves his worth, Sorin thought. "If we lose, she will have a much greater chance of survival away from Oakbridge."

"We won't lose. And even if we did, what's left for her then? Presumably we would both be dead, Jakium too. That's her entire family."

"Except Ren," Sorin said, before he could really think better of it.

Vladimir shot right to his feet, clearly furious. "The prince," he bit out, "is *not* Anica's family."

"You counted Jakium and legally, he is far less family than Ren, now that he's an adult." Despite the fact he kept his words even and calm, deeply ingrained instincts screamed at him to run *now*.

If his brother could have struck him dead with looks alone, Sorin would have been flat on the floor. "How *dare* you," Vladimir hissed.

"You have no one else who would dare, so that leaves me," Sorin said flatly, clenching his fists at his sides. "Vlad, I didn't come here to fight."

"And yet you started one," Vladimir snapped.

That wasn't fair at all. He'd just stated the truth to Vladimir's delusions. Vladimir had always been the one who wanted Ren and Ani married. Sorin had not agreed until it had become clear to him that Ren at least liked Ani – even he hadn't predicted what their relationship would truly become. But these things were convenient to forget, clearly. "I just wanted to see how you're doing. It's been days since I'd last seen you." Mostly because Vladimir was rarely in Oakbridge.

"I'm fine," he minced out, still gripping his desk with white fingers.

"Good, I'm glad," Sorin said openly, even if he didn't believe it. "Do you need me to do anything? Are you going to be around a while? I heard that you ordered the garrison that's been going with you to stand down."

"They'll come to us," Vladimir said, gaze not focused on anything in the room. "They'll come to us and we'll crush them like the insignificant pests they are."

Once, Sorin would have argued that he needed to pay attention to the Freedom Fighters, that they were more of a danger than Vladimir let himself see, but that time was past. He had argued and lost and soon, it would be over.

"Vlad," he said quietly, seeing a fleeting weariness in his brother's face and hoping to use it as an opening.

"Get out," Vladimir growled.

Sorin couldn't stop his instincts this time, taking a step back. The weariness was gone in a flash, replaced by an almost feral look. Sorin made a note to check Ren's guard roster and make sure he put exactly the right people there to ensure the prince stayed safe. "Vlad?"

"Get out. Go do your job and let me do mine."

He took a slow breath and released it. "Very well. Let me know if I can do anything for you," he said then backed out of the room, not quite daring to take his eyes off his brother. Only once he'd pulled the door shut did he turn and hurry away.

So be it.

Chapter Forty

We knew that the rest of the Freedom Fighters would come from three directions – the front gates, which always stood open during daylight hours, and the two smaller auxiliary gates which weren't used as often and generally kept closed, unless there was a scheduled arrival. Individuals could get in and out via the gatehouse and a small single door there. We would need it open by the time our forces arrived. Colin had put himself in charge of assisting at the front gates, and had taken Stella among others for assistance. Jay and I were given the north gate, which was where Beau would be attacking. Bri and Kira, gods help us, were in charge of the southern gate. Despite warnings we wanted the gate intact, I had a feeling that might not be possible with Bri.

Jay and I had spent two days scouting our gate every free moment we had. Its usual complement was eight soldiers with two of those in the guardhouse and a further two outside of the walls. Two more watched the city from the ground, flanking the gate and the final two stood on the wall and watched the farmland that stretched away from Oakbridge.

In the hour before dawn, the morning of the attack, we had taken our usual vantage point to wait. Just before we knew the dawn watch change would occur, we heard the distinct hooting of an owl, from a little deeper into the city. I looked at Jay and nodded. We slid down out of the abandoned building and to the street, pressing close into the walls and keeping to the shadows as we crept closer, hands on our sword hilts.

When the change came, there were only six guards, as had been previously organized.

"What's going on?" one of the men from the guardhouse asked as he emerged.

"Higher ups said we've got other stuff to do today, so only a six man complement."

The first man, a sergeant from his uniform, frowned at the lesser ranked replacement. "I'll have two of mine stay while I go investigate."

I held my breath. Six men, especially with a surprise attack, Jay and I could take. More than that, and we'd need our back-up, including our friendly 'owl' but the quicker we could do this and keep it quiet, the better. Still, it wouldn't be the end of the world if two more stayed, especially since those two would be half-asleep.

Jay shifted and pointed. While I'd been pondering, the sergeant had gestured for two of his men to stay – neither looked the least bit happy – and was marching off with five other relieved men.

The replacement rolled his eyes. "Go take a load off in the guardhouse until Sergeant Wilkes is content with the orders. We've got the other six posts," he said. "You'd think with our bosses, he wouldn't bother questioning this stuff anymore." If only he knew.

"Thank you, sir," the two men who had been on watch all night said and disappeared into the guardhouse in double time. Two more, who would be posted outside, followed.

That was our signal. Now, before this Wilkes could throw a kink in the plans.

I nudged Jay with my elbow and he cupped his hands around his mouth and let out two long hoots. I began counting to twenty. That would give our back-up enough time to receive the message and be ready. While I counted, Jay unslung his bow from his shoulder and fit an arrow to it, holding it at ready by his side, watching me. Across the main road, somewhere out of sight but parallel to us, our support was doing the same. I palmed a small throwing knife. While my bow skills were still good, I was also better than Jay at knife throwing so I'd chosen to take one of the guard standing on the ground facing into the city, leaving the men on the wall as the target of others. As I reached five, Jay slid next to me. If the men looked right, they would be able to see him. A slow bit of movement in my peripheral vision told me his mirror was doing the same. I reached zero.

Jay drew back the string, sighted more accurately on the wall guard closest to us and let fly. At the same time, I raised my arm and threw. Then I raced forward. Depending on how accurate our various shots had been would determine how quickly we needed to get to those in the guardhouse. I saw almost immediately that my throw had been off. It hit the man, but on the wrong side of his chest. He reeled back but didn't go down. Still, by the time his brain had processed not only the pain but what had caused it, I'd reached him. I had another knife ready and I drove it at him.

He twisted, trying to avoid the blow as he fumbled to draw his sword. I almost felt sorry for him and his lack of smaller, more easily drawn weapon. This time my knife hit the mark. His eyes went wide and he gasped silently, looking surprised by the turn of events. Then I pulled my knife out, stepping back, and his body sagged against the wall to crumple in a heap.

Jay had reached me, bow slung back over his shoulder and knife drawn. To my right, an Oakbridge Freedom Fighter - recruited by my brother - finished off the other guard inside.

"Wall?" I asked Jay.

"Both dead," he reported as we turned together to the guardhouse, whose door stood only about two yards away.

Before we could reach it, though, one of the tired guards poked his head out. "What's," he began before Jay pounced.

This time, I really did feel sorry for the man. It was only his bad luck that he'd been chosen to stay behind and wasn't happily headed to bed back at the castle, where he might have only been taken captive and survived the upcoming - no, the current - battle for Oakbridge and all of Tira.

Jay caught him in the gut and sort of bearhugged him, pulling him from the open doorway. I darted around him, but paused before crossing into view of the remaining guard in the guardhouse. It was much darker in there than it was even in the early dawn light of the street. It turned out my hesitation worked in my favor, because the second man emerged a moment later. I thrust my knife into his gut and pulled, cutting him open. He dropped almost immediately, grasping at his stomach.

"We planned, so this should be easy, but why do I still feel weird about it?" Jay asked as we both paused for a second to catch our breath. We couldn't wait too long in case either Wilkes came back with possible reinforcements - it would depend on who he ran into first at the castle - or someone else spotted us and sent up an alarm.

To my surprise, it was Russ who answered. I hadn't even known that Russ was one of our assistants. My brother and I would have words next time I saw him. "Because it's rare plans go to form," he said dryly. "C'mon, we've still got two outside who might notice their buddies from above are no longer there. And for all we know, they have another way of sending up an alarm."

"Thanks for that positive thought," Jay muttered, but led the way into the guardhouse. Russ and I followed. The fourth Freedom Fighter, when I glanced at her, just said, "Isabelle."

I nodded acknowledgement.

At the far end of the small guardhouse, which was barely longer than the thick defensive wall itself, Jay placed his hand on the doorknob and opened it at an entirely normal pace, stepping outside as he did, drawn knife in his other hand. Only then did I realize he'd stolen one of the helmets from the soldiers we'd already killed. I could follow his reasoning - in the early morning air, he might gain crucial seconds before the two soldiers outside realized he was not otherwise dressed in the livery that had apparently been designed by Vladimir's father a long time ago, according to Sorin. I made a vague note to ask him about the symbolism on the uniforms if we got the chance.

Jay moved swiftly out of view, presumably towards the closest guard and I realized that the last one would have time to prepare so I burst out after him, bolting towards that last guard in an attempt to get to him before he was fully alert to the threat bearing down on him. Russ was right behind me but Isabelle stayed in the guardhouse. As Jay engaged the startled guard, the gate started to rise with a rumble of chains and wood and I realized why. The whole point of the plan was to get the gate open and hold it as our people reached it.

The guard I was after - the last damn one - reacted in good time, sword already drawn by the time I reached him. I offered a quick slash at his arm before having to dart back to avoid the longer reach of his sword. The man hesitated, clearly debating his best move.

Russ made the decision for him. "Jez, drop," he ordered crisply.

I did not hesitate, dropping straight to the ground. As I caught my weight smoothly, I heard a grunt and glanced up to see an arrow protruding out of the man's chest. It was buried deep due to proximity of the shot. I scrambled back to my feet. "Good thinking."

By then, Isabelle had gotten the gate open to my waist and Jay was already heading back in to help her.

"Thanks," he said and then pointed out away from the castle. "Looks like the troops are here."

I looked up too. Relief spread through me. "Thank the gods for that," I said and raised my hand in a wave, even as I squinted to see if I could spot Beau. Sure enough, my heart lifted further as I recognized the figure who came sprinting towards us. A moment later, Beau's arms were around me, hugging me tightly. "Hi," I managed, returning it fiercely, despite the bloody knife in my hand.

"You okay?"

I smiled and didn't bother to answer. He knew.

Our hug did not last nearly as long as I would have preferred, but we both knew we didn't have the time. So, we parted, Beau kissing me briefly on the cheek and smiling at Russ, which was my cue for introductions. I did so quickly, and we retreated to the guardhouse and I did the same with Isabelle. She nodded curtly as she and Jay focused on getting the gate fully up. As they did, two things happened: the rest of the group caught up and distant bells started in the city. Someone, somewhere, had caught on to the invasion. Fine by me. We'd known from the beginning that the element of surprise would only last as long as it took to get everyone in and had planned accordingly.

Beau quickly detailed four others to stay with Isabelle at the gate, leaving the local woman in charge. He then split the rest of us into smaller groups - each would take one of the roads stretching away from the gate, making it quicker for us to sweep the city. Each group had enough for two rows of Freedom Fighters to completely block the road. It took us a bit to encounter any resistance. The soldiers were disorganized and came in such small batches that they were no match for us. With Vladimir presumably hiding in the castle, his men didn't put up a good defense. But I couldn't help feeling impressed at how Sorin had called his brother's reaction. It would also hopefully cause the castle to be an easier fight. The Three's soldiers only fought through the first few casualties before surrendering. As much as I hated having to waste our people to watch them, none of us were killers without reason and it was strangely reassuring not to have to kill any more than absolutely necessary. We'd figure out what to do with the prisoners later.

Before I knew it, we had reached the main road. We looked towards the castle and could see the wall bristling with troops. "Not yet," I told Beau.

"We'll clear the city first," he agreed. We all knew Sorin couldn't make his move too early.

Oakbridge, as I'd discovered, was loosely grid-based, while the city walls formed approximately a circle. The castle sat on the eastern end of the city. The main street flowed straight from the castle's entry courtyard down to the gates from east to west. The road in from each of the side gates ran straight into the main street, but at two different points. The group with Bri and Jessie should come in on a street west of us. We'd come from the north. Beyond the basic cross that set up, there were smaller streets that ran both parallel and perpendicular to the main street, but many of the alleys and small roads were less than straight and some of the oldest parts of the city were a complete warren of alleys and dead ends. In many ways, clearing the city of opposition in a timely fashion was not something I was looking forward to.

Russ and Jay joined us, Jay wiping his sword on his pants irreverently. "What now?"

Our forces had spread out but were coalescing again now that we were at the main street so instead of answering directly, Beau raised his voice so everyone could hear him. Other than the continued ringing of a few bells and the fairly distant sounds of conflict, the city was quiet. No one was abroad on the streets, except the occasional darting form but none came close to us. Beau glanced towards the fighting but we all knew that unless there was an emergency, we were to stick to our jobs.

"All right, we're going to break into smaller groups. We'll spread out from here on our side of main street and clear out any opposition. Remember, civilians are off-limits. Any damage that's done to any building should be kept to a minimum. These are *our* people, the same as any of you here, so act responsibility." The split happened seamlessly and I realized Beau had prepared for this earlier to save time.

"And us?" I asked him, indicating myself, Jay, and Russ.

Beau offered a quick, crooked smile. "I might have saved room on my team. Good for it?"

"I'm just surprised you want me by your side in such a moment of triumph," Jay said with a loud and fake sniff. "I am truly honored. Although I am also aware you consider me chopped liver and really just did this so you would have an excuse to stick close to our lovely Jasmine."

"James," Beau and I growled, pretty much in concert.

He grinned. "Shall we?"

Beau sighed. Russ punched Jay in the shoulder, far more gently than I would have if I had been close enough.

"You're learning too fast," Jay whined at him even as Beau gestured to our group and headed back into the side streets. We encountered little resistance at first. Just the occasional pocket of soldiers who didn't even seem to be aware we were there. But, as we worked through the backstreets towards the castle, they got smarter. Or bolder.

The twenty or so of us in Beau's group had just turned a corner when a yell stopped us. Ahead, a group of approximately the same number of the Three's soldiers stood by a house. One held a knife to a small girl's throat while another stood by the door with a torch. All of the houses in these back roads were wooden and no doubt highly flammable.

"Come any closer and I'll kill the girl. Keep it up and we'll torch the house. It's got the rest of the family inside. Three generations," the soldier called.

We froze. Beau spread his hands slightly, without really lowering his sword. "You're losing," he said. "There's no need for innocents to be hurt."

"Hurting innocents is exactly how we can start winning," the man retorted.

"Russ?" Jay murmured behind me. His hand lightly touched my back then trailed down to where one of my throwing knives rested on my hip.

"If we hit the one with the torch, he'll drop it and we risk the family inside," Russ replied softly. He was further away from me.

"Then what do you want?" Beau said. I knew he could hear our compatriots but acted like he hadn't heard anything. I did my best to split my focus without seeming that way.

"Hit the torch?" Jay suggested.

"Stall them," Russ said. "I have an idea. You'll know when to act."

I felt a shift behind me, although Jay was still there, slowly pulling the knife from my belt. It was genius, actually, using me to block the soldiers' view of him while he got a weapon he could use, since his bow was slung over his shoulder and any attempts to use that would be far too obvious. "Russ?" I asked without moving my lips.

"Gone," Jay said.

I'd missed the soldier's response but could see Beau's frustration at the stand-off.

"I want you all to lay down your weapons and put your hands on your heads," the man ordered.

"This won't stop us. We're all over the city now."

The soldier's lip curled in a sneer. "You think I don't know who you and your friend are?" he asked. "You're the other Highcastle bastard and she's Jasmine. You'll be all the leverage we need to stop your friends."

"Actually," I said cheerfully, "by virtue of the fact he is a Highcastle he's not a bastard. But yes, I'm Jasmine."

The man scowled. "Put down your weapons."

The girl, maybe eight years old, stood very still in his grasp, staring at us with wide, dry eyes. I shot her what I hoped was a reassuring smile.

"Now," he added, pressing the dagger closer to the girl's throat.

"Okay, okay," Beau said. Jay had the knife free from my belt as Beau and I made a show of lowering our swords - very, very slowly - towards the ground.

The soldier grinned in triumph, not seeming to even care that we were both being ridiculously slow or that the others were being just as slow in drawing or lowering weapons. It really couldn't have been more obvious that we were stalling, but he somehow, gods be thanked, didn't see it.

As it turned out, there was absolutely no doubt about when to act. A large cascade of water - at least a good-sized bucket full - tumbled down on the man holding the torch, soaking him and putting out the flame. By the time the water hit, I spun aside, still clutching my sword, and Jay let the knife fly. It caught the man in the throat, mere inches above the little girl's head. Somehow, the child had the presence of mind to shove his hand away before he could slit her throat in his slide to death. Then she scrambled towards us. I scooped her up and out of the way of our charging fighters, holding her close as she shook, wrapping her arms around my neck tightly.

The two sides clashed and only then did the child let out a tiny screech of terror.

"It's all right," I told her. "It's all right now. We've got you." I backed further from the fray and bumped straight into a solid body near the mouth of the alley beside the threatened house. I jumped and spun, ready to somehow defend both of us, but Russ held up his hands.

"It's just me."

"Oh, thank the gods," I said. "Wasn't sure how I was going to fight like this."

He peered past me, sword drawn. "Looks like our folks have it covered."

I looked that way too and could tell the force of our attack had overwhelmed the soldiers and they were battling on their heels. "That was genius," I told him. "What made you think of it?"

He jerked a thumb over his shoulder. "Saw the pump down here and getting on the vast majority of roofs in Oakbridge is easy. I'm just glad I could do it in time."

"Us too. We couldn't have done it much longer."

"I'm sure you would have thought of something," he said.

I nodded. "Your family in that house?" I asked the little girl, not sure I'd get a response.

"Yes," she whispered.

"Any of them hurt?"

"My uncle tried to stop them."

"We'll get him taken care of."

Beau was coming our way, bloody sword in his grip. He thanked Russ, shaking his hand with more energy than necessary - Russ winced a little - then turned to the girl and me. "Let's get you back to your family," he told her gently.

When we reached the house, Jay was already talking to an older gentleman in the doorway, who was wringing my friend's hand with enthusiasm. A woman broke from them and raced over to take the girl from my arms. "Thank you," she said tearfully.

"Our pleasure," I told her, even if it occurred to me that their family wouldn't have even been in trouble if it hadn't been for us. At least it had ended well.

The older man had switched to shaking Beau's hand and Russ smirked at Beau's slight wince.

"Ann's in there treating the uncle. She said it didn't look serious and we'll be good to go in a couple minutes," Jay told me as he appeared at my side.

"Perfect."

The little girl picked up her head from where it was buried in her mother's shirt. "Thank you," she said shyly.

"You're welcome," I replied. "We weren't going to let him hurt you. You were incredibly brave."

"The soldiers are big bullies," she said with a little more confidence. "They like it when you cry so I told myself I couldn't."

I smiled. "After today, you won't have to worry about the soldiers anymore."

"Really?"

"Yes, we're here to get rid of them."

"Then the rumors are true?" her mother asked, eyes lighting. "We're really going to have a Highcastle back on the throne?"

My gaze darted to Beau. "That's the plan."

She beamed in pure relief. "Oh thank the gods. We've hoped this day might come since they announced that Prince Renier was still alive. Things have gotten so bad around here, it's all we can do to afford our house."

"We'll do our best to get things back to pre-Three as soon as possible."

She smiled. "Of course you will, dear, and we'll be patient." She freed a hand and offered it to me. "We appreciate everything you folks have done for those of us who weren't in the position to do the same."

"It's our deepest pleasure," I told her sincerely.

Her expression softened further. "Oh, I don't doubt that, but I also know to be where you are means you've sacrificed a lot and we won't forget that."

My cheeks warmed. "Thank you," I said quietly, just as I spotted Ann exit the house. She and Beau exchanged a few quick words then Beau patted the old man's hand.

"Time to move out!" he called.

The Three's soldiers had fought to the last man, so our people had spread out to protect in case of follow-up attack from another group. We fully regrouped and, with waves and well wishes from our side and the extended family, we headed further down the streets.

A little while later, as we headed back towards the main street to hopefully meet up with the rest of the Freedom Fighters, I fell in step with Beau. "Too few," I murmured.

He nodded grimly. "I'm hoping everyone else saw more fighting, but more likely the castle will be a bloodbath."

I did some quick math, taking the approximate number of soldiers we'd fought and tripling them before comparing the numbers to what Sorin said was stationed in Oakbridge. "Well, the garrison for the city is on the south side of Main. Vladimir shouldn't have had time to pull them back to the castle."

As I said this, we reached the street and instantly Nathaniel, Reardon's assistant, came rushing up. "Sir! We need help."

"The garrison?" Beau asked, giving me a look.

"Don't shoot the messenger," I muttered.

Nathaniel looked a little alarmed at that, not realizing I meant me, and hastened to explain. "Yes, sir. They've really dug in."

"Lead the way, Nathaniel," Beau said after stationing some of our troops to meet Colin and Mick.

Nathaniel took off at a jog, leading us through a winding path. The garrison, as it turned out, sat close to the castle - so close soldiers on the wall could lay down covering fire. Our men were a block or two back, keeping them as pinned down as possible but not actively engaging. I looked around for any of our group as Beau beelined after Nathaniel, heading for Reardon. Before I'd really even glanced about, I was hit with a hug that almost knocked me off my feet. "Where's Jay?" Bri demanded.

"Right here," his brother said, hugging Kira. "Why are you bleeding?"

"I'm not any more, duh," Bri said but pulled back to show off a large bandage peeking out from under his shirt along his shoulder. "I was aiming for a matching facial scar but the guy had poor aim."

I slugged him in the other arm as hard as I could. "*Not* funny."

He grinned, although it held a pained twinge much to my satisfaction. "You've thought all my other dead jokes were funny."

"When we all weren't potentially about to die," I protested.

"Hm, point."

"How do you stand him?" I asked Kira.

She shrugged. "Honestly, I have no idea. Are you two okay?"

"Just fine," I said, quickly filling her in. "You didn't get Jessie and Ry?"

"No, Dunkin and his crew. Jessie and Ry are apparently with Mick and your brother." That reminded me to speak to Beau about not following my advice and making sure someone was watching his back on the initial approach to the city.

"Are you hurt?" I asked her.

"No, but we've got a lot who are."

"Reardon's flagging us," Jay said.

As we reached them, Reardon spread his hands. "I don't know what to do. We can't get to them because of the archers."

"We've got another hour until Sorin's move and we need to be elsewhere then," Russ said.

"Your archers can't get to them?" Beau asked, frowning.

"We've gotten a couple but not enough to make a difference."

"Why not?" Jay asked. "The angles?"

"Exactly. Between the fact we have to shoot up and the wind, it's been near impossible to land them right."

Jay held up a hand, pointing, squinting along it as he measured distances and arcs. I mentally did the same. "Yeah, I see the problem. Well, we'll just need to get level with them."

"Windows?" I asked, looking around, but none of the buildings close to the wall were more than a story or a story and a half tall. Roofs would not give nearly enough coverage for our people.

Jay gave a knowing grin and shifted his finger. "The wall. It's not perfect because the protection on the inside is not as tall, but it's better than the rooftops."

Beau glanced at Reardon, who shrugged. "It might just work. We've got the city walls cleared and between the fortifications and the buildings, ours shouldn't be too exposed."

"That still leaves the issues of the fortified and heavily defended garrison. Going in there will mean a lot of loss of life," Kira said, "even without the archers."

"Fire arrows," Jay said promptly.

"Boom," Bri said approvingly and gave his brother a high five.

"Smoke them out," Reardon said. "I like it."

"Keep two archers back for fire arrows," Jay said, "I'll take the rest up to the wall. Where's the nearest access?"

"I'll show you," Bri told him.

Reardon took the brothers to round up the archers while Russ went to help Ann with some of the injured.

"How close can we get?" Beau asked Kira.

"I'll show you." She led us halfway down the block until we could just see the garrison and had clearly reached the edge of our line. "Any closer and you're in easy sight and range of the archers."

Beau looked between us and the defended building - it had makeshift barricades surrounding much of it and the occasional head popped up to check on us. "Close enough," he said and raised his voice. "To those in the garrison, can you hear me?"

There was a pause as a couple heads peeked out at us. "Yeah, we can, so what of it, traitor?" someone finally yelled back.

"I am Beau Highcastle, prince of Tira," Beau called. "In the name of my brother, the rightful king, I am giving you the opportunity to surrender peacefully before more lives are lost."

A longer pause and more heads this time, all peering in our direction. Clearly Sorin had not passed his suspicions on to the common soldier. The one with the little girl must've been a higher rank, or smarter, than I'd realized.

"Bullshit," the same voice called. "There's only one Highcastle left."

"And that's their biggest hang-up," Kira muttered.

I snorted.

"Regardless of if you believe me or not, I am giving you one last chance to end this before further bloodshed."

"Pal, you can't get to us, so why don't *you* surrender to *us*?" he yelled.

"You have one minute and then we will come in."

"Fine, then the bloodshed'll be on your side."

"Any of the men who want to surrender will be accepted as prisoners of war until after Tira is once again in Highcastle hands," Beau said calmly.

Two Freedom Fighters armed with bows edged up near us, another carried a torch.

"The archers have left, sir. Jay says give them about five minutes to be in position."

"Sounds good," Beau replied without taking his eyes off the garrison.

"They're not going to surrender."

He pursed his lips and shook his head slightly. "I don't honestly know if that's a good thing or not. No matter who they fight for, we're all Tirans."

I put my hand on his shoulder.

After a minute, the soldier shouted. "Coming at us yet?"

"Thought I'd give you a couple more to think it through," Beau yelled back.

Other than a few bobbing heads, no one seemed to pay us much attention from the barracks until the first volley from our forces cut through the archers on the castle wall. There was instantly a mad scramble up there as they tried to figure out where the attack came from. The men on the ground also popped up to try and see as well. Jay's group spared a half volley down at them and they dropped instantly, although we couldn't tell how many were injured.

The enemy archers regrouped and returned fire. I winced at the couple screams from our side.

"Excuse us, sir," said the archers on the ground, both having lit their arrows.

We slid back to allow them a better aim and they let fly. One fell short but the other hit the wooden building. Almost immediately, they let loose another volley. We could hear indistinct yelling at the barracks. Jay's group were firing as soon as they reloaded to keep a steady stream of arrows heading to the adjoining wall. It seemed to be doing its job of keeping the Three's archers down.

Beau shifted impatiently as our two archers launched fire arrow after fire arrow. I peeked past them and watched with satisfaction as the first tendrils of flame sprouted from the roof in multiple places. It wasn't long before the soldiers began streaming out the door, caught between flames and arrows.

Reardon had brought the rest of the combined forces forward once the assault started. Beau held up a hand to pause them, but we all drew our weapons. I took a deep breath. Then he brought the hand down. In the garrison's confusion, our charge went unnoticed until we were almost upon them. We swarmed the barricade - in some places just pushing through it - and drove into them. I cut down my first opponent before he had time to adequately defend himself. My second parried my blow and attacked back ferociously. I blocked and focused on holding my ground as the fighting raged around us.

What followed was a good stretch of fierce fighting. By then, sweat was dripping perilously down my forehead and I was panting. My opponent had gotten in two minor cuts but I'd managed to dodge backwards in time to prevent any more damage. Slowly, though, he was pushing me back towards the barricade. I knew I had to act before then. I lashed out with my foot, snapping his knee straight. He yowled, stumbling back. I pressed the advantage, slicing at any part of him that was exposed. He fumbled, hopping awkwardly. I ducked a swing from his sword, pushing it further out of the way with my blade. Then I brought mine sweeping back, cutting deep into his stomach. His mouth opened but no sound came out. He went down.

I engaged two others but neither lasted long, then the way in front of me was clear. I kept my guard up, scanning the area, but this part of the battle was over. Most of the remaining soldiers had surrendered and the barracks were burning merrily. Reardon was already gathering together prisoners and some of our people to get to work putting the flames out.

It took another minute of searching to spot the others. Besides Beau, they were all together. Jay was getting patched up and blood dripped from a wound on Kira's forehead as she waited her turn. Bri's bandage had bled through and he pressed fresh bandages to it. Russ was untouched, standing nearby, ever watchful. I made my way over to them. "Beau?"

"Talking to the head of the garrison. He said he'd be back in a minute and then we should head out once we've got everyone back in one piece," Russ said.

"Everyone all right?"

"Nothing serious," Kira said. The others all agreed in varying ways.

"Same," I said at Jay's inquisitive look.

Kira moved to help Bri get a fresh bandage on his arm and he, in turn, patched up her head as the rest of us got ourselves taken care of as well.

By then, Beau was making his way back over and looking us all over critically. "Everyone okay to go on?"

Jay and Bri cocked identical eyebrows at him.

"Ditto," I said, jerking a thumb towards them.

"All right. Reardon's going to stay here and organize things. It's time for us to hit the castle."

"Let's go," I said.

Beau raised a hand and gathered the troops that would be accompanying us and we headed out, leaving Reardon and a section of his group behind to keep an eye on the garrison and prisoners. I hoped Vladimir could see the smoke and know his time was coming too.

We set off for the main road again. I spotted Colin before he spotted me and I sprinted forward, breaking from the others to hug him. His right arm was in a temporary sling - I noticed in the instant before I connected to hug him - but he looked healthy enough otherwise.

"Hey, little sis," he said, hugging me a little awkwardly with his other arm, which held his sword.

"What did you do to yourself?" I demanded, shoving him back.

"Nothing permanent," he promised. "We should be just on time," he added over my shoulder as Beau and the others caught up.

"Perfect. You good to go on?"

My brother shot him a foul look. "Would you and Mick lay off?"

"Not in our nature," Beau replied lightly. Then he moved off to join Mick.

"Jez!!" Before I could even ask after Jessie and Ry, the duo came racing up. Ry appeared to not have a scratch while Jessie had a couple bandages, like the rest of us.

"I see where we rate," Jay said dryly.

"Really low," Bri agreed. "I was your friend first, kids." That wasn't strictly true in the case of Ry but I let him have it.

Ry grinned at him. "But not nearly as special."

"Ouch! That cuts deep, Ry. Deep."

Stella had appeared much more quietly than the others and she had her arms tightly wrapped around Jay, who was now speaking quietly to her. She nodded and then spotted me looking and managed a faint smile and a thumbs up.

She was interrupted from replying by Beau calling for everyone's attention. He gave a quick recap of what was to come, separated a few groups off to support those we'd left at the gates to the city. Then, we turned and headed for the castle. We stayed towards the front and Beau and Mick worked their way through to join us after a minute.

I had no idea how Sorin did it and it was more than we had planned, but the gates to the castle stood wide open. He was only supposed to have managed a side gate and not to clear the courtyard, although the area through the gates looked empty and almost forlorn. Still, Beau split people up. Some were sent to gain the walls and cover us and others were to be second and third waves. We were in the first wave, but waited until word reached us we had cover before we split further and inched in along the walls. The large courtyard looked freshly abandoned. Items lay around - not particularly out of order but as if just left when their owners wandered off. It provided us with additional cover. It took only a minute, though, before the first arrows came at us from the far end of the courtyard. They too were using the cover but there didn't seem to be many of them.

We worked our way from item to item, firing our own cover fire back as we moved. The second group made their way into the courtyard.

"Side door," Russ said suddenly and gestured. Although more than our group had come in with the first wave, we'd instinctively stayed clustered together.

There was, in fact, a small door to our left.

"They wouldn't have not covered it," Beau said.

"Maybe not, but it's there."

Beau hesitated.

"I'll take charge of things out here. I'm less effective than I should be with only one arm. Don't let Opalin escape," Colin said, flagging down another group. "Go." I didn't like to leave him, but in many ways, his job was probably safer and I had to trust he'd be careful.

Jessie and Ry moved before anyone else could. Jessie raised her sword as Ry shoved the door open hard, giving Jessie a free shot. There were two young soldiers on the other side, who looked shocked to find someone barreling down on them. With only a second's hesitation, they threw their swords on the ground and held up their hands. Jessie smirked and beckoned them forward, handing them over to my brother and the others who had come to join him.

Then, we were actually in the castle and moving down the hall. The place was simpler than I had expected, but then, we were in some of the normal hallways, not the places that the royal family was usually likely to go.

At the first major intersection, Beau stopped us. "We have two options as I see it," he said, glancing at Mick for confirmation. "One, we push our way through and do only what we need to get to the upper levels where we might find those of higher rank, including my brother. Or we clear it out room by room and do it slowly and figure the other groups will slowly catch up to us."

We all exchanged glances and then looked back at Beau. As far as I saw it, our choice was simple because of who we had. I felt sure the others were in agreement.

"Your choice, Beau," Mick said, "but I think you know where we're all leaning."

"Then we push forward as quickly as we can. But nothing foolhardy."

"We're never foolhardy, how could you say such a thing?" Bri asked, but Beau pinned him with a look.

"I'm not kidding."

"Neither are we," I assured him. "You know this is just how we handle things."

He took a deep breath. "Yeah, I know."

We had only cursory knowledge of the castle and its layout. Mick had been a toddler - it was hard to picture Mick that little and Beau confirmed he hadn't acted a lot different - the last time he'd been there and the rest of us in our group had never been. My oldest brother, Kent, had visited but the rest of us hadn't. Reardon was one of the handful of Freedom Fighters who had, but he was busy at the garrison. Hindsight.

Still, we hopefully knew enough. There were seven floors and except for the grand staircase that went straight from the ground floor and switchbacked its way through galleries to the fifth floor where the grand ballroom was, the staircases through the regular levels were staggered and made it harder for an invading force like ours to make their way through the castle. Still, it wasn't impossible, especially when the castle was mostly deserted.

Sorin had done an amazing job of getting all the everyday people and servants out of the castle. Or at least in concentrated areas where the majority of our people could fight them. We made it to the third floor without much resistance. Though we hit occasional small pocket of soldiers, they were ill-prepared to face us. Most gave in with only a brief attempt at fighting back. Not one of those groups didn't fold after the first injury to one of their own. After some of the fighting in the streets, it was a strange sort of letdown. We took their weapons and left them, not really having any other recourse.

Of course, almost as soon as the thought crossed my mind, we hit soldiers who did not cave so easily. In fact, it was the exact opposite. Word had somehow gotten ahead of us and the ambush caught us completely without warning. Thankfully, we were on our guard or it might have been much worse.

Not surprisingly, the soldiers had the advantage of knowing the castle much better than we did. Although we had to blunder a bit to find each successive stairwell, they knew every nook and cranny. As we hit an intersection, they appeared almost out of nowhere from all three directions. Our only saving grace was the fact that only so many could come at us at a time. I tried to keep my focus on my fight, which I found harder when everyone around me was someone I cared deeply about. Of course, I found it easier to focus when my opponent almost split me in half while I was momentarily distracted by a yell to my left. I managed to deflect most of the blow at the last second but it still left a shallow cut across my chest, neatly slicing through my shirt.

I shoved his blade away and pressed the attack, blocking and slicing until I finally slipped within his guard and drive my blade deep into his side. He gasped and fell back as I drew my sword out and brought it back around to finish him off. For a second, I had no opponents and I scanned the surging crowd of fighters. My brain registered everyone as still whole, quicker than I could really fully catalogue, and I had to trust that instinct as another soldier appeared to take a swing at me. I parried and pressed the attack, finding myself back to back with someone as we fought. A lightning quick glance confirmed it was Jay, fighting two soldiers. I pushed my opponent back and then spun and felt my sword go deep into one of his before I had to turn back to deflect the next nasty strike.

Distantly, I heard the continued clang of metal on metal and the shouts of battle, but could do nothing more than note them until I managed to cut down the soldier in front of me. Once done, I searched for which of my friends I could help.

It happened almost the instant my eyes found Beau, who fought near Mick. I don't know if the soldiers had identified him as a Highcastle or just our leader but Beau and Mick battled four soldiers between them. Then, one of the soldiers broke from Mick, spinning at Beau's unprotected back. I screamed.

Time seemed to ground to a halt as the blade arced in.

Then Mick was there.

Once Sorin arranged to have the main gate opened, the courtyard emptied, and all non-essentials and civilians evacuated to the main ballroom - all of which was far too easy, where was Vladimir to countermand him? - his next stop was the armory. It took only a minute to find what he was looking for: King Patrick Highcastle's sword. It had been passed down through generations and hung on a wall behind the desk, the scabbard on a peg beside it.

Sorin stared at it. Russ and Colin had smuggled Ani out of Oakbridge and supposedly given her detailed instructions to Dean's location. Colin, via Russ, had assured him that no one in the Freedom Fighters besides himself and Russ knew where Ani and Dean were. Sorin hoped at least one of them survived so that Ren had the option to follow through on his word of bringing her back once it was safe. Sorin supposed Dean would end up living here too as he knew his sister well enough to know she wouldn't leave the boy behind. If the Freedom Fighters didn't kill him - which was well deserved - maybe Dean could...

He shook his head to shake the thought loose. He had two more jobs to do. Possibly only one. It depended on how quick Beau Highcastle was, he suspected.

With a silent apology to the previous owner, Sorin plucked the sword off the wall followed by the scabbard. Then he turned away and, taking the nearest staircase two steps at a time, he made his way up to Ren's room. He hadn't ordered the guard away but the stretch of hallway was empty. He had a momentary panic as he hurried forward and threw the door open - the fact it had still been locked was a little reassuring.

Ren spun from the window.

They locked gazes.

"They're going to win?"

Sorin offered out the sheathed sword on his palms. "Let's finish this." He figured that was answer enough.

Ren's eyes went wide, and he stepped forward to place a hand on the blade reverently.

"It's yours."

"Vlad?"

"Don't know, but I plan to find him," Sorin said grimly, his own hand dropped to the hilt of his sword as Ren finally lifted his father's blade and began to buckle it around his waist. "I assume you remember how to use that thing?"

Ren favored him with a ghost of a smile. "Give me a little credit. I was not only heir but my father knew danger was coming." He drew the sword, testing its balance. "I'd always looked forward to the day this would become mine."

"I'm sure I wasn't your first choice for grantor."

"No, but you made the effort to get it and not just any blade."

Again, their eyes met, with all their complicated history. And Sorin knew that Ren understood. Sorin had to do this for himself, for Ani, for his son, for *Vlad,* and he had to do it alone. "If I fail, I expect you to finish the job," he said.

Ren nodded.

"They should be within the castle now. Find your brother."

"I saw them in the courtyard a few minutes ago."

Still, for another instant, the two just stood there. Then, Sorin offered a slight bow from the waist. "My liege."

Ren stepped forward and gripped his upper arm. "No matter what happens today, as long as I'm alive, you've got a brother."

Sorin didn't deserve it. He knew he didn't, but he wanted it. Gods, but the world was a fucked up place. So he just nodded and slipped out the door, heading for the stairs up, while Ren went the other way, heading down. At the corner, Sorin glanced back. Ren would be okay.

Now for the last job.

Although he had told Ren he didn't know where Vladimir was, he had a strong suspicion. His brother would be aware enough to realize this was the end. He would want to make a statement. He would also expect it to be Ren coming after him. It wouldn't be the grand ballroom but there was a location on the top floor that would be just as iconic for his brother. The large audience chamber that had been rarely used during the Highcastle times but had become Vladimir's favorite place due to making everyone come to him at the top.

Sorin felt no surprise at finding the audience chamber doors flung wide open with two guards standing on either side. He ignored them, stepping into the open doorway.

Vladimir sat at the far end in one of the thrones. There was a pause as they stared at each other, Vladimir rising. "Sorin?" he asked.

Without looking at the guards, Sorin spoke in a low voice. "You two are dismissed. Make your decision wisely." Then he slowly made his way down the gap between the riser seats.

He watched the understanding dawn on his brother's face. "Even you?" he spat as Sorin reached the end of the seats and stopped.

"There's still time, Vlad."

637

Vlad didn't seem to hear him. "Did you do this? Let them into our castle?"

"It's not ours. It never really was. We just stole it for a few years."

"We are *not* caretakers."

"No, because we didn't take care of it," Sorin said with a feeling of faint amusement. "We were nothing more than invaders and it's over now. They're within the castle grounds and it won't take them long to make it here. It's over, Vlad, but this, this doesn't have to happen." He spread his arms. "You're my brother. I don't want to fight you."

"You're the one who turned traitor," Vlad snarled.

Sorin let out a laugh. "You don't see the irony of this at all, do you? I'm making what we did right again! We're the traitors!"

"Why? Because Renier supposedly loves our sister?"

"Because it's the gods-be-damned right thing to do! How can you not see that?" Sorin said, a bit desperately. He would make this right, but he didn't have to like it. It was his last job and then the Freedom Fighters - the right side - could hang him or lock him deep in a hole and things would be okay again for Tira. And, as an added bonus, Dean got the best of their family to take care of him.

As Vladimir pulled his sword, Sorin was at peace. He had always been the better swordsman. Still, he tried one more time, because he had known Vlad for his entire life, for better or worse, even if Vlad had ended up on Edward's side, so perfectly Edward's blood. "Vlad, *please.*"

"What did they offer you? Whatever they said, they will hang you and laugh as they do," Vlad said. "You will die by their hand but without being able to defend yourself. I will not go the same way."

"So be it. We deserve no less for what we've done," Sorin said and drew his sword.

Vlad stepped off the dais and began to circle. Sorin instinctively matched him, step for step. "Do you really think you can kill me?"

Sorin took a deep breath and let it out slowly. "I know I have to."

Vlad drove forward.

Chapter Forty-one

AT THE LAST POSSIBLE SECOND, Mick threw himself between Beau's back and the plunging blade. The rest of the world seemed to freeze as the sword drove deep into Mick's chest. In his dive to protect Beau, he'd had no time to protect himself.

Beau spun, swinging at the soldier before the scene had registered for him. I think it was mostly in reaction to my scream and I realized, in a split second, that while I had possibly saved Beau's life temporarily, maybe I'd also done more harm than good. Beau's other two opponents were now at his back.

I surged forward but before I could reach them, one of the soldiers stiffened and a newcomer shoved him aside to engage the second one. I slid to a stop next to Beau and Mick, figuring the new person could hold their own as I crouched on Mick's other side. Beau cradled his lifelong best friend, ally when allies were scarce, and bodyguard in his lap, rocking slightly. I reached out, trying to figure out where to put my hands to try and stop the rivers of blood. Before I could even begin, though, Mick's hand gripped my arm. I started, since his eyes were closed and he was already deathly pale.

"Jez. Don't," he murmured.

"We can," I started but I didn't know how I would finish it. There was so much blood. We all had a few supplies on us but most of the others were still fighting and our gear was rudimentary. This cut, I could tell, went deep. Too deep.

His fingers tightened. "I was wrong about you. At the beginning. I'm sorry. You take care of him, you hear?" The words were firm but contained a hint of noise I did not like. Something deep inside him.

"I promise," I managed around a tight throat, my hands still hanging uselessly over him. It felt like lifetimes ago that Mick had judged me against my upbringing and expected me to be lacking. Lifetimes since I had worked so hard to gain his approval. Lifetimes since I had, but not in the ways either of us had ever expected. I had come to the realization, at almost the same time that I'd admitted my feelings for Beau, that they were a matched pair. That if I was going to be with Beau, Mick would always be near, keeping us both safe. But now...but now everything was wrong.

"Beau," he said, shifting his head and actually opening his eyes, although they were glossy with pain.

Beau's head was bowed over Mick and he didn't seem to react other than to tighten his grip on his best friend.

Mick let go of me to take Beau's hand. "I always had faith in you. You did this and don't ever forget it. Always be the best of you."

I put my hand over his and Beau's gently, tears sliding down my face.

"I won't forget," Beau whispered, voice cracking.

A moment later, he relaxed against Beau's legs. Swallowing hard, I reached over with my free hand and slid his eyelids shut. Neither of us moved. I was aware of the noise of the fighting at my back but it was dying down.

Then, someone stepped up behind Beau. None of our people should've come from that direction so it was enough to make me reach for my discarded sword, even as I looked up. As soon as I met the man's eyes and took in his face, my grip on the hilt relaxed.

Renier Highcastle nodded to me, but didn't break our silence. His gaze skittered past me and I felt as much as heard the others join us. Russ stayed a step back near Renier out of respect, since he had only met Mick a couple hours before. Hands on my shoulders and Beau's linked us around Mick's body as we paid our own silent homage to a friend we had all respected. A man who had wholeheartedly dedicated his entire life to something that, much of the time, must have felt like a lost cause or, for the many years before the Three had actually taken the throne, a useless one.

Finally, Beau stirred and wiped at his eyes with the back of his arm. "We need to keep going. Mick would want that."

"I know a place where his body will be safe until you return," Renier offered hesitantly as our other friends began to step away, cleaning weapons and wiping their own eyes.

Beau started at the unfamiliar voice and twisted to look, for the first time, into the face of his brother. They stared at each other until Beau nodded. "Thank you."

"It's the least I can do," Renier said softly.

I helped Beau heft Mick up as Jay snagged my sword for me. Renier led the way down the hall to a small antechamber where we were able to lay Mick out. Once the door was shut, Beau took a deep breath, straightened his shoulders and turned back to his brother. "We're looking for Opalin."

"Sorin's already gone after him."

"Sorin?" Beau repeated, startled.

I wasn't surprised, not after recent events. He had been determined to make it right. I absently cleaned my returned sword on my pants.

"I suspect they're both in the formal audience chamber, on the top floor. It's where Ani and I were married. I would guess Vlad likes the symbolism."

"Show us the way?" Beau asked.

He nodded and turned. Beau hesitated, glancing at me. I went to him, took his hand, and we caught up to Renier. The others fell in behind us. The prince looked at us, seeming nervous. "So, um," he said, clearing his throat, "I'm sorry about your friend. I'm...sorry I didn't get there sooner."

"It wasn't your fault."

Renier shrugged self-consciously.

"How did you find us?"

"Sorin let me out and armed me," the prince said, "then he went after Vlad and I thought I should maybe try and find you. In case...in case you needed help?"

"It did help. Your timing was really good, actually," I pointed out. "You took out the two soldiers at Beau's back."

"Thank you," Beau said immediately.

"You're welcome," Renier replied.

There was a moment of silence as the brothers regarded each other. I let the silence stand, listening to the others talk quietly behind us as we hit the next staircase up. As the youngest of five, and the only girl, I was well aware that siblings had to find their own equilibrium. I couldn't make or force a relationship.

"It's nice to meet you," Renier said finally. "My, *our*, father never told me about you. I mean, not directly. I didn't know until Sorin got suspicious that the head of the Freedom Fighters was using methods he recognized from Father's younger days."

Beau nodded. "Mom said he wouldn't, because it was safer if you didn't know. If something did happen, you wouldn't be able to tell about me if they tried to get it out of you."

"Is she...dead too?" Renier asked.

I pressed my lips together. It hadn't occurred to me that, while Beau knew full well both his parents were dead - and had for a while thought Renier was too - Renier had probably lived with a slight hope their mother was still alive once he had known about Beau.

"She got sick and died when I was ten. I'm sorry," Beau said quietly.

Renier took a deep breath and nodded. "No, don't be. It's certainly not your fault. I'm glad you had her while you did."

Any more conversation was briefly cut off as we ran into another disorganized group of soldiers. Still, we had to fight them off, thankfully without any further serious injury. Then, with Renier in the lead, we made our way up to the next set of stairs, reaching the fifth floor.

Only two to go.

We encountered a couple more pockets of resistance but nothing of note. Each time, we pulled out a few more bandages but none would even require stitches, I didn't think. Renier helped patch people up and I was amazed by the very similar down-to-earth nature of both Highcastles in trying circumstances, despite having never met until that day. It'd remain to see how far Renier's extended when people weren't trying to murder us.

The closer we got to the seventh floor, the more deserted the castle appeared. Beau and I exchanged looks and moved closer to Renier, fully expecting another ambush. Instead, we made it up the last staircase without issue. There, only a few feet away, was a hunched body, propped against the wall. Hair fell into the face, one knee pulled up towards the chest and other leg straight. One hand rested splayed over a sword.

Renier gasped and threw himself forward.

The body moved.

Not much, but a general tensing as the fingers tried to wrap around the hilt. And the head lifted enough for my heart to lurch in surprise as I recognized the face.

"Sorin?" Renier said as he dropped to his knees beside the other man. "Where…?"

"I got him, Ren" Sorin said, lulling his head back against the wall so he could look at Renier.

Ren. That's right. That's what Russ had said.

"And he got you," Renier said lightly. "Where did he get you?"

Sorin waved a hand weakly at him. "Better this way."

"I don't think your son would say the same thing."

Son??

"Or Ani," Renier added.

At least that nickname made sense.

Sorin shrugged with one shoulder.

"Where, Sorin?" Renier repeated firmly.

"Chest and others."

"Let me see."

Sorin lowered his arm from his chest as Beau and I dropped down next to Renier. I winced at the obviously deep cut across his chest, which probably went down to bone and certainly needed stitches. Renier held out a hand for bandages and we both gave him what we had left. I scooted around to Sorin's other side to help wrap the bandages around him. Sorin didn't make a sound, as if he was used to pain or being bandaged, or both.

Sorin finally shoved slightly at Renier's shoulder. "Go. Go make sure and end this war."

"Will they stop then?"

"Tell them Vlad's dead. You're king. Or will be, as soon as things can be made official." Sorin's eyes had closed, but his breathing was still fairly steady. He might make it, if we could get him real medical assistance soon enough.

"I'll stay with him," Russ said. "Do a bit more work. Go on."

I straightened and offered my hand to Beau to pull him up. Renier hesitated, putting a hand on Sorin's shoulder. "Don't, for a minute, think you don't have things to live for, got it?"

Sorin squinted, focusing on Renier's face and scanning it. "Got it," he said finally.

Renier now stood too. "Let's go." Without a backward glance, he strode onwards. We fell in behind him.

This time Beau walked next to him. "He has a son?"

Renier nodded. "He's six. Colin smuggled Ani out to join him a few days ago." I knew about Ani but Beau might not yet.

I let out a quiet whistle. I had not expected that Sorin had a child. Still, we didn't have much time to debate it because we turned the corner to the formal audience chamber and found ourselves facing a wall of more soldiers than we'd yet come upon. At least a dozen stood between us and the entrance to the chamber in two rows.

Renier put a hand on Beau's arm and stepped forward. "I have it on good authority that Vladimir Opalin is dead. This is over. The Highcastle line will be restored," he said calmly but firmly.

The soldiers said nothing, watching our group until two men, one old and the other a short man I knew better than I'd ever wanted, shuffled between their ranks to face Renier with scornful looks. "You are nothing but a puppet," the old man said dismissively. Dayton sneered at me from his side.

"Stand down, Bert," Renier said flatly. "Your leader is dead. You already know this if you're here. It's time to face the facts and stand down. You and all the others will be treated fairly. You have my word as prince and future king."

A few of the soldiers shifted their weight, starting to look dubious about continuing the fight.

Dayton and Bert exchanged a look. Then Dayton grinned, showing all his teeth. "That's if you can catch us. Get them!" he squealed, pointing at us as he and Bert quickly backed behind the double wall of soldiers.

The moment when none of the rest of us moved stretched into a second heartbeat. Then a third.

"Stand *down*," Renier repeated, in a loud voice of command I knew well from Beau.

The wall of soldiers collapsed. Some turned to flee, a few dropped their weapons and raised their hands and a couple charged us. I drew my sword and stepped closer to Renier as Beau did the same on his other side. With the soldiers so split, it took little work to disarm or kill the few who attacked. Leaving us to deal with the rest, Renier bolted towards the audience chamber. I glanced for Beau but he had his back to Renier as he spoke to a soldier and Jay. I raced after the prince.

I skidded to a halt just inside the large room. Renier stood near the dais, staring down at a body. After a quick scan confirmed there was no one else about, I made my way up the aisle towards him. As I approached, he glanced up and gestured me forward to his side.

The body at his feet had been mutilated, the face slashed in multiple places, but it was clearly male and wore clothes of a fine weave.

"He's dead," Renier said.

"So it's him."

"Yes. Same build, same clothes, same hair," he said. "I doubt the face gashes were Sorin, but who knows what Bert and the other one might've done for whatever reason."

I nodded.

"You and Beau?" he asked after a brief pause.

"Yes."

"Good." He took a deep breath and then looked up again, meeting my eyes. The furrows in his brow slowly loosened, making him look years younger. "Then it's truly over."

My heart stuttered for a second at those words, so simple and yet so full of meaning. It was over. Tira was free and, as Renier had said, the Highcastle line would be restored. We could turn our concentration outward. To fixing what Vladimir, and Sorin, had damaged and to making sure the neighboring countries returned to respecting our longstanding borders. Both Alyia and Nerius had pushed in towards Oakridge since the Three had turned so much of their attention inward to fight us and keep the peace during the transition and following.

We could rebuild.

I heard the scuff of feet behind us and we both turned. Beau stood in the doorway. "It's done."

Chapter Forty-two

THE BATTLE HAD TAKEN MOST OF the day and yet there was still so much work left to do. We followed Beau out and went to retrieve Sorin. I helped Russ, Jessie, and Ry get him downstairs to the infirmary. Bri and Jay went to retrieve Mick's body while Beau, Ren, and the others went to speak to those gathered in the main ballroom. Reports started to come in as we met up with other groups of Freedom Fighters that the city was ours. Smaller rebellions in other cities, orchestrated from afar by Colin and a handful of our representatives at each, had gone successfully too. We knew for a fact that Greensward was once again under Highcastle control and there was no doubt the others would fall. Any possible holdouts would buckle as soon as they heard that Opalin was dead and Oakbridge ours.

In the meantime, people were dispatched to gather the prisoners and lock them away until Ren could speak to them. We hoped not all would be irredeemable. I assisted Russ with taking care of Sorin and the other wounded who had been brought to the infirmary until Ann and the castle doctors came in and took over. Russ left at that point and returned with a fairly hefty tray of bread, cheese and fruit. At the sight, my stomach grumbled loudly and those of us volunteering let the experts take over while we washed our hands and ate. Once we were done, I slipped away and went to wash off the rest of the blood and grime, although there was no helping my clothes. Like I'd summoned him, Jay appeared down the hall as I headed out, carrying bags. He brightened and waved one at me. "Your things from the safehouse," he said.

"You are a lifesaver," I told him.

He grinned. "I know. Clearly you own me one."

"Clearly," I agreed, since there was no use arguing with him. Instead, I ruffled his hair with my relatively clean hand.

He wrinkled his nose at me but passed the bag over. "Also, word is, bonfire in the courtyard and around the city at dusk. We're all meeting in the courtyard around then."

"I'll be there," I promised.

"There are bunkrooms on this floor too, where we're all going to stay for now." He sketched out directions. I repeated them back and he nodded in satisfaction. "I trust you can manage from here," he said with a wink and skipped off.

I rolled my eyes and found a small side room in which to change. Then, I went back to the washrooms and washed a second time. I snuck a glance out a window as I passed and realized there wasn't much time until dusk. The sun was already dipping below Oakbridge's walls. Trying to keep up with the maze of corridors in the castle, I made my way downstairs and eventually, after having to ask a passing person, found my way to the courtyard.

Three bonfires burned across the wide courtyard. I squinted against the flames at the backlit figures before finally recognizing Colin's form and making my way over. Not only were my usual circle of friends there, but also some of the early Freedom Fighters from Cavern Hall. Reardon, I knew, was in the infirmary, although likely to make it, but his apprentice, Nathaniel, had not survived the fighting. Dunkin and Kilo were there, along with many other faces I knew well. Beau and Renier were not yet, though. When I asked Colin, he said the two had disappeared to talk. I subtly crossed my fingers, hoping it went well. There was no reason it wouldn't, considering I knew that Beau would be much happier without having to take the throne.

More faces joined until almost all of our original group – those who had fought in that first big battle and lived – had joined us, filling the area with laughter and conversation, not to mention remembrances of those now gone. As sweet as victory was, there existed a bittersweet undercurrent and I kept expecting to see Mick striding out of the deepening night to join us. Not only that, but it felt strange not to have Dave, Iris, and the others who had stayed behind.

Our smaller group gathered to one side of the fire automatically. Kira leaned her head on Bri's shoulder. Stella sat with her back against Jay's side.

Colin sat with Ben, who I hadn't seen all day. The young noble was deep in conversation with Jessie and Ry. My brother's arm thankfully was still in his sling. I had half expected him to ditch it. Russ had joined us, but sat a few feet away, at least until Colin motioned him over and started talking quietly to him.

Finally, Stella shushed us. "It's Beau and the king!"

"It's Beau and Ren," Bri said sagely.

I glanced at him. "Ren?" I repeated.

"Sorin called him that," Jay said.

"Sorin, for all the other issues, also knows him a hell of a lot better than we do," I pointed out.

Bri just grinned. "C'mon, who wants to get treated with deference *all* the time? I nominate us to keep him grounded."

Colin groaned. "Bri, I'm pretty sure the last couple years will keep the prince plenty grounded."

Any more potential argument was cut off as Beau and Renier came to stand within the light of the flames. Beau looked around the group and smiled, clearly recognizing every face and appreciating the fact we'd come together on our own.

"I'm glad you're all here," he said, which pretty effectively stopped all remaining conversation. "It's so good to see your faces after today. I only wish there were certain others here too. But as trite as it may sound, their sacrifices were not in vain and we will not forget them or what they did for Tira. I am so proud of you and everything we've managed to accomplish together. This may well mark the last time we're all in the same spot. Many of you have places to return to, to help Tira rebuild and find its way again. Many of you, I also know, do not and you are welcome to stay and help us here. But, before we look forward, there's something I need to do."

Renier had been standing a step or two behind him, aware that these were Beau's people.

Beau caught my eye and smiled before he turned and dropped to one knee in front of his brother. "I, Beau Highcastle, do hereby swear allegiance to my brother, Renier Highcastle, our true and rightful king. I follow him willingly." He bowed his head.

Renier reached down and drew Beau back to his feet. "I accept your allegiance and look forward to working with you to make Tira better in the years to come." Then he turned to all of us, putting a hand on Beau's shoulder. "I look forward to working with all of you in the days, months, and years to come. Without you, I would still be a prisoner in the castle and Tira would be looking at a much darker future. I will never forget what you all have done for me and our country."

There was a momentary pause before Bri let out a whoop and Jay yelled, "bravo!" A dam broke as other calls and cheers went up.

"I hope," Beau called, once they started to die down, "that you'll all treat Ren with the same loyalty, respect, and confidence that you treated me all these years."

"See, he calls him Ren," Jay whispered to me.

I rolled my eyes.

"Damn, Beau, you and the prince had better both hope he gets treated with a hell of a lot more respect than you ever have," Bri called.

There was scattered laughter and applause.

"Oh, no, that's just you lot," Beau said pleasantly. "And if you don't shape up, I see a lot of border duty in your futures."

"You wouldn't do that to Jez!" Jay said.

"You better believe I would," Beau said, winking at me.

I laughed.

"Only if you went too," Ry said. "You wouldn't survive without her that long. You barely survived the time she was in Greensward!"

"Touché," Beau said, amused.

He and Renier joined our group and Beau settled next to me, wrapping an arm around my waist. Renier sat on his other side, near Colin. "Hey, good job with all that," I told him.

He smiled. "It might've been planned, but I will say it was my idea. I didn't want there to be any question about the line of succession. Tira doesn't need that and I don't want it."

I leaned up to kiss him. "Works for me," I murmured.

We were only distracted when I heard something hit the fire. "Richard Malden," Dunkin said.

I felt a jolt in my stomach and looked around. What did this mean? I didn't spot Richard. Others were already standing, Ry among them. She tossed another branch on. "Bean Schid."

Ben and Kira were right behind her. "Melinda Walters."

"Robert Walters," Ben added and nodded to his sister before moving back to their spots.

That was when it fully kicked it. This was our best attempt at a memorial, our funeral, for all those lost in the fight against the Three. I hadn't even realized that Richard Malden, Dunk and Kilo's friend, had died. I took a deep breath. I was lucky. I wouldn't need to stand and add a branch. We had lost Mick but that was mostly Beau's loss. Even Bri had come back from the dead somehow. I glanced now at the Dall brothers, who waited to add their parents' names to the list.

It took far too long to work our way through the list of names; friends and family adding their branches. Stella stood and added two, one for her mother and one for George and I wished Dave could have been there. Maybe it would have helped the boy too.

The prince joined in halfway through, saying his father's name.

Finally, Beau stood and stepped forward, tossing a branch on. "Elizabeth Highcastle. Mick Sanders. And so many more." We all sat in a moment of silence before he spoke again. "And as much as we've sacrificed so far, we have to remember that the fight is not over. As I said earlier, if you have families or towns to return to, don't feel you have to stay. We each need to help with the rebuilding in the way we best see fit, but for those of you who can, Nerius and Alyia have taken advantage of our civil war and unrest to poach our borders, pushing in from the west and south. We need to keep things moving and get out there to push them back. As such, I have two announcements before I'll leave you to your evening."

I frowned, glancing around, but only Colin and Renier seemed to know what he was talking about.

"Well, the first is more the asking of a favor," Beau amended with a smile. "We find ourselves in need of a leader for our national army. Reardon declined and offered to help, but had another suggestion in mind who I think might work out quite nicely for many reasons. Ry?"

Ry blinked and stood as he gestured. "Yes?"

"Would you do Ren and me the honor of being the first commander of our new army?"

Her eyes bulged. "What? Me? Why?"

"Reardon pointed out that although you're not the best at any particular weapon, you have an incredibly solid grasp of all of them. Not only that but you have a natural flair for leadership and, I suspect our neighbors might be prone to underestimating you, due to both your gender and age."

Ry glanced at the rest of us questioningly.

"Of course we'll help however you need," Jessie said firmly and we all nodded, chorusing our agreement.

She took a deep breath. "Yes, I'll take it, but you're allowed to take it away when you realize I'm terrible at it," she said.

Beau smiled. "I doubt that will happen but I'll keep that in mind. The other has to do with Colin and a project he has up his sleeve. I believe Russ will be helping him with that as well. Colin?"

My brother stood. "We've worked up a good network of informants, spies, and other sneaky people already and I'd like to expand on that. In the coming weeks and months, I'll be officially forming The King's Information Network, or KIN for short, whose aim will be to keep not only our royal family secure, but also all the citizens of Tira. We'll be working behind the scenes and underground for the most part, as well as in conjunction with the army." Here he nodded to Ry with a crooked grin. "If anyone's interested in joining, come talk to me and we'll figure things out. For the immediate future, we'll be based out of Oakbridge, but I don't expect that to last. Ry, I was thinking we might want to chat with the men and women we've got locked up and see if some would like to serve for a while in return for amnesty."

Ry brightened. "That's brilliant!"

Beau grinned. "I'll leave you two to your planning. And that concludes my announcements. If you want to help either endeavor, talk to Ry and Colin in the coming days." He offered everyone a quick bow then rejoined Renier and me. I settled back in against him and returned my gaze to the flames. As they slowly dwindled down to coals, I was confident that Tira would be okay, even if we still had some long days, weeks, months, and maybe years ahead of us.

Sorin was given his own room off the infirmary in which to begin the process of healing. He knew it wasn't out of a particular concern for his health over others, but merely because he knew from Russ that they were keeping his survival of the Battle for Oakbridge quiet, at least for now.

Also, as prisons went, it wasn't half bad. The room was small, fitting not much more than a dresser, bed and stool for a visitor, but considering he was confined to bed until further notice, it actually felt almost airy. A large, unbarred window sat on the wall by his bedside and he could see the castle gardens and beyond them to the city wall.

On top of that, he received an almost endless train of interesting visits in the days following the Freedom Fighters' successful bid for the country – he tried not to think too hard about the fact that he'd killed his own brother but his sleeping mind wouldn't let him forget it. Not only did Russ appoint himself Sorin's personal nurse and gossip-bringer, and visited multiple times a day, but there was a steady stream of others. In some ways, he appreciated Russ's the most. The younger man had interested him while acting as Sorin's contact with the Freedom Fighters before the attack. Russ carried a pain deep inside him that Sorin instinctively understood, even if he didn't know the reasoning behind it, and they continued to get along surprisingly well.

Nonetheless, some of his other meetings were incredibly fascinating – and got passed along, in turn, to Russ. The first two to show up, late the morning after the battle, were Colin Lockholme and a young woman, who eyed him curiously, like he was an interesting specimen of a potentially dangerous animal. She stayed by the door, leaning against it with one leg bent and her hand near her sword. Colin approached, though, and perched on the stool beside it. "Word is you'll make a full recovery given time," he said.

"That's what I've been told," Sorin agreed, glancing instinctively at his wrist, which was surprisingly free of cuffs. Even as injured as he was, they should have done *something*.

"You're not a prisoner," Colin said. "Nor are most of the soldiers who were fighting for you anymore. Ry and I conscripted many of them this morning."

Sorin's eyebrows rose and he glanced at the woman. That name he knew, but only by reputation via Jakium. Rylia offered a curt bow and a half smile. "I'm the new commander of the Tiran army."

"Congratulations," he said, a bit neutrally. "What does this have to do with me? Why am I not under arrest for what I did?"

Colin grinned with an edge of mischief that Sorin usually only saw on Ani's face. "Well, here's the thing. First of all, Renier doesn't really want us to. You *are* his brother-in-law. But more importantly, I have a much better preposition for you. You were in charge of the Three's spy and informant network, right?"

It was a dumb question. Colin knew that full well. Sorin nodded slowly anyway.

Colin's grin widened. "How would you like to join forces?"

Sorin said yes almost before Colin finished his explanation of KIN. It would be the perfect atonement to try and help fix what his brother had started. His one caveat was that Russell be asked too. Colin just laughed and admitted he was asking Russ next and had basically already conscripted him.

The next interesting visit was Ren himself, later that evening, after Russ had come and gone with dinner. Ren plunked himself down on the stool and sighed, leaning against the bed frame. "Being in charge is exhausting," he announced without any preamble.

Sorin let out a laugh and regretted it as his chest throbbed in protest. For a moment, he saw stars around the edge of his vision.

"Sorry," Ren said.

Sorin waved him off. "You knew it would be hard. At least you have Beau."

He sighed again and then brightened a little. "You've met him, right? In Lockholme?"

"Yes."

"It's amazing! I mean, I thought all my family was dead. And even after we knew about him, I didn't fully believe it. He's great," he said happily. And then paused. "Um, right, probably shouldn't talk about the amazingness of brothers."

Sorin raised his eyebrows, barely holding in another burst of laughter. "Ren, you're punch drunk. Go to bed. I'm fully aware of who and what Vlad had become. You're also more than allowed to be excited about having family alive," he added, a touch guiltily. Patrick's murder would never not pull at his sense of shame and guilt.

Ren nodded. "How goes the healing?"

"Good, I guess. I'm not dead. Nor am I likely to be soon, if I behave myself."

The prince sat up a little, pinning him with a look.

Sorin sighed. "I plan on behaving myself, never fear, Your Majesty."

Ren flinched a little. "Please don't. I'm pretty sure you're the only one, besides Beau, who is willing to call me Ren."

"And the irony of that isn't incredible or anything," Sorin said dryly.

Ren grinned. "Right now, I'll take it. I set my coronation date. One week from yesterday."

"That's too soon for any other nations to send delegates," he replied carefully.

"That is *exactly* what Beau said." Maybe someday, Sorin mused, he and the younger Highcastle could find common ground in reacting to Ren the same way. "And I don't care. Gilan might anyway and Nerius and Alyia aren't invited, frankly," Ren said. "Not after they refused to help the Freedom Fighters and poached our borders while we were weakened. They can send presents later."

"Fair enough. It should be enough time for all the nobles to get here," Sorin said. "And a test of who doesn't come and begs off."

"That's what I said!" Ren said, looking proud of himself.

Sorin felt himself smile a little. "You should get some rest. Tomorrow will be another long day."

Ren nodded, stretching and yawning, before slumping back down on the stool. "I miss her."

He didn't need to ask who. "I do too. Are...?" he started before reminding himself it was none of his business.

"Am I going to bring her back? I'd like to obviously, but I don't know how the country will feel. Colin says he's sending you and Russ her and Dean's way once you're well enough."

Sorin's stomach clenched and not because of the deep gash across his chest for once. "He hadn't told me that yet."

"Do you not want to?" Ren asked, sitting up a little and meeting his gaze.

Sorin gave a twitching shrug, since anything deeper hurt.

"Do you think he doesn't want you to?"

Sorin eyed him. "Are you filling in for my sister deliberately or what?"

He smiled. "Someone has to and Ani's not here to do it. She trained me well."

He sighed. If Ren was channeling Ani, he might as well answer as truthfully as he could. "I don't know."

"If it's the latter, you can bet Ani will fill him full of all the stories before you get there. He'd be crazy not to want to meet you." With that, Ren stood and patted his shoulder. "Goodnight, Sorin."

He watched him go and shook his head slightly. Still, he slept a little better that night.

After that, Ren was almost as regular as Russ, appearing after dinner each night to talk briefly, mostly about policy, like Sorin's voice might matter or even make sense. Still, as weird as it was, it was nice to feel wanted.

Beau and Jez visited a couple times, maintaining a certain distance but seeming open to at least brief conversations. Ry came by herself, or with another woman who introduced herself as Jessie, a couple times to start establishing a few things, since apparently Colin was out and about. She was also a great source of information, even if her delivery seemed more accidental than purposeful.

By the time the night of the coronation came, Sorin felt better. He'd been allowed to sit all the way up and even walk that morning, although nothing more than one circuit around his tiny room before Russ herded him back to bed. Russ appeared that night for dinner early and dressed in what were clearly his best clothes.

"The coronation's tonight so I'll have to be quick," he said.

"Actually, I have a favor to ask in relation to that."

Russ raised his eyebrows. The dresser had been stocked with Sorin's own things, thanks to Ren, and he knew there were a couple nicer outfits in there.

"I want to go to the coronation."

"You can barely walk," Russ said instantly. "And we're supposed to keep you quiet until things can be explained. Until tempers and emotions die down."

"I don't need to be part of it," Sorin countered. "I can stay in the very back and leave before anyone will notice me. I'll wear a hood. I just…I need to be there. I need to see that what we did was not entirely irreversible."

Russ frowned at him. "I'm not sure you'll make it."

"It's in the main ballroom. I can make it," he said firmly and more confidently than he really felt, but he was determined.

The other man sighed. "Do you need help getting dressed?"

"Just the last bits, buckles and buttons."

"Yell when you're ready," he said and helped him over to the dresser before disappearing out the door. Sorin got dressed slowly then Russ assisted him with the last bits. "Give me as much as weight as you need," Russ told him. "You're lucky there aren't many people on duty in the infirmary right now and none that outrank me."

Sorin smiled slightly. "I am that," he agreed softly as he slowly walked out, leaning against Russ.

By the time they arrived at the coronation, it was about to start, which is what Sorin had wanted. The room was packed but Russ managed to find a bit of wall space at the very back for both of them. Luckily, everyone's attention was on the two men at the front of the room. Ren sat in what had been Patrick's throne, while Beau sat in a slightly smaller, less ornate one, looking pale but determined.

A noise at the back made everyone turn, Sorin included. In the doorway, stood a man who had to be Benton Walters, considering he looked just like his father. Benton held a pillow that contained the large, fancy crown, which would be Ren's to wear on special occasions. Next to him stood, to Sorin's slight surprise, Jez Lockholme. Upon quick reflection, it perhaps shouldn't have been so odd. Jez and Beau were together and she was a noble. Patrick and her father, Denham, had had a very close relationship for many years. Jez carried another pillow with a much simpler crown. It also meant the younger prince, who, by the accounts Sorin had gotten over the past week, seemed uncertain about taking his place officially as royalty, wouldn't bolt or shy away at this stage, no matter how nervous he was.

Benton and Jez paced their way forward solemnly, surrounded by an almost utterly silent crowd except the occasional murmur, probably identifying one or both of them. Finally, the pair came to a stop in front of the thrones. They stepped off to either side of Beau and Ren. Both placed their pillows on small tables near the thrones.

"Renier Highcastle, please stand and face your people," Benton said and the words carried the weight of generations.

Ren stood fluidly, back straight, gaze on the crowd in front of him.

"Do you," Benton began, "in the name of your people, accept the burdens, joys and responsibilities of being the king and ruling monarch?"

"I do."

"Do you, Renier Highcastle, swear and promise that you will treat every person, rich or poor, with equal justice, fairness, and loving care?"

"I do."

"Do you agree that you have said this in front of and to a representation of your people? And that it is only fair that they hold you to the standards of which your family has followed for generations, and of which you have just sworn yourself?"

"I do. It is only fair."

"Then kneel."

Ren did, dropping to one knee. Benton carefully scooped up the crown and, stepping behind Ren, set it gently on his head.

"Stand, Your Majesty, so that your people may pay their respects."

Around them, those gathered bowed their heads or dipped in light curtseys. Sorin followed suit.

Only once Ren was reseated on his throne and Benton back in his original position did Jez move. "Beau Highcastle. Stand and face your people."

The younger Highcastle did so, still pale but resolute, gaze darting to Jez's and then he smiled just a little.

"Do you," Jez continued, "as younger sibling to the king, accept your duties and responsibilities as Crown Prince of Tira?"

"I do."

"Do you recognize that you are first in line for the throne, until such time as the king may have heirs?"

"I do."

"And, in case of any unforeseen accident, you will be required to take over all duties as king?"

"I do."

"Then kneel."

Beau did, hands clasped, and Jez stepped beside him to set the crown on his head. Her hand dipped briefly to his shoulder to squeeze before he rose and the crowd offered their silent respect to him as well.

"King Renier," Jez said, even as she slipped back to the side, "if you would stand as well."

Ren did as ordered as Benton and Jez faced the crowd solemnly. Jez spoke first, "Do you, the people of Tira, accept these two as your rulers hence forth..."

"Through thick and thin, to defend your borders, and support you in all your endeavors?" Benton finished smoothly.

"Yes!" came the firm and enthusiastic call from the gathered crowd.

"Then it is official," they said together and Jez grinned.

"Let it be henceforth known that today marks the beginning of the rule of King Renier Highcastle of Tira. May your reign be long and prosperous."

Sorin flinched slightly. Once upon a time, someone had said that to Beau and Ren's father. Russ glanced at him with concern, but Sorin shook his head slightly.

Applause exploded across the room, almost deafening as it echoed back off the walls and ceiling.

"I should go," Sorin murmured in Russ's ear, but his gaze drifted back to the brothers at the front of the room. Maybe not all mistakes had to be permanent. Looking at the future stretching in front of all of them, Sorin felt, for the first time in a very long time, that just possibly things would be okay.

Acknowledgements

Like all good authors, I have a pile of people to thank. Nothing is Ever Easy has been in the works since August of 2003. After posting a few initial bits on LiveJournal (lol yes), I learned about fictionpress.com and posted the rest of the book there as I wrote it. To the handful of anonymous but faithful readers on fictionpress for the couple years it took to finish, thank you so much for your kind words and encouragement, even if you'll never see this. Also, the Museland crew, thank you for all the help fleshing out the characters!

Two people from those times deserve their own personal thanks. First, De. My "twin" and long-time internet bestie. I'm so glad our friendship has lasted and that we've happily adapted to "in real life" friendship! Your encouragement and never-ending shipping have been a delight for years and years.

And Marina! From reviewing buddies on fictionpress, to cowriters, to roommates (and cowriters), I most certainly would've never finished NiEE let alone any of what come since without you! Thank you so much for being my writing buddy and best friend for 20 years now.

Whew, transitions don't get any easier even in the acknowledgements. So, I'm going to thank the Mighty Pens next who have been my writing friends now since 2017. Thanks so much for all the encouragement, laughs, insanity, and all-around good time for the last five years. Our Discord is one of my favorite places to spend time! Special thanks to the year-round regulars: Rochelle, Abigail, Misty, Leaves, Asteria, and Kaite (sorry anyone I forgot!) and our founders: Kat Brauer and Susan Dennard.

And most especially to Mel, who without their pestering, this book would not be anything other than a Word file on my harddrive. Your yelling and flailing and invaluable help in all things Indie publishing knowledge (and don't you dare edit this!) means so, so much to me. As nerve-wracking as this all is, I'm glad you have a physical copy for your shelf. (I'm not promising anything beyond this, though).

This was never a NaNo book, but most of the sequels were written in November and I've met so many wonderful writers who have encouraged me, including Rachel, Kristen, and Morgan, who read the first chapter of NiEE, were confused, suggested ways to totally rewrite the book, and who I politely ended up ignoring (sorry, not sorry, friends!).

I would be remiss to not thank Lin for being my other best friend, cowriter (of 20+ years of Star Wars fanfiction!) and roommate. Thanks for letting me read this chunk of a book out loud to you! You're the best and I wouldn't be the same without you.

And finally, my family. To my mom, Jody, who read a weirdly formatted version of the first draft and went: this is not my usual genre but it was great and when are you publishing it? To my dad, Steve, who has never read it, but listened to me wax poetic in the early stages of the first draft and then went: but what about the villains? (I bet you all can figure out how that ended). To my brother, Tim, who was my first storytelling partner, and sister-in-law, Chelsea, who might not even know I write but will always talk fantasy with me. And finally, the still tiny nieces, Freya and Tali, who were not even a thought when I started writing this. Love you, kiddos.